Jirel of Joiry

She is a commander of warriors. Fierce. Proud. Relentless. Her red hair and yellow eyes burning like fire, her armour streaked with blood, she stands tall before her enemies. Bold. Defiant. Simmering with rage. And in the deepest dungeons of a castle under siege, she bids farewell to the world of treacherous men – and walks, by her own will, through a forbidden door into Hell itself. For freedom. For justice. *For Revenge* …

Northwest of Earth

From the crumbling temples of forgotten gods on Venus to the seedy pleasure halls of old Mars, the thirteen stories in Northwest of Earth blaze a trail through the underbelly of the solar system. The quick-drawing smuggler of the spaceways who would become the model for countless science fiction heroes, Northwest Smith is SF's original outlaw.

Judgment Night: A Selection of Science Fiction

Five novellas from the pages of John W. Campbell, Jr.'s *Astounding Science Fiction* magazine: 'Judgment Night'; 'The Code'; 'Promised Land'; 'Heir Apparent'; and 'Paradise Street'. Chosen by the author herself as the best of her longer-form writing, these stories show a gifted wordsmith working at the height of her talents.

Also by C. L. Moore

Novels

Earth's Last Citadel (1943) (with Henry Kuttner)
The Mask of Circe (1948) (with Henry Kuttner)
Doomsday Morning (1957)

Collections

Beyond Earth's Gates (1949)
Judgment Night (1952)
Shambleau and Others (1953)
Northwest of Earth (1954)
No Boundaries (with Henry Kuttner (1955))

C.L. Moore

SF GATEWAY OMNIBUS

JIREL OF JOIRY
NORTHWEST OF EARTH
JUDGMENT NIGHT: A SELECTION OF SCIENCE FICTION

GOLLANCZ
LONDON

First published in Great Britain in 2014 by
Gollancz
An imprint of the Orion Publishing Group
Orion House, 5 Upper St Martin's Lane,
London WC2H 9EA

An Hachette UK Company

A CIP catalogue record for this book is available from the British Library

ISBN 978 0 575 11932 1

1 3 5 7 9 10 8 6 4 2

Typeset by Input Data Services Ltd,
Bridgwater, Somerset

Printed and bound by
CPI Group (UK) Ltd, Croydon CR0 4YY

The Orion Publishing Group's policy is to use papers that are natural, renewable and recyclable products and made from wood grown in sustainable forests. The logging and manufacturing processes are expected to conform to the environmental regulations of the country of origin.

www.orionbooks.co.uk
www.gollancz.co.uk

CONTENTS

ENTER THE SF GATEWAY . . .

Towards the end of 2011, in conjunction with the celebration of fifty years of coherent, continuous science fiction and fantasy publishing, Gollancz launched the SF Gateway.

Over a decade after launching the landmark SF Masterworks series, we realised that the realities of commercial publishing are such that even the Masterworks could only ever scratch the surface of an author's career. Vast troves of classic SF and fantasy were almost certainly destined never again to see print. Until very recently, this meant that anyone interested in reading any of those books would have been confined to scouring second-hand bookshops. The advent of digital publishing changed that paradigm for ever.

Embracing the future even as we honour the past, Gollancz launched the SF Gateway with a view to utilising the technology that now exists to make available, for the first time, the entire backlists of an incredibly wide range of classic and modern SF and fantasy authors. Our plan, at its simplest, was – and still is! – to use this technology to build on the success of the SF and Fantasy Masterworks series and to go even further.

The SF Gateway was designed to be the new home of classic science fiction and fantasy – the most comprehensive electronic library of classic SFF titles ever assembled. The programme has been extremely well received and we've been very happy with the results. So happy, in fact, that we've decided to complete the circle and return a selection of our titles to print, in these omnibus editions.

We hope you enjoy this selection. And we hope that you'll want to explore more of the classic SF and fantasy we have available. These are wonderful books you're holding in your hand, but you'll find much, much more . . . through the SF Gateway.

www.sfgateway.com

INTRODUCTION

from The Encyclopedia of Science Fiction

Catherine Lucille Moore (1911–1987) was a US writer, collaborator with Henry Kuttner whom she married in 1940, and with whom she had collaborated since 1937. Before her intimate working association with Kuttner, she had, however, already achieved fame with her first story, 'Shambleau' for *Weird Tales* in 1933, a *femme fatale* tale of a psychic Vampire set on a Planetary Romance version of Mars, continuing during the 1930s to chronicle the exploits of its hero Northwest Smith, much of the series being assembled in *Shambleau and Others* (1953) and *Northwest of Earth* (1954).

Most of Moore's and Kuttner's works between 1940 and his death in 1958 were to some extent collaborations; each writer reportedly being able to pick up any story where the other had left off, and it has proved futile to attempt to determine who may have been the sole or senior author of many tales published under their own or their several shared names. It has seemed safe to assume that many titles signed as by Kuttner alone are collaborations, though somewhat less safe to assume that the reverse applies, for much of her work has a texture and emotional intensity that seems hard to think of as collaborative; and a gradual consensus has been established that Moore was in fact the stronger writer of the two. In any case, Kuttner's wit, deftly audacious deployment of ideas and neat exposition well complemented Moore's greater lyrical fluency and the power to evoke a Sense of Wonder in the past-haunted interstellar venues that were her specialty.

When Kuttner and Moore became part of the stable of writers working for John W. Campbell Jr's *Astounding Science-Fiction* during World War Two they devised their two most famous pseudonyms, Lewis Padgett and Laurence O'Donnell, under which they did much of their best work. Kuttner *may* have been the primary user of the Padgett name but the O'Donnell stories were more often Moore's. These include the remarkable Keeps sequence – comprising *Clash by Night* (1943) and *Fury* (1950) – which was collaborative (though it has been reprinted as by Kuttner alone, Moore signed copies of the book); the stories are set in City-sized Keeps located Under the Seas of Venus after nuclear war has destroyed life on Earth.

Some titles seem mainly by Moore, for instance *Judgment Night: A Selection of Science Fiction* (1952), in which four O'Donnell stories are combined with the remarkable titular novel, originally published as 'Judgment Night'

(1943). The tale is set during the death throes of a Galactic Empire that occupies its capital planet by the grace and favour of resident godlike 'ancients', possible survivors of a Forerunner race whose origins lie inconceivably deep in time; the martial fervour of the story seems at first simply to evoke Space Opera conventions, though with an injection of Sex as a war-trained wilful princess and the leader of a vast rebellion vie recklessly with each other over various ancient Weapons. It gradually becomes clear that their sex-charged, impetuous, savagely dysfunctional quarrel – which causes the death of a pleasure planetoid, for starters – is so far beyond their capacity to control or analyze that their behaviour is enough to convince the ancients that human civilization has lost the right to survive: not because of sex itself, which Moore treats with (muffled) respect, but because *Homo sapiens* is ungovernably blind to its own nature. The novel ends with a new, non-human species being selected for Uplift by the forerunners. The darkness of the tale, its use of the conventions of Genre SF to expose the tragic failure of the human species to understand itself, and its weighting towards a deep, engendering past against which present actors seem shallow puppets dancing on a darkening stage, marks it as a significant predecessor to (and probable direct influence upon) a wide range of writers, including Leigh Brackett, Margaret St Clair, Jack Vance, Gene Wolfe, and later figures like Michael Moorcock.

Other stories that seem essentially Moore's include the excellent 'The Children's Hour' (1944) as by Lawrence O'Donnell, and of course all the stories astutely assembled in *The Best of C. L. Moore* (1975) edited by Lester del Rey, which includes the classic *Vintage Season* (1946), about time-travelling tourists who delectate the Disaster of a meteor strike whose impact will cause a deadly plague; the passionate sexual emotions aroused in its protagonist by one of the visitors are an early representation in SF of the human dream that Exogamy and Paradise are somehow linked. Also in *The Best of C. L. Moore* is 'No Woman Born' (1944) as Moore, about a badly burned dancer who is given a Robot body and becomes a Cyborg. In these stories Moore's sometimes extravagant style is carefully controlled and combined with an earnest emotionality which was underappreciated at the time.

In the late 1940s, Moore and Kuttner wrote a series of novels for *Startling Stories* which, continuing the colourful tradition of the Northwest Smith stories, became archetypes of the hybrid genre of Science Fantasy, neatly fusing the strengths of Moore's romanticism and Kuttner's vigorous plotting. *The Dark World* (1965 as by Kuttner) is a pastiche of A. Merritt's *Dwellers in the Mirage* (1932) and was itself pastiched in Marion Zimmer Bradley's *Falcons of Narabedla* (1964).

In 1950 Kuttner and Moore went to study at the University of Southern California; although they wrote a number of mystery novels, there were few more SF stories. Moore did one solo SF novel in this period, *Doomsday Morning* (1957), a futuristic thriller which did not exploit her greatest strengths as a writer. Moore wrote no fiction after Kuttner's death in 1958, though she did write some Television scripts – as by Catharine Kuttner – for such series as *Maverick* and *77 Sunset Strip*. She remarried in 1963 and abandoned writing for good. In 1981 she received the World Fantasy Award for life achievement, and posthumously in 2004, with Kuttner, the Cordwainer Smith Rediscovery Award. She was posthumously inducted into the Science Fiction Hall of Fame in 1998.

Two of the three books here brought together, *Jirel of Joiry* and *Northwest of Earth* are historical or planetary romances from a time, now a few generations back, when writers could invest great emotional energy in romanticized visions of the past or other planets, without apology. It is certainly the case that Moore, whose early use of feminine protagonists in heroic roles significantly changed the rules of the game for many male readers, never felt any need to repudiate her first stories, written in the tough 1930s, when women needed moments of imaginary freedom as much as the men who could no longer 'provide' for them. The great energy of these tales, and the almost synaesthetic intensity of their telling, can still rouse the reader into dreams. They are deeply healthy for the human imagination. *Judgment Night* (see discussion above) is something else. It may be the first space opera story written by an American to enforce the lesson that fun and fisticuffs in a space opera might not seem the same in the real world (where war had again broken out across the planet). Here, on Earth, that sort of fun led to the death camps. *Judgment Night*, which is a compelling reading experience, may also be the earliest example of an American SF story that seems genuinely wise to what the future would cost us.

For a more detailed version of the above, see C. L. Moore's author entry in *The Encyclopedia of Science Fiction*: http://sf-encyclopedia.com/entry/moore_c_l

Some terms above are capitalised when they would not normally be so rendered; this indicates that the terms represent discrete entries in *The Encyclopedia of Science Fiction*.

JIREL OF JOIRY

BLACK GOD'S KISS

1

They brought in Joiry's tall commander, struggling between two men-at-arms who tightly gripped the ropes which bound their captive's mailed arms. They picked their way between mounds of dead as they crossed the great hall towards the dais where the conqueror sat, and twice they slipped a little in the blood that splattered the flags. When they came to a halt before the mailed figure on the dais, Joiry's commander was breathing hard, and the voice that echoed hollowly under the helmet's confines was hoarse with fury and despair.

Guillaume the conqueror leaned on his mighty sword, hands crossed on its hilt, grinning down from his height upon the furious captive before him. He was a big man, Guillaume, and he looked bigger still in his spattered armour. There was blood on his hard, scarred face, and he was grinning a white grin that split his short, curly beard glitteringly. Very splendid and very dangerous he looked, leaning on his great sword and smiling down upon fallen Joiry's lord, struggling between the stolid men-at-arms.

'Unshell me this lobster,' said Guillaume in his deep, lazy voice. 'We'll see what sort of face the fellow has who gave us such a battle. Off with his helmet, you.'

But a third man had to come up and slash the straps which held the iron helmet on, for the struggles of Joiry's commander were too fierce, even with bound arms, for either of the guards to release their hold. There was a moment of sharp struggle; then the straps parted and the helmet rolled loudly across the flagstones.

Guillaume's white teeth clicked on a startled oath. He stared. Joiry's lady glared back at him from betwen her captors, wild red hair tousled, wild lion-yellow eyes ablaze.

'God curse you!' snarled the lady of Joiry between clenched teeth. 'God blast your black heart!'

Guillaume scarcely heard her. He was still staring, as most men stared when they first set eyes upon Jirel of Joiry. She was tall as most men, and as savage as the wildest of them, and the fall of Joiry was bitter enough to break her heart as she stood snarling curses up at her tall conqueror. The face above her mail might not have been fair in a woman's head-dress, but in the steel setting of her armour it had a biting, sword-edge beauty as keen as the flash of blades. The red hair was short upon her high defiant head, and the yellow blaze of her eyes held fury as a crucible holds fire.

Guillaume's stare melted into a slow smile. A little light kindled behind his eyes as he swept the long, strong lines of her with a practised gaze. The smile broadened, and suddenly he burst into full-throated laughter, a deep bull bellow of amusement and delight.

'By the Nails!' he roared. 'Here's welcome for the warrior! And what forfeit d'ye offer, pretty one, for your life?'

She blazed a curse at him.

'So? Naughty words for a mouth so fair, my lady. Well, we'll not deny you put up a gallant battle. No man could have done better, and many have done worse. But against Guillaume –' He inflated his splendid chest and grinned down at her from the depths of his jutting beard. 'Come to me, pretty one,' he commanded. 'I'll wager your mouth is sweeter than your words.'

Jirel drove a spurred heel into the shin of one guard and twisted from his grip as he howled, bringing up an iron knee into the abdomen, of the other. She had writhed from their grip and made three long strides towards the door before Guillaume caught her. She felt his arms closing about her from behind, and lashed out with both spiked heels in a futile assault upon his leg armour, twisting like a maniac, fighting with her knees and spurs, straining hopelessly at the ropes which bound her arms. Guillaume laughed and whirled her round, grinning down into the blaze of her yellow eyes. Then deliberately he set a fist under her chin and tilted her mouth up to his. There was a cessation of her hoarse curses.

'By heaven, that's like kissing a sword-blade,' said Guillaume, lifting his lips at last.

Jirel choked something that was mercifully muffled as she darted her head sidewise, like a serpent striking, and sank her teeth into his neck. She missed the jugular by a fraction of an inch.

Guillaume said nothing, then. He sought her head with a steady hand, found it despite her wild writhing, sank iron fingers deep into the hinges of her jaw, forcing her teeth relentlessly apart. When he had her free he glared down into the yellow hell of her eyes for an instant. The blaze of them was hot enough to scorch his scarred face. He grinned and lifted his ungauntleted hand, and with one heavy blow in the face he knocked her half-way across the room. She lay still upon the flags.

2

Jirel opened her yellow eyes upon darkness. She lay quiet for a while, collecting her scattered thoughts. By degrees it came back to her, and she muffled upon her arm a sound that was half curse and half sob. Joiry had fallen. For a time she lay rigid in the dark, forcing herself to the realization.

The sound of feet shifting on stone near by brought her out of that particular misery. She sat up cautiously, feeling about her to determine in what part of Joiry its liege lady was imprisoned. She knew that the sound she had heard must be a sentry, and by the dank smell of the darkness that she was underground. In one of the little dungeon cells, of course. With careful quietness she got to her feet, muttering a curse as her head reeled for an instant and then began to throb. In the utter dark she felt around the cell. Presently she came to a little wooden stool in a corner, and was satisfied. She gripped one leg of it with firm fingers and made her soundless way around the wall until she had located the door.

The sentry remembered, afterward, that he had heard the wildest shriek for help which had ever rung in his ears, and he remembered unbolting the door. Afterward, until they found him lying inside the locked cell with a cracked skull, he remembered nothing.

Jirel crept up the dark stairs of the north turret, murder in her heart. Many little hatreds she had known in her life, but no such blaze as this. Before her eyes in the night she could see Guillaume's scornful face laughing, the little jutting beard split-with the whiteness of his mirth. Upon her mouth she felt the remembered weight of his, about her the strength of his arms. And such a blast of hot fury came over her that she reeled a little and clutched at the wall for support. She went on in a haze of red anger, and something like madness burning in her brain as a resolve slowly took shape out of the chaos of her hate. When that thought came to her she paused again, mid-step upon the stairs, and was conscious of a little coldness blowing over her. Then it was gone, and she shivered a little, shook her shoulders and grinned wolfishly, and went on.

By the stars she could see through the arrow-slits in the wall it must be near to midnight. She went softly on the stairs, and she encountered no one. Her little tower room at the top was empty. Even the straw pallet where the serving-wench slept had not been used that night. Jirel got herself out of her armour alone, somehow, after much striving and twisting. Her doeskin shirt was stiff with sweat and stained with blood. She tossed it disdainfully into a corner. The fury in her eyes had cooled now to a contained and secret flame. She smiled to herself as she slipped a fresh shirt of doeskin over her tousled red head and donned a brief tunic of link-mail. On her legs she buckled the greaves of some forgotten legionary, relic of the not long past days when Rome still ruled the world. She thrust a dagger through her belt and took her own long two-handed sword bare-bladed in her grip. Then she went down the stairs again.

She knew there must have been revelry and feasting in the great hall that night, and by the silence hanging so heavily now she was sure that most of her enemies lay still in drunken slumber, and she experienced a swift regret for the gallons of her good French wine so wasted. And the thought flashed through her head that a determined woman with a sharp sword might work some little damage among the drunken sleepers before she was overpowered. But she put that idea by, for Guillaume would have posted sentries to spare, and she must not give up her secret freedom so fruitlessly.

Down the dark stairs she went, and crossed one corner of the vast centre hall whose darkness she was sure hid wine-deadened sleepers, and so into the lesser dimness of the rough little chapel that Joiry boasted. She had been sure she would find Father Gervase there, and she was not mistaken. He rose from his knees before the altar, dark in his robe, the starlight through the narrow window shining upon his tonsure.

'My daughter!' he whispered. 'My daughter! How have you escaped? Shall I find you a mount? If you can pass the sentries you should be in your cousin's castle by daybreak.'

She hushed him with a lifted hand.

'No,' she said. 'It is not outside I go this night. I have a more perilous journey even than that to make. Shrive me, father.'

He stared at her. 'What is it?'

She dropped to her knees before him and gripped the rough cloth of his habit with urgent fingers.

'Shrive me, I say! I go down into hell tonight to pray the devil for a weapon, and it may be I shall not return.'

Gervase bent and gripped her shoulders with hands that shook.

'Look at me!' he demanded. 'Do you know what you're saying? You go—'

'Down!' She said it firmly. 'Only you and I know that passage, father – and not even we can be sure of what lies beyond. But to gain a weapon against the man I would venture into perils even worse than that.'

'If I thought you meant it,' he whispered, 'I would waken Guillaume now and give you into his arms. It would be a kinder fate, my daughter.'

'It's that I would walk through hell to escape,' she whispered back fiercely. 'Can't you see? Oh, God knows I'm not innocent of the ways of light loving – but to be any man's fancy, for a night or two, before he snaps my neck or sells me into slavery – and above all, if that man were Guillaume! Can't you understand?'

'That would be shame enough,' nodded Gervase. 'But think, Jirel! For that shame there is atonement and absolution, and for that death the gates of heaven open wide. But this other – Jirel, Jirel, never through all eternity may you come out, body or soul, if you venture – down!'

She shrugged.

'To wreak my vengeance upon Guillaume I would go if I knew I should burn in hell for ever.'

'But Jirel, I do not think you understand. This is a worse fate than the deepest depths of hell-fire. This is – this is beyond all the bounds of the hells we know. And I think Satan's hottest flames were the breath of paradise, compared to what may befall you there.'

'I know. Do you think I'd venture down if I could not be sure? Where else would I find such weapons as I need, save outside God's dominion?'

'Jirel, you shall not!'

'Gervase, I go! Will you shrive me?' The hot yellow eyes blazed into his, lambent in the starlight.

After a moment he dropped his head. 'You are my lady. I will give you God's blessing, but it will not avail you – there.'

3

She went down into the dungeons again. She went down a long way through utter dark, over stones that were oozy and odorous with moisture, through blackness that had never known the light of day. She might have been a little afraid at other times, but that steady flame of hatred burning behind her eyes was a torch to light the way, and she could not wipe from her memory the feel of Guillaume's arms about her, the scornful press of his lips on her mouth. She whimpered a little, low in her throat, and a hot gust of hate went over her.

In the solid blackness she came at length to a wall, and she set herself to pulling the loose stones from this with her free hand, for she would not lay down the sword. They had never been laid in mortar, and they came out easily. When the way was clear she stepped through and found her feet upon a downward-sloping ramp of smooth stone. She cleared the rubble away from the hole in the wall, and enlarged it enough for a quick passage; for when she came back this way – if she did – it might well be that she would come very fast.

At the bottom of the slope she dropped to her knees on the cold floor and felt about. Her fingers traced the outline of a circle, the veriest crack in the stone. She felt until she found the ring in its centre. That ring was of the coldest metal she had ever known, and the smoothest. She could put no name to it. The daylight had never shone upon such metal.

She tugged. The stone was reluctant, and at last she took her sword in her teeth and put both hands to the lifting. Even then it taxed the limit of her strength, and she was strong as many men. But at last it rose, with the strangest sighing sound, and a little prickle of goose-flesh rippled over her.

Now she took the sword back into her hand and knelt on the rim of the invisible blackness below. She had gone this path once before and once only, and never thought to find any necessity in life strong enough to drive her down again. The way was the strangest she had ever known. There was, she thought, no such passage in all the world save here. It had not been built for human feet to travel. It had not been built for feet at all. It was a narrow, polished shaft that cork-screwed round and round. A snake might have slipped in it and gone shooting down, round and round in dizzy circles – but no snake on earth was big enough to fill that shaft. No human travellers had worn the sides of the spiral so smooth, and she did not care to speculate on what creatures had polished it so, through what ages of passage.

She might never have made that first trip down, nor anyone after her, had not some unknown human hacked the notches which made it possible to descend slowly; that is, she thought it must have been a human. At any rate, the notches were roughly shaped for hands and feet, and spaced not too far apart; but who and when and how she could not even guess. As to the beings who made the shaft, in long-forgotten ages – well, there were devils on earth before man, and the world was very old.

She turned on her face and slid feet-first into the curving tunnel. That first time she and Gervase had gone down in sweating terror of what lay below, and with devils tugging at their heels. Now she slid easily, not bothering to find toeholds, but slipping swiftly round and round the long spirals with only her hands to break the speed when she went too fast. Round and round she went, round and round.

It was a long way down. Before she had gone very far the curious dizziness she had known before came over her again, a dizziness not entirely induced by the spirals she whirled around, but a deeper atomic unsteadiness as if not only she but also the substances around her were shifting. There was something queer about the angles of those curves. She was no scholar in geometry or aught else, but she felt intuitively that the bend and slant of the way she went were somehow outside any other angles or bends she had ever known. They led into the unknown and the dark, but it seemed to her obscurely that they led into deeper darkness and mystery than the merely physical, as if, though she could not put it clearly even into thoughts, the peculiar and exact lines of the tunnel had been carefully angled to lead through poly-dimensional space as well as through the underground – perhaps through time, too. She did not know she was thinking such things; but all about her was a blurred dizziness as she shot down and round, and she knew that the way she went took her on a stranger journey than any other way she had ever travelled.

Down, and down. She was sliding fast, but she knew how long it would be. On that first trip they had taken alarm as the passage spiralled so endlessly and with thoughts of the long climb back had tried to stop before it was too late. They had found it impossible. Once embarked, there was no halting. She had tried, and such waves of sick blurring had come over her that she came near to unconsciousness. It was as if she had tried to halt some inexorable process of nature, half finished. They could only go on. The very atoms of their bodies shrieked in rebellion against a reversal of the change.

And the way up, when they returned, had not been difficult. They had had visions of a back-breaking climb up interminable curves, but again the uncanny difference of those angles from those they knew was manifested. In a queer way they seemed to defy gravity, or perhaps led through some way outside the power of it. They had been sick and dizzy on the return, as on the way down, but through the clouds of that confusion it had seemed to them that they slipped as easily up the shaft as they had gone down; or perhaps that, once in the tunnel, there was neither up nor down.

The passage levelled gradually. This was the worst part for a human to travel, though it must have eased the speed of whatever beings the shaft was made for. It was too narrow for her to turn in, and she had to lever herself face down and feet first, along the horizontal smoothness of the floor, pushing with her hands. She was glad when her questioning heels met open space and she slid from the mouth of the shaft and stood upright in the dark.

Here she paused to collect herself. Yes, this was the beginning of the long passage she and Father Gervase had travelled on that long-ago journey of exploration. By the veriest accident they had found the place, and only the veriest bravado had brought them thus far. He had gone on a greater distance than she – she was younger then, and more amenable to authority – and had come back white-faced in the torchlight and hurried her up the shaft again.

She went on carefully, feeling her way, remembering what she herself had seen in the darkness a little farther on, wondering in spite of herself, and with a tiny catch at her heart, what it was that had sent Father Gervase so hastily back. She had never been entirely satisfied with his explanations. It had been about here – or was it a little farther on? The stillness was like a roaring in her ears.

Then ahead of her the darkness moved. It was just that – a vast, imponderable shifting of the solid dark. Jesu! This was new! She gripped the cross at her throat with one hand and her sword-hilt with the other. Then it was upon her, striking like a hurricane, whirling her against the walls and shrieking in her ears like a thousand wind-devils – a wild cyclone of the dark that buffeted her mercilessly and tore at her hair and raved in her ears with the myriad voices of all lost things crying in the night. The voices were piteous in their terror and loneliness. Tears came to her eyes even as she shivered with nameless dread, for the whirlwind was alive with a dreadful instinct, an animate thing sweeping through the dark of the underground; an unholy thing that made her flesh crawl even though it touched her to the heart with its pitiful little lost voices wailing in the wind where no wind could possibly be.

And then it was gone. In that one flash of an instant it vanished, leaving no whisper to commemorate its passage. Only in the heart of it could one hear the sad little voices wailing or the wild shriek of the wind. She found herself standing stunned, her sword yet gripped futilely in one hand and the tears running down her face. Poor little lost voices, wailing. She wiped the tears away with a shaking hand and set her teeth hard against the weakness of reaction that flooded her. Yet it was a good five minutes before she could force herself on. After a few steps her knees ceased to tremble.

The floor was dry and smooth underfoot. It sloped a little downward, and she wondered into what unplumbed deeps she had descended by now. The silence had fallen heavily again, and she found herself straining for some other sound than the soft padding of her own boots. Then her foot slipped in sudden wetness. She bent, exploring fingers outstretched, feeling without reason that the wetness would be red if she could see it. But her fingers traced the immense outline of a footprint – splayed and three-toed like a frog's, but of monster size. It was a fresh footprint. She had a vivid flash of memory – that thing she had glimpsed in the torchlight on the other trip down. But she had had light then, and now she was blind in the dark, the creature's natural habitat …

For a moment she was not Jirel of Joiry, vengeful fury on the trail of a devilish weapon, but a frightened woman alone in the unholy dark. That memory had been so vivid … Then she saw Guillaume's scornful, laughing face again, the little beard dark along the line of his jaw, the strong teeth white with his laughter; and something hot and sustaining swept over her like a thin flame, and she was Jirel again, vengeful and resolute. She went on more slowly, her sword swinging in a semicircle before every third step, that she might not be surprised too suddenly by some nightmare monster clasping her in, smothering her arms. But the flesh crept upon her unprotected back.

The smooth passage went on and on. She could feel the cold walls on either hand, and her upswung sword grazed the roof. It was like crawling through some worm's tunnel, blindly under the weight of countless tons of earth. She felt the pressure of it above and about her, overwhelming, and found herself praying that the end of this tunnel-crawling might come soon, whatever the end might bring.

But when it came it was a stranger thing than she had ever dreamed. Abruptly she felt the immense, imponderable oppression cease. No longer was she conscious of the tons of earth pressing about her. The walls had fallen away and her feet struck a sudden rubble instead of the smooth floor. But the darkness that had bandaged her eyes was changed too, indescribably. It was no longer darkness, but void; not an absence of light, but nothingness. Abysses opened around her, yet she could see nothing. She only knew that she stood at the threshold of some immense space, and sensed nameless things about her, and battled vainly against that nothingness which was all her straining eyes could see. And at her throat something constricted painfully.

She lifted her hand and found the chain of her crucifix taut and vibrant around her neck. At that she smiled a little grimly, for she began to understand. The crucifix. She found her hand shaking despite herself, but she unfastened the chain and dropped the cross to the ground. Then she gasped.

All about her, as suddenly as the awakening from a dream, the nothingness had opened out into undreamed-of distances. She stood high on a hilltop under a sky spangled with strange stars. Below she caught glimpses of misty plains and valleys, with mountain peaks rising far away. And at her feet a ravening circle of small, slavering, blind things leaped with clashing teeth.

They were obscene and hard to distinguish against the darkness of the hillside, and the noise they made was revolting. Her sword swung up of itself, almost, and slashed furiously at the little dark horrors leaping up around her legs. They died squashily, splattering her bare thighs with unpleasantness, and after a few had gone silent under the blade, the rest fled into the dark with quick, frightened pantings, their feet making a queer splashing noise on the stones.

Jirel gathered a handful of the coarse grass which grew there and wiped her legs of the obscene splatters, looking about with quickened breath upon this land so unholy that one who bore a cross might not even see it. Here, if anywhere, one might find a weapon such as she sought. Behind her in the hillside was the low tunnel opening from which she had emerged. Overhead the strange stars shone. She did not recognize a single constellation, and if the brighter sparks were planets they were strange ones, tinged with violet and green and yellow. One was vividly crimson, like a point of fire. Far out over the rolling land below she could discern a mighty column of light. It did not blaze, nor illuminate the dark about. It cast no shadows. It simply was a great pillar of luminance towering high in the night. It seemed artificial – perhaps man-made, though she scarcely dared hope for men here.

She had half expected, despite her brave words, to come out upon the storied and familiar red-hot pave of hell, and this pleasant, starlit land surprised her and made her more wary. The things that built the tunnel could not have been human. She had no right to expect men here. She was a little stunned by finding open sky so far underground, though she was intelligent enough to realize that however she had come, she was not underground now. No cavity in the earth could contain this starry sky. She came of a credulous age, and she accepted her surroundings without too much questioning, though she was a little disappointed if the truth were known, in the pleasantness of the mistily starlit place. The fiery streets of hell would have been a likelier locality in which to find a weapon against Guillaume.

When she had cleansed her sword on the grass and wiped her legs clean, she turned slowly down the hill. The distant column beckoned her, and after a moment of indecision she turned towards it. She had no time to waste, and this was the likeliest place to find what she sought.

The coarse grass brushed her legs and whispered round her feet. She stumbled now and then on the rubble, for the hill was steep, but she reached the bottom without mishap, and struck out across the meadows towards that blaze of far-away brilliance. It seemed to her that she walked more lightly, somehow. The grass scarcely bent underfoot, and she found she could take long sailing strides like one who runs with wings on his heels. It felt like a dream. The gravity pull of the place must have been less than she was accustomed to, but she only knew that she was skimming over the ground with amazing speed.

Travelling so, she passed through the meadows over the strange, coarse grass, over a brook or two that spoke endlessly to itself in a curious language that was almost speech, certainly not the usual gurgle of earth's running water. Once she ran into a blotch of darkness, like some pocket of void in the air, and struggled through gasping and blinking outraged eyes. She was beginning to realize that the land was not so innocently normal as it looked.

On and on she went, at that surprising speed, while the meadows skimmed past beneath her flying feet, and gradually the light grew nearer. She saw now that it was a round tower of sheeted luminance, as if walls of solid flame rose up from the ground. Yet it seemed to be steady, nor did it cast any illumination upon the sky.

Before much time had elapsed, with her dream-like speed she had almost reached her goal. The ground was becoming marshy underfoot, and presently the smell of swamps rose in her nostrils and she saw that between her and the light stretched a belt of unstable ground tufted with black reedy grass. Here and there she could see dim white blotches moving. They might be beasts, or only wisps of mist. The starlight was not very illuminating.

She began to pick her way carefully across the black, quaking morasses. Where the tufts of grass rose she found firmer ground, and she leaped from clump to clump with that amazing lightness, so that her feet barely touched the black ooze. Here and there slow bubbles rose through the mud and broke thickly. She did not like the place.

Half-way across, she saw one of the white blotches approaching her with slow, erratic movements. It bumped along unevenly, and at first she thought it might be inanimate, its approach was so indirect and purposeless. Then it blundered nearer, with that queer bumpy gait, making sucking noises in the ooze and splashing as it came. In the starlight she saw suddenly what it was, and for an instant her heart paused and sickness rose overwhelmingly in her throat. It was a woman – a beautiful woman whose white bare body had the curves and loveliness of some marble statue. She was crouching like a frog, and as Jirel watched in stupefaction she straightened her legs abruptly and leaped as a frog leaps, only more clumsily, falling forward into the ooze a little distance beyond the watching woman. She did not seem to see Jirel. The mud-spattered face was blank. She blundered on through the mud in awkward leaps. Jirel watched until the woman was no more than a white wandering blur in the dark, and above the shock of that sight pity was rising, and uncomprehending resentment against whatever had brought so lovely a creature into this – into blundering in frog leaps aimlessly through the mud, with empty mind and blind staring eyes. For the second time that night she knew the sting of unaccustomed tears as she went on.

The sight, though, had given her reassurance. The human form was not unknown here. There might be leathery devils with hoofs and horns, such as she still half expected, but she would not be alone in her humanity; though if all the rest were as piteously mindless as the one she had seen – she did not follow that thought. It was too unpleasant. She was glad when the marsh was past and she need not see any longer the awkward white shapes bumping along through the dark.

She struck out across the narrow space which lay between her and the tower. She saw now that it was a building, and that the light composed it. She could not understand that, but she saw it. Walls and columns outlined the tower, solid sheets of light with definite boundaries, not radiant. As she came nearer she saw that it was in motion, apparently spurting up from some source underground as if the light illuminated sheets of water rushing upward under great pressure. Yet she felt intuitively that it was not water, but incarnate light.

She came forward hesitantly, gripping her sword. The area around the tremendous pillar was paved with something black and smooth that did not reflect the light. Out of it sprang the uprushing walls of brilliance with their sharply defined edges. The magnitude of the things dwarfed her to infinitesimal size. She stared upward with undazzled eyes, trying to understand. If there could be such a thing as solid, non-radiating light, this was it.

4

She was very near under the mighty tower before she could see the details of the building clearly. They were strange to her – great pillars and arches around the base, and one stupendous portal, all moulded out of the rushing, prisoned light. She turned towards the opening after a moment, for the light had a tangible look. She did not believe she could have walked through it even had she dared.

When that tremendous portal arched over her she peered in, affrighted by the very size of the place. She thought she could hear the hiss and spurt of the light surging upward. She was looking into a mighty globe inside, a hall shaped like the interior of a bubble, though the curve was so vast she was scarcely aware of it. And in the very centre of the globe floated a light. It glowed there in mid-air with a pale, steady flame that was somehow alive and animate, and brighter than the serene illumination of the building, for it hurt her eyes to look at it directly.

She stood on the threshold and stared, not quite daring to venture in. And as she hesitated a change came over the light. A flash of rose tinged its pallor. The rose deepened and darkened until it took on the colour of blood. And the shape underwent strange changes. It lengthened, drew itself out narrowly, split at the bottom into two branches, put out two tendrils from the top. The blood-red paled again, and the light somehow lost its brilliance, receded into the depths of the thing that was forming. Jirel clutched her sword and forgot to breathe, watching. The light was taking on the shape of a human being – of a woman – of a tall woman in mail, her red hair tousled and her eyes staring straight into the duplicate eyes at the portal …

'Welcome,' said the Jirel suspended in the centre of the globe, her voice deep and resonant and clear in spite of the distance between them. Jirel at the door held her breath, wondering and afraid. This was herself, in every detail, a mirrored Jirel – that was it, Jirel mirrored upon a surface which blazed and smouldered with barely repressed light, so that the eyes gleamed with it and the whole figure seemed to hold its shape by an effort, only by that effort restraining itself from resolving into pure, formless light again. But the voice was not her own. It shook and resounded with a knowledge as alien as the light-built walls. It mocked her. It said:

'Welcome! Enter into the portals, woman!'

She looked up warily at the rushing walls about her. Instinctively she drew back.

'Enter, enter!' urged that mocking voice from her own mirrored lips. And there was a note in it she did not like.

'Enter!' cried the voice again, this time a command.

Jirel's eyes narrowed. Something intuitive warned her back, and yet – she drew the dagger she had thrust in her belt and with a quick motion she tossed it into the great globe-shaped hall. It struck the floor without a sound, and a brilliant light flared up around it, so brilliant she could not look upon what was happening; but it seemed to her that the knife expanded, grew large and nebulous, and ringed with dazzling light. In less time than it takes to tell, it had faded out of sight as if the very atoms which composed it had flown apart and dispersed in the golden glow of that mighty bubble. The dazzle faded with the knife, leaving Jirel staring dazedly at a bare floor.

That other Jirel laughed, a rich, resonant laugh of scorn and malice.

'Stay out, then,' said the voice. 'You've more intelligence than I thought. Well, what would you here?'

Jirel found her voice with an effort.

'I seek a weapon,' she said, 'a weapon against a man I so hate that upon earth there is none terrible enough for my need.'

'You so hate him, eh?' mused the voice.

'With all my heart!'

'With all your heart!' echoed the voice, and there was an undernote of laughter in it that Jirel did not understand. The echoes of that mirth ran round and round the great globe. Jirel felt her cheeks burn with resentment against some implication in the derision which she could not put a name to. When the echoes of the laugh had faded the voice said indifferently, 'Give the man what you find at the black temple in the lake. I make you a gift of it.'

The lips that were Jirel's twisted into a laugh of purest mockery; then all about that figure so perfectly her own the light flared out. She saw the outlines melting fluidly as she turned her dazzled eyes away. Before the echoes of that derision had died, a blinding, formless light burned once more in the midst of the bubble.

Jirel turned and stumbled away under the mighty column of the tower, a hand to her dazzled eyes. Not until she had reached the edge of the black, unreflecting circle that paved the ground around the pillar did she realize that she knew no way of finding the lake where her weapon lay. And not until then did she remember how fatal it is said to be to accept a gift from a demon. Buy it, or earn it, but never accept the gift. Well – she shrugged and stepped out upon the grass. She must surely be damned by now, for having ventured down of her own will into this curious place for such a purpose as hers. The soul can be lost but once.

She turned her face up to the strange stars and wondered in what direction her course lay. The sky looked blankly down upon her with its myriad meaningless eyes. A star fell as she watched, and in her superstitious soul she took it for an omen, and set off boldly over the dark meadows in the direction where the bright streak had faded. No swamps guarded the way here, and she was soon skimming along over the grass with that strange, dancing gait that the lightness of the place allowed her. And as she went she was remembering, as from long ago in some other far world, a man's arrogant mirth and the press of his mouth on hers. Hatred bubbled up hotly within her and broke from her lips a little savage laugh of anticipation. What dreadful thing awaited her in the temple in the lake, what punishment from hell to be loosed by her own hands upon Guillaume? And though her soul was the price it cost her, she would count it a fair bargain if she could drive the laughter from his mouth and bring terror into the eyes that mocked her.

Thoughts like these kept her company for a long way upon her journey. She did not think to be lonely or afraid in the uncanny darkness across which no shadows fell from that mighty column behind her. The unchanging meadows flew past underfoot, lightly as meadows in a dream. It might almost have been that the earth moved instead of herself, so effortlessly did she go. She was sure now that she was heading in the right direction, for two more stars had fallen in the same arc across the sky.

The meadows were not untenanted. Sometimes she felt presences near her in the dark, and once she ran full-tilt into a nest of little yapping horrors like those on the hilltop. They lunged up about her with clicking teeth, mad with a blind ferocity, and she swung her sword in frantic circles, sickened by the noise of them lunging splashily through the grass and splattering her sword with their deaths. She beat them off and went on, fighting her own sickness, for she had never known anything quite so nauseating as these little monstrosities.

She crossed a brook that talked to itself in the darkness with that queer murmuring which came so near to speech, and a few strides beyond it she paused suddenly, feeling the ground tremble with the rolling thunder of hoofbeats approaching. She stood still, searching the dark anxiously, and presently the earth-shaking beat grew louder and she saw a white blur flung wide across the dimness to her left, and the sound of hoofs deepened and grew. Then out of the night swept a herd of snow-white horses. Magnificently they ran, manes tossing, tails streaming, feet pounding a rhythmic, heart-stirring roll along the ground. She caught her breath at the beauty of their motion. They swept by a little distance away, tossing their heads, spurning the ground with scornful feet.

But as they came abreast of her she saw one blunder a little and stumble against the next, and that one shook his head bewilderedly; and suddenly she realized that they were blind – all running so splendidly in a deeper dark than even she groped through. And she saw, too, their coats were roughened with sweat, and foam dripped from their lips, and their nostrils were flaring pools of scarlet. Now and again one stumbled from pure exhaustion. Yet they ran, frantically, blindly through the dark, driven by something outside their comprehension.

As the last one of all swept by her, sweat-crusted and staggering, she saw him toss his head high, spattering foam, and whinny shrilly to the stars. And it seemed to her that the sound was strangely articulate. Almost she heard the echoes of a name – 'Julienne! Julienne!' – in that high, despairing sound. And the incongruity of it, the bitter despair, clutched at her heart so sharply that for the third time that night she knew the sting of tears.

The dreadful humanity of that cry echoed in her ears as the thunder died away. She went on, blinking back the tears for that beautiful blind creature, staggering with exhaustion, calling a girl's name hopelessly from a beast's throat into the blank darkness wherein it was for ever lost.

Then another star fell across the sky, and she hurried ahead, closing her mind to the strange, incomprehensible pathos that made an undernote of tears to the starry dark of this land. And the thought was growing in her mind that, though she had come into no brimstone pit where horned devils pranced over flames, yet perhaps it was after all a sort of hell through which she ran.

Presently in the distance she caught a glimmer of something bright. The ground dipped after that and she lost it, and skimmed through a hollow, where pale things wavered away from her into the deeper dark. She never knew what they were, and was glad. When she came up on to higher ground again she saw it more clearly, an expanse of dim brilliance ahead. She hoped it was a lake, and ran more swiftly.

It *was* a lake – a lake that could never have existed outside some obscure hell like this. She stood on the brink doubtfully, wondering if this could be the place the light devil had meant. Black, shining water stretched out before her, heaving gently with a motion unlike that of any water she had ever seen before. And in the depths of it, like fireflies caught in ice, gleamed myriad small lights. They were fixed there immovably, not stirring with the motion of the water. As she watched, something hissed above her and a streak of light split the dark air. She looked up in time to see something bright curving across the sky to fall without a splash into the water, and small ripples of phosphorescence spread sluggishly toward the shore, where they broke at her feet with the queerest whispering sound, as if each succeeding ripple spoke the syllable of a word.

She looked up, trying to locate the origin of the falling lights, but the strange stars looked down upon her blankly. She bent and stared down into the centre of the spreading ripples, and where the thing had fallen she thought a new light twinkled through the water. She could not determine what it was, and after a curious moment she gave the question up and began to cast about for the temple the light-devil had spoken of. After a moment she thought she saw something dark in the centre of the lake, and when she had stared for a few minutes it gradually became clearer, an arch of darkness against the starry background of the water. It might be a temple. She strolled slowly along the brim of the lake, trying to get a closer view of it, for the thing was no more than a darkness against the spangles of light, like some void in the sky where no stars shine. And presently she stumbled over something in the grass.

She looked down with startled yellow eyes, and saw a strange, indistinguishable darkness. It had solidity to the feel but scarcely to the eye, for she could not quite focus upon it. It was like trying to see something that did not exist save as a void, a darkness in the grass. It had the shape of a step, and when she followed with her eyes she saw that it was the beginning of a dim bridge stretching out over the lake, narrow and curved and made out of nothingness. It seemed to have no surface, and its edges were difficult to distinguish from the lesser gloom surrounding it. But the thing was tangible – an arch carved out of the solid dark – and it led out in the direction she wished to go. For she was naively sure now that the dim blot in the centre of the lake was the temple she was searching for. The falling stars had guided her, and she could not have gone astray.

So she set her teeth and gripped her sword and put her foot upon the bridge. It was rock-firm under her, but scarcely more than a foot or so wide, and without rails. When she had gone a step or two she began to feel dizzy; for under her the water heaved with a motion that made her head swim, and the stars twinkled eerily in its depths. She dared not look away for fear of missing her footing on the narrow arch of darkness. It was like walking a bridge flung across the void, with stars underfoot and nothing but an unstable strip of nothingness to bear her up. Half-way across, the heaving of the water and the illusion of vast, constellated spaces beneath and the look her bridge had of being no more than empty space ahead, combined to send her head reeling; and as she stumbled on, the bridge seemed to be wavering with her, swinging in gigantic arcs across the starry void below.

Now she could see the temple more closely, though scarcely more clearly than from the shore. It looked to be no more than an outlined emptiness against a star-crowded brilliance behind it, etching its arches and columns of blankness upon the twinkling waters. The bridge came down in a long dim swoop to its doorway. Jirel took the last few yards at a reckless run and stopped breathless under the arch that made the temple's vague doorway. She stood there panting and staring about narrow-eyed, sword poised in her hand. For though the place was empty and very still, she felt a presence even as she set her foot upon the floor of it.

She was staring about a little space of blankness in the starry lake. It seemed to be no more than that. She could see the walls and columns where they were outlined against the water and where they made darknesses in the star-flecked sky, but where there was only dark behind them she could see nothing. It was a tiny place, no more than a few square yards of emptiness upon the face of the twinkling waters. And in its centre an image stood.

She stared at it in silence, feeling a curious compulsion growing within her, like a vague command from something outside herself. The image was of some substance of nameless black, unlike the material which composed the building, for even in the dark she could see it clearly. It was a semi-human figure, crouching forward with outthrust head, sexless and strange. Its one central eye was closed as if in rapture, and its mouth was pursed for a kiss. And though it was but an image and without even the semblance of life, she felt unmistakably the presence of something alive in the temple, something so alien and innominate that instinctively she drew away.

She stood there for a full minute, reluctant to enter the place where so alien a being dwelt, half conscious of that voiceless compulsion growing up within her. And slowly she became aware that all the lines and angles of the half-seen building were curved to make the image their centre and focus. The very bridge swooped its long arc to complete the centring. As she watched, it seemed to her that through the arches of the columns even the stars in lake and sky were grouped in patterns which took the image for their focus. Every line and curve in the dim world seemed to sweep round towards the squatting thing before her with its closed eye and expectant mouth.

Gradually the universal focusing of lines began to exert its influence upon her. She took a hesitant step forward without realizing the motion. But that step was all the dormant urge within her needed. With her one motion forward the compulsion closed down upon her with whirlwind impetuosity. Helplessly she felt herself advancing, helplessly with one small, sane portion of her mind she realized the madness that was gripping her, the blind, irresistible urge to do what every visible line in the temple's construction was made to compel. With stars swirling around her she advanced across the floor and laid her hands upon the rounded shoulders of the image – the sword, forgotten, making a sort of accolade against its hunched neck – lifted her red head and laid her mouth blindly against the pursed lips of the image.

In a dream she took that kiss. In a dream of dizziness and confusion she seemed to feel the iron-cold lips stirring under hers. And through the union of that kiss – warmblooded woman with image of nameless stone – through the meeting of their mouths something entered into her very soul; something cold and stunning; something alien beyond any words. It lay upon her shuddering soul like some frigid weight from the void, a bubble holding something unthinkably alien and dreadful. She could feel the heaviness of it upon some intangible part of her that shrank from the touch. It was like the weight of remorse or despair, only far colder and stranger and – somehow – more ominous, as if this weight were but the egg from which things might hatch too dreadful to put even into thoughts.

The moment of the kiss could have been no longer than a breath's space, but to her it was timeless. In a dream she felt the compulsion falling from her at last. In a dim dream she dropped her hands from its shoulders, finding the sword heavy in her grasp and staring dully at it for a while before clarity began its return to her cloudy mind. When she became completely aware of herself once more she was standing with slack body and dragging head before the blind, rapturous image, that dead weight upon her heart as dreary as an old sorrow, and more coldly ominous than anything she could find words for.

And with returning clarity the most staggering terror came over her, swiftly and suddenly—terror of the image and the temple of darkness, and the coldly spangled lake and of the whole, wide, dim, dreadful world about her. Desperately she longed for home again, even the red fury of hatred and the press of Guillaume's mouth and the hot arrogance of his eyes again. Anything but this. She found herself running without knowing why. Her feet skimmed over the narrow bridge lightly as a gull's wings dipping the water. In a brief instant the starry void of the lake flashed by beneath her and the solid earth was underfoot. She saw the great column of light far away across the dark meadows and beyond it a hill-top rising against the stars. And she ran.

She ran with terror at her heels and devils howling in the wind her own speed made. She ran from her own curiously alien body, heavy with its weight of inexplicable doom. She passed through the hollow where pale things wavered away, she fled over the uneven meadows in a frenzy of terror. She ran and ran, in those long light bounds the lesser gravity allowed her, fleeter than a deer, and her own panic choked in her throat and that weight upon her soul dragged at her too drearily for tears. She fled to escape it, and could not; and the ominous certainty she carried something too dreadful to think of grew and grew.

For a long while she skimmed over the grass, tirelessly, wing-heeled, her red hair flying. The panic died after a while, but that sense of heavy disaster did not die. She felt somehow that tears would ease her, but something in the frigid darkness of her soul froze her tears in the ice of that grey and alien chill.

And gradually, through the inner dark, a fierce anticipation took form in her mind. Revenge upon Guillaume! She had taken from the temple only a kiss, so it was that which she must deliver to him. And savagely she exulted in the thought of what that kiss would release upon him, unsuspecting. She did not know, but it filled her with fierce joy to guess.

She had passed the column and skirted the morass where the white, blundering forms still bumped along awkwardly through the ooze, and was crossing the coarse grass towards the nearing hill when the sky began to pale along the horizon. And with that pallor a fresh terror took hold upon her, a wild horror of daylight in this unholy land. She was not sure if it was the light itself she so dreaded, or what that light would reveal in the dark stretches she had traversed so blindly – what unknown horrors she had skirted in the night. But she knew instinctively that if she valued her sanity she must be gone before the light had risen over the land. And she redoubled her efforts, spurring her wearying limbs to yet more skimming speed. But it would be a close race, for already the stars were blurring out, and a flush of curious green was broadening along the sky, and around her the air was turning to a vague, unpleasant grey.

She toiled up the steep hillside breathlessly. When she was half-way up, her own shadow began to take form upon the rocks, and it was unfamiliar and dreadfully significant of something just outside her range of understanding. She averted her eyes from it, afraid that at any moment the meaning might break upon her outraged brain.

She could see the top of the hill above her, dark against the paling sky, and she toiled up in frantic haste, clutching her sword and feeling that if she had to look in the full light upon the dreadful abominations that had snapped around her feet when she first emerged she would collapse into screaming hysteria.

The cave-mouth yawned before her, invitingly black, a refuge from the dawning light behind her. She knew an almost irresistible desire to turn and look back from this vantage-point across the land she had traversed, and gripped her sword hard to conquer the perversive longing. There was a scuffling in the rocks at her feet, and she set her teeth in her underlip and swung viciously in brief arcs, without looking down. She heard small squeakings and the splashy sound of feet upon the stones, and felt her blade shear thrice through semi-solidity, to the click of little vicious teeth. Then they broke and ran off over the hillside, and she stumbled on, choking back the scream that wanted so fiercely to break from her lips.

She fought that growing desire all the way up to the cave-mouth, for she knew that if she gave way she would never cease shrieking until her throat went raw.

Blood was trickling from her bitten lip with the effort at silence when she reached the cave And there, twinkling upon the stones, lay something small and bright and dearly familiar. With a sob of relief she bent and snatched up the crucifix she had torn from her throat when she came out into this land. And as her fingers shut upon it a vast, protecting darkness swooped around her. Gasping with relief, she groped her way the step or two that separated her from the cave.

Dark lay like a blanket over her eyes, and she welcomed it gladly, remembering how her shadow had lain so awfully upon the hillside as she climbed, remembering the first rays of savage sunlight beating upon her shoulders. She stumbled through the blackness, slowly getting control again over her shaking body and labouring lungs, slowly stilling the panic that the dawning day had roused so inexplicably within her. And as the terror died, the dull weight upon her spirit became strong again. She had all but forgotten it in her panic, but now the impending and unknown dreadfulness grew heavier and more oppressive in the darkness of the underground, and she groped along in a dull stupor of her own depression, slow with the weight of the strange doom she carried.

Nothing barred her way. In the dullness of her stupor she scarcely realized it, or expected any of the vague horrors that peopled the place to leap out upon her. Empty and unmenacing, the way stretched before her blindly stumbling feet. Only once did she hear the sound of another presence – the rasp of hoarse breathing and the scrape of a scaly hide against the stone – but it must have been outside the range of her own passage, for she encountered nothing.

When she had come to the end and a cold wall rose up before her, it was scarcely more than automatic habit that made her search along it with groping hand until she came to the mouth of the shaft. It sloped gently up into the dark. She crawled in, trailing her sword, until the rising incline and lowering roof forced her down upon her face. Then with toes and fingers she began to force herself up the spiral, slippery way.

Before she had gone very far she was advancing without effort, scarcely realizing that it was against gravity she moved. The curious dizziness of the shaft had come over her, the strange feeling of change in the very substance of her body, and through the cloudy numbness of it she felt herself sliding round and round the spirals, without effort. Again, obscurely, she had the feeling that in the peculiar angles of this shaft was neither up nor down. And for a long while the dizzy circling went on.

When the end came at last, and she felt her fingers gripping the edge of that upper opening which lay beneath the floor of Joiry's lowest dungeons, she heaved herself up warily and lay for a while on the cold floor in the dark, while slowly the clouds of dizziness passed from her mind, leaving only that ominous weight within. When the darkness had ceased to circle about her, and the floor steadied, she got up dully and swung the cover back over the opening, her hands shuddering from the feel of the cold, smooth ring which had never seen daylight.

When she turned from this task she was aware of the reason for the lessening in the gloom around her. A guttering light outlined the hole in the wall from which she had pulled the Stones – was it a century ago? The brilliance all but blinded her after her long sojourn through blackness, and she stood there awhile, swaying a little, one hand to her eyes, before she went out into the familiar torchlight she knew waited her beyond. Father Gervase, she was sure, anxiously waiting her return. But even he had not dared to follow her through the hole in the wall, down to the brink of the shaft.

Somehow she felt that she should be giddy with relief at this safe homecoming, back to humanity again. But as she stumbled over the upward slope toward light and safety she was conscious of no more than the dullness of whatever unreleased horror it was which still lay so ominously upon her stunned soul.

She came through the gaping hole in the masonry into the full glare of torches awaiting her, remembering with a wry inward smile how wide she had made the opening in anticipation of flight from something dreadful when she came back that way. Well, there was no flight from the horror she bore within her. It seemed to her that her heart was slowing, too, missing a beat now and then and staggering like a weary runner.

She came out into the torchlight, stumbling with exhaustion, her mouth scarlet from the blood of her bitten lip and her bare greaved legs and bare sword-blade foul with the deaths of those little horrors that swarmed around the cave-mouth. From the tangle of red hair her eyes stared out with a bleak, frozen inward look, as of one who had seen nameless things. That keen, steel-bright beauty which had been hers was as dull and fouled as her sword-blade, and at the look in her eyes Father Gervase shuddered and crossed himself.

5

They were waiting for her in an uneasy group – the priest anxious and dark, Guillaume splendid in the torchlight, tall and arrogant, a handful of men-at-arms holding the guttering lights and shifting uneasily from one foot to the other. When she saw Guillaume the light that flared up in her eyes blotted out for a moment the bleak dreadfulness behind them, and her slowing heart leaped like a spurred horse, sending the blood riotously through her veins. Guillaume, magnificent in his armour, leaning upon his sword and staring down at her from his scornful height, the little black beard jutting. Guillaume, to whom Joiry had fallen. Guillaume.

That which she carried at the core of her being was heavier than anything else in the world, so heavy she could scarcely keep her knees from bending, so heavy her heart laboured under its weight. Almost irresistibly she wanted to give way beneath it, to sink down and down under the crushing load, to lie prone and vanquished in the ice-grey, bleak place she was so dimly aware of through the clouds that were rising about her. But there was Guillaume, grim and grinning, and she hated him so very bitterly – she must make the effort. She must, at whatever cost, for she was coming to know that death lay in wait for her if she bore this burden long, that it was a two-edged weapon which could strike at its wielder if the blow were delayed too long. She knew this through the dim mists that were thickening in her brain, and she put all her strength into the immense effort it cost to cross the floor toward him. She stumbled a little, and made one faltering step and then another, and dropped her sword with a clang as she lifted her arms to him.

He caught her strongly, in a hard, warm clasp, and she heard his laugh triumphant and hateful as he bent his head to take the kiss she was raising her mouth to offer. He must have seen, in that last moment before their lips met, the savage glare of victory in her eyes, and been startled. But he did not hesitate. His mouth was heavy upon hers.

It was a long kiss. She felt him stiffen in her arms. She felt a coldness in the lips upon hers, and slowly the dark weight of what she bore lightened, lifted, cleared away from her cloudy mind. Strength flowed back through her richly. The whole world came alive to her once more. Presently she loosed his slack arms and stepped away, looking up into his face with a keen and dreadful triumph upon her own.

She saw the ruddiness of him draining away, and the rigidity of stone coming over his scarred features. Only his eyes remained alive, and there was torment in them, and understanding. She was glad – she had wanted him to understand what it cost to take Joiry's kiss unbidden. She smiled thinly into his tortured eyes, watching. And she saw something cold and alien seeping through him, permeating him slowly with some unnamable emotion which no man could ever have experienced before. She could not name it, but she saw it in his eyes – some dreadful emotion never made for flesh and blood to know, some iron despair such as only an unguessable being from the grey, formless void could have felt before – too hideously alien for any human creature to endure. Even she shuddered from the dreadful, cold bleakness looking out of his eyes, and knew as she watched that there must be many emotions and many fears and joys too far outside man's comprehension for any being of flesh to undergo, and live. Greyly she saw it spreading through him, and the very substance of his body shuddered under that iron weight.

And now came a visible, physical change. Watching, she was aghast to think that in her own body and upon her own soul she had borne the seed of this dreadful flowering, and did not wonder that her heart had slowed under the unbearable weight of it. He was standing rigidly with arms half bent, just as he stood when she slid from his embrace. And now great shudders began to go over him, as if he were wavering in the torchlight, some grey-faced wraith in armour with torment in his eyes. She saw the sweat beading his forehead. She saw a trickle of blood from his mouth, as if he had bitten through his lip in the agony of this new, incomprehensible emotion. Then a last shiver went over him violently, and he flung up his head, the little curling beard jutting ceilingward and the muscles of his strong throat corded, and from his lips broke a long, low cry of such utter, inhuman strangeness that Jirel felt coldness rippling through her veins and she put up her hands to her ears to shut it out. It meant something – it expressed some dreadful emotion that was neither sorrow nor despair nor anger, but infinitely alien and infinitely sad. Then his long legs buckled at the knees and he dropped with a clatter of mail and lay still on the stone floor.

They knew he was dead. That was unmistakable in the way he lay. Jirel stood very still, looking down upon him, and strangely it seemed to her that all the lights in the world had gone out. A moment before he had been so big and vital, so magnificent in the torchlight – she could still feel his kiss upon her mouth, and the hard warmth of his arms …

Suddenly and blindingly it came upon her what she had done. She knew now why such heady violence had flooded her whenever she thought of him – knew why the light-devil in her form had laughed so derisively – knew the price she must pay for taking a gift from a demon. She knew that there was no light anywhere in the world, now that Guillaume was gone.

Father Gervase took her arm gently. She shook him off with an impatient shrug and dropped to one knee beside Guillaume's body, bending her head so that the red hair fell forward to hide her tears.

BLACK GOD'S SHADOW

Through Jirel's dreams a faraway voice went wailing. She opened yellow eyes upon darkness and lay still for a while, wondering what had waked her and staring into the gloom of her tower chamber, listening to the familiar night sounds of the sentry on the battlements close overhead, the rattle of armour and the soft shuffle of feet in the straw laid down to muffle the sound so that Joiry's lady might sleep in peace.

And as she lay there in the dark, quite suddenly the old illusion came over her again. She felt the pressure of strong mailed arms and the weight of a bearded mouth insolently upon hers, and she closed her red lips on an oath at her own weakness and knew again the sting of helpless tears behind her eyelids.

She lay quiet, remembering. Guillaume – so hatefully magnificent in his armour, grinning down upon her from her own dais in her own castle hall where her own dead soldiers lay scattered about upon the bloody flags. Guillaume, his arms hard about her, his mouth heavy upon her own. Even now anger swept like a flame across her memory in answer to the arrogance and scorn of that conqueror's kiss. Yet was it anger? – was it hatred? And how had she to know, until he lay dead at last at her vengeful feet, that it was not hate which bubbled up so hotly whenever she remembered the insolence of his arms, or that he had defeated her men and conquered unconquerable Joiry? For she had been the commander of the strongest fortress in the kingdom and called no man master, and it was her proudest boast that Joiry would never fall, and that no lover dared lay hands upon her save in answer to her smile.

No, it had not been hatred which answered Guillaume's overwhelming arrogance. Not hate, though the fire and fury of it had gone storming like madness through her. So many loves had blown lightly through her life before – how was she to know this surge of heady violence for what it was, until too late? Well, it was ended now.

She had gone down the secret way that she and one other knew, down into that dark and nameless hell which none who wore a cross might enter, where God's dominion ended at the portals, and who could tell what strange and terrible gods held sway instead? She remembered the starry darkness of it, and the voices that cried along the wind, and the brooding perils she could not understand. No other thing than the flame of her – hatred? – could have driven her down and nothing but its violence could have sustained her along the dark ways she went seeking a weapon worthy to slay Guillaume.

Well, she had found it. She had taken the black god's kiss. Heavy and cold upon her soul she had carried it back, feeling the terrible weight bearing down upon some intangible part of her that shuddered and shrank from the touch. She had fouled her very soul with that burden, but she had not guessed what terrible potentialities it bore within her, like some egg of hell's spawning to slay the man she loved.

Her weapon was a worthy one. She smiled grimly, triumphantly he had accepted that kiss from hell, not understanding ... Again she saw the awful fruition of her vengeance, as the chill of her soul's burden shifted, through the meeting of their mouths, from her soul to his. Again she saw the spreading of that nameless emotion from Beyond through his shuddering body, an iron despair which no flesh and blood could endure.

Yes, a worthy weapon. She had perilled her soul in the seeking of it, and slain him with a god-cursed kiss, and known too late that she would never love another man. Guillaume – tall and splendid in his armour, the little black beard split by the whiteness of his grin, and arrogance sneering from his scarred and scornful face. Guillaume – whose kiss would haunt her all the nights of her life. Guillaume – who was dead. In the dark she hid her face upon her bent arm, and the red hair fell forward to smother her sobs.

When sleep came again she did not know. But presently she was alone in a dim, formless place through whose mists the faraway voice wailed fretfully. It was a familiar voice with strange, plaintive overtones – a sad little lost voice wailing through the dark.

'Oh, Jirel,' it moaned reedily, the tiniest thread of sound. 'Oh, Jirel – my murderess....'

And in the dream her heart stood still, and – though she had killed more men than one – she thought she knew that voice, tiny and thin though it was in the bodiless dark of her sleep. And she held her breath, listening. It came again, 'Oh, Jirel! It is Guillaume calling – Guillaume, whom you slew. Is there no end to your vengeance? Have mercy, oh my murderess! Release my soul from the dark god's torment, Oh Jirel – Jirel – I pray your mercy!'

Jirel awoke wet-eyed and lay there staring into the dark, recalling that pitiful little reedy wail which had once been Guillaume's rich, full-throated voice. And wondering. The dark god? True, Guillaume had died unshriven, with all his sins upon him, and because of this she had supposed that his soul plunged straight downward to the gates of hell.

Yet – could it be? By the power of that infernal kiss which she had braved the strange dark place underground to get as a weapon against him – by the utter strangeness of it, and the unhuman death he died, it must be that now his naked soul wandered, lost and lonely, through that nameless hell lit by strange stars, where ghosts moved in curious forms through the dark. And he asked her mercy – Guillaume, who in life had asked mercy of no living creature.

She heard the watch changing on the battlements above, and dropped again into an uneasy slumber, and once more entered the dim place where the little voice cried through the mist, wailing piteously for mercy from her vengeance. Guillaume – the proud Guillaume, with his deep voice and scornful eyes. Guillaume's lost soul wailing through her dreams … 'Have mercy upon me, oh my murderess!' … and again she woke with wet eyes and started up, staring wildly around her in the gloom and thinking that surely she heard yet the echo of the little lost voice crying. And as the sound faded from her ears she knew that she must go down again.

For a while she lay there, shivering a little and forcing herself into the knowledge. Jirel was a brave woman and a savage warrior, and the most reckless soldier of all her men-at-arms. There was not a man for miles about who did not fear and respect Joiry's commander – her sword-keen beauty and reckless courage and her skill at arms. But at the thought of what she must do to save Guillaume's soul the coldness of terror blew over her and her heart contracted forebodingly. To go down again – down into the perilous, star-lit dark among dangers more dreadful than she could put words to – dared she? Dared she go?

She rose at last, cursing her own weakness. The stars through the narrow windows watched her pull on her doeskin shirt and the brief tunic of linked mail over it. She buckled the greaves of a long-dead Roman legionary on her slim, strong legs, and, as on that unforgettable night not long since when she had dressed for this same journey, she took her two-edged sword unsheathed in her hand.

Again she went down through the dark of the sleeping castle. Joiry's dungeons are deep, and she descended a long way through the oozing, dank corridors underground, past cells where the bones of Joiry's enemies rotted in forgotten chains. And she, who feared no living man, was frightened in that haunted dark, and gripped her sword closer and clutched the cross at her neck with nervous fingers. The silence hurt her ears with its weight, and the dark was like a bandage over her straining eyes.

At the end of the last oozing passage, far underground, she came to a wall. With her free hand she set to work pulling the unmortared stones from their places, making an opening to squeeze through – trying not to remember that upon this spot that dreadful night tall Guillaume had died, with the black god's kiss burning upon his mouth and unnamable torment in his eyes. Here upon these stones. Against the darkness vividly she could see that torch-lit scene, and Guillaume's long, mailed body sprawled across the floor. She would never forget that. Perhaps even after she died she would remember the smoky, acrid smell of the torches, and the coldness of the stones under her bare knees as she knelt beside the body of the man she had killed; the choke in her throat, and the brush of the red hair against her cheek, falling forward to mask her tears from the stolid men-at-arms. And Guillaume – Guillaume ...

She took her lip between her teeth resolutely, and turned her mind to the pulling out of stones. Presently there was a hole big enough for her slim height, and she pushed through into the solid dark beyond. Her feet were upon a ramp, and she went down cautiously, feeling her way with exploring toes. When the floor levelled she dropped to her knees and felt for the remembered circle in the pavement. She found that, and the curious cold ring in its centre, of some nameless metal which daylight had never shone upon, metal so smooth and cold and strange that her fingers shuddered as she gripped it and heaved. That lid was heavy. As before, she had to take her sword in her teeth, for she dared not lay it down, and use both hands to lift the stone circle. It rose with an odd little sighing sound, as if some suction from below had gripped it and were released.

She sat on the edge for a moment, swinging her feet in the opening and gathering all her courage for the plunge. When she dared hesitate no longer, for fear she would never descend if she delayed another instant, she caught her breath and gripped her sword hard and plunged.

It must have been the strangest descent that the world has known – not a shaft but a spiral twisting down in smooth, corkscrew loops, a spiral made for no human creature to travel, yet into whose sides in some forgotten era a nameless human had cut notches for hands and feet, so that Jirel went down more slowly than if she had had to take an unbroken plunge. She slipped smoothly along down the spirals, barely braking her passage now and again by grasping at the notches in the wall when she felt herself sliding too fast.

Presently the familiar sickness came over her – that strange, inner dizziness as if the spiral were taking her not only through space but through dimensions, and the very structure of her body was altering and shifting with the shifting spirals. And it seemed, too, that down any other shaft she would have fallen more swiftly. This was not a free glide downward – she scarcely seemed to be falling at all. In the spiral there was neither up nor down, and the sickness intensified until in the whirling loops and the whirling dizziness she lost all count of time and distance, and slid through the dark in a stupor of her own misery.

At long last the spiral straightened and began to incline less steeply, and she knew that she approached the end. It was hard work then, levering herself along the gentle slope on hands and knees, and when she came out at last into open darkness she scrambled to her feet and stood panting, sword in hand, straining her eyes against the impenetrable dark of this place that must be without counterpart anywhere in the world, or outside it. There were perils here, but she scarcely thought of them as she set out through the dark, for remembering those greater perils beyond.

She went forward warily for all that, swinging her sword in cautious arcs before her that she might not run full-tilt into some invisible horror. It was an unpleasant feeling, this groping through blackness, knowing eyes upon her, fettling presences near her, watching. Twice she heard hoarse breathing, and once the splat of great wet feet upon stone, but nothing touched her or tried to bar her passage.

Nevertheless she was shaking with tension and terror when at last she reached the end of the passage. There was no visible sign to tell her that it was ended, but as before, suddenly she sensed the oppression of those vast weights of earth on all sides had lifted. She was standing at the threshold of some mighty void. The very darkness had a different quality – and at her throat something constricted.

Jirel gripped her sword a little more firmly and felt for the crucifix at her neck – found it – lifted the chain over her head.

Instantly a burst of blinding radiance smote her dark-accustomed eyes more violently than a blow. She stood at a cave mouth, high on the side of a hill, staring out over the most blazing day she had ever seen. Heat and light shimmered in the dazzle: strangely coloured light, heat that danced and shook. Day, over a dreadful land.

Jirel cried out inarticulately and clapped a hand over her outraged eyes, groping backward step by step into the sheltering dark of the cave. Night in this land was terrible enough, but day – no, she dared not look upon the strange hell save when the darkness veiled it. She remembered that other journey, when she had raced the dawn up the hillside, shuddering, averting her eyes from the terror of her own misshapen shadow forming upon the stones. No, she must wait, how long she could not guess; for though it had been night above ground when she left, here was broad day, and it might be that day in this land was of a different duration from that she knew.

She drew back farther into the cave, until that dreadful day was no more than a blur upon the darkness, and sat down with her back to the rock and the sword across her bare knees, waiting. That blurred light upon the walls had a curious tinge of colour such as she had never seen in any earthly daylight. It seemed to her that it shimmered – paled and deepened and brightened again as if the illumination were not steady. It had almost the quality of firelight in its fluctuations.

Several times something seemed to pass across the cave-mouth, blotting out the light for an instant, and once she saw a great, stooping shadow limned upon the wall, as if something had paused to peer within the cave.

And at the thought of what might rove this land by day Jirel shivered as if in a chill wind, and groped for her crucifix before she remembered that she no longer wore it.

She waited for a long while, clasping cold hands about her knees, watching that blur upon the wall in fascinated anticipation. After a time she may have dozed a little, with the light, unresting sleep of one poised to wake at the tiniest sound or motion. It seemed to her that eternities went by before the light began to pale upon the cave wall.

She watched it fading. It did not move across the wall as sunlight would have done. The blur remained motionless, dimming slowly, losing its tinge of unearthly colour, taking on the blueness of evening. Jirel stood up and paced back and forth to limber her stiffened body. But not until that blur had faded so far that no more than the dimmest glimmer of radiance lay upon the stone did she venture out again towards the cave mouth.

Once more she stood upon the hilltop, looking out over a land lighted by strange constellations that sprawled across the sky in pictures whose outlines she could not quite trace, though there was about them a dreadful familiarity. And, looking up upon the spreading patterns in the sky, she realized afresh that this land, whatever it might be, was no underground cavern of whatever vast dimensions. It was open air she breathed, and stars in a celestial void she gazed upon, and however she had come here, she was no longer under the earth.

Below her the dim country spread. And it was not the same landscape she had seen on that other journey. No mighty column of shadowless light swept skyward in the distance. She caught the glimmer of a broad river where no river had flowed before, and the ground here and there was patched and checkered with pale radiance, like luminous fields laid out orderly upon the darkness.

She stepped down the hill delicately, poised for the attack of those tiny, yelping horrors that had raved about her knees once before. They did not come. Surprised, hoping against hope that she was to be spared that nauseating struggle, she went on. The way down was longer than she remembered. Stones turned under her feet, and coarse grass slashed at her knees. She was wondering as she descended where her search was to begin, for in all the dark, shifting land she saw nothing to guide her, and Guillaume's voice was no more than a fading memory from her dream. She could not even find her way back to the lake where the black god crouched, for the whole landscape was changed unrecognizably.

So when, unmolested, she reached the foot of the hill, she set off at random over the dark earth, running as before with that queer dancing lightness, as if the gravity pull of this place were less than that to which she was accustomed, so that the ground seemed to skim past under her flying feet. It was like a dream, this effortless glide through the darkness, fleet as the wind.

Presently she began to near one of those luminous patches that resembled fields, and saw now that they were indeed a sort of garden. The luminosity rose from myriads of tiny, darting lights planted in even rows, and when she came near enough she saw that the lights were small insects, larger than fireflies, and with luminous wings which they beat vainly upon the air, darting from side to side in a futile effort to be free. For each was attached to its little stem as if they had sprung living from the soil. Row upon row of them stretched into the dark.

She did not even speculate upon who had sown such seed here, or toward what strange purpose. Her course led her across a corner of the field, and as she ran she broke several of the stems, releasing the shining prisoners. They buzzed up around her instantly, angrily as bees, and wherever a luminous wing brushed her a hot pain stabbed. She beat them off after a while and ran on, skirting other fields and new wariness.

She crossed a brook that spoke to itself in the dark with a queer, whispering sound so near to speech that she paused for an instant to listen, then thought she had caught a word or two of such dreadful meaning that she ran on again, wondering if it could have been only an illusion.

Then a breeze sprang up and brushed the red hair from her ears, and it seemed to her that she caught the faintest, far wailing. She stopped deadstill, listening, and the breeze stopped too. But she was almost certain she had heard that voice again, and after an instant's hesitation she turned in the direction from which the breeze had blown.

It led towards the river. The ground grew rougher, and she began to hear water running with a subdued, rushing noise, and presently again the breeze brushed her face. Once more she thought she could hear the dimmest echo of the voice that had cried in her dreams.

When she came to the brink of the water she paused for a moment, looking down to where the river rushed between steep banks. The water had a subtle difference in appearance from water in the rivers she knew – somehow thicker, for all its swift flowing. When she leaned out to look, her face was mirrored monstrously upon the broken surface, in a way that no earthly water would reflect, and as the image fell upon its torrent the water broke there violently, leaping upward and slashing as if some hidden rock had suddenly risen in its bed. There was a hideous eagerness about it, as if the water were ravening for her, rising in long, hungry leaps against the rocky walls to splash noisily and run back into the river. But each leap came higher against the wall, and Jirel started back in something like alarm, a vague unease rising within her at the thought of what might happen if she waited until the striving water reached high enough.

At her withdrawal the tumult lessened instantly, and after a moment or so she knew by the sound that the river had smoothed over its broken place and was flowing on undisturbed. Shivering a little, she went on upstream whence the fitful breeze seemed to blow.

Once she stumbled into a patch of utter darkness and fought through in panic fear of walking into the river in her blindness, but she won free of the curious air-pocket without mishap. And once the ground under her skimming feet quaked like jelly, so that she could scarcely keep her balance as she fled on over the unstable section. But ever the little breeze blew and died away and blew again, and she thought the faint echo of a cry was becoming clearer. Almost she caught the far-away sound of 'Jirel—' moaning upon the wind, and quickened her pace.

For some while now she had been noticing a growing pallor upon the horizon, and wondering uneasily if night could be so short here, and day already about to dawn. But no – for she remembered that upon that other terrible dawn which she had fled so fast to escape, the pallor had ringed the whole horizon equally as if day rose in one vast circle on the edge of the sky which showed that unpleasant, dawning light. It was faintly tinged with green that strengthened as she watched, and presently above the hills in the distance rose the rim of a vast green moon. The stars paled around it. A cloud floated across its face, writhed for an instant as if in some skyey agony then puffed into a mist and vanished, leaving the green face clear again.

And it was a mottled face across which dim things moved very slowly. Almost it might have had an atmosphere of its own, and dark clouds floating sluggishly; and if that were so it must have been self-luminous, for these slow masses dimmed its surface and it cast little light despite its hugeness. But there was light enough so that in the land through which Jirel ran great shadows took shape upon the ground, writhing and shifting as the moon-clouds obscured and revealed the green surface, and the whole night scene was more baffling and unreal than a dream. And there was something about the green luminance that made her eyes ache.

She waded through shadows as she ran now, monstrous shadows with a hideous dissimilarity to the thing that cast them, and, no two alike, however identical the bodies which gave them shape. Her own shadow, keeping pace with her along the ground, she did not look at after one shuddering glance. There was something so unnatural about it, and yet – yet it was like her, too, with a dreadful likeness she could not fathom. And more than once she saw great shadows drifting across the ground without any visible thing to cast them – nothing but the queerly shaped blurs moving soundlessly past her and melting into the farther dark. And that was the worst of all.

She ran on upwind, ears straining for a repetition of the far crying, skirting the shadows as well as she could and shuddering whenever a great dark blot drifted noiselessly across her path. The moon rose slowly up the sky, tinting the night with a livid greenness, bringing it dreadfully to life with moving shadows. Sometimes the sluggishly moving darknesses across its face clotted together and obscured the whole great disc, and she ran on a few steps thankfully through the unlighted dark before the moon-clouds parted again and the dead green face looked blankly down once more, the cloud-masses crawling across it like corruption across a corpse's face.

During one of these darknesses something slashed viciously at her leg, and she heard the grate of teeth on the greave she wore. When the moon unveiled again she saw a long bright scar along the metal, and a drip of phosphorescent venom trickling down. She gathered a handful of grass to wipe it off before it reached her unprotected foot, and the grass withered in her hand when the poison touched it.

All this while the river had been rushing past her and away, and as she ran it began to narrow and diminish; so she knew she must be approaching its head. When the wind blew she was sure now that she heard her own name upon it, in the small wail which had once been Guillaume's scornful voice. Then the ground began to rise, and down the hillside she mounted, the river fell tinkling, and a little thread of water: no larger than a brook.

The tinkling was all but articulate now. The river's rush had been no more than a roaring threat, but the voice of the brook was deliberately clear, a series of small, bright notes like syllables, saying evil things. She tried not to listen, for fear of understanding.

The hill rose steeper, and the brook's voice sharpened and clarified and sang delicately in its silvery poisonous tones, and above her against the stars she presently began to discern something looming on the very height of the hill, something like a hulking figure motionless as the hill it crowned. She gripped her sword and slackened her pace a little, skirting the dark thing warily. But when she came near enough to make it out in the green moonlight she saw that it was no more than an image crouching there, black as darkness, giving back a dull gleam from its surface where the lividness of the moon struck it. Its shadow moved uneasily upon the ground.

The guiding wind had fallen utterly still now. She stood in a breathless silence before the image, and the stars sprawled their queer patterns across the sky and the sullen moonlight poured down upon her and nothing moved anywhere but those quivering shadows that were never still.

The image had the shape of a black, shambling thing with shallow head sunk between its shoulders and great arms dragging forward on the ground. But something about it, something indefinable and obscene, reminded her of Guillaume. Some aptness of line and angle parodied in the ugly hulk the long, clear lines of Guillaume, the poise of his high head, the scornful tilt of his chin. She could not put a finger on any definite likeness, but it was unmistakably there. And it was all the ugliness of Guillaume – she saw it as she stared. All his cruelty and arrogance and brutish force. The image might have been a picture of Guillaume's sins, with just enough of his virtues left in to point its dreadfulness.

For an instant she thought she could see behind the black parody, rising from it and irrevocably part of it, a nebulous outline of the Guillaume she had never known, the scornful face twisted in despair, the splendid body writhing futilely away from that obscene thing which was himself – Guillaume's soul, rooted in the ugliness which the image personified. And she knew his punishment – so just, yet so infinitely unjust.

And what subtle torment the black god's kiss had wrought upon him! To dwell in the full, frightful realization of his own sins, chained to the actual manifestation, suffering eternally in the obscene shape that was so undeniably himself – his worst and lowest self. It was just, in a way. He had been a harsh and cruel man in life. But the very fact that such punishment was agony to him proved a higher self within his complex soul – something noble and fine which writhed away from the unspeakable thing – himself. So the very fineness of him was a weapon to torture his soul, turned against him even as his sins were turned.

She understood all this in the timeless moment while she stood there with eyes fixed motionless upon the hulking shape of the image, wringing from it the knowledge of what its ugliness meant And something in her throat swelled and swelled, and behind her eyelids burnt the sting of tears. Fiercely she fought back the weakness, desperately cast about for some way in which she might undo what she had unwittingly inflicted upon him.

And then all about her something intangible and grim began to form. Some iron presence that manifested itself only by the dark power she felt pressing upon her, stronger and stronger. Something coldly inimical to all things human. The black god's presence. The black god, come to defend his victim against one who was so alien to all his darkness – one who wept and trembled, and was warm with love and sorrow and desperate with despair.

She felt the inexorable force tightening around her, freezing her tears, turning the warmth and tenderness of her into grey ice, rooting her into a frigid immobility. The air dimmed about her, grey with cold, still with the utter deadness of the black god's unhuman presence. She had a glimpse of the dark place into which he was drawing her – a moveless, twilight place, deathlessly still. And an immense weight was pressing her down. The ice formed upon her soul, and the awful, iron despair which has no place among human emotions crept slowly through the fibres of her innermost self.

She felt herself turning into something cold and dark and rigid – a black image of herself – a black, hulking image to prison the spark of consciousness that still burned.

Then, as from a long way off in another time and world, came the memory of Guillaume's arms about her and the scornful press of his mouth over hers. It had not happened to her. It had happened to someone else, someone human and alive, in a faraway place. But the memory of it shot like fire through the rigidness of the body she had almost forgotten was hers, so cold and still it was – the memory of that curious, raging fever which was both hate and love. It broke the ice that bound her, for a moment only, and in that moment she fell to her knees at the dark statue's feet and burst into shuddering sobs, and the hot tears flowing were like fire to thaw her soul.

Slowly that thawing took place. Slowly the ice melted and the rigidity gave way, and the awful weight of the despair which was no human emotion lifted by degrees. The tears ran hotly between her fingers. But all about her she could feel, as tangibly as a touch, the imminence of the black god, waiting. And she knew her humanity, her weakness and transcience, and the eternal, passionless waiting she could never hope to outlast. Her tears must run dry – and then—

She sobbed on, knowing herself in hopeless conflict with the vastness of death and oblivion, a tiny spark of warmth and life fighting vainly against the dark engulfing it; the perishable spark, struggling against inevitable extinction. For the black god was all death and nothingness, and the powers he drew upon were without limit – and all she had to fight him with was the flicker within her called life.

But suddenly in the depths of her despair she felt something stirring. A long, confused blurring passed over her, and another, and another, and the strangest emotions tumbled through her mind and vanished. Laughter and mirth, sorrow and tears and despair, love, envy, hate. She felt somehow a lessening in the oppressive peril about her, and she lifted her face from her hands.

Around the dark image a mist was swirling. It was tenuous and real by turns, but gradually she began to make out a ring of figures – girl's figures, more unreal than a vision – dancing girls who circled the crouching statue with flying feet and tossing hair – girls who turned to Jirel her own face in as many moods as there were girls. Jirel laughing, Jirel weeping, Jirel convulsed with fury, Jirel honey-sweet with love. Faster they swirled, a riot of flashing limbs, a chaos of tears and mirth and all humanity's moods. The air danced with them in shimmering waves, so that the land was blurred behind them and the image seemed to shiver within itself.

And she felt those waves of warmth and humanity beating insistently against the hovering chill which was the black god's presence. Life and warmth, fighting back the dark nothingness she had thought unconquerable. She felt it wavering about her as a canopy wavers in the wind. And slowly she felt it melting. Very gradually it lifted and dissipated, while the wild figures of gaiety and grief and all kindred emotions whirled about the image and the beat of their aliveness pulsed through in the air in heatwaves against the greyness of the god's cold.

And something in Jirel knew warmly that the image of life as a tiny spark flickering out in limitless black was a false one – that without light there can be no darkness – that death and life are interdependent, one upon the other. And that she, armoured in the warmth of her aliveness, was the black god's equal, and a worthy foe. It was an even struggle. She called up the forces of life within her, feeling them hurled against the darkness, beating strongly upon the cold and silence of oblivion. Strength flowed through her, and she knew herself immortal in the power of life.

How long this went on she never knew. But she felt victory pulsing like wine through her veins even before the cold pall lifted, And it lifted quite suddenly. In a breath, without warning, the black god's presence was not. In that breath the swirling dancers vanished, and the night was empty about her, and the singing of triumph ran warmly through her body.

But the image – the image! The queerest change was coming over it. The black, obscene outlines were unstable as mist. They quavered and shook, and ran together and somehow melted … The green moon veiled its face again with clouds, and when the light returned the image was no more than a black shadow running fluidly upon the ground; a shadow which bore the outlines of Guillaume – or what might have been Guillaume …

The moon-shadows moved across the livid disc, and the shadow on the ground moved too, a monstrous shadow latent with a terrible implication of the horrors dormant within the being which cast the shadow, dreadful things that Guillaume might have been and done. She knew then why the misshapen shadows were so monstrous. They were a dim, leering hinting at what might have been – what might yet be – frightful suggestions of the dreadfulnesses dormant within every living being. And the insane suggestions they made were the more terrible because, impossible beyond nightmares though they seemed, yet the mind intuitively recognized their truth …

A little breeze sprang up fitfully, and the shadow moved, slipping over the stones without a sound. She found herself staggering after it on legs that shook, for the effort of that battle with the god had drained her of all strength. But the shadow was gliding faster now, and she dared not lose it. It floated on without a sound, now fast, now slow, its monstrous outline shifting continually into patterns each more terribly significant than the last. She stumbled after it, the sword a dead weight in her hand, her head hanging.

In five minutes she had lost all sense of direction. Beyond the hilltop the river ceased. The moving moonlight confused her and the stars traced queer pictures across the sky, from which she could get no bearings. The moon was overhead by now, and in those intervals when its clouds obscured the surface and the night was black around her, Guillaume's misshapen shadow vanished with the rest, and she suffered agonies of apprehension before the light came out again and she took up the chase anew.

The dark blot moving now over a rolling meadowland dotted with queerly shaped trees. The grass over which she ran was velvet-soft, and she caught whiffs of perfume now and again from some tree that billowed with pale bloom in the moonlight. The shadow wavering ahead of her moved forward to pass one tall tree a little apart from the rest, its branches hanging in long, shaking streamers from its central crown. She saw the dark shape upon the ground pause as it neared the tree, and shiver a little, and then melt imperceptibly into the shadow cast by its branches. The tree-shadow, until Guillaume's touched it, had borne the shape of a monster with crawling tentacles and flattened, thrusting head, but at the moment of conjunction the two melted into one – all the tentacles leaped forward to embrace the newcomer, and the two merged into an unnamably evil thing that lay upon the ground and heaved with a frightful aliveness of its own.

Jirel paused at its edge, looking down helplessly. She disliked to set her foot even upon the edge of that hideous black shape, though she knew intuitively that it could not harm her. The joined shadows were alive with menace and evil, but only to things in their own plane. She hesitated under the tree, wondering vainly how to part her lover's shade from the thing that gripped it. She felt somehow that his shadow had not joined the other altogether willingly. It was rather as if the evil instinct in the tree-shape had reached out to the evil in Guillaume, and by that evil held him, though the fineness that was still his revolted to the touch.

Then something brushed her shoulder gently and lapped around her arm, and she leaped backward in a panic, too late. The tree's swinging branches had writhed round towards her, and one already was wrapped about her body. That shadow upon the ground had been clear warning of the danger dormant within the growth, had she only realized it before – a tentacled monster, lying in wait. Up swung her sword in a flash of green-tinged moonlight, and she felt the gripping branch yield like rubber under the blow. It gave amazingly and sprang back again, jerking her almost off her feet. She turned the blade against it, hewing desperately as she saw other branches curling around towards her. One had almost come within reach of her sword-arm, and was poising for the attack, when she felt her blade bite into the rubbery surface at last. Then with a root-deep shudder through all its members the tree loosed its hold and the severed limb fell writhing to the ground. Thick black sap dripped from the wound. And all the branches hung motionless, but upon the ground the shadow flung wildly agonized tentacles wide, and from the released grip Guillaume's shadow sprang free and glided away over the grass. Shaking with reaction, Jirel followed.

She gave more attention to the trees they passed now. There was one little shrub whose leaves blew constantly in shivering ripples, even when there was no wind, and its shadow was the shadow of a small leaping thing that hurled itself time and again against some invisible barrier and fell back, only to leap once more in panic terror. And one slim, leafless tree writhed against the stars with a slow, unceasing motion. It made ho sound, but its branches twisted together and shuddered and strained in an agony more eloquent than speech. It seemed to wring its limbs together, agonized, dumb, with a slow anguish that never abated. And its shadow, dimly, was the shadow of a writhing, woman.

And one tree, a miracle of bloom in the moonlight swayed its ruffled branches seductively, sending out wave upon wave of intoxicating perfume and making a low, delightful humming, somehow like the melody of bees. Its shadow upon the ground was the shadow of a coiled serpent, lifting to strike.

Jirel was glad when they left the region of the trees and curved to the left down a long hill slope across which other shadows, without form, blew unceasingly with nothing to cast them. They raced noiselessly by, like wind-driven clouds. Among them she lost and found and lost again the shape she followed, until she grew dizzy from trying to keep her footing upon a ground that quavered with the blowing shadows so that she never knew upon what her feet were stepping, and the dim thing she followed was a nothingness that threaded its way in and out of the cloud-shapes bafflingly.

She had the idea now that the shadow of her lover was heading towards some definite goal. There was purpose in its dim gliding, and she looked ahead for some sign of the place it aimed towards. Below the hill the land stretched away featurelessly, cloud-mottled in the livid moonlight. Drifts of mist obscured it, and there were formless dark patches and pale blotches upon the night, and here and there a brook crawled across the blackness. She was completely lost now, for the river had long since vanished and she saw no hill which might have been the one upon which she had emerged.

They crossed another belt of quaking land, and the shadow gained upon her as she staggered over the jelly-like surface. They came to a pale brook across which the shadow glided without a pause. It was a narrow, swift brook whose water chuckled thickly to itself in the dark. One stepping-stone broke the surface in the centre of the stream, and she held her breath and leaped for it, not daring to slacken her pace. The stone gave under her foot like living flesh, and she though she heard a groan, but she had gained the farther bank and did not pause to listen.

Then they were hurrying down another slope, the shadow gliding faster now, and more purposefully. And the slope went down and down, steeply, until it became the side of a ravine and the rocks began to roll under her stumbling feet. She saw the fleeting shadow slip over a ledge and down a steep bank and then plunge into the darkness which lay like water along the bottom of the gully, and she gave a little sob of despair, for she knew now that she had lost it. But she struggled on into the dark that swallowed her up.

It was like wading deeper and deeper into a tangible oblivion. The blackness closed over her head, and she was groping through solid night. It filled the hollow in a thick flood, and in the depths of it she could not even see the stars overhead. There was a moment of this blindness and groping, and then the moon rose.

Like a great leprous face it swung over the ravine's edge, the moon-clouds crawling across its surface. And that green light was an agony to her eyes, obscurely, achingly. It was like no mortal moonlight. It seemed endowed with a poisonous quality that was essentially a part of the radiance, and that unearthly, inexplicable light had an effect upon the liquid dark in the gully's bottom which no earthly moonlight could have had. It penetrated the blackness, broke it up into myriad struggling shadows that did not lie flat upon the ground, as all shadows should, but stood upright and three-dimensional and danced about her in a dizzy riot of nothingness taken shape. They brushed by her and through her without meeting obstruction, because for all their seeming solidity they were no more than shadows, without substance.

Among them danced the shape of Guillaume, and the outlines of it made her faint with terror, they were so like – and so dreadfully unlike – the Guillaume she had known, so leeringly suggestive of all the evil in him, and all the potential evil of mankind. The other shapes of things whose real form she did not know, so that the implications latent in them she did not understand. But she missed no subtle half-tone of the full dreadfulness which was Guillaume, and her mind staggered with the suggestions the shadow-form made.

'Guillaume—' she heard herself sobbing, 'Guillaume!' and realized that it was the first articulate sound which had passed her lips since she entered here. At her voice the reeling shadow slowed a little and hesitated, and then very reluctantly began to drift towards her through the spinning shades.

And then without warning something immeasurably cold and still closed down around her once more. The black god's presence. Again she felt herself congealing, through and through, as the ice of eternal nothingness thickened upon her soul and the grey, dim, formless place she remembered took shape about her and the immense weight of that iron despair descended again upon her shuddering spirit. If she had had warning she could have struggled but it came so suddenly that before she could marshal her forces for the attack she was frigid to the core with the chill of unhumanity, and her body did not belong to her, and she was turning slowly into a black shadow that reeled among shadows in a dreadful, colourless void ...

Sharply through this stabbed the fire-hot memory that had wakened upon hers, the grip of his mailed arms, And again she knew the flash of violence that might have been hate or love, and warmth flowed through her again in a sustaining tide.

And she fought. All the deeps of warmth and humanity in her she drew upon to fight the cold, all the violence of emotion to combat the terrible apathy which had gripped her once and was stretching out again for her soul.

It was not an easy victory. There were moments when the chill all but conquered, and moments when she felt herself drawn tenuously out of the congealing body which was hers to reel among the other shadows – a dim thing whose shape hinted at unspeakable possibilities, a shadow with form and depth and no reality. She caught remote beats of the insane harmony they danced to, and though her soul was fainting, her unreal shade went whirling on with the rest. She shared their torment for long minutes together.

But always she pulled herself free again. Always she fought back somehow into the ice-fettered body and shook off the frigid apathy that bound it, and hurled her weapons of life and vitality against the dark god's frosty presence.

And though she knew she would win this time, a little creeping doubt had entered her mind and would not be ousted. She could beat the god off, but she could never destroy him. He would always return. She dared not destroy him – a vision of her thought-picture came back to her, of the tiny life-spark burning against eternal darkness. And though if there were no light there could be no dark, yet it was true in reverse too, and if the power upon which the black god drew were destroyed – if the dark were dissipated, then there would be no light. No life. Interdependence, and eternal struggle ...

All this she was realizing with a remote part of herself and she fought. She realized it very vaguely, for her mind had not been trained to such abstractions. With her conscious self she was calling up the memories of love and hate and terror, the exultation of battle, the exaltation of joy. Everything that was alive and pulsing and warm she flung against the black god's chill, feeling her thoughts rise up in a protecting wall about her, to shut out all menace.

Victory, as before, came very suddenly. Without warning a blaze of light sprang up around her. The dark presence melted into oblivion. In that abrupt glare she closed her dazzled eyes, and when she opened them again familiar moonlight was flooding the glen. The fluid dark had vanished, the shadows no longer danced. That light had blasted them out of existence, and as it died she stared round the dim ravine with startled eyes, searching for the thing that was all she had seen of Guillaume. It was gone with the rest. The tangible dark which had brimmed the place was utterly gone. Not a shadow moved anywhere. But on the wind that was blowing down the ravine a small voice wailed.

And so again the weary chase went on. But she had less than ever to guide her now – only a fitful crying in the dark. 'Jirel –' it wailed, 'Jirel – Jirel –' and by that calling she followed. She could see nothing. Guillaume was no more than a voice now, and she could follow him by ear alone. Emptily the landscape stretched before her.

She had come out of the ravine's end upon a broad fan-shaped slope which tilted downward into darkness. Water was falling somewhere near, but she could not see it. She ran blindly, ears strained for the small wailing cry. It led out over the slope and skirted the foot of a hill and passed by the place where water fell in a thin cascade down a cliffside, and whispered evilly to itself as it fell.

The sound obscured the sound she followed, and when she had passed beyond the whisper of the falls she had to stop and listen for a long time, while her heart thudded and the land around her crept with small, inexplicable noises, before she caught the far-away wail, 'Jirel – Jirel—'

She set off in the direction from which the sound came, and presently heard it again more clearly, 'Jirel! Jirel, my murderess!'

It was a heart-breaking course she ran, with no more than a fitful wailing to guide her and unknown perils lurking all about in the dark, and her own body and soul so drained of all strength by that second struggle with the god that the misty darkness wavered before her eyes and the ground underfoot heaved up to meet her time after time.

Once she fell, and lay still for a second to catch her struggling breath. But it seemed to her that the ground against her body was too warm, somehow, and moving gently as if with leisured breathing. So she leaped up again in swift alarm, and went skimming on with that dream-like speed over the dark grass.

It seemed to her that, as the shadow she had pursued had fled through the shadowy places where she all but lost it time and again, now the fleeing voice led her through noisy places where she could scarcely hear it above the talking of brooks and the rush of falls and the blowing of the wind. She heard sounds she had never heard before – small, tenuous voices murmuring in the wind, the whispering of grass saying things in a murmurous language, the squeak of insects brushing past her face and somehow almost articulate. She had heard no birds here, though once a great, dark, shapeless thing flapped heavily through the air a little distance ahead. But there were frog voices from the swamps she skirted, and hearing these she remembered what she had met in another swamp on her first visit here, and a little chill went down her back.

In every sound she heard ran the thread of evil inextricably tangled with a thread of purest despair – a human despair even through the grasses' rustling and in the murmur of the wind – voices wailing so hopelessly that more than once tears started unbidden to her eyes, but so indistinctly that she could never be sure she had heard. And always through the wailing rippled the chuckle of dim evils without any names in human languages. And with all these sounds she heard many others that meant nothing to her and upon whose origins she dared not speculate.

Through this welter of incomprehensible noises she followed the one far crying that had meaning for her. It led in a long arc across rolling ground, over muttering brooks that talked morbidly in the dark. Presently she began to catch the faint strains of the most curious music. It did not have the quality of composition, or even unity, but seemed to consist of single groups of notes, like sprays of music, each unrelated to the rest, as if thousands of invisible creatures were piping tiny, primitive tunes, every one deaf to the songs of his fellows. The sound grew louder as she advanced, and she saw that she was coming to a luminous patch upon the dark ground. When she reached the edge she paused in wonder.

The music was rising from the earth, and it rose visibly. She could actually see the separate strains wavering upward through the still air. She could never have described what she saw, for the look of that visible music was beyond any human words. Palely the notes rose, each singing its tiny, simple tune. There seemed to be no discords, for all the non-unity of the sounds. She had the mad fancy that the music was growing – that if she wished she could wade through the ranks of it and gather great sheaves of sound – perhaps bouquets, which, if they were carefully selected, would join together and play a single complex melody.

But it was not music she dared listen to long. There was in it the queerest little gibbering noise, and as she lingered that sound intensified and ran through her brain in small, giggling undernotes, and she caught herself laughing senselessly at nothing at all. Then she took fright, and listened for the voice that was Guillaume. And terrifyingly she heard it strongly in the very midst of the little mad jingles. It deepened and grew, and drowned out the smaller sounds, and the whole field was one vast roar of insane laughter that thundered through her head in destroying waves – a jarring laughter that threatened to shake her irresistibly and wrung tears from her eyes even as she laughed.

'Guillaume!' she called again in the midst of her agony. 'Oh Guillaume!' and at the sound of her voice all laughter ceased and a vast, breathless silence fell upon the whole dark world. Through that silence the tiniest wail threaded itself reedily, 'Jirel –' Then other sounds came back to life, and the wind blew and the wail diminished in the distance. Again the chase went on.

By now the moon's dead, crawling face had sunk nearly to the horizon, and the shadows lay in long patterns across the ground. It seemed to her that around the broad ring of the sky a pallor was rising. In her weariness and despair she did not greatly care now, knowing though she did that should day catch her here it meant a death more terrible than any man can die on earth, and an eternity, perhaps, of torment in one of the many shapes she had seen and recognized as the spirits of the damned. Perhaps a writhing tree – or imprisonment in an obscenely revelatory image, like Guillaume – or no more than a wailing along the wind for ever. She was too tired to care. She stumbled on hopelessly, hearing the voice that cried her name grow fainter and fainter in the distance.

The end of the chase came very suddenly. She reached a stream that flowed smoothly under the arch of a low, dark bridge, and crossed over it, seeing her face look up at her from the water with a wild mouthing of soundless cries, though her own lips were closed. She met her acutest agony in their depths, and saw her own face writhing all out of familiarity with anguish and hopelessness. It was a frightful vision, but she scarcely saw it, and ran on without heeding the image in the water or the landscape around her or even the broadening dawn around the horizon.

Then close ahead of her sounded the thin small voice she followed, and she woke out of her stupor and stared around. That bridge had not ended upon the far side of the brook, but somehow had arched up its sides and broadened its floor and become a dark temple round whose walls ran a more bestial sculpture than anything imagined even in dreams. Here in this carved and columned building was the epitome of the whole dim hell through which she had been running. Here in these sculptures she read all the hideous things the shadows had hinted at, all the human sorrow and despair and hopelessness she had heard in the wind's crying, all the chuckling evil that the water spoke. In the carvings she could trace the prisoned souls of men and beasts, tormented in many ways, some of which she had already seen, but many that she had not, and which she mercifully could not understand. It was not clear for what they were punished, save that the torture was tinged just enough with justice so that it seemed the more hideously unjust in its exaggerations. She closed her eyes and stood swaying a little, feeling the triumphant evil of the temple pulsing around her, too stunned and sick even to wonder what might come next.

Then the small voice was beating around her head. Almost she felt the desperate hammering of wings, as if some little, frantic bird were flying against her face. 'Jirel – Jirel!' it cried in the purest agony, over and over, a final, wild appeal. And she did not know what to do. Helplessly she stood there, feeling it beating round her head, feeling the temple's obscene triumph surging through her.

And without warning, for the third time the black god's presence folded like a cloak about her. Almost she welcomed it. Here was something she knew how to fight. As from a long distance away she heard the small voice crying in diminishing echoes, and the frigid twilight was forming about her, and the grey ice thickened upon her soul. She called up the memories of hate and love and anger to hurl against it, thinking as she did so that perhaps one who had lived less violently than herself and had lesser stores of passions to recall might ever be able to combat the god's death-chill. She remembered laughter, and singing and gaiety – she remembered slaughter and blood and the wild clang of mail – she remembered kisses in the dark, and the hard grip of men's arms about her body.

But she was weary, and the dawn was breaking terribly along the sky, and the dark god's power was footed in a changeless oblivion that never faltered. And she began to realize failure. The memories she flung out had no power against the grey pall of that twilight place wherein he dwelt, and she knew the first seeping of the iron despair through her brain. Gradually the will to struggle congealed with her congealing body, until she was no longer a warm, vital thing of flesh and blood, but something rigid and icebound, dwelling bodilessly in the twilight.

There was one small spark of her that the god could not freeze. She felt him assailing it. She felt him driving it out of the cold thing that had been her body – drawing it forth irresistibly – she was a thin, small crying in the dark ... Helplessly she felt herself whirling to and fro upon currents she had never felt before, and dashing against unseen obstacles, wailing wordlessly. She had no substance, and the world had faded from around her. She was aware of other things – dim, vague, like beating pulses, that were whirling through the dark, small lost things like herself, bodiless and unprotected, buffeted by every current that blew; little wailing things, shrieking through the night.

Then one of the small vaguenesses blew against her and through her, and in the instant of its passage she caught the faint vibration of her name, and knew that this was the voice that had summoned her out of her dreams, the voice she had pursued: Guillaume. And with that instant's union something as sustaining as life itself flashed through her wonderfully, a bright spark that swelled and grew and blazed, and—

She was back again in her body amidst the bestial carvings of the temple – a thawing, warming body from which the shackles of icy silence were falling, and that hot blaze was swelling still, until all of her being was suffused and pulsing with it, and the frigid pall of dark melted away unresistingly before the hot, triumphant blaze that dwelt within her.

In her ecstasy of overwhelming warmth she scarcely realized her victory. She did not greatly care. Something very splendid was happening . . .

Then the air trembled, and all about her small, thin sounds went shivering upward, as if ribbons of high screams were rippling past her across a background of silence. The blaze within her faded slowly, paled, imperceptibly died away and the peace of utter emptiness flooded into her soul. She turned wearily backward across the bridge. Behind her the temple stood in a death-like quiet. The evil that had beat in long pulses through it was stilled for a while by something stunningly splendid which had no place in the starry hell; something human and alive, something compounded of love and longing, near-despair and sacrifice and triumph.

Jirel did not realize how great a silence she left behind, nor very clearly what she had done. Above her against the paling sky she saw a familiar hilltop, and dimly knew that in all her long night of running she had been circling round towards her starting-place. She was too numb to care. She was beyond relief or surprise.

She began the climb passionlessly, with no triumph in the victory she knew was hers at last. For she had driven Guillaume out of the image and into the shadow, and out of the shadow into the voice, and out of the voice into clean death, perhaps. She did not know. But he had found peace, for his insistences no longer beat upon her consciousness. And she was content.

Above her the cave mouth yawned. She toiled up the slope, dragging her sword listlessly, weary to the very soul, but quite calm now, with a peace beyond all understanding.

JIREL MEETS MAGIC

Over Guischard's fallen drawbridge thundered Joiry's warrior lady, sword swinging, voice shouting hoarsely inside her helmet. The scarlet plume of her crest rippled in the wind. Straight into the massed defenders at the gate she plunged, careering through them by the very impetuosity of the charge, the weight of her mighty warhorse opening up a gap for the men at her heels to widen. For a while there was tumult unspeakable there under the archway, the yells of fighters and the clang of mail on mail and the screams of stricken men. Jirel of Joiry was a shouting battle-machine from which Guischard's men reeled in bloody confusion as she whirled and slashed and slew in the narrow confines of the gateway, her great stallion's iron hoofs weapons as potent as her own whistling blade.

In her full armor she was impregnable to the men on foot, and the horse's armor protected him from their vengeful blades, so that alone, almost, she might have won the gateway. By sheer weight and impetuosity she carried the battle through the defenders under the arch. They gave way before the mighty war-horse and his screaming rider. Jirel's swinging sword and the stallion's trampling feet cleared a path for Joiry's men to follow, and at last into Guischard's court poured the steel-clad hordes of Guischard's conquerors.

Jirel's eyes were yellow with blood-lust behind the helmet bars, and her voice echoed savagely from the steel cage that confined it. 'Giraud! Bring me Giraud! A gold piece to the man who brings me the wizard Giraud!'

She waited impatiently in the courtyard, reining her excited charger in mincing circles over the flags, unable to dismount alone in her heavy armor and disdainful of the threats of possible arbalesters in the arrow-slits that looked down upon her from Guischard's frowning gray walls. A crossbow shaft was the only thing she had to fear in her impregnable mail.

She waited in mounting impatience, a formidable figure in her bloody armor, the great sword lying across her saddlebow and her eager, angry voice echoing hoarsely from the helmet, 'Giraud! Make haste, you varlets! Bring me Giraud!'

There was such bloodthirsty impatience in that hollowly booming voice that the men who were returning from searching the castle hung back as they crossed the court toward their lady in reluctant twos and threes, failure eloquent upon their faces.

'What!' screamed Jirel furiously. 'You, Giles! Have you brought me Giraud? Watkin! Where is that wizard Giraud? Answer me, I say!'

'We've scoured the castle, my lady,' said one of the men fearfully as the angry voice paused. 'The wizard is gone.'

'Now God defend me!' groaned Joiry's lady. 'God help a poor woman served by fools! Did you search among the slain?'

'We searched everywhere, Lady Jirel. Giraud has escaped us.'

Jirel called again upon her Maker in a voice that was blasphemy itself.

'Help me down, then, you hell-spawned knaves,' she grated. 'I'll find him myself. He must be here!'

With difficulty they got her off the sidling horse. It took two men to handle her, and a third to steady the charger. All the while they struggled with straps and buckles she cursed them hollowly, emerging limb by limb from the casing of steel and swearing with a soldier's fluency as the armor came away. Presently she stood free on the bloody flagstones, a slim, straight lady, keen as a blade, her red hair a flame to match the flame of her yellow eyes. Under the armor she wore a tunic of link-mail from the Holy Land, supple as silk and almost as light, and a doeskin shirt to protect the milky whiteness of her skin.

She was a creature of the wildest paradox, this warrior lady of Joiry, hot as a red coal, chill as steel, satiny of body and iron of soul. The set of her chin was firm, but her mouth betrayed a tenderness she would have died before admitting. But she was raging now.

'Follow me, then, fools!' she shouted. 'I'll find that God-cursed wizard and split his head with this sword if it takes me until the day I die. I swear it. I'll teach him what it costs to ambush Joiry men. By heaven, he'll pay with his life for my ten who fell at Massy Ford last week. The foul spell-brewer! He'll learn what it means to defy Joiry!'

Breathing threats and curses, she strode across the court, her men following reluctantly at her heels and casting nervous glances upward at the gray towers of Guischard. It had always borne a bad name this ominous castle of the wizard Giraud, a place where queer things happened, which no man entered uninvited and whence no prisoner had ever escaped, though the screams of torture echoed often from its walls. Jirel's men would have followed her straight through the gates of hell, but they stormed Guischard at her heels with terror in their hearts and no hope of conquest.

She alone seemed not to know fear of the dark sorcerer. Perhaps it was because she had known things so dreadful that mortal perils held no terror for her – there were whispers at Joiry of their lady, and of things that had happened there which no man dared think on. But when Guischard fell, and the wizard's defenders fled before Jirel's mighty steed and the onrush of Joiry's men, they had plucked up heart, thinking that perhaps the ominous tales of

Giraud had been gossip only, since the castle fell as any ordinary lord's castle might fall. But now – there were whispers again, and nervous glances over the shoulder, and men huddled together as they re-entered Guischard at their lady's hurrying heels. A castle from which a wizard might vanish into thin air, with all the exits watched, must be a haunted place, better burned and forgotten. They followed Jirel reluctantly, half ashamed but fearful.

In Jirel's stormy heart there was no room for terror as she plunged into the gloom of the archway that opened upon Guischard's great central hall. Anger that the man might have escaped her was a torch to light the way, and she paused in that door with eager anticipation, sweeping the corpse-strewn hall at a glance, searching for some clue to explain how her quarry had disappeared.

'He can't have escaped,' she told herself confidently. 'There's no way out. He *must* be here somewhere.' And she stepped into the hall, turning over the bodies she passed with a careless foot to make sure that death had not robbed her of vengeance.

An hour later, as they searched the last tower, she was still telling herself that the wizard could not have gone without her knowledge. She had taken special pains about that. There was a secret passage to the river, but she had had that watched. And an underwater door opened into the moat, but he could not have gone that way without meeting her men. Secret paths lay open; she had found them all and posted a guard at each, and Giraud had not left the castle by any door that led out. She climbed the stairs of the last tower wearily, her confidence shaken.

An iron-barred oaken door closed the top of the steps, and Jirel drew back as her men lifted the heavy crosspieces and opened it for her. It had not been barred from within. She stepped into the little round room inside, hope fading completely as she saw that it too was empty, save for the body of a page-boy lying on the uncarpeted floor. Blood had made a congealing pool about him, and as Jirel looked she saw something which roused her flagging hopes. Feet had trodden in that blood, not the mailed feet of armed men, but the tread of shapeless cloth shoes such as surely none but Giraud would have worn when the castle was besieged and falling, and every man's help needed. Those bloody tracks led straight across the room toward the wall, and in that wall – a window.

Jirel stared. To her a window was a narrow slit deep in stone, made for the shooting of arrows, and never covered save in the coldest weather. But this window was broad and low, and instead of the usual animal pelt for hangings a curtain of purple velvet had been drawn back to disclose shutters carved out of something that might have been ivory had any beast alive been huge enough to yield such great unbroken sheets of whiteness. The shutters were unlatched, swinging slightly ajar, and upon them Jirel saw the smear of bloody fingers.

With a little triumphant cry she sprang forward. Here, then, was the secret way Giraud had gone. What lay beyond the window she could not guess. Perhaps an unsuspected passage, or a hidden room. Laughing exultantly, she swung open the ivory shutters.

There was a gasp from the men behind her. She did not hear it. She stood quite still, staring with incredulous eyes. For those ivory gates had opened upon no dark stone hiding-place or secret tunnel. They did not reveal the afternoon sky outside, nor did they admit the shouts of her men still subduing the last of the defenders in the court below. Instead she was looking out upon a green woodland over which brooded a violet day like no day she had ever seen before. In paralyzed amazement she looked down, seeing not the bloody flags of the courtyard far below, but a mossy carpet at a level with the floor. And on that moss she saw the mark of bloodstained feet. This window might be a magic one, opening into strange lands, but through it had gone the man she swore to kill, and where he fled she must follow.

She lifted her eyes from the tracked moss and stared out again through the dimness under the trees. It was a lovelier land than anything seen even in dreams; so lovely that it made her heart ache with its strange, unearthly enchantment – green woodland hushed and brooding in the hushed violet day. There was a promise of peace there, and forgetfulness and rest. Suddenly the harsh, shouting, noisy world behind her seemed very far away and chill She moved forward and laid her hand upon the ivory shutters, staring out.

The shuffle of scared men behind her awakened Jirel from the enchantment that had gripped her. She turned. The dreamy magic of the woodland loosed its hold as she faced the men again, but its memory lingered. She shook her red head a little, meeting their fearful eyes. She nodded toward the open window.

'Giraud has gone out there,' she said. 'Give me your dagger, Giles. This sword is too heavy to carry far.'

'But lady – Lady Jirel – dear lady – you can't – can't go out there – Saint Guilda save us! Lady Jirel!'

Jirel's crisp voice cut short the babble of protest.

'Your dagger, Giles. I've sworn to slay Giraud, and slay him I shall, in whatever land he hides. Giles!'

A man-at-arms shuffled forward with averted face, handing her his dagger. She gave him the sword she carried and thrust the long-bladed knife into her belt. She turned again to the window. Green and cool and lovely, the woodland lay waiting. She thought as she set her knee upon the sill that she must have explored this violet calm even had her oath not driven her; for there was an enchantment about the place that drew her irresistibly. She pulled up her other knee and jumped lightly. The mossy ground received her without a jar.

For a few moments Jirel stood very still, watching, listening. Bird songs trilled intermittently about her, and breezes stirred the leaves. From very far away she thought she caught the echoes of a song when the wind blew, and there was something subtly irritating about its simple melody that seemed to seesaw endlessly up and down on two notes. She was glad when the wind died and the song no longer shrilled in her ears.

It occurred to her that before she ventured far she must mark the window she had entered by, and she turned curiously, wondering how it looked from this side. What she saw sent an inexplicable little chill down her back. Behind her lay a heap of moldering ruins, moss-grown, crumbling into decay. Fire had blackened the stones in ages past. She could see that it must have been a castle, for the original lines of it were not yet quite lost. Only one low wall remained standing now, and in it opened the window through which she had come. There was something hauntingly familiar about the lines of those moldering stones, and she turned away with a vague unease, not quite understanding why. A little path wound away under the low-hanging trees, and she followed it slowly, eyes alert for signs that Giraud had passed this way. Birds trilled drowsily in the leaves overhead, queer, unrecognizable songs like the music of no birds she knew. The violet light was calm and sweet about her.

She had gone on in the bird-haunted quiet for many minutes before she caught the first hint of anything at odds with the perfect peace about her. A whiff of wood-smoke drifted to her nostrils on a vagrant breeze. When she rounded the next bend of the path she saw what had caused it. A tree lay across the way in a smother of shaking leaves and branches. She knew that she must skirt it, for the branches were too tangled to penetrate, and she turned out of the path, following the trunk toward its broken base.

She had gone only a few steps before the sound of a curious sobbing came to her ears. It was the gasp of choked breathing, and she had heard sounds like that too often before not to know that she approached death in some form or another. She laid her hand on her knife-hilt and crept forward softly.

The tree trunk had been severed as if by a blast of heat, for the stump was charred black and still smoking. Beyond the stump a queer tableau was being enacted, and she stopped quite still, staring through the leaves.

Upon the moss a naked girl was lying, gasping her life out behind the hands in which her face was buried. There was no mistaking the death-sound in that failing breath, although her body was unmarked. Hair of a strange green-gold pallor streamed over her bare white body, and by the fragility and tenuosity of that body Jirel knew that she could not be wholly human.

Above the dying girl a tall woman stood. And that woman was a magnet for Jirel's fascinated eyes. She was generously curved, sleepy-eyed. Black hair bound her head sleekly, and her skin was like rich, dark, creamy velvet. A violet robe wrapped her carelessly, leaving arms and one curved shoulder bare, and her girdle was a snake of something like purple glass. It might have been carved from some vast jewel, save for its size and unbroken clarity. Her feet were thrust bare into silver sandals. But it was her face that held Jirel's yellow gaze.

The sleepy eyes under heavily drooping lids were purple as gems, and the darkly crimson mouth curled in a smile so hateful that fury rushed up in Jirel's heart as she watched. That lazy purple gaze dwelt aloofly upon the gasping girl on the moss. The woman was saying in a voice as rich and deep as thick-piled velvet:

'—nor will any other of the dryad folk presume to work forbidden magic in my woodlands for a long, long while to come. Your fate shall be a deadly example to them, Irsla. You dared too greatly. None who defy Jarisme live. Hear me, Irsla!'

The sobbing breath had slowed as the woman spoke, as if life were slipping fast from the dryad-girl on the moss; and as she realized it the speaker's arm lifted and a finger of white fire leaped from her outstretched hand, stabbing the white body at her feet. And the girl Irsla started like one shocked back into life.

'Hear me out, dryad! Let your end be a warning to—'

The girl's quickened breath slowed again as the white brilliance left her, and again the woman's hand rose, again the light-blade stabbed. From behind her shielding hands the dryad gasped:

'Oh, mercy, mercy, Jarisme! Let me die!'

'When I have finished. Not before. Life and death are mine to command here, and I am not yet done with you. Your stolen magic—'

She paused, for Irsla had slumped once more upon the moss, breath scarcely stirring her. As Jarisme's light-dealing hand rose for the third time Jirel leapt forward. Partly it was intuitive hatred of the lazy-eyed woman, partly revolt at this cat-and-mouse play with a dying girl for a victim. She swung her arm in an arc that cleared the branches from her path, and called out in her clear, strong voice:

'Have done, woman! Let her die in peace.'

Slowly Jarisme's purple eyes rose. They met Jirel's hot yellow glare. Almost physical impact was in that first meeting of their eyes, and hatred flashed between them instantly, like the flash of blades – the instinctive hatred of total opposites, born enemies. Each stiffened subtly, as cats do in the instant before combat. But Jirel thought she saw in the purple gaze, behind all its kindling anger, a faint disquiet, a nameless uncertainty.

'Who are you?' asked Jarisme, very softly, very dangerously.

Something in that unsureness behind her angry eyes prompted Jirel to answer boldly:

'Jirel of Joiry. I seek the wizard Giraud, who fled me here. Stop tormenting that wretched girl and tell me where to find him. I can make it worth your while.'

Her tone was imperiously mandatory, and behind Jarisme's drooping lips an answering flare of anger lighted, almost drowning out that faint unease.

'You do not know me,' she observed, her voice very gentle. 'I am the sorceress Jarisme, and high ruler over all this land. Did you think to buy me, then, earth-woman?'

Jirel smiled her sweetest, most poisonous smile.

'You will forgive me,' she purred. 'At the first glance at you I did not think your price could be high ...'

A petty malice had inspired the speech, and Jirel was sorry as it left her lips, for she knew that the scorn which blazed up in Jarisme's eyes was justified. The sorceress made a contemptuous gesture of dismissal.

'I shall waste no more of my time here,' she said. 'Get back to your little lands, Jirel of Joiry, and tempt me no further.'

The purple gaze rested briefly on the motionless dryad at her feet, flicked Jirel's hot eyes with a glance of scorn which yet did not wholly hide that curious uncertainty in its depths. One hand slid behind her, oddly as if she were seeking a door-latch in empty air. Then like a heat-shimmer the air danced about her, and in an instant she was gone.

Jirel blinked. Her ears had deceived her as well as her eyes, she thought, for as the sorceress vanished a door closed softly somewhere. Yet look though she would, the green glade was empty, the violet air untroubled. No Jarisme anywhere – no door. Jirel shrugged after a moment's bewilderment. She had met magic before.

A sound from the scarcely breathing girl upon the moss distracted her, and she dropped to her knees beside the dying dryad. There was no mark or wound upon her, yet Jirel knew that death could be only a matter of moments. And dimly she recalled that, so legend said, a tree-sprite never survived the death of its tree. Gently she turned the girl over, wondering if she were beyond help.

At the feel of those gentle hands the dryad's lips quivered and rose. Brook-brown eyes looked up at Jirel, with green swimming in their deeps like leaf-reflection in a woodland pool.

'My thanks to you,' faltered the girl in a ghostly murmur. 'But get you back to your home now – before Jarisme's anger slays you.'

Jirel shook her red head stubbornly.

'I must find Giraud first, and kill him, as I have sworn to do. But I will wait. Is there anything I can do?'

The green-reflecting eyes searched hers for a moment. The dryad must have read resolution there, for she shook her head a little.

'I must die – with my tree. But if you are determined – hear me. I owe you – a debt. There is a talisman – braided in my hair. When I – am dead – take it. It is Jarisme's sign. All her subjects wear them. It will guide you to her – and to Giraud. He is ever beside her. I know. I think it was her anger at you – that made her forget to take it from me, after she had dealt me my death. But why she did not slay you – I do not know. Jarisme is quick – to kill. No matter – listen now. If you must have Giraud – you must take a risk that no one here – has ever taken – before. Break this talisman – at Jarisme's feet. I do not know – what will happen then. Something – very terrible. It releases powers – even she can not control. It may – destroy you too. But – it is – a chance. May you – have – all good—'

The faltering voice failed. Jirel, bending her head, caught only meaningless murmurs that trailed away to nothing. The green-gold head dropped suddenly forward on her sustaining arm. Through the forest all about her went one long, quivering sigh, as if an intangible breeze ruffled the trees. Yet no leaves stirred.

Jirel bent and kissed the dryad's forehead, then laid her very gently back on the moss. And as she did so her hand in the masses of strangely colored hair came upon something sharp and hard. She remembered the talisman. It tingled in her fingers as she drew it out – an odd little jagged crystal sparkling with curious aliveness from the fire burning in its heart.

When she had risen to her feet, leaving the dead dryad lying upon the moss which seemed so perfectly her couch, she saw that the inner brilliance streaming in its wedge-shaped pattern through the crystal was pointing a quivering apex forward and to the right. Irsla had said it would guide her. Experimentally she twisted her hand to the left. Yes, the shaking light shifted within the crystal, pointing always toward the right, and Jarisme.

One last long glance she gave to the dryad on the moss. Then she set off again down the path, the little magical thing stinging her hand as she walked. And as she went she wondered. This strong hatred which had flared so instinctively between her and the sorceress was not enough to burn any trace of fear from her mind, and she remembered that look of uncertainty in the purple gaze that had shot such hatred at her. Why? Why had she not been slain as Irsla was slain, for defiance of this queer land's ruler?

For a while she paced unheedingly along under the trees. Then abruptly the foliage ceased and a broad meadow lay before her, green in the clear, violet day. Beyond the meadow the slim shaft of a tower rose dazzingly white, and toward it in steady radiance that magical talisman pointed.

From very far away she thought she still caught the echoes of that song when the wind blew, an irritating monotony that made her ears ache. She was glad when the wind died and the song no longer shrilled in her ears.

Out across the meadow she went. Far ahead she could make out purple mountains like low clouds on the horizon, and here and there in the distances clumps of woodland dotted the meadows. She walked on more rapidly now, for she was sure that the white tower housed Jarisme, and with her Giraud. And she must have gone more swiftly than she knew, for with almost magical speed the shining shaft drew nearer.

She could see the arch of its doorway, bluely violet within. The top of the shaft was battlemented, and she caught splashes of color between the teeth of the stone scarps, as if flowers were massed there and spilling blossoms against the whiteness of the tower. The singsong music was louder than ever, and much nearer. Jirel's heart beat a bit heavily as she advanced, wondering what sort of a sorceress this Jarisme might be, what dangers lay before her in the path of her vow's fulfillment. Now the white tower rose up over her, and she was crossing the little space before the door, peering in dubiously. All she could see was dimness and violet mist.

She laid her hand upon the dagger, took a deep breath and stepped boldly in under the arch. In the instant her feet left the solid earth she saw that this violet mist filled the whole shaft of the tower, that there was no floor. Emptiness engulfed her, and all reality ceased.

She was falling through clouds of violet blackness, but in no recognizable direction. It might have been up, down, or sidewise through space. Everything had vanished in the violet nothing. She knew an endless moment of vertigo and rushing motion; then the dizzy emptiness vanished in a breath and she was standing in a gasping surprise upon the roof of Jarisme's tower.

She knew where she was by the white battlements ringing her round, banked with strange blossoms in muted colors. In the center of the circular, marble-paved place a low couch, cushioned in glowing yellow, stood in the midst of a heap of furs. Two people sat side by side on the couch. One was Giraud. Black-robed, dark-visaged, he stared at Jirel with a flicker of disquiet in his small, dull eyes. He said nothing.

Jirel dismissed him with a glance, scarcely realizing his presence. For Jarisme had lowered from her lips a long, silver flute. Jirel realized that the queer, maddening music must have come from that gleaming length, for it no longer echoed in her ears. Jarisme was holding the instrument now in midair, regarding Jirel over it with a purple-eyed gaze that was somehow thoughtful and a little apprehensive, though anger glowed in it, too.

'So,' she said richly, in her slow, deep voice. 'For the second time you defy me.'

At these words Giraud turned his head sharply and stared at the sorceress' impassive profile. She did not return his gaze, but after a moment he looked quickly back at Jirel, and in his eyes too she saw that flicker of alarm, and with it a sort of scared respect. It puzzled her, and she did not like being puzzled. She said a little breathlessly:

'If you like, yes. Give me that skulking potion-brewer beside you and set me down again outside this damned tower of trickery. I came to kill your pet spellmonger here for treachery done me in my own world by this creature who dared not stay to face me.'

Her peremptory words hung in the air like the echoes of a gong. For a while no one spoke. Jarisme smiled more subtly than before, an insolent, slow smile that made Jirel's pulses hammer with the desire to smash it down the woman's lush, creamy throat. At last Jarisme said, in a voice as rich and deep as thick-piled velvet:

'Hot words, hot words, soldier-woman! Do you really imagine that your earthly squabbles matter to Jarisme?'

'What matters to Jarisme is of little moment to me,' Jirel said contemptuously. 'All I want is this skulker here, whom I have sworn to kill.'

Jarisme's slow smile was maddening. 'You demand it of me – Jarisme?' She asked with soft incredulity. 'Only fools offend me, woman, and they but once. None commands me. You will have to learn that.'

Jirel smiled thinly. 'At what price, then, do you value your pet cur?'

Giraud half rose from the couch at that last insult, his dark face darker with a surge of anger. Jarisme pushed him back with a lazy hand.

'This is between your – friend – and me,' she said. 'I do not think, soldier' – the appellation was the deadliest of insults in the tone she used – 'that any price you could offer would interest me.'

'And yet your interest is very easily caught.' Jirel flashed a contemptuous glance at Giraud, restive under the woman's restraining hand.

Jarisme's rich pallor flushed a little. Her voice was sharper as she said:

'Do not tempt me too far, earthling.'

Jirel's yellow eyes defied her. 'I am not afraid.'

The sorceress' purple gaze surveyed her slowly. When Jarisme spoke again a tinge of reluctant admiration lightened the slow scorn of her voice.

'No – you are not afraid. And a fool not to be. Fools annoy me, Jirel of Joiry.'

She laid the flute down on her knee and lazily lifted a ringless hand. Anger was glowing in her eyes now, blotting out all trace of that little haunting fear. But Giraud caught the rising hand, bending, whispering urgently in her ear. Jirel caught a part of what he said: '—what happens to those who tamper with their own destiny—' And she saw the anger fade from the sorceress' face as apprehension brightened there again. Jarisme looked at Jirel with a long, hard look and shrugged her ample shoulders.

'Yes,' she murmured. 'Yes, Giraud. It is wisest so.' And to Jirel, 'Live then, earthling. Find your way back to your own land if you can, but I warn you, do not trouble me again. I shall not stay my hand if our paths ever cross in the future.'

She struck her soft, white palms together sharply. And at the sound the roof-top and the violet sky and the banked flowers at the parapets whirled around Jirel in dizzy confusion. From very far away she heard that clap of peremptory hands still echoing, but it seemed to her that the great, smokily colored blossoms were undergoing an inexplicable transformation. They quivered and spread and thrust upward from the edges of the tower to arch over her head. Her feet were pressing a mossy ground, and the sweet, earthy odors of a garden rose about her. Blinking, she stared around as the world slowly steadied.

She was no longer on the roof-top. As far as she could see through the tangled stems, great flowering plants sprang up in the gloaming of a strange, enchanted forest. She was completely submerged in greenery, and the illusion of under-water filled her eyes, for the violet light that filtered through the leaves was diffused and broken into a submarine dimness. Uncertainly she began to grope her way forward, staring about to see what sort of a miracle had enfolded her.

It was a bower in fairyland. She had come into a tropical garden of great, muted blooms and jungle silences. In the diffused light the flowers nodded sleepily among the leaves, hypnotically lovely, hypnotically soporific with their soft colors and drowsy, never-ending motion. The fragrance was overpowering. She went on slowly, treading moss that gave back no sound. Here under the canopy of leaves was a little separate world of color and silence and perfume. Dreamily she made her way among the flowers.

Their fragrance was so strongly sweet that it went to her head, and she walked in a waking dream. Because of this curious, scented trance in which she went she was never quite sure if she had actually seen that motion among the leaves, and looked closer, and made out a huge, incredible serpent of violet transparency, a giant replica of the snake that girdled Jarisme's waist, but miraculously alive, miraculously supple and gliding, miraculously twisting its soundless way among the blossoms and staring at her with impassive, purple eyes.

While it glided along beside her she had other strange visions too, and could never remember just what they were, or why she caught familiar traces in the tiny, laughing faces that peered at her from among the flowers, or half believed the wild, impossible things they whispered to her, their laughing mouths brushing her ears as they leaned down among the blossoms.

The branches began to thin at last, as she neared the edge of the enchanted place. She walked slowly, half conscious of the great transparent snake like a living jewel writhing along soundlessly at her side, her mind vaguely troubled in its dream by the fading remembrance of what those little, merry voices had told her. When she came to the very edge of the bowery jungle and broke out into clear daylight again she stopped in a daze, staring round in the brightening light as the perfumes slowly cleared from her head.

Sanity and realization returned to her at last. She shook her red head dizzily and looked round, half expecting, despite her returning clarity, to see the great serpent gliding across the grass. But there was nothing. Of course she had dreamed. Of course those little laughing voices had not told her that – that – she clutched after the vanishing tags of remembrance, and caught nothing. Ruefully she laughed and brushed away the clinging memories, looking round to see where she was.

She stood at the crest of a little hill. Below her the flower-fragrant jungle nodded, a little patch of enchanted greenery clothing the slopes of the hill. Beyond and below green meadows stretched away to a far-off line of forest which she thought she recognized as that in which she had first met Jarisme. But the white tower which had risen in the midst of the meadows was magically gone. Where it had stood, unbroken greenery lay under the violet clarity of the sky.

As she stared round in bewilderment a faint prickling stung her palm, and she glanced down, remembering the talisman clutched in her hand. The quivering light was streaming in a long wedge toward some point behind her. She turned. She was in the foothills of those purple mountains she had glimpsed from the edge of the woods. High and shimmering, they rose above her. And, hazily in the heat-waves that danced among their heights, she saw the tower.

Jirel groaned to herself. Those peaks were steep and rocky. Well, no help for it. She must climb. She growled a soldier's oath in her throat and turned wearily toward the rising slopes. They were rough and deeply slashed with ravines. Violet heat beat up from the reflecting rocks, and tiny, brilliantly colored things scuttled from her path – orange lizards and coral red scorpions and little snakes like bright blue jewels.

It seemed to her as she stumbled upward among the broken stones that the tower was climbing too. Time after time she gained upon it, and time after time when she lifted her eyes after a grueling struggle up steep ravines, that mocking flicker of whiteness shimmered still high and unattainable on some distant peak. It had the mistiness of unreality, and if her talisman's guide had not pointed steadily upward she would have thought it an illusion to lead her astray.

But after what seemed hours of struggle, there came the time when, glancing up, she saw the shaft rising on the topmost peak of all, white as snow against the clear violet sky. And after that it shifted no more. She took heart now, for at last she seemed to be gaining. Every laborious step carried her nearer that lofty shining upon the mountain's highest peak.

She paused after a while, looking up and wiping the moisture from her forehead where the red curls clung. As she stood there something among the rocks moved, and out from behind a boulder a long, slinking feline creature came. It was not like any beast she had ever seen before. Its shining pelt was fabulously golden, brocaded with queer patterns of darker gold, and down against its heavy jaws curved two fangs whiter than ivory. With a grace as gliding as water it paced down the ravine toward her.

Jirel's heart contracted. Somehow she found the knife-hilt in her hand, though she had no recollection of having drawn it. She was staring hard at the lovely and terrible cat, trying to understand the haunting familiarity about its eyes. They were purple, like jewels. Slowly recognition dawned. She had met that purple gaze before, insolent under sleepy lids. Jarisme's eyes. Yes, and the snake in her dream had watched her with a purple stare too. Jarisme?

She closed her hand tightly about the crystal, knowing that she must conceal from the sorceress her one potent weapon, waiting until the time came to turn it against its maker. She shifted her knife so that light glinted down the blade. They stood quite still for a moment, yellow-eyed woman and fabulous, purple-eyed cat, staring at each other with hostility eloquent in every line of each. Jirel clenched her knife tight, warily eyeing the steel-clawed paws on which the golden beast went so softly. They could have ripped her to ribbons before the blade struck home.

She saw a queer expression flicker across the somber purple gaze that met hers, and the beautiful cat crouched a little, tail jerking, lip twitched back to expose shining fangs. It was about to spring. For an interminable moment she waited for that hurtling golden death to launch itself upon her, tense, rigid, knife steady in her hand…

It sprang. She dropped to one knee in the split second of its leaping, instinctively hiding the crystal, but thrusting up her dagger in defense. The great beast sailed easily over her head. As it hurtled past, a peal of derisive laughter rang in her ears, and she heard quite clearly the sound of a slamming door. She scrambled up and whirled in one motion, knife ready.

The defile was quite empty in the violet day. There was no door anywhere. Jarisme had vanished.

A little shaken, Jirel sheathed her blade. She was not afraid. Anger burned out all trace of fear as she remembered the scorn in that ringing laugh. She took up her course again toward the tower, white and resolute, not looking back.

The tower was drawing near again. She toiled upward. Jarisme showed no further sign of her presence, but Jirel felt eyes upon her, purple eyes, scornful and sleepy. She could see the tower clearly, just above her at the crest of the highest peak, up to which a long arc of steps curved steeply. They were very old, these steps, so worn that many were little more than irregularities on the stone. Jirel wondered what feet had worn them so, to what door they had originally led.

She was panting when she reached the top and peered in under the arch of the door. To her surprise she found herself staring into a broad, semicircular hallway, whose walls were lined with innumerable doors. She remembered the violet nothingness into which she had stepped the last time she crossed the sill, and wondered as she thrust a tentative foot over it if the hall were an illusion and she were really about to plunge once more into that cloudy abyss of falling. But the floor was firm.

She stepped inside and paused, looking round in some bewilderment and wondering where to turn now. She could smell peril in the air. Almost she could taste the magic that hovered like a mist over the whole enchanted place. Little warning prickles ran down her back as she went forward very softly and pushed open one of those innumerable doors. Behind it a gallery stretched down miles of haze-shrouded extent. Arrow-straight it ran, the arches of the ceiling making an endless parade that melted into violet distance. And as she stood looking down the cloudy vista, something like a puff of smoke obscured her vision for an instant – smoke that eddied and billowed and rolled away from the shape of that golden cat which had vanished in the mountain ravine.

It paced slowly down the hall toward her, graceful and lovely, muscles rippling under the brocaded golden coat and purple eyes fixed upon her in a scornful stare. Jirel's hand went to the knife in her belt, hatred choking up in her throat as she met the purple eyes. But in the corridor a voice was echoing softly, Jarisme's voice, saying:

'Then it is war between us, Jirel of Joiry. For you have defied my mercy, and you must be punished. Your punishment I have chosen – the simplest, and the subtlest, and the most terrible of all punishments, the worst that could befall a human creature. Can you guess it? No? Then wonder for a while, for I am not prepared yet to administer it fully … or shall I kill you now? Eh-h-h? …'

The curious, long-drawn query melted into a purring snarl, and the great cat's lip lifted, a flare of murderous light flaming up in the purple eyes. It had been pacing nearer all the while that light voice had echoed in the air. Now its roar crescendoed into a crashing thunder that rang from the walls, and the steel springs of its golden body tightened for a leap straight at Jirel's throat. Scarcely a dozen paces away, she saw the brocaded beauty of it crouching, taut and poised, saw the powerful body quiver and tighten – and spring. In instinctive panic she leaped back and slammed the door in its face.

Derisive laughter belled through the air. A cloud of thin smoke eddied through the crack around the door and puffed in her face with all the insolence of a blow. Then the air was clear again. The red mist of murder swam before Jirel's eyes. Blind with anger, breath beating thickly in her throat, she snatched at the door again, ripping the dagger from her belt. Through that furious haze she glared down the corridor. It was empty. She closed the door a second time and leaned against it, trembling with anger, until the mist had cleared from her head and she could control her shaking hand well enough to replace the dagger.

When she had calmed a little she turned to scan the hall, wondering what to do next. And she saw that there was no escape now, even had she wished, for the door she had entered by was gone. All about her now closed the door-studded walls, enigmatic, imprisoning. And the very fact of their presence was an insult, suggesting that Jarisme had feared she would flee if the entrance were left open. Jirel forced herself into calmness again. She was not afraid, but she knew herself in deadly peril.

She was revolving the sorceress' threat as she cast about for some indication to guide her next step. The simplest and subtlest and most terrible of punishments – what could it be? Jirel knew much of the ways of torture – her dungeons were as blood-stained as any of her neighbors' – but she knew too that Jarisme had not meant only the pain of the flesh. There was a subtler menace in her words. It would be a feminine vengeance, and more terrible than anything iron and fire could inflict. She knew that. She knew also that no door she could open now would lead to freedom, but she could not stay quiet, waiting. She glanced along the rows of dark, identical panels. Anything that magic could contrive might lie behind them. In the face of peril more deadly than death she could not resist the temptation to pull open the nearest one and peer within.

A gust of wind blew in her face and rattled the door. Dust was in that wind, and bitter cold. Through an inner grille of iron, locked across the opening, she saw a dazzle of whiteness like sun on snow in the instant before she slammed the door shut on the piercing gust. But the incident had whetted her curiosity. She moved along the wall and opened another.

This time she was looking through another locked grille into a dimness of gray smoke shot through with flame. The smell of burning rose in her nostrils, and she could hear faintly, as from vast distances, the sound of groans and the shivering echo of screams. Shuddering, she closed the door.

When she opened the next one she caught her breath and stared. Before her a thick crystal door separated her from bottomless space. She pressed her face to the cold glass and stared out and down. Nothingness met her gaze. Dark and silence and the blaze of unwinking stars. It was day outside the tower, but she looked into fathomless night. And as she stared, a long streak of light flashed across the blackness and faded. It was not a shooting star. By straining her eyes she could make out something like a thin sliver of silver flashing across the dark, its flaming tail fading behind it in the sky. And the sight made her ill with sudden vertigo. Bottomless void reeled around her, and she fell back into the hallway, slamming the door upon that terrifying glimpse of starry nothingness.

It was several minutes before she could bring herself to try the next door. When she did, swinging it open timorously, a familiar sweetness of flower perfume floated out and she found herself gazing through a grille of iron bars deep into that drowsy jungle of blossoms and scent and silence which she had crossed at the mountain's foot. A wave of remembrance washed over her. For an instant she could hear those tiny, laughing voices again, and she felt the presence of the great snake at her side, and the wild, mirth-ridden secrets of the little gay voices rang in her ears. Then she was awake again, and the memory vanished as dreams do, leaving nothing but tantalizing fragments of forgotten secrets drifting through her mind. She knew as she stared that she could step straight into that flowery fairyland again if the bars would open. But there was no escape from this magical place, though she might look through any number of opening doors into far lands and near.

She was beginning to understand the significance of the hall. It must be from here that Jarisme by her magical knowledge journeyed into other lands and times and worlds through the doors that opened between her domain and those strange, outland places. Perhaps she had sorcerer friends there, and paid them visits and brought back greater knowledge, stepping from world to world, from century to century, through her enchanted doorways. Jirel felt certain that one of these enigmatic openings would give upon that mountain pass where the golden cat with its scornful purple eyes had sprung at her, and vanished, and laughed backward as the door slammed upon it, and upon the woodland glade where the dryad died. But she knew that bars would close these places away even if she could find them.

She went on with her explorations. One door opened upon a steamy fern-forest of gigantic growths, out of whose deeps floated musky, reptilian odors, and the distant sound of beasts bellowing hollowly. And another upon a gray desert stretching flat and lifeless to the horizon, wan under the light of a dim red sun.

But at last she came to one that opened not into alien lands but upon a stairway winding down into solid rock whose walls showed the mark of the tools that had hollowed them. No sound came up the shaft of the stairs, and a gray light darkened down their silent reaches. Jirel peered in vain for some hint of what lay below. But at last, because inactivity had palled upon her and she knew that all ways were hopeless for escape, she entered the doorway and went slowly down the steps. It occurred to her that possibly she might find Jarisme below, engaged in some obscure magic in the lower regions, and she was eager to come to grips with her enemy.

The light darkened as she descended, until she was groping her way through obscurity round and round the curving stairs. When the steps ended at a depth she could not guess, she could tell that she had emerged into a low-roofed corridor only by feeling the walls and ceiling that met her exploring hands, for the thickest dark hid everything. She made her slow way along the stone hall, which wound and twisted and dipped at unexpected angles until she lost all sense of direction. But she knew she had gone a long way when she began to see the faint gleam of light ahead.

Presently she began to catch the faraway sound of a familiar song – Jarisme's monotonous little flute melody on two notes, and she was sure then that her intuition had been true, that the sorceress was down here somewhere. She drew her dagger in the gloom and went on more warily.

An arched opening ended the passage. Through the arch poured a blaze of dancing white luminance. Jirel paused, blinking and trying to make out what strange place she was entering. The room before her was filled with the baffling glitter and shimmer and mirage of reflecting surfaces so bewilderingly that she could not tell which was real and which mirror, and which dancing light. The brilliance dazzled in her face and dimmed into twilight and blazed again as the mirrors shifted. Little currents of dark shivered through the chaos and brightened into white sparkle once more. That monotonous music came to her through the quivering lights and reflections, now strongly, now faintly in the distance.

The whole place was a chaos of blaze and confusion. She could not know if the room were small or large, a cavern or a palace hall. Queer reflections danced through the dazzle of it. She could see her own image looking back at her from a dozen, a score, a hundred moving planes that grotesquely distorted her and then flickered out again, casting a blaze of light in her blinded eyes. Dizzily she blinked into the reeling wilderness of planes.

Then she saw Jarisme in her violet robe watching her from a hundred identical golden couches reflected upon a hundred surfaces. The figure held a flute to its lips, and the music pulsed from it in perfect time with the pulsing of the sorceress' swelling white throat. Jirel stared round in confusion at the myriad Jarismes all piping the interminable monotones. A hundred sensual, dreamy faces turned to her, a hundred white arms dropped as the flute left a hundred red mouths that Jarisme might smile ironic welcome a hundredfold more scornful for its multiplicity.

When the music ceased, all the flashing dazzle suddenly stilled. Jirel blinked as the chaos resolved itself into shining order, the hundred Jarismes merging into one sleepy-eyed woman lounging upon her golden couch in a vast crystal-walled chamber shaped like the semicircular half of a great, round, domed room. Behind the couch a veil of violet mist hung like a curtain shutting off what would have formed the other half of the circular room:

'Enter,' said the sorceress with the graciousness of one who knows herself in full command of the situation. 'I thought you might find the way here. I am preparing a ceremony which will concern you intimately. Perhaps you would like to watch? This is to be an experiment, and for that reason a greater honor is to be yours than you can ever have known before; for the company I am assembling to watch your punishment is a more distinguished one than you could understand. Come here, inside the circle.'

Jirel advanced, dagger still clenched in one hand, the other closed about her bit of broken crystal. She saw now that the couch stood in the center of a ring engraved in the floor with curious, cabalistic symbols. Beyond it the cloudy violet curtain swayed and eddied within itself, a vast, billowing wall of mist. Dubiously she stepped over the circle and stood eyeing Jarisme, her yellow gaze hot with rigidly curbed emotion. Jarisme smiled and lifted the flute to her lips again.

As the irritating two notes began their seesawing tune Jirel saw something amazing happen. She knew then that the flute was a magic one, and the song magical too. The notes took on a form that overstepped the boundaries of the aural and partook in some inexplicable way of all the other senses too. She could feel them, taste them, smell them, see them. In a queer way they were visible, pouring in twos from the flute and dashing outward like little needles of light. The walls reflected them, and those reflections became swifter and brighter and more numerous until the air was full of flying slivers of silvery brilliance, until shimmers began to dance among them and over them, and that bewildering shift of mirrored planes started up once more. Again reflections crossed and dazzled and multiplied in the shining air as the flute poured out its flashing double notes.

Jirel forgot the sorceress beside her, the music that grated on her ears, even her own peril, in watching the pictures that shimmered and vanished in the mirrored surfaces. She saw flashes of scenes she had glimpsed through the doors of Jarisme's hallway. She saw stranger places than that, passing in instant-brief snatches over the silvery planes. She saw jagged black mountains with purple dawns rising behind them and stars in unknown figures across the dark skies; she saw gray seas flat and motionless beneath gray clouds; she saw smooth meadows rolling horizonward under the glare of double suns. All these and many more awoke to the magic of Jarisme's flute, and melted again to give way to others.

Jirel had the strange fancy, as the music went on; that it was audible in those lands whose brief pictures were flickering across the background of its visible notes. It seemed to be piercing immeasurable distances, ringing across the cloudy seas, echoing under the durable suns, calling insistently in strange lands and far, unknown places, over deserts and mountains that man's feet had never trod, reaching other worlds and other times and crying its two-toned monotony through the darkness of interstellar space. All of this, to Jirel, was no more than a vague realization that it must be so. It meant nothing to her, whose world was a flat plane arched by the heaven-pierced bowl of the sky. Magic, she told herself, and gave up trying to understand.

Presently the tempo of the fluting changed. The same two notes still shrilled endlessly up and down, but it was no longer a clarion call ringing across borderlands into strange worlds. Now it was slower, statelier. And the notes of visible silver that had darted crazily against the crystal walls and reflected back again took on an order that ranked them into one shining plane. Upon that plane Jirel saw the outlines of a familiar scene gradually take shape. The great door-lined hall above mirrored itself in faithful replica before her eyes. The music went on changelessly.

Then, as she watched, one of those innumerable doors quivered. She held her breath. Slowly it swung open upon that gray desert under the red sun which she had seen before she closed it quickly away behind concealing panels. Again as she looked, that sense of utter desolation and weariness and despair came over her, so uncannily dreary was the scene. Now the door stood wide, its locked grille no longer closing it, and as the music went on she could see a dazzle like a jagged twist of lightning begin to shimmer in its aperture. The gleam strengthened. She saw it quiver once, twice, then sweep forward with blinding speed through the open doorway. And as she tried to follow it with her eyes another moving door distracted her.

This time the steamy fern-forest was revealed as the panels swung back. But upon the threshold sprawled something so frightful that Jirel's free hand flew to her lips and a scream beat up in her throat. It was black – shapeless and black and slimy. And it was alive. Like a heap of putrescently shining jelly it heaved itself over the doorsill and began to flow across the floor, inching its way along like a vast blind ameba. But she knew without being told that it was horribly wise, horribly old. Behind it a black trail of slime smeared the floor.

Jirel shuddered and turned her eyes away. Another door was swinging open. Through it she saw a place she had not chanced upon before, a country of bare red rock strewn jaggedly under a sky so darkly blue that it might have been black, with stars glimmering in it more clearly than stars of earth. Across this red, broken desert a figure came striding that she knew could be only a figment of magic, so tall it was, so spidery-thin, so grotesquely human despite its bulbous head and vast chest. She could not see it clearly, for about it like a robe it clutched a veil of blinding light. On those incredibly long, thin legs it stepped across the door-sill, drew its dazzling garment closer about it, and strode forward. As it neared, the light was so blinding that she could not look upon it. Her averted eyes caught the motion of a fourth door.

This time she saw that flowery ravine again, dim in its underwater illusion of diffused light. And out from among the flowers writhed a great serpent-creature, not of the transparent crystal she had seen in her dream, but irridescently scaled. Nor was it entirely serpent, for from the thickened neck sprang a head which could not be called wholly unhuman. The thing carried itself as proudly as a cobra, and as it glided across the threshold its single, many-faceted eye caught Jirel's in the reflection. The eye flashed once, dizzyingly, and she reeled back in sick shock, the violence of that glance burning through her veins like fire. When she regained control of herself many other doors were standing open upon scenes both familiar and strange. During her daze other denizens of those strange worlds must have entered at the call of the magic flute.

She was just in time to see an utterly indescribable thing flutter into the hall from a world which so violated her eyes that she got no more than a glimpse of it as she flung up outraged hands to shut it out. She did not lower that shield until Jarisme's amused voice said in an undertone: 'Behold your audience, Jirel of Joiry,' and she realized that the music had ceased and a vast silence was pressing against her ears. Then she looked out, and drew a long breath. She was beyond surprise and shock now, and she stared with the dazed incredulity of one who knows herself in a nightmare.

Ranged outside the circle that enclosed the two women sat what was surely the strangest company ever assembled. They were grouped with a queer irregularity which, though meaningless to Jirel, yet gave the impression of definite purpose and design. It had a symmetry so strongly marked that even though it fell outside her range of comprehension she could not but feel the rightness of it.

The light-robed dweller in the red barrens sat there, and the great black blob of shapeless jelly heaved gently on the crystal floor. She saw others she had watched enter, and many more. One was a female creature whose robe of peacock iridescence sprang from her shoulders in great drooping wings and folded round her like a bat's leathery cloak. And her neighbor was a fat gray slug of monster size, palpitating endlessly. One of the crowd looked exactly like a tall white lily swaying on a stalk of silver pallor, but from its chalice poured a light so ominously tinted that she shuddered and turned her eyes away.

Jarisme had risen from her couch. Very tall and regal in her violet robe, she rose against the back-drop of mist which veiled the other half of the room. As she lifted her arms, the incredible company turned to her with an eager expectancy. Jirel shuddered. Then Jarisme's flute spoke softly. It was a different sort of music from the clarion that called them together, from the stately melody which welcomed them through the opening doors. But it harped still on the two seesawing notes, with low, rippling sounds so different from the other two that Jirel marveled at the range of the sorceress' ability on the two notes.

For a few moments as the song went on, nothing happened. Then a motion behind Jarisme caught Jirel's eye. The curtain of violet mist was swaying. The music beat at it and it quivered to the tune. It shook within itself, and paled and thinned, and from behind it a light began to glow. Then on a last low monotone it dissipated wholly and Jirel was staring at a vast globe of quivering light which loomed up under the stupendous arch that soared outward to form the second half of the chamber.

As the last clouds faded she saw that the thing was a huge crystal sphere, rising upon the coils of a translucent purple base in the shape of a serpent. And in the heart of the globe burned a still flame, living, animate, instinct with a life so alien that Jirel stared in utter bewilderment. It was a thing she knew to be alive – yet she knew it could *not* be alive. But she recognized even in her daze of incomprehension its relation to the tiny fragment of crystal she clutched in her hand. In that too the still flame burned. It stung her hand faintly in reminder that she possessed a weapon which could destroy Jarisme, though it might destroy its wielder in the process. The thought gave her a sort of desperate courage.

Jarisme was ignoring her now. She had turned to face the great globe with lifted arms and shining head thrown back. And from her lips a piercingly sweet sound fluted, midway between hum and whistle. Jirel had the wild fancy that she could see that sound arrowing straight into the heart of the vast sphere bulking so high over them all. And in the heart of that still, living flame a little glow of red began to quiver.

Through the trembling air shrilled a second sound. From the corner of her eye Jirel could see that a dark figure had moved forward into the circle and fallen to its knees at the sorceress' side. She knew it for Giraud. Like two blades the notes quivered in the utter hush that lay upon the assembly, and in the globe that red glow deepened.

One by one, other voices joined the chorus, queer, uncanny sounds some of them, from throats not shaped for speech. No two voices blended. The chorus was one of single, unrelated notes. As each voice struck the globe, the fire burned more crimson, until its still pallor had flushed wholly into red. High above the rest soared Jarisme's knife-keen fluting. She lifted her arms higher, and the voices rose in answer. She lowered them, and the blade-like music swooped down an almost visible arc to a lower key. Jirel felt that she could all but see the notes spearing straight from each singer into the vast sphere that dwarfed them all. There was no melody in it, but a sharply definite pattern as alien and unmistakable as the symmetry of their grouping in the room. And as Jarisme's arms rose, lifting the voices higher, the flame burned more deeply red, and paled again as the voices fell.

Three times that stately, violet-robed figure gestured with lifted arms, and three times the living flame deepened and paled. Then Jarisme's voice soared in a high, triumphant cry and she whirled with spread arms, facing the company. In one caught breath, all voices ceased. Silence fell upon them like a blow. Jarisme was no longer priestess, but goddess, as she fronted them in that dead stillness with exultant face and blazing eyes. And in one motion they bowed before her as corn bows under wind. Alien things, shapeless monsters, faceless, eyeless, unrecognizable creatures from unknowable dimensions, abased themselves to the crystal floor before the splendor of light in Jarisme's eyes. For a moment of utter silence the tableau held. Then the sorceress' arms fell.

Ripplingly the company rose. Beyond Jarisme the vast globe had paled again into that living, quiet flame of golden pallor. Immense, brooding, alive, it loomed up above them. Into the strained stillness Jarisme's low voice broke. She was speaking in Jirel's native tongue, but the air, as she went on, quivered thickly with something like waves of sound that were pitched for other organs than human ears. Every word that left her lips made another wave through the thickened air. The assembly shimmered before Jirel's eyes in that broken clarity as a meadow quivers under heat waves.

'Worshippers of the Light,' said Jarisme sweetly, 'be welcomed from your far dwellings into the presence of the Flame. We who serve it have called you to the worship, but before you return, another sort of ceremony is to be held, which we have felt will interest you all. For we have called it truly the simplest and subtlest and most terrible of all punishments for a human creature.

'It is our purpose to attempt a reversal of this woman's physical and mental self in such a way as to cause her body to become rigidly motionless while her mind – her soul – looks eternally backward along the path it has traveled. You who are human, or have known humanity, will understand what deadly torture that can be. For no human creature, by the laws that govern it, can have led a life whose intimate review is anything but pain. To be frozen into eternal reflections, reviewing all the futility and pain of life, all the pain that thoughtless or intentional acts have caused others, all the spreading consequences of every act – that, to a human being, would be the most dreadful of all torments.'

In the silence that fell as her voice ceased, Giraud laid a hand on Jarisme's arm. Jirel saw terror in his eyes.

'Remember,' he uttered, 'remember, for those who tamper with their known destiny a more fearful thing may come than—'

Jarisme shrugged off the restraining hand impatiently. She turned to Jirel.

'Know, earthling,' she said in a queerly strained voice, 'that in the books of the future it is written that Jarisme the Sorceress must die at the hands of the one human creature who defies her thrice – and that human creature a woman. Twice I have been weak, and spared you. Once in the forest, once on the roof-top, you cast your puny defiance in my face, and I stayed my hand for fear of what is written. But the third time shall not come. Though you are my appointed slayer, you shall not slay. With my own magic I break Fate's sequence, now, and we shall see!'

In the blaze of her purple eyes Jirel saw, that the moment had come. She braced herself, fingers closing about the fragment of crystal in her hand uncertainly as she hesitated, wondering if the time had come for the breaking of her talisman at the sorceress' feet. She hesitated too long, though her waiting was only a split second in duration. For Jarisme's magic was more supremely simple than Jirel could have guessed. The sorceress turned a blazing purple gaze upon her and sharply snapped her plump fingers in the earthwoman's face.

At the sound Jirel's whole world turned inside out about her. It was the sheerest physical agony. Everything vanished as that terrible shift took place. She felt her own body being jerked inexplicably around in a reversal like nothing that any living creature could ever have experienced before. It was a backward-facing in a direction which could have had no existence until that instant. She felt the newness in the second before sight came to her – a breathless, soundless, new-born *now* in which she was the first dweller, created simultaneously with the new plane of being. Then sight broke upon her consciousness.

The thing spread out before her was so stupendous that she would have screamed if she had possessed an animate body. All life was open to her gaze. The sight was too immeasurable for her to grasp it fully – too vast for her human consciousness to look upon at all save in flashing shutter-glimpses without relation or significance. Motion and immobility existed simultaneously in the thing before her. Endless activity shuttling to and fro – yet the whole vast panorama was frozen in a timeless calm through which a mighty pattern ran whose very immensity was enough to strike terror into her soul. Threaded through it the backward trail of her own life stretched. As she gazed upon it such floods of conflicting emotion washed over her that she could not see anything clearly, but she was fiercely insisting to her inner consciousness that she would not – *would not* – look back, dared not, could not – and all the while her sight was running past days and weeks along the path which led inexorably toward the one scene she could not bear to think of.

Very remotely, as her conscious sight retraced the backward way, she was aware of overlapping planes of existence in the stretch of limitless activity before her. Shapes other than human, scenes that had no meaning to her, quivered and shifted and boiled with changing lives – yet lay motionless in the mighty pattern. She scarcely heeded them. For her, of all that panoramic impossibility one scene alone had meaning – the one scene toward which her sight was racing now, do what she would to stop it – the one scene that she knew she could never bear to see again.

Yet when her sight reached that place the pain did not begin at once. She gazed almost calmly upon that little interval of darkness and flaring light, the glare of torches shining upon a girl's bent red head and on a man's long body sprawled motionless upon flagstones. In the deepest stillness she stared. She felt no urge to look farther, on beyond the scene into the past. This was the climax, the center of all her life – this torch-lit moment on the flagstones. Vividly she was back again in the past, felt the hardness of the cold flags against her knees, and the numbness of her heart as she stared down into a dead man's face. Timelessly she dwelt upon that long-ago heartbreak, and within her something swelled unbearably.

That something was a mounting emotion too great to have name, too complexly blending agony and grief and hatred and love – and rebellion; so strong that all the rest of the stupendous thing before her was blotted out in the gathering storm of what seethed in her innermost consciousness. She was aware of nothing but that overwhelming emotion. And it was boiling into one great unbearable explosion of violence in which rage took precedence over all. Rage at life for permitting such pain to be. Rage at Jarisme for forcing her into memory. Such rage that everything shook before it, and melted and ran together in a heat of rebellion, and – something snapped. The panorama reeled and shivered and collapsed into the dark of semi-oblivion.

Through the clouds of her half-consciousness the agony of change stabbed at her. Half understanding, she welcomed it, though the piercing anguish of that reversal was so strong it dragged her out of her daze again and wrung her anew in the grinding pain of that change which defied all natural laws. In heedless impatience she waited for the torture to pass. Exultation was welling up in her for she knew that her own violence had melted the spell by which Jarisme held her. She knew what she must do when she stood free again, and conscious power flowed intoxicatingly through her.

She opened her eyes. She was standing rigidly before the great fire-quickened globe. The amazing company was grouped around her intently, and Jarisme, facing her, had taken one angry, incredulous step forward as she saw her own spell break. Upon that tableau Jirel's hot yellow eyes opened, and she laughed in grim exultation and swung up her arm. Violet light glinted upon crystal.

In the instant Jarisme saw what she intended, convulsive terror wiped all other expression from her face. A cry of mingled inarticulatenesses thundered up from the transfixed crowd. Giraud started forward from among them, frantic hands clawing out toward her.

'No, no!' shrieked Jarisme. 'Wait!'

It was too late. The crystal dashed itself from Jirel's down-swinging arm, the light in it blazing. With a splintering crash it struck the floor at the sorceress's sandaled feet and flew into shining fragments.

For an instant nothing happened. Jirel held her breath, waiting. Giraud had flung himself flat on the shining floor, reaching out for her in a last desperate effort. His hands had flown out to seize her, and found only her ankles. He clung to them now with a paralyzed grip, his face hidden between his arms. Jarisme cowered motionless, arms clasped about her head as if she were trying to hide. The motley throng of watchers was rigid in fatalistic quiet. In tense silence they waited.

Then in the great globe above them the pale flame flickered. Jarisme's gaspingly caught breath sounded loud in the utter quiet. Again the flame shook. And again. Then abruptly it went out. Darkness stunned them for a moment; then a low muttering roar rumbled up out of the stillness, louder and deeper and stronger until it pressed unbearably upon Jirel's ears and her head was one great aching surge of sound. Above that roar a sharply crackling noise broke, and the crystal walls of the room trembled, reeled dizzily – split open in long jagged rents through which the violet day poured in thin fingers of light. Overhead the shattering sound of falling walls roared loud. Jarisme's magic tower was crumbling all around them. Through the long, shivering cracks in the walls the pale violet day poured more strongly, serene in the chaos.

In that clear light Jirel saw a motion among the throng. Jarisme had risen to her full height. She saw the sleek black head go up in an odd, defiant, desperate poise, and above the soul-shaking tumult she heard the sorceress' voice scream:

'Urda! Urda-sla!'

In the midst of the roar of the falling walls for the briefest instant a deathly silence dropped. And out of that silence, like an answer to the sorceress' cry, came a Noise, an indescribable, intolerable loudness like the crack of cyclopean thunder. And suddenly in the sky above them, visible through the crumbling crystal walls, a long black wedge opened. It was like a strip of darkest midnight splitting the violet day, a midnight through which stars shone unbearably near, unbearably bright.

Jirel stared up in dumb-surprise at that streak of starry night cleaving the daylit sky. Jarisme stood rigid, arms outstretched, defiantly fronting the thunderous dark whose apex was drawing nearer and nearer, driving downward like a vast celestial spear. She did not flinch as it reached toward the tower. Jirel saw the darkness sweep forward like a racing shadow. Then it was upon them, and the earth shuddered under her feet, and from very far away she heard Jarisme scream.

When consciousness returned to her, she sat up painfully and stared around. She lay upon green grass, bruised and aching, but unharmed. The violet day was serene and unbroken once more. The purple peaks had vanished. No longer was she high among mountains. Instead, the green meadow where she had first seen Jarisme's tower stretched about her. In its dissolution it must have returned to its original site, flashing back along the magical ways it had traveled as the sorceress' magic was broken. For the tower too was gone. A little distance away she saw a heap of marble blocks outlining a rough circle, where that white shaft had risen. But the stones were weathered and cracked like the old, old stones of an ancient ruin.

She had been staring at this for many minutes, trying to focus her bewildered mind upon its significance, before the sound of groaning which had been going on for some time impressed itself on her brain. She turned. A little way off, Giraud lay in a tangle of torn black robes. Of Jarisme and the rest she saw no sign. Painfully she got to her feet and staggered to the wizard, turning him over with a disdainful toe. He opened his eyes and stared at her with a cloudy gaze into which recognition and realization slowly crept.

'Are you hurt?' she demanded.

He pulled himself to a sitting position and flexed his limbs experimentally. Finally he shook his head, more in answer to his own investigation than to her query, and got slowly to his feet. Jirel's eyes sought the weapon at his hip.

'I am going to kill you now,' she said calmly. 'Draw your sword, wizard.'

The little dull eyes flashed up to her face. He stared. Whatever he saw in the yellow gaze must have satisfied him that she meant what she said, but he did not draw, nor did he fall back. A tight little smile drew his mouth askew, and he lifted his black-robed arms. Jirel saw them rise, and her gaze followed the gesture automatically. Up they went, up. And then in the queerest fashion she lost all control of her own eyes, so that they followed some invisible upward line which drew her on and on skyward until she was rigidly staring at a fixed point of invisibility at the spot where the lines of Giraud's arms would have crossed, were they extended to a measureless distance. Somehow she actually saw that point, and could not look away. Gripped in the magic of those lifted arms, she stood rigid, not even realizing what had happened, unable even to think in the moveless magic of Giraud.

His little mocking chuckle reached her from immeasurably far away.

'Kill me?' he was laughing thickly. 'Kill me, Giraud? Why, it was you who saved me, Joiry! Why else should I have clung to your ankles so tightly? For I knew that when the Light died, the only one who could hope to live would be the one who slew it – nor was that a certainty, either. But I took the risk, and well I did, or I would be with Jarisme now in the outer dark whence she called up her no-god of the void to save her from oblivion. I warned her what would happen if she tampered with Fate. And I would rather – yes, much rather – be here, in this violet land which I shall rule alone now. Thanks to you, Joiry! Kill me, eh? I think not!'

That thick, mocking chuckle reached her remotely, penetrated her magic-stilled mind. It echoed round and round there, for a long while, before she realized what it meant. But at last she remembered, and her mind woke a little from its inertia, and such anger swept over her that its heat was an actual pain. Giraud, the runaway sorcerer, laughing at Joiry! Holding Jirel of Joiry in his spell! Mocking her! Blindly she wrenched at the bonds of magic, blindly urged her body forward. She could see nothing but that non-existent point where the lifted arms would have crossed, in measureless distances, but she felt the dagger-hilt in her hand, and she lunged forward through invisibility, and did not even know when the blade sank home.

Sight returned to her then in a stunning flood. She rubbed dazed eyes and shook herself and stared round the green meadow in the violet day uncomprehendingly, for her mind was not yet fully awake. Not until she looked down did she remember.

Giraud lay there. The black robes were furled like wings over his quiet body, but red in a thick flood was spreading on the grass, and from the tangled garments her dagger-hilt stood up. Jirel stared down at him, emotionless, her whole body still almost asleep from the power of the dead man's magic. She could not even feel triumph. She pulled the blade free automatically and wiped it on his robes. Then she sat down beside the body and rested her head in her hands, forcing herself to awaken.

After a long while she looked up again, the old hot light rising in her eyes, life flushing back into her face once more. Shaking off the last shreds of the spell, she got to her feet, sheathing the dagger. About her the violet-misted meadows were very still. No living creature moved anywhere in sight. The trees were motionless in the unstirring air. And beyond the ruins of the marble tower she saw the opening in the woods out of which path had come, very long ago.

Jirel squared her shoulders and turned her back upon her vow fulfilled, and without a backward glance set off across the grass toward the tree-hid ruins which held the gate to home.

THE DARK LAND

In her great bed in the tower room of Joiry Castle, Jirel of Joiry lay very near to death. Her red hair was a blaze upon the pillow above the bone-whiteness of her face, and the lids lay heavy over the yellow fire of her eyes. Life had gushed out of her in great scarlet spurts from the pike-wound deep in her side, and the whispering women who hovered at the door were telling one another in hushed murmurs that the Lady Jirel had led her last battle charge. Never again would she gallop at the head of her shouting men, swinging her sword with all the ferocity that had given her name such weight among the savage warrior barons whose lands ringed hers. Jirel of Joiry lay very still upon her pillow.

The great two-edged sword which she wielded so recklessly in the heat of combat hung on the wall now where her yellow eyes could find it if they opened, and her hacked and battered armor lay in a heap in one corner of the room just as the women had flung it as they stripped her when the grave-faced men-at-arms came shuffling up the stairs bearing the limp form of their lady, heavy in her mail. The room held the hush of death. Nothing in it stirred. On the bed Jirel's white face lay motionless among the pillows.

Presently one of the women moved forward and gently pulled the door to against their watching.

'It is unseemly to stare so,' she reproved the others. 'Our lady would not desire us to behold her thus until Father Gervase has shriven her sins away.'

And the coifed heads nodded assent, murmurous among themselves. In a moment or two more a commotion on the stairs forced the massed watchers apart, and Jirel's serving-maid came up the steps holding a kerchief to her reddened eyes and leading Father Gervase. Someone pushed open the door for them, and the crowd parted to let them through.

The serving-maid stumbled forward to the bedside, mopping her eyes blindly. Behind her something obscurely wrong was happening. After a moment she realized what it was. A great stillness had fallen stunningly upon the crowd. She lifted a bewildered gaze toward the door. Gervase was staring at the bed in the blankest amazement.

'My child,' he stammered, 'where is your lady?'

The girl's head jerked round toward the bed. It was empty.

The sheets still lay exactly as they had covered Jirel, not pushed back as one pushes the blankets on arising. The hollow where her body had lain still held its shape among the yet warm sheets, and no fresh blood spattered the floor; but of the Lady of Joiry there was no sign.

Gervase's hands closed hard on his silver crucifix and under the fringe of gray hair his face crumpled suddenly into grief.

'Our dear lady has dabbled too often in forbidden things,' he murmured to himself above the crucifix. 'Too often ...'

Behind him trembling hands signed the cross, and awed whispers were already passing the word back down the crowded stairs: 'The devil himself has snatched Jirel of Joiry body and soul out of her deathbed.'

Jirel remembered shouts and screams and the din of battle, and that stunning impact in her side. Afterward nothing but dimness floating thickly above a bedrock of savage pain, and the murmur of voices from very far away. She drifted bodiless and serene upon a dark tide that was ebbing seaward, pulling her out and away while the voices and the pain receded to infinite distances, and faded and ceased.

Then somewhere a light was shining. She fought the realization weakly, for the dark tide pulled seaward and her soul desired the peace it seemed to promise with a longing beyond any words to tell. But the light would not let her go. Rebellious, struggling, at last she opened her eyes. The lids responded sluggishly, as if they had already forgotten obedience to her will. But she could see under the fringe of lashes, and she lay motionless, staring quietly while life flowed back by slow degrees into the body it had so nearly left.

The light was a ring of flames, leaping golden against the dark beyond them. For a while she could see no more than that circlet of fire. Gradually perception returned behind her eyes, and reluctantly the body that had hovered so near to death took up the business of living again. With full comprehension she stared, and as she realized what it was she looked upon, incredulity warred with blank amazement in her dazed mind.

Before her a great image sat, monstrous and majestic upon a throne. Throne and image were black and shining. The figure was that of a huge man, wide-shouldered, tremendous, many times life size. His face was bearded, harsh with power and savagery, and very regal, haughty as Lucifer's might have been. He sat upon his enormous black throne staring arrogantly into nothingness. About his head the flames were leaping. She looked harder, unbelieving. How could she have come here? What was it, and where? Blank-eyed, she stared at that flaming crown that circled the huge head, flaring and leaping and casting queer bright shadows over the majestic face below them.

Without surprise, she found that she was sitting up. In her stupor she had not known the magnitude of her hurt, and it did not seem strange to her that no pain attended the motion, or that her pike-torn side was whole again beneath the doeskin tunic which was all she wore. She could not have known that the steel point of the pike had driven the leather into her flesh so deeply that her women had not dared to remove the garment lest they open the wound afresh and their lady die before absolution came to her. She only knew that she sat here naked in her doeskin tunic, her bare feet on a fur rug and cushions heaped about her. And all this was so strange and inexplicable that she made no attempt to understand.

The couch on which she sat was low and broad and black, and that fur rug in whose richness her toes were rubbing luxuriously was black too, and huger than any beast's pelt could be outside dreams.

Before her, across an expanse of gleaming black floor the mighty image rose, crowned with flame. For the rest, this great, black, dim-lighted room was empty. The flame-reflections danced eerily in the shining floor. She lifted her eyes, and saw with a little start of surprise that there was no ceiling. The walls rose immensely overhead, terminating in jagged abruptness above which a dark sky arched, sown with dim stars.

This much she had seen and realized before a queer glittering in the air in front of the image drew her roving eyes back. It was a shimmer and dance like the dance of dust motes in sunshine, save that the particles which glittered in the darkness were multicolored, dazzling. They swirled and swarmed before her puzzled eyes in a queer dance that was somehow taking shape in the light of the flames upon the image's head. A figure was forming in the midst of the rainbow shimmer A man's figure, a tall, dark-visaged, heavy-shouldered man whose outlines among the dancing motes took on rapid form and solidarity, strengthening by moments until in a last swirl the gaily colored dazzle dissipated and the man himself stood wide-legged before her, fists planted on his hips, grinning darkly down upon the spell-bound Jirel.

He was the image. Save that he was of flesh and blood, life size, and the statue was of black stone and gigantic, there was no difference. The same harsh, arrogant, majestic face turned its grim smile upon Jirel. From under scowling black brows, eyes that glittered blackly with little red points of intolerable brilliance blazed down upon her. She could not meet that gaze. A short black beard outlined the harshness of his jaw, and through it the white flash of his smile dazzled her.

This much about the face penetrated even Jirel's dazed amazement, and she caught her breath in a sudden gasp, sitting up straighter among her cushions and staring. The dark stranger's eyes were eager upon the long, lithe lines of her upon the couch. Red sparkles quickened in their deeps, and his grin widened.

'Welcome,' he said, in a voice so deep and rich that involuntarily a little burr of answer rippled along Jirel's nerves. 'Welcome to the dark land of Romne.'

'Who brought me here?' Jirel found her voice at last. 'And why?'

'I did it,' he told her. 'I – Pav, king of Romne. Thank me for it, Jirel of Joiry. But for Pav you had lain among the worms tonight. It was out of your deathbed I took you, and no power but mine could have mended the pike-hole in your side or put back into you the blood you spilled on Triste battlefield. Thank me, Jirel!'

She looked at him levelly, her yellow eyes kindling a little in rising anger as she met the laughter in his.

'Tell me why you brought me here.'

At that he threw back his head and laughed hugely, a bull bellow of savage amusement that rang in deep echoes from the walls and beat upon her ears with the sound of organ notes. The room shook with his laughter; the little flames around the image's head danced to it.

'To be my bride, Joiry!' he roared. 'That look of defiance ill becomes you, Jirel! Blush, lady, before your bridegroom!'

The blankness of the girl's amazement was all that saved her for the moment from the upsurge of murderous fury which was beginning to seethe below the surface of her consciousness. She could only stare as he laughed down at her, enjoying to the full her mute amaze.

'Yes,' he said at last, 'you have traveled too often in forbidden lands, Jirel of Joiry, to be ignored by us who live in them. And there is in you a hot and savage strength which no other woman in any land I know possesses. A force to match my own, Lady Jirel. None but you is fit to be my queen. So I have taken you for my own.'

Jirel gasped in a choke of fury and found her voice again.

'Hell-dwelling madman!' she spluttered. 'Black beast out of nightmares! Let me waken from this crazy dream!'

'It is no dream,' he smiled infuriatingly. 'As you died in Joiry Castle I seized you out of your bed and snatched you body and soul over the space-curve that parts this land from yours. You have awakened in your own dark kingdom, O Queen of Romne!' And he swept her an, ironical salute, his teeth glittering in the darkness of his beard.

'By what right—' blazed Jirel.

'By a lover's right,' he mocked her. 'Is it not better to share Romne with me than to reign among the worms, my lady? For death was very near to you just now. I have saved your lovely flesh from a cold bed, Jirel, and kept your hot soul rooted there for you. Do I get no thanks for that?'

Yellow fury blazed in her eyes.

'The thanks of a sword-edge, if I had one,' she flared. 'Do you think to take Joiry like some peasant wench to answer to your whims? I'm Joiry, man! You must be mad!'

'I'm Pav,' he answered her somberly, all mirth vanishing in a breath from his heavy voice. 'I'm king of Romne and lord of all who dwell therein. For your savageness I chose you, but do not try me too far, Lady Jirel!'

She looked up into the swart, harsh face staring down on her, and quite suddenly the nearest thing she had ever known to fear of a human being came coldly over her; perhaps the fear that if any man alive could tame her fierceness, this man could. The red prickles had gone out of his eyes, and something in her shuddered a little from that black, unpupiled stare. She veiled the hawk-yellow of her own gaze and set her lips in a straight line.

'I shall call your servants,' said Pav heavily. 'You must be clothed as befits a queen, and then I shall show you your land of Romne.'

She saw the black glare of his eyes flick sidewise as if in search, and in the instant his gaze sought them there appeared about her in the empty air the most curious phenomenon she had ever seen. Queer, shimmering bluenesses swarm shoulder-high all around her, blue and translucent like hot flames, and like flames their outlines flickered. She never saw them clearly, but their touch upon her was like the caress a flame might give if it bore no heat: swift, brushing, light.

All about her they seethed, moving too quickly for the eyes to follow; all over her the quick, flickering caresses ran. And she felt queerly exhausted as they moved, as if strength were somehow draining out of her while the blue flames danced. When their bewildering ministrations ceased the strange weariness abated too, and Jirel in blank surprise looked down at her own long, lovely body sheathed in the most exquisite velvet she had ever dreamed of. It was black as a starless night, softer than down, rich and lustrous as it molded her shining curves into sculptured beauty. There was a sensuous delight in the soft swirl of it around her feet as she moved, in the dark caress of it upon her flesh when motion stirred the silken surfaces against her skin. For an instant she was lost in pure feminine ecstasy.

But that lasted only for an instant. Then she heard Pav's deep voice saying: 'Look!' and she lifted her eyes to a room whose outlines were melting away like smoke. The great image faded, the gleaming floor and the jagged, roofless walls turned translucent and misty, and through their melting surfaces mountains began to loom in the distance, dark trees and rough, uneven land. Before the echoes of Pav's deeply vibrant 'Look!' had shivered wholly into silence along her answering nerves, the room had vanished and they two stood alone in the midst of the dark land of Romne.

It was a dark land indeed. As far as she could see, the air swallowed up every trace of color, so that in somber grays and blacks the landscape stretched away under her eyes. But it had a curious clarity, too, in the dark, translucent air. She could see the distant mountains black and. clear beyond the black trees. Beyond them, too, she caught a gleam of still black water, and under her feet the ground was black and rocky. And there was a curiously circumscribed air about the place. Somehow she felt closed in as she stared, for the horizon seemed nearer than it should be, and its dark circle bound the little world of grayness and blackness and clear, dark air into a closeness she could not account for.

She felt prisoned in and a little breathless, for all the wide country spreading so clearly, so darkly about her. Perhaps it was because even out at the far edge of the sky everything was as distinct in the transparent darkness of the air as the rocks at her very feet, so that there was no sense of distance here at all.

Yes, it was a dark land, and a strange land, forbidding, faintly nightmarish in the color-swallowing clarity of its air, the horizons too near and too clear in the narrowness of their circle.

'This,' said Pav beside her, in his nerve-tingling voice that sent unconquerable little shudders of answer along her resounding nerves, 'this is your land of Romne, O Queen! A land wider than it looks, and one well befitted to your strength and loveliness, my Jirel. A strange land, too, by all earthly standards. Later you must learn how strange. The illusion of it—'

'Save your breath, King of Romne,' Jirel broke in upon his deep-voiced speech. 'This is no land of mine, and holds no interest for me save in its way out. Show me the gate back into my own world, and I shall be content never to see Romne or you again.'

Pav's big hand shot out and gripped her shoulder ungently. He swung her round in a swirl of velvet skirts and a toss of fire-colored hair, and his dark, bearded face was savage with anger. The little red dazzles danced in his unpupiled black eyes until she could not focus her own hot yellow gaze upon them, and dropped her eyes from his in helpless fury.

'You are mine!' he told her in a voice so deep and low that her whole body tingled to its vibration. 'I took you out of Joiry and your death-bed and the world you knew, and you are mine from this moment on. Strong you may be, but not so strong as I, Jirel of Joiry, and when I command, henceforth obey!'

Blind with fury, Jirel ripped his hand away and fell back one step in a swirl of black skirts. She tossed her head up until the curls upon it leaped like flames, and the scorching anger in her voice licked up in matching flames, so hotly that her speech was broken and breathless as she choked in a half-whisper.

'Never touch me again, you black hell-dweller! Before God, you'd never, have dared if you'd left me a knife to defend myself with! I swear I'll tear the eyes out of your head if I feel the weight of your hand on me again! Yours, you filthy wizard? You'll never have me – never, if I must die to escape you! By my name I swear it!'

She choked into silence, not for lack of words but because the mounting fury that seethed up in her throat drowned out all further sound. Her eyes were blazing yellow with scorching heat, and her fingers flexed like claws eager for blood.

The King of Romne grinned down at her, thumbs hooked in his belt and derision gleaming whitely in the whiteness of his smile. The little beard jutted along his jaw, and red lights were flickering in the fathomless darkness of his eyes.

'You think so, eh, Joiry!' he mocked her, deep-voiced. 'See what I *could* do!'

He did not shift a muscle, but even through her blinding fury she was aware of a sudden altering in him, a new power and command. His red-gleaming eyes were hot upon hers, and with sick anger she realized anew that she could not sustain that gaze. There was something frightening in the unpupiled blackness of it, the blazing, unbearable strength that beat out from it in heavy command. It was a command all out of proportion to his moveless silence, a command that wrenched at her intolerably. She must obey – she must ...

Suddenly a fresh wave of soul-scorching heat surged over her blindingly, terribly, in such a burst that the whole dark land of Romne blazed into nothingness and she lost all grip upon reality. The rocky ground swirled sidewise and vanished. The dark world dissolved around her. She was not flesh and blood but a white-hot incandescence of pure rage. Through the furnace heat of it, as through a shimmer of flame, she saw the body that her own violence had wrenched her out of. It stood straight in its gown of velvety blackness, facing Pav's unmoving figure defiantly. But as she watched, a weakening came over it. The stiffness went out of its poise, the high red head drooped. Helplessly she watched her own forsaken body moving forward step by reluctant step, as if the deserted flesh itself resented the subjection so forced upon it. She saw herself come to Pav's feet. She saw her black-sheathed body bend submissively, ripple pliantly to its knees. In a stillness beyond any ultimate climax of incarnate fury, she saw herself abased before Pav, her head bowed, her body curving into lines of warm surrender at his feet.

And she was afraid. For from somewhere a power was beating of such intolerable magnitude that even the inferno of her fury was abashed before it. Her body's obedience lost all significance in the rush of that terrible force. She would have thought that it radiated from Pav had it been possible for any human creature to sustain such an incredible force as that she was so fleetingly aware of.

For the briefest instant the knowledge of that power was all around her, terrifyingly, thunderously. It was too tremendous a thing to endure in her state of unbodied vulnerability. It scorched her like strong flame. And she was afraid – for Pav was the center of that inferno's might, and he could be no human thing who radiated such an infinity of power. What was he? What *could* he be—?

In that instant she was horribly afraid – soul-naked in the furnace blast of something too tremendous ... too terrible ...

Then the moment of separation ceased. With a rush and a dazzle she was back in her kneeling body, and the knowledge of that power faded from about her and the humiliation of her pose burned again hotly in her throat. Like a spring released she leaped to her feet, starting back and blazing into Pav's smiled face so hotly that her whole body seemed incandescent with the rage that flooded back into it. That moment of terror was fuel to feed the blaze, for she was not naked now, not bodiless and undefended from the force she had so briefly sensed, and anger that she had been exposed to it, that she had felt terror of it, swelled with the fury of her abasement before Pav. She turned eyes like two pits of hell-blaze upon her tormentor. But before she could speak:

'I admit your power,' said Pav in a somewhat surprised voice. 'I could conquer your body thus, but only by driving out the blaze that is yourself. I have never known before a mortal creature so compounded that my will could not conquer his. It proves you a fit mate for Pav of Romne. But though I could force you to my command, I shall not. I desire no woman against her will. You are a little human thing, Jirel, and your fullest strength against mine is like a candle in the sun – but in these last few minutes I have learned respect for you. Will you bargain with me?'

'I'd bargain sooner with the Devil,' she whispered hotly. 'Will you let me go, or must I die to be free?'

Somberly he looked down at her. The smile had vanished from his bearded mouth, and a dark majesty was brooding upon the swarthy face turned down to hers. His eyes flashed red no longer. They were black with so deep a blackness that they seemed two holes of fathomless space, two windows into infinity. To look into them sent something in Jirel sick with sudden vertigo. Somehow, as she stared, her white-blazing fury cooled a little. Again she felt subtly that here was no human thing into whose eyes she gazed. A quiver of fright struggled up through her fading anger. At last he spoke.

'What I take I do not lightly give up. No, there is in you a heady violence that I desire, and will not surrender. But I do not wish you against your will.'

'Give me a chance then, at escape,' said Jirel. Her boiling anger had died almost wholly away under his somber, dizzying gaze, in the memory of that instant when inferno itself had seemed to beat upon her from the power of his command. But there had not abated in her by any fraction of lessening purpose the determination not to yield. Indeed, she was strengthened against him by the very knowledge of his more than human power – the thing which in her unbodied nakedness had burned like a furnace blast against the defenseless soul of her was terrible enough even in retrospect to steel all her resolution against surrender. She said in a steady voice:

'Let me seek through your land of Romne, the gateway back into my own world. If I fail—'

'You cannot but fail. There is no gateway by which you could pass.'

'I am unarmed,' she said desperately, grasping at straws in her determination to find some excuse to leave him. 'You have taken me helpless and weaponless into your power, and I shall not surrender. Not, until you have shown yourself my master – and I do not think you can. Give me a weapon and let me prove that!'

Pav smiled down on her as a man smiles on a rebellious child.

'You have no idea what you ask,' he said. 'I am not' – he hesitated – 'perhaps not wholly as I seem to you. Your greatest skill could not prevail against me.'

'Then let me find a weapon!' Her voice trembled a little with the anxiety to be free of him, to find somehow an escape from the intolerable blackness of his eyes, the compulsion of his presence. For every moment that those terrible eyes beat so hotly upon her she felt her resistance weaken more, until she knew that if she did not leave him soon all strength would melt away in her and her body of its own will sink once more into surrender at his feet. To cover her terror she blustered, but her voice was thick. 'Give me a weapon! There is no man alive who is not somehow vulnerable. I shall learn your weakness, Pav of Romne, and slay you with it. And if I fail – then take me.'

The smile faded slowly from Pav's bearded lips. He stood in silence, looking down at her, and the fathomless darkness of his eyes radiated power like heat in such insupportable strength that her own gaze fell before it and she stared down at her velvet shirt-hem on the rocks. At last he said:

'Go, then. If that will content you, seek some means to slay me. But when you fail, remember – you have promised to acknowledge me your lord.'

'If I fail!' Relief surged up in Jirel's throat. '*If* I fail!'

He smiled again briefly, and then somehow all about his magnificent dark figure a swirl of rainbow dazzle was dancing. She stared, half afraid, half in awe, watching the tall, black tangibility of him melting easily into that multicolored whirling she had seen before, until nothing was left but the dazzling swirl that slowed and faded and dissipated upon the dark air – and she was alone.

She drew a deep breath as the last of the rainbow shimmer faded into nothing. It was a heavenly relief not to feel the unbearable power of him beating unceasingly against her resistance, not to keep tense to the breaking-point all the strength that was in her. She turned away from the spot where he had vanished and scanned the dark land of Romne, telling herself resolutely that if she found no gateway, no weapon, then death itself must open the way out of Romne. There was about Pav's terrible strength something that set the nerves of her humanity shuddering against it. In her moment of soul-nakedness she had sensed that too fully ever to surrender. The inferno of the *thing* that was Pav burning upon her unbodied consciousness had been the burning of something so alien that she knew with every instinct in her that she would die if she must, rather than submit. Pav's body was the body of a man, but it was not – she sensed it intuitively – as a man alone that he desired her, and from surrender to the dark intensity of what lay beyond the flesh her whole soul shuddered away.

She looked about helplessly. She was standing upon stones, her velvet skirts sweeping black jagged rock that sloped down toward the distant line of trees. She could see the shimmer of dark water between them, and above and beyond their swaying tops the black mountains loomed. Nowhere was there any sign of the great chamber where the image sat. Nowhere could she see anything but deserted rocks, empty meadows, trees where no birds sang. Over the world of grayness and blackness she stood staring.

And again she felt that sense of imprisonment in the horizon's dark, close bounds. It was a curiously narrow land, this Romne. She felt it intuitively, though there was no visible barrier closing her in. In the clear, dark air even the mountains' distant heights were distinct and colorless and black.

She faced them speculatively, wondering how far away their peaks lay. A dark thought was shadowing her mind, for it came to her that if she found no escape from Romne and from Pav the mountains alone offered that final escape which she was determined to take if she must. From one of those high, sheer cliffs she could leap …

It was not tears that blurred the black heights suddenly. She stared in bewilderment, lifted dazed hands to rub her eyes, and then stared again. Yes, no mistake about it, the whole panorama of the land of Romne was melting like mist about her. The dark trees with their glint of lake beyond, the rocky foreground, everything faded and thinned smokily, while through the vanishing contours those far mountains loomed up near and clear overhead. Dizzy with, incomprehension, she found herself standing amid the shreds of dissipating landscape at the very foot of those mountains which a moment before had loomed high and far on the edge of the horizon. Pav had been right indeed – Romne was a strange land. What had he said – about the illusion of it?

She looked up, trying to remember, seeing the dark slopes tilting over her head. High above, on a ledge of outcropping stone, she could see gray creepers dropping down the rocky sides, the tips of tall trees waving. She stared upward toward the ledge whose face she could not see, wondering what lay beyond the vine-festooned edges. And:

In a thin, dark fog the mountainside melted to her gaze. Through it, looming darkly and more darkly as the fog thinned, a level plateau edged with vines and thick with heavy trees came into being before her. She stood at the very edge of it, the dizzy drop of the mountain falling sheer behind her. By no path that feet can tread could she have come to this forested plateau.

One glance she cast backward and down from her airy vantage above the dark land of Romne. It spread out below her in a wide horizon-circle of black rock and black waving tree-tops and colorless hills, clear in the clear, dark air of Romne. Nowhere was anything but rock and hills and trees, clear and distinct out to the horizon in the color-swallowing darkness of the air. No sight of man's occupancy anywhere broke the somberness of its landscape. The great black hall where the image burned might never have existed save in dreams. A prison land it was, narrowly bound by the tight circle of the sky.

Something insistent and inexplicable tugged at her attention then, breaking off abruptly that scanning of the land below. Not understanding why, she answered the compulsion to turn. And when she had turned she stiffened into rigidity, one hand halting in a little futile reach after the knife that no longer swung at her side; for among the trees a figure was approaching.

It was a woman – or could it be? White as leprosy against the blackness of the trees, with a whiteness that no shadows touched, so that she seemed like some creature out of another world reflecting in dazzling pallor upon the background of the dark, she paced slowly forward. She was thin – deathly thin, and wrapped in a white robe like a winding-sheet. The black hair lay upon her shoulders as snakes might lie.

But it was her face that caught Jirel's eyes and sent a chill of sheer terror down her back. It was the face of Death itself, a skull across which the white, white flesh was tightly drawn. And yet it was not without a certain stark beauty of its own, the beauty of bone so finely formed that even in its death's-head nakedness it was lovely.

There was no color upon that face anywhere. White-lipped, eyes shadowed, the creature approached with a leisured swaying of the long robe, a leisured swinging of the long black hair lying in snake-strands across the thin white shoulders. And the nearer the – the woman? – came the more queerly apart from the land about her she seemed. Bone-white, untouched by any shadow save in the sockets of her eyes, she was shockingly detached from even the darkness of the air. Not all of Romne's dim, color-veiling atmosphere could mask the staring whiteness of her, almost blinding in its unshadowed purity.

As she came nearer, Jirel sought instinctively for the eyes that should be fixed upon her from those murky hollows in the scarcely fleshed skull. If they were there, she could not see them. An obscurity clouded the dim sockets where alone shadows clung, so that the face was abstract and sightless – not blind, but more as if the woman's thoughts were far away and intent upon something so absorbing that her surroundings held nothing for the hidden eyes to dwell on.

She paused a few paces from the waiting Jirel and stood quietly, not moving. Jirel had the feeling that from behind those shadowy hollows where the darkness clung like cobwebs a close and critical gaze was analyzing her, from red head to velvet-hidden toes. At last the bloodless lips of the creature parted and from them a voice as cool and hollow as a tomb fell upon Jirel's ears in queer, reverberating echoes, as if the woman spoke from far away in deep caverns underground, coming in echo upon echo out of the depths of unseen vaults, though the air was clear and empty about her. Just as her shadowless whiteness gave the illusion of a reflection from some other world, so the voice seemed also to come from echoing distances. Its hollowness said slowly:

'So here is the mate Pav chose. A red woman, eh? Red as his own flame. What are you doing here, bride, so far from your bridegroom's arms?'

'Seeking a weapon to slay him with!' said Jirel hotly. 'I am not a woman to be taken against her will, and Pav is no choice of mine.'

Again she felt that hidden scrutiny from the pits of the veiled eyes. When the cool voice spoke it held a note of incredulity that sounded clearly even in the hollowness of its echo from the deeps of invisible tombs.

'Are you mad? Do you not know what Pav is? You actually seek to *destroy* him?'

'Either him or myself,' said Jirel angrily. 'I know only that I shall never yield to him, whatever he may be.'

'And you came – here. Why? How did you know? How did you dare?' The voice faded and echoes whispered down vaults and caverns of unseen depth ghostily, '—did you dare – did you dare – you dare ...'

'Dare what?' demanded Jirel uneasily. 'I came here because – because when I gazed upon the mountains, suddenly the world dissolved around me and I was – was here.'

This time she was quite sure that a long, deep scrutiny swept her from head to feet, boring into her eyes as if it would read her very thoughts, though the cloudy pits that hid the woman's eyes revealed nothing. When her voice sounded again it held a queer mingling of relief and amusement and stark incredulity as it reverberated out of its hollow, underground places.

'Is this ignorance or guile, woman? Can it be that you do not understand even the secret of the land of Romne, or why, when you gazed at the mountains, you found yourself here? Surely even you must not have imagined

Romne to be – as it seems. Can you possibly have come here unarmed and alone, to my very mountain – to my very grove – to my very face? You say you seek destruction?' The cool voice murmured into laughter that echoed softly from unseen walls and caverns in diminishing sounds, so that when the woman spoke again it was to the echoes of her own fading mirth. 'How well you have found your way! Here is death for you – here at my hands! For you must have known that I shall surely kill you!'

Jirel's heart leaped thickly under her velvet gown. Death she had sought, but not death at the hands of such a thing as this. She hesitated for words, but curiosity was stronger even than her sudden jerk of reflexive terror, and after a moment she contrived to ask, in a voice of rigid steadiness:

'Why?'

Again the long, deep scrutiny from eyeless sockets. Under it Jirel shuddered, somehow not daring to take her gaze from that leprously white, skull-shaped face, though the sight of it sent little shivers of revulsion along her nerves. Then the bloodless lips parted again and the cool, hollow voice fell echoing on her ears:

'I can scarcely believe that you do not know. Surely Pav must be wise enough in the ways of women – even such as I – to know what happens when rivals meet. No, Pav shall not see his bride again, and the white witch will be queen once more. Are you ready for death, Jirel of Joiry?'

The last words hung hollowly upon the dark air, echoing and re-echoing from invisible vaults. Slowly the arms of the corpse-creature lifted, trailing the white robe in great pale wings, and the hair stirred upon her shoulders like living things. It seemed to Jirel that a light was beginning to glimmer through the shadows that clung like cobwebs to the skullface's sockets, and somehow she knew chokingly that she could not bear to gaze upon what was dawning there if she must throw herself backward off the cliff to escape it. In a voice that strangled with terror she cried:

'Wait!'

The pale-winged arms hesitated in their lifting; the light which was dawning behind the shadowed eye-sockets for a moment ceased to brighten through the veiling. Jirel plunged on desperately:

'There is no need to slay me. I would very gladly go if I knew the way out.'

'No,' the cold voice echoed from reverberant distances. 'There would be the peril of you always, existing and waiting. No, you must die or my sovereignty is at an end.'

'Is it sovereignty or Pav's love that I peril, then?' demanded Jirel, the words tumbling over one another in her breathless eagerness lest unknown magic silence her before she could finish.

The corpse-witch laughed a cold little echo of sheer scorn.

'There is no such thing as love,' she said, '—for such as I.'

'Then,' said Jirel quickly, a feverish hope beginning to rise behind her terror, 'then let me be the one to slay. Let me slay Pav as I set out to do, and leave this land kingless, for your rule alone.'

For a dreadful moment the half-lifted arms of the figure that faced her so terribly hesitated in midair; the light behind the shadows of her eyes flickered. Then slowly the winged arms fell, the eyes dimmed into cloud-filled hollows again. Blind-faced, impersonal, the skull turned toward Jirel. And curiously, she had the idea that calculation and malice and a dawning idea that spelled danger for her were forming behind that expressionless mask of white-fleshed bone. She could feel tensity and peril in the air – a subtler danger than the frank threat of killing. Yet when the white witch spoke there was nothing threatening in her words. The hollow voice sounded as coolly from its echoing caverns as if it had not a moment before been threatening death.

'There is only one way in which Pav can be destroyed,' she said slowly. 'It is a way I dare not attempt, nor would any not already under the shadow of death. I think not even Pav knows of it. If you—' The hollow tones hesitated for the briefest instant, and Jirel felt, like the breath of a cold wind past her face, the certainty that there was a deeper danger here, in this unspoken offer, than even in the witch's scarcely stayed death-magic. The cool voice went on, with a tingle of malice in its echoing.

'If you dare risk this way of clearing my path to the throne of Romne, you may go free.'

Jirel hesitated, so strong had been that breath of warning to the danger-accustomed keenness of her senses. It was not a genuine offer – not a true path of escape. She was sure of that, though she could not put her finger on the flaw she sensed so strongly. But she knew she had no choice.

'I accept, whatever it is,' she said, 'my only hope of winning back to my own land again. What is this thing you speak of?'

'The – the flame,' said the witch half hesitantly, and again Jirel felt a sidelong scrutiny from the cobwebbed sockets, almost as if the woman scarcely expected to be believed. 'The flame that crowns Pav's image. If it can be quenched, Pav – dies.' And queerly she laughed as she said it, a cool little ripple of scornful amusement. It was somehow like a blow in the face, and Jirel felt the blood rising to her cheeks as if in answer to a tangible slap. For she knew that the scorn was directed at herself, though she could not guess why.

'But how?' she asked, striving to keep bewilderment out of her voice.

'With flame,' said the white witch quickly. 'Only with flame can that flame be quenched. I think Pav must at least once have made use of those little blue fires that flicker through the air about your body. Do you know them?'

Jirel nodded mutely.

'They are the manifestations of your own strength, called up by him. I can explain it no more clearly to you than that. You must have felt a momentary exhaustion as they moved. But because they are essentially a part of your own human violence, here in this land of Romne, which is stranger and more alien than you know, they have the ability to quench Pav's flame. You will not understand that now. But when it happens, you will know why. I cannot tell you.

'You must trick Pav into calling forth the blue fire of your own strength, for only he can do that. And then you must concentrate all your forces upon the flame that burns around the image. Once it is in existence, you can control the blue fire, send it out to the image. You must do this. Will you? Will you?'

The tall figure of the witch leaned forward eagerly, her white skull-face thrusting nearer in an urgency that not even the veiled, impersonal eye-sockets could keep from showing. And though she had imparted the information that the flame held Pav's secret life in a voice of hollow reverberant mockery, as if the statement were a contemptuous lie, she told of its quenching with an intensity of purpose that proclaimed it unmistakable truth. 'Will you?' she demanded again in a voice that shook a little with nameless violence.

Jirel stared at the white-fleshed skull in growing disquiet. There was a danger here that she could feel almost tangibly. And somehow it centered upon this thing which the corpse-witch was trying to force her into promising. Somehow she was increasingly sure of that. And rebellion suddenly flamed within her. If she must die, then let her do it now, meeting death face to face and not in some obscurity of cat's-paw witchcraft in the attempt to destroy Pav. She would not promise.

'No,' she heard her own voice saying in sudden violence. 'No, I will not!'

Across the skull-white face of the witch convulsive fury swept. It was the rage of thwarted malice, not the disappointment of a plotter. The hollow voice choked behind grinning lips, but she lifted her arms like great pale wings again, and a glare of hell-fire leaped into being among the shadows that clung like cobwebs to her eye-sockets. For a moment she stood towering, white and terrible, above the earthwoman, in a tableau against the black woods of unshadowed bone-whiteness, dazzling in the dark air of Romne, terrible beyond words in the power of her gathering magic.

Then Jirel, rigid with horror at the light brightening so ominously among the shadows of these eyeless sockets, saw terror sweep suddenly across the convulsed face, quenching the anger in a cold tide of deadly fear.

'Pav!' gasped the chill voice hollowly. 'Pav comes!'

Jirel swung round toward the far horizon, seeking what had struck such fear into the leprously white skull-face, and with a little gasp of reprieve saw the black figure of her abductor enormous on the distant skyline. Through the clear dark air she could see him plainly, even to the sneering arrogance upon his bearded face, and a flicker of hot rebellion went through her. Even in the knowledge of his black and terrible power, the human insolence of him struck flame from the flint of her resolution, and she began to burn with a deep-seated anger which not even his terror could quench, not even her amazement at the incredible size of him.

For he strode among the tree-tops like a colossus, gigantic, heaven-shouldering, swinging in league-long strides across the dark land spread out panorama-like under that high ledge where the two women stood. He was nearing in great distance-devouring steps, and it seemed to Jirel that he diminished in stature as the space between them lessened. Now the tree-tops were creaming like black surf about his thighs. She saw anger on his face, and she heard a little gasp behind her. She whirled in quick terror, for surely now the witch would slay her with no more delay, before Pav could come near enough to prevent.

But when she turned she saw that the pale corpse-creature had forgotten her in the frantic effort to save herself. And she was working a magic that for an instant wiped out from Jirel's wondering mind even her own peril, even the miraculous oncoming of Pav. She had poised on her toes, and now in a swirl of shroud-like robes and snaky hair she began to spin. At first she revolved laboriously, but in a few moments the jerky whirling began to smooth out and quicken and she was revolving without effort, as if she utilized a force outside Jirel's understanding, as if some invisible whirlwind spun her faster and faster in its vortex, until she was a blur of shining, unshadowed whiteness wrapped in the dark snakes of her hair – until she was nothing but a pale mist against the forest darkness – until she had vanished utterly.

Then, as Jirel stared in dumb bewilderment, a little chill wind that somehow seemed to blow from immeasurably far distances, from cool, hollow, underground places, brushed her cheek briefly, without ruffling a single red curl. It was not a tangible wind. And from empty air a hand that was bone-hard dealt her a stinging blow in the face. An incredibly tiny, thin, far-away voice sang in her ear as if over gulfs of measurable vastness:

'That for watching my spell, red woman! And if you do not keep our bargain, you shall feel the weight of my magic. Remember!'

Then in a great gush of wind and a trample of booted feet Pav was on the ledge beside her, and no more than life-size now, tall, black, magnificent as before, radiant with arrogance and power. He stared hotly, with fathomless blackness in his eyes, at the place where the mist that was the witch had faded. Then he laughed contemptuously.

'She is safe enough – there,' he said. 'Let her stay. You should not have come here, Jirel of Joiry.'

'I didn't come,' she said in sudden, childish indignation against everything that had so mystified her, against his insolent voice and the arrogance and power of him, against the necessity for owing to him her rescue from the witch's magic. 'I didn't come. The – the mountain came! All I did was look at it, and suddenly it was here.'

His deep bull-bellow of laughter brought the blood angrily to her cheeks.

'You must learn that secret of your land of Romne,' he said indulgently. 'It is not constructed on the lines of your old world. And only by slow degrees, as you grow stronger in the magic which I shall teach you, can you learn the full measure of Romne's strangeness. It is enough for you to know now that distances here are measured in different terms from those you know. Space and matter are subordinated to the power of the mind, so that when you desire to reach a place you need only concentrate upon it to bring it into focus about you, succeeding the old landscape in which you stood.

'Later you must see Romne in its true reality, walk through Romne as Romne really is. Later, when you are my queen.'

The old hot anger choked up in Jirel's throat. She was not so afraid of him now, for a weapon was in her hands which even he did not suspect. She knew his vulnerability. She cried defiantly:

'Never, then! I'd kill you first.'

His scornful laughter broke into her threat.

'You could not do that,' he told her, deep-voiced. 'I have said before that there is no way. Do you think I could be mistaken about that?'

She glared at him with hot, yellow eyes, indiscretion hovering on her lips. Almost she blurted it out, but not quite. In a choke of anger she turned her face away, going prickly and hot at the deep laughter behind her.

'Have you had your fill of seeking weapons against me?' he went on, still in that voice of mingling condescension and arrogance.

She hesitated a moment. Somehow she must get them both back into the hall of the image. In a voice that trembled she said at last:

'Yes.'

'Shall we go back then, to my palace, and prepare for the ceremony which will make you queen?'

The deep voice was still shuddering along her nerves as the mountain behind them and the great dark world below melted together in a mirage through which, as through a veil, a flame began to glow; the flame about an image's head – an image gigantic in a great black hall whose unroofed walls closed round them in a magical swiftness. Jirel stared, realizing bewilderedly that without stirring a step she had somehow come again into the black hall where she had first opened her eyes.

A qualm of remembrance came over her as she recalled how fervently she had sworn to herself to die somehow, rather than return here into Pav's power. But now she was armed. She need have no fear now. She looked about her.

Black and enormous, the great image loomed up above them both. She lifted a gaze of new respect to that leaping diadem of flame which crowned the face that was Pav's. She did not understand what it was she must do now, or clearly how to do it, but the resolve was hot in her to take any way out that might lie open rather than submit to the dark power that dwelt in the big, black man at her side.

Hands fell upon her shoulders then, heavily. She whirled in a swirl of velvet skirts into Pav's arms, tight against his broad breast. His breath was hot in her face, and upon her like the beating of savage suns burned the intolerable blackness of his eyes. She could no more meet their heat than she could have stared into a sun. A sob of pure rage choked up in her throat as she thrust hard with both hands against the broad black chest to which she was crushed. He loosed her without a struggle. She staggered with the suddenness of it, and then he had seized her wrist in an iron grip, twisting savagely. Jirel gasped in a wrench of pain and dropped helplessly to one knee. Above her the heavy and ominous voice of Romne's king said in its deepest, most velvety burr, so that she shook to the very depths in that drum-beat of savage power.

'Resist me again and – things can happen here too dreadful for your brain to grasp even if I told you. Beware of me, Jirel, for Pav's anger is a terrible thing. You have found no weapon to conquer me, and now you must submit to the bargain you yourself proposed. Are you ready, Jirel of Joiry?'

She bent her head so that her face was hidden, and her mouth curved into a twist of fiercely smiling anticipation.

'Yes,' she said softly.

Then abruptly, amazingly, upon her face a cold wind blew, heavy with the odor of chill hollowness underground, and in her ears was the thin and tiny coldness of a voice she knew, echoing from reverberant vaults over gulfs unthinkable:

'Ask him to clothe you in bridal dress. Ask him! Ask him now!'

Across the screen of her memory flashed a face like a white-fleshed skull to whose eye-sockets cobwebby shadows clung, whose pale mouth curled in a smile of bitter scorn, maliciously urging her on. But she dared not disobey, for she had staked everything now on the accomplishment of the witch's bargain. Dangerous it might be, but there was worse danger waiting here and now, in Pav's space-black eyes. The thin shrill ceased and the tomb-smelling wind faded, and she heard her own voice saying:

'Let me up, then. Let me up – I am ready. Only am I to have no bridal dress for my wedding? For black ill becomes a bride.'

He could not have heard that thin, far-calling echo of a voice, for his dark face did not change and there was no suspicion in his eyes. The iron clutch of his fingers loosened. Jirel swung to her feet lithely and faced him with downcast eyes, not daring to unveil the yellow triumph that blazed behind her lashes.

'My wedding gown,' she reminded him, still in that voice of strangled gentleness.

He laughed, and his eyes sought in empty air. It was the most imperiously regal thing conceivable, that assured glance into emptiness for what, by sheer knowledge of his own power, must materialize in answer to the king of Romne's questing. And all about her, glowing into existence under the sun-hot blackness of Pav's eyes, the soft blue flames were suddenly licking.

Weakness crawled over her as the blueness seethed about her body, brushing, caressing, light as fire-tongues upon her, murmurous with the soft flickering sounds of quiet flame. A weariness like death was settling into her very bones, as if life itself were draining away into the caressing ministrations of those blue and heatless flames. She exulted in her very weakness, knowing how much of her strength must be incarnate, then, in the flames which were to quench Pav's flame. And they would need strength – all she had.

Then again the cold wind blew from hollow tombs, as if through an opened door, and upon the intangible breath of it that did not stir one red curl upon her cheek, though she felt its keenness clearly, the thin, small echo of the corpse-witch's voice cried, tiny and far over spaces beyond measurement.

'Focus them on the Flame – now, now! Quickly! Ah – fool!'

And the ghost of a thin, cool laugh, stinging with scorn, drifting through the measureless voids. Reeling with weakness, Jirel obeyed. The derision in that tiny, far-away voice was like a spur to drive her, though ready anger surged up in her throat against that strange scorn for which she could find no reason. As strongly as before she felt the breath of danger when the corpse-witch spoke, but she ignored it now, knowing in her heart that Pav must die if she were ever to know peace again, let his dying cost her what it might.

She set her teeth in her red underlip and in the pain of it drove all her strength into a strong focusing upon the flame that burned around the great imaged Pav's head. What would happen she did not know, but in the fog of her weakness, stabbed by her bitten lip's pain, she fought with all the force she had to drive those flames curling like caresses about her body straight toward the flame-crown on the image's majestic brow.

And presently, in little tentative thrusts, the blue tongues that licked her so softly began to turn away from the velvety curves of her own body and reach out toward the image. Sick with weakness as the strength drained out of her into the pulling flames, she fought on, and in an arc that lengthened and stretched away the flames began to forsake her and reach flickeringly out toward the great black statue that loomed overhead.

From far away she heard Pav's deep voice shouting on a note of sudden panic:

'Jirel, Jirel! Don't! Oh, little fool, don't do it!'

It seemed to her that his voice was not that of a man afraid for his own life, but rather as if it was peril to herself he would avert. But she could pay him no heed at all now. Nothing was real but the sharp necessity to quench the image's flame, and she poured all the strength that was left to her into the rainbow of flickering blueness that was arching up toward the image.

'Jirel, Jirel!' the deep voice of Pav was storming from somewhere in the fog of her weakness. 'Stop! You don't know—'

A blast of cold wind drowned the rest of his words, and:

'S-s-s! Go on!' hissed the corpse-witch's voice tinily in her ear. 'Don't listen to him! Don't let him stop you! He can't touch you while the blue flames burn! Go on! Go on!'

And she went on. Half fainting, wholly blind now to everything but that stretching arc of blue, she fought. And it lengthened as she poured more and more of her strength into it, reached up and out and grew by leaping degrees until the blue flames were mingling with the red, and over that blazing crown a dimness began to fall. From somewhere in the blind mist of her exhaustion Pav's voice shouted with a note of despair in its shudderingly vibrant depths:

'Oh, Jirel, Jirel! What have you done?'

Exultation surged up in her. The hot reserves of her anger against him flooded over and strength like wine boiled up through her body. In one tremendous burst of fierce energy she hurled every ounce of her newly-won power against the flame. Triumphantly she saw it flicker. There was a moment of guttering twilight; then abruptly the light went out and red flame and blue vanished in a breath. A crashing darkness like the weight of falling skies dropped thunderously about her.

Sick to the very soul with reactionary weakness as the tremendous effort relaxed at last, she heard from reeling distances Pav's voice call wordlessly. All about her the dark was heavy, with a crushing weight that somehow made her whole body ache as if with the pressure of deep seas. In the heaviness of it she scarcely realized that the voice was shouting at all; but even through the dimness of her failing senses she-knew that there was something tremendously wrong with it. In a mighty effort she rallied herself, listening.

Yes – he was trying to speak, trying to tell her something that she knew intuitively was of infinite importance. But his voice was ceasing, to be a human voice, becoming less and less articulate and more and more a mighty roaring like the voice of incalculable power. In such a voice a typhoon might speak, or a dynamo more tremendous than any man ever made.

'Jirel – Jirel – why did you …' So much she made out before the words rushed together and melted into that thunderous roar which was the very voice of infinity itself. The darkness was full of it – one with it – intolerable violence upon her ears, intolerable pressure of the black dark upon her body.

Through the roaring void a keen wind blew hollow with the smell of tombs. Jirel, trying to whirl to face it, found herself incapable of motion, a finite and agonized thing in the midst of crashing black thunder whose sound was torment in her brain, whose weight was crushing her very atoms in upon themselves until consciousness flickered within her like a guttering candle flame.

But there was no need to turn. Directions had ceased to be. The wind smote her turned cheek, but before her, as if through an opened door from which coldness streamed, she was aware of a white-shrouded figure floating upon the blackness; an unshadowed figure, staringly white, not touched by anything the blackness could muster against it. Even through the terrible roaring of pure power the corpse-witch's voice struck low and cool in its echo from reverberant caverns; even through the blinding dark her skull-face gleamed, the cob-webbed eyes lurid in the depths of their clinging shadows with a light that glowed from deep within the leprosy-white skull. The witch was laughing.

'O fool!' she lilted in a hollow ripple of scorn as cool as caverns underground. 'Poor, presumptuous fool! Did you really think to bargain with us of the outer worlds? Did you really believe that Pav – *Pav!* – could die? No – in your little human brain how could you have known that all the Romne you saw was illusion, that Pav's human body was no real thing? Blind, hot, earthly woman, with your little hates and vengeances, how could you have reigned queen over a Romne that is Darkness itself – as you see it now? For this roaring night which engulfs you, without dimensions, without form, lightless, inchoate – this is Romne! And Romne is Pav. The land that you walked through, the mountains and plains you saw – all these were no less Pav than the human body he assumed. Nor was his height and black-bearded arrogance any more Pav himself than were the rocks and trees and black waters of Romne. Pav is Romne, and Romne is Pav – one terrible whole out of which all you saw was wrought.

'Yes, shudder, and presently, when I am through with you – die. For no human thing could live in the Romne that is real. When in your foolish vengeance you quenched the flame that burned on the image's head, you sealed your own doom. Only in the power of that flame could the illusion of the land of Romne hold itself steady about you. Only that flame in its tangible light held Romne and Pav in the semblance of reality to you, or kept the weight of the Dark from crushing your puny soul in the soft white flesh you call a body. Only the sound of my voice does it now. When I cease to speak, when the breath of my tomb-breeze ceases to blow around you – then you die.'

The cool voice broke into soft and scornful laughter while darkness reeled about Jirel and the roaring was a tumult unbearable in her very brain. Was it indeed the voice of what had been Pav? Then the low, chill voice echoed on:

'But before you die I would have you look upon what you sought to slay. I would have you *see* the Darkness that is Pav and Romne, clearly and visibly, so that you might understand what manner of lover I had. And you thought to rival me! Do you think, in your pride of human endurance, you could so much as gaze for one instant upon the inferno that is – Pav!'

In that one ringing word the chill wind ceased, the voice echoed into silence from its heights of scorn, and in the darkness, black upon the black, with no sense that human flesh possesses – neither sight nor hearing nor touch – yet with hideous clarity, she saw.

She saw the Darkness. It was tremendous beyond the power of any human perceptions to endure save in the brief flash she had of it. A thunderous Darkness whose roar was vaster than anything like mere sound. The inferno of it was too hot to bear. The human Pav's eyes had blazed like black suns, intolerably, but that had been only a reflection of this infinite might. This Darkness was the incarnate blaze, and all her consciousness reeled and was in agony before it.

She thought she could not endure to look – even to exist so near to that terrible heat of darkness, but no closing of eyes could shut it out. In the fleeting instant while she saw – through closed eyes and numbed senses, conscious in every fiber of the blaze so close – a vibration from the great Thing that was beyond shape and size and matter shivered through her in a scorch of heat too hot to touch her flesh, though her soul shuddered fainting away. It was not anything like a voice, but there was intelligence in it. And in her brain she received dimly what it said.

'Sorry – would have had you – could have loved you – but go now – go instantly, before you die ...'

And somehow, in a way that left her mind blank with the tremendous power of it, that infinite force was commanding obedience even out of the stunning Dark. For the Darkness was Romne, and Romne was Pav, and the command ran like a shudder of dark lightning from edge to edge, expelling her from its heart in an explosion of black inferno.

Instantly, blindingly, in the numb shock of that thunderous power, the darkness ceased to engulf her. Light in a dazzle that stunned her very brain burst all around. She was spun by forces so mighty that their very tremendousness saved her from destruction, as an insect might pass unharmed through a tornado. Infinity was a whirlpool around her, and—

Flagstones pressed cool and smooth against her bare feet. She blinked dizzily. Joiry's chapel walls were rising grayly about her, familiar and dun in the dim light of dawn. She stood here in her doeskin tunic upon the flagstones and breathed in deep gusts, staring about her with dazed eyes that dwelt like lingering caresses upon the familiar things of home.

QUEST OF THE STARSTONE

By C. L. Moore and Henry Kuttner

Jirel of Joiry is riding down with a score of men at her hack,
For none is safe in the outer lands from Jirels outlaw pack;
The vaults of the wizard are over-full, and locked with golden key,
And Jirel says, 'If he hath so much, then he shall share with me!'
And fires flame high on the altar fane in the lair of the wizard folk,
And magic crackles and Jirels name goes whispering through the smoke.
But magic fails in the stronger spell that the Joiry outlaws own:
The splintering crash of a broadsword blade that shivers against the bone,
And blood that bursts through a warlock's teeth can strangle a half-voiced spell
Though it rises hot from the blistering coals on the red-hot floor of Hell!

The rivet-studded oaken door crashed open, splintering from the assault of pike-butts whose thunderous echoes still rolled around the walls of the tiny stone room revealed beyond the wreck of the shattered door. Jirel, the warrior-maid of Joiry, leaped through the splintered ruins, dashing the red hair from her eyes, grinning with exertion, gripping her two-edged sword. But in the ruin of the door she paused. The mail-clad men at her heels surged around her in the doorway like a wave of blue-bright steel, and then paused too, staring.

For Franga the warlock was kneeling in his chapel, and to see Franga on his knees was like watching the devil recite a paternoster. But it was no holy altar before which the wizard bent. The black stone of it bulked huge in this tiny, bare room echoing still with the thunder of battle, and in the split second between the door's fall and Jirel's crashing entry through its ruins Franga had crouched in a last desperate effort at – at what?

His bony shoulders beneath their rich black robe heaved with frantic motion as he fingered the small jet bosses that girdled the altar's block. A slab in the side of it fell open abruptly as the wizard, realizing that his enemy was almost within sword's reach, whirled and crouched like a feral thing. Blazing light, cold and unearthly, streamed out from the gap in the altar.

'So that's where you've hidden it!' said Jirel with a savage softness.

Over his shoulder Franga snarled at her, pale lips writhed back from discolored teeth. Physically he was terrified of her, and his terror paralyzed him. She saw him hesitate, evidently between his desire to snatch into safety what was hidden in the altar and his panic fear of her sword that dripped blood upon the stones.

Jirel settled his indecision.

'You black devil!' she blazed, and lunged like lightning, the dripping blade whistling as it sheared the air.

Franga screamed hoarsely, flinging himself sidewise beneath the sword. It struck the altar with a shivering shock that numbed Jirel's arm, and as she gasped a sound that was half a sob of pain and fury, half a blistering curse, he scurried crabwise into a corner, his long robe giving him a curiously amorphous look. Recovering herself, Jirel stalked after him, rubbing her numbed arm but gripping that great wet sword fast, the highlights of murder still blazing in her yellow eyes.

The warlock flattened himself against the wall, skinny arms outstretched.

'Werhi-yu-io!' he screamed desperately. *'Werhi! Werhi-yu!'*

'What devil's gibberish is that, you dog?' demanded Jirel angrily. 'I'll—'

Her voice silenced abruptly, the red lips parted. She stared at the wall behind the wizard, and something like awe was filming the blood-lust in her eyes. For over that corner in which Franga crouched a shadow had been drawn as one draws a curtain.

'*Werhil*!' screamed the warlock again, in a cracked and strained voice, and – how could she not have seen before that door against whose panels he pressed, one hand behind him pushing it open upon darkness beyond? Here was black magic, devil's work.

Doubtfully Jirel stared, her sword lowering. She did not know it, but her free hand rose to sign her breast with the church's guard against evil. The door creaked a little, then swung wide. The blackness within was blinding as too much light is blinding – a dark from which she blinked and turned her eyes away. One last glimpse she had of the gaunt, pale face of Franga, grinning, contorted with hate. The door creaked shut.

The trance that had gripped Jirel broke with the sound. Fury flooded back in the wake of awe. Choking on hot soldier-curses she sprang for the door, swinging up her sword in both hands, spitting hatred and bracing herself for the crash of the heavy blade through those oaken panels so mysteriously veiled in the shadow that clung about that corner.

The blade clanged shiveringly against stone. For the second time, the agonizing shock of steel swung hard against solid rock shuddered up the blade and racked Jirel's shoulders. The door had vanished utterly. She dropped the sword from nerveless hands and reeled back from the empty corner, sobbing with fury and pain.

'C-coward!' she flung at the unanswering stone. 'H-hide in your hole, then, you fiend-begotten runaway, and watch me take the Starstone!'

And she whirled to the altar.

Her men had shrunk back in a huddle beyond the broken door, their magic-dazzled eyes following her in fascinated dread.

'You womanish knaves!' she flared at them over her shoulder as she knelt where the wizard had knelt. 'Womanish, did I say? Ha! You don't deserve the flattery! Must I go the whole way alone? Look then – here it is!'

She plunged her bare hand into the opening in the altar from which streamed that pale, unearthly light, gasped a little, involuntarily, and then drew out what looked like a block of living flame.

In her bare hand as she knelt she held it, and for minutes no one moved. It was pale, this Starstone, cold with unearthly fire, many-faceted yet not glittering. Jirel thought of twilight above the ocean, when the land is darkening and the smooth water gathers into its surface all the glimmering light of sea and sky. So this great stone gleamed, gathering the chapel's light into its pale surface so that the room seemed dark by contrast, reflecting it again transmuted into that cold, unwavering brilliance.

She peered into the translucent depths of it so near her face. She could see her own fingers cradling the gem distorted as if seen through water – and yet somehow there was a motion between her hand and the upper surface of the jewel. It was like looking down into water in whose depths a shadow stirred – a living shadow – a restlessly moving shape that beat against the prisoning walls and sent a flicker through the light's cold blue-white gleaming. It was—

No, it was the Starstone, nothing more. But to have the Starstone! To hold it here in her hands at last, after weeks of siege, weeks of desperate battle! It was triumph itself she cradled in her palm. Her throat choked with sudden ecstatic laughter as she sprang to her feet, brandishing the great gem toward that empty corner through whose wall the wizard had vanished.

'Ha, behold it!' she screamed to the unanswering stone. 'Son of a fiend, behold it! The luck of the Starstone is mine, now a better man has wrested it from you! Confess Joiry your master, you devil-deluder! Dare you show your face? Dare you?'

Over that empty corner the shadow swept again, awesomely from nowhere. Out of the sudden darkness creaked a door's hinges, and the wizard's voice called in a choke of fury.

'Bel's curse on you, Joiry! Never think you've triumphed over me! I'll have it back if I – if I—'

'If you – what? D'ye think I fear you, you hell-spawned warlock? If you – what?'

'Me you may not fear, Joiry,' the wizard's voice quavered with fury, 'but by Set and Bubastis, I'll find one who'll tame you if I must go to the ends of space to find him – to the ends of time itself! And then – beware!

'Bring on your champion!' Jirel's laughter was hot with scorn. 'Search hell itself and bring out the chiefest devil! I'll lift the head from his shoulders as I'd have lifted yours, with one sweep, had you not fled.'

But she got for answer only the creak of a closing door in the depths of that shadow. And now the shadow faded again, and once more empty stone walls stared at her enigmatically.

Clutching the Starstone that – so legend had it – carried luck and wealth beyond imagination for its possessor, she shrugged and swung round to her soldiers.

'Well, what are you gaping at?' she flared. 'Before heaven, I'm the best man here! Out – out – pillage the castle – there's rich loot of that devil's servant, Franga! What are you waiting for?' and with the flat of her sword she drove them from the chapel.

'By Pharol, Smith, have you lost your taste for *segir*? I'd as soon have expected old Marnak here to sprout legs!'

Yarol's cherubic face was puzzled as he nodded toward the waiter who was moving quickly about the little private drinking booth of polished steel in the back of the Martian tavern, placing fresh drinks before the two men, regardless of his artificial limbs – lost, some said, during an illicit amorous visit to the forbidden dens of the spider women.

Northwest Smith frowned moodily, pushing the glass away. His scarred dark face, lighted with the pallor of steel-colored eyes, was morose. He drew deeply on the brown Martian cigarette that smoked between his fingers.

'I'm getting rusty, Yarol,' he said. 'I'm sick of this whole business. Why can't something really worth the effort turn up? Smuggling – gun-running – I'm sick of it, I tell you! Even *segir* doesn't taste the same.'

'That's old age creeping up,' Yarol advised him owlishly above the rim of his glass. 'Tell you what you need, N.W., a snort of the green Mingo liqueur old Marnak keeps on his top shelf. It's distilled from *pani*-berries, and one shot of it will have you prancing like a pup. Wait a minute, I'll see what I can do.'

Smith hunched over his folded arms and stared at the shining steel wall behind Yarol's vacant chair as the little Venusian slid out of the booth. Hours like these were the penalty of the exiled and the outlaw. Even the toughest of them knew times when the home planet called almost intolerably across the long voids of the spaceways, and all other places seemed flat and dull. Homesickness he would not have admitted to anyone alive, but as he sat there alone, morosely facing his dim reflection in the steel wall, he found himself humming that old sweet song of all Earth's exiled people, 'The Green Hills of Earth':

Across the seas of darkness
The good green Earth is bright—
Oh, star that was my homeland
Shine down on me tonight ...

Words and tune were banal, but somehow about them had gathered such a halo of association that the voices which sang them went sweeter and softer as they lingered over the well-remembered phrases, the well-remembered scenes of home. Smith's surprisingly good baritone took on undernotes of a homesick sweetness which he would have died rather than admit:

My heart turns home in longing
Across the voids between,
To know beyond the spaceways
The hills of Earth are green ...

What wouldn't he give just now, to be free to go home again? Home without a price on his head, freedom to rove the blue seas of Earth, the warm garden continents of the sun's loveliest planet? He hummed very softly to himself,

—and count the losses worth
To see across the darkness
The green hills of Earth ...

and then let the words die on his lips unnoticed as he narrowed steel-colored eyes at the polished wall in which a moment before his dim reflection had faced him. It was darkening now, a shadow quivering across the bright surfaces, thickening, clouding his mirrored face. And the wall – was it metal, or – or stone? The shadow was too thick to tell, and unconsciously he rose to his feet, bending across the table, one hand hovering back toward the heat-gun on his thigh. A door creaked open in the dimness – a heavy door, half seen, opening upon darkness beyond too black to gaze on – darkness, and a face.

'Are your services for hire, stranger?' quavered a cracked voice speaking in a tongue that despite himself sent Smith's pulse quickening in recognition. French, Earth's French, archaic and scarcely intelligible, but unquestionably a voice from home.

'For a price,' he admitted, his fingers closing definitely on his gun. 'Who are you and why do you ask? And how in the name of—'

'It will reward you to ask no questions,' said the cracked quaver. 'I seek a fighting-man of a temper strong enough for my purpose, and I think you are he. Look, does this tempt you?'

A claw-like hand extended itself out of the shadow, dangling a double rope of such blue-white pearls as Smith had never dreamed of. 'Worth a king's ransom,' croaked the voice. 'And all for the taking. Will you come with me?'

'Come where?'

'To the planet Earth – to the land of France – to the year of 1500.'

Smith gripped the table-edge with one frantic hand, wondering if the *segir* he had drunk could somehow have sent him into paroxysms of dream. By no stretch of imagination could he really be standing here, in this drinking-booth in a Martian tavern, while out of a door that opened upon darkness a cracked voice beckoned him into the past. He was dreaming, of course, and in a dream it could do no harm to push back his chair, skirt the table, step closer to that incredible door thick-hung with shadows, take the outstretched hand over whose wrist the luminous pearls hung gleaming . . .

The room staggered and whirled into darkness. From somewhere far away he heard Yarol's voice shouting frantically, 'N.W.! Wait! N.W., where're you going—' And then night too black to gaze on blinded his dark-dazzled eyes and cold unthinkable flamed through his brain, and – and—

He stood on a green hilltop whose gentle slope rolled downward to a meadow where a brook wound with a sound of rippling water. Beyond, on a high upthrust of craggy rock, a great gray castle loomed. The sky was blessedly blue, the air fresh in his nostrils with the sweetness of green growing things. And all about him rolled grassy uplands. He took a deep, deep breath. 'The Green Hills of Earth!'

'N.W., what in – by Pharol, I – hell's blazes, man, what's happened?' Yarol's spluttering amazement jolted him out of his delight.

Smith turned. The little Venusian stood on the soft grass beside him, two small glasses full of pale green liquid in his hands and a look of almost idiotic bewilderment on his good-looking, cherubic face. 'I come back into the booth with the *pani*-juice' he was muttering dazedly, 'and there you are stepping through a door that – damn it! – that wasn't there when I left! And when I try to pull you back I – I – well, what *did* happen?'

'You stumbled through the Gateway – uninvited,' said a cracked voice ominously behind them.

Both men whirled, hands dropping to their guns. For a dazed moment

Smith had forgotten the voice that had lured him into the past. Now for the first time he saw his host – a small man, wizened, dark, stooping under his robe of rich black velvet as if the evil reflected on his seamed face were too heavy to bear upright. Dark wisdom glinted in the eyes that stared malevolently at Yarol.

'What's he saying, N.W.?' demanded the little Venusian.

'French – he's speaking French,' muttered Smith distractedly, his gaze on the lined and evil face of their host. And then to the warlock, *'Qui êtes-vous, m'sieur? Pourquoi—'*

'I am Franga,' interrupted the old man impatiently. 'Franga, the warlock. And I am displeased with this blundering stranger who followed us through the door. His speech is as uncouth as his manners. Were it not for my magic I could not guess his meaning. Has he never learned a civilized tongue? Well, no matter – no matter.

'Listen, now. I have brought you here to avenge my defeat at the hands of the lady of Joiry whose castle you see on yonder hilltop. She stole my magical jewel, the Starstone, and I have vowed to find a man who could tame her if I had to search outside my own world and time to do it. I am too old myself, too feeble now. Once when I was as young and lusty as you I won the jewel from a rival as it must be won, bloodily in battle, or its magic is void to the possessor. Too, it may be given freely and maintain its power. But by neither method can I take it from Joiry, and so you must go up to the castle and in your own way win the stone.

'I can help you – a little. This much I can do – I can put you beyond the reach of the pikes and swords of Joiry's men.'

Smith lifted an eyebrow and laid his hand lightly on his heat-gun, a blast of whose deadly violence could have mowed down a charging army like wheat ripe for the scythe.

'I'm armed,' he said shortly.

Franga frowned. 'Your arms would not avail you against a dagger in the back. No, you must do as I say. I have my reasons. You must go – beyond the Gateway.'

Cold, pale eyes met the wizard's veiled stare for a moment. Then Smith nodded.

'It doesn't matter – my gun burns as straight in any land. What's your plan?'

'You must get the lady of Joiry through the Gateway – that same Gateway by which you came hither. But it will take you into another land, where – where' – he hesitated – 'where there are – powers – favorable to me, and therefore to you. Make no mistake; it will not be easy to wrest the Starstone from Joiry. She has learned much of the dark lore.'

'How shall we open the Gateway?'

Franga's left hand rose in a swift, strangely archaic gesture. 'By this sign – learn it well – thus, and thus.'

Smith's gun-callused brown hand imitated the queer motion. 'Thus?'

'Yes – and the spell must be learned as well.' Franga mouthed something queer and garbled, Smith echoing him with twisted tongue, for the words were as strange as he had ever spoken.

'Good.' The warlock nodded, and again the strange syllables came incoherently from his lips, again his hand moved, giving the gestures an oddly cadenced rhythm. 'When you voice the spell again the Gateway will open for you – as it opens now for me!'

Silently a shadow swept down upon them, dimming the sunlit hill. In its midst a blacker oblong darkened, the creak of a door sounded faintly as if from enormous distances.

'Bring Joiry through the Gateway,' the wizard whispered, vicious lights crawling in his cold eyes, 'and follow. Then you may seize the Starstone, for the powers in this – this other land will fight with you. But not here, not in Joiry. You must follow me ... As for this little man who blundered through my door of darkness—'

'He is my friend,' said Smith hastily. 'He will help me.'

'Eh – well, let his life be hostage then to your success. Win me the stone, and I stay my wrath at his stupid interference. But remember – the sword of my magic hovers at your throat ...'

A shadow quivered over the wizard's black-robed form. His image quivered with it as a reflection in troubled water shakes, and abruptly shadow and man were gone.

'By great Pharol,' articulated Yarol in measured syllables, 'will you tell me what this is all about? Drink this – you look as though you need it. As for me' – he thrust a small glass into Smith's hand, and drained his own drink at a gulp – 'if all this is a dream, I hope there's liquor in it. Will you kindly explain—'

Smith threw back his head and tossed the *pani*-spirits down his grateful throat. In crisp sentences he outlined the situation, but though his words were brisk his eyes lingered like a caress over the warm, sweet-scented hills of home.

'Um-m,' said Yarol, when he had finished. 'Well, why are we waiting? Who knows, there may be a wine-cellar in that cozy-looking castle over there.' He licked his lips reflectively, tasting the last of the green liquor. 'Let's get going. The sooner we meet the woman the sooner she'll offer us a drink.'

So they went down the long hill, Earth's green grass springing under their spaceman's boots, Earth's warm June breezes caressing their Mars-burned faces.

*

The gray heights of Joiry loomed above the two before life stirred anywhere in the sunny midday silences of this lost century. Then high in the buttresses a man shouted, and presently, with a rattling of hooves and a jangle of accoutrements, two horsemen came thundering across the lowered drawbridge. Yarol's hand went to his heat-gun, and a smile of ineffable innocence hovered on his face. The Venusian never looked so much like a Raphael cherub as when death was trembling on his trigger finger. But Smith laid a restraining hand on his arm.

'Not yet.'

The horsemen bore down on them, visors lowered. For a moment Smith thought they would trample them down, and his hand hovered ever so lightly over his gun, but the men reined to a halt beside the two and one of them, glaring down through his helmet bars, roared a threatening question.

'We're strangers,' Smith told him haltingly at first, and then more easily as long-forgotten French flowed back into his memory. 'From another land. We come in peace.'

'Few come in peace to Joiry,' snapped the man, fingering his sword-hilt, 'and we do not love strangers here. Have you, perhaps' – a covetous gleam brightened the eyes half hidden by the vizor – 'gold? Or gems?'

'Your lady can judge of that, fellow.' Smith's voice was as cold as the steel-gray eyes that caught the man's gaze in a stare of sudden savagery. 'Take us to her.'

The man hesitated for an instant, uncertainty eloquent in the eyes behind the vizor. Here was a dusty stranger, afoot, swordless, unarmed, such a fellow Joiry's men might ride down on the highway and never notice twice. But his eyes were the eyes of – of – he had never seen such eyes. And command spoke in his cold, clipped voice. The soldier shrugged inside his mail and spat through the bars of the helmet.

'There's always room in Joiry's dungeons for one more varlet, if our lady doesn't fancy you,' he said philosophically. 'Follow me, then.'

Yarol, plodding across the drawbridge, murmured, 'Was he speaking a language, N.W. – or merely howling like a wolf?'

'Shut up,' muttered Smith. 'I'm trying to think. We've got to have a good story ready for this – this amazon.'

'Some brawny wench with a face like a side of beef,' speculated Yarol.

So they entered Joiry, over the drawbridge, under the spiked portcullis, into the high-vaulted, smoke-blackened banquet hall where Jirel sat at midday table. Blinking in the dimness Smith looked up to the dais at the head of the great T-shaped board where the lady of Joiry sat. Her red mouth glistened with the grease of a mutton-bone she had been gnawing, and the bright hair fell flaming on her shoulders.

She looked into Smith's eyes.

Clear and pale and cold as steel they were, and Joiry's yellow gaze met them with a flash like the spark of meeting blades. For a long moment there was silence between them, and a curious violence flamed in the silent stare. A great mastiff loped to Smith's knee, fangs bared, a growl rumbling in its furry throat. Without looking down, Smith's hand found the beast's head and the dog sniffed for a moment and let the man rough its shaggy fur. Then Jirel broke the silence.

'*Tigre – ici*!' Her voice was strong and suddenly deeper in timbre, as if emotions she would not acknowledge were stirring in her. The mastiff went to her chair and lay down, finding a well-gnawed bone to crack. But Jirel's eyes were still fast on Smith's, and a slow flush was mounting her face.

'Pierre – Voisin,' she said. 'Who is he?'

'I bring you news of treasure,' said Smith before they could speak. 'My name is Smith, and I come from a – a far land.'

'Smeet,' she murmured. 'Smeet . . . Well, what of this treasure?'

'I would speak to you alone of that,' he said guardedly. 'There are jewels and gold, guarded by thieves but ripe for harvesting. And I think Joiry – harvests well.'

'*C'est vrai*. With the luck of the Starstone—' She hesitated, wiping her mouth on the back of a narrow hand. 'Are you lying to me? You who come so curiously clad, who speak our language so strangely – always before I have seen the lie in the eyes of the man who tells it. But you—'

Suddenly, and so quickly that despite himself Smith blinked, she had flung herself across the table, leaning there on one knee while the slender blade of her dagger flickered in the air. She laid the point of it against Smith's bare brown throat, just where a strong pulse stirred sunburnt flesh. He watched her without a quiver of expression, without a twitch of muscle.

'I cannot read your eyes – Smeet . . . Smeet . . . But if you are lying to me' – the point dented the full swell of his muscular throat – 'if you are, I'll strip the skin from your carcass in Joiry's dungeons. Know that!'

The blade fell to her side. Something wet trickled stickily down Smith's neck inside the leather collar. So keen was that blade he had not known himself scratched. He said coldly,

'Why should I lie? I can't get the treasure alone – you can help me win it. I came to you for aid.'

Unsmilingly she bent toward him across the table, sheathing her dagger. Her body was one sweep of flowing grace, of flowing strength, slim as a sword-blade, as she half knelt among the broken meats upon the board. Her yellow eyes were cloudy with doubt.

'I think there is something more,' she said softly, 'something you have left untold. And I have a memory now of a yelling warlock who fled from my blade, with certain – threats …'

The yellow eyes were cold as polar seas. She shrugged at last and stood up, her gaze sweeping down over the long table where men and women divided their time between feasting and fascinated staring at the tableau by the tablehead.

'Bring him up to my apartment,' she said to Smith's captors. 'I'd learn more of this – treasure.'

'Shall we stay to guard him?'

Jirel's lips curled scornfully.

'Is there a man here who can best me with steel – or anything else?' she demanded. 'Guard yourselves, you cravens! If you brought him in without getting a poniard in the belly, I can safely talk to him in the heart of Joiry's stronghold. Well, don't stand there gaping – go!'

Smith shrugged off the heavy hand laid on his shoulder.

'Wait!' he said crisply. 'This man goes with me.'

Jirel's eyes dwelt on Yarol with a velvety, menacing appraisal. Yarol's sidelong black stare met hers eloquently.

'Brawny wench, did I say?' he murmured in the liquid cadences of High Venusian. '*Aie* – the Minga maidens were not more luscious. I'll kiss that pretty mouth of yours before I go back to my own time, lady! I'll—'

'What is he saying – he gurgles like a brook!' Jirel broke in impatiently. 'He is your friend? Take them both, then, Voisin.' Jirel's apartment lay in the top of the highest tower of Joiry, at the head of a winding stone stairway. Lofty-roofed, hung with rich tapestries, carpeted with furs, the place seemed to Smith at once alien and yet dearly familiar with a strange, heart-warming familiarity. Separated from his own time by dusty centuries, yet it was earth-sprung, earth-born, reared on the green hills of his home planet.

'What I need,' said Yarol carefully, 'is some more Minga-liqueur. Did you see how that hell-cat looked me over? Black Pharol, I don't know if I'd sooner kiss her or kill her! Why, the damned witch would run her sword through my gullet on a whim – for the sheer deviltry of it!'

Smith chuckled deep in his throat. 'She's dangerous. She—'

Jirel's voice behind him said confidently,

'Wait beyond the door, Voisin. These two strangers may visit our dungeons, after all. This little one – how are you named?'

'He's called Yarol,' Smith said curtly.

'Yes – Yarol. Well, we may find means to make you a taller man, Yarol. You would like that, eh? We have a little device – a ladder which I got from the Count of Görz when he visited me last summer – and the Count is clever in these things.'

'He does not speak your tongue,' Smith interrupted.

'No? It is not strange – he looks as though he came from a far land indeed. I have never seen a man like him.' Her eyes were puzzled. She half turned her shoulders to them, toying with a sword that lay on a table at her side, and said without looking up, 'Well, your story. Let's have it. And – yes, I'll give you one more chance at living – if you're lying, go now. None will stop you. You are strangers. You do not know Joiry – or Joiry's vengeance.'

Over her shoulder she slanted into Smith's eyes a level glance that burnt like the stab of lightnings. Hell-fires flickered in it, and despite himself Smith knew a sudden crawl of unease. Yarol, though he did not understand the words, whistled between his teeth. For the heartbeat no one spoke. Then very softly in Smith's ear a voice murmured, 'She has the Starstone. Say the spell of the Gateway!'

Startled, he glanced around. Jirel did not stir. Her lion-yellow eyes were still brooding on him with a gaze that smoldered. Yarol was watching her in fascination. And Smith realized abruptly that he alone had heard the cracked quaver of command in – yes, in Franga's voice! Franga, the warlock, whispering through some half-opened door into infinity. Without glancing aside at Yarol he said in the ripples of High Venusian, 'Get ready – watch the door and don't let her out.'

Jirel's face changed. She swung around from the table, her brows a straight line of menace. 'What are you muttering? What devil's work are you at?'

Smith ignored her. Almost involuntarily his left hand was moving in the queer, quick gesture of the spell. Phrases in the unearthly tongue that Franga had taught him burned on his lips with all the ease of his mother-tongue. Magic was all about him, guiding his lips and hands.

Alarm blazed up in Jirel's yellow eyes. An oath smoked on her lips as she lunged forward, the sword she had been toying with a gleam in her fist. Yarol grinned. The heat-gun danced in his hand, and a white-hot blast traced a trail of fire on the rug at Jirel's feet. She shut her red lips on a word half uttered, and twisted in midair, flinging herself back in swift terror from this sudden gush of hell-flame. Behind her the door burst open and men in armor clanged into the room, shouting, dragging at their swords.

And then – down swept the shadow over the noisy room. Cloudy as the sweep of the death-angel's wings it darkened the sunny air so that the ray from Yarol's gun blazed out in dazzling splendor through the gloom. As if in the misted depths of a mirror Smith saw the men in the door shrink back, mouths agape, swords clattering from their hands. He scarcely heeded them, for in the far wall where a moment before a tall, narrow window had opened upon sunlight and the green hills of Earth – was a door. Very slowly, very quietly it was swinging open, and the black of utter infinity lay beyond its threshold.

'*Hai – s'leli* – Smith!' Yarol's warning voice yelled in the darkness, and

Smith threw himself back in a great leap as he felt a sword-blade prick his shoulder. Jirel sobbed a furious curse and plunged forward, her sword and sword-arm a single straight bar. In the dimness Yarol's gun hand moved, and a thin beam of incandescence burned bright. Jirel's sword hissed in midair, glowed blindingly and then dripped in a shower of white-hot drops to the stone floor. Her momentum carried her forward with a hilt and a foot of twisted steel still gripped in her stabbing hand, so that she lunged against Smith's broad chest thrusting with the stump of the ruined sword.

His arms prisoned her, a writhing fury that sobbed wild oaths and twisted like a tiger against him. He grinned and tightened his arms until the breath rushed out of her crushed lungs and he felt her ribs give a little against his chest.

Then vertigo was upon him. Dimly he realized that the girl's arms had gone round his neck in a frantic grip as the room swayed – tilted dizzily, amazingly, revolving as through on a giant axis – or as if the black depths of the Gateway were opening under him ... he could not tell, nor was he ever to understand, just what happened in that fantastic instant when nature's laws were warped by strange magic. The floor was no longer solid beneath his feet. He saw Yarol twisting like a small sleek cat as he stumbled and fell – fell into oblivion with his gun hand upflung. He was falling himself, plunging downward through abysses of dark, clasping a frightened girl whose red hair streamed wildly in the wind of their falling.

Stars were swirling about them. They were dropping slowly through stars while the air danced and dazzled all around them. Smith had time to catch his breath and flex the muscles of his gun thigh to be sure the comforting weight pressed there before a spongy ground received them softly. They fell like people in a nightmare, slowly and easily, with no jar, upon the strange dim surface of the land beyond the Gateway. Yarol landed on his feet like the cat he was, gun still gripped and ready, black eyes blinking in the starry dark. Smith, hampered by the terrified Jirel, sank with nightmare ease to the ground and rebounded a little from its sponginess. The impact knocked the stump of sword from the girl's hand, and he pitched it away into the blinding shimmer of the star-bright dark before he helped her to her feet.

For once Joiry was completely subdued. The shock of having her sword melted by hell-fire in her very grasp, the dizzying succession of manhandling and vertigo and falling into infinity had temporarily knocked all violence out of her, and she could only gasp and stare about this incredible starlit darkness, her red lips parted in amazement.

As far as they could see the mist of stars quivered and thickened the dim air, tiny points of light that danced all around them as if thousands of fireflies were winking all at once. Half blinded by that queer, shimmering dazzle, they could make out no familiar topography of hills or valleys, only that spongy dark ground beneath them, that quiver of stars blinding the dim air.

Motion swirled the shimmer a little distance away, and Jirel snarled as Franga's dark-robed form came shouldering through the stars, spinning them behind him in the folds of his cloak as he moved forward. His withered features grimaced into a grin when he saw the dazed three.

'Ah – you have her!' he rasped. 'Well, what are you waiting for? Take the stone! She carries it on her.'

Smith's pale eyes met the warlock's through the star-shimmer, and his firm lips tightened. Something was wrong. He sensed it unmistakably – danger whispered in the air. For why should Franga have brought them here if the problem was no more complex than the mere wrestling of a jewel from a woman? No – there must be some other reason for plunging them into this starry dimness. What had Franga hinted – powers here that were favorable to him? Some dark, nameless god dwelling among the stars?

The warlock's eyes flared at Jirel in a flash of pure murder, and suddenly Smith understood a part of the puzzle. She was to die, then, when the jewel could no longer protect her. Here Franga could wreak vengeance unhampered, once the Starstone was in his hands. Here Joiry was alone and helpless – and the flame of hatred in the wizard's eyes could be quenched by no less than the red flood of her bloody death.

Smith glanced back at Jirel, white and shaken with recent terror, but snarling feebly at the warlock in invincible savagery that somehow went to his heart as no helplessness could have done. And suddenly he knew he could not surrender her up to Franga's hatred. The shift of scene had shifted their relations, too, so that three mortals – he could not think of Franga as wholly human – stood together against Franga and his malice and his magic. No, he could not betray Jirel.

His gaze flicked Yarol's with a lightning message more eloquent than a warning shout. It sent a joyous quiver of tautening along the little Venusian's body, and both men's gun hands dropped to their sides with simultaneous casualness.

Smith said, 'Return us to Joiry and I'll get the stone for you: Here – no.'

That black glare of murder shifted from Jirel to Smith, bathing him in hatred.

'Take if from her now – or die!'

A smothered sound like the snarl of an angry beast halted Smith's reflexive snatch at his gun. Past him Jirel lunged, her red hair streaming with stars, her fingers flexed into claws as she leaped bare-handed at the warlock. Rage had drowned out her momentary terror, and soldier's curses tumbled blistering from her lips as she sprang.

Franga stepped back; his hand moved intricately and between him and the charging fury the starlight thickened – solidified into a sheet like heavy glass. Jirel dashed herself against it and was hurled back as if she had plunged into a stone wall. The silvery mist of the barrier dissolved as she reeled back, gasping with rage, and Franga laughed thinly.

'I am in my own place now, vixen,' he told her. 'I do not fear you or any man here. It is death to refuse me – bloody death. Give me the stone.'

'I'll tear you to rags with my bare nails!' sobbed Joiry. 'I'll have the eyes out of your head, you devil! Ha – even here you fear me! Come out from behind your rampart and let me slay you!'

'Give me the stone.' The wizard's voice was calm.

'Return us all to Joiry and I think she'll promise to let you have it.' Smith fixed a meaning stare upon Jirel's blazing yellow eyes. She shrugged off the implied advice furiously.

'Never! Yah – wait!' She leaped to Yarol's side and, as he shied nervously away, his eyes mistrustfully on her pointed nails, snatched from his belt the small knife he carried. She set the blade against the full, high swell of her bosom and laughed in Franga's face. 'Now – kill me if you can!' she taunted, her face a blaze of defiance. 'Make one move to slay me – and I slay myself! And the jewel is lost to you for ever!'

Franga bit his lip and stared at her through the mist of stars, fury glaring in his eyes. There was no hesitancy in her, and he knew it. She would do as she threatened, and—

'The stone has no virtue if not taken by violence or given freely,' he admitted. 'Lifted from a suicide's corpse, it would lose all value to anyone. I will bargain with you then, Joiry.'

'You'll not! You'll set me free or lose the jewel for ever.'

Franga turned goaded eyes on Smith. 'Either way I lose it, for once in her own land Joiry would die before surrendering it, even as she would here. You! Fulfill your bargain – get me the Starstone!'

Smith shrugged. 'Your meddling's spoiled everything now. There's little I can do.'

The angry black eyes searched for a long moment, evil crawling in their deeps. They flicked to Yarol. Both men stood on the spongy ground with feet braced, bodies balanced in the easy tautness which characterizes the gunman, hands light on their weapons, eyes very steady, very deadly. They were two very dangerous men, and Smith realized that even here Franga was taking no chances with their strange weapons. Behind them Jirel snarled like an angry cat, her fingers flexing themselves involuntarily. And suddenly the wizard shrugged.

'Stay here then, and rot!' he snapped, swinging his cloak so that the stars swirled about him in a blinding shower. 'Stay here and starve and thirst until you'll surrender. I'll not bargain with you longer.'

*

They blinked in the sudden eddy of that starry mist, and when their vision cleared the bent black figure had vanished. Blankly they looked at one another through the drifting stars.

'Now what?' said Yarol. '*Shar*, but I could drink! Why did he have to mention thirst!'

Smith blinked about him in the swirling brightness. For once he was utterly at a loss. The wizard had every advantage over them in this dim, blinding outland where his god reigned supreme.

'Well, what have we to lose?' he shrugged at last. 'He's not through with us, but there's nothing we can do. I'm for exploring a bit, anyhow.'

Yarol raked the starry dark with a dubious gaze. 'We couldn't be worse off,' he admitted.

'*Comment*?' demanded Jirel, suspicious eyes shifting from one to the other. Smith said briefly,

'We're going to explore. Franga's got some trick in mind, we think. We'd be fools to wait here for him to come back. We – oh, wait!' He snapped his fingers involuntarily and turned a startled face on the surprised two. The Gateway! He knew the spell that opened it – Franga had taught him that. Why not voice the invocation now and see what happened? He drew a quick breath and opened his mouth to speak – and then faltered with the remembered words fading from his very tongue-tip. His fingers rose halfheartedly in the intricate gestures of the spell, groping after the vanished memory as if it could be plucked out of the starmisted air. No use. His mind was as blank of the magical remembrance as if it had never been. Franga's magic worked well indeed.

'Are you crazy?' demanded Yarol, regarding his hesitating ally with an amazed gaze. Smith grinned ruefully.

'I thought I had an idea,' he admitted. 'But it's no good. Come on.'

The spongy ground was wicked to walk on. They stumbled against one another, swearing in a variety of tongues at the blinding air they groped through, the hard going under foot, the wretched uncertainty that kept their eyes scanning the dazzle as they walked.

It was Jirel who first caught sight of the shrunken brown thing. Indeed, she almost stumbled over it, a mummified body, curled up on its side so that its bony knees nearly touched the brown fleshless forehead. Smith turned at her little gasp, saw the thing, and paused to bend over it wonderingly.

It was not pleasant to see. The skin stretched tightly over the bony frame, was parchment-brown, hideously rough in texture, almost as if the hide of some great lizard had been stretched over the skeleton of a man. The face was hidden, but the hands were slender claws, whitish in places where the granulated skin had been stripped from the bone. Wisps of straw-like hair still clung to the wrinkled scalp.

'Well, come along,' said Yarol impatiently. 'Certainly *he* can't help us, or harm us either.'

Silently assenting, Smith swung on his heel. But some instinct – the little tingling danger-note that whispers in the back of a spaceman's head – made him turn. The position of the recumbent figure had changed. Its head was lifted, and it was staring at him with swollen, glazed eyes.

Now the thing should have been dead. Smith knew that, somehow, with a dreadful certainty. The face was a brown skull-mask, with a vaguely canine cast, and the nose, although ragged and eaten away in places, protruded with a shocking resemblance to a beast's muzzle.

The limbs of the horror twitched and moved slowly, and the skeletal, tattered body arose. It dragged itself forward among the whirling star-motes, and instinctively Smith recoiled. There was something so unutterably dreary about it, despite the dreadful attitude of hunger that thrust its beast's head forward, that he sickened a little as he stared. From Jirel came a little cry of repugnance, quickly muffled.

'We'd better get out of here,' said Smith harshly.

Yarol did not speak for a moment. Then he murmured, 'There are more of the things, N.W. See?'

Hidden by the starry mists close to the ground, the ghastly things must have been closing in upon them with that hideous dreary slowness for the past several minutes. They came on, scores of them veiled in stars, moving with a dreadful deliberation, and none of them stood upright. From all sides they were converging, and the dancing motes lent them a curious air of nightmare unreality, like carven gargoyles seen through a fog.

For the most part they came on hands and knees, withered brown skull-faces and glaring bulbous eyes staring blindly at the three. For it seemed to Smith that the beings were blind; the swollen eyes were quite whitish and pupilless. There was nothing about them that savored of the breathing flesh which they so hideously caricatured save the terrible hunger of their approach, made doubly hideous by the fact that those rotting jaws and parchment-dry bellies could never satisfy it by any normal means.

The deformed muzzles of some of them were twitching, and Smith realized abruptly what instinct had led them here. They hunted, apparently, by scent. And their circle was closing in, so that the three humans, recoiling before that creeping, dryly rustling approach, stood very close together now, shoulder to shoulder. Smith felt the girl shudder against him, and then give him a swift sidelong glance, hot with anger that she should have betrayed weakness even for a moment.

A little hesitantly he drew his heat-gun. There was something a bit incongruous about the very thought of shooting at these already dead things. But they were coming closer, and the prospect of contact with those brown, scaling bodies was so repulsive that his finger pressed the trigger almost of its own volition.

One of the approaching horrors toppled over, the left arm completely burned from its body. Then it regained its balance and crawled onward with a crab-like sidewise motion, the severed arm forgotten behind it, although the skeleton fingers writhed and clawed convulsively. The creature made no outcry, and no blood flowed from the wound.

'*Shar*!' breathed Yarol. 'Can't they – die?' His gun jarred and bucked in his hand. The head of the nearest horror became a blackened, cindery stub, but the thing betrayed no pain. It crawled on slowly, the nimbus of swirling stars like a malefic halo about the burned remnant of a head.

'Yarol!' said Smith sharply. 'Double strength – we'll cut a path through them. Follow us, Jirel.' Without waiting for an acknowledgment he flicked over a lever on his heat-gun's muzzle, and sent the searing ray flaming through the dark.

The stars danced more swiftly, troubled. Smith sensed a quick, intangible menace in their aroused motion. It was as though something, drowsy and dreaming, had awakened suddenly from slumber to confront the intruders in this strange land. Yet nothing happened; the stars raced back from the heat-ray's beam, but the crawling monsters paid it no attention, even though they blackened into cinders as they crept. The dry, rustling hordes of them advanced straight into the heat-gun's path, and crisped into ruin – and crunched under the feet of their destroyers into fragments that twitched and squirmed with unquenchable animation too hideous to be called life.

Yarol and Smith and Jirel moved forward over brittle black things that still moved and crunched and crept beneath their feet. The two heat-guns hissed softly, mowing a path. Jirel's yellow eyes dwelt speculatively on Smith's brawny back, and once she touched Yarol's dagger sheathed at her side. But she made no hostile move.

So they won free at last from the withered brown horrors, although until the thickening star-mist hid them Smith could see the nightmare horde crawling behind them, slowly, inexorably. And ever the stars danced and swung in their oddly patterned orbits, seeming to watch with detached and sardonic amusement as the three moved on.

The misty brilliance thickened about them sometimes until they could not see each other's faces; sometimes it thinned so that distances were visible, long corridors of emptiness stretched through the stars. Along one of these aisles at last they caught a glimpse of rising ground, and turned toward it in some hopeless hope of escape.

The spongy earth became firmer as they advanced, until by the time they reached the upland they were walking on black, splintered rock from which a sort of star-veiled mountain rose into the misty upper air. Here the stars thickened about them again, so that they could see nothing, but they stumbled up the jagged slope blindly, clutching at the rock with slipping fingers as they helped one another from ledge to ledge.

In Smith, as he mounted the difficult slopes, a fever of exploration had begun to burn so hotly that their danger retired to the back of his mind. What lay ahead, what unimaginable heights rearing among the stars, what lands beyond the mountain? He was not to know, then or ever.

The slope had grown steeper and more rugged at every step. There was no progress save by painful climbing. And now, as Smith braced his back against a rocky outcropping, straining upward to his full height as he supported Yarol's scrambling boots which a moment before had left his shoulders, his arms encountered a queer, thick obstruction in the starry mist overhead. Full of the desire to know what lay ahead, his mind intent on helping Yarol to a foothold above, he scarcely heeded it until the obstruction had thickened until he could hardly move his hands.

Then the shock of memory jarred him sickeningly awake as he recalled the wall of mist that had solidified between Franga and Jirel. He moved with whiplash swiftness to jerk his arms down, but not quite swiftly enough. That thickening mist had turned to strong steel about his wrists, and after a moment of surging struggle against it, while the veins stood out on his forehead and the blood thundered in his ears, he relaxed against the stone, stretched painfully to full height so that he almost swung from his prisoned wrists, and blinked about him in the dazzling dim air, searching for Franga.

He knew now, with a sick regretfulness, that danger had never been farther from them in the mist than they had been from one another. Franga must have moved invisibly at their sides, waiting patiently for the men's hands to stretch far enough from their guns so that his shackles could prison them before they could reach the weapons. Well, he had them now.

From above, Yarol's voice, muffled in the starry mist, spoke passionately of gods and devils. Smith heard boots thrashing upon the rock and realized that the little Venusian must be struggling with bonds like his own. As for himself, he stood spread-eagled with his back to the mountain and his face to the starry void, boots braced on a long slope of rising stone.

He saw Jirel's back as she loitered below them on the slope, waiting for their call that the next highest ledge had been reached. He said quietly, 'Joiry!' and met her gaze with a small rueful grin.

'Well – what?' She was at his side before the question was out of her mouth, a blaze smoldering in her yellow eyes as she saw what had happened. Then she said viciously, 'Good! This comes of trafficking with warlocks! May you hang there till you rot!'

'Heh!' came a dry chuckle from behind her. 'He'll do just that, Joiry, if he doesn't obey my commands!' Franga came shuffling up the slope, emerging from the stars as from a thick fog, his malice-bright eyes gloating on the prisoned men. From above, Yarol's voice poured smoking Venusian curses upon the wizard's unheeding head.

Jirel matched his fervor with a hot French oath and spun toward Franga purposefully. He smiled crookedly and stepped back, his hands weaving in the air between them. And once more, the cloudy barrier thickened in the dimness. Through it, in a triumphant voice, Franga called to Smith,

'Now will you fulfill your bargain and wrest the jewel from Jirel?'

'Not until you return us to Joiry.'

The warlock's eyes were on his, and in the baffled fury glaring there Smith thought he read suddenly the full reason why they had been brought here. Franga had no thought of paying the debt he had contracted, nor of letting any of the three escape alive. Once the stone was surrendered they would die here, in some unimaginable way, and their bones would whiten until Judgment Day in the darkness at the mountain's foot. Their only hope of salvation lay in their ability to bargain with Franga over the Starstone. So he shut his lips on the refusal and shifted his shoulders to ease his already aching arms. The weight of the gun on his leg was a tantalization almost unbearable, so near and yet so hopelessly far from his shackled hands.

Franga said:

'I think I can change your mind.'

His hands behind the barrier moved cryptically, and there came a stirring in the stars that danced between him and Smith. They moved as if fireflies were swarming there, moved toward Smith and swirled about him dizzyingly, blindly, so that the eye despaired of following their motion. They turned into streaks of flame spinning about him, and now the nearest brushed across his cheek.

At the touch he started involuntarily, jerking back his head from the flame. For it was hot with a heat that sent pain stabbing deeper than a ray-burn through his flesh. Above him he heard Yarol's sharply caught breath, and knew that the hot pain was upon him too. He set his teeth and stared through the swirl at the warlock, his eyes pale and deadly. The spinning flames closed in, brushing his body with scores of tiny tongues, and at every touch the white-hot pain of their torment leaped through him until it seemed to him that every inch of his body flamed with deep-running agony.

Through the blinding pain and the blinding shimmer Franga's voice rasped, 'Will you do my bidding?'

Stubbornly Smith shook his head, clinging even in the hot torture of the flames to the desperate hope which was all that remained to him – that so long as Franga had not the Starstone he dared not kill them. Smith had endured pain before; he could endure it now long enough to hold Franga to his bargain. And Yarol must endure it with him for a while. The Venusian had a shameless sort of bravery against physical pain for the simple reason that he could not endure it, quietly fainted and was out of it if called upon to suffer long. Smith hoped he reached that point soon. He said, 'No,' shortly, between clenched teeth, and pressed his head back against the rock, feeling sweat gather on his forehead as the flashing streaks of flame seared by him, every touch sending deep agony flaming through his flesh.

Franga laughed in a brief, hard cackle and gestured with one hand. And the star-swirls began to flash like knives before Smith's eyes. If they had flamed before, now they dazzled too blindingly to follow. The deep, hot torture of their flickering roared over him in a storm of agony, so that the torment wiped out all thought of Franga or Jirel or Yarol, or anything but his own racked flesh flaming with ray-hot pain. He did not know that his fists were clenched above the shackles, or that the muscles stood out in ridges along his jaws as he fought to keep the agony voiceless behind his teeth. The world was a hell of unbearable torment that swept him on a white-hot tide of pain deep into blazing oblivion. He did not even feel the drag on his wrists as his knees gave way beneath him.

Jirel had been watching with mingling emotions as the stars began to swirl into flames about her tall enemy. Triumph was foremost among them, as resentment and fury were foremost among her thoughts just then. But somehow, she who had looked hardily on torture many times before now felt a queer, hot weakness rising in her as the stars become brushing flames and she saw the sweat beading Smith's forehead and his fists clench against the rock.

Then Franga's hateful voice demanded that he rob her by violence of her jewel and she had tensed herself involuntarily to the struggle before she heard Smith's tortured but resolute 'No.' She stared at him then half in amazement, her mind whirling with wonder at his motives. And a small, reluctant admiration was coloring her resentment of him as she watched. Jirel was a connoisseur of torture, and she could not remember a man who had endured it more resolutely than Smith. Nor was there a sound from Yarol, half hidden in the starry mist above them, though the small flames streaked the dimness even there.

Then she saw the tenseness melting from Smith's racked body as his long legs buckled at the knees, saw him collapse against the mountainside, swinging by his wrists from the shackles. And a sudden fury of sympathy and hot emotion rushed over her, a sudden gust of pain in his pain. Without realizing how it had happened she found herself beating with clenched fists against the barrier that parted her from Franga, heard her own voice crying,

'Stop it! Stop! Let him go free – I give you the Starstone!'

In the deeps of his pain-flaming oblivion Smith heard that high, passionate cry. The significance of it jolted him back into the memory that a world existed outside the burning circle of his agony, and with infinite effort he lifted his sagging head, found a footing on the rocky slope once more, struggled back into consciousness and flaming anguish. He called in a voice as hoarse as if it had screamed itself raw,

'Jirel! Jirel, you fool, don't do it! He'll kill us all! Jirel!'

If she heard him she did not heed. She was wrenching with both hands at the doeskin tunic buckled at her throat, and Franga, the barrier dissolving, leaned eagerly forward with clawed hands outstretched.

'Don't – Jirel, don't!' yelled Smith despairingly through the dazzle of the flames as the leather parted, and suddenly, blindingly, the Starstone flamed in her hands.

Even his own hot pain was blotted for a moment from Smith's mind as he stared. Franga bent forward, breath sucked in, eyes riveted upon the great pale glory of the jewel. There was utter silence in the strange, dim place as the Starstone blazed through the dusk, its cold, still pallor burning in Jirel's fingers like a block of frozen flame. Looking down, she saw again her own fingers distorted through its translucency, saw again that queer, moving flicker as if a shadow stirred in the deeps of the stone.

For a moment it seemed to her as if these smooth, cool surfaces against her hands enclosed a space as vast as the heavens. In a moment of sudden vertigo she might have been staring deep into an infinity through whose silences moved a something that filled it from edge to edge. Was it a world she held here, as vast in its own dimension as space itself, even though her narrow hands cradled it between them? And was there not a Dweller in that vast, glowing place – a moving shadow that—

'Jirel!' Smith's pain-hoarse voice startled her out of her dreaming daze. She lifted her head and moved toward him, half visible in the swirl of his torture, holding the jewel like a lamp in her hands. 'Don't – don't do it!' begged Smith, gripping hard at his ebbing consciousness as the flames stabbed through him.

'Free him!' she commanded Franga, feeling her own throat constrict inexplicably as she saw the pain etched upon Smith's scarred face.

'You surrender the stone willingly?' The warlock's eyes were ravenous upon her hands.

'Yes – yes, only free him!'

Smith choked on his own desperation as he saw her holding out the jewel. At any cost he knew he must keep in from Franga's clutches, and to his pain-dazed brain there seemed only one way for that. How it would help he did not stop to think, but he put all his weight on his prisoned wrists, swinging his long body through the burning stars in an arc as he kicked the jewel from Jirel's outstretched hands.

She gasped; Franga screamed in a thin, high note that quivered with terror as the Starstone was dashed from her hands against the jagged rock of the mountainside. There was a cracking sound that tinkled like broken glass, and then—

And then a pale, bright glory rolled up in their faces as if the light that dwelt in the jewel were pouring out of its shattered prison. The winking stars were swallowed up in its splendor, the dim air glowed and brightened, the whole mountainside was bathed in the calm, still glory that a moment before had blazed in the Starstone's deeps.

Franga was muttering frantically, twisting his hands in spells that accomplished nothing, gabbling in a cracked voice incantations that evoked no magic. It was as if all his power had melted with the melting stars, the vanished dimness, and he stood unprotected in the full glow of this alien light.

Smith was scarcely heeding it. For as the great pale glory billowed up about him the flashing torment of the stars vanished as their flames vanished and the utter bliss of peace after pain left him so weak with relief that as the shackles dissolved about his wrists he could only reel back against the rock while waves of near-oblivion washed over him.

A rattling and scuffling sounded above him, and Yarol's small form slid to the ground at his feet in the complete relaxation of unconsciousness. There was a silence while Smith breathed deeply and slowly, gathering strength again, while Yarol stirred in the beginnings of awakening and Franga and Jirel stared about them in the broadening light from the Starstone.

Then down about them swept a thing that can be called only a shadow of light – a deeper brilliance in the glory of the pale day about them. Smith found himself staring directly into its blazing heart, unblended, although he could make out no more than the shadowy outlines of a being that hung above them inhuman, utterly alien – but not terrible, not menacing. A presence as tangible as flame – and as intangible.

And somehow he sensed a cool and impersonal regard, an aloof, probing gaze that seemed to search the depths of his mind and soul. He strained his eyes, staring into the heart of the white blaze, trying to make out the nature of the being that regarded him. It was like the graceful whorl of a nautilus – and yet he sensed that his eyes could not fully comprehend the unearthly curves and spirals that followed a fantastic, non-Euclidean system of some alien geometry. But the beauty of the thing he could recognize, and there was a deep awe within him, and a feeling of fathomless delight in the wonder and beauty of the being he gazed on.

Franga was screaming thinly and hoarsely, falling to his knees to hide his eyes from the deep splendor. The air quivered, the shadow of brilliance quivered, and a thought without words quivered too through the minds of the three at the mountain's foot.

'For this release We are grateful,' said a voiceless voice as deep and still and somehow flaming as the light that made it manifest. 'We whom strong magic prisoned in the Starstone ages ago would grant one last favor before We return to Our own planet again. Ask it of Us.'

'Oh, return us home again!' gasped Jirel before Smith could speak. 'Take us out of this terrible place and send us home!'

Abruptly, almost instantaneously, the shadow of light enveloped them, swept blindingly about them all. The mountain dropped away underfoot, the glory-bright air swept sidewise into nothingness. It was as if the walls of space and time opened up all around them.

Smith heard Franga's shriek of utter despair – saw Jirel's face whirled by him with a sudden, desperate message blazing in her yellow eyes, the red hair streaming like a banner in the wind – and then that dazzle all about him was the dulled gleam of steel walls, and a cold steel surface was smooth against his cheek.

He lifted his head heavily and stared into silence into Yarol's eyes across the table in the little Martian drinking-booth he had left an eon ago. In silence the Venusian returned that long stare.

Then Yarol leaned back in his chair and called, 'Marnak! Liquor – quick!' and swung round and began to laugh softly, crazily.

Smith groped for the glass of *segir*-whisky he had pushed away when he rose from this table, ages past. He threw back his head and tossed the liquid down his throat with a quick, stiff-wristed gesture, closing his eyes as the familiar warmth burned through him. Behind the closed lids flashed the remembrance of a keen, pale face whose eyes blazed with some sudden violence of emotion, some message he would never know – whose red streaming hair was a banner on the wind. The face of a girl dead two thousand years in time, light-years of space away, whose very dust was long lost upon the bright winds of earth.

Smith shrugged and drained his glass.

HELLSGARDE

Jirel of Joiry drew rein at the edge of the hill and sat awhile in silence, looking out and down. So this was Hellsgarde. She had seen it many times in her mind's eye as she saw it now from the high hill in the yellow light of sunset that turned every pool of the marshes to shining glass. The long causeway to the castle stretched out narrowly between swamps and reeds up to the gate of that grim and eery fortress set alone among the quicksands. This same castle in the marshes, seen at evening from the high hilltop, had haunted her dreams for many nights now.

'You'll find it by sunset only, my lady,' Guy of Garlot had told her with a sidelong grin marring his comely dark face. 'Mists and wilderness ring it round, and there's magic in the swamps about Hellsgarde. Magic – and worse, if legends speak truth. You'll never come upon it save at evening.'

Sitting her horse now on the hilltop, she remembered the grin in his black eyes and cursed him in a whisper. There was such a silence over the whole evening world that by instinct she dared not speak aloud. Dared not? It was no normal silence. Bird-song did not break it, and no leaves rustled. She huddled her shoulders together a little under the tunic of link-mail she wore and prodded her horse forward down the hill.

Guy of Garlot – Guy of Garlot! The hoofbeats thumped out the refrain all the way downhill. Black Guy with his thinly smiling lips and his slanted dark eyes and his unnatural comeliness – unnatural because Guy, within, was ugly as sin itself. It seemed no design of the good God that such sinfulness should wear Guy's dark beauty for a fleshly garment.

The horse hesitated at the head of the causeway which stretched between the marsh pools toward Hellsgarde. Jirel shook the reins impatiently and smiled a one-sided smile downward at his twitching ears.

'I go as loath as you,' she told him. 'I go wincing under spurs too, my pretty. But go I must, and you too.' And she cursed Guy again in a lingering whisper as the slow hoofbeats reverberated upon the stone arches of the causeway.

Beyond it loomed Hellsgarde, tall and dark against the sunset. All around her lay the yellow light of evening, above her in the sky, below her in the marshy pools beneath which quicksands quivered. She wondered who last had ridden this deserted causeway in the yellow glow of sunset, under what dreadful compulsion.

For no one sought Hellsgarde for pleasure. It was Guy of Garlot's slanting grin that drove Jirel across the marshes this evening – Guy and the knowledge that a score of her best men-at-arms lay shivering tonight in his dripping dungeons with no hope of life save the hope that she might buy their safety. And no riches could tempt Black Guy, not even Jirel's smoothly curving beauty and the promise of her full-lipped smile. And Garlot Castle, high on its rocky mountain peak, was impregnable against even Jirel's masterfully planned attacks. Only one thing could tempt the dark lord of Garlot, and that a thing without a name.

'It lies in Hellsgarde, my lady,' he had told her with that hateful smooth civility which his sleek grin so belied. 'And it is indeed Hell-guarded. Andred of Hellsgarde died defending it two hundred years ago, and I have coveted it all my life. But I love living, my lady! I would not venture into Hellsgarde for all the wealth in Christendom. If you want your men back alive, bring me the treasure that Andred died to save.'

'But what is it, coward?'

Guy had shrugged. 'Who knows? Whence it came and what it was no man can say now. You know the tale as well as I, my lady. He carried it in a leather casket locked with an iron key. It must have been small – but very precious. Precious enough to die for, in the end – as I do not propose to die, my lady! You fetch it for me and buy twenty lives in the bargain.'

She had sworn at him for a coward, but in the end she had gone. For after all, she was Joiry. Her men were hers to bully and threaten and command, but they were hers to die for too, if need be. She was afraid, but she remembered her men in Garlot's dungeons with the rack and the boot awaiting them, and she rode on.

The causeway was so long. Sunset had begun to tarnish a little in the bright pools of the marsh, and she could look up at the castle now without being blinded by the dazzle beyond. A mist had begun to rise in level layers from the water, and the smell of it was not good in her nostrils.

Hellsgarde – Hellsgarde and Andred. She did not want to remember the hideous old story, but she could not keep her mind off it this evening. Andred had been a big, violent man, passionate and wilful and very cruel. Men hated him, but when the tale of his dying spread abroad even his enemies pitied Andred of Hellsgarde.

For the rumor of his treasure had drawn at last besiegers whom he could not overcome. Hellsgarde gate had fallen and the robber nobles who captured the castle searched in vain for the precious casket which Andred guarded. Torture could not loosen his lips, though they tried very terribly to make him speak. He was a powerful man, stubborn and brave. He lived a long while under torment, but he would not betray the hiding-place of his treasure.

They tore him limb from limb at last and cast his dismembered body into the quicksands, and came away empty-handed. No one ever found Andred's treasure.

Since then for two hundred years Hellsgarde had lain empty. It was a dismal place, full of mists and fevers from the marsh, and Andred did not lie easy in the quicksands where his murderers had cast him. Dismembered and scattered broadcast over the marshes, yet he would not lie quiet. He had treasured his mysterious wealth with a love stronger than death itself, and legend said he walked Hellsgarde as jealously in death as in life.

In the two hundred years searchers had gone fearfully to ransack the empty halls of Hellsgarde for that casket – gone and vanished. There was magic in the marshes, and a man could come upon the castle only by sunset, and after sunset Andred's violent ghost rose out of the quicksands to guard the thing he died for. For generations now no one had been so foolhardy as to venture upon the way Jirel rode tonight.

She was drawing near the gateway. There was a broad platform before it, just beyond the place where Andred's drawbridge had once barred the approach to Hellsgarde. Long ago the gap in the causeway had been filled in with rubble by searchers who would reach the castle on horseback, and Jirel had thought of passing the night upon that platform under the gate arch, so that dawn might find her ready to begin her search.

But – the mists between her and the castle had thickened, and her eyes might be playing her false – but were not those the shapes of men drawn up in a double row before the doorway of Hellsgarde? Hellsgarde, that had stood empty and haunted these two hundred years? Blinking through the dazzle of sun on water and the thickening of the mists, she rode on toward the gateway. She could feel the horse trembling between her knees, and with every step he grew more and more reluctant to go on. She set her teeth and forced him ahead resolutely, swallowing her own terror.

They *were* the figures of men, two rows of them, waiting motionless before the gate. But even through the mist and the sun-dazzle she could see that something was wrong. They were so still – so unearthly still as they faced her. And the horse was shying and trembling until she could scarcely force him forward.

She was quite near before she saw what was wrong, though she knew that at every forward step the obscure frightfulness about these guardsmen grew greater. But she was almost upon them before she realized why. They were all dead.

The captain at their front stood slumped down upon the great spear that propped him on his feet, driven through his throat so that the point stood out above his neck as he sagged there, his head dragging forward until his cheek lay against the shaft which transfixed him.

And so stood all the rest, behind him in a double row, reeling drunkenly upon the spears driven through throat or chest or shoulder to prop them on their feet in the hideous semblance of life.

So the company of dead men kept guard before the gateway of Hellsgarde. It was not unfitting – dead men guarding a dead castle in the barren deadlands of the swamp.

Jirel sat her horse before them for a long moment in silence, feeling the sweat gather on her forehead, clenching her hands on the pommel of the saddle. So far as she knew, no other living person in decades had ridden the long causeway to Hellsgarde; certainly no living man had dwelt in these haunted towers in generations. Yet – here stood the dead men reeling against the spears which had slain them but would not let them fall. Why? – how? – when? …

Death was no new thing to Jirel. She had slain too many men herself to fear it. But the ghastly unexpectedness of this dead guard! It was one thing to steel oneself to enter an empty ruin, quite another to face a double row of standing dead men whose blood still ran in dark rivulets, wetly across the stones at their feet. Still wet – they had died today, then. Today while she struggled cursing through the wilderness something had slain them here, something had made a jest of death as it propped them on their dead feet with their dead faces toward the causeway along which she must come riding. Had that something expected her? Could the dead Andred have known—?

She caught herself with a little shudder and shrugged beneath the mail, clenching her fingers on the pommel, swallowing hard. (Remember your men – remember Guy of Garlot – remember that you are Joiry!) The memory of Guy's comely face, bright with mockery, put steel into her and she snapped her chin up with a murmured oath. These men were dead – they could not hinder her …

Was that motion among the ghastly guard? Her heart leaped to her throat and she gripped the saddle between nervous knees with a reflex action that made the horse shudder. For one of the men in the row before her was slipping silently toward the flagstones. Had the spear-butt slid on the bloody tiles? Had a breeze dislodged his precarious balance? There was no breeze. But with a curious little sigh from collapsing lungs he folded gently downward to his knees, to his side, to a flattened proneness on the stones. And a dark stream of blood trickled from his mouth to snake across the pavement as he lay there.

Jirel sat frozen. It was a nightmare. Only in nightmares could such things happen. This unbearable silence in the dying sunset, no breeze, no motion, no sound. Not even a ripple upon the mirroring waters lying so widely around her below the causeway, light draining from their surfaces. Sky and water were paling as if all life receded from about her, leaving only Jirel on her trembling horse facing the dead men and the dead castle. She scarcely dared move lest the thump of her mount's feet on the stones dislodge the balance of another man. And she thought she could not bear to see motion again among those motionless ranks. She could not bear it, and yet – and yet if something did not break the spell soon the screams gathering in her throat would burst past her lips and she knew she would never stop screaming.

A harsh scraping sounded beyond the dead guardsmen. Her heart squeezed itself to a stop. And then the blood began to thunder through her veins and her heart leaped and fell and leaped again in a frenzied pounding against the mail of her tunic.

For beyond the men the great door of Hellsgarde was swinging open. She gripped her knees against the saddle until her thighs ached, and her knuckles were bone-white upon the pommel. She made no move toward the great sword at her side. What use is a sword against dead men?

But it was no dead man who looked out under the arch of the doorway, stooped beneath his purple tunic with the heartening glow of firelight from beyond reddening his bowed shoulders. There was something odd about his pale, pinched face upturned to hers across the double line of dead defenders between them. After a moment she recognized what it was – he had the face of a hunchback, but there was no deformity upon his shoulders. He stooped a little as if with weariness, but he carried no hump. Yet it was the face of a cripple if she had ever seen one. His back was straight, but could his soul be? Would the good God have put the sign of deformity upon a human creature without cause? But he was human – he was real. Jirel sighed from the bottom of her lungs.

'Good evening to you, my lady,' said the hunchback (but he was not humped) in a flat, ingratiating voice.

'*These* – did not find it good,' said Jirel shortly, gesturing. And the man grinned.

'My master's jest,' he said.

Jirel looked back to the rows of standing dead, her heart quieting a little. Yes, a man might find a grim sort of humor in setting such a guard before his door. If a living man had done it, for an understanding reason, then the terror of the unknown was gone. But the man—

'Your master?' she echoed.

'My lord Alaric of Hellsgarde – you did not know?'

'Know what?' demanded Jirel flatly. She was beginning to dislike the fellow's sidelong unctuousness.

'Why, that my lord's family has taken residence here after many generations away.'

'Sir Alaric is of Andred's kin?'

'He is.'

Jirel shrugged mentally. It was God's blessing to feel the weight of terror lift from her, but this would complicate matters. She had not known that Andred left descendants, though it might well be so. And if they lived here, then be sure they would already have ransacked the castle from keep to dungeon for that nameless treasure which Andred had died to save and had not yet forsaken, were rumor true. Had they found it? There was only one way to learn that.

'I am nighted in the marshes,' she said as courteously as she could manage. 'Will your master give me shelter until morning?'

The hunchback's eyes – (but he was no hunchback, she must stop thinking of him so!) – his eyes slid very quickly, yet very comprehensively, from her tanned and red-lipped face downward over the lifting curves of her under the molding chainmail, over her bare brown knees and slim, steel-greaved legs. There was a deeper unctuousness in his voice as he said:

'My master will make you very welcome, lady. Ride in.'

Jirel kicked her horse's flank and guided him, snorting and trembling, through the gap in the ranks of dead men which the falling soldier had left. He was a battle-charger, he was used to dead men; yet he shuddered as he minced through these lines.

The courtyard within was warm with the light of the great fire in its center. Around it a cluster of loutish men in leather jerkins looked up as she passed.

'Wat, Piers – up, men!' snapped the man with the hunchback's face. 'Take my lady's horse.'

Jirel hesitated a moment before she swung from the saddle, her eyes dubious upon the faces around her. She thought she had never seen such brutish men before, and she wondered at the lord who dared employ them. Her own followers were tough enough, reckless, hard fellows without fear or scruple. But at least they were men. These louts around the fire seemed scarcely more than beasts; let greed or anger stir them and no man alive could control their wildness. She wondered with what threats of punishment the lord Alaric held sway here, what sort of man he must be to draw his guard from the very dregs of humanity.

The two who took her horse stared at her under shaggy beetle-brows. She flashed them a poison glance as she turned to follow the purple cloak of her guide. Her eyes were busy. Hellsgarde had been a strong fortress in Andred's day; under Alaric it was well manned, but she thought she sensed a queer, hovering sullenness in the very air as she followed her guide across the courtyard, down a passageway, under an arch into the great hall.

The shadows of two hundred haunted years hovered under the lofty roof-beams. It was cold here, damp with the breath of the swamps outside, dark with two centuries of ugly legend and the terrible tradition of murder. But

Alaric before the fire in his scarlet tunic seemed pleasantly at home. The great blaze roaring up the chimney from six-foot logs drove back the chill and the dark and the damp a little in a semicircle about the fireplace, and in that semicircle a little company of brightly clad people sat silent, watching Jirel and her guide cross the echoing flags of the great hall toward them.

It was a pleasant scene, warm and firelit and bright with color, but even at a distance, something was wrong – something in the posture of the people crouching before the blaze, something in their faces. Jirel knew a moment of wild wonder if all this were real. Did she really walk a haunted ruin empty two hundred years? Were the people flesh and blood, or only the bright shadows of her own imagination that had so desperately longed for companionship in the haunted marsh?

But no, there was nothing illusive about Alaric in his high-backed chair, his face a pale oval watching her progress. A humped dwarf leaned above his shoulder, fingers suspended over his lute-strings as he stared. On cushions and low benches by the fire a handful of women and girls, two young boys in bright blue, a pair of greyhounds with the firelight scarlet in their eyes – these made up the rest of the company.

Jirel's narrow yellow gaze summed them up as she crossed the hall. Striding smoothly in her thigh-length hauberk, she knew she was a figure on which a man's eyes must linger. Her supple height, the pleasant smooth curves of her under mail, the long, shapely legs bare beneath the linked metal of her hauberk, the swinging of the long sword whose weight upon its belt pulled in her waist to tigerish slimness – Alaric's eyes missed nothing of all these. Deliberately she tossed the dark cloak back over her shoulders, letting the firelight take the sleek mailed curves of her in a bright glimmer, flash from the shining greaves that clasped her calves. It was not her way to postpone the inevitable. Let Alaric learn in his first long stare how splendid a creature was Joiry's lady. And as for those women at his feet – well, let them know too.

She swaggered to a halt before Alaric, resting a hand on her sword-hilt, tossing back the cloak that had swirled about her as she swung to a stop. His face, half in the shadow of the chair, tilted up to her leanly. Here was no burly brute of a man such as she had half expected on the evidence of the men-at-arms he kept. He was of middle years, his face deeply grooved with living, his nose a hawk-beak, his mouth a sword-gash.

And there was something oddly wrong with his features, a queer cast upon them that made him seem akin to the purple-clad courtier hovering at Jirel's elbow, to the grinning jester who peered across the chair-back. With a little twist of the heart she saw what it was. There was no physical likeness between master and men in any feature, but the shadow of deformity lay upon all three faces, though only the hunchback wore it honestly. Looking at those faces, one would have sworn that each of the trio went limping through life under the burden of a crooked spine. Perhaps, Jirel thought involuntarily, with a small shudder, the master and the courtier as well as the fool did indeed carry a burden, and if they did she thought she would prefer the jester's to theirs. His at least was honest and of the flesh. But theirs must be of the spirit, for surely, she thought again, God in His wisdom does not for nothing mark a whole and healthy man with a cripple's face. It was a deformity of the soul that looked out of the eyes meeting hers.

And because the thought frightened her she swung her shoulders until the cape swirled wide, and flashed her white teeth in a smile more boldly reckless than the girl behind it felt.

'You must not crave the company of strangers, sir – you keep a discouraging guard before your gate!'

Alaric did not smile. 'Honest travelers are welcome here,' he said very smoothly. 'But the next robbers who ride our causeway will think twice before they storm the gates. We have no gallows here where thieves may swing in chains, but I think the guard before my castle will be warning enough to the next raiders who come.'

'A grisly sort of warning,' said Jirel. And then, with belated courtesy, 'I am Jirel of Joiry. I missed my way in the marsh tonight – I shall be grateful for your hospitality.'

'And we for your presence, Lady Jirel.'

Alaric's voice was oily, but his eyes raked her openly. She felt other eyes upon her back too, and her red hair stiffened a little at the roots with a prickling uneasiness. 'We keep a small court here at Hellsgarde,' went on Alaric's voice. 'Damara, Ettard, Isoud, Morgaine – all of you, make our guest welcome!'

Jirel swung round with a swirl of her long cloak to face the women, wondering at the subtle slight to their dignity, for Alaric made no effort to introduce them separately.

She thought they crouched a little on their low seats by the fire, looking up with the queer effect of women peering fearfully from under lowered brows, though she could not have said why they seemed so, for they met her eyes squarely. And upon these faces too lay that strange shadow of deformity, not so definitely as upon the men's, but visible in the firelight. All of them were thin creatures with big eyes showing a rather shocking space of whiteness around the staring irises. Their cheek-bones were sharp in the firelight, so that shadows stood hollowly beneath.

The woman who had risen when Alaric said 'Damara' was as tall as Jirel, strongly made under her close green gown, but her face too had that queer hollow look and her eyes stared too whitely under wide-open lids. She said in a tight voice:

'Sit down by the fire and warm yourself, lady. We dine in a few minutes.'

Jirel sank to the low cushioned stool she dragged forward, one leg doubled under her for instant rising, her sword-hilt and sword-hand free. There was something wrong here. She could feel it in the air.

The two dogs growled a little and shifted away from her on the floor, and even that was – wrong. Dogs had fawned on her always – until now. And the firelight was so red in their eyes …

Looking away uneasily from those unnaturally red eyes, she saw the boys' features clearly for the first time, and her heart contracted a little. For naked evil was upon these two young faces. The others wore their shadow of deformity elusively, a thing more sensed than seen. It might be only a trick of her legend-fed imagination that put evil there. But the two young lads had the faces of devils, long faces with high cheekbones and slitted, lusterless eyes. Jirel shuddered a little inwardly. What sort of company had she stumbled into, where the very children and dogs wore evil like a garment?

She drew a deep breath and glanced around the circle of still faces that watched her wordlessly, with an intentness like that of – of beasts of prey? Her pride rebelled at that. Joiry was ever the predator, not the prey! She squared her cleft chin and said with determined casualness:

'You have dwelt here long?'

She could have sworn a look went round the semicircle before the fire, a swift, amused glance from face to face as if they shared a secret. Yet not an eye wavered from hers. Only the two boys leaned together a little, and the look of evil brightened upon their wicked young faces. Alaric answered after the briefest possible pause:

'Not long. Nor will we stay long – now.' There was a subtle menace in it, though Jirel could not have said why. And again that feeling of knowledge shared ran like a strong current around the circle, a little quiver as if a dreadful amusement were almost stirring in the air. But not a face changed or turned. The eyes were still eager – almost avid – upon the bright, strong face of Jirel with the firelight warming her golden tan and touching her red curls to flame and trembling upon the soft curve of her under-lip. For all the bright clothes of the company around her, she had the sudden feeling that dark robes and dark eyes and dark faces hemmed her in – like shadows around a fire.

The conversation had come to a full stop; the eyes never wavered from her. She could not fathom this strange interest, for it was queer Alaric had not asked anything at all about her coming. A woman alone in this wilderness at night was sufficiently unusual to arouse interest, yet no one seemed concerned to ask how she had come there. Why, then, this concerted, deep interest in the sight of her?

To conquer the little tremor she could not quite ignore she said boldly:

'Hellsgarde of the Marshes has an ugly reputation, my lord. I wonder you dare dwell here – or do you know the old tale?'

Unmistakably this time that quiver of amusement flashed around the circle, though not an eye left hers. Alaric's voice was dry as he answered:

'Yes – yes, we know the tale. We are – not afraid.'

And suddenly Jirel was quite sure of a strange thing. Something in his voice and his words told her very surely that they had not come in spite of the terrible old legend, but *because of it.*

No normal people would deliberately seek out a haunted and blood-stained ruin for a dwelling-place, yet there could be no mistaking the implication in Alaric's voice, in the unspoken mirth at her words that ran like a whisper around the circle. She remembered those dead men at the door. What normal person could make a joke so grisly? No, no – this company was as definitely abnormal as a company of monsters. One could not sit with them long even in silence without sensing that. The look of abnormality upon their faces did not lie – it was a sure sign of a deformity of the soul.

The conversation had stopped again. To break the nerve-racking silence Jirel said:

'We hear many strange tales of Hellsgarde' – and knew she was talking too much, but could not stop – anything was better than that staring silence – 'tales of treasure and – and – is it true that one can come upon Hellsgarde Castle only in the sunset – as I did?'

Alaric paused deliberately for a moment before he answered with as deliberate evasiveness. 'There are stranger tales than that of Hellsgarde – and who can say how much of truth is in them? Treasure? There may well be treasure here. Many have come seeking it – and remained, for ever.'

Jirel remembered the dead men at the door, and she shot Alaric a yellow glare that would have clanged like the meeting of blades with his stare – had he met it. He was looking up into the shadows of the ceiling, and he was smiling a little. Did he suspect her errand? He had asked no questions ... Jirel remembered Guy of Garlot's smile as he sent her on this quest, and a murderous wonder began to take shape in her mind. If Guy had known – if he had deliberately sent her into this peril – she let herself sink for a moment into a luxury of picturing that comely smile smashed in by the handle of her sword ...

They were watching her. She came back with a jerk and said at random:

'How cold the marshes are after sunset!' And she shivered a little, not until that moment realizing the chill of the great hall.

'We find it – pleasant,' murmured Alaric, watching her.

The others were watching too, and again she sensed that ripple of subtle amusement running around the circle that closed her out of a secret shared. They were here for a purpose. She knew it suddenly: a strange, unfathomable purpose that bound them together with almost one mind, so that thoughts seemed to flow soundlessly from brain to brain; a purpose that included her now, and in no pleasant way. Danger was in the air, and she alone here by night in the deserted marshes, among these queer, abnormal people who watched her with an avid and unwavering eagerness. Well, she had been in peril before, and hewed her way out again.

A slovenly wench in a ragged smock tiptoed clumsily out of the shadows to murmur in Damara's ear, and Jirel felt with conscious relief the removal of at least one pair of staring eyes as the woman turned to nod. Jirel's gaze was scornful on the girl. A queer household they kept here – the bestial retainers, the sluttish wench in her soiled gown.

Not even Joiry's kitchen maids were so slovenly clad.

Damara turned back to the fire. 'Shall we dine now?' she asked.

Every face around the fire brightened magically, and Jirel was conscious of a little loosening of the tension in her own mind. The very fact that the thought of food pleased them made the whole group seem more normal. And yet – she saw it in a moment – this was not even a normal eagerness. There was something a little horrid about the gleam in every eye, the avid hunger on every face. For a little while the thought of food supplanted herself in their interest, and that terrible battery of watchfulness forsook her. It was like an actual weight lifted. She breathed deeper.

Frowsy kitchen scullions and a pair of unwashed girls were carrying in the planks and trestles for the table, setting it up by the fire.

'We dine alone,' Alaric was explaining as the group around the fire reshifted itself to make way. It seemed a witless sort of fastidiousness to Jirel, particularly since they let themselves be served by such shamefully unkempt lackeys. Other households dined all together, from lord to stable hands, at the long T-shaped tables where the salt divided noblesse from peasantry. But perhaps Alaric dared not allow those beast-wild men of his even that familiarity. And she was conscious of a tiny disappointment that the company of these staring, strange-faced people was not to be leavened even by the brutish earthiness of their retainers. The men-at-arms seemed scarcely human, but at least it was a normal, open sort of brutality, something she could understand.

When the table was ready Alaric seated her at his right hand, beside the two evil-faced youngsters who sat preternaturally quiet. Young lads of that age were scufflers and squirmers at table in the company she knew. It was another count of eeriness against them that they scarcely moved save to reach for food.

Who were they? she wondered. Alaric's sons? Pages or squires from some noble family? She glanced around the table in deepening bewilderment, looking for signs of kinship on the shadowed faces, finding nothing but that twist of deformity to link the company together. Alaric had made no attempt to introduce any of them, and she could not guess what relationship bound them all together in this close, unspoken communion. She met the eyes of the dwarf at Alaric's elbow and looked quickly away again, angry at his little comprehending grin. He had been watching her.

There was no conversation after the meat was brought in. The whole company fell upon it with such a starved eagerness that one might think they had not dined in weeks before now. And not even their food tasted right or normal.

It looked well enough, but there was a subtle seasoning about it that made Jirel gag and lay down her knife after the first taste – a flavor almost of decay, and a sort of burning bitterness she could not put a name to, that lingered on the tongue long after the food itself was swallowed. Everything stank of it, the roast, the bread, the few vegetables, even the bitter wine.

After a brave effort, for she was hungry, Jirel gave up and made not even the pretense of eating. She sat with her arms folded on the table edge, right hand hanging near her sword, watching the ravenous company devour their tainted food. It was no wonder, she realized suddenly, that they ate alone. Surely not even the dull palates of their retainers could accept this revoltingly seasoned meat.

Alaric sat back at last in his high-backed chair, wiping his dagger on a morsel of bread.

'You do not hunger, Lady Jirel?' he asked, tilting a brow at her still-heaped trencher. She could not help her little grimace as she glanced down.

'Not now,' she said, with wry humor.

Alaric did not smile. He leaned forward to pick up upon his dagger the thick slab of roast before her, and tossed it to the hearth. The two greyhounds streaked from beneath the table to growl over it hungrily, and Alaric glanced obliquely at Jirel, with a hint of a one-sided smile, as he wiped the knife again and sheathed it.

If he meant her to understand that the dogs were included in this queer closed circle of his she caught it. Obviously there had been a message in that act and smile.

When the table had been cleared away and the last glimmer of sunset had faded from the high, narrow slits of the windows, a sullen fellow in frieze went around the hall with a long pole-torch, lighting the cressets.

'Have you visited Hellsgarde before, my lady?' inquired Alaric. And as Jirel shook her head, 'Let me show you the hall then, and my forefathers' arms and shields. Who knows? – you may find quarterings of your own among our escutcheons.'

Jirel shuddered at the thought of discovering even a remote kinship with Hellsgarde's dwellers, but she laid her hand reluctantly on the arm he offered and let him lead her away from the fire out under the echoing vaults of the hall where cressets brought the shadows to life.

The hall was as Andred's murderers must have left it two centuries ago. What shields and armor had not fallen from the walls were thick with rust in the damp air of the marshes, and the tatters of pennons and tapestries had long ago taken on a uniform color of decay. But Alaric seemed to savor the damp and the desolation as a normal man might savor luxury. Slowly he led her around the hall, and she could feel the eyes of the company, who had resumed their seats by the fire, follow her all the way with one unwinking stare.

The dwarf had taken up his lute again and struck occasional chords in the echoing silence of the hall, but except for that there was no sound but the fall of their feet on the rushless flagstones and the murmur of Alaric's voice pointing out the vanished glories of Hellsgarde Castle.

They paused at the side of the big room farthest from the fire, and Alaric said in an unctuous voice, his eyes seeking Jirel's with curious insistence:

'Here on this spot where we stand, lady, died Andred of Hellsgarde two hundred years ago.'

Jirel looked down involuntarily. Her feet were planted on the great blotch of a spreading stain that had the rough outline of a beast with questing head and paws outsprawled. It was a broad, stain, black and splattered upon the stone. Andred must have been a big man. He had bled terribly on that day two centuries past.

Jirel felt her host's eyes on her face full of a queer anticipation, and she caught her breath a little to speak, but before she could utter a sound, quite suddenly there was a riot of wind all about them, shrieking out of nowhere in a whirlwind gust that came ravening with such fury that the cressets went out all together in one breath and darkness like a blow fell upon the hall.

In the instant of that blackness, while the whole great hall was black and vocal and bewildering with storm-wind, as if he had been waiting avidly for this moment all evening a man's arm seized Jirel in a grip like death and a mouth came down upon hers in a more savagely violent and intimate kiss than she had ever known before. It all burst upon her so quickly that her impressions confused and ran together into one gust of terrible anger against Alaric as she struggled helplessly against that iron arm and ravenous mouth, while the storm-wind shrieked in the darkness. She was conscious of nothing but the arm, the mouth, the insolent hand. She was not pressed against a man's body, but the strength of the arm was like steel about her.

And in the same moment of the seizure the arm was dragging her violently across the floor with irresistible force, never slackening its crushing grip, the kiss in all its revolting intimacy still ravaging her muted mouth. It was as if the kiss, the crush of the arm, the violence of the hand, the howl of the wind and the drag across the room were all but manifestations of a single vortex of violence.

It could not have lasted more than seconds. She had an impression of big, square, wide-spaced teeth against her lips and the queer violence behind them manifest not primarily in the savageness of the kiss or the embrace, or the wild drag across the room, but more as if all these were mere incidents to a burning vehemence behind them that beat like heat all around her.

Choking with impotent fury, she tried to struggle, tried to scream. But there was no chest to push for leverage and no body to arch away from, and she could not resist. She could only make dumb animal sounds in her throat, sealed in behind the storming violation of that mouth.

She had scarcely time to think, it happened so quickly. She was too stunned by the violence and suddenness of the attack even to wonder at the absence of anything but the mouth, the arm, the hand. But she did have the distinct impression of walls closing in around her, as if she were being dragged out of the great open hall into a narrow closet. It was somehow as if that violence beating all about her were confined and made more violent by the presence of close walls very near.

It was all over so quickly that even as that feeling of closing walls dawned upon her she heard the little amazed cries of the others as the cressets were blown out all together. It was as if time had moved faster for her than for them. In another instant someone must have thrown brush on the fire, for the great blaze in the cavern of the chimney roared up with a gush of light and sound, for a moment beating back the darkness in the hall.

And Jirel was staggering alone in the center of the big room. No one was near her, though she could have sworn upon the cross-hilt of her sword that a split second before the heavy mouth had crushed her muted lips. It was gone now as if it had never been. Walls did not enclose her; there was no wind, there was no sound in the great hall.

Alaric stood over the black blotch of Andred's blood at the other side of the hall. She thought she must have known subconsciously after the first moment that it was not he whose lips ravaged her bruised mouth. That flaming vehemence was not in him. No, though he had been the only man near her when the dark closed down, he was not the man whose outrageous kiss still throbbed on her mouth.

She lifted an unsteady hand to those bruised lips and stared around her wildly, gasping for lost breath, half sobbing with fury.

The others were still around the fire, half the width of the room away. And as the light from the replenished blaze leaped up, she saw the blankness of their momentary surprise vanish before one leaping flame of avid hope that for an instant lit every face alike. With long running strides Alaric reached her side. In her dazed confusion she felt his hands on her arms shaking her eagerly, heard him gabbling in a tongue she did not know:

'G'hasta-est? Tai g'hasta? Tai g'hasta?'

Angrily, she shook him off as the other closed round her in an eagerly excited group, babbling all together, *'G'hasta tai? Est g'hasta?'*

Alaric recovered his poise first. In a voice shaking with the first emotion she had heard from him he demanded with almost desperate eagerness.

'What was it? What happened? Was it – was it—?' But he seemed scarcely to dare name the thing his whole soul longed for, though the tremble of hope was in his voice.

Jirel caught herself on the verge of answering. Deliberately she paused to fight down the dizzy weakness that still swam in her brain, drooping her lids to hide the calculation that came up like a flame behind her yellow eyes. For the first time she had a leverage over these mysterious people. She knew something they frantically desired to know, and she must make full use of the knowledge she scarcely knew she had.

'H-happened?' The stammer was not entirely feigned. 'There was a – a wind, and darkness – I don't know – it was all over so quickly.' And she glanced up into the gloom with not wholly assumed terror. Whatever that thing had been – it was no human agency. She could have sworn that the instant before the light flared up, walls were closing around her as tightly as a tomb's walls; yet they had vanished more lightly than mist in the glow of the fire. But that mouth upon hers, those big, squarely spaced teeth against her lips, the crush of the brutal arm – nothing could have been more tangible. Yet there had been only the arm, the mouth, the hand. No body … With a sudden shudder that made the goose-flesh ripple along her limbs she remembered that Andred had been dismembered before they flung him into the quicksands … Andred …

She did not know she had said it aloud, but Alaric pounced like a cat on the one word that left her lips.

'Andred? Was it Andred?'

Jirel recovered herself with a real effort, clenching her teeth to stop their chattering.

'Andred? He died two hundred years ago!'

'He will never die until—' One of the young boys with the evil faces said that much before Alaric whirled on him angrily, yet with curious deference.

'Silence! … Lady Jirel, you asked me if the legends of Hellsgarde are true. Now I tell you that the tale of Andred is. We believe he still walks the halls where his treasure lies hid, and we – we—' He hesitated, and Jirel saw a strong look of calculation dawn upon his face. He went on smoothly, 'We believe there is but one way to find that treasure. Only the ghost of Andred can lead us there. And Andred's ghost has been – elusive, until now.'

She could have sworn that he had not meant to say just that when he began to speak. She was surer of it when she saw the little flicker of communication ripple around the circle of faces closing her in. Amusement at a subtle jest in which she did not share ... it was on every face around her, the hollow-cheeked women's white-rimmed staring eyes brightened, the men's faces twitched a little with concealed mirth. Suddenly she felt smothered by abnormality and mystery and that subtle, perilous amusement without reason.

She was more shaken by her terrifying experience than she would have cared to admit. She had little need to feign weakness as she turned away from them toward the fire, eager to escape their terrible company even though it meant solitude in this haunted dark. She said:

'Let me – rest by the fire. Perhaps it – it – he won't return.'

'But he must return!' She thought that nearly every voice around her spoke simultaneously, and eager agreement was bright upon every face. Even the two dogs had thrust themselves forward among the legs of the little crowd around Jirel, and their shadowed eyes, still faintly aglow as if with borrowed firelight, followed the conversation from face to face as if they too understood. Their gazes turned redly up to Alaric now as he said:

'For many nights we have waited in vain for the force that was Andred to make itself known to us. Not until you come does he create that vortex which – which is necessary if we are to find the treasure.' Again, at that word, Jirel thought she felt a little current of amusement ripple from listener to listener. Alaric went on in his smooth voice, 'We are fortunate to find one who has the gift of summoning Andred's spirit to Hellsgarde. I think there must be in you a kindred fierceness which Andred senses and seeks. We must call him out of the dark again – and we must use your power to do it.'

Jirel stared around her incredulously. 'You would call – *that* – up again?'

Eyes gleamed at her with a glow that was not of the firelight. 'We would indeed,' murmured the evil-faced boy at her elbow. 'And we will not wait much longer ...'

'But – God's Mercy!' said Jirel, '—are all the legends wrong? They say Andred's spirit swoops down with sudden death on all who trespass in Hellsgarde. Why do you talk as if only I could evoke it? Do you want to die so terribly? I do not! I won't endure *that* again if you kill me for it. I'll have no more of Andred's kisses!'

There was a pulse of silence around the circle for a moment. Eyes met and looked away again. Then Alaric said:

'Andred resents only outsiders in Hellsgarde, not his own kinsmen and their retainers. Moreover, those legends you speak of are old ones, telling tales of long-ago trespassers in this castle.

'With the passage of years the spirits of the violent dead draw farther and farther away from their death-scenes. Andred is long dead, and he revisits Hellsgarde Castle less often and less vindictively as the years go by. We have striven a long while to draw him back – but you alone succeeded. No, lady, you must endure Andred's violence once again, or—'

'Or what?' demanded Jirel coldly, dropping her hand to her sword.

'There is no alternative.' Alaric's voice was inflexible. 'We are many to your one. We will hold you here until Andred comes again.'

Jirel laughed. 'You think Joiry's men will let her vanish without a trace? You'll have such a storming about Hellsgarde walls as—'

'I think not, lady. What soldiers will dare follow when a braver one than any of them was vanished in Hellsgarde? No, Joiry, your men will not seek you here. You—'

Jirel's sword flamed in the firelight as she sprang backward, dragging it clear. The blade flashed once – and then arms like iron pinioned her from behind. For a dreadful moment she thought they were Andred's, and her heart turned over. But Alaric smiled, and she knew. It was the dwarf who had slipped behind her at an unspoken message from his master, and if his back was weak his arms were not. He had a bear's grip upon her and she could not wrench herself free.

Struggling, sobbing curses, kicking hard with her steel-spurred heels, she could not break his hold. There was a murmurous babble all around her of that strange, haunting tongue again, *'L'vraista! Tai g' hasta vrai! El vraist' tai lau!'* And the two devil-faced boys dived for her ankles. They clung like ghoulishly grinning apes, pinning her feet to the floor. And Alaric stepped forward to wrench the sword from her hand. He murmured something in their queer speech, and the crowd scattered purposefully.

Fighting hard, Jirel was scarcely aware of their intention before it was accomplished. But she heard the sudden splash of water on blazing logs and the tremendous hissing of steam as the fire went out and darkness fell like a blanket upon the shadowy hall. The crowd had melted away from her into the dark, and now the grip on her ankles suddenly ceased and the great arms that held her so hard heaved in a mighty swing.

Choking with fury, she reeled into the darkness. There was nothing to stop her, and those mighty arms had thrown her hard. She fell and slid helplessly across bare flagstones in black dark, her greaves and empty scabbard clanging upon stone. When she came to a halt, bruised and scratched and breathless, it was a moment before she could collect her senses enough to scramble up, too stunned even for curses.

'Stay where you are Jirel of Joiry,' Alaric's voice said calmly out of the blackness. 'You cannot escape this hall – we guard every exit with drawn swords. Stand still – and wait.'

Jirel got her breath and launched into a blasphemous survey of his ancestry and possible progeny with such vehemence that the dark for several minutes throbbed with her fury. Then she recalled Alaric's suggestion that violence in herself might attract a kindred violence in that strange force called Andred, and she ceased so abruptly that the silence was like a blow upon the ears.

It was a silence full of tense waiting. She could almost feel the patience and the anticipation that beat out upon her from the circle of invisible jailers, and at the thought of what they wanted her blood ran chilly. She looked up blindly into the darkness overhead, certain for a long and dreadful moment that the familiar blast of storm-wind was gathering there to churn the night into chaos out of which Andred's arm would reach …

After a while she said in a voice that sounded unexpectedly small in the darkness:

'Y-you might throw me a pillow. I'm tired of standing and this floor's cold.'

To her surprise footsteps moved softly and quite surely across stone, and after a moment a pillow hurtled out of the darkness to thump softly at her feet. Jirel sank upon it thankfully, only to stiffen an instant later and glare about her in the dark, the hair prickling on her neck. So – they could see in the darkness! There had been too much certainty in those footsteps and the accurate toss of the pillow to doubt it. She huddled her shoulders together a little and tried not to think.

The darkness was enormous above her. Age upon age went by, with no sound except her own soft breathing to break that quiet pulsing with waiting and anticipation. Her terror grew. Suppose that dreadful storm-wind should come whooping through the hall again; suppose the bodiless arm should seize her and the mouth come ravening down upon her lips once more … Coldness crept down her spine.

Yes, and suppose it did come again. What use, for her? These slinking abnormalities who were her jailers would never share the treasure with her which they were so avid to find – so avid that they dared evoke this terror by night and brave a death which legend whispered fearfully of, simply that they might possess it. *It* – did they know, then, what lay in Andred's terribly guarded box? What conceivable thing could be so precious that men would dare *this* to have it?

And what hope at all for her? If the monstrous thing called Andred did not come tonight – then he would come again some other night, sooner or later, and all nights would find her isolated here as bait for the monster that haunted Hellsgarde. She had boasted without hope when she said her men would follow. They were brave men and they loved her – but they loved living more. No, here was not a man in Joiry who would dare follow where she had failed. She remembered Guy of Garlot's face, and let violence come flooding up in her for a moment. That handsome coward, goading her into this that he might possess the nameless thing he coveted ... Well, she would ruin his comely face for him with the crosshilt of her sword – if she lived! She was forgetting ...

Slowly the stars wheeled by the arrow-slit windows high up in the darkness of the walls. Jirel sat hugging her knees and watching them. The darkness sighed above her with vagrant drafts, any one of which might be Andred roaring down out of the night ...

Well, her captors had made one mistake. How much it might avail her she did not know, but they thought they had disarmed her, and Jirel hugged her greave-sheathed legs in the darkness and smiled a wicked smile, knowing they had not.

It must have been after midnight, and Jirel dozing uneasily with her head on her knees, when a long sigh from the darkness made her start awake. Alaric's voice, heavy with weariness and disappointment, spoke in his nameless language. It occurred to Jirel to wonder briefly that though this seemed to be their mother tongue (for they spoke it under stress and among themselves), yet their speech with her had no taint of accent. It was strange – but she was beyond wondering long about the monstrous folk among whom she had fallen.

Footsteps approached her, walking unerringly. Jirel shook herself awake and stood up, stretching cramped limbs. Hands seized her arms from both sides – at the first grasp, with no groping, though even her dark-accustomed eyes could see nothing. No one bothered to translate Alaric's speech to her, but she realized that they had given up their vigil for the night. She was too drugged with sleep to care. Even her terror had dulled as the endless night hours dragged by. She stumbled along between her captors, making no effort to resist. This was not the time to betray her hidden weapon, not to these people who walked the dark like cats. She could wait until the odds were evener.

No one troubled to strike a light. They went swiftly and unhesitatingly through the blackness, and when stairs rose unexpectedly underfoot Jirel was the only one who stumbled. Up steps, along a cold and echoing hall – and then a sudden thrust that sent her staggering. A stone wall caught her and a door slammed at her back. She whirled, a hot Norman oath smoking on her lips, and knew that she was alone.

Groping, she made out the narrow confines of her prison. There was a cot, a jug of water, a rough door through whose chinks light began to glimmer even as she ran questing hands across its surface. Voices spoke briefly outside, and in a moment she understood. Alaric had summoned one of his apish men to watch her while he and his people slept. She knew it must be a man-at-arms and not one of Alaric's company, for the fellow had brought a lantern with him. She wondered if the guardsmen knew how unerringly their masters walked the darkness – or if they cared. But it no longer seemed strange to her that Alaric dared employ such brutish men. She knew well enough now with what ease he could control them – he and his night-sight and his terrible fearlessness.

Silence fell outside. Jirel smiled a thin smile and leaned into the nearest corner, drawing up one knee. The long, thin-bladed knife she carried between greave and leg slid noiselessly from its sheath. She waited with feline patience, her eyes upon the lighted chinks between the door's planks.

It seemed a long while before the guard ceased his muffled pacing, yawned loudly, tested the bar that fastened the door from without. Jirel's thin smile widened. The man grunted and – she had prayed he would – settled down at last on the floor with his back against the panels of her door. She knew he meant to sleep awhile in the certainty that the door could not be opened without waking him. She had caught her own guards at that trick too often not to expect it now.

Still she waited. Presently the even breath of slumber reached her ears, and she licked her lips and murmured, 'Gentle Jesu, let him not wear mail' and leaned to the door. Her knife was thin enough to slide easily between the panels ... He was not wearing mail – and the blade was razor-keen. He must scarcely have felt it, or known when he died. She felt the knife grate against bone and gave it an expert twist to clear the rib it had grazed, and heard the man give a sudden, startled grunt in his sleep, and then a long sigh ... He must never have awakened. In a moment blood began to gush through the panels of the door in heavy spurts, and Jirel smiled and withdrew her knife.

It was simple enough to lift the bar with that narrow blade. The difficulty was in opening the door against the dead weight of the man outside, but she accomplished that too, without too much noise – and then the lantern sat waiting for her and the hall was long and empty in the half-dark. She could see the arch of the stairway and knew the way she had come. And she did not hesitate on the way down. She had thought it all out carefully in the darkness of the hall downstairs while she crouched on the cushion and waited for Andred's ravenous storm-blast to come shrieking down above her bent shoulders.

There was no way out. She knew that. Other castles had posterns and windows from which a fugitive might escape, but quicksands surrounded Hellsgarde and the only path to freedom lay along the causeway where Alaric's guard would be watching tonight. And only in minstrels' romances does a lone adventurer escape through a guarded courtyard and a guarded gate.

And too – she had come here for a purpose. It was her duty to find that small treasured box which alone would buy the twenty lives depending on her. She would do that, or die. And perhaps, after all, it was fortunate that the castle had not been empty when she came. Without Alaric, it might never have occurred to her to dare the power of Andred's ghost in order to reach her goal. She realized now that it might well be the only way she would ever succeed. Too many searchers in the past had ransacked Hellsgarde Castle to leave her much hope unless great luck attended her. But Alaric had said it: there was a way – a terrible and deadly perilous way, but the only hope.

And after all, what chance did she have? To sit supinely waiting, a helpless decoy, until the night when Andred's power swooped down to claim her again – or to seek him out deliberately and challenge him to the duel. The end would be the same – she must suffer his presence again, either way. But tonight there was a bare chance for her to escape with the treasure-casket, or at least to find it alone and if she lived to hide it and bargain with Alaric for freedom.

It was a forlorn and futile hope, she knew well. But it was not in her to sit waiting for death, and this way there was at least a bare hope for success. She gripped her bloody knife in one hand and her lantern in the other and went on down the stairs, cat-footed and quick.

Her little circle of light moving with her across the cold flags was so tenuous a defense against the dark. One gust of Andred's storm-wind would puff it out and the darkness would smash in upon her like a blow. And there were other ghosts here than Andred's – small, cold things in the dark just beyond her lantern light. She could feel their presence as she picked her way across the great hall, past the quenched logs of the fireplace, past the crumbling ruins of armor and tapestry, toward the one spot where she thought she might be surest of summoning up the dreadful thing she sought.

It was not easy to find. She ranged back and forth for many minutes with her little circle of light before a corner of that great black splotch she hunted moved into the light; beast-shaped, dark as murder itself upon the flagstones Andred's life-blood spilled two hundred years ago.

Here once before that ravening ghost had taken her; here if anywhere, surely he would come again. She had her underlip firmly between her teeth as she stepped upon that stain, and she was holding her breath without realizing it. She must have stood there for a full minute, feeling the goose-flesh shudder along her limbs, before she could nerve herself for the thing she must do next. But she had come too far to fail herself now. She drew a deep breath and blew out the lifted lantern.

Darkness crashed upon her with the impact of a physical blow, almost squeezing the breath from her body. And now suddenly fright was past and the familiar wing exultation of tension before battle rushed along her limbs and she looked up into the darkness defiantly and shouted to the great vaults of the ceiling, 'Come out of Hell, dead Andred! Come if you dare, Andred the Damned!'

Wind – wind and storm and violence! It snatched the words from her lips and the breath from her throat in one tremendous whirling gust that came rushing out of nowhere. And in the instant of its coming, while the wild challenge still echoed on her lips, a ravenous mouth came storming down to silence hers and a great arm smacked down around her shoulders in a blow that sent her reeling as iron fingers dug agonizingly into her arm – a blow that sent her reeling but would not let her fall, for that terrible drag again was sweeping her across the floor with a speed that ran faster than time itself.

She had ducked her head instinctively when she felt the arm seize her, but not soon enough. The heavy mouth had hers, and again the square, wide-set teeth were bruising her lips and the violence of the monstrous kiss made fury bubble up in her sealed throat as she fought in vain against it.

This time the thing was not such a stunning surprise, and she could sense more clearly what was happening to her. As before, the whole violent fury of the attack burst upon her at once – the mouth seized hers and the arm swept her almost off her feet in the same instant. In that instant the unslackening grip around her shoulders rushed her across the dark floor, blinded in the blackness, deafened by the raving wind, muted and dazed by the terrible vehemence of the mouth and the pain of her iron-clawed arm. But she could sense dimly again that walls were closing around her, closer and closer, like a tomb's walls. And as before she was aware of a tremendous force beating about her, a greater violence than any one manifestation of it upon her body; for the mouth, the gripping hand, the arm, the sweeping drag itself were all but parts of that vortex.

And it was indeed a vortex – it was somehow spinning and narrowing as if the whole force that was Andred were concentrating into one tornado-whirl of savage power. Perhaps it was that feeling of narrowing and vortexing rotation which made walls seem to draw close about her. It was all too dimly sensed a thing to put clearly into words, and yet it was terribly real. Jirel, breathless and bruised and stunned with pain and violence, still knew clearly that here in the midst of the great open hall walls were drawing prison-tight about her.

Savagely she slashed at the arm around her shoulders, at the steel-fingered hand digging her arm to the bone. But the angle was an awkward one and she was too dazed to know if she cut flesh or simply stabbed at disembodied force. And the grip did not slacken; the storming mouth still held hers in a kiss so wild and infuriating that she could have sobbed with pure rage.

Those walls were very near … her stumbling knees touched stone. She groped dizzily with her free hand and felt walls dripping-damp, close around her. The forward motion had ceased, and the power which was Andred whirled in one concentrated cone of violence that stopped her breath and sent the darkness reeling around her.

Through the haze of her confusion she knew that this, then, must be his own place to which he had dragged her, a place of stone and damp and darkness somewhere *outside* – for they had reached it too quickly for it to be a real place – and yet it was tangible … Stone walls cold against her hands, and what were these round and slipping things underfoot? – things that rattled a little as she stumbled among them – bones? Dear God, the bones of other seekers after treasure, who had found what they sought? For she thought the treasure-box must be here, surely, if it were anywhere at all – here in this darkness unreachable save through the very heart of the whirlwind …

Her senses were failing and the whirl that was like the whirl in a tornado's heart seemed to create a vacuum which drew her out of her body in one thin, protesting wisp of self that had no strength to fight …

Somewhere a long way off was her body, hanging limp in the clutch of the iron arm, gasping for breath under a kiss that made reality faint about her, still struggling feebly in some tomb-smelling, narrow place where stone walls dripped and bones turned underfoot – the bones of those who had come before her …

But she was not there. She was a wispy wraith rooted only tenuously in that fainting body, a wraith that reeled out and out in a thin skein to spin on the whirls of tornado-violence pulling her farther and farther and farther away … The darkness was slipping sidewise – the stone walls were a prison no longer, for she was moving up along the great expanding whirl that sucked her out of her body, up and out around widening circles into night-time distances where space and time were not …

Somewhere infinitely far away a foot that was not hers stumbled over something small and square, and a body that was not hers slid to its knees among wet, rattling bones, and a bosom that was not hers bruised itself on the corner of that square something as the tenantless body fell forward among bones upon a wet stone floor. But upon the widening whorls of the vortex the wisp that was Jirel rebelled in its spinning. She must go back – she must remember – there was something – something …

For one fleeting instant she was in her body again, crumpled down upon the stones, arms sprawled about a small square thing that was slimy to the touch. A box – a wet leather box thick with fungus, bound with iron. Andred's box, that for two hundred years searchers had hunted in vain. The box that Andred had died for and that she would die for too – was dying for now in the darkness and the damp among the bones, with violence ravening down to seize her again …

Dimly, as her senses left her for the second time, she heard a dog bark, high and hysterically, from far above. And another dog answered, and then she heard a man's voice shouting in a tongue she did not know, a wild, exultant shout, choking with triumph. But after that the dizziness of the whirlwind which snatched her out of her body made everything blur, until – until—

Queerly, it was music that brought her back. A lute's strings singing as if madness itself swept wild chords across them. The dwarfed jester's lute, shrieking with music that wakened her out of nowhere into her own fallen body in the dampness and the dark where that hard box-corner bruised her bosom.

And the whirlwind was – uncoiling – from about her. The walls widened until she was no longer aware of their prison closeness and the smell of damp and decay faded from her nostrils. In a dizzy flash of realization she clasped the wet casket to her breast just as the walls faded altogether and she sat up unsteadily, blinking into the dark.

The whirlwind still raved around her, but somehow, strangely, it did not touch her now. No, there was something outside it – some strong force against which it battled – a force that – that—

She was in the dark hall again. Somehow she knew it. And the wild lute-music shrilled and sang, and in some queer way – she saw. It was dark still – but she saw. For a luminous glow was generating itself in a ring around her and by its ghostlight she was aware – scarcely through sight – of familiar faces spinning past her in a wide, whirling ring. A witch dance, round and round ... Alaric's lined face flashed by, blazing with exultation; Damara's white-ringed eyes glared blindly into the dark. She saw the two boys whirl past, the light of hell itself luminous on their faces. There was a wild bark, and one of the greyhounds loped by her and away, firelight from no earthly flame glaring in its eyes, its tongue lolling in a canine grin of ecstasy. Round and round her through that luminous glow which was scarcely light the mad circle spun. And ever the lute-strings wailed and sang with a wilder music than strings can ever have sung before, and the terrible joy on every face – yes, even upon the dogs' – was more frightening than even Andred's menace had been.

Andred – Andred ... The power of his volcano-force spun above her now, with a strength that stirred the red hair against her cheeks and a raving of wind through which the lute music screamed high. But it was not the dull force that had overwhelmed her. For this manic dance that spun round and round through the dark was building up a climax of cumulative strength that she could feel as she knelt there, hugging the slimy box. She thought the very air sang with tension and stress. That circle was reeling counterwise to the spin of Andred's vortexing force, and Andred was weakening. She could feel him slackening above her in the dark. The music shrieked louder above the failing storm-wind and the fearful joy upon those faces whirling past told her why. Somehow they were overpowering him. Something in the dwarf's mad lute-strings, something in the spinning of their dance was breaking down the strength of Andred's centuries-old violence. She could feel it weakening as she crouched there with the casket hugged bruisingly to her bosom.

And yet – was it this precious casket that they fought for? No one had a glance to spare for the crouching girl or the burden she hugged. Every face was lifted raptly, every eye stared blindly and exultantly into the upper dark as if the thing that was Andred was visible and – and infinitely desirable. It was a lust for that thing upon their faces that made joy so vivid there. Jirel's brain had almost ceased recording sensation in the bewilderment of what she watched.

When the dance ended she scarcely knew it. Lulled into a dizzy trance by the mad spinning of the dancers, she was almost nodding on her knees in their center, feeling her brain whirl with their whirling – feeling the motion slow about her so imperceptibly that nothing but the whirl itself registered on her mind. But the dancers were slackening – and with them, the whirl above. The wind no longer raved through the dark; it was a slow sigh now, growing softer and gentler as the circle of dancers ceased to spin …

And then there was a great, soft, puffing sigh from the darkness above her that blew out her awareness like a candleflame …

Daylight fingering through the arrow-slits touched Jirel's closed lids. She awoke painfully, blinking in the light. Every muscle and bone of her supple body ached from the buffeting of last night's storm and violence, and the cold stones were hard beneath her. She sat up, groping by instinct for her knife. It lay a little distance off, rusting with last night's blood. And the casket – the casket! …

Panic swelling in her throat quieted in an instant as she saw that precious, molding thing lying on its side at her elbow. A little thing, its iron hinges rusty, its leather whitened and eaten with rot from two centuries in a nameless, dripping place; but safe, unopened. She picked it up, shaking it experimentally. And she heard the softest shifting within, a sound and weight like finest flour moving gently.

A rustle and a sigh from beyond brought her head up, and she stared around her in the shadows of the halls. In a broad, uneven circle the bodies of last night's dancers lay sprawled. Dead? No, slow breathing stirred them as they lay, and upon the face of the nearest – it was Damara – was a look of such glutted satiety that Jirel glanced away in disgust. But they all shared it. She had seen revelers asleep after a night of drunken feasting with not half such surfeit, such almost obscene satisfaction upon their faces as Alaric's drugged company wore now. Remembering that obscure lusting she had seen in their eyes last night, she wondered what nameless satiety they had achieved in the dark after her own consciousness went out ...

A footfall sounded upon stone behind her and she spun halfway round, rising on one knee and shifting the knife-hilt firmer in her fist. It was Alaric, a little unsteady on his feet, looking down upon her with a sort of half-seeing abstraction. His scarlet tunic was dusty and rumpled as if he had slept in it all night upon the floor and had only just risen. He ran a hand through his ruffled hair and yawned, and looked down at her with a visible effort at focusing his attention.

'I'll have your horse brought up,' he said, his eyes sliding indifferently away from her even as he spoke. 'You may go now.'

Jirel gaped up at him, her lips parting in amazement over white teeth. He was not watching her. His eyes had shifted focus and he was staring blindly into some delightful memory that had blotted out Jirel's very existence. And upon his face that look of almost obscene satiety relaxed every feature until even his sword-gash mouth hung loose.

'B-but—' Jirel blinked and clutched at the mildewed box she had risked her life for. He came back into focus for an impatient instant to say carelessly:

'Oh – that! Take the thing.'

'You – you know what it is? I thought you wanted—'

He shrugged. 'I could not have explained to you last night what it was I wanted of – Andred. So I said it was the treasure we sought – you could understand that. But as for that rotting little box – I don't know or care what lies inside. I've had – a better thing ...' And his remembering eyes shifted again to escape hers and stare blissfully into the past.

'Then why did you – save me?'

'Save you?' He laughed. 'We had no thought of you or your treasure in what we – did – last night. You have served your purpose – you may go free.'

'Served – what purpose?'

Impatiently for an instant he brought himself wholly back out of his remembering dream to say:

'You did what we were holding you for – called up Andred into our power. Lucky for you that the dogs sensed what happened after you had slipped off to dare the ghost alone. And lucky for us, too. I think Andred might not have come even to take you, had he sensed our presence. Make no doubt of it – he feared us, and with good reason.'

Jirel looked up at him for a long instant, a little chill creeping down her spine, before she said in a shaken whisper:

'What – are you?' And for a moment she almost hoped he would not answer. But he smiled, and the look of deformity deepened upon his face.

'A hunter of undeath,' he said softly. 'A drinker of undeath, when I can find it ... My people and I lust after that dark force which the ghosts of the violent dead engender, and we travel far sometimes between – feastings.' His eyes escaped hers for an instant to stare gloatingly into the past. Still looking with that unfocused gaze, in a voice she had not heard before from him, he murmured, 'I wonder if any man who has not tasted it could guess the utter ecstasy of drinking up the undeath of a strong ghost … a ghost as strong as Andred's … feeling that black power pouring into you in deep drafts as you suck it down – a thirst that strengthens as you drink – feel – darkness – spreading through every vein more sweetly than wine, more intoxicating … To be drunk on undeath – a joy almost unbearable.'

Watching him, Jirel was aware of a strong shudder that rose in the pit of her stomach and ran strongly and shakingly along her limbs. With an effort she tore her gaze away. The obscene ecstasy that Alaric's inward-looking eyes dwelt upon was a thing she would not see even in retrospect, through another's words and eyes. She scrambled to her feet, cradling the leather box in her arm, averting her eyes from his.

'Let me go, then,' she said in a lowered voice, obscurely embarrassed as if she had looked inadvertently upon something indescribable. Alaric glanced up at her and smiled.

'You are free to go,' he said, 'but waste no time returning with your men for vengeance against the force we imposed on you.' His smile deepened at her little twitch of acknowledgment, for that thought had been in her mind. 'Nothing holds us now at Hellsgarde. We will leave today on – another search. One thing before you go – we owe you a debt for luring Andred into our power, for I think he would not have come without you. Take a warning away with you, lady.'

'What is it?' Jirel's gaze flicked the man's briefly and fell again. She would not look into his eyes if she could help it. 'What warning?'

'Do not open that box you carry.'

And before she could get her breath to speak he had smiled at her and turned away, whistling for his men. Around her on the floor Jirel heard a rustling and a sigh as the sleepers began to stir. She stood quiet for an instant longer, staring down in bewilderment at the small box under her arm, before she turned to follow Alaric into the outer air.

Last night was a memory and a nightmare to forget. Not even the dead men still on their ghastly guard before the door could mar her triumph now.

Jirel rode back across the causeway in the strong light of morning, moving like a rider in a mirage between blue skies and blue reflecting waters. Behind her Hellsgarde Castle was a vision swimming among the mirroring pools of the marsh. And as she rode, she remembered.

The vortex of violence out of which she had snatched this box last night – the power and terror of the thing that had treasured it so long … what lay within? Something akin to – Andred? Alaric might not know, but he had guessed ... His warning still sounded in her ears.

She rode awhile with bent brows, but presently a wicked little smile began to thin the red lips of Joiry's sovereign lady. Well ... she had suffered much for Guy of Garlot, but she thought now that she would not smash in his handsome, grinning face with her sword-hilt as she had dreamed so luxuriously of doing. No ... she would have a better vengeance ...

She would hand him a little iron-bound leather box.

Acknowledgements

NORTHWEST OF EARTH

SHAMBLEAU

Man has conquered Space before. You may be sure of that. Somewhere beyond the Egyptians, in that dimness out of which come echoes of half-mythical names – Atlantis, Mu – somewhere back of history's first beginnings there must have been an age when mankind, like us today, built cities of steel to house its star-roving ships and knew the names of the planets in their own native tongues – heard Venus's people call their wet world 'Sha-ardol' in that soft, sweet, slurring speech and mimicked Mars's guttural 'Lakkdiz' from the harsh tongues of Mars's dryland dwellers. You may be sure of it. Man has conquered Space before, and out of that conquest faint, faint echoes run still through a world that has forgotten the very fact of a civilization which must have been as mighty as our own. There have been too many myths and legends for us to doubt it. The myth of the Medusa, for instance, can never have had its roots in the soil of Earth. That tale of the snake-haired Gorgon whose gaze turned the gazer to stone never originated about any creature that Earth nourished. And those ancient Greeks who told the story must have remembered, dimly and half believing, a tale of antiquity about some strange being from one of the outlying planets their remotest ancestors once trod.

'Shambleau! Ha ... Shambleau!' The wild hysteria of the mob rocketed from wall to wall of Lakkdarol's narrow streets and the storming of heavy boots over the slag-red pavement made an ominous undernote to that swelling bay, 'Shambleau! Shambleau!'

Northwest Smith heard it coming and stepped into the nearest doorway, laying a wary hand on his heat-gun's grip, and his colorless eyes narrowed. Strange sounds were common enough in the streets of Earth's latest colony on Mars – a raw, red little town where anything might happen, and very often did. But Northwest Smith, whose name is known and respected in every dive and wild outpost on a dozen wild planets, was a cautious man, despite his reputation. He set his back against the wall and gripped his pistol, and heard the rising shout come nearer and nearer.

Then into his range of vision flashed a red running figure, dodging like a hunted hare from shelter to shelter in the narrow street. It was a girl – a berry-brown girl in a single tattered garment whose scarlet burnt the eyes with its brilliance. She ran wearily, and he could hear her gasping breath from where he stood. As she came into view he saw her hesitate and lean one hand against the wall for support, and glance wildly around for shelter. She must not have seen him in the depths of the doorway, for as the bay of the mob grew louder and the pounding of feet sounded almost at the corner she gave a despairing little moan and dodged into the recess at his very side.

When she saw him standing there, tall and leather-brown, hand on his heat-gun, she sobbed once, inarticulately, and collapsed at his feet, a huddle of burning scarlet and bare, brown limbs.

Smith had not seen her face, but she was a girl, and sweetly made and in danger; and though he had not the reputation of a chivalrous man, something in her hopeless huddle at his feet touched that chord of sympathy for the underdog that stirs in every Earthman, and he pushed her gently into the corner behind him and jerked out his gun, just as the first of the running mob rounded the corner.

It was a motley crowd, Earthmen and Martians and a sprinkling of Venusian swampmen and strange, nameless denizens of unnamed planets – a typical Lakkdarol mob. When the first of them turned the corner and saw the empty street before them there was a faltering in the rush and the foremost spread out and began to search the doorways on both sides of the street.

'Looking for something?' Smith's sardonic call sounded clear above the clamor of the mob.

They turned. The shouting died for a moment as they took in the scene before them – tall Earthman in the space-explorer's leathern garb, all one color from the burning of savage suns save for the sinister pallor of his no-colored eyes in a scarred and resolute face, gun in his steady hand and the scarlet girl crouched behind him, panting.

The foremost of the crowd – a burly Earthman in tattered leather from which the Patrol insignia had been ripped away – stared for a moment with a strange expression of incredulity on his face overspreading the savage exultation of the chase. Then he let loose a deep-throated bellow, 'Shambleau!' and lunged forward. Behind him the mob took up the cry again. 'Shambleau! Shambleau! Shambleau!' and surged after.

Smith, lounging negligently against the wall, arms folded and gun-hand draped over his left forearm, looked incapable of swift motion, but at the leader's first forward step the pistol swept in a practiced half-circle and the dazzle of blue-white heat leaping from its muzzle seared an arc in the slag pavement at his feet. It was an old gesture, and not a man in the crowd misunderstood it. The foremost recoiled swiftly against the surge of those in the rear, and for a moment there was confusion as the two tides met and struggled. Smith's mouth curled into a grim curve as he watched. The man in the mutilated Patrol uniform lifted a threatening fist and stepped to the very edge of the deadline, while the crowd rocked to and fro behind him.

'Are you crossing that line?' queried Smith in an ominously gentle voice.

'We want that girl!'

'Come and get her!' Recklessly Smith grinned into his face. He saw danger there, but his defiance was not the foolhardy gesture it seemed. An expert psychologist of mobs from long experience, he sensed no murder here. Not a gun had appeared in any hand in the crowd. They desired the girl with an inexplicable bloodthirstiness he was at a loss to understand, but toward himself he sensed no such fury. A mauling he might expect, but his life was in no danger. Guns would have appeared before now if they were coming out at all. So he grinned in the man's angry face and leaned lazily against the wall.

Behind their self-appointed leader the crowd milled impatiently, and threatening voices began to rise again. Smith heard the girl moan at his feet.

'What do you want with her?' he demanded.

'She's Shambleau! Shambleau, you fool! Kick her out of there – we'll take care of her!'

'I'm taking care of her,' drawled Smith.

'She's Shambleau, I tell you! Damn your hide, man, we never let those things live! Kick her out here!'

The repeated name had no meaning to him, but Smith's innate stubbornness rose defiantly as the crowd surged forward to the very edge of the arc, their clamor growing louder. 'Shambleau! Kick her out here! Give us Shambleau! Shambleau!'

Smith dropped his indolent pose like a cloak and planted both feet wide, swinging up his gun threateningly. 'Keep back!' he yelled. 'She's mine! Keep back!'

He had no intention of using that heat-beam. He knew by now that they would not kill him unless he started the gunplay himself, and he did not mean to give up his life for any girl alive. But a severe mauling he expected, and he braced himself instinctively as the mob heaved within itself.

To his astonishment a thing happened then that he had never known to happen before. At his shouted defiance the foremost of the mob – those who had heard him clearly – drew back a little, not in alarm but evidently surprised. The ex-Patrolman said, 'Yours! She's *yours?*' in a voice from which puzzlement crowded out the anger.

Smith spread his booted legs wide before the crouching figure and flourished his gun.

'Yes,' he said. 'And I'm keeping her! Stand back there!'

The man stared at him wordlessly, and horror and disgust and incredulity mingled on his weather-beaten face. The incredulity triumphed for a moment and he said again,

'Yours!'

Smith nodded defiance.

The man stepped back suddenly, unutterable contempt in his very pose. He waved an arm to the crowd and said loudly, 'It's – his!' and the press melted away, gone silent, too, and the look of contempt spread from face to face.

The ex-Patrolman spat on the slag-paved street and turned his back indifferently. 'Keep her, then,' he advised briefly over one shoulder. 'But don't let her out again in this town!'

Smith stared in perplexity almost open-mouthed as the suddenly scornful mob began to break up. His mind was in a whirl. That such bloodthirsty animosity should vanish in a breath he could not believe. And the curious mingling of contempt and disgust on the faces he saw baffled him even more. Lakkdarol was anything but a puritan town – it did not enter his head for a moment that his claiming the brown girl as his own had caused that strangely shocked revulsion to spread through the crowd. No, it was something deeper-rooted than that. Instinctive, instant disgust had been in the faces he saw – they would have looked less so if he had admitted cannibalism or Pharol-worship.

And they were leaving his vicinity as swiftly as if whatever unknowing sin he had committed were contagious. The street was emptying as rapidly as it had filled. He saw a sleek Venusian glance back over his shoulder as he turned the corner and sneer, 'Shambleau!' and the word awoke a new line of speculation in Smith's mind. Shambleau! Vaguely of French origin, it must be. And strange enough to hear it from the lips of Venusian and Martian drylanders, but it was their use of it that puzzled him more. 'We never let those things live,' the ex-Patrolman had said. It reminded him dimly of something … an ancient line from some writing in his own tongue … 'Thou shalt not suffer a witch to live.' He smiled to himself at the similarity, and simultaneously was aware of the girl at his elbow.

She had risen soundlessly. He turned to face her, sheathing his gun and stared at first with curiosity and then in the entirely frank openness with which men regard that which is not wholly human. For she was not. He knew it at a glance, though the brown, sweet body was shaped like a woman's and she wore the garment of scarlet – he saw it was leather – with an ease that few unhuman beings achieve toward clothing. He knew it from the moment he looked into her eyes, and a shiver of unrest went over him as he met them. They were frankly green as young grass, with slit-like, feline pupils that pulsed unceasingly, and there was a look of dark, animal wisdom in their depths – that look of the beast which sees more than man.

There was no hair upon her face – neither brows nor lashes, and he would have sworn that the tight scarlet turban bound around her head covered baldness. She had three fingers and a thumb, and her feet had four digits apiece too, and all sixteen of them were tipped with round claws that sheathed back into the flesh like a cat's. She ran her tongue over her lips – a thin, pink, flat tongue as feline as her eyes – and spoke with difficulty. He felt that that throat and tongue had never been shaped for human speech.

'Not – afraid now,' she said softly, and her little teeth were white and pointed as a kitten's.

'What did they want you for?' he asked her curiously. 'What have you done? Shambleau … is that your name?'

'I – not talk your – speech,' she demurred hesitantly.

'Well, try to – I want to know. Why were they chasing you? Will you be safe on the street now, or hadn't you better get indoors somewhere? They looked dangerous.'

'I – go with you.' She brought it out with difficulty.

'Say you!' Smith grinned. 'What are you, anyhow? You look like a kitten to me.'

'Shambleau.' She said it somberly.

'Where d'you live? Are you a Martian?'

'I come from – from far – from long ago – far country—'

'Wait!' laughed Smith. 'You're getting your wires crossed. You're not a Martian?'

She drew herself up very straight beside him, lifting the turbaned head, and there was something queenly in the pose of her.

'Martian?' she said scornfully. 'My people – are – are – you have no word. Your speech – hard for me.'

'What's yours? I might know it – try me.'

She lifted her head and met his eyes squarely, and there was in hers a subtle amusement – he could have sworn it.

'Some day I – speak to you in – my own language,' she promised, and the pink tongue flicked out over her lips, swiftly, hungrily.

Approaching footsteps on the red pavement interrupted Smith's reply. A dryland Martian came past, reeling a little and exuding an aroma of *segir*-whisky, the Venusian brand. When he caught the red flash of the girl's tatters he turned his head sharply, and as his *segir*-steeped brain took in the fact of her presence he lurched toward the recess unsteadily, bawling, 'Shambleau, by Pharol! Shambleau!' and reached out a clutching hand.

Smith struck it aside contemptuously.

'On your way, drylander,' he advised.

The man drew back and stared, bleary-eyed.

'Yours, eh?' he croaked. '*Zut!* You're welcome to it!' And like the ex-Patrolman before him he spat on the pavement and turned away, muttering harshly in the blasphemous tongue of the drylands.

Smith watched him shuffle off, and there was a crease between his colorless eyes, a nameless unease rising within him.

'Come on,' he said abruptly to the girl. 'If this sort of thing is going to happen we'd better get indoors. Where shall I take you?'

'With – you,' she murmured.

He stared down into the flat green eyes. Those ceaselessly pulsing pupils disturbed him, but it seemed to him, vaguely, that behind the animal shallows of her gaze was a shutter – a closed barrier that might at any moment open to reveal the very deeps of that dark knowledge he sensed there.

Roughly he said again, 'Come on, then,' and stepped down into the street.

She pattered along a pace or two behind him, making no effort to keep up with his long strides, and though Smith – as men know from Venus to Jupiter's moons – walks as softly as a cat, even in spaceman's boots, the girl at his heels slid like a shadow over the rough pavement, making so little sound that even the lightness of his footsteps was loud in the empty street.

Smith chose the less frequented ways of Lakkdarol, and somewhat shamefacedly thanked his nameless gods that his lodgings were not far away, for the few pedestrians he met turned and stared after the two with that by now familiar mingling of horror and contempt which he was as far as ever from understanding.

The room he had engaged was a single cubicle in a lodging-house on the edge of the city. Lakkdarol, raw camptown that it was in those days, could have furnished little better anywhere within its limits, and Smith's errand there was not one he wished to advertise. He had slept in worse places than this before, and knew that he would do so again.

There was no one in sight when he entered, and the girl slipped up the stairs at his heels and vanished through the door, shadowy, unseen by anyone in the house. Smith closed the door and leaned his broad shoulders against the panels, regarding her speculatively.

She took in what little the room had to offer in a glance – frowsy bed, rickety table, mirror hanging unevenly and cracked against the wall, unpainted chairs – a typical camptown room in an Earth settlement abroad. She accepted its poverty in that single glance, dismissed it, then crossed to the window and leaned out for a moment, gazing across the low roof-tops toward the barren countryside beyond, red slag under the late afternoon sun.

'You can stay here,' said Smith abruptly, 'until I leave town. I'm waiting here for a friend to come in from Venus. Have you eaten?'

'Yes,' said the girl quickly. 'I shall – need no – food for – a while.'

'Well – ' Smith glanced around the room. 'I'll be in sometime tonight. You can go or stay just as you please. Better lock the door behind me.'

With no more formality than that he left her. The door closed and he heard the key turn, and smiled to himself. He did not expect, then, ever to see her again.

He went down the steps and out into the late-slanting sunlight with a mind so full of other matters that the brown girl receded very quickly into the background. Smith's errand in Lakkdarol, like most of his errands, is better not spoken of. Man lives as he must, and Smith's living was a perilous affair outside the law and ruled by the ray-gun only. It is enough to say that the shipping-port and its cargoes outbound interested him deeply just now, and that the friend he awaited was Yarol the Venusian, in that swift little Edsel ship the *Maid* that can flash from world to world with a derisive speed that laughs at Patrol boats and leaves pursuers floundering in the ether far behind. Smith and Yarol and the *Maid* were a trinity that had caused the Patrol leaders much worry and many gray hairs in the past, and the future looked very bright to Smith himself that evening as he left his lodging-house.

Lakkdarol roars by night, as Earthmen's camptowns have away of doing on every planet where Earth's outposts are, and it was beginning lustily as Smith went down among the awakening lights toward the center of town. His business there does not concern us. He mingled with the crowds where the lights were brightest, and there was the click of ivory counters and the jingle of silver, and red *segir* gurgled invitingly from black Venusian bottles, and much later Smith strolled homeward under the moving moons of Mars, and if the street wavered a little under his feet now and then – why, that is only understandable. Not even Smith could drink red *segir* at every bar from the *Martian Lamb* to the *New Chicago* and remain entirely steady on his feet. But he found his way back with very little difficulty – considering – and spent a good five minutes hunting for his key before he remembered he had left it in the inner lock for the girl.

He knocked then, and there was no sound of footsteps from within, but in a few moments the latch clicked and the door swung open. She retreated soundlessly before him as he entered, and took up her favorite place against the window, leaning back on the sill and outlined against the starry sky beyond. The room was in darkness.

Smith flipped the switch by the door and then leaned back against the panels, steadying himself. The cool night air had sobered him a little and his head was clear enough – liquor went to Smith's feet, not his head, or he would never have come this far along the lawless way he had chosen. He lounged against the door now and regarded the girl in the sudden glare of the bulbs, blinding a little as much at the scarlet of her clothing as at the light.

'So you stayed,' he said.

'I waited,' she answered softly, leaning farther back against the sill and clasping the rough wood with slim, three-fingered hands, pale brown against the darkness.

'Why?'

She did not answer that, but her mouth curved into a slow smile. On a woman it would have been reply enough – provocative, daring. On Shambleau there was something pitiful and horrible in it – so human on the face of one half-animal. And yet … that sweet brown body curving so softly from the tatters of scarlet leather – the velvety texture of that brownness – the white-flashing smile … Smith was aware of a stirring excitement within him. After all – time would be hanging heavy now until Yarol came … Speculatively he allowed the steel-pale eyes to wander over her, with a slow regard that missed nothing. And when he spoke he was aware that his voice had deepened a little …

'Come here,' he said.

She came forward slowly, on bare clawed feet that made no slightest sound on the floor, and stood before him with downcast eyes and mouth trembling in that pitifully human smile. He took her by the shoulders – velvety soft shoulders, of a creamy smoothness that was not the texture of human flesh. A little tremor went over her, perceptibly, at the contact of his hands. Northwest Smith caught his breath suddenly and dragged her to him … sweet yielding brownness in the circle of his arms … heard her own breath catch and quicken as her velvety arms closed about his neck. And then he was looking down into her face, very near, and the green animal eyes met his with the pulsing pupils and the flicker of – something – deep behind their shallows – and through the rising clamor of his blood, even as he stooped his lips to hers, Smith felt something deep within him shudder away – inexplicable, instinctive, revolted. What it might be he had no words to tell, but the very touch of her was suddenly loathsome – so soft and velvet and unhuman – and it might have been an animal's face that lifted itself to his mouth – the dark knowledge looked hungrily from the darkness of those slit pupils – and for a mad instant he knew that same wild, feverish revulsion he had seen in the faces of the mob …

'God!' he gasped, a far more ancient invocation against evil than he realized, then or ever, and he ripped her arms from his neck, swung her away with such a force that she reeled half across the room. Smith fell back against the door, breathing heavily, and stared at her while the wild revolt died slowly within him.

She had fallen to the floor beneath the window, and as she lay there against the wall with bent head he saw, curiously, that her turban had slipped – the turban that he had been so sure covered baldness – and a lock of scarlet hair fell below the binding leather, hair as scarlet as her garment, as unhumanly red as her eyes were unhumanly green. He stared, and shook his head dizzily and stared again, for it seemed to him that the thick lock of crimson had moved, *squirmed* of itself against her cheek.

At the contact of it her hands flew up and she tucked it away with a very human gesture and then dropped her head again into her hands. And from the deep shadow of her fingers he thought she was staring up at him covertly.

Smith drew a deep breath and passed a hand across his forehead. The inexplicable moment had gone as quickly as it came – too swiftly for him to understand or analyze it. 'Got to lay off the *segir*,' he told himself unsteadily. Had he imagined that scarlet hair? After all, she was no more than a pretty brown girl-creature from one of the many half-human races peopling the planets. No more than that, after all. A pretty little thing, but animal … He laughed, a little shakily.

'No more of that,' he said. 'God knows I'm no angel, but there's got to be a limit somewhere. Here.' He crossed to the bed and sorted out a pair of blankets from the untidy heap tossing them to the far corner of the room. 'You can sleep there.'

Wordlessly she rose from the floor and began to rearrange the blankets, the uncomprehending resignation of the animal eloquent in every line of her.

*

Smith had a strange dream that night. He thought he had awakened to a room full of darkness and moonlight and moving shadows, for the nearer moon of Mars was racing through the sky and everything on the planet below her was endued with a restless life in the dark. And something … some nameless, unthinkable thing … was coiled about his throat … something like a soft snake, wet and warm. It lay loose and light about his neck … and it was moving gently, very gently, with a soft, caressive pressure that sent little thrills of delight through every nerve and fiber of him, a perilous delight – beyond physical pleasure, deeper than joy of the mind. That warm softness was caressing the very roots of his soul and with a terrible intimacy. The ecstasy of it left him weak, and yet he knew – in a flash of knowledge born of this impossible dream – that the soul should not be handled … And with that knowledge a horror broke upon him, turning the pleasure into a rapture of revulsion, hateful, horrible – but still most foully sweet. He tried to lift his hands and tear the dream-monstrosity from his throat – tried but half-heartedly; for though his soul was revolted to its very deeps, yet the delight of his body was so great that his hands all but refused the attempt. But when at last he tried to lift his arms a cold shock went over him and he found that he could not stir … his body lay stony as marble beneath the blankets, a living marble that shuddered with a dreadful delight through every rigid vein.

The revulsion grew strong upon him as he struggled against the paralyzing dream – a struggle of soul against sluggish body – titanically, until the moving dark was streaked with blankness that clouded and closed about him at last and he sank back into the oblivion from which he had awakened.

Next morning, when the bright sunlight shining through Mars's clear thin air awakened him, Smith lay for a while trying to remember. The dream had been more vivid than reality, but he could not now quite recall … only that it had been more sweet and horrible than anything else in life. He lay puzzling for a while, until a soft sound from the corner aroused him from his thoughts and he sat up to see the girl lying in a cat-like coil on her blankets, watching him with round, grave eyes. He regarded her somewhat ruefully.

'Morning,' he said. 'I've just had the devil of a dream … Well, hungry?'

She shook her head silently, and he could have sworn there was a covert gleam of strange amusement in her eyes.

He stretched and yawned, dismissing the nightmare temporarily from his mind.

'What am I going to do with you?' he inquired, turning to more immediate matters. 'I'm leaving here in a day or two and I can't take you along, you know. Where'd you come from in the first place?'

Again she shook her head.

'Not telling? Well, it's your business. You can stay here until I give up the room. From then on you'll have to do your own worrying.'

He swung his feet to the floor and reached for his clothes.

Ten minutes later, slipping the heat-gun into its holster at his thigh, Smith turned to the girl. 'There's food-concentrate in that box on the table. It ought to hold you until I get back. And you'd better lock the door again after I've gone.'

Her wide, unwavering stare was his only answer, and he was not sure she had understood, but at any rate the lock clicked after him as before, and he went down the steps with a faint grin on his lips.

The memory of last night's extraordinary dream was slipping from him, as such memories do, and by the time he had reached the street the girl and the dream and all of yesterday's happenings were blotted out by the sharp necessities of the present.

Again the intricate business that had brought him here claimed his attention. He went about it to the exclusion of all else, and there was a good reason behind everything he did from the moment he stepped out into the street until the time when he turned back again at evening; though had one chosen to follow him during the day his apparently aimless rambling through Lakkdarol would have seemed very pointless.

He must have spent two hours at the least idling by the spaceport, watching with sleepy, colorless eyes the ships that came and went, the passengers, the vessels lying at wait, the cargoes – particularly the cargoes. He made the rounds of the town's saloons once more, consuming many glasses of varied liquors in the course of the day and engaging in idle conversation with men of all races and worlds, usually in their own languages, for Smith was a linguist of repute among his contemporaries. He heard the gossip of the spaceways, news from a dozen planets of a thousand different events. He heard the latest joke about the Venusian Emperor and the latest report on the Chino-Aryan war and the latest song hot from the lips of Rose Robertson, whom every man on the civilized planets adored as 'the Georgia Rose.' He passed the day quite profitably, for his own purposes, which do not concern us now, and it was not until late evening, when he turned homeward again, that the thought of the brown girl in his room took definite shape in his mind, though it had been lurking there, formless and submerged, all day.

He had no idea what comprised her usual diet, but he bought a can of New York roast beef and one of Venusian frog-broth and a dozen fresh canal-apples and two pounds of that Earth lettuce that grows so vigorously in the fertile canal-soil of Mars. He felt that she must surely find something to her liking in this broad variety of edibles, and – for his day had been very satisfactory – he hummed 'The Green Hills of Earth' to himself in a surprisingly good baritone as he climbed the stairs.

The door was locked, as before, and he was reduced to kicking the lower panels gently with his boot, for his arms were full. She opened the door with that softness that was characteristic of her and stood regarding him in the semidarkness as he stumbled to the table with his load. The room was unlit again.

'Why don't you turn on the lights?' he demanded irritably after he had barked his shin on the chair by the table in an effort to deposit his burden there.

'Light and – dark – they are alike – to me,' she murmured.

'Cat eyes, eh? Well, you look the part. Here, I've brought you some dinner. Take your choice. Fond of roast beef? Or how about a little frog-broth?'

She shook her head and backed away a step.

'No,' she said. 'I can not – eat your food.'

Smith's brows wrinkled. 'Didn't you have any of the food tablets?'

Again the red turban shook negatively.

'Then you haven't had anything for – why, more than twenty-four hours! You must be starved.'

'Not hungry,' she denied.

'What can I find for you to eat, then? There's time yet if I hurry. You've got to eat, child.'

'I shall – eat,' she said softly. 'Before long – I shall – feed. Have no – worry.'

She turned away then and stood at the window, looking out over the moonlit landscape as if to end the conversation. Smith cast her a puzzled glance as he opened the can of roast beef. There had been an odd undernote in that assurance that, undefinably, he did not like. And the girl had teeth and tongue and presumably a fairly human digestive system, to judge from her human form. It was nonsense for her to pretend that he could find nothing that she could eat. She must have had some of the food concentrate after all, he decided, prying up the thermos lid of the inner container to release the long-sealed savor of the hot meat inside.

'Well, if you won't eat you won't,' he observed philosophically as he poured hot broth and diced beef into the dish-like lid of the thermos can and extracted the spoon from its hiding-place between the inner and outer receptacles. She turned a little to watch him as he pulled up a rickety chair and sat down to the food, and after a while the realization that her green gaze was fixed so unwinkingly upon him made the man nervous, and he said between bites of creamy canal-apple, 'Why don't you try a little of this? It's good.'

'The food – I eat is – better,' her soft voice told him in its hesitant murmur, and again he felt rather than heard a faint undernote of unpleasantness in the words. A sudden suspicion struck him as he pondered on that last remark – some vague memory of horror-tales told about campfires in the past – and he swung round in the chair to look at her, a tiny, creeping fear unaccountably arising. There had been that in her words – in her unspoken words, that menaced ...

She stood up beneath his gaze demurely, wide green eyes with their pulsing pupils meeting his without a falter. But her mouth was scarlet and her teeth were sharp ...

'What food do you eat?' he demanded. And then, after a pause, very softly, 'Blood?'

She stared at him for a moment, uncomprehending; then something like amusement curled her lips and she said scornfully, 'You think me – vampire, eh? No – I am Shambleau!'

Unmistakably there were scorn and amusement in her voice at the suggestion, but as unmistakably she knew what he meant – accepted it as a logical suspicion – vampires! Fairy-tales – but fairy-tales this unhuman, outland creature was most familiar with. Smith was not a credulous man, nor a superstitious one, but he had seen too many strange things himself to doubt that the wildest legend might have a basis of fact. And there was something namelessly strange about her ...

He puzzled over it for a while between deep bites of the canal-apple. And though he wanted to question her about a great many things, he did not, for he knew how futile it would be.

He said nothing more until the meat was finished and another canal-apple had followed the first, and he had cleared away the meal by the simple expedient of tossing the empty can out of the window. Then he lay back in the chair and surveyed her from half-closed eyes, colorless in a face tanned like saddle-leather. And again he was conscious of the brown, soft curves of her, velvety – subtle arcs and planes of smooth flesh under the tatters of scarlet leather. Vampire she might be, unhuman she certainly was, but desirable beyond words as she sat submissive beneath his low regard, her red-turbaned head bent, her clawed fingers lying in her lap. They sat very still for a while, and the silence throbbed between them.

She was so like a woman – an Earth woman – sweet and submissive and demure, and softer than soft fur, if he could forget the three-fingered claws and the pulsing eyes – and that deeper strangeness beyond words … (Had he dreamed that red lock of hair that moved? Had it been *segir* that woke the wild revulsion he knew when he held her in his arms? Why had the mob so thirsted for her?) He sat and stared, and despite the mystery of her and the half-suspicions that thronged his mind – for she was so beautifully soft and curved under those revealing tatters – he slowly realized that his pulses were mounting, became aware of a kindling within … brown girl-creature with downcast eyes … and then the lids lifted and the green flatness of a cat's gaze met his, and last night's revulsion woke swiftly again, like a warning bell that clanged as their eyes met – animal, after all, too sleek and soft for humanity, and that inner strangeness …

Smith shrugged and sat up. His failings were legion, but the weakness of the flesh was not among the major ones. He motioned the girl to her pallet of blankets in the corner and turned to his own bed.

From deeps of sound sleep he awoke much later. He awoke suddenly and completely, and with that inner excitement that presages something momentous. He awoke to brilliant moonlight, turning the room so bright that he could see the scarlet of the girl's rags as she sat up on her pallet. She was awake, she was sitting with her shoulder half turned to him and her head bent, and some warning instinct crawled coldly up his spine as he watched what she was doing. And yet it was a very ordinary thing for a girl to do – any girl, anywhere. She was unbinding her turban …

He watched, not breathing, a presentiment of something horrible stirring in his brain, inexplicably … The red folds loosened, and – he knew then that he had not dreamed – again a scarlet lock swung down against her cheek … a hair, was it? A lock of hair? … thick as a thick worm it fell, plumply, against that smooth cheek ... more scarlet than blood and thick as a crawling worm ... and like a worm it crawled.

Smith rose on an elbow, not realizing the motion, and fixed an unwinking stare, with a sort of sick, fascinated incredulity, on that – that lock of hair. He had not dreamed. Until now he had taken it for granted that it was the *segir* which had made it seem to move on that evening before. But now ... it was lengthening, stretching, moving of itself. It must be hair, but it crawled; with a sickening life of its own it squirmed down against her cheek, caressingly, revoltingly, impossibly ... Wet, it was, and round and thick and shining ...

She unfastened the last fold and whipped the turban off. From what he saw then Smith would have turned his eyes away – and he had looked on dreadful things before, without flinching – but he could not stir. He could only lie there on elbow staring at the mass of scarlet, squirming – worms, hairs, what? – that writhed over her head in a dreadful mockery of ringlets. And it was lengthening, falling, somehow growing before his eyes, down over her shoulders in a spilling cascade, a mass that even at the beginning could never have been hidden under the skull-tight turban she had worn. He was beyond wondering, but he realized that. And still it squirmed and lengthened and fell, and she shook it out in a horrible travesty of a woman shaking out her unbound hair – until the unspeakable tangle of it – twisting, writhing, obscenely scarlet – hung to her waist and beyond, and still lengthened, an endless mass of crawling horror that until now, somehow, impossibly, had been hidden under the tight-bound turban. It was like a nest of blind, restless red worms ... it was – it was like naked entrails endowed with an unnatural aliveness, terrible beyond words.

Smith lay in the shadows, frozen without and within in a sick numbness that came of utter shock and revulsion.

She shook out the obscene, unspeakable tangle over her shoulder, and somehow he knew that she was going to turn in a moment and that he must meet her eyes. The thought of that meeting stopped his heart with dread, more awfully than anything else in this nightmare horror; for nightmare it must be, surely. But he knew without trying that he could not wrench his eyes away – the sickened fascination of that sight held him motionless, and somehow there was a certain beauty ...

Her head was turning. The crawling awfulness rippled and squirmed at the motion, writhing thick and wet and shining over the soft brown shoulders about which they fell now in obscene cascades that all but hid her body. Her head was turning. Smith lay numb. And very slowly he saw the round of her cheek foreshorten and her profile come into view, all the scarlet horrors twisting ominously, and the profile shortened in turn and her full face came slowly round toward the bed – moonlight shining brilliantly as day on the pretty girl-face, demure and sweet, framed in tangled obscenity that crawled ...

The green eyes met his. He felt a perceptible shock, and a shudder rippled down his paralyzed spine, leaving an icy numbness in its wake. He felt the goose-flesh rising. But that numbness and cold horror he scarcely realized, for the green eyes were locked with his in a long, long look that somehow presaged nameless things – not altogether unpleasant things – the voiceless voice of her mind assailing him with little murmurous promises ...

For a moment he went down into a blind abyss of submission; and then somehow the very sight of that obscenity in eyes that did not then realize they saw it, was dreadful enough to draw him out of the seductive darkness ... the sight of her crawling and alive with unnamable horror.

She rose, and down about her in a cascade fell the squirming scarlet of – of what grew upon her head. It fell in a long, alive cloak to her bare feet on the floor, hiding her in a wave of dreadful, wet, writhing life. She put up her hands and like a swimmer she parted the waterfall of it, tossing the masses back over her shoulders to reveal her own brown body, sweetly curved. She smiled exquisitely, and in starting waves back from her forehead and down about her in a hideous background writhed the snaky wetness of her living tresses. And Smith knew that he looked upon Medusa.

The knowledge of that – the realization of vast backgrounds reaching into misted history – shook him out of his frozen horror for a moment, and in that moment he met her eyes again, smiling, green as glass in the moonlight, half hooded under drooping lids. Through the twisting scarlet she held out her arms. And there was something soul-shakingly desirable about her, so that all the blood surged to his head suddenly and he stumbled to his feet like a sleeper in a dream as she swayed toward him, infinitely graceful, infinitely sweet in her cloak of living horror.

And somehow there was beauty in it, the wet scarlet writhings with moonlight sliding and shining along the thick, worm-round tresses and losing itself in the masses only to glint again and move silvery along writhing tendrils – an awful, shuddering beauty more dreadful than any ugliness could be.

But all this, again, he but half realized, for the insidious murmur was coiling again through his brain, promising, caressing, alluring, sweeter than honey; and the green eyes that held his were clear and burning like the depths of a jewel, and behind the pulsing slits of darkness he was staring into a greater dark that held all things ... He had known – dimly he had known when he first gazed into those flat animal shallows that behind them lay this – all beauty and terror, all horror and delight, in the infinite darkness upon which her eyes opened like windows, paned with emerald glass.

Her lips moved, and in a murmur that blended indistinguishably with the silence and the sway of her body and the dreadful sway of her – her hair – she whispered – very softly, very passionately, 'I shall – speak to you now – in my own tongue – oh, beloved!'

And in her living cloak she swayed to him, the murmur swelling seductive and caressing in his innermost brain – promising, compelling, sweeter than sweet. His flesh crawled to the horror of her, but it was a perverted revulsion that clasped what it loathed. His arms slid round her under the sliding cloak, wet, wet and warm and hideously alive – and the sweet velvet body was clinging to his, her arms locked about his neck – and with a whisper and a rush the unspeakable horror closed about them both.

In nightmares until he died he remembered that moment when the living tresses of Shambleau first folded him in their embrace. A nauseous, smothering odor as the wetness shut around him – thick, pulsing worms clasping every inch of his body, sliding, writhing, their wetness and warmth striking through his garments as if he stood naked to their embrace.

All this in a graven instant – and after that a tangled flash of conflicting sensation before oblivion closed over him for he remembered the dream – and knew it for nightmare reality now, and the sliding, gently moving caresses of those wet, warm worms upon his flesh was an ecstasy above words – that deeper ecstasy that strikes beyond the body and beyond the mind and tickles the very roots of the soul with unnatural delight. So he stood, rigid as marble, as helplessly stony as any of Medusa's victims in ancient legends were, while the terrible pleasure of Shambleau thrilled and shuddered through every fiber of him; through every atom of his body and the intangible atoms of what men call the soul, through all that was Smith the dreadful pleasure ran. And it was truly dreadful. Dimly he knew it, even as his body answered to the root-deep ecstasy, a foul and dreadful wooing from which his very soul shuddered away – and yet in the innermost depths of that soul some grinning traitor shivered with delight. But deeply, behind all this, he knew horror and revulsion and despair beyond telling, while the intimate caresses crawled obscenely in the secret places of his soul – knew that the soul should not be handled – and shook with the perilous pleasure through it all.

And this conflict and knowledge, this mingling of rapture and revulsion all took place in the flashing of a moment while the scarlet worms coiled and crawled upon him, sending deep, obscene tremors of that infinite pleasure into every atom that made up Smith. And he could not stir in that slimy, ecstatic embrace – and a weakness was flooding that grew deeper after each succeeding wave of intense delight, and the traitor in his soul strengthened and drowned out the revulsion – and something within him ceased to struggle as he sank wholly into a blazing darkness that was oblivion to all else but that devouring rapture . . .

*

The young Venusian climbing the stairs to his friend's lodging-room pulled out his key absent-mindedly, a pucker forming between his fine brows. He was slim, as all Venusians are, as fair and sleek as any of them, and as with most of his countrymen the look of cherubic innocence on his face was wholly deceptive. He had the face of a fallen angel, without Lucifer's majesty to redeem it; for a black devil grinned in his eyes and there were faint lines of ruthlessness and dissipation about his mouth to tell of the long years behind him that had run the gamut of experiences and made his name, next to Smith's, the most hated and the most respected in the records of the Patrol.

He mounted the stairs now with a puzzled frown between his eyes. He had come into Lakkdarol on the noon liner – the *Maid* in her hold very skillfully disguised with paint and otherwise – to find in lamentable disorder the affairs he had expected to be settled. And cautious inquiry elicited the information that Smith had not been seen for three days. That was not like his friend – he had never failed before, and the two stood to lose not only a large sum of money but also their personal safety by the inexplicable lapse on the part of Smith. Yarol could think of one solution only: fate had at last caught up with his friend. Nothing but physical disability could explain it.

Still puzzling, he fitted his key in the lock and swung the door open.

In that first moment, as the door opened, he sensed something very wrong . . . The room was darkened, and for a while he could see nothing, but at the first breath he scented a strange, unnamable odor, half sickening, half sweet. And deep stirrings of ancestral memory awoke within him – ancient swamp-born memories from Venusian ancestors far away and long ago . . .

Yarol laid his hand on his gun, lightly, and opened the door wider. In the dimness all he could see at first was a curious mound in the far corner . . . Then his eyes grew accustomed to the dark, and he saw it more clearly, a mound that somehow heaved and stirred within itself . . . A mound of – he caught his breath sharply – a mound like a mass of entrails, living, moving, writhing with an unspeakable aliveness. Then a hot Venusian oath broke from his lips and he cleared the door-sill in a swift stride, slammed the door and set his back against it, gun ready in his hand, although his flesh crawled – for he *knew* . . .

'Smith!' he said softly, in a voice thick with horror.

The moving mass stirred – shuddered – sank back into crawling quiescence again.

'Smith! Smith!' The Venusian's voice was gentle and insistent, and it quivered a little with terror.

An impatient ripple went over the whole mass of aliveness in the corner.

It stirred again, reluctantly, and then tendril by writhing tendril it began to part itself and fall aside, and very slowly the brown of a spaceman's leather appeared beneath it, all slimed and shining.

'Smith! Northwest!' Yarol's persistent whisper came again, urgently, and with a dream-like slowness the leather garments moved … a man sat up in the midst of the writhing worms, a man who once, long ago, might have been Northwest Smith. From head to foot he was slimy from the embrace of the crawling horror about him. His face was that of some creature beyond humanity – dead-alive, fixed in a gray stare, and the look of terrible ecstasy that overspread it seemed to come from somewhere far within, a faint reflection from immeasurable distances beyond the flesh. And as there is mystery and magic in the moonlight which is after all but a reflection of the everyday sun, so in that gray face turned to the door was a terror unnamable and sweet, a reflection of ecstasy beyond the understanding of any who have known only earthly ecstasy themselves. And as he sat there turning a blank, eyeless face to Yarol the red worms writhed ceaselessly about him, very gently, with a soft, caressive motion that never slacked.

'Smith … come here! Smith … get up … Smith, Smith!' Yarol's whisper hissed in the silence, commanding, urgent – but he made no move to leave the door.

And with a dreadful slowness, like a dead man rising, Smith stood up in the nest of slimy scarlet. He swayed drunkenly on his feet, and two or three crimson tendrils came writhing up his legs to the knees and wound themselves there, supportingly, moving with a ceaseless caress that seemed to give him some hidden strength, for he said then, without inflection,

'Go away. Go away. Leave me alone.' And the dead ecstatic face never changed.

'Smith!' Yarol's voice was desperate. 'Smith, listen! Smith, can't you hear me?'

'Go away,' the monotonous voice said. 'Go away. Go away. Go—'

'Not unless you come too. Can't you hear? Smith! Smith! I'll—'

He hushed in mid-phrase, and once more the ancestral prickle of race-memory shivered down his back, for the scarlet mass was moving again, violently, rising …

Yarol pressed back against the door and gripped his gun, and the name of a god he had forgotten years ago rose to his lips unbidden. For he knew what was coming next, and the knowledge was more dreadful than any ignorance could have been.

The red, writhing mass rose higher, and the tendrils parted and a human face looked out – no, half human, with green cat-eyes that shone in that dimness like lighted jewels, compellingly …

Yarol breathed 'Shar!' again, and flung up an arm across his face, and the tingle of meeting that green gaze for even an instant went thrilling through him perilously.

'Smith!' he called in despair. 'Smith, can't you hear me?'

'Go away,' said that voice that was not Smith's. 'Go away.'

And somehow, although he dared not look, Yarol knew that the – the other – had parted those worm-thick tresses and stood there in all the human sweetness of the brown, curved woman's body, cloaked in living horror. And he felt the eyes upon him, and something was crying insistently in his brain to lower that shielding arm … He was lost – he knew it, and the knowledge gave him that courage which comes from despair. The voice in his brain was growing, swelling, deafening him with a roaring command that all but swept him before it – command to lower that arm – to meet the eyes that opened upon darkness – to submit – and a promise, murmurous and sweet and evil beyond words, of pleasure to come …

But somehow he kept his head – somehow, dizzily, he was gripping his gun in his upflung hand – somehow, incredibly, crossing the narrow room with averted face, groping for Smith's shoulder. There was a moment of blind fumbling in emptiness, and then he found it, and gripped the leather that was slimy and dreadful and wet – and simultaneously he felt something loop gently about his ankle and a shock of repulsive pleasure went through him, and then another coil, and another, wound about his feet …

Yarol set his teeth and gripped the shoulder hard, and his hand shuddered of itself, for the feel of that leather was slimy as the worms about his ankles, and a faint tingle of obscene delight went through him from the contact.

That caressive pressure on his legs was all he could feel, and the voice in his brain drowned out all other sounds, and his body obeyed him reluctantly – but somehow he gave one heave of tremendous effort and swung Smith, stumbling, out of that nest of horror. The twining tendrils ripped loose with a little sucking sound, and the whole mass quivered and reached after, and then Yarol forgot his friend utterly and turned his whole being to the hopeless task of freeing himself. For only a part of him was fighting, now – only a part of him struggled against the twining obscenities, and in his innermost brain the sweet, seductive murmur sounded, and his body clamored to surrender …

'*Shar! Shar y'anis … Shar mor'la-rol—*' prayed Yarol, gasping and half unconscious that he spoke, boy's prayers that he had forgotten years ago, and with his back half turned to the central mass he kicked desperately with his heavy boots at the red, writhing worms about him. They gave back before him, quivering and curling themselves out of reach, and though he knew that more were reaching for his throat from behind, at least he could go on struggling until he was forced to meet those eyes …

He stamped and kicked and stamped again, and for one instant he was free of the slimy grip as the bruised worms curled back from his heavy feet, and he lurched away dizzily, sick with revulsion and despair as he fought off the coils, and then he lifted his eyes and saw the cracked mirror on the wall. Dimly in its reflection he could see the writhing scarlet horror behind him, cat face peering out with its demure girl-smile, dreadfully human, and all the red tendrils reaching after him. And remembrance of something he had read long ago swept incongruously over him, and the gasp of relief and hope that he gave shook for a moment the grip of the command in his brain.

Without pausing for a breath he swung the gun over his shoulder, the reflected barrel in line with the reflected horror in the mirror, and flicked the catch.

In the mirror he saw its blue flame leap in a dazzling spate across the dimness, full into the midst of that squirming, reaching mass behind him. There was a hiss and a blaze and a high, thin scream of inhuman malice and despair – the flame cut a wide arc and went out as the gun fell from his hand, and Yarol pitched forward to the floor.

Northwest Smith opened his eyes to Martian sunlight streaming thinly through the dingy window. Something wet and cold was slapping his face, and the familiar fiery sting of *segir*-whisky burnt his throat.

'Smith!' Yarol's voice was saying from far away. 'N.W.! Wake up, damn you! Wake up!'

'I'm – awake,' Smith managed to articulate thickly. 'Wha's matter?'

Then a cup-rim was thrust against his teeth and Yarol said irritably, 'Drink it, you fool!'

Smith swallowed obediently and more of the fire-hot *segir* flowed down his grateful throat. It spread a warmth through his body that awakened him from the numbness that had gripped him until now, and helped a little toward driving out the all-devouring weakness he was becoming aware of slowly. He lay still for a few minutes while the warmth of the whisky went through him, and memory sluggishly began to permeate his brain with the spread of the *segir*. Nightmare memories … sweet and terrible … memories of—

'God!' gasped Smith suddenly, and tried to sit up. Weakness smote him like a blow, and for an instant the room wheeled as he fell back against something firm and warm – Yarol's shoulder. The Venusian's arm supported him while the room steadied, and after a while he twisted a little and stared into the other's black gaze.

Yarol was holding him with one arm and finishing the mug of *segir* himself, and the black eyes met his over the rim and crinkled into sudden laughter, half hysterical after that terror that was passed.

'By Pharol!' gasped Yarol, choking into his mug. 'By Pharol, N.W.! I'm never gonna let you forget this! Next time you have to drag me out of a mess I'll say—'

'Let it go,' said Smith. 'What's been going on? How—'

'Shambleau,' Yarol's laughter died. 'Shambleau! What were you doing with a thing like that?'

'What was it?' Smith asked soberly.

'Mean to say you didn't know? But where'd you find it? How—'

'Suppose you tell me first what you know,' said Smith firmly. 'And another swig of that *segir*, too. I need it.'

'Can you hold the mug now? Feel better?'

'Yeah – some. I can hold it – thanks. Now go on.'

'Well – I don't know just where to start. They call them Shambleau—'

'Good God, is there more than one?'

'It's a – a sort of race, I think, one of the very oldest. Where they come from nobody knows. The name sounds a little French, doesn't it? But it goes back beyond the start of history. There have always been Shambleau.'

'I never heard of 'em.'

'Not many people have. And those who know don't care to talk about it much.'

'Well, half this town knows. I hadn't any idea what they were talking about, then. And I still don't understand—'

'Yes, it happens like this, sometimes. They'll appear, and the news will spread and the town will get together and hunt them down, and after that – well, the story doesn't get around very far. It's too – too unbelievable.'

'But – my God, Yarol! – what was it? Where'd it come from? How—'

'Nobody knows just where they come from. Another planet – maybe some undiscovered one. Some say Venus – I know there are some rather awful legends of them handed down in our family – that's how I've heard about it. And the minute I opened that door, awhile back – I – I think I knew that smell ...'

'But – what *are* they?'

'God knows. Not human, though they have the human form. Or that may be only an illusion ... or maybe I'm crazy. I don't know. They're a species of the vampire – or maybe the vampire is a species of – of them. Their normal form must be that – that mass, and in that form they draw nourishment from the – I suppose the life-forces of men. And they take some form – usually a woman form, I think, and key you up to the highest pitch of emotion before they – begin. That's to work the life-force up to intensity so it'll be easier ... And they give, always, that horrible, foul pleasure as they – feed. There are some men who, if they survive the first experience, take to it like a drug – can't give it up – keep the thing with them all their lives – which isn't long – feeding it for that ghastly satisfaction. Worse than smoking *ming* or – or "praying to Pharol."'

'Yes,' said Smith. 'I'm beginning to understand why that crowd was so surprised and – and disgusted when I said – well, never mind. Go on.'

'Did you get to talk to – to it?' asked Yarol.

'I tried to. It couldn't speak very well. I asked it where it came from and it said – "from far away and long ago" – something like that.'

'I wonder. Possibly some unknown planet – but I think not. You know there are so many wild stories with some basis of fact to start from, that I've sometimes wondered – mightn't there be a lot more of even worse and wilder superstitions we've never even heard of? Things like this, blasphemous and foul, that those who know have to keep still about? Awful, fantastic things running around loose that we never hear rumors of at all!'

'These things – they've been in existence for countless ages. No one knows when or where they first appeared. Those who've seen them, as we saw this one, don't talk about it. It's just one of those vague, misty rumors you find half hinted at in old books sometimes . . . I believe they are an older race than man, spawned from ancient seed in times before ours, perhaps on planets that have gone to dust, and so horrible to man that when they are discovered the discoverers keep still about it – forget them again as quickly as they can.

'And they go back to time immemorial. I suppose you recognized the legend of Medusa? There isn't any question that the ancient Greeks knew of them. Does it mean that there have been civilizations before yours that set out from Earth and explored other planets? Or did one of the Shambleau somehow make its way into Greece three thousand years ago? If you think about it long enough you'll go off your head! I wonder how many other legends are based on things like this – things we don't suspect, things we'll never know.'

'The Gorgon, Medusa, a beautiful woman with – with snakes for hair, and a gaze that turned men to stone, and Perseus finally killed her – I remembered this just by accident, N.W., and it saved your life and mine – Perseus killed her by using a mirror as he fought to reflect what he dared not look at directly. I wonder what the old Greek who first started that legend would have thought if he'd known that three thousand years later his story would save the lives of two men on another planet. I wonder what that Greek's own story was, and how he met the thing, and what happened . . .'

'Well, there's a lot we'll never know. Wouldn't the records of that race of – of *things*, whatever they are, be worth reading! Records of other planets and other ages and all the beginnings of mankind! But I don't suppose they've kept any records. I don't suppose they've even any place to keep them – from what little I know, or anyone knows about it, they're like the Wandering

Jew, just bobbing up here and there at long intervals, and where they stay in the meantime I'd give my eyes to know! But I don't believe that terribly hypnotic power they have indicates any superhuman intelligence. It's their means of getting food – just like a frog's long tongue or a carnivorous flower's odor. Those are physical because the frog and the flower eat physical food. The Shambleau uses a – a mental reach to get mental food. I don't quite know how to put it. And just as a beast that eats the bodies of other animals acquires with each meal greater power over the bodies of the rest, so the Shambleau, stoking itself up with the life-forces of men, increases its power over the minds and the souls of other men. But I'm talking about things I can't define – things I'm not sure exist.'

'I only know that when I felt – when those tentacles closed around my legs – I didn't want to pull loose, I felt sensations that – that – oh, I'm fouled and filthy to the very deepest part of me by that – pleasure – and yet—'

'I know,' said Smith slowly. The effect of the *segir* was beginning to wear off, and weakness was washing back over him in waves, and when he spoke he was half meditating in a low voice, scarcely realizing that Yarol listened. 'I know it – much better than you do – and there's something so indescribably awful that the thing emanates, something so utterly at odds with everything human – there aren't any words to say it. For a while I was a part of it, literally, sharing its thoughts and memories and emotions and hungers, and – well, it's over now and I don't remember very clearly, but the only part left free was that part of me that was all but insane from the – the obscenity of the thing. And yet it was a pleasure so sweet – I think there must be some nucleus of utter evil in me – in everyone – that needs only the proper stimulus to get complete control; because even while I was sick all through from the touch of those – things – there was something in me that was – was simply gibbering with delight … Because of that I saw things – and knew things – horrible, wild things I can't quite remember – visited unbelievable places, looked backward through the memory of that – creature – I was one with, and saw – God, I wish I could remember!'

'You ought to thank your God you can't,' said Yarol soberly. His voice roused Smith from the half-trance he had fallen into, and he rose on his elbow, swaying a little from weakness. The room was wavering before him, and he closed his eyes, not to see it, but he asked, 'You say they – they don't turn up again? No way of finding – another?'

Yarol did not answer for a moment. He laid his hands on the other man's shoulders and pressed him back, and then sat staring down into the dark, ravaged face with a new, strange, undefinable look upon it that he had never seen there before – whose meaning he knew, too well.

'Smith,' he said finally, and his black eyes for once were steady and serious, and the little grinning devil had vanished from behind them, 'Smith,

I've never asked your word on anything before, but I've – I've earned the right to do it now, and I'm asking you to promise me one thing.'

Smith's colorless eyes met the black gaze unsteadily. Irresolution was in them, and a little fear of what that promise might be. And for just a moment Yarol was looking, not into his friend's familiar eyes, but into a wide gray blankness that held all horror and delight – a pale sea with unspeakable pleasures sunk beneath it. Then the wide stare focused again and Smith's eyes met his squarely and Smith's voice said, 'Go ahead. I'll promise.'

'That if you ever should meet a Shambleau again – ever, anywhere – you'll draw your gun and burn it to hell the instant you realize what it is. Will you promise me that?'

There was a long silence. Yarol's somber black eyes bored relentlessly into the colorless ones of Smith, not wavering. And the veins stood out on Smith's tanned forehead. He never broke his word – he had given it perhaps half a dozen times in his life, but once he had given it, he was incapable of breaking it. And once more the gray seas flooded in a dim tide of memories, sweet and horrible beyond dreams. Once more Yarol was staring into blankness that hid nameless things. The room was very still.

The gray tide ebbed. Smith's eyes, pale and resolute as steel, met Yarol's levelly.

'I'll – try,' he said. And his voice wavered.

BLACK THIRST

Northwest Smith leaned his head back against the warehouse wall and stared up into the black night-sky of Venus. The waterfront street was very quiet tonight, very dangerous. He could hear no sound save the eternal slap-slap of water against the piles, but he knew how much of danger and sudden death dwelt here voiceless in the breathing dark, and he may have been a little homesick as he stared up into the clouds that masked a green star hanging lovely on the horizon – Earth and home. And if he thought of that he must have grinned wryly to himself in the dark, for Northwest Smith had no home, and Earth would not have welcomed him very kindly just then.

He sat quietly in the dark. Above him in the warehouse wall a faintly lighted window threw a square of pallor upon the wet street. Smith drew back into his angle of darkness under the slanting shaft, hugging one knee. And presently he heard footsteps softly on the street.

He may have been expecting footsteps, for he turned his head alertly and listened, but it was not a man's feet that came so lightly over the wooden quay, and Smith's brow furrowed. A woman, here, on this black waterfront by night? Not even the lowest class of Venusian street-walker dared come along the waterfronts of Ednes on the nights when the space-liners were not in. Yet across the pavement came clearly now the light tapping of a woman's feet.

Smith drew farther back into the shadows and waited. And presently she came, a darkness in the dark save for the triangular patch of pallor that was her face. As she passed under the light falling dimly from the window overhead he understood suddenly how she dared walk here and who she was. A long black cloak hid her, but the light fell upon her face, heart-shaped under the little three-cornered velvet cap that Venusian women wear, fell on ripples of half-hidden bronze hair; and by that sweet triangular face and shining hair he knew her for one of the Minga maids – those beauties that from the beginning of history have been bred in the Minga stronghold for loveliness and grace, as race-horses are bred on Earth, and reared from earliest infancy in the art of charming men. Scarcely a court on the three planets lacks at least one of these exquisite creatures, long-limbed, milk-white, with their bronze hair and lovely brazen faces – if the lord of that court has the wealth to buy them. Kings from many nations and races have poured their riches into the Minga gateway, and girls like pure gold and ivory have gone forth to grace a thousand palaces, and this has been so since Ednes first rose on the shore of the Greater Sea.

This girl walked here unafraid and unharmed because she wore the beauty that marked her for what she was. The heavy hand of the Minga stretched out protectingly over her bronze head, and not a man along the wharf-fronts but knew what dreadful penalties would overtake him if he dared so much as to lay a finger on the milk-whiteness of a Minga maid – terrible penalties, such as men whisper of fearfully over *segir*-whisky mugs in the waterfront dives of many nations – mysterious, unnamable penalties more dreadful then any knife or gun-flash could inflict.

And these dangers, too, guarded the gates of the Minga castle. The chastity of the Minga girls was proverbial, a trade boast. This girl walked in peace and safety more sure than that attending the steps of a nun through slum streets by night on Earth.

But even so, the girls went forth very rarely from the gates of the castle, never unattended. Smith had never seen one before, save at a distance. He shifted a little now, to catch a better glimpse as she went by, to look for the escort that must surely walk a pace or two behind, though he heard no footsteps save her own. The slight motion caught her eye. She stopped. She peered closer into the dark, and said in a voice as sweet and smooth as cream,

'How would you like to earn a gold piece, my man?'

A flash of perversity twisted Smith's reply out of its usual slovenly dialect, and he said in his most cultured voice, in his most perfect High Venusian,

'Thank you, no.'

For a moment the woman stood quite still, peering through the darkness in a vain effort to reach his face. He could see her own, a pale oval in the window light, intent, surprised. Then she flung back her cloak and the dim light glinted on the case of a pocket flash as she flicked the catch. A beam of white radiance fell blindingly upon his face.

For an instant the light held him – lounging against the wall in his spaceman's leather, the burns upon it, the tatters, ray-gun in its holster low on his thigh, and the brown scarred face turned to hers, eyes the colorless color of pale steel narrowed to the glare. It was a typical face. It belonged here, on the waterfront, in these dark and dangerous streets. It belonged to the type that frequents such places, those lawless men who ride the spaceways and live by the rule of the ray-gun, recklessly, warily outside the Patrol's jurisdiction. But there was more than that in the scarred brown face turned to the light. She must have seen it as she held the flash unwavering, some deep-buried trace of breeding and birth that made the cultured accents of the High Venusian not incongruous. And the colorless eyes derided her.

'No,' she said, flicking off the light. 'Not one gold piece, but a hundred. And for another task than I meant.'

'Thank you,' said Smith, not rising. 'You must excuse me.'

'Five hundred,' she said without a flicker of emotion in her creamy voice.

In the dark Smith's brows knit. There was something fantastic in the situation. Why—?

She must have sensed his reaction almost as he realized it himself, for she said,

'Yes, I know. It sounds insane. You see – I knew you in the light just now. Will you? – can you? – I can't explain here on the street ...'

Smith held the silence unbroken for thirty seconds, while a lightning debate flashed through the recesses of his wary mind. Then he grinned to himself in the dark and said, 'I'll come.' Belatedly he got to his feet. 'Where?'

'The Palace Road on the edge of the Minga. Third door from the central gate, to the left. Say to the door-warden – "Vaudir."'

'That is – ?'

'Yes, my name. You will come, in half an hour?'

An instant longer Smith's mind hovered on the verge of refusal. Then he shrugged.

'Yes.'

'At the third bell, then.' She made the little Venusian gesture of parting and wrapped her cloak about her. The blackness of it, and the softness of her footfalls, made her seem to melt into the darkness without a sound, but Smith's trained ears heard her footsteps very softly on the pavement as she went on into the dark.

He sat there until he could no longer detect any faintest sound of feet on the wharf. He waited patiently, but his mind was a little dizzy with surprise. Was the traditional inviolability of the Minga a fraud? Were the close-guarded girls actually allowed sometimes to walk unattended by night, making assignations as they pleased? Or was it some elaborate hoax? Tradition for countless centuries had declared the gates in the Minga wall to be guarded so relentlessly by strange dangers that not even a mouse could slip through without the knowledge of the Alendar, the Minga's lord. Was it then by order of the Alendar that the door would open to him when he whispered 'Vaudir' to the warden? Or would it open? Was the girl perhaps the property of some Ednes lord, deceiving him for obscure purposes of her own? He shook his head a little and grinned to himself. After all, time would tell.

He waited a while longer in the dark. Little waves lapped the piles with sucking sounds, and once the sky lit up with the long, blinding roar of a space-ship splitting the dark.

At last he rose and stretched his long body as if he had been sitting there for a good while. Then he settled the gun on his leg and set off down the black street. He walked very lightly in his spaceman's boots.

A twenty-minute walk through dark byways, still and deserted, brought him to the outskirts of that vast city-within-a-city called the Minga. The dark, rough walls of it towered over him, green with the lichen-like growths of the Hot Planet. On the Palace Road one deeply-sunk central gateway opened upon the mysteries within. A tiny blue light burned over the arch. Smith went softly through the dimness to the left of it, counting two tiny doors half hidden in deep recesses. At the third he paused. It was painted a rust green, and a green vine spilling down the wall half veiled it, so that if he had not been searching he would have passed it by.

Smith stood for a long minute, motionless, staring at the green panels deep-sunk in rock. He listened. He even sniffed the heavy air. Warily as a wild beast he hesitated in the dark. But at last he lifted his hand and tapped very lightly with his fingertips on the green door.

It swung open without a sound. Pitch-blackness confronted him, an archway of blank dark in the dimly seen stone wall. And a voice queried softly, *'Qu'a lo' val?'*

'Vaudir,' murmured Smith, and grinned to himself involuntarily. How many romantic youths must have stood at these doors in nights gone by, breathing hopefully the names of bronze beauties to doormen in dark archways! But unless tradition lied, no man before had ever passed. He must be the first in many years to stand here invited at a little doorway in the Minga wall and hear the watchman murmur, 'Come.'

Smith loosened the gun at his side and bent his tall head under the arch. He stepped into blackness that closed about him like water as the door swung shut. He stood there with quickened heart-beats, hand on his gun, listening. A blue light, dim and ghostly, flooded the place without warning and he saw the doorman had crossed to a switch at the far side of the tiny chamber wherein he stood. The man was one of the Minga eunuchs, a flabby creature, splendid in crimson velvet. He carried a cloak of purple over his arm, and made a splash of royal colors in the dimness. His sidelong eyes regarded Smith from under lifted brows, with a look that the Earthman could not fathom. There was amusement in it, and a touch of terror and a certain reluctant admiration.

Smith looked about him in frank curiosity. The little entry was apparently hollowed out of the enormously thick wall itself. The only thing that broke its bareness was the ornate bronze door set in the far wall. His eyes sought the eunuch's in mute inquiry.

The creature came forward obsequiously, murmuring, 'Permit me—' and flung the purple cloak he carried over Smith's shoulder. Its luxurious folds, faintly fragrant, swept about him like a caress. It covered him, tall as he was, to the very boot-soles. He drew back in faint distaste as the eunuch lifted his hands to fasten the jeweled clasp at his throat. 'Please to draw up the hood also,' murmured the creature without apparent resentment, as Smith snapped the fastening himself. The hood covered his sun-bleached hair and fell in thick folds about his face, casting it into deep shadow.

The eunuch opened the bronze inner door and Smith stared down a long hallway curving almost imperceptibly to the right. The paradox of elaborately decorated simplicity was illustrated in every broad polished panel of the wall, so intricately and exquisitely carved that it gave at first the impression of a strange, rich plainness.

His booted feet sank sensuously into the deep pile of the carpet at every step as he followed the eunuch down the hall. Twice he heard voices murmuring behind lighted doors, and his hand lay on the butt of the ray-gun under the folds of his robe, but no door opened and the hall lay empty and dim before them. So far it had been amazingly easy. Either tradition lied about the impregnability of the Minga, or the girl Vaudir had bribed with incredible lavishness or – that thought again, uneasily – it was with the Alendar's consent that he walked here unchallenged. But why?

They came to a door of silver grille at the end of the curved corridor, and passed through it into another hallway slanting up, as exquisitely voluptuous as the first. A flight of stairs wrought from dully gleaming bronze curved at the end of it. Then came another hall lighted with rosy lanterns that swung from the arched ceiling, and beyond another stairway, this time of silvery metal fretwork, spiraling down again.

And in all that distance they met no living creature. Voices hummed behind closed doors, and once or twice strains of music drifted faintly to Smith's ears, but either the corridors had been cleared by a special order, or incredible luck was attending them. And he had the uncomfortable sensation of eyes upon his back more than once. They passed dark hallways and open, unlighted doors, and sometimes the hair on his neck bristled with the feeling of human nearness, inimical, watching.

For all of twenty minutes they walked through curved corridors and up and down spiral stairs until even Smith's keen senses were confused and he could not have said at what height above the ground he was, or in what direction the corridor led into which they at last emerged. At the end of that time his nerves were tense as steel wire and he restrained himself only by force from nervous, over-the-shoulder glances each time they passed an open door. An air of languorous menace brooded almost visibly over the place, he thought. The sound of soft voices behind doors, the feel of eyes, of whispers in the air, the memory of tales half heard in waterfront dives about the secrets of the Minga, the nameless dangers of the Minga …

Smith gripped his gun as he walked through the splendor and the dimness, every sense assailed by voluptuous appeals, but his nerves strained to wire and his flesh crawled as he passed unlighted doors. This was too easy. For so many centuries the tradition of the Minga had been upheld, a byword of impregnability, a stronghold guarded by more than sword, by greater danger than the ray-gun – and yet here he walked, unquestioned, into the deepest heart of the place, his only disguise a velvet cloak, his only weapon a holstered gun, and no one challenged him, no guards, no slaves, not even a passer-by to note that a man taller than any dweller here should be striding unquestioned through the innermost corridors of the inviolable Minga. He loosened the ray-gun in its sheath.

The eunuch in his scarlet velvet went on confidently ahead. Only once did he falter. They had reached a dark passageway, and just as they came opposite its mouth the sound of a soft, slithering scrape, as of something over stones, draggingly, reached their ears. He saw the eunuch start and half glance back, and then hurry on at a quicker pace, nor did he slacken until they had put two gates and a length of lighted corridor between them and that dark passage.

So they went on, through halls half lighted, through scented air and empty dimness where the doorways closed upon murmurous mysteries within or opened to dark and the feel of watching eyes. And they came at last, after endless, winding progress, into a hallway low-ceilinged and paneled in mother-of-pearl, pierced and filigreed with carving, and all the doors were of silver grille. And as the eunuch pushed open the silver gate that led into this corridor the thing happened that his taut nerves had been expecting ever since the start of the fantastic journey. One of the doors opened and a figure stepped out and faced them.

Under the robe Smith's gun slid soundlessly from its holster. He thought he saw the eunuch's back stiffen a little, and his step falter, but only for an instant: It was a girl who had come out, a slave-girl in a singe white garment, and at the first glimpse of the tall, purple-robed figure with hooded face, towering over her, she gave a little gasp and slumped to her knees as if under a blow. It was obeisance, but so shocked and terrified that it might have been a faint. She laid her face to the very carpet, and Smith, looking down in amazement on the prostrate figure, saw that she was trembling violently.

The gun slid back into its sheath and he paused for a moment over her shuddering homage. The eunuch twisted round to beckon with soundless violence, and Smith caught a glimpse of his face for the first time since their journey began. It was glistening with sweat, and the sidelong eyes were bright and shifting, like a hunted animal's. Smith was oddly reassured by the sight of the eunuch's obvious panic. There was danger then – danger of discovery, the sort of peril he knew and could fight. It was that creeping sensation of eyes watching, of unseen things slithering down dark passages, that had strained his nerves so painfully. And yet, even so, it had been too easy . . .

The eunuch had paused at a silver door halfway down the hall and was murmuring something very softly, his mouth against the grille. A panel of green brocade was stretched across the silver door on the inside, so they could see nothing within the room, but after a moment a voice said, 'Good!' in a breathing whisper, and the door quivered a little and swung open six inches. The eunuch genuflected in a swirl of scarlet robes, and Smith caught his eye swiftly, the look of terror not yet faded, but amusement there too, and a certain respect. And then the door opened wider and he stepped inside.

He stepped into a room green as a sea-cave. The walls were paneled in green brocade, low green couches circled the room, and, in the center, the blazing bronze beauty of the girl Vaudir. She wore a robe of green velvet cut in the startling Venusian fashion to loop over one shoulder and swathe her body in tight, molten folds, and the skirt of it was slit up one side so that at every other motion the long white leg flashed bare.

He saw her for the first time in a full light, and she was lovely beyond belief with her bronze hair cloudy on her shoulders and the pale, lazy face smiling. Under deep lashes the sidelong black eyes of her race met his.

He jerked impatiently at the hampering hood of the cloak. 'May I take this off?' he said. 'Are we safe here?'

She laughed with a short, metallic sound. 'Safe!' she said ironically. 'But take it off if you must. I've gone too far now to stop at trifles.'

And as the rich folds parted and slid away from his leather brownness she in turn stared in quickened interest at what she had seen only in a half-light before. He was almost laughably incongruous in this jewel-box room, all leather and sunburn and his scarred face keen and wary in the light of the lantern swinging from its silver chain. She looked a second time at that face, its lean, leathery keenness and the scars that ray-guns had left, and the mark of knife and talon, and the tracks of wild years along the spaceways. Wariness and resolution were instinct in that face, there was ruthlessness in every line of it, and when she met his eyes a little shock went over her. Pale, pale as bared steel, colorless in the sunburnt face. Steady and clear and no-colored, expressionless as water. Killer's eyes.

And she knew that this was the man she needed. The name and fame of Northwest Smith had penetrated even into these mother-of-pearl Minga halls. In its way it had spread into stranger places than this, by strange and devious paths and for strange, devious reasons. But even had she never heard the name (nor the deed she connected it with, which does not matter here), she would have known from this scarred face, these cold and steady eyes, that here stood the man she wanted, the man who could help her if any man alive could.

And with that thought, others akin to it flashed through her mind like blades, crossing, and she dropped her milk-white lids over the sword-play to hide its deadliness, and said, 'Northwest … Smith,' in a musing murmur.

'To be commanded,' said Smith in the idiom of her own tongue, but a spark of derision burned behind the courtly words.

Still she said nothing, but looked him up and down with slow eyes. He said at last.

'Your desire – ?' and shifted impatiently.

'I had need of a wharfman's services,' she said, still in that breathing whisper. 'I had not seen you, then … There are many wharfmen along the sea-front, but only one of you, oh man of Earth—' and she lifted her arms and swayed toward him exactly as a reed sways to a lake breeze, and her arms lay lightly on his shoulders and her mouth was very near …

Smith looked down into the veiled eyes. He knew enough of the breed of Venus to guess the deadly sword-flash of motive behind anything a Venusian does, and he had caught a glimpse of that particular sword-flash before she lowered her lids. And if her thoughts were sword-play, his burnt like heat-beams straight to their purpose. In the winking of an eye he knew a part of her motive – the most obvious part. And he stood there unanswering in the circle of her arms.

She looked up at him, half incredulous not to feel a leather embrace tighten about her.

'Quh lo'val?' she murmured whimsically. 'So cold, then, Earthman? Am I not desirable?'

Wordlessly he looked down at her, and despite himself the blood quickened in him. Minga girls for too many centuries had been born and bred to the art of charming men for Northwest Smith to stand here in the warm arms of one and feel no answer to the invitation in her eyes. A subtle fragrance rose from her brazen hair, and the velvet molded a body whose whiteness he could guess from the flash of the long bare thigh her slashed skirt showed. He grinned a little crookedly and stepped away, breaking the clasp of her hands behind his neck.

'No,' he said. 'You know your art well, my dear, but your motive does not flatter me.'

She stood back and regarded him with a wry, half-appreciative smile.

'What do you mean?'

'I'll have to know much more about all this before I commit myself as far as – that.'

'You fool,' she smiled. 'You're in over your head now, as deeply as you could ever be. You were the moment you crossed the door-sill at the outer wall. There is no drawing back.'

'Yet it was so easy – so very easy, to come in,' murmured Smith.

She came forward a step and looked up at him with narrowed eyes, the pretense of seduction dropped like a cloak.

'You saw that, too?' she queried in a half-whisper. 'It seemed so – to you? Great Shar, if I could be *sure* …' And there was terror in her face.

'Suppose we sit down and you tell me about it,' suggested Smith practically.

She laid a hand – white as cream, soft as satin – on his arm and drew him to the low divan that circled the room. There was inbred, generations-old coquetry in the touch, but the white hand shook a little.

'What is it you fear so?' queried Smith curiously as they sank to the green velvet. 'Death comes only once, you know.'

She shook her bronze head contemptuously.

'Not that,' she said. 'At least – no, I wish I knew just what it is I do fear – and that is the most dreadful part of it. But I wish – I wish it had not been so easy to get you here.'

'The place was deserted,' he said thoughtfully. 'Not a soul along the halls. Not a guard anywhere. Only once did we see any other creature, and that was a slave-girl in the hall just outside your door.'

'What did she – do?' Vaudir's voice was breathless.

'Dropped to her knees as if she'd been shot. You might have thought me the devil himself by the way she acted.'

The girl's breath escaped in a sigh.

'Safe, then,' she said thankfully. 'She must have thought you the – the Alendar.' Her voice faltered a little over the name, as if she half feared to pronounce it. 'He wears a cloak like that you wore when he comes through the halls. But he comes so very seldom …'

'I've never seen him,' said Smith, 'but, good Lord, is he such a monster? The girl dropped as if she'd been hamstrung.'

'Oh, hush, hush!' Vaudir agonized. 'You mustn't speak of him so. He's – he's – of course she knelt and hid her face. I wish to heaven I had …'

Smith faced her squarely and searched the veiled dark eyes with a gaze as bleak as empty seas. And he saw very clearly behind the veils the stark, nameless terror at their depths.

'What is it?' he demanded.

She drew her shoulders together and shivered a little, and her eyes were furtive as she glanced around the room.

'Don't you feel it?' she asked in that half-whisper to which her voice sank so carelessly. And he smiled to himself to see how instinctively eloquent was the courtesan in her – alluring gestures though her hands trembled, soft voice huskily seductive even in its terror. ' – always, always!' she was saying. 'The soft, hushed, hovering menace! It haunts the whole place. Didn't you feel it as you came in?'

'I think I did,' Smith answered slowly. 'Yes – that feel of something just out of sight, hiding in dark doorways … a sort of tensity in the air …'

'Danger,' she whispered, 'terrible, nameless danger … oh, I feel it wherever

I go … it's soaked into me and through me until it's a part of me, body and soul …'

Smith heard the note of rising hysteria in her voice, and said quickly.

'Why did you come to me?'

'I didn't, consciously.' She conquered the hysteria with an effort and took up her tale a little more calmly. 'I was really looking for a wharfman, as I said, and for quite another reason than this. It doesn't matter, now. But when you spoke, when I flashed my light and saw your face, I knew you. I'd heard of you, you see, and about the – the Lakkmanda affair, and I knew in a moment that if anyone alive could help me, it would be you.'

'But what is it? Help you in what?'

'It's a long story,' she said, 'and too strange, almost, to believe, and too vague for you to take seriously. And yet I *know* … Have you heard the history of the Minga?'

'A little of it. It goes back very far.'

'Back into the beginning – and farther. I wonder if you can understand. You see, we on Venus are closer to our beginnings than you. Life here developed faster, of course, and along lines more different than Earthmen realize. On Earth, civilization rose slowly enough for the – the elementals – to sink back into darkness. On Venus – oh, it's bad, *bad* for men to develop too swiftly! Life rises out of dark and mystery and things too strange and terrible to be looked upon. Earth's civilization grew slowly, and by the time men were civilized enough to look back they were sufficiently far from their origins not to see, not to know. But we here who look back see too clearly, sometimes, too nearly and vividly the black beginning … Great Shar defend me, what I have seen!'

White hands flashed up to hide sudden terror in her eyes, and hair in a brazen cloud fell fragrantly over her fingers. And even in that terror was an inbred allure as natural as breathing.

In the little silence that followed, Smith caught himself glancing furtively over his shoulder. The room was ominously still …

Vaudir lifted her face from her hands, shaking back her hair. The hands trembled. She clasped them on her velvet knee and went on.

'The Minga,' she said, and her voice was resolutely steady, 'began too long ago for anyone to name the date. It began before dates. When Far-thursa came out of the seafog with his men and founded this city at the mountain's foot he built it around the walls of a castle already here. The Minga castle. And the Alendar sold Minga girls to the sailors and the city began. All that is myth, but the Minga had always been here.

'The Alendar dwelt in his stronghold and bred his golden girls and trained them in the arts of charming men, and guarded them with – with strange weapons – and sold them to kings at royal prices. There has always been an Alendar. I have seen him, once …'

'He walks the halls on rare occasions, and it is best to kneel and hide one's face when he comes by. Yes, it is best … But I passed him one day, and – and – he is tall, tall as you, Earthman, and his eyes are like – the space between the worlds. I looked into his eyes under the hood he wore – I was not afraid of devil or man, then. I looked him in the eyes before I made obeisance, and I – I shall never be free of fear again. I looked into evil as one looks into a pool. Blackness and blankness and raw evil. Impersonal, not malevolent. Elemental … the elemental dreadfulness that life rose from. And I know very surely, now, that the first Alendar sprang from no mortal seed. There were races before man … Life goes back very dreadfully through many forms and evils, before it reaches the well-spring of its beginning. And the Alendar had not the eyes of a human creature, and I met them – and I am damned!'

Her voice trailed softly away and she sat quiet for a space, staring before her with remembering eyes.

'I am doomed and damned to a blacker hell than any of Shar's priests threaten,' she resumed. 'No, wait – this is not hysteria. I haven't told you the worst part. You'll find it hard to believe, but it's truth – truth – Great Shar, if I could hope it were not!'

'The origin of it is lost in legend. But why, in the beginning, did the first Alendar dwell in the misty sea-edge castle, alone and unknown, breeding his bronze girls? – not for sale, then. Where did he get the secret of producing the invariable type? And the castle, legend says, was age-old when Farthursa found it. The girls had a perfected, consistent beauty that could be attained only by generations of effort. How long had the Minga been built, and by whom? Above all, why? What possible reason could there be for dwelling there absolutely unknown, breeding civilized beauties in a world half-savage? Sometimes I think I have guessed the reason …'

Her voice faded into a resonant silence, and for a while she sat staring blindly at the brocaded wall. When she spoke again it was with a startling shift of topic.

'Am I beautiful, do you think?'

'More so than any I have ever seen before,' answered Smith without flattery.

Her mouth twisted.

'There are girls here now, in this building, so much lovelier than I that I am humbled to think of them. No mortal man has ever seen them, except the Alendar, and he – is not wholly mortal. No mortal man will ever see them. They are not for sale. Eventually they will disappear …'

'One might think that feminine beauty must reach an apex beyond which it cannot rise, but this is not true. It can increase and intensify until – I have no words. And I truly believe that there is no limit to the heights it can reach, in the hands of the Alendar. And for every beauty we know and hear of, through the slaves that tend them, gossip says there are as many more, too immortally lovely for mortal eyes to see. Have you ever considered that beauty might be refined and intensified until one could scarcely bear to look upon it? We have tales here of such beauty, hidden in some of the secret rooms of the Minga.'

'But the world never knows of these mysteries. No monarch on any planet known is rich enough to buy the loveliness hidden in the Minga's innermost rooms. It is not for sale. For countless centuries the Alendars of the Minga have been breeding beauty, in higher and higher degrees, at infinite labor and cost – beauty to be locked in secret chambers, guarded most terribly, so that not even a whisper of it passes the outer walls, beauty that vanishes, suddenly, in a breath – like that! Where? Why? How? No one knows.'

'And it is that I fear. I have not a fraction of the beauty I speak of, yet a fate like that is written for me – somehow I know. I have looked into the eyes of the Alendar, and – I know. And I am sure that I must look again into those blank black eyes, more deeply, more dreadfully … I know – and I am sick with terror of what more I shall know, soon …'

'Something dreadful is waiting for me, drawing nearer and nearer. To-morrow, or the next day, or a little while after, I shall vanish, and the girls will wonder and whisper a little, and then forget. It has happened before. Great Shar, what shall I do?'

She wailed it, musically and hopelessly and sank into a little silence. And then her look changed and she said reluctantly,

'And I have dragged you in with me. I have broken every tradition of the Minga in bringing you here, and there has been no hindrance – it has been too easy, too easy. I think I have sealed your death. When you first came I was minded to trick you into committing yourself so deeply that perforce you must do as I asked to win free again. But I know now that through the simple act of asking you here I have dragged you in deeper than I dreamed. It is a knowledge that has come to me somehow, out of the air tonight. I can feel knowledge beating upon me – compelling me. For in my terror to get help I think I have precipitated damnation upon us both. I know now – I have known in my soul since you entered so easily, that you will not go out alive – that – *it* – will come for me and drag you down too … Shar, Shar, what have I done!'

'But what, what?' Smith struck his knee impatiently. 'What is it we face? Poison? Guards? Traps? Hypnotism? Can't you give me even a guess at what will happen?'

He leaned forward to search her face commandingly, and saw her brows knit in an effort to find words that would cloak the mysteries she had to tell. Her lips parted irresolutely.

'The Guardians,' she said. 'The – Guardians ...'

And then over her hesitant face swept a look of such horror that his hand clenched on his knee and he felt the hairs rise along his neck. It was not horror of any material thing, but an inner dreadfulness, a terrible awareness. The eyes that had met his glazed and escaped his commanding stare without shifting their focus. It was as if they ceased to be eyes and became dark windows – vacant. The beauty of her face set like a mask, and behind the blank window, behind the lovely set mask, he could sense dimly the dark command flowing in ...

She put out her hands stiffly and rose. Smith found himself on his feet, gun in hand, while his hackles lifted shudderingly and something pulsed in the air as tangibly as the beat of wings. Three times that nameless shudder stirred the air, and then Vaudir stepped forward like an automaton and faced the door. She walked in her dream of masked dreadfulness, stiffly, through the portal. As she passed him he put out a hesitant hand and laid it on her arm, and a little stab of pain shot through him at the contact, and once more he thought he felt the pulse of wings in the air. Then she passed by without hesitation, and his hands fell.

He made no further effort to arouse her, but followed after on cat-feet, delicately as if he walked on eggs. He was crouching a little, unconsciously, and his gun-hand held a tense finger on the trigger.

They went down the corridor in a breathing silence, an empty corridor where no lights showed beyond closed doors, where no murmur of voices broke the live stillness. But little shudders seemed to shake in the air somehow, and his heart was pounding suffocatingly.

Vaudir walked like a mechanical doll, tense in a dream of horror. When they reached the end of the hall he saw that the silver grille stood open, and they passed through without pausing. But Smith noted with a little qualm that a gateway opening to the right was closed and locked, and the bars across it were sunk firmly into wall-sockets. There was no choice but to follow her.

The corridor slanted downward. They passed others branching to right and left, but the silver gateways were closed and barred across each. A coil of silver stairs ended the passage, and the girl went stiffly down without touching the rails. It was a long spiral, past many floors, and as they descended, the rich, dim light lessened and darkened and a subtle smell of moisture and salt invaded the scented air. At each turn where the stairs opened on successive floors, gates were barred across the outlets; and they passed so many of these that Smith knew, as they went down and down, that however high the green jewel-box room had been, by now they were descending deep into the earth. And still the stair wound downward. The stories that opened beyond the bars like honeycomb layers became darker and less luxurious, and at last ceased altogether and the silver steps wound down through a well of rock, lighted so dimly at wide intervals that he could scarcely see the black polished walls circling them in. Drops of moisture began to appear on the dark surface, and the smell was of black salt seas and dank underground.

And just as he was beginning to believe that the stairs went on and on into the very black, salt heart of the planet, they came abruptly to the bottom. A flourish of slim, shining rails ended the stairs, at the head of a hallway, and the girl's feet turned unhesitatingly to follow its dark length. Smith's pale eyes, searching the dimness, found no trace of other life than themselves; yet eyes were upon him – he knew it surely.

They came down the black corridor to a gateway of wrought metal set in bars whose ends sank deep into the stone walls. She went through, Smith at her heels raking the dark with swift, unresting eyes like a wild animal's, wary in a strange jungle. And beyond the great gates a door hung with sweeping curtains of black ended the hall. Somehow Smith felt that they had reached their destination. And nowhere along the whole journey had he had any choice but to follow Vaudir's unerring, unseeing footsteps. Grilles had been locked across every possible outlet. But he had his gun ...

Her hands were white against the velvet as she pushed aside the folds. Very bright she stood for an instant – all green and gold and white – against the blackness. Then she passed through and the folds swept to behind her – candle-flame extinguished in dark velvet. Smith hesitated the barest instant before he parted the curtains and peered within.

He was looking into a room hung in black velvet that absorbed the light almost hungrily. That light radiated from a single lamp swinging from the ceiling directly over an ebony table. It shone softly on a man – a very tall man.

He stood darkly under it, very dark in the room's darkness, his head bent, staring up from under level black brows. His eyes in the half-hidden face were pits of blackness, and under the lowered brows two pinpoint gleams stabbed straight – not at the girl – but at Smith hidden behind the curtains. It held his eyes as a magnet holds steel. He felt the narrow glitter plunging blade-like into his very brain, and from the keen, burning stab something within him shuddered away involuntarily. He thrust his gun through the curtains, stepped through quietly, and stood meeting the sword-gaze with pale, unwavering eyes.

Vaudir moved forward with a mechanical stiffness that somehow could not hide her grace – it was as if no power existing could ever evoke from that lovely body less than loveliness. She came to the man's feet and stopped there. Then a long shudder swept her from head to foot and she dropped to her knees and laid her forehead to the floor.

Across the golden loveliness of her the man's eyes met Smith's, and the man's voice, deep, deep, like black waters flowing smoothly, said, 'I am the Alendar.'

'Then you know me,' said Smith, his voice harsh as iron in the velvet dimness.

'You are Northwest Smith,' said the smooth, deep voice dispassionately. 'An outlaw from the planet Earth. You have broken your last law, Northwest Smith. Men do not come here uninvited – and live. You perhaps have heard tales ...'

His voice melted into silence, lingeringly.

Smith's mouth curled into a wolfish grin, without mirth, and his gun hand swung up. Murder flashed bleakly from his steel-pale eyes. And then with stunning abruptness the world dissolved about him. A burst of coruscations flamed through his head, danced and wheeled and drew slowly together in a whirling darkness until they were two pinpoint sparks of light – a dagger stare under level brows ...

When the room steadied about him he was standing with slack arms, the gun hanging from his fingers, an apathetic numbness slowly with-drawing from his body. A dark smile curved smoothly on the Alendar's mouth.

The stabbing gaze slid causally away, leaving him dizzy in sudden vertigo, and touched the girl prostrate on the floor. Against the black carpet her burnished bronze curls sprayed out exquisitely. The green robe folded softly back from the roundness of her body, and nothing in the universe could have been so lovely as the creamy whiteness of her on the dark floor. The pit-black eyes brooded over her impassively. And then, in his smooth, deep voice the Alendar asked, amazingly, matter-of-factly, 'Tell me, do you have such girls on Earth?'

Smith shook his head to clear it. When he managed an answer his voice had steadied, and in the receding of that dizziness even the sudden drop into causal conversation seemed not unreasonable.

'I have never seen such a girl anywhere,' he said calmly.

The sword-gaze flashed up and pierced him.

'She has told you,' said the Alendar.' You know I have beauties here that outshine her as the sun does a candle. And yet ... she has more than beauty, this Vaudir. You have felt it, perhaps?'

Smith met the questioning gaze, searching for mockery, but finding none. Not understanding – a moment before the man had threatened his life – he took up the conversation.

'They all have more than beauty. For what other reason do kings buy the Minga girls?'

'No – not that charm. She has it too, but something more subtle than fascination, much more desirable than loveliness. She has courage, this girl.

She has intelligence. Where she got it I do not understand. I do not breed my girls for such things. But I looked into her eyes once, in the hallway, as she told you – and saw there more arousing things than beauty. I summoned her – and you come at her heels. Do you know why? Do you know why you did not die at the outer gate or anywhere along the hallways on your way in?'

Smith's pale stare met the dark one questioningly. The voice flowed on.

'Because there are – interesting things in your eyes too. Courage and ruthlessness and a certain – power, I think. Intensity is in you. And I believe I can find a use for it, Earthman.'

Smith's eyes narrowed a little. So calm, so matter-of-fact, this talk. But death was coming. He felt it in the air – he knew that feel of old. Death – and worse things than that, perhaps. He remembered the whispers he had heard.

On the floor the girl moaned a little, and stirred. The Alendar's quiet, pin-point eyes flicked her, and he said softly, 'Rise.' And she rose, stumbling, and stood before him with bent head. The stiffness was gone from her. On an impulse Smith said suddenly, 'Vaudir!' She lifted her face and met his gaze, and a thrill of horror rippled over him. She had regained consciousness, but she would never be the same frightened girl he had known. Black knowledge looked out of her eyes, and her face was a strained mask that covered horror barely – barely! It was the face of one who has walked through a blacker hell than any of humanity's understanding, and gained knowledge there that no human soul could endure knowing and live.

She looked him full in the face for a long moment, silently, and then turned away to the Alendar again. And Smith thought, just before her eyes left his, he had seen in them one wild flash of hopeless, desperate appeal ...

'Come,' said the Alendar.

He turned his back – Smith's gun-hand trembled up and then fell again. No, better wait. There was always a bare hope, until he saw death closing in all around.

He stepped out over the yielding carpet at the Alendar's heels. The girl came after with slow steps and eyes downcast in a horrible parody of meditation, as if she brooded over the knowledge that dwelt so terribly behind her eyes.

The dark archway at the opposite end of the room swallowed them up. Light failed for an instant – a breathstopping instant while Smith's gun leaped up involuntarily, like a live thing in his hand, futilely against invisible evil, and his brain rocked at the utter blackness that enfolded him. It was over in the wink of an eye, and he wondered if it had ever been as his gun-hand fell again. But the Alendar said across one shoulder.

'A barrier I have placed to guard my – beauties. A mental barrier that would have been impassable had you not been with me, yet which – but you understand now, do you not, my Vaudir?' And there was an indescribable leer in the query that injected a note of monstrous humanity into the inhuman voice.

'I understand,' echoed the girl in a voice as lovely and toneless as a sustained musical note. And the sound of those two inhuman voices proceeding from the human lips of his companions sent a shudder thrilling along Smith's nerves.

They went down the long corridor thereafter in silence, Smith treading soundlessly in his spaceman's boots, every fiber of him tense to painfulness. He found himself wondering, even in the midst of his strained watchfulness, if any other creature with a living human soul had ever gone down this corridor before – if frightened golden girls had followed the Alendar thus into blackness, or if they too had been drained of humanity and steeped in that nameless horror before their feet followed their master through the black barrier.

The hallway led downward, and the salt smell became clearer and the light sank to a glimmer in the air, and in a silence that was not human they went on.

Presently the Alendar said – and his deep, liquid voice did nothing to break the stillness, blending with it softly so that not even an echo roused,

'I am taking you into a place where no other man than the Alendar has ever set foot before. It pleases me to wonder just how your unaccustomed senses will react to the things you are about to see. I am reaching an – an age' – he laughed softly – 'where experiment interests me. Look!'

Smith's eyes blinked shut before an intolerable blaze of sudden light. In the streaked darkness of that instant while the glare flamed through his lids he though he felt everything shift unaccountably about him, as if the very structure of the atoms that built the walls were altered. When he opened his eyes he stood at the head of a long gallery blazing with a soft, delicious brilliance. How he had got there he made no effort even to guess.

Very beautifully it stretched before him. The walls and floor and ceiling were of sheeny stone. There were low couches along the walls at intervals, and a blue pool broke the floor, and the air sparkled unaccountably with golden light. And figures were moving through that champagne sparkle …

Smith stood very still, looking down the gallery. The Alendar watched him with a subtle anticipation upon his face, the pinpoint glitter of his eyes sharp enough to pierce the Earthman's very brain. Vaudir with bent head brooded over the black knowledge behind her drooping lids. Only Smith of the three looked down the gallery and saw what moved through the golden glimmer of the air.

They were girls. They might have been goddesses – angels haloed with bronze curls, moving leisurely through a golden heaven where the air sparkled like wine. There must have been a score of them strolling up and down the gallery in twos and threes, lolling on the couches, bathing in the pool. They wore the infinitely graceful Venusian robe with its looped shoulder and slit skirt, in soft, muted shades of violet and blue and jewel-green, and the beauty of them was breath-stopping as a blow. Music was in every gesture they made, a flowing, singing grace that made the heart ache with its sheer loveliness.

He had thought Vaudir lovely, but here was beauty so exquisite that it verged on pain. Their sweet, light voices were pitched to send little velvety burrs along his nerves, and from a distance the soft sounds blended so musically that they might have been singing together. The loveliness of their motion made his heart contract suddenly, and the blood pounded in his ears . . .

'You find them beautiful?' The Alendar's voice blended into the humming lilt of voices as perfectly as it had blended with silence. His dagger-glitter of eyes was fixed piercingly on Smith's pale gaze, and he smiled a little faintly. 'Beautiful? Wait!'

He moved down the gallery, tall and very dark in the rainbow light. Smith, following after, walked in a haze of wonder. It is not given to every man to walk through heaven. He felt the air tingle like wine, and a delicious perfume caressed him and the haloed girls drew back with wide, amazed eyes fixed on him in his stained leather and heavy boots as he passed. Vaudir paced quietly after, her head bent, and from her the girls turned away their eyes, shuddering a little.

He saw now that their faces were as lovely as their bodies, languorously, colorfully. They were contented faces, unconscious of beauty, unconscious of any other existence than their own – soulless. He felt that instinctively. Here was beauty incarnate, physically, tangibly; but he had seen in Vaudir's face – before – a sparkle of daring, a tenderness of remorse at having brought him here, that gave her an indefinable superiority over even this incredible beauty, soulless.

They went down the gallery in a hush as the musical voices fell silent from very amazement. Apparently the Alendar was a familiar figure here, for they scarcely glanced at him, and from Vaudir they turned away in a shuddering revulsion that preferred not to recognize her existence. But Smith was the first man other than the Alendar whom they had ever seen, and the surprise of it struck them dumb.

They went on through the dancing air, and the last lovely, staring girls fell behind, and an ivory gateway opened before them without a touch. They went downstairs from there, and along another hallway, while the tingle died in the air and a hum of musical voices sprang up behind them. They passed beyond the sound. The hallway darkened until they were moving again through dimness.

Presently the Alendar paused and turned.

'My more costly jewels,' he said, 'I keep in separate settings. As here—'

He stretched out his arm, and Smith saw that a curtain hung against the wall. There were others, farther on, dark blots against the dimness. The Alendar drew back black folds, and light from beyond flowed softly through a pattern of bars to cast flowery shadows on the opposite wall. Smith stepped forward and stared.

He was looking through a grille window down into a room lined with dark velvet. It was quite plain. There was a low couch against the wall opposite the window, and on it – Smith's heart gave a stagger and paused – a woman lay. And if the girls in the gallery had been like goddesses, this woman was lovelier than men have ever dared to imagine even in legends. She was beyond divinity – long limbs white against the velvet, sweet curves and planes of her rounding under the robe, bronze hair spilling like lava over one shoulder, and her face calm as death with closed eyes. It was a passive beauty, like alabaster shaped perfectly. And charm, a fascination all but tangible, reached out from her like a magic spell. A sleeping charm, magnetic, powerful. He could not wrench his eyes away. He was like a wasp caught in honey...

The Alendar said something across Smith's shoulder, in a vibrant voice that thrilled the air. The closed lids rose. Life and loveliness flowed into the calm face like a tide, lighting it unbearably. That heady charm wakened and brightened to a dangerous liveness – tugging, pulling ... She rose in one long glide like a wave over rocks; she smiled (Smith's senses reeled to the beauty of that smile) and then sank in a deep salaam, slowly, to the velvet floor, her hair rippling and falling all about her, until she lay abased in a blaze of loveliness under the window.

The Alendar let the curtain fall, and turned to Smith as the dazzling sight was blotted out. Again the pinpoint glitter stabbed into Smith's brain. The Alendar smiled again.

'Come,' he said, and moved down the hall.

They passed three curtains, and paused at a fourth. Afterward Smith remembered that the curtain must have been drawn back and he must have bent forward to stare through the window bars, but the sight he saw blasted every memory of it from his mind. The girl who dwelt in this velvet-lined room was stretching on tiptoe just as the drawn curtain caught her, and the beauty and grace of her from head to foot stopped Smith's breath as a ray-stab to the heart would have done. And the irresistible, wrenching charm of her drew him forward until he was clasping the bars with white-knuckled hands, unaware of anything but her compelling, soul-destroying desirability...

She moved, and the dazzle of grace that ran like a song through every motion made his sense ache with its pure, unattainable loveliness. He knew, even in his daze of rapture, that he might hold the sweet, curved body in his arms for ever, yet hunger still for the fulfillment which the flesh could never wring from her. Her loveliness aroused a hunger in the soul more maddening than the body's hunger could ever be. His brain rocked with the desire to possess that intangible, irresistible liveliness that he knew he could never possess, never reach with any sense that was in him. That bodiless desire raged like madness through him, so violently that the room reeled and the white outlines of the beauty unattainable as the stars wavered before him. He caught his breath and choked and drew back from the intolerable, exquisite sight.

The Alendar laughed and dropped the curtain.

'Come,' he said again, the subtle amusement clear in his voice, and Smith in a daze moved after him down the hall.

They went a long way, past curtains hanging at regular intervals along the wall. When they paused at last, the curtain before which they stopped was faintly luminous about the edges, as if something dazzling dwelt within. The Alendar drew back the folds.

'We are approaching,' he said, 'a pure clarity of beauty, hampered only a little by the bonds of flesh. Look.'

One glance only Smith snatched of the dweller within. And the exquisite shock of that sight went thrilling like torture through every nerve of him. For a mad instant his reason staggered before the terrible fascination beating out from that dweller in waves that wrenched at his very soul – incarnate loveliness tugging with strong fingers at every sense and every nerve and intangibly, irresistibly, at deeper things than these, groping among the roots of his being, dragging his soul out …

Only one glance he took, and in the glance he felt his soul answer that dragging, and the terrible desire tore futilely through him. Then he flung up an arm to shield his eyes and reeled back into the dark, and a wordless sob rose to his lips and the darkness reeled about him.

The curtain fell. Smith pressed the wall and breathed in long shuddering gasps, while his heart-beats slowed gradually and the unholy fascination ebbed from about him. The Alendar's eyes were glittering with a green fire as he turned from the window, and a nameless hunger lay shadowy on his face. He said,

'I might show you others, Earthman. But it could only drive you mad, in the end – you were very near the brink for a moment just now – and I have another use for you … I wonder if you begin to understand, now, the purpose of all this?'

The green glow was fading from that dagger-sharp gaze as the Alendar's eyes stabbed into Smith's. The Earthman gave his head a little shake to clear away the vestiges of that devouring desire, and took a fresh grip on the butt of his gun. The familiar smoothness of it brought him a measure of reassurance, and with it a reawakening to the peril all around. He knew now that there could be no conceivable mercy for him, to whom the innermost secrets of the Minga had been unaccountably revealed. Death was waiting – strange death, as soon as the Alendar wearied of talking – but if he kept his ears open and his eyes alert it might not – please God – catch him so quickly that he died alone. One sweep of that blade-blue flame was all he asked, now. His eyes, keen and hostile, met the dagger-gaze squarely. The Alendar smiled and said.

'Death in your eyes, Earthman. Nothing in your mind but murder. Can that brain of yours comprehend nothing but battle? Is there no curiosity there? Have you no wonder of why I brought you here? Death awaits you, yes. But a not unpleasant death, and it awaits all, in one form or another. Listen, let me tell you – I have reason for desiring to break through that animal shell of self-defense that seals in your mind. Let me look deeper – if there are depths. Your death will be – useful, and in a way, pleasant. Otherwise – well, the black beasts hunger. And flesh must feed them, as a sweeter drink feeds me … Listen.'

Smith's eyes narrowed. A sweeter drink … Danger, danger – the smell of it in the air – instinctively he felt the peril of opening his mind to the plunging gaze of the Alendar, the force of those compelling eyes beating like strong lights into his brain …

'Come,' said the Alendar softly, and moved off soundlessly through the gloom. They followed, Smith painfully alert, the girl walking with lowered, brooding eyes, her mind and soul afar in some wallowing darkness whose shadow showed so hideously beneath her lashes.

The hallway widened to an arch, and abruptly, on the other side, one wall dropped away into infinity and they stood on the dizzy brink of a gallery opening on a black, heaving sea. Smith bit back a startled oath. One moment before the way had led through low-roofed tunnels deep underground; the next instant they stood on the shore of a vast body of rolling darkness, a tiny wind touching their faces with the breath of unnamable things.

Very far below, the dark waters rolled. Phosphorescence lighted them uncertainly, and he was not even sure it was water that surged there in the dark. A heavy thickness seemed to be inherent in the rollers, like black slime surging.

The Alendar looked out over the fire-tinged waves. He waited for an instant without speaking, and then, far out in the slimy surges, something broke the surface with an oily splash, something mercifully veiled in the dark, then dived again, leaving a wake of spreading ripples over the surface.

'Listen,' said the Alendar, without turning his head. 'Life is very old. There are older races than man. Mine is one. Life rose out of the black slime of the sea-bottoms and grew toward the light along many diverging lines. Some reached maturity and deep wisdom when man was still swinging through the jungle trees.

'For many centuries, as mankind counts time, the Alendar has dwelt here, breeding beauty. In later years he has sold some of his lesser beauties, perhaps to explain to mankind's satisfaction what it could never understand were it told the truth. Do you begin to see? My race is very remotely akin to those races which suck blood from man, less remotely to those which drink his life-forces for nourishment. I refine taste even more than that. I drink – beauty. I live on beauty. Yes, literally.'

'Beauty is as tangible as blood, in a way. It is a separate, distinct force that inhabits the bodies of men and women. You must have noticed the vacuity that accompanies perfect beauty in so many women ... the force so strong that it drives out all other forces and lives vampirishly at the expense of intelligence and goodness and conscience and all else.'

'In the beginning, here – for our race was old when this world began, spawned on another planet, and wise and ancient – we woke from slumber in the slime, to feed on the beauty-force inherent in mankind even in cave-dwelling days. But it was meager fare, and we studied the race to determine where the greatest prospects lay, then selected specimens for breeding, built this stronghold and settled down to the business of evolving mankind up to its limit of loveliness. In time we weeded out all but the present type. For the race of man we have developed the ultimate type of loveliness. It is interesting to see what we have accomplished on other worlds, with utterly different races ...'

'Well, there you have it. Women, bred as a spawning-ground for the devouring force of beauty on which we live.'

'But – the fare grows monotonous, as all food must without change. Vaudir I took because I saw in her a sparkle of something that except in very rare instances has been bred out of the Minga girls. For beauty, as I have said, eats up all other qualities but beauty. Yet somehow intelligence and courage survived latently in Vaudir. It decreases her beauty, but the tang of it should be a change from the eternal sameness of the rest. And so I thought until I saw you.'

'I realized then how long it had been since I tasted the beauty of man. It is so rare, so different from female beauty, that I had all but forgotten it existed. And you have it, very subtly, in a raw, harsh way ...'

'I have told you all this to test the quality of that – that harsh beauty in you. Had I been wrong about the deeps of your mind, you would have gone to feed the black beast, but I see that I was not wrong. Behind your animal shell of self-preservation are depths of that force and strength which nourish the roots of male beauty. I think I shall give you a while to let it grow, under the forcing methods I know, before I – drink. It will be delightful . . .'

The voice trailed away in a murmurous silence, the pinpoint glitter sought Smith's eyes. And he tried half-heartedly to avoid it, but his eyes turned involuntarily to the stabbing gaze, and the alertness died out of him, gradually, and the compelling pull of those glittering points in the pits of darkness held him very still.

And as he stared into the diamond glitter he saw its brilliance slowly melt and darken, until the pinpoints of light had changed to pools that dimmed, and he was looking into black evil as elemental and vast as the space between the worlds, a dizzying blankness wherein dwelt unnamable horror . . . deep, deep . . . all about him the darkness was clouding. And thoughts that were not his own seeped into his mind out of that vast, elemental dark . . . crawling, writhing thoughts . . . until he had a glimpse of that dark place where Vaudir's soul wallowed, and something sucked him down and down into a waking nightmare he could not fight . . .

Then somehow the pull broke for an instant. For just that instant he stood again on the shore of the heaving sea and gripped a gun with nerveless fingers – then the darkness closed about him again, but a different, uneasy dark that had not quite the all-compelling power of that other nightmare – it left him strength enough to fight.

And he fought, a desperate, moveless, soundless struggle in a black sea of horror, while worm-thoughts coiled through his straining mind and the clouds rolled and broke and rolled again about him. Sometimes, in the instants when the pull slackened, he had time to feel a third force struggling here between that black, blind downward suck that dragged at him and his own sick, frantic effort to fight clear, a third force that was weakening the black drag so that he had moments of lucidity when he stood free on the brink of the ocean and felt the sweat roll down his face and was aware of his laboring heart and how gaspingly breath tortured his lungs, and he knew he was fighting with every atom of himself, body and mind and soul, against the intangible blackness sucking him down.

And then he felt the force against him gather itself in a final effort – he sensed desperation in that effort – and come rolling over him like a tide. Bowled over, blinded and dumb and deaf, drowning in utter blackness, he floundered in the deeps of that nameless hell where thoughts that were alien and slimy squirmed through his brain. Bodiless he was, and unstable, and as he wallowed there in the ooze more hideous than any earthly ooze, because it came from black, inhuman souls and out of ages before man, he became aware that the worm-thoughts a-squirm in his brain were forming slowly into monstrous meanings – knowledge like a formless flow was pouring through his bodiless brain, knowledge so dreadful that consciously he could not comprehend it, though subconsciously every atom of his mind and soul sickened and writhed futilely away. It was flooding over him, drenching him, permeating him through and through with the very essence of dreadfulness – he felt his mind melting away under the solvent power of it, melting and running fluidly into new channels and fresh molds – horrible molds …

And just at that instant, while madness folded around him and his mind rocked on the verge of annihilation, something snapped, and like a curtain the dark rolled away, and he stood sick and dizzy on the gallery above the black sea. Everything was reeling about him, but they were stable things that shimmered and steadied before his eyes, blessed black rock and tangible surges that had form and body – his feet pressed firmness and his mind shook itself and was clean and his own again.

And then through the haze of weakness that still shrouded him a voice was shrieking wildly, 'Kill! … kill!' and he saw the Alendar staggering against the rail, all his outlines unaccountably blurred and uncertain, and behind him Vaudir with blazing eyes and face wrenched hideously into life again, screaming 'Kill!' in a voice scarcely human.

Like an independent creature his gun-hand leaped up – he had gripped that gun through everything that happened – and he was dimly aware of the hardness of it kicking back against his hand with the recoil, and of the blue flash flaming from its muzzle. It struck the Alendar's dark figure full, and there was a hiss and a dazzle …

Smith closed his eyes tight and opened them again, and stared with a sick incredulity; for unless that struggle had unhinged his brain after all, and the worm-thoughts still dwelt slimily in his mind, tingeing all he saw with unearthly horror – unless this was true, he was looking not at a man just rayed through the lungs, and who should be dropping now in a bleeding, collapsed heap to the floor, but at – at – God, what *was* it? The dark figure had slumped against the rail, and instead of blood gushing, a hideous, nameless, formless black poured sluggishly forth – a slime like the heaving sea below. The whole dark figure of the man was melting, slumping farther down into the pool of blackness forming at his feet on the stone floor.

Smith gripped his gun and watched in numb incredulity, and the whole body sank slowly down and melted and lost all form – hideously, gruesomely – until where the Alendar had stood a heap of slime lay viscidly on the gallery floor, hideously alive, heaving and rippling and striving to lift itself into a semblance of humanity again. And as he watched, it lost even that form, and the edges melted revoltingly and the mass flattened and slid down into a pool of utter horror, and he became aware that it was pouring slowly through the rails into the sea. He stood watching while the whole rolling, shimmering mound melted and thinned and trickled through the bars, until the floor was clear again, and not even a stain marred the stone.

A painful constriction of his lungs roused him, and he realized he had been holding his breath, scarcely daring to realize. Vaudir had collapsed against the wall, and he saw her knees give limply, and staggered forward on uncertain feet to catch her as she fell.

'Vaudir, Vaudir!' he shook her gently. 'Vaudir, what's happened? Am I dreaming? Are we safe now? Are you – awake again?'

Very slowly her white lids lifted, and the black eyes met his. And he saw shadowily there the knowledge of that wallowing void he had dimly known, the shadow that could never be cleared away. She was steeped and foul with it. And the look of her eyes was such that involuntarily he released her and stepped away. She staggered a little and then regained her balance and regarded him from under bent brows. The level inhumanity of her gaze struck into his soul, and yet he thought he saw a spark of the girl she had been, dwelling in torture amid the blackness. He knew he was right when she said, in a far-away, toneless voice,

'Awake? ... No, not ever now, Earthman. I have been down too deeply into hell ... he had dealt me a worse torture than he knew, for there is just enough humanity left within me to realize what I have become, and to suffer ...'

'Yes, he is gone, back into the slime that bred him. I have been a part of him, one with him in the blackness of his soul, and I know. I have spent eons since the blackness came upon me, dwelt for eternities in the dark, rolling seas of his mind, sucking in knowledge ... and I was one with him, and he now gone, so shall I die; yet I will see you safely out of here if it is in my power, for it was I who dragged you in. If I can remember – if I can find the way ...'

She turned uncertainly and staggered a step back along the way they had come. Smith sprang forward and slid his free arm about her, but she shuddered away from the contact.

'No, no – unbearable – the touch of clean human flesh – and it breaks the chord of my remembering ... I can not look back into his mind as it was when I dwelt there, and I must, I must ...'

She shook him off and reeled on, and he cast one last look at the billowing sea, and then followed. She staggered along the stone floor on stumbling feet, one hand to the wall to support herself, and her voice was whispering gustily, so that he had to follow close to hear, and then almost wished he had not heard.

'—black slime – darkness feeding on light – everything wavers so – slime, slime and a rolling sea – he rose out of it, you know, before civilization began here – he is age-old – there never has been but one Alendar ... And somehow – I could not see just how, or remember why – he rose from the rest, as some of his race on other planets had done, and took the man-form and stocked his breeding-pens ...'

They went on up the dark hallway, past curtains hiding incarnate loveliness, and the girl's stumbling footsteps kept time to her stumbling, half-incoherent words.

'—has lived all these ages here, breeding and devouring beauty – vampire-thirst, a hideous delight in drinking in that beauty-force – I felt it and remembered it when I was one with him – wrapping black layers of primal slime about – quenching human loveliness in ooze, sucking – blind black thirst ... And his wisdom was ancient and dreadful and full of power – so he could draw a soul out through the eyes and sink it in hell, and drown it there, as he would have done mine if I had not had, somehow, a difference from the rest. Great Shar, I wish I had not! I wish I were drowned in it and did not feel in every atom of me the horrible uncleanness of – what I know. But by virtue of that hidden strength I did not surrender wholly, and when he had turned his power to subduing you I was able to struggle, there in the very heart of his mind, making a disturbance that shook him as he fought us both – making it possible to free you long enough for you to destroy the human flesh he was clothed in – so that he lapsed into the ooze again. I do not quite understand why that happened – only that his weakness with you assailing him from without and me struggling strongly in the very center of his soul was such that he was forced to draw on the power he had built up to maintain himself in the man form, and weakened it enough so that he collapsed when the man form was assailed. And he fell back into the slime again – whence he rose – black slime – heaving – oozing ...'

Her voice trailed away in murmurs, and she stumbled, all but falling. When she regained her balance she went on ahead of him at a greater distance, as if his very nearness were repugnant to her, and the soft babble of her voice drifted back in broken phrases without meaning.

Presently the air began to tingle again, and they passed the silver gate and entered that gallery where the air sparkled like champagne. The blue pool lay jewel-clear in its golden setting. Of the girls there was no sign.

When they reached the head of the gallery the girl paused, turning to him a face twisted with the effort at memory.

'Here is the trail,' she said urgently. 'If I can remember—' She seized her head in clutching hands, shaking it savagely. 'I haven't the strength, now – can't – can't—' the piteous little murmur reached his ears incoherently. Then she straightened resolutely, swaying a little, and faced him, holding out her hands. He clasped them hesitantly, and saw a shiver go through her at the contact, and her face contort painfully, and then a shudder communicated itself through that clasp and he too winced in revolt. He saw her eyes go blank and her face strain in lines of tensity, and a fine dew broke out on her forehead. For a long moment she stood so, her face like death, and strong shudders went over her body and her eyes were blank as the void between the planets.

And as each shudder swept her it went unbroken through the clasping of their hands to him, and they were black waves of dreadfulness, and again he saw the heaving sea and wallowed in the hell he had fought out of on the gallery, and he knew for the first time what torture she must be enduring who dwelt in the very deeps of that uneasy dark. The pulses came faster, and for moments together he went down into the blind blackness and the slime, and felt the first wriggling of the worm-thoughts tickling the roots of his brain …

And then suddenly a clean darkness closed round them and again everything shifted unaccountably, as if the atoms of the gallery were changing, and when Smith opened his eyes he was standing once more in the dark, slanting corridor with the smell of salt and antiquity heavy in the air.

Vaudir moaned softly beside him, and he turned to see her reeling against the wall and trembling so from head to foot that he looked to see her fall the next moment.

'Better – in a moment,' she gasped. 'It took – nearly all my strength to – to get us through – wait …'

So they halted there in the darkness and the dead salt air, until the trembling abated a little and she said, 'Come,' in her little whimpering voice. And again the journey began. It was only a short way, now, to the barrier of black blankness that guarded the door into the room where they had first seen the Alendar. When they reached the place she shivered a little and paused, then resolutely held out her hands. And as he took then he felt once more the hideous slimy waves course through him, and plunged again into the heaving hell. And as before the clean darkness flashed over them in a breath, and then she dropped his hands and they were standing in the archway looking into the velvet-hung room they had left – it seemed eons ago.

He watched as waves of blinding weakness flooded over her from that supreme effort. Death was visible in her face as she turned to him at last.

'Come – oh, come quickly,' she whispered, and staggered forward.

At her heels he followed, across the room, past the great iron gateway, down the hall to the foot of the silver stairs. And here his heart sank, for he felt sure she could never climb the long spiral distances to the top. But she set her foot on the step and went upward resolutely, and as he followed he heard her murmuring to herself.

'Wait – oh, wait – let me reach the end – let me undo this much – and then – no, no! Please Shar, not the black slime again … Earthman, Earthman!'

She paused on the stair and turned to face him, and her haggard face was frantic with desperation and despair.

'Earthman, promise – do not let me die like this! When we reach the end, ray me! Burn me clean, or I shall go down for eternity into the black sinks from which I dragged you free. Oh, promise!'

'I will,' Smith's voice said quietly. 'I will.'

And they went on. Endlessly the stairs spiraled upward and endlessly they climbed. Smith's legs began to ache intolerably, and his heart was pounding like a wild thing, but Vaudir seemed not to notice weariness. She climbed steadily and no more unsurely than she had come along the halls. And after eternities they reached the top.

And there the girl fell. She dropped like a dead woman at the head of the silver spiral. Smith thought for a sick instant that he had failed her and let her die uncleansed, but in a moment or two she stirred and lifted her head and very slowly dragged herself to her feet.

'I will go on – I will, I will,' she whispered to herself, '—come this far – must finish—' and she reeled off down the lovely, rosily-lit hallway paneled in pearl.

He could see how perilously near she was to her strength's end, and he marveled at the tenacity with which she clung to life though it ebbed away with every breath and the pulse of darkness flowed in after it. So with bulldog stubbornness she made her wavering way past door after door of carven shell, under rosy lights that flushed her face with a ghastly mockery of health, until they reached the silver gateway at the end. The lock had been removed from it by now, and the bar drawn.

She tugged open the gate and stumbled through.

And the nightmare journey went on. It must be very near morning, Smith thought, for the halls were deserted, but did he not sense a breath of danger in the still air? …

The girl's gasping voice answered that half-formed query as if, like the Alendar, she held the secret of reading men's minds.

'The – Guardians – still rove the halls, and unleashed now – so keep your ray-gun ready, Earthman …'

After that he kept his eyes alert as they retraced, stumbling and slow, the steps he had taken on his way in. And once he heard distinctly the soft slither of – something – scraping over the marble pavement, and twice he smelt with shocking suddenness in this scented air a whiff of salt, and his mind flashed back to a rolling black sea … But nothing molested them.

Step by faltering step the hallways fell behind them, and he began to recognize landmarks, and the girl's footsteps staggered and hesitated and went on gallantly, incredibly, beating back oblivion, fighting the dark surges rolling over her, clinging with tenacious fingers to the tiny spark of life that drove her on.

And at long last, after what seemed hours of desperate effort, they reached the blue-lit hallway at whose end the outer door opened. Vaudir's progress down it was a series of dizzy staggers, interspersed with pauses while she hung to the carven doors with tense fingers and drove her teeth into a bloodless lip and gripped that last flicker of life. He saw the shudders sweep over her, and knew what waves of washing dark must be rising all about her, and how the worm-thoughts writhed through her brain ... But she went on. Every step now was a little tripping, as if she fell from one foot to the other, and at each step he expected that knee to give way and pitch her down into the black deeps that yawned for her. But she went on.

She reached the bronze door, and with a last spurt of effort she lifted the bar and swung it open. Then that tiny spark flickered out like a lamp. Smith caught one flash of the rock room within – and something horrible on the floor – before he saw her pitch forward as the rising tide of slimy oblivion closed at last over her head. She was dying as she fell, and he whipped the ray-gun up and felt the recoil against his palm as a blue blaze flashed forth and transfixed her in midair. And he could have sworn her eyes lighted for a flickering instant and the gallant girl he had known looked forth, cleansed and whole, before death – clean death – glazed them.

She slumped down in a huddle at his feet, and he felt a sting of tears beneath his eyelids as he looked down on her, a huddle of white and bronze on the rug. And as he watched, a film of defilement veiled the shining whiteness of her – decay set in before his eyes and progressed with horrible swiftness, and in less time than it takes to tell he was staring with horrified eyes at a pool of black slime across which green velvet lay bedraggled.

Northwest Smith closed his pale eyes, and for a moment struggled with memory, striving to wrest from it the long-forgotten words of a prayer learned a score of years ago on another planet. Then he stepped over the pitiful, horrible heap on the carpet and went on.

In the little rock room of the outer wall he saw what he had glimpsed when Vaudir opened the door. Retribution had overtaken the eunuch. The body must have been his, for tatters of scarlet velvet lay about the floor, but there was no way to recognize what its original form had been. The smell of salt was heavy in the air, and a trail of black slime snaked across the floor toward the wall. The wall was solid, but it ended there ...

Smith laid his hand on the outer door, drew the bar, swung it open. He stepped out under the hanging vines and filled his lungs with pure air, free, clear, untainted with scent or salt. A pearly dawn was breaking over Ednes.

SCARLET DREAM

1

Northwest Smith bought the shawl in the Lakkmanda Markets of Mars. It was one of his chiefest joys to wander through the stalls and stands of that greatest of marketplaces whose wares are drawn from all the planets of the solar system, and beyond. So many songs have been sung and so many tales written of that fascinating chaos called the Lakkmanda Markets that there is little need to detail it here.

He shouldered his way through the colorful cosmopolitan throng, the speech of a thousand races beating in his ears, the mingled odors of perfume and sweat and spice and food and the thousand nameless smells of the place assailing his nostrils. Vendors cried their wares in the tongues of a score of worlds.

As he strolled through the thick of the crowd, savoring the confusion and the odors and the sights from lands beyond counting, his eye was caught by a flash of that peculiar geranium scarlet that seems to lift itself bodily from its background and smite the eye with all but physical violence. It came from a shawl thrown carelessly across a carved chest, typically Martian drylander work by the exquisite detail of that carving, so oddly at variance with the characteristics of the harsh dryland race. He recognized the Venusian origin of the brass tray on the shawl, and knew the heap of carved ivory beasts that the tray held as the work of one of the least known races on Jupiter's largest moon, but from all his wide experience he could draw no remembrance of any such woven work as that of the shawl. Idly curious, he paused at the booth and asked of its attendant,

'How much for the scarf?'

The man – he was a canal Martian – glanced over his shoulder and said carelessly, 'Oh, that. You can have it for half a *cris* – gives me a headache to look at the thing.'

Smith grinned and said, 'I'll give you five dollars.'

'Ten.'

'Six and a half, and that's my last offer.'

'Oh, take the thing.' The Martian smiled and lifted the tray of ivory beasts from the chest.

Smith drew out the shawl. It clung to his hands like a live thing, softer and lighter than Martian 'lamb's-wool.' He felt sure it was woven from the hair of some beast rather than from vegetable fiber, for the electric clinging of it sparkled with life. And the crazy pattern dazzled him with its utter strangeness. Unlike any pattern he had seen in all the years of his far wanderings, the wild, leaping scarlet threaded its nameless design in one continuous, tangled line through the twilight blue of the background. That dim blue was clouded exquisitely with violet and green – sleepy evening colors against which the staring scarlet flamed like something more sinister and alive than color. He felt that he could almost put his hand between the color and the cloth, so vividly did it start up from its background.

'Where in the universe did this come from?' he demanded of the attendant.

The man shrugged.

'Who knows? It came in with a bale of scrap cloth from New York. I was a little curious about it myself, and called the market-master there to trace it. He says it was sold for scrap by the down-and-out Venusian who claimed he'd found it in a derelict ship floating around one of the asteroids. He didn't know what nationality the ship had been – a very early model, he said, probably one of the first space-ships, made before the identification symbols were adopted. I've wondered why he sold the thing for scrap. He could have got double the price, anyhow, if he'd made any effort.'

'Funny.' Smith stared down at the dizzy pattern writhing through the cloth in his hands. 'Well, it's warm and light enough. If it doesn't drive me crazy trying to follow the pattern, I'll sleep warm at night.'

He crumpled it in one hand, the whole six-foot square of it folding easily into his palm, and stuffed the silky bundle into his pocket – and thereupon forgot it until after his return to his quarters that evening.

He had taken one of the cubical steel rooms in the great steel lodging-houses the Martian government offers for a very nominal rent to transients. The original purpose was to house those motley hordes of spacemen that swarm every port city of the civilized planets, offering them accommodations cheap and satisfactory enough so that they will not seek the black byways of the town and there fall in with the denizens of the Martian underworld whose lawlessness is a byword among space sailors.

The great steel building that housed Smith and countless others was not entirely free from the influences of Martian byways, and if the police had actually searched the place with any degree of thoroughness a large percentage of its dwellers might have been transferred to the Emperor's prisons – Smith almost certainly among them, for his activities were rarely within the law and though he could not recall at the moment any particularly flagrant sins committed in Lakkdarol, a charge could certainly have been found against him by the most half-hearted searcher. However, the likelihood of a police raid was very remote, and Smith, as he went in under the steel portals of the great door, rubbed shoulders with smugglers and pirates and fugitives and sinners of all the sins that keep the spaceways thronged.

In his little cubicle he switched on the light and saw a dozen blurred replicas of himself, reflected dimly in the steel walls, spring into being with the sudden glow. In that curious company he moved forward to a chair and pulled out the crumpled shawl. Shaking it in the mirror-walled room produced a sudden wild writhing of scarlet patterns over walls and floor and ceiling, and for an instant the room whirled in an inexplicable kaleidoscope and he had the impression that the four-dimensional walls had opened suddenly to undreamed-of vastnesses where living scarlet in wild, unruly patterns shivered through the void.

Then in a moment the walls closed in again and the dim reflections quieted and became only the images of a tall, brown man with pale eyes, holding a curious shawl in his hands. There was a strange, sensuous pleasure in the clinging of the silky wool to his fingers, the lightness of it, the warmth. He spread it out on the table and traced the screaming scarlet pattern with his finger, trying to follow that one writhing line through the intricacies of its path, and the more he stared the more irritatingly clear it became to him that there must be a purpose in that whirl of color, that if he stared long enough, surely he must trace it out …

When he slept that night he spread the bright shawl across his bed, and the brilliance of it colored his dreams fantastically …

That threading scarlet was a labyrinthine path down which he stumbled blindly, and at every turn he looked back and saw himself in myriad replicas, always wandering lost and alone through the pattern of the path. Sometimes it shook itself under his feet, and whenever he thought he saw the end it would writhe into fresh intricacies …

The sky was a great shawl threaded with scarlet lightning that shivered and squirmed as he watched, then wound itself into the familiar, dizzy pattern that became one mighty Word in a nameless writing, whose meaning he shuddered on the verge of understanding, and woke in icy terror just before the significance of it broke upon his brain …

He slept again, and saw the shawl hanging in a blue dusk the color of its background, stared and stared until the square of it melted imperceptibly into the dimness and the scarlet was a pattern incised lividly upon a gate … a gate of strange outline in a high wall, half seen through that curious, cloudy twilight blurred with exquisite patches of green and violet, so that it seemed no mortal twilight, but some strange and lovely evening in a land where the air was suffused with colored mists, and no winds blew. He felt himself moving forward, without effort, and the gate opened before him …

He was mounting a long flight of steps. In one of the metamorphoses of dreams it did not surprise him that the gate had vanished, or that he had no remembrance of having climbed the long flight stretching away behind him. The lovely colored twilight still veiled the air, so that he could see but dimly the steps rising before him and melting into the mist.

And now, suddenly, he was aware of a stirring in the dimness, and a girl came flying down the stairs in headlong, stumbling terror. He could see the shadow of it on her face, and her long, bright-colored hair streamed out behind her, and from head to foot she was dabbled with blood. In her blind flight she must not have seen him, for she came plunging downward three steps at a time and blundered full into him as he stood undecided, watching. The impact all but unbalanced him, but his arms closed instinctively about her and for a moment she hung in his embrace, utterly spent, gasping against his broad leather breast and too breathless even to wonder who had stopped her. The smell of fresh blood rose to his nostrils from her dreadfully spattered garments.

Finally she lifted her head and raised a flushed, creamy-brown face to him, gulping in air through lips the color of holly berries. Her dabbled hair, so fantastically golden that it might have been almost orange, shivered about her as she clung to him with lifted, lovely face. In that dizzy moment he saw that her eyes were sherry-brown with tints of red, and the fantastic, colored beauty of her face had a wild tinge of something utterly at odds with anything he had ever known before. It might have been the look in her eyes …

'Oh!' she gasped. 'It – it has her! Let me go! … Let me—' Smith shook her gently.

'What has her?' he demanded. 'Who? Listen to me! You're covered with blood, do you know it? Are you hurt?'

She shook her head wildly.

'No – no – let me go! I must – not my blood – hers …'

She sobbed on the last word, and suddenly collapsed in his arms, weeping with a violet intensity that shook her from head to foot. Smith gazed helplessly about over the orange head, then gathered the shaking girl in his arms and went up the steps through the violent gloaming.

He must have climbed for all of five minutes before the twilight thinned a little and he saw that the stairs ended at the head of a long hallway, high-arched like a cathedral aisle. A row of low doors ran down one side of the hall, and he turned aside at random into the nearest. It gave upon a gallery whose arches opened into blue space. A low bench ran along the wall under the gallery windows, and he crossed it, gently setting down the sobbing girl and supporting her against his shoulder.

'My sister,' she wept. 'It has her – oh, my sister!'

'Don't cry, don't cry,' Smith heard his own voice saying, surprisingly. 'It's all a dream, you know. Don't cry – there never was any sister – you don't exist at all – don't cry so.'

She jerked her head up at that, startled out of her sobs for a moment, and stared at him with sherry-brown eyes drowned in tears. Her lashes clung together in wet, starry points. She stared with searching eyes, taking in the leather-brownness of him, his spaceman's suit, his scarred dark face and eyes paler than steel. And then a look of infinite pity softened the strangeness of her face, and she said gently,

'Oh … you come from – from – you still believe that you dream!'

'I *know* I'm dreaming,' persisted Smith childishly. 'I'm lying asleep in Lakkdarol and dreaming of you, and all this, and when I wake—'

She shook her head sadly.

'You will never wake. You have come into a more deadly dream than you could ever guess. There is no waking from this land.'

'What do you mean? Why not?' A little absurd pity was starting up in his mind at the sorrow and the pity in her voice, the sureness of her words. Yet this was one of those rare dreams wherein he knew quite definitely that he dreamed. He could not be mistaken …

'There are many dream countries,' she said, 'many nebulous, unreal half-lands where the souls of sleepers wander, places that have an actual, tenuous existence, if one knows the way … But here – it has happened before, you see – one may not blunder without passing a door that opens one way only. And he who has the key to open it may come through, but he can never find the way into his own waking land again. Tell me – what key opened the door to you?'

'The shawl,' Smith murmured. 'The shawl … of course. That damnable red pattern, dizzy—'

He passed a hand across his eyes, for the memory of it, writhing, alive, searingly scarlet, burned behind his eyelids.

'What was it?' she demanded, breathlessly, he thought, as if a half-hopeless eagerness forced the question from her lips. 'Can you remember?'

'A red pattern,' he said slowly, 'a thread of bright scarlet woven into a blue shawl – nightmare pattern – painted on the gate I came by … but it's only a dream, of course. In a few minutes I'll wake …'

She clutched his knee excitedly.

'Can you remember?' she demanded. 'The pattern – the red pattern? The Word?'

'Word?' he wondered stupidly. 'Word – in the sky? No – no, I don't want to remember – crazy pattern, you know. Can't forget it – but no, I couldn't tell you what it was, or trace it for you. Never was anything like it – thank God. It was on that shawl …'

'Woven on a shawl,' she murmured to herself. 'Yes, of course. But how you ever came by it, in your world – when it – when *it* – oh!'

Memory of whatever tragedy had sent her flying down the stairs swept back in a flood, and her face crumbled into tears again. 'My sister!'

'Tell me what happened.' Smith woke from his daze at the sound of her sob. 'Can't I help? Please let me try – tell me about it.'

'My sister,' she said faintly. 'It caught her in the hall – caught her before my eyes – spattered me with her blood. Oh! ...'

'It?' puzzled Smith. 'What? Is there danger?' and his hand moved instinctively toward his gun.

She caught the gesture and smiled a little scornfully through her tears.

'It,' she said. 'The – the Thing. No gun can harm it, no man can fight it – It came, and that was all.'

'But what is it? What does it look like? Is it near?'

'It's everywhere. One never knows – until the mist begins to thicken and the pulse of red shows through – and then it's too late. We do not fight it, or think of it overmuch – life would be unbearable. For it hungers and must be fed, and we who feed it strive to live as happily as we may know before the Thing comes for us. But one can never know.'

'Where did it come from? What is it?'

'No one knows – it has always been there – always will be ... too nebulous to die or be killed – a Thing out of some alien place we couldn't understand, I suppose – somewhere so long ago, or in some such unthinkable dimension that we will never have any knowledge of its origin. But as I say, we try not to think.'

'If it eats flesh,' said Smith stubbornly, 'it must be vulnerable – and I have my gun.'

'Try if you like,' she shrugged. 'Others have tried – and it still comes. It dwells here, we believe, if it dwells anywhere. We are – taken – more often in these halls than elsewhere. When you are weary of life you might bring your gun and wait under this roof. You may not have long to wait.'

'I'm not ready to try the experiment just yet,' Smith grinned. 'If the Thing lives here, why do you come?'

She shrugged again, apathetically. 'If we do not, it will come after us when it hungers. And we come here for – for our food.' She shot him a curious glance from under lowered lids. 'You wouldn't understand. But as you say, it's a dangerous place. We'd best go now – you will come with me, won't you? I shall be lonely now.' And her eyes brimmed again.

'Of course. I'm sorry, my dear. I'll do what I can for you – until I wake.' He grinned at the fantastic sound of this.

'You will not wake,' she said quietly. 'Better not to hope, I think. You are trapped here with the rest of us and here you must stay until you die.'

He rose and held out his hand.

'Let's go, then,' he said. 'Maybe you're right, but – well, come on.'

*

She took his hand and jumped up. The orange hair, too fantastically colored for anything outside a dream, swung about her brilliantly. He saw now that she wore a single white garment, brief and belted, over the creamy brownness of her body. It was torn now, and hideously stained. She made a picture of strange and vivid loveliness, all white and gold and bloody, in the misted twilight of the gallery.

'Where are we going?' she asked Smith. 'Out there?' And he nodded toward the blueness beyond the windows.

She drew her shoulders together in a little shudder of distaste. 'Oh, no,' she said.

'What is it?'

'Listen.' She took him by the arms and lifted a serious face to his. 'If you must stay here – and you must, for there is only one way out save death, and that is a worse way even than dying – you must learn to ask no questions about the – the Temple. This is the Temple. Here it dwells. Here we – feed.

'There are halls we know, and we keep to them. It is wiser. You saved my life when you stopped me on those stairs – no one has ever gone down into that mist and darkness, and returned. I should have known, seeing you climb them, that you were not of us … for whatever lies beyond, wherever that stairway leads – it is better not to know. It is better not to look out the windows of this place. We have learned that, too. For from the outside the Temple looks strange enough, but from the inside, looking out, one is liable to see things it is better not to see … What that blue space is, on which this gallery opens, I do not know – I have no wish to know. There are windows here opening on stranger things than this – but we turn our eyes away when we pass them. You will learn …'

She took his hand, smiling a little.

'Come with me, now.'

And in silence they left the gallery opening on space and went down the hall where the blue mist floated so beautifully with its clouds of violet and green confusing the eye, and a great stillness all about.

The hallways led straight, as nearly as he could see, for the floating clouds veiled it, toward the great portals of the Temple. In the form of a mighty triple arch it opened out of the clouded twilight upon a shining day like no day he had ever seen on any planet. The light came from no visible source, and there was a lucid quality about it, nebulous but unmistakable, as if one were looking through the depths of a crystal, or through clear water that trembled a little now and then. It was diffused through the translucent day from a sky as shining and unfamiliar as everything else in this amazing dreamland.

They stood under the great arch of the Temple, looking out over the shining land beyond. Afterward he could never quite remember what had made it so unutterably strange, so indefinably dreadful. There were trees, feathery masses of green and bronze above the bronze-green grass; the bright air shimmered, and through the leaves he caught the glimmer of water not far away. At first glance it seemed a perfectly normal scene – yet tiny details caught his eyes that sent ripples of coldness down his back. The grass, for instance …

When they stepped down upon it and began to cross the meadow toward the trees beyond which water gleamed, he saw that the blades were short and soft as fur, and they seemed to cling to his companion's bare feet as she walked. As he looked out over the meadow he saw that long waves of it, from every direction, were rippling toward them as if the wind blew from all sides at once toward the common center that was themselves. Yet no wind blew.

'It – it's alive,' he stammered, startled. 'The grass!'

'Yes, of course,' she said indifferently.

And then he realized that though the feathery fronds of the trees waved now and then, gracefully together, there was no wind. And they did not sway in one direction only, but by twos and threes in many ways, dipping and rising with a secret, contained life of their own.

When they reached the belt of woodland he looked up curiously and heard the whisper and rustle of leaves above him, bending down as if in curiosity as the two passed beneath. They never bent far enough to touch them, but a sinister air of watchfulness, of aliveness, brooded over the whole uncannily alive landscape, and the ripples of the grass followed them wherever they went.

The lake, like that twilight in the Temple, was a sleepy blue clouded with violet and green, not like real water, for the colored blurs did not diffuse or change as it rippled.

On the shore, a little above the water line, stood a tiny, shrine-like building of some creamy stone, its walls no more than a series of arches open to the blue, translucent day. The girl led him to the doorway and gestured within negligently.

'I live here,' she said.

Smith stared. It was quite empty save for two low couches with a blue coverlet thrown across each. Very classic it looked, with its whiteness and austerity, the arches opening on a vista of woodland and grass beyond.

'Doesn't it ever get cold?' he asked. 'Where do you eat? Where are your books and food and clothes?'

'I have some spare tunics under my couch,' she said. 'That's all. No books, no other clothing, no food. We feed at the Temple. It is never any colder or warmer than this.'

'But what do you do?'

'Do? Oh, swim in the lake, sleep and rest and wander through the woods. Times passes very quickly.'

'Idyllic,' murmured Smith, 'But rather tiresome, I should think.'

'When one knows,' she said, 'that the next moment may be one's last, life is savored to the full. One stretches the hours out as long as possible. No, for us it is not tiresome.'

'But have you no cities? Where are the other people?'

'It is best not to collect in crowds. Somehow they seem to draw – it. We live in twos and threes – sometimes alone. We have no cities. We do nothing – what purpose in beginning anything when we know we shall not live to end it? Why even think too long of one thing? Come down to the lake.'

She took his hand and led him across the clinging grass to the sandy brink of the water, and they sank in silence on the narrow beach. Smith looked out over the lake where vague colors misted the blue, trying not to think of the fantastic things that were happening to him. Indeed, it was hard to do much thinking, here, in the midst of the blueness and the silence, the very air dreamy about them ... the cloudy water lapping the shore with tiny, soft sounds like the breathing of a sleeper. The place was heavy with the stillness and the dreamy colors, and Smith was never sure, afterward, whether in his dream he did not sleep for a while; for presently he heard a stir at his side and the girl reseated herself, clad in a fresh tunic, all the blood washed away. He could not remember her having left, but it did not trouble him.

The light had for some time been sinking and blurring, and imperceptibly a cloudy blue twilight closed about them, seeming somehow to rise from the blurring lake, for it partook of that same dreamy blueness clouded with vague colors. Smith thought that he could be content never to rise again from that cool sand, to sit here for ever in the blurring twilight and the silence of his dream. How long he did sit there he never knew. The blue peace enfolded him utterly, until he was steeped in its misty evening colors and permeated through and through with the tranced quiet.

The darkness had deepened until he could no longer see any more than the nearest wavelets lapping the sand. Beyond, and all about, the dream-world melted into the violet-misted blueness of the twilight. He was not aware that he had turned his head, but presently he found himself looking down on the girl beside him. She was lying on the pale sand, her hair a fan of darkness to frame the pallor of her face. In the twilight her mouth was dark too, and from the darkness under her lashes he slowly became aware that she was watching him unwinkingly.

For a long while he sat there, gazing down, meeting the half-hooded eyes in silence. And presently, with the effortless detachment of one who moves in a dream, he bent down to meet her lifting arms. The sand was cool and sweet, and her mouth tasted faintly of blood.

2

There was no surprise in that land. Lucid day brightened slowly over the breathing landscape, and grass and trees stirred with wakening awareness, rather horribly in the beauty of the morning. When Smith woke, he saw the girl coming up from the lake, shaking blue water from her orange hair. Blue droplets clung to the creaminess of her skin, and she was laughing and flushed from head to foot in the glowing dawn.

Smith sat up on his couch and pushed back the blue coverlet.

'I'm hungry,' he said. 'When and what do we eat?'

The laughter vanished from her face in a breath. She gave her hair a troubled shake and said doubtfully,

'Hungry?'

'Yes, starved! Didn't you say you get your food at the Temple? Let's go up there.'

She sent him a sidelong, enigmatic glance from under her lashes as she turned aside.

'Very well,' she said.

'Anything wrong?' He reached out as she passed and pulled her to his knee, kissing the troubled mouth lightly. And again he tasted blood.

'Oh, no.' She ruffled his hair and rose. 'I'll be ready in a moment, and then we'll go.'

And so again they passed the belt of woods where the trees bent down to watch, and crossed the rippling grassland. From all directions long waves of it came blowing toward them as before, and the fur-like blades clung to their feet. Smith tried not to notice. Everywhere, he was seeing this morning, an undercurrent of nameless unpleasantness ran beneath the surface of this lovely land.

As they crossed the live grass a memory suddenly returned to him, and he said, 'What did you mean, yesterday, when you said that there was a way – out – other than death?'

She did not meet his eyes as she answered, in that troubled voice, 'Worse than dying, I said. A way out we do not speak of here.'

'But if there's any way at all, I must know of it,' he persisted. 'Tell me.'

She swept the orange hair like a veil between them, bending her head and saying indistinctly, 'A way out you could not take. Away too costly. And – and I do not wish you to go, now . . .'

'I must know,' said Smith relentlessly.

She paused then, and stood looking up at him, her sherry-colored eyes disturbed.

'By the way you came,' she said at last. 'By virtue of the Word. But that gate is impassable.'

'Why?'

'It is death to pronounce the Word. Literally. I do not know it now, could not speak it if I would. But in the Temple there is one room where the Word is graven in scarlet on the wall, and its power is so great that the echoes of it ring for ever round and round that room. If one stands before the graven symbol and lets the force of it beat upon his brain he will hear, and know – and shriek the awful syllables aloud – and so die. It is a word from some tongue so alien to all our being that the spoken sound of it, echoing in the throat of a living man, is disrupting enough to rip the very fibers of the human body apart – to blast its atoms asunder, to destroy body and mind as utterly as if they had never been. And because the sound is so disruptive it somehow blasts open for an instant the door between your world and mine. But the danger is dreadful, for it may open the door to other worlds too, and let things through more terrible than we can dream of. Some say it was thus that the Thing gained access to our land eons ago. And if you are not standing exactly where the door opens, on the one spot in the room that is protected, as the center of a whirlwind is quiet, and if you do not pass instantly out of the sound of the Word, it will blast you asunder as it does the one who has pronounced it for you. So you see how impos—' Here she broke off with a little scream and glanced down in half-laughing annoyance, then took two or three little running steps and turned.

'The grass,' she explained ruefully, pointing to her feet. The brown bareness of them was dotted with scores of tiny bloodspots. 'If one stands too long in one place, barefoot, it will pierce the skin and drink – stupid of me to forget. But come.'

Smith went on at her side, looking round with new eyes upon the lovely, pellucid land, too beautiful and frightening for anything outside a dream. All about them the hungry grass came hurrying in long, converging waves as they advanced. Were the trees, then, flesh-eating too? Cannibal trees and vampire grass – he shuddered a little and looked ahead.

The Temple stood tall before them, a building of some nameless material as mistily blue as far-off mountains on the Earth. The mistiness did not condense or clarify as they approached, and the outlines of the place were mysteriously hard to fix in mind – he could never understand, afterward, just why. When he tried too hard to concentrate on one particular corner or tower or window it blurred before his eyes as if the focus were at fault – as if the whole strange, veiled building stood just on the borderland of another dimension.

From the immense triple arch of the doorway, as they approached – a triple arch like nothing he had ever seen before, so irritatingly hard to focus upon that he could not be sure just wherein its difference lay – a pale blue mist issued smokily. And when they stopped within they walked into that twilight dimness he was coming to know so well.

The great hall lay straight and veiled before them, but after a few steps the girl drew him aside and under another archway, into a long gallery through whose drifting haze he could see rows of men and women kneeling against the wall with bowed heads, as if in prayer. She led him down the line to the end, and he saw then that they knelt before small spigots curving up from the wall at regular intervals. She dropped to her knees before one and, motioning him to follow, bent her head and laid her lips to the up-curved spout. Dubiously he followed her example.

Instantly with the touch of his mouth on the nameless substance of the spigot something hot and, strangely, at once salty and sweet flowed into his mouth. There was an acridity about it that gave a curious tang, and the more he drank the more avid he became. Hauntingly delicious it was, and warmth flowed through him more strongly with every draft. Yet somewhere deep within him memory stirred unpleasantly … somewhere, somehow, he had known this hot, acrid, salty taste before, and – suddenly suspicions struck him like a bludgeon, and he jerked his lips from the spout as if it burnt. A tiny thread of scarlet trickled from the wall. He passed the back of one hand across his lips and brought it away red. He knew that odor, then.

The girl knelt beside him with closed eyes, rapt avidity in every line of her. When he seized her shoulder she twitched away and opened protesting eyes, but did not lift her lips from the spigot. Smith gestured violently, and with one last long draft she rose and turned a half-angry face to his, but laid a finger on her reddened lips.

He followed her in silence past the kneeling lines again. When they reached the hall outside he swung upon her and gripped her shoulders angrily.

'What was that?' he demanded.

Her eyes slid away. She shrugged.

'What were you expecting? We feed as we must, here. You'll learn to drink without a qualm – if it does not come for you too soon.'

A moment longer he stared angrily down into her evasive, strangely lovely face. Then he turned without a word and strode down the hallway through the drifting mists toward the door. He heard her bare feet pattering along behind hurriedly, but he did not look back. Not until he had come out into the glowing day and half crossed the grasslands did he relent enough to glance around. She paced at his heels with bowed head, the orange hair swinging about her face and unhappiness eloquent in every motion. The submission of her touched him suddenly, and he paused for her to catch up, smiling down half reluctantly on the bent orange head.

She lifted a tragic face to his, and there were tears in the sherry eyes. So he had no choice but to laugh and lift her up against his leather-clad breast and kiss the drooping mouth into smiles again. But he understood, now, the faintly acrid bitterness of her kisses.

'Still,' he said, when they had reached the little white shrine among the trees, 'there must be some other food than – that. Does no grain grow? Isn't there any wild life in the woods? Haven't the trees fruit?'

She gave him another sidelong look from under dropped lashes, warily.

'No,' she said. 'Nothing but the grass grows here. No living thing dwells in this land but man – and it. And as for the fruit of the trees – give thanks that they bloom but once in a lifetime.'

'Why?'

'Better not to – speak of it,' she said.

The phrase, the constant evasion, was beginning to wear on Smith's nerves. He said nothing of it then, but he turned from her and went down to the beach, dropping to the sand and striving to recapture last night's languor and peace. His hunger was curiously satisfied, even from the few swallows he had taken, and gradually the drowsy content of the day before began to flow over him in deepening waves. After all, it was a lovely land …

That day drew dreamily to a close, and darkness rose in a mist from the misty lake, and he came to find in kisses that tasted of blood a certain tang that but pointed their sweetness. And in the morning he woke to the slowly brightening day, swam with the girl in the blue, tingling waters of the lake – and reluctantly went up through the woods and across the ravenous grass to the Temple, driven by a hunger greater than his repugnance. He went up with a slight nausea rising within him, and yet strangely eager …

Once more the Temple rose veiled and indefinite under the glowing sky, and once more he plunged into the eternal twilight of its corridors, turned aside as one who knows the way, knelt of his own accord in the line of drinkers along the wall …

With the first draft that nausea rose within him almost overwhelmingly, but when the warmth of the drink had spread through him the nausea died and nothing was left but hunger and eagerness, and he drank blindly until the girl's hand on his shoulder roused him.

A sort of intoxication had wakened within him with the burning of that hot, salt drink in his veins, and he went back across the hurrying grass in a half-daze. Through most of the pellucid day it lasted, and the slow dark was rising from the lake before clearness returned to him.

3

And so life resolved itself into a very simple thing. The days glowed by and the blurred darknesses came and went. Life held little any more but the bright clarity of the day and the dimness of the dark, morning journeys to drink at the Temple fountain and the bitter kisses of the girl with the orange hair. Time had ceased for him. Slow day followed slow day, and the same round of living circled over and over, and the only change – perhaps he did not see it then – was the deepening look in the girl's eyes when they rested upon him, her growing silences.

One evening just as the first faint dimness was clouding the air, and the lake smoked hazily, he happened to glance off across its surface and thought he saw through the rising mists the outline of very far mountains.

He asked curiously, 'What lies beyond the lake? Aren't those mountains over there?'

The girl turned her head quickly and her sherry-brown eyes darkened with something like dread.

'I don't know,' she said. 'We believe it best not to wonder what lies – beyond.'

And suddenly Smith's irritation with the old evasions woke and he said violently, 'Damn your beliefs! I'm sick of that answer to every question I ask! Don't you even wonder about anything? Are you all so thoroughly cowed by this dread of something unseen that every spark of your spirit is dead?'

She turned the sorrowful, sherry gaze upon him.

'We learn by experience,' she said. 'Those who wonder – those who investigate – die. We live in a land alive with danger, incomprehensible, intangible, terrible. Life is bearable only if we do not look too closely – only if we accept conditions and make the most of them. You must not ask questions if you would live.

'As for the mountains beyond, and all the unknown country that lies over the horizons – they are as unreachable as a mirage. For in a land where no food grows, where we must visit the Temple daily or starve, how could an explorer provision himself for a journey? No, we are bound here by unbreakable bonds, and we must live here until we die.'

Smith shrugged. The languor of the evening was coming upon him, and the brief flare of irritation had died as swiftly as it rose.

Yet from that outburst dated the beginning of his discontent. Somehow, despite the lovely languor of the place, despite the sweet bitterness of the Temple fountains and the sweeter bitterness of the kisses that were his for the asking, he could not drive from his mind the vision of those far mountains veiled in rising haze. Unrest had wakened within him, and like some sleeper arising from a lotus-dream his mind turned more and more frequently to the desire for action, adventure, some other use for his danger-hardened body than the exigencies of sleep and food and love.

On all sides stretched the moving, restless woods, farther than the eye could reach. The grasslands rippled, and over the dim horizon the far mountains beckoned him. Even the mystery of the Temple and its endless twilight began to torment his waking moments. He dallied with the idea of exploring those hallways which the dwellers in this lotus-land avoided, of gazing from the strange windows that opened upon inexplicable blue. Surely life, even here, must hold some more fervent meaning than that he followed now. What lay beyond the wood and grasslands? What mysterious country did those mountains wall?

He began to harry his companion with questions that woke more and more often the look of dread behind her eyes, but he gained little satisfaction. She belonged to a people without history, without ambition, their lives bent wholly toward wringing from each moment its full sweetness in anticipation of the terror to come. Evasion was the keynote of their existence, perhaps with reason. Perhaps all the adventurous spirits among them had followed their curiosity into danger and death, and the only ones left were the submissive souls who led their bucolically voluptuous lives in this Elysium so shadowed with horror.

In this colored lotus-land, memories of the world he had left grew upon him more and more vividly: he remembered the hurrying crowds of the planets' capitals, the lights, the noise, the laughter. He saw space-ships cleaving the night sky with flame, flashing from world to world through the star-flecked darkness. He remembered sudden brawls in saloons and space-sailor dives when the air was alive with shouts and tumult, and heat-guns slashed their blue-hot blades of flame and the smell of burnt flesh hung heavy. Life marched in pageant past his remembering eyes, violent, vivid, shoulder to shoulder with death. And nostalgia wrenched at him for the lovely, terrible, brawling worlds he had left behind.

Daily the unrest grew upon him. The girl made pathetic little attempts to find some sort of entertainment that would occupy his ranging mind. She led him on timid excursions into the living woods, even conquered her horror of the Temple enough to follow him on timorous tiptoe as he explored a little way down the corridors which did not arouse in her too anguished a terror. But she must have known from the first that it was hopeless.

One day as they lay on the sand watching the lake ripple bluely under a crystal sky, Smith's eyes, dwelling on the faint shadow of the mountains, half unseeingly, suddenly narrowed into a hardness as bright and pale as steel.

Muscle ridged his abruptly set jaw and he sat upright with a jerk, pushing away the girl who had been leaning on his shoulder.

'I'm through,' he said harshly, and rose.

'What – what is it?' The girl stumbled to her feet.

'I'm going away – anywhere. To those mountains, I think. I'm leaving now!'

'But – you wish to die, then?'

'Better the real thing than a living death like this,' he said. 'At least I'll have a little more excitement first.'

'But, what of your food? There's nothing to keep you alive, even if you escape the greater dangers. Why, you'll dare not even lie down on the grass at night – it would eat you alive! You have no chance at all to live if you leave this grove – and me.'

'If I must die, I shall,' he said. 'I've been thinking it over, and I've made up my mind. I could explore the Temple and so come on *it* and die. But do *something* I must, and it seems to me my best chance is in trying to reach some country where food grows before I starve. It's worth trying. I can't go on like this.'

She looked at him miserably, tears brimming her sherry eyes. He opened his mouth to speak, but before he could say a word her eyes strayed beyond his shoulder and suddenly she smiled, a dreadful, frozen little smile.

'You will not go,' she said. 'Death has come for us now.'

She said it so calmly, so unafraid that he did not understand until she pointed beyond him. He turned.

The air between them and the shrine was curiously agitated. As he watched, it began to resolve itself into a nebulous blue mist that thickened and darkened ... blurry tinges of violet and green began to blow through it vaguely, and then by imperceptible degrees a flush of rose appeared in the mist – deepened, thickened, contracted into burning scarlet that seared his eyes, pulsed alively – and he knew that it had come.

An aura of menace seemed to radiate from it, strengthening as the mist strengthened, reaching out in hunger toward his mind. He felt it as tangibly as he saw it – cloudy danger reaching out avidly for them both.

The girl was not afraid. Somehow he knew this, though he dared not turn, dared not wrench his eyes from that hypnotically pulsing scarlet ... She whispered very softly from behind him.

'So I die with you, I am content.' And the sound of her voice freed him from the snare of the crimson pulse.

He barked a wolfish laugh, abruptly – welcoming even this diversion from the eternal idyl he had been living – and the gun leaping to his hand spurted a long blue flame so instantly that the girl behind him caught her breath. The steel-blue dazzle illumined the gathering mist lividly, passed through it without obstruction and charred the ground beyond. Smith set his teeth and swung a figure-eight pattern of flame through and through the mist, lacing it with blue heat. And when that finger of fire crossed the scarlet pulse the impact jarred the whole nebulous cloud violently, so that its outlines wavered and shrank, and the pulse of crimson sizzled under the heat – shriveled – began to fade in desperate haste.

Smith swept the ray back and forth along the redness, tracing its pattern with destruction, but it faded too swiftly for him. In little more than an instant it had paled and disembodied and vanished save for a fading flush of rose, and the blue-hot blade of his flame sizzled harmlessly through the disappearing mist to sear the ground beyond. He switched off the heat, then, and stood breathing a little unevenly as the death-cloud thinned and paled and vanished before his eyes, until no trace of it was left and the air glowed lucid and transparent once more.

The unmistakable odor of burning flesh caught at his nostrils, and he wondered for a moment if the Thing had indeed materialized a nucleus of matter, and then he saw that the smell came from the seared grass his flame had struck. The tiny, furry blades were all writhing away from the burnt spot, straining at their roots as if a wind blew them back and from the blackened area a thick smoke rose, reeking with the odor of burnt meat. Smith, remembering their vampire habits, turned away, half nauseated.

The girl had sunk to the sand behind him, trembling violently now that the danger was gone.

'Is – it dead?' she breathed, when she could master her quivering mouth.

'I don't know. No way of telling. Probably not.'

'What will – will you do now?'

He slid the heat-gun back into its holster and settled the belt purposefully.

'What I started out to do.'

The girl scrambled up in desperate haste.

'Wait!' she gasped, 'wait!' and clutched at his arm to steady herself. And he waited until the trembling had passed. Then she went on, 'Come up to the Temple once more before you go.'

'All right. Not a bad idea. It may be a long time before my next – meal.'

And so again they crossed the fur-soft grass that bore down upon them in long ripples from every part of the meadow.

The Temple rose dim and unreal before them, and as they entered blue twilight folded them dreamily about. Smith turned by habit toward the gallery of the drinkers, but the girl laid upon his arms a hand that shook a little, and murmured, 'Come this way.'

He followed in growing surprise down the hallway through the drifting mists and away from the gallery he knew so well. It seemed to him that the mist thickened as they advanced, and in the uncertain light he could never be sure that the walls did not waver as nebulously as the blurring air. He felt a curious impulse to step through their intangible barriers and out of the hall into – what?

Presently steps rose under his feet, almost imperceptibly, and after a while the pressure on his arm drew him aside. They went in under a low, heavy arch of stone and entered the strangest room he had ever seen. It appeared to be seven-sided, as nearly as he could judge through the drifting mist, and curious, converging lines were graven deep in the floor.

It seemed to him that forces outside his comprehension were beating violently against the seven walls, circling like hurricanes through the dimness until the whole room was a maelstrom of invisible tumult.

When he lifted his eyes to the wall, he knew where he was. Blazoned on the dim stone, burning through the twilight like some other-dimensional fire, the scarlet pattern writhed across the wall.

The sight of it, somehow, set up a commotion in his brain, and it was with whirling head and stumbling feet that he answered to the pressure on his arm. Dimly he realized that he stood at the very center of those strange, converging lines, feeling forces beyond reason coursing through him along paths outside any knowledge he possessed.

Then for one moment arms clasped his neck and a warm, fragrant body pressed against him, and a voice sobbed in his ear.

'If you must leave me, then go back through the Door, beloved – life without you – more dreadful even than a death like this …' A kiss that stung of blood clung to his lips for an instant; then the clasp loosened and he stood alone.

Through the twilight he saw her dimly outlined against the Word. And he thought, as she stood there, that it was as if the invisible current beat bodily against her, so that she swayed and wavered before him, her outlines blurring and forming again as the forces from which he was so mystically protected buffeted her mercilessly.

And he saw knowledge dawning terribly upon her face, as the meaning of the Word seeped into her mind. The sweet brown face twisted hideously, the blood-red lips writhed apart to shriek a Word – in a moment of clarity he actually saw her tongue twisting incredibly to form the syllables of the unspeakable thing never meant for human lips to frame. Her mouth opened into an impossible shape … she gasped in the blurry mist and shrieked aloud …

4

Smith was walking along a twisting path so scarlet that he could not bear to look down, a path that wound and unwound and shook itself under his feet so that he stumbled at every step. He was groping through a blinding mist clouded with violet and green, and in his ears a dreadful whisper rang – the first syllable of an unutterable Word … Whenever he neared the end of the path it shook itself under him and doubled back, and weariness like a drug was sinking into his brain, and the sleepy twilight colors of the mist lulled him, and—

'He's waking up!' said an exultant voice in his ear.

Smith lifted heavy eyelids upon a room without walls – a room wherein multiple figures extending into infinity moved to and fro in countless hosts …

'Smith! N.W.! Wake up!' urged that familiar voice from somewhere near.

He blinked. The myriad diminishing figures resolved themselves into the reflections of two men in a steel-walled room, bending over him. The friendly, anxious face of his partner, Yarol the Venusian, leaned above the bed.

'By Pharol, N.W.,' said the well-remembered, ribald voice, 'you've been asleep for a week! We thought you'd never come out of it – must have been an awful brand of whisky!'

Smith managed a feeble grin – amazing how weak he felt – and turned an inquiring gaze upon the other figure.

'I'm a doctor,' said that individual, meeting the questing stare. 'Your friend called me in three days ago and I've been working on you ever since. It must have been all of five or six days since you fell into this coma – have you any idea what caused it?'

Smith's pale eyes roved the room. He did not find what he sought, and though his weak murmur answered the doctor's question, the man was never to know it.

'Shawl?'

'I threw the damned thing away,' confessed Yarol. 'Stood it for three days and then gave up. That red pattern gave me the worst headache I've had since we found that case of black wine on the asteroid. Remember?'

'Where—?'

'Gave it to a space-rat checking out for Venus. Sorry. Did you really want it? I'll buy you another.'

Smith did not answer, the weakness was rushing up about him in gray waves. He closed his eyes, hearing the echoes of that first dreadful syllable whispering through his head … whisper from a dream … Yarol heard him murmur softly,

'And – I never even knew – her name …'

DUST OF GODS

1

'Pass the whisky, N.W.,' said Yarol the Venusian persuasively.

Northwest Smith shook the black bottle of Venusian *segir*-whisky tentatively, evoked a slight gurgle, and reached for his friend's glass. Under the Venusian's jealous dark gaze he measured out exactly half of the red liquid. It was not very much.

Yarol regarded his share of the drink disconsolately.

'Broke again,' he murmured. 'And me so thirsty.' His glance of cherubic innocence flashed along the temptingly laden counters of the Martian saloon wherein they sat. His face with its look of holy innocence turned to Smith's, the wise black gaze meeting the Earthman's pale-steel look questioningly. Yarol lifted an arched brow.

'How about it?' he suggested delicately. 'Mars owes us a drink anyhow, and I just had my heat-gun recharged this morning. I think we could get away with it.'

Under the table he laid a hopeful hand on his gun. Smith grinned and shook his head.

'Too many customers,' he said. 'And you ought to know better than to start anything here. It isn't healthful.'

Yarol shrugged resigned shoulders and drained his glass with a gulp.

'Now what?' he demanded.

'Well, look around. See anyone here you know? We're open for business – any kind.'

Yarol twirled his glass wistfully and studied the crowded room from under his lashes. With those lashes lowered he might have passed for a choir boy in any of Earth's cathedrals. But too dark a knowledge looked out when they rose for that illusion to continue long.

It was a motley crowd the weary black gaze scrutinized – hard-faced Earthmen in space-sailors' leather, sleek Venusians with their sidelong, dangerous eyes, Martian drylanders muttering the blasphemous gutturals of their language, a sprinkling of outlanders and half-brutes from the wide-flung borders of civilization. Yarol's eyes returned to the dark, scarred face across the table. He met the pallor of Smith's no-colored gaze and shrugged.

'No one who'd buy us a drink,' he sighed. 'I've seen one or two of 'em before, though. Take those two space-rats at the next table: the little red-faced Earthman – the one looking over his shoulder – and the drylander with an eye gone. See? I've heard they're hunters.'

'What for?'

Yarol lifted his shoulders in the expressive Venusian shrug. His brows rose too, quizzically.

'No one knows what they hunt – but they run together.'

'Hm-m.' Smith turned a speculative stare toward the neighboring table. 'They look more hunted than hunting, if you ask me.'

Yarol nodded. The two seemed to share one fear between them, if over-the-shoulder glances and restless eyes spoke truly. They huddled together above their *segir* glasses, and though they had the faces of hard men, inured to the spaceway dangers, the look on those faces was curiously compounded of many unpleasant things underlying a frank, unreasoning alarm. It was a look Smith could not quite fathom – a haunted, uneasy dread with nameless things behind it.

'They do look as if Black Pharol were one jump behind,' said Yarol. 'Funny, too. I've always heard they were pretty tough, both of 'em. You have to be, in their profession.'

Said a husky half-whisper in their very ears, 'Perhaps they found what they were hunting.'

It produced an electric stillness. Smith moved almost imperceptibly sidewise in his chair, the better to clear his gun, and Yarol's slim fingers hovered above his hip. They turned expressionless faces toward the speaker.

A little man sitting alone at the next table had bent forward to fix them with a particularly bright stare. They met it in silence, hostile and waiting, until the husky half-whisper spoke again.

'May I join you? I couldn't help overhearing that – that you were open for business.'

Without expression Smith's colorless eyes summed up the speaker, and a puzzlement clouded their paleness as he looked. Rarely does one meet a man whose origin and race are not apparent even upon close scrutiny. Yet here was one whom he could not classify. Under the deep burn of the man's skin might be concealed a fair Venusian pallor or an Earthman bronze, canal-Martian rosiness or even a leathery dryland hide. His dark eyes could have belonged to any race, and his husky whisper, fluent in the jargon of the spaceman, effectively disguised its origin. Little and unobtrusive, he might have passed for native on any of the three planets.

Smith's scarred, impassive face did not change as he looked, but after a long moment of scrutiny he said, 'Pull up,' and then bit off the words as if he had said too much.

The brevity must have pleased the little man, for he smiled as he compiled, meeting the passively hostile stare of the two without embarrassment. He folded his arms on the table and leaned forward. The husky voice began without preamble, 'I can offer you employment – if you're not afraid. It's dangerous work, but the pay's good enough to make up for it – if you're not afraid.'

'What is it?'

'Work they – those two – failed at. They were – hunters – until they found what they hunted. Look at them now.'

Smith's no-colored eyes did not swerve from the speaker's face, but he nodded. No need to look again upon the fear-ridden faces of the neighboring pair. He understood.

'What's the job?' he said.

The little man hitched his chair closer and sent a glance round the room from under lowered lids. He scanned the faces of his two companions half doubtfully. He said, 'There have been many gods since time's beginning,' then paused and peered dubiously into Smith's face.

Northwest nodded briefly. 'Go on,' he said.

Reassured, the little man took up his tale, and before he had gone far enthusiasm drowned out the doubtfulness in his husky voice, and a tinge of fanaticism crept in.

'There were gods who were old when Mars was a green planet, and a verdant moon circled an Earth blue with steaming seas, and Venus, molten-hot, swung round a younger sun. Another world circled in space then, between Mars and Jupiter where its fragments, the planetoids, now are. You will have heard rumors of it – they persist in the legends of every planet. It was a mighty world, rich and beautiful, peopled by the ancestors of mankind. And on that world dwelt a mighty Three in a temple of crystal, served by strange slaves and worshipped by a world. They were not wholly abstract, as most modern gods have become. Some say they were from beyond, and real, in their way, as flesh and blood.'

'Those three gods were the origin and beginning of all other gods that mankind has known. All modern gods are echoes of them, in a world that has forgotten the very name of the Lost Planet. Saig they called one, and Lsa was the second. You will never have heard of them – they died before your world's hot seas had cooled. No man knows how they vanished, or why, and no trace of them is left anywhere in the universe we know. But there was a Third – a mighty Third set above these two and ruling the Lost Planet; so mighty a Third that even today, unthinkably long afterward, his name has not died from the lips of man. It has become a byword now – his name, that once no living man dared utter! I heard you call upon him not ten minutes past – Black Pharol!'

His husky voice sank to a quiver as it spoke the hackneyed name. Yarol gave a sudden snort of laughter, quickly hushed, and said, 'Pharol! Why—'

'Yes, I know. Pharol, today, means unmentionable rites to an ancient no-god of utter darkness. Pharol has sunk so low that his very name denotes nothingness. But in other days – ah, in other days! Black Pharol has not always been a blur of dark worshipped with obscenity. In other days men knew what things that darkness hid, nor dared pronounce the name you laugh at, lest unwittingly they stumble upon that secret twist of its inflection which opens the door upon the dark that is Pharol. Men have been engulfed before now in that utter blackness of the god, and in that dark have seen fearful things. I know' – the raw voice trailed away into a murmur – 'such fearful things that a man might scream his throat hoarse and never speak again above a whisper ...'

Smith's eyes flicked Yarol's. The husky murmur went on after a moment.

'So you see the old gods have not died utterly. They can never die as we know death: they come from too far Beyond to know either death or life as we do. They came from so very far that to touch us at all they had to take a visible form among mankind – to incarnate themselves in a material body through which, as through a door, they might reach out and touch the bodies and minds of men. The form they chose does not matter now – I do not know it. It was a material thing, and it has gone to dust so long ago that they very memory of its shape has vanished from the minds of men. But that dust still exists. Do you hear me? That dust which was once the first and the greatest of all gods, still exists! It was that which those men hunted. It was that they found, and fled in deadly terror of what they saw there. You look to be made of firmer stuff. Will you take up the search where they left it?'

Smith's pale stare met Yarol's black one across the table. Silence hung between them for a moment. Then Smith said, 'Any objection to us having a little talk with those two over there?'

'None at all,' answered the hoarse whisper promptly. 'Go now, if you like.'

Smith rose without further words. Yarol pushed back his chair noiselessly and followed him. They crossed the floor with the spaceman's peculiar, shifting walk and slid into opposite chairs between the huddling two.

The effect was startling. The Earthman jerked convulsively and turned a pasty face, eloquent with alarm, toward the interruption. They drylander stared from Smith's face to Yarol's in dumb terror. Neither spoke.

'Know that fellow over there?' inquired Smith abruptly, jerking his head toward the table they had quitted.

After a moment's hesitation the two heads turned as one. When they faced around again the terror on the Earthman's face was giving way to a dawning comprehension. He said from a dry throat, 'He – he's hiring you, eh?'

Smith nodded. The Earthman's face crumpled into terror again and he cried, 'Don't do it. For God's sake, you don't know!'

'Know what?'

The man glanced furtively round the room and licked his lips uncertainly. A curious play of conflicting emotions flickered across his face.

'Dangerous—' he mumbled. 'Better leave well enough alone. We found that out.'

'What happened?'

The Earthman stretched out a shaking hand for the *segir* bottle and poured a brimming glass. He drained it before he spoke, and the incoherence of his speech may have been due to the glasses that had preceded it.

'We went up toward the polar mountains, where he said. Weeks … it was cold. The nights get dark up there … dark. Went into the cave that goes through the mountain – a long way … Then our lights went out – full-charged batteries in new super-Tomlinson tubes, but they went out like candles, and in the dark – in the dark the white thing came …'

A shudder went over him strongly. He reached out shaking hands for the *segir* bottle, and poured another glass, the rim clicking against his teeth as he drank. Then he set down the glass hard and said violently,

'That's all. We left. Don't remember a thing about getting out – or much more than starving and freezing in the saltlands for a long time. Our supplies ran low – hadn't been for him' – nodding across the table – 'we'd both have died. Don't know how we did get out finally – but we're out, understand? Out! Nothing could hire us to go back – we've seen enough. There's something about it that – that makes your head ache – we saw … never mind. But—'

He beckoned Smith closer and sank his voice to a whisper. His eyes rolled fearfully.

'It's after us. Don't ask me what … I don't know. But – feel it in the dark, watching – watching in the dark …'

The voice sank to a mumble and he reached again for the *segir* bottle.

'It's here now – waiting – if the lights go out – watching – mustn't let the lights go out – more *segir* …'

The bottle clinked on the glass-rim, the voice trailed away into drunken mutterings.

Smith pushed back his chair and nodded to Yarol. The two at the table did not seem to notice their departure. The drylander was clutching the *segir* bottle in turn and pouring out red liquid without watching the glass – an apprehensive one-eyed stare turned across his shoulder.

Smith laid a hand on his companion's shoulder and drew him across the room toward the bar. Yarol scowled at the approaching bartender and suggested, 'Suppose we get an advance for drinks, anyhow.'

'Are we taking it?'

'Well, what d'you think?'

'It's dangerous. You know, there's something worse than whisky wrong with those two. Did you notice the Earthman's eyes?'

'Whites showed all around,' nodded Yarol. 'I've seen madmen look like that.'

'I thought of that, too. He was drunk, of course, and probably wouldn't be so wild-sounding, sober – but from the looks of him he'll never be sober again till he dies. No use trying to find out anything more from him. And the other – well, did you ever try to find out anything from a drylander? Even a sober one?'

Yarol lifted expressive shoulders. 'I know. If we go into this, we go blind. Never dig any more out of those drunks. But something certainly scared them.'

'And yet,' said Smith, 'I'd like to know more about his. Dust of the gods – and all that. Interesting. Just what does he want with this dust, anyhow?'

'Did you believe that yarn?'

'Don't know – I've come across some pretty funny things here and there. He does act half-cracked, of course, but – well, those fellows back there certainly found *something* out of the ordinary, and they didn't go all the way at that.'

'Well, if he'll buy us a drink I say let's take the job,' said Yarol. 'I'd as soon be scared to death later as die of thirst now. What do you say?'

'Good enough,' shrugged Smith. 'I'm thirsty, too.'

The little man looked up hopefully as they reseated themselves at the table.

'If we can come to terms,' said Smith, 'we'll take it. And if you can give us some idea of what we're looking for, and why.'

'The dust of Pharol,' said the husky voice impatiently. 'I told you that.'

'What d'you want with it?'

'We're risking our necks for it, aren't we?'

Again the bright, small eyes bored into the Earthman's. The husky voice fell lower, to the very echo of a whisper, and he said, secretly,

'I'll tell you, then. After all, why not? You don't know how to use it – it's of no value to anyone but me. Listen, then – I told you that the Three incarnated themselves into a material form to use as a door through which they could reach humanity. They had to do it, but it was a door that opened both ways – through it, if one dared, man could reach the Three. No one dared in those days – the power beyond was too terrible. It would have been like walking straight through a gateway into hell. But time has passed since then. The gods have drawn away from humanity into farther realms. The terror that was Pharol is only an echo in a forgetful world. The spirit of the god has gone – but not wholly. While any remnant of that shape which was once incarnate Pharol exists, Pharol can be reached. For the man who could lay hands on that dust, knowing the requisite rites and formulae, all knowledge, all power would lie open like a book. To enslave a god!'

The raw whisper rasped to a crescendo; fanatic lights flared in the small, bright eyes. He had forgotten them entirely – his piercing stare fixed on some shining future, and his hands on the table clenched into white-knuckled fists.

Smith and Yarol exchanged dubious glances. Obviously the man was mad . . .

'Fifty thousand dollars to your account in any bank you choose,' the hoarse voice, eminently sane, broke in abruptly upon their dubiety. 'All expenses, of course, will be paid. I'll give you charts and tell you all I know about how to get there. When can you start?'

Smith grinned. Touched the man might be, but just then Smith would have stormed the gates of hell, at any madman's request, for fifty thousand Earth dollars.

'Right now,' he said laconically. 'Let's go.'

2

Northward over the great curve of Mars, red slag and red dust and the reddish, low-lying dryland vegetation gave way to the saltlands around the Pole. Scrub grows there, and sparse, coarse grass, and the snow that falls by night lies all the cold, thin day among the tough grass-roots and in the hillocks of the dry salt soil.

'Of all the God-forsaken countries,' said Northwest Smith, looking down from his pilot seat at the gray lands slipping past under the speed of their plane, 'this must be the worst. I'd sooner live on Luna or one of the asteroids.'

Yarol tilted the *segir* bottle to his lips and evoked an eloquent gurgle from its depths.

'Five days of flying over this scenery would give anyone the jitters,' he pronounced. 'I'd never have thought I'd be glad to see a mountain range as ugly as that, but it looks like Paradise now,' and he nodded toward the black, jagged slopes of the polar mountains that marked their journey's end so far as flying was concerned; for despite their great antiquity the peaks were jagged and rough as mountains new-wrenched from a heaving world.

Smith brought the plane down at the foot of the rising black slopes. There was a triangular gap there with a streak of white down its side, a landmark he had been watching for, and the plane slid quietly into the shelter to lie protected under the shelving rock. From here progress must be made afoot and painfully through the mountains. There was no landing-place any nearer their goal than this. Yet in measure of distance they had not far to go.

The two climbed stiffly out. Smith stretched his long legs and sniffed the air. It was bitterly cold, and tinged with that nameless, dry salt smell of eon-dead seas which is encountered nowhere in the known universe save in the northern saltlands of Mars. He faced the mountains doubtfully. From their beginnings here, he knew, they rolled away, jagged and black and deadly, to the very Pole. Snow lay thickly upon them in the brief Martian winter, unmarked by any track until it melted for the canals, carving deeper runnels into the already jig-sawed peaks.

Once in the very long-past days, so the little whispering fanatic had said, Mars was a green world. Seas had spread here, lapping the feet of gentler mountains, and in the slopes of those hills a mighty city once lay – a nameless city, so far as the present generations of man remembered, and a nameless star shone down upon it from a spot in the heavens now empty – the Lost Planet, shining on a lost city. The dwellers there must have seen the catastrophe which blasted that sister planet from the face of the sky. And if the little man were right, the gods of that Lost Planet had been saved from the wreckage and spirited across the void to a dwelling-place in this greatly honored city of the mountains that is not even a memory today.

And time passed, so the story went. The city aged – the gods aged – the planet aged. At last, in some terrible catastrophe, the planet heaved under the city's foundations, the mountains shook it into ruins and folded themselves into new and dreadful shapes. The seas receded, the fertile soil sloughed away from the rocks and time swallowed up the very memory of that city which once had been the dwelling-place of gods – which was still, so the hoarse whisper had told them, the dwelling-place of gods.

'Must have been right around here somewhere,' said Smith, 'that those two found the cave.'

'Out around the slope to the left,' agreed Yarol. 'Let's go.' He squinted up at the feeble sun. 'Not very long past dawn. We ought to be back again by dark if things go right.'

They left the ship in its shelter and struck out across the salt drylands, the harsh scrub brushing about their knees and their breath clouding the thin air as they advanced. The slope curved away to the left, rising in rapid ascent to black peaks that were unscalable and forbidding. The only hope of penetrating that wall lay in finding the cavern that their predecessors had fled … and in that cavern – Smith loosened the heat-gun in its holster at his side.

They had plodded for fifteen minutes through the scrub, dry snow rising under their feet and the harsh salt air frosting their breath, before the mouth of the cave they were hunting appeared darkly under the overhanging rock they had been told of.

The two peered in doubtfully. That jagged floor might never have known the tread of human feet, so far as one might know by the look of it. Powdered snow lay undisturbed in the deep crannies, and daylight did not penetrate very far into the forbidding dark beyond. Smith drew his gun, took a deep breath and plunged into the blackness and the cold, with Yarol at his heels.

It was like leaving everything human and alive for some frosty limbo that had never known life. The cold struck sharply through their leather garments. They took out their Tomlinson tubes before they had gone more than twenty paces, and the twin beams illumined a scene of utter desolation, more dead than death, for it seemed never to have known life.

For perhaps fifteen minutes they stumbled through the cold dark. Smith kept his beam focused on the floor beneath them; Yarol's roved the walls and pierced the blackness ahead. Rough walls and ragged ceiling and teeth of broken stone projecting from the floor to slash at their boots – no sound but their footsteps, nothing but the dark and the frost and the silence. Then Yarol said, 'It's foggy in here,' and something clouded the clear beams of the lights for an instant; then darkness folded round them as suddenly and completely as the folds of a cloak.

Smith stopped dead-still, tense and listening. No sound. He felt the lens of his light-tube and knew that it still burned – it was warm, and the faint vibration under the glass told him that the tubes still functioned. But something intangible and strange blotted it out at the source … a thick, stifling blackness that seemed to muffle their senses. It was like a bandage over the eyes – Smith, holding the burning light-lens to his eyes, could not detect even its outline in that all-cloaking dark.

For perhaps five minutes that dead blackness held them. Vaguely they knew what to expect, but when it came, the shock of it took their breath away. There was no sound, but quite suddenly around a bend of the cavern came a figure of utter whiteness, seen at first fragmentarily through a screen of rock-toothed jags, then floating full into view against the background of the dark. Smith thought he had never seen whiteness before until his incredulous eyes beheld this creature – if creature it could be. Somehow he thought it must be partly below the level of the floor along which it moved; for though in that blind black he had no way of gauging elevation, it seemed to him that the apparition, moving with an effortless glide, advanced unopposed through the solid rock of the floor. And it was whiter than anything living or dead had ever been before – so white that it sickened him, somehow, and the flesh crept along his spine. Like a cut-out figure of paper, it blazed against the flat black beyond. The dark did not affect it, no shadows lay upon its surface; in two arbitrary dimensions only, blind white superimposed upon blind dark, it floated toward them. And it was tall, and somehow man-formed, but of no shape that words could describe.

Smith heard Yarol catch his breath in a gasp behind him. He heard no other sound, though the whiteness floated swiftly forward *through* the rocky floor. He was sure of that now – a part of it extended farther down than his feet, and they were planted upon solid rock. And though his skin crawled with unreasoning terror, and the hair on his neck prickled with the weird, impossible approach of the impossible thing, he kept his head enough to see that it was apparently solid, yet somehow milkily translucent; that it had form and depth, though no shadows of that darkness lay upon it; that from where no face should have been a blind, eyeless visage fronted him impassively. It was very close now, and though the extremities of it trailed below the floor line, its height lifted far above his head.

And a nameless, blind force beat out from it and assailed him, a force that somehow seemed to be driving him into unnamable things – an urge to madness, beating at his brain with the reasonless buffeting of insanity, but a wilder, more incomprehensible insanity than the sane mind could understand.

Something frantic within him clamored for instant, headlong flight – he heard Yarol's breathing panicky behind him and knew that he too wavered on the verge of bolting – but something insistent at the roots of his brain held him firm before the whiteness bearing down in its aura of madness – something that denied the peril, that hinted at solution …

Scarcely realizing that he had moved, he found the heat-gun in his hand, and on a sudden impulse jerked his arm up and sent a long, blue-hot streamer of flame straight at the advancing apparition. For the briefest of instants the blue dazzle flashed a light-blade through the dark. It struck the floating whiteness full – vanished – Smith heard a faint crackle of sparks on the invisible floor beyond and knew that it had passed through the creature without meeting resistance. And in that flashing second while the blue gaze split the thickness of the dark he saw it shine luridly upon a splinter of rock in its path, but not upon the white figure. No blaze of blueness affected the deathly pallor of it – he had a sudden conviction that though a galaxy of colored lights were played upon it no faintest hint of color could ever tinge it with any of man's hues. Fighting the waves of madness that buffeted at his brain, he realized painfully that it must be beyond the reach of men – and therefore—

He laughed unsteadily and holstered his gun.

'Come on,' he yelled to Yarol, reaching out blindly to grasp his comrade's arm, and – suppressing a tingle of terror – plunged straight through that towering horror.

There was an instant of blaze and blinding whiteness, a moment of turmoil while dizziness swirled round him and the floor rocked under his feet and a maelstrom of mad impulses battered through his brain; then everything was black again and he was plunging recklessly ahead through the dark, dragging a limply acquiescent Yarol behind him.

After a while of stumbling progress, punctuated with falls, while the white horror dropped away behind them, not following, though the muffling dark still sealed their eyes – the almost forgotten light in Smith's hand suddenly blazed forth again. In its light he faced Yarol, blinking at the abrupt illumination. The Venusian's face was a mask of question, his black eyes bright with inquiry.

'What happened? What was it? How did you – how could we—'

'It can't have been real,' said Smith with a shaky grin. 'I mean, not material in the sense that we know. Looked awful enough, but – well, there were too many things about it that didn't hitch up. Notice how it seemed to trail through the solid floor? And neither light nor dark affected it – it had no shadows, even in that blackness, and the flash of my gun didn't even give it a blue tinge. Then I remembered what that little fellow had told us about his three gods: that, though they had real existence, it was on such a widely different plane from ours that they couldn't touch us except by providing themselves with a material body. I think this thing was like that also: visible, but too other-dimensional to reach us except through sight. And when I saw that the floor didn't offer any resistance to it I thought that maybe, conversely, it wouldn't affect us either. And it didn't. We're through.'

Yarol drew a deep breath.

'The master-mind,' he gibed affectionately. 'Wonder if anyone else ever figured that out, or are we the first to get through?'

'Don't know. Don't get the idea it was just a scarecrow, though. I think we moved none too soon. A minute or two longer and – and – I felt as if someone were stirring my brains with a stick. Nothing seemed – right. I think I know now what was wrong with those other two – they waited too long before they ran. Good thing we moved when we did.'

'But what about that darkness?'

'I suppose we'll never really know. Must have had some relation to the other – the white thing, possibly some force or element out of that other dimension; because just as dark couldn't touch the whiteness of that thing, so light had no effect on the dark. I got the impression, somehow, that the dark space is a fixed area there, as if a section out of the other world has been set down in the cave, for the white thing to roam about it – a barrier of blackness across the way. And I don't suppose that it can move outside the darkness. But I may be wrong – let's go!'

'Right behind you!' said Yarol. 'Get along.'

The cave extended for another fifteen-minute walk, cold and silent and viciously rough underfoot, but no further mishap broke the journey. Tomlinson-lights gleaming, they traversed it, and the glow of cold day at the far end looked like the gleam of paradise after that journey through the heart of the dead rock.

They looked out upon the ruins of that city where once the gods had dwelt – ragged rock, great splintered teeth of stone upflung, the bare black mountainside folded and tortured into wild shapes of desolation. Here and there, buried in the debris of ages, lay huge six-foot blocks of hewn stone, the only reminder that here had stood Mars' holiest city, once, very long ago.

After five minutes of search Smith's eyes finally located the outline of what might, millions of years ago, have been a street. It led straight away from the slope at the cave-mouth, and the blocks of hewn stone, the crevices and folded ruins of earthquake choked it, but the course it once had run was not entirely obliterated even yet. Palaces and temples must have lined it once. There was no trace of them now save in the blocks of marble lying shattered among the broken stones. Time had erased the city from the face of Mars almost as completely as from the memories of man. Yet the trace of this one street was all they needed now to guide them.

The going was rough. Once down among the ruins it was difficult to keep in the track, and for almost an hour they clambered over broken rock and jagged spikes of stone, leaping the crevices, skirting great mounds of ruin. Both were scratched and breathless by the time they came to the first landmark they recognized – a black, leaning needle of stone, half buried in fragments of broken marble. Just beyond it lay two blocks of stone, one upon the other, perhaps the only two in the whole vast ruin which still stood as the hands of man had laid them hundreds of centuries ago.

Smith paused beside them and looked at Yarol, breathing a little heavily from exertion.

'Here it is,' he said. 'The old boy was telling the truth after all.'

'So far,' amended Yarol dubiously, drawing his heat-gun. 'Well, we'll see.'

The blue pencil of flame hissed from the gun's muzzle to splatter along the crack between the stones. Very slowly Yarol traced that line, and in spite of himself excitement quickened within him. Two-thirds of the way along the line the flame suddenly ceased to spatter and bit deep. A blackening hole appeared in the stone. It widened swiftly, and smoke rose, and there came a sound of protesting rock wrenched from its bed of eons as the upper stone slowly ground half around on the lower, tottered a moment and then fell.

The lower stone was hollow. The two bent over curiously, peering down. A tiny breath of unutterable antiquity rose in their faces out of that darkness, a little breeze from a million years ago. Smith flashed his light-tube downward and saw level stone a dozen feet below. The breeze was stronger now, and dust danced up the shaft from the mysterious depths – dust that had lain there undisturbed for unthinkably long ages.

'We'll give it a while to air out,' said Smith, switching off his light. 'Must be plenty of ventilation, to judge from that breeze, and the dust will probably blow away before long. We can be rigging up some sort of ladder while we wait.'

By the time a knotted rope had been prepared and anchored about a near-by needle of rock the little wind was blowing cleanly up the shaft, still laden with that indefinable odor of ages, but breathable. Smith swung over first, lowering himself cautiously until his feet touched the stone. Yarol, when he came down, found him swinging the Tomlinson-beam about a scene of utter lifelessness. A passageway stretched before them, smoothly polished as to walls and ceiling, with curious, unheard-of frescoes limned in dim colors under the glaze. Antiquity hung almost tangibly in the air. The little breeze that brushed past their faces seemed sacrilegiously alive in this tomb of dead dynasties.

That glazed and patterned passageway led downward into the dark. They followed it dubiously, feet stirring in the dust of a dead race, light-beams violating the million-years night of the underground. Before they had gone very far the circle of light from the shaft disappeared from sight beyond the up-sloping floor behind them, and they walked through antiquity with nothing but the tiny, constant breeze upon their faces to remind them of the world above.

They walked a very long way. There was no subterfuge about the passage, no attempt to confuse the traveler. No other halls opened from it – it led straight forward and down through the stillness, the dark, the odor of very ancient death. And when at long last they reached the end, they had passed no other corridor-mouth, no other openings at all save the tiny ventilation holes at intervals along the ceiling.

At the end of that passage a curving wall of rough, unworked stone bulged like the segment of a sphere, closing the corridor. It was a different stone entirely from that under the patterned glaze of the way along which they had come. In the light of their Tomlinson tubes they saw a stone door set flush with the slightly bulging wall that held it. And in the door's very center a symbol was cut deep and vehement and black against the gray background. Yarol, seeing it, caught his breath.

'Do you know that sign?' he said softly, his voice reverberating in the stillness of the underground, and echoes whispered behind him down the darkness, '*—know that sign … know that sign?*'

'I can guess,' murmured Smith, playing his light on the black outline of it.

'The symbol of Pharol,' said the Venusian in a near-whisper, but the echoes caught it and rolled back along the passage in diminishing undertones, '*—Pharol … Pharol … Pharol!*'

'I saw it once carved in the rock of an asteroid,' whispered Yarol. 'Just a bare little fragment of dead stone whirling around and around through space. There was one smooth surface on it, and this same sign was cut there. The Lost Planet must really have existed, N.W., and that must have been a part of it once, with the god's name cut so deep that even the explosion of a world couldn't wipe it out.'

Smith drew his gun. 'We'll soon know,' he said. 'This will probably fall, so stand back.'

The blue pencil of heat traced the door's edges, spattering against the stone as Yarol's had in the city above. And as before, in its course it encountered the weak place in the molding and the fire bit deep. The door trembled as Smith held the beam steady; it uttered an ominous creaking and began slowly to tilt outward at the top. Smith snapped off his gun and leaped backward, as the great stone slab tottered outward and fell. The mighty crash of it reverberated through the dark, and the concussion of its fall shook the solid floor and flung both men staggering against the wall.

They reeled to their feet again, shielding blinded eyes from the torrent of radiance that poured forth out of the doorway. It was a rich, golden light, somehow thick, yet clear, and they saw almost immediately, as their eyes became accustomed to the sudden change from darkness, that it was like no light they had ever known before. Tangibly it poured past them down the corridor in hurrying waves that lapped one another and piled up and flowed as a gas might have done. It was light which had an unnamable body to it, a physical, palpable body which yet did not affect the air they breathed.

They walked forward into a sea of radiance, and that curious light actually eddied about their feet, rippling away from the forward motion of their bodies as water might have done. Widening circles spread away through the air as they advanced, breaking soundlessly against the wall, and behind them a trail of bright streaks streamed away like the wake of a ship in water.

Through the deeps of that rippling light they walked a passage hewn from ragged stone, a different stone from that of the outer corridor, and somehow older. Tiny speckles of brightness glinted now and again on the rough walls, and neither could remember ever having seen just such mottled, bright-flecked rock before.

'Do you know what I think this is?' demanded Smith suddenly, after a few minutes of silent progress over the uneven floor. 'An asteroid! That rough wall bulging into the corridor outside was the outer part of it. Remember, the three gods were supposed to have been carried away from the catastrophe on the other world and brought here. Well, I'll bet that's how it was managed – a fragment of that planet, enclosing a room, possibly, where the gods' images stood, was somehow detached from the Lost Planet and hurled across space to Mars. Must have buried itself in the ground here, and the people of this city tunneled in to it and built a temple over the spot. No other way, you see, to account for that protruding wall and the peculiar formation of this rock. It must have come from the lost world – never saw anything like it anywhere, myself.'

'Sounds logical,' admitted Yarol, swinging his foot to start an eddy of light toward the wall. 'And what do you make of this funny light?'

'Whatever other-dimensional place those gods came from, we can be pretty sure that light plays funny tricks there. It must be nearly material – physical. You saw it in that white thing in the cave, and in the dark that smothered our tubes. It's as tangible as water, almost. You saw how it flowed out into the passage when the door fell, not as real light does, but in succeeding waves, like heavy gas. Yet I don't notice any difference in the air. I don't believe – say! Look at that!'

He stopped so suddenly that Yarol bumped into him from behind and muttered a mild Venusian oath. Then across Smith's shoulder he saw it too, and his hand swept downward to his gun. Something like an oddly shaped hole opening onto utter dark had appeared around the curve of the passage. And as they stared, it moved. It was a Something blacker than anything in human experience could ever have been before – as black as the guardian of the cave had been white – so black that the eye refused to compass it save as a negative quality, an emptiness. Smith, remembering the legends of Pharol the No-God of utter nothingness, gripped his gun more firmly and wondered if he stood face to face with one of the elder gods.

The Thing had shifted its shape, flowing to a stabler outline and standing higher from the floor. Smith felt that it must have form and thickness – at least three dimensions and probably more – but try though he would, his eyes could not discern it save as a flat outline of nothingness against the golden light.

And as from the white dweller in darkness, so from this black denizen of the light there flowed a force that goaded the brain to madness. Smith felt it battering in blind waves at the foundations of his mind – but he felt more than the reasonless urge in this force assailing him. He sensed a struggle of some sort, as if the black guardian were turning only a part of its attention to him – as if it fought against something unseen and powerful. Feeling this, he began to see signs of that combat in the black outlines of the thing. It rippled and flowed, its shape shifted fluidly, it writhed in protest against something he could not comprehend. Definitely now he felt that it fought a desperate battle with some unseen enemy, and a little shudder crawled down his back as he watched.

Quite suddenly it dawned upon him what was happening. Slowly, relentlessly, the black nothingness was being drawn down the passage. And it was – it must be – the flow of the golden radiance that drew it, as a fish might be carried forward down a stream. Somehow the opening of the door must have freed the pent-up lake of light, and it was flowing slowly out down the passage as water flows, draining the asteroid, if asteroid it was. He could see now that though they had halted the wake of rippling illumination behind them did not cease. Past them in a bright tide streamed the light. And on that outflowing torrent the black guardian floated, struggling but helpless.

It was closer now, and the beat of insistent impulses against Smith's brain was stronger, but he was not greatly alarmed by it. The panic of the thing must be deep, and the waves of force that washed about him were dizzying but not deep-reaching. Because of this increasing dizziness, as the thing approached, he was never sure afterward just what had happened. Rapidly it drew nearer, until he could have put out his hand and touched it – though instinctively he felt that, near as it seemed, it was too far away across dimensional gulfs for him ever to lay hand upon it. The blackness of it, at close range, was stupefying, a blackness that the eye refused to comprehend – that could not be, and was.

With the nearness of it his brain seemed to leave its moorings and plunge in mad, impossible curves through a suddenly opened space wherein the walls of the passage were shadows dimly seen and his own body no more than a pillar of mist in a howling void. The black thing must have rolled over him in passing, and engulfed him in its reasonless and incredible dark. He never knew. When his plunging brain finally ceased its lunges through the void and returned reluctantly to his body, the horror of nothingness had receded past then down the corridor, still struggling, and the waves of its blinding force weakened with the distance.

Yarol was leaning against the wall, wide-eyed and gasping. 'Did it get you, too?' he managed to articulate after several attempts to control his hurrying breath.

Smith found his own lungs laboring. He nodded breathless.

'I wonder,' he said when he had recovered a measure of normality, 'if that thing would look as white in the dark as it did dark in the light? I'll bet it would. And do you suppose it can't exist outside the light? Reminded me of a jelly-fish caught in a mill-race. Say, if the light's flowing out that fast, d'you think it may go entirely? We'd better be moving.'

Under their feet the passage sloped downward still. And when they reached the end of their quest, it came very suddenly. The curve of the passage sharpened to an angle, and round the bend the corridor ended abruptly at the threshold of a great cavity in the heart of the asteroid.

In the rich golden light it glittered like the center of a many-faceted diamond – that vast crystal room. The light brimmed it from wall to wall, from floor to ceiling. And it was strange that in the mellow flood of radiance the boundaries of the room seemed hard to define – somehow it looked limitless, though the walls were clear to be seen.

All this, though, they were realizing only subconsciously. Their eyes met the throne in the center of the crystal vault and clung there, fascinated. It was a crystal throne, and it had been fashioned for no human occupant. On this the mighty Three of measureless antiquity had sat. It was not an altar – it was a throne where incarnate godhood reigned once, too long ago for the mind to comprehend. Roughly triform, it glittered under the great arch of the ceiling. There was no knowing from the shape of it now, what form the Three had worn who sat upon it. But the forms must; have been outside modern comprehension – nothing the two explorers had ever seen in all their wanderings could have occupied it.

Two of the pedestals were empty. Saig and Lsa had vanished as completely as their names from man's memory. On the third – the center and the highest ... Smith's breath caught in his throat suddenly. Here then, on the great throne before them, lay all that was left of a god – the greatest of antiquity's deities. This mound of gray dust. The oldest thing upon three worlds – older than the mountains that held it, older than the very old beginnings of the mighty race of man. Great Pharol – dust upon a throne.

'Say, listen,' broke in Yarol's matter-of-fact voice. 'Why did the image turn to dust when the room and the throne didn't? The whole room must have come from that crystal temple on the other world. You'd think—'

'The image must have been very old long before the temple was built,' said Smith softly. He was thinking how dead it looked, lying there in a soft gray mound on a crystal. How dead! how immeasurably old! – yet if the little man spoke truly, life still dwelt in these ashes of forgotten deity. Could he indeed forge from the gray dust a cable that would reach out irresistibly across the gulfs of time and space, into dimensions beyond man's understanding, and draw back the vanished entity which had once been Great Pharol? Could he? And if he could – suddenly doubt rose up in Smith's mind. What man, with a god to do his bidding, would stop short of domination over the worlds of space – perhaps of godhood for himself? And if that man were half mad? ...

He followed Yarol across the shining floor in silence. It took them longer to reach the throne than they had expected – there was something deceptive about the crystal of that room, and the clarity of the brimming golden light. The translucent heights of the triumvirate structure that had enthroned gods towered high over their heads. Smith looked upward toward that central pedestal bearing its eon-old burden, wondering what men had stood here before him at the foot of the throne, what men of nameless races and forgotten worlds, worshipping the black divinity that was Pharol. On this crystal floor the feet of—

A scrambling sound interrupted his wondering. The irreverent Yarol, his eyes on the gray dust above them, was climbing the crystal throne. It was slippery, and never meant for mounting, and his heavy boots slid over the smoothness of it. Smith stood watching with a half-smile. For long ages no living man had dared approach this place save in reverence, on his knees, not venturing so much as to lift his eyes to that holy of holies where sat incarnate godhood. Now – Yarol's foot slipped on the last step of the ascent and he muttered under his breath, reaching out to clutch the pedestal where Great Pharol, first of the living gods, had ruled a mightier world than any men inhabit now.

At the summit he paused, looking down from an eminence whence no eyes save those of gods had ever looked before. And he frowned in a puzzled way as he looked.

'Something wrong here, N.W.,' he said. 'Look up. What's going on around the ceiling?'

Smith's pale gaze rose. For a moment he stared in utter bewilderment. For the third time that day his eyes were beholding something so impossible that they refused to register the fact upon an outraged brain. Something dark and yet not dark was closing down upon them. The roof seemed to lower – and panic stirred within him briefly. The ceiling, coming down to crush them? Some further guardian of the gods descending like a blanket over their heads? What?

And then understanding broke upon him, and his laugh of sheer relief echoed almost blasphemously in the silence of the place.

'The light's running out,' he said. 'Like water, just draining away. That's all.'

And the incredible thing was true. That shining lake of light which brimmed the crystal hollow was ebbing, pouring through the door, down the passage, out into the upper air, and darkness, literally, was flowing in behind it. And it was flowing fast.

'Well,' said Yarol, casting an imperturbable glance upward, 'we'd better be moving before it all runs out. Hand me up the box, will you?'

Hesitantly, Smith unslung the little lacquered steel box they had been given. Suppose they brought him back the dust to weld it from – what then? Such limitless power even in the hands of an eminently wise, eminently sane and balanced man would surely be dangerous. And in the hands of the little whispering fanatic—

Yarol, looking down from his height, met the troubled eyes and was silent for a moment. Then he whistled softly and said, though Smith had not spoken,

'I never thought of that … D'you suppose it really could be done? Why, the man's half crazy!'

'I don't know,' said Smith. 'Maybe he couldn't – but he told us the way here, didn't he? He knew this much – I don't think we'd better risk his not knowing any more. And suppose he did succeed, Yarol – suppose he found some way to bring this – this monster of the dark – through into our dimension – turned it loose on our worlds. Do you think he could hold it? He talked about enslaving a god, but could he? I haven't much doubt that he knows some way of opening a door between dimensions to admit the thing that used to be Pharol – it can be done. It has been done. But once he gets it opened, can he close it? Could he keep the thing under control? You know he couldn't! You know it'd break loose, and – well, anything could happen then.'

'I hadn't thought of that,' said Yarol again. 'Gods! Suppose—'

He broke off, staring in fascination at the gray dust that held such terrible potentialities. And there was silence for a while in the crystal place.

Smith, looking upward at the throne and his friend, saw that the dark was flowing in faster and faster. And the light thinned about them, and long streaks of brilliance wavered out behind him as the light ebbed by a racing torrent.

'Suppose we don't take it back, then,' said Yarol suddenly. 'Say we couldn't find the place – or that it was buried under debris or something. Suppose we – gods, but it's getting dark in here!'

The line of light was far down the walls now. Above them the black night of the underground brimmed in relentlessly. They watched in half-incredulous wonder as the tidemark of radiance ebbed down and down along the crystal. Now it touched the level of the throne, and Yarol gasped as he was plunged head and shoulders into blackness, starring down as into a sea of light in which his own lower limbs moved shimmeringly, sending long ripples outward as they stirred.

Very swiftly the tide-race ran. Fascinated, they watched it ebb away, down Yarol's legs, down beyond him entirely, so that he perched in darkness above the outrunning tide, down the heights of the throne, down to touch Smith's tall head with blackness. Uncannily he stood in the midst of a receding sea, shoulder-deep – waist-deep – knee-deep …

The light that so short a time before – for so many countless ages before – had brimmed this chamber lay in a shallow, gleaming sea ankle-deep on the floor. For the first time in eons the throne of the Three stood in darkness.

Not until the last dregs of illumination were snaking along a black floor in rivulets that ran swiftly, like fiery snakes, toward the door, did the two men awake from their wonder. The last of the radiance that must have been lighted on a lost world millions of years ago, perhaps by the hands of the first gods – ebbed doorward. Smith drew a deep breath and turned in the blackness toward the spot where the throne must be standing in the first dark it had known for countless ages. Those snakes of light along the floor did not seem to give out any radiance – the place was blacker than any night above ground. Yarol's light-tube suddenly stabbed downward, and Yarol's voice said from the dark, 'Whew! Should have bottled some of that to take home. Well, what d'you say, N.W.? Do we leave with the dust or without it?'

'Without it,' said Smith slowly. 'I'm sure of that much, anyhow. But we can't leave it here. The man would simply send others, you know. With blasting material, maybe, if we said the place was buried. But he'd get it.'

Yarol's beam shifted, a white blade in the dark, to the gray, enigmatic mound beside him. In the glare of the Tomlinson tube it lay inscrutably, just as it had lain for all the eons since the god forsook it – waiting, perhaps, for this moment. And Yarol drew his gun.

'Don't know what that image was made of,' he said, 'but rock or metal or anything else will melt into nothing in the full-power heat of a gun.'

And in a listening silence he flicked the catch. Blue-white and singing, the flame leaped irresistibly from is muzzle – struck full in an intolerable violence of heat upon that gray mound which had been a god. Rocks would have melted under the blast. Rocket-tube steel would have glowed molten. Nothing that the hands of man can fashion could have resisted the heat-blast of a ray-gun at full strength. But in its full blue glare the mound of dust lay motionless.

Above the hissing of the flame Smith heard Yarol's muttered *'Shar!'* of amazement. The gun muzzle thrust closer into the gray heap, until the crystal began to glow in the reflected heat and blue sparks spattered through the darkness. And very slowly the edges of the mound began to turn red and sullen. The redness spread. A little blue flame licked up; another.

Yarol flipped off the gun-catch and sat watching as the dust began to blaze. Presently, as the brilliance of it grew stronger, he slid down from his pedestal and made his precarious way along the slippery crystal to the floor. Smith scarcely realized that he had come. His eyes were riveted on the clear, burning flame that was once a god. It burned with a fierce, pale light flickering with nameless evanescent colors – the dust that had been Pharol of the utter darkness burning slowly away in a flame of utter light.

And as the minutes passed and the flame grew stronger, the reflections of it began to dance eerily in the crystal walls and ceiling, sending long wavers downward until the floor was carpeted with dazzles of flame. An odor of unnamable things very faintly spread upon the air – smoke of dead gods ... It went to Smith's head dizzily, and the reflections wavered and ran together until he seemed to be suspended in a space while all about him pictures of flame went writhing through the dark – pictures of flame – nebulous, unreal pictures waving across the walls and vanishing – flashing by uncertainly overhead, running under his feet, circling him round from wall to wall in reeling patterns, as if reflections made eons ago on another world and buried deep in the crystal were waking to life at the magic touch of the burning god.

With the smoke eddying dizzily in his nostrils he watched – and all about him, overhead, underfoot, the strange, wild pictures ran blurrily through the crystal and vanished. He thought he saw mighty landscapes ringed by such mountains as none of today's world know ... he thought he saw a whiter sun than has shone for eons, lighting a land where rivers thundered between green banks ... thought he saw many moons parading across a purple night wherein shone constellations that haunted him with familiarity in the midst of their strangeness ... saw a green star where red Mars should be, and a far pin-prick of white where the green point that is Earth hangs. Cities reeled past across the crystal darkness in shapes stranger than any that history records. Peaks and spires and angled domes towered high and shining under the hot white sun – strange ships riding the airways ... He saw battles – weapons that have no names today blasting the tall towers into ruins, wiping great smears of blood across the crystal – saw triumphant marches where creatures that might have been the forerunners of men paraded in a blaze of color through shining streets ... strange, sinuous creatures, half seen, that were men, yet not men ... Nebulously the history of a dead and forgotten world flared by him in the dark.

He saw the man-things in their great shining cities bowing down before a – something – of darkness that spread monstrously across the white-lit heavens ... saw the beginnings of Great Pharol ... saw the crystal throne in a room of crystal where the sinuous, man-formed beings lay face down in worshipping windrows about a great triple pedestal toward which, for the dazzle and the darkness of it, he could not turn his eyes. And then without warning, in a mighty blast of violence, all the wild pictures in the flickering flamelight ran together and shivered before his dizzied eyes, and a great burst of blinding light leaped across the walls until the whole great chamber once more for an instant blazed with radiance but a radiance so searing that it did not illuminate but stunned, blinded, exploded in the very brains of the two men who watched ...

In the flash of an instant before oblivion overtook him, Smith knew they had looked upon the death of a world. Then, with blinded eyes and reeling brain, he stumbled and sank into darkness.

Blackness was all about them when they opened their eyes again. The fire on the throne had burnt away into eternal darkness. Stumblingly they followed the white guidance of their tube-lights down the long passage and out into the upper air. The pale Martian day was darkening over the mountains.

JULHI

The tale of Smith's scars would make a saga. From head to foot his brown and sunburnt hide was scored with the marks of battle. The eye of a connoisseur would recognize the distinctive tracks of knife and talon and ray-burn, the slash of the Martian drylander *cring*, the clean, thin stab of the Venusian stiletto, the crisscross lacing of Earth's penal whip. But one or two scars that he carried would have baffled the most discerning eye. That curious, convoluted red circlet, for instance, like some bloody rose on the left side of his chest just where the beating of his heart stirred the sun-darkened flesh ...

In the starless dark of the thick Venusian night Northwest Smith's pale steel eyes were keen and wary. Save for those restless eyes he did not stir. He crouched against a wall that his searching fingers had told him was stone, and cold; but he could see nothing and he had no faintest idea of where he was or how he had come there. Upon this dark five minutes ago he had opened puzzled eyes, and he was still puzzled. The dark-piercing pallor of his gaze flickered restlessly through the blackness, searching in vain for some point of familiarity. He could find nothing. The dark was blurred and formless around him, and though his keen senses spoke to him of enclosed spaces, yet there was a contradiction even in that, for the air was fresh and blowing.

He crouched motionless in the windy dark, smelling earth and cold stone, and faintly – very faintly – a whiff of something unfamiliar that made him gather his feet under him noiselessly and poise with one hand against the chill stone wall, tense as a steel spring. There was motion in the dark. He could see nothing, hear nothing, but he felt that stirring come cautiously nearer. He stretched out exploring toes, found the ground firm underfoot, and stepped aside a soundless pace or two, holding his breath. Against the stone where he had been leaning an instant before he heard the soft sound of hands fumbling, with a queer, sucking noise, as if they were sticky. Something exhaled with a small, impatient sound. In a lull of the wind he heard quite distinctly the slither over stone of something that was neither feet nor paws nor serpent-coils, but akin to all three.

Smith's hand sough his hip by instinct, and came away empty. Where he was and how he came there he did not know, but his weapons were gone and he knew that their absence was not accidental. The something that was pursuing him sighed again, queerly, and the shuffling sound over the stones moved with sudden, appalling swiftness, and something touched him that stung like an electric shock. There were hands upon him, but he scarcely realized it, or that they were no human hands, before the darkness spun around him and the queer, thrilling shock sent him reeling into a blurred oblivion.

When he opened his eyes again he lay once more upon cold stone in the unfathomable dark to which he had awakened before. He lay as he must have fallen when the searcher dropped him, and he was unhurt. He waited, tense and listening, until his ears ached with the strain and the silence. So far as his blade-keen senses could tell him, he was quite alone. No sound broke the utter stillness, no sensation of movement, no whiff of scent. Very cautiously he rose once more, supporting himself against the unseen stones and flexing his limbs to be sure that he was unhurt.

The floor was uneven underfoot. He had the idea now that he must be in some ancient ruins, for the smell of stone and chill and desolation was clear to him, and the breeze moaned a little through unseen openings. He felt his way along the broken wall, stumbling over fallen blocks and straining his senses against the blanketing gloom around him. He was trying vainly to recall how he had come here, and succeeding in recapturing only vague memories of much red *segir*-whisky in a nameless dive, and confusion and muffled voices thereafter, and wide spaces of utter blank – and then awakening here in the dark. The whisky must have been drugged, he told himself defensively, and a slow anger began to smolder within him at the temerity of whoever it was who had dared lay hands upon Northwest Smith.

Then he froze into stony quiet, rigid in mid-step, at the all but soundless stirring of something in the dark near by. Blurred visions of the unseen thing that had seized him ran through his head – some monster whose gait was a pattering glide and whose hands were armed with the stunning shock of an unknown force. He stood frozen, wondering if it could see him in the dark.

Feet whispered over the stone very near him, and something breathed pantingly, and a hand brushed his face. There was a quick suck of indrawn breath, and then Smith's arms leaped out to grapple the invisible thing to him. The surprise of that instant took his breath, and then he laughed deep in his throat and swung the girl round to face him in the dark.

He could not see her, but he knew from the firm curves of her under his hands that she was young and feminine, and from the sound of her breath that she was near to fainting with fright.

'Sh-h-h,' he whispered urgently, his lips at her ear and her hair brushing his cheek fragrantly. 'Don't be afraid. Where are we?'

It might have been reaction from her terror that relaxed the tense body he held, so that she went limp in his arms and the sound of her breathing almost ceased. He lifted her clear of the ground – she was light and fragrant and he felt the brush of velvet garments against his bare arms as unseen robes swept him – and carried her across to the wall. He felt better with something solid at his back. He laid her down there in the angle of the stones and crouched beside her, listening, while she slowly regained control of herself.

When her breathing was normal again, save for the faint hurrying of excitement and alarm, he heard the sound of her sitting up against the wall, and bent closer to catch her whisper.

'Who are you?' she demanded.

'Northwest Smith,' he said under his breath, and grinned at her softly murmured 'Oh-h!' of recognition. Whoever she was she had heard that name before. Then, 'There has been a mistake,' she breathed, half to herself. 'They never take any but the – space-rats and the scum of the ports for Julhi to – I mean, to bring here. They must not have known you, and they will pay for that mistake. No man is brought here who might be searched for – afterward.'

Smith was silent for a moment. He had thought her lost like himself, and her fright had been too genuine for pretense. Yet she seemed to know the secrets of this curious, unlit place. He must go warily.

'Who are you?' he murmured. 'Why were you so frightened? Where are we?'

In the dark her breath caught in a little gasp, and went on unevenly.

'We are in the ruins of Vonng,' she whispered. 'I am Apri, and I am condemned to death. I thought you were death coming for me, as it will come at any instant now.' Her voice failed on the last syllables, so that she spoke in a fading gasp as if terror had her by the throat and would not let her breathe. He felt her trembling against his arm.

Many questions crowded up to his lips, but the most urgent found utterance.

'What will come?' he demanded. 'What is the danger?'

'The haunters of Vonng,' she whispered fearfully. 'It is to feed them that Julhi's slaves bring men here. And those among us who are disobedient must feed the haunters too. I have suffered her displeasure – and I must die.'

'The haunters – what are they? Something with a touch like a live wire had me awhile ago, but it let me loose again. Could that have been—'

'Yes, one of them. My coming must have disturbed it. But as to what they are, I don't know. They come in the darkness. They are of Julhi's race, I think, but not flesh and blood, like her. I – I can't explain.'

'And Julhi – ?'

'Is – well, simply Julhi. You don't know?'

'A woman? Some queen, perhaps? You must remember I don't even know where I am.'

'No, not a woman. At least, not as I am. And much more than queen. A great sorceress, I have thought, or perhaps a goddess. I don't know. It makes me ill to think, here in Vonng. It makes me ill to – to – oh, I couldn't bear it! I think I was going mad! It's better to die than go mad, isn't it? But I'm so afraid—'

Her voice trailed away incoherently, and she cowered shivering against him in the dark.

Smith had been listening above her shuddering whispers for any tiniest sound in the night. Now he turned his mind more fully to what she had been saying, though with an ear still alert for any noises about them.

'What do you mean? What was it you did?'

'There is a – a light,' murmured Apri vaguely. 'I've always seen it, even from babyhood, whenever I closed my eyes and tried to make it come. A light, and queer shapes and shadows moving through it, like reflections from somewhere I never saw before. But somehow it got out of control, and then I began to catch the strangest thought-waves beating through, and after a while Julhi came – through the light. I don't know – I can't understand. But she makes me summon up the light for her now, and then queer things happen inside my head, and I'm ill and dizzy, and – and I think I'm going mad. But she makes me do it. And it grows worse, you know, each time worse, until I can't bear it. Then she's angry, and that dreadful still look comes over her face – and this time she sent me here. The haunters will come, now—'

Smith tightened his arm comfortingly about her, thinking that she was perhaps a little mad already.

'How can we get out of here?' he demanded, shaking her gently to call back her wandering mind. 'Where are we?'

'In Vonng. Don't you understand? On the island where Vonng's ruins are.'

He remembered then. He had heard of Vonng, somewhere. The ruins of an old city lost in the tangle of vines upon a small island a few hours off the coast of Shann. There were legends that it had been a great city once, and a strange one. A king with curious powers had built it, a king in league with beings better left unnamed, so the whispers ran. The stone had been quarried with unnamable rites, and the buildings were very queerly shaped, for mysterious purposes. Some of its lines ran counter-wise to the understanding even of the men who laid them out, and at intervals in the streets, following a pattern certainly not of their own world, medallions had been set, for reasons known to none but the king. Smith remembered what he had heard of the strangeness of fabulous Vonng, and of the rites that attended its building, and that as last some strange plague had overrun it, driving men mad … something about ghosts that flickered through the streets at mid-day; so that at last the dwellers there had deserted it, and for centuries it had stood here, slowly crumbling into decay. No one ever visited the place now, for civilization had moved inland since the days of Vonng's glory, and uneasy tales still ran through men's minds about the queer things that had happened there once.

'Julhi lives in these ruins?' he demanded.

'Julhi lives here but not in a ruined Vonng. Her Vonng is a splendid city. I have seen it, but I could never enter.'

'Quite mad,' thought Smith compassionately. And aloud, 'Are there no boats here? No way to escape at all?'

Almost before the last words had left his lips he heard something like the humming of countless bees begin to ring in his ears. It grew and deepened and swelled until his head was filled with sound, and the cadences of that sound said, 'No. No way. Julhi forbids it.'

In Smith's arms the girl startled and clung to him convulsively.

'It is Julhi!' she gasped. 'Do you feel her, singing in your brain? Julhi!'

Smith heard the voice swelling louder, until it seemed to fill the whole night, humming with intolerable volume.

'Yes, my little Apri. It is I. Do you repent your disobedience, my Apri?'

Smith felt the girl trembling against him. He could hear her heart pounding, and the breath rushed chokingly through her lips.

'No – no, I do not,' he heard her murmur, very softly. 'Let me die, Julhi.'

The voice hummed with a purring sweetness.

'Die, my pretty? Julhi could not be so cruel. Oh no, little Apri, I but frightened you for punishment. You are forgiven now. You may return to me and serve me again, my Apri. I would not let you die.' The voice was cloyingly sweet.

Apri's voice crescendoed into hysterical rebellion.

'No, no! I will not serve you! Not again, Julhi! Let me die!'

'Peace, peace my little one.' That humming was hypnotic in its soothing lilt. 'You will serve me. Yes, you will obey me as before, my pretty. You have found man there, haven't you, little one? Bring him with you, and come.'

Apri's unseen hands clawed frantically at Smith's shoulders, tearing herself free, pushing him away.

'Run, run!' she gasped. 'Climb this wall and run! You can throw yourself over the cliff and be free. Run, I say, before it's too late. Oh, *Shar, Shar*, if I were free to die!'

Smith prisoned the clawing hands in one of his and shook her with the other.

'Be still!' he snapped. 'You're hysterical. Be still!'

He felt the shuddering slacken. The straining hands fell quiet. By degrees her panting breath evened.

'Come,' she said at last, and in quite a different voice. 'Julhi commands it. Come.'

Her fingers twined firmly in his, and she stepped forward without hesitation into the dark. He followed, stumbling over debris, bruising himself against the broken walls. How far they went he did not know, but the way turned and twisted and doubled back upon itself, and he had, somehow, the curious idea that she was not following a course through corridors and passages which she knew well enough not to hesitate over, but somehow, under the influence of Julhi's sorcery, treading a symbolic pattern among the stones, tracing it out with unerring feet – a witch-pattern that, when it was completed, would open a door for them which no eyes could see, no hands unlock.

It may have been Julhi who put that certainty in his mind, but he was quite sure of it as the girl walked on along her intricate path, threading silently in and out among the unseen ruins, nor was he surprised when without warning the floor became smooth underfoot and the walls seemed to fall away from about him, the smell of cold stone vanished from the air. Now he walked in darkness over a thick carpet, through sweetly scented air, warm and gently moving with invisible currents. In that dark he was somehow aware of eyes upon him. Not physical eyes, but a more all-pervading inspection. Presently the humming began again, swelling through the air and beating in his ears in sweetly pitched cadences.

'Hm-m-m … have you brought me a man from Earth, my Apri? Yes, an Earthman, and a fine one. I am pleased with you, Apri, for saving me this man. I shall call him to me presently. Until then let him wander, for he can not escape.'

The air fell quiet again, and about him Smith gradually became aware of a dawning light. It swelled from no visible source, but it paled the utter dark to a twilight through which he could see tapestries and richly glowing columns about him, and the outlines of the girl Apri standing at his side. The twilight paled in turn, and the light grew strong, and presently he stood in full day among the queer, rich furnishings of the place into which he had come.

He stared round in vain for signs of the way they had entered. The room was a small cleared space in the midst of a forest of shining pillars of polished stone. Tapestries were stretched between some of them, swinging down in luxuriant folds. But as far as he could see in all directions the columns reached away in diminishing aisles, and he was quite sure that they had not made their way to this place through the clustering pillars. He would have been aware of them. No, he had stepped straight from Vonng's stonestrewn ruins upon this rug which carpeted the little clear space, through some door invisible to him.

He turned to the girl. She had sunk upon one of the divans which stood between the columns around the edge of the circular space. She was paler than the marble, and very lovely, as he had known she would be. She had the true Venusian's soft, dark, sidelong eyes, and her mouth was painted coral, and her hair swept in black, shining clouds over her shoulders. The tight-swathed Venusian robe clung to her in folds of rose-red velvet, looped to leave one shoulder bare, and slit, as all Venusian's women's garments are, to let one leg flash free with every other step. It is the most flattering dress imaginable for any woman to wear, but Apri needed no flattery to make her beautiful. Smith's pale eyes were appreciative as he stared.

She met his gaze apathetically. All rebellion seemed to have gone out of her, and a strange exhaustion had drained the color from her face.

'Where are we now?' demanded Smith.

She gave him an oblique glance.

'This is the place Julhi uses for a prison,' she murmured, almost indifferently. 'Around us I suppose her slaves are moving, and the halls of her palace stretch. I can't explain it to you, but at Julhi's command anything can happen. We could be in the midst of her palace and never suspect it, for there is no escape from here. We can do nothing but wait.'

'Why?' Smith nodded toward the columned vistas stretching away all around them. 'What's beyond that?'

'Nothing. It simply extends like that until – until you find yourself back here again.'

Smith glanced at her swiftly under lowered lids, wondering just how mad she really was. Her white, exhausted face told him nothing.

'Come along,' he said at last. 'I'm going to try anyhow.'

She shook her head.

'No use. Julhi can find you when she is ready. There is no escape from Julhi.'

'I'm going to try,' he said again, stubbornly. 'Are you coming?'

'No. I'm – tired. I'll wait here. You'll come back.'

He turned without further words and plunged at random into the wilderness of pillars surrounding the little carpeted room. The floor was slippery under his boots, and dully shining. The pillars, too, shone along all their polished surfaces, and in the queer light diffused throughout the place no shadows fell; so that a dimension seemed to be lacking and a curious flatness lay over all the shining forest. He went on resolutely, looking back now and again to keep his course straight away from the little clear space he had left. He watched it dwindle behind him and lose itself among the columns and vanish, and he wandered on through endless wilderness, to the sound of his own echoing footsteps, with nothing to break the monotony of the shining pillars until he thought he glimpsed a cluster of tapestries far ahead through the unshadowed vistas and began to hurry, hoping against hope that he had found at least a way out of the forest. He reached the place at last, and pulled aside the tapestry, and met Apri's wearily smiling eyes. The way somehow had doubled back upon him.

He snorted disgustedly at himself and turned again to plunge into the columns. This time he had wandered for no more than ten minutes before he found himself coming back once more into the clearing. He tried a third time, and it seemed had taken no more than a dozen steps before the way twisted under his feet and catapulted him back again into the room he had just left. Apri smiled as he flung himself upon one of the divans and regarded her palely from under knit brows.

'There is no escape,' she repeated. 'I think this place is built upon some different plan from any we know, with all its lines running in a circle whose center is this room. For only a circle had boundaries, yet no end, like this wilderness around us.'

'Who is Julhi?' asked Smith abruptly. '*What* is she?'

'She is – a goddess, perhaps. Or a devil from hell. Or both. And she comes from the place beyond the light – I can't explain it to you. It was I who opened the door for her, I think, and through me she looks back into the light that I must call up for her when she commands me. And I shall go mad – mad!'

Desperation flamed from her eyes suddenly and faded again, leaving her face whiter than before. Her hands rose in a small, futile gesture and dropped to her lap again. She shook her head.

'No – not wholly mad. She would never permit me even that escape, for then I could not summon up the light and so open the window for her to look backward into that land from which she came. That land—'

'Look!' broke in Smith. 'The light—'

Apri glanced up and nodded almost indifferently.

'Yes. It's darkening again. Julhi will summon you now, I think.'

Rapidly the illumination was failing all about them, and the columned forests melted into dimness, and dark veiled the long vistas, and presently everything clouded together and black night fell once more. This time they did not move, but Smith was aware, remotely, of a movement all about them, subtle and indescribable, as if the scenes were being shifted behind the curtain of the dark. The air quivered with motion and change. Even under his feet the floor was shifting, not tangibly but with an inner metamorphosis he could put no name to.

And then the dark began to lift again. Light diffused slowly through it, paling the black, until he stood in a translucent twilight through whose veil he could see that the whole scene had changed about him. He saw Apri from the corner of his eye, heard her quickened breathing beside him, but he did not turn his head. Those columned vistas were gone. The limitless aisles down which he had wandered were closed now by great walls uplifting all around.

His eyes rose to seek the ceiling, and as the dusk lightened into day once more he became aware of a miraculous quality about those walls. A curious wavy pattern ran around them in broad bands, and as he stared he realized that the bands were not painted upon the surface, but were integrally part of the walls themselves, and that each successive band lessened in density. Those along the base of the walls were heavily dark, but the rising patterns paled and became less solid as they rose, until at half-way up the wall they were like layers of patterned smoke, and farther up still bands of scarcely discernible substance more tenuous than mist. Around the heights they seemed to melt into pure light, to which he could not lift his eyes for the dazzling brilliance of it.

In the center of the room rose a low black couch, and upon it – Julhi. He knew that instinctively the moment he saw her, and in that first moment he realized nothing but her beauty. He caught his breath at the sleek and shining loveliness of her, lying on her black couch and facing him with a level, unwinking stare. Then he realized her unhumanity, and a tiny prickling ran down his back – for she was one of that very ancient race of one-eyed beings about which whispers persist so unescapably in folklore and legend, though history has forgotten them for ages. One-eyed. A clear eye, uncolored, centered in the midst of a fair, broad forehead. Her features were arranged in a diamond-shaped pattern instead of humanity's triangle, for the slanting nostrils of her low-bridged nose were set so far apart that they might have been separate features, tilting and exquisitely modeled. Her mouth was perhaps the queerest feature of her strange yet somehow lovely face. It was perfectly heartshaped, in an exaggerated cupid's-bow, but it was not a human mouth. It did not close, ever. It was a beautifully arched orifice, the red lip that rimmed it compellingly crimson, but fixed and moveless in an unhinged jaw. Behind the bowed opening he could see the red, fluted tissue of flesh within.

Above that single, clear, deep-lashed eye something sprang backward from her brow in a splendid sweep, something remotely feather-like, yet no such feather as was ever fledged upon any bird alive. It was exquisitely iridescent, and its fronds shivered with blowing color at the slight motion of her breathing.

For the rest – well, as the lines of a lap-dog travesty the clean, lean grace of a racing greyhound, so humanity's shape travestied the serpentine loveliness of her body. And it was definitely humanity that aped her form, not herself aping humanity. Somehow she was so *right* in every flowing, curving line, so unerringly fashioned toward some end he could not guess, yet to which instinctively he conceded her perfect fitness.

There was a fluidity about her, a litheness that partook more of the serpent's rippling flow than of any warm-blooded creature's motion, but her body was not like any being, warm-blooded or cold, that he had ever seen before. From the waist up she was human, but below all resemblance ended. And yet she was so breath-takingly lovely. Any attempt to describe the alien beauty of her lower limbs would sound grotesque, and she was not grotesque even in her unnamable shape, even in the utter weirdness of her face.

That clear, unwinking eye turned its gaze upon Smith. She lay there luxuriously upon her black couch, ivory-pale against the darkness of it, the indescribable strangeness of her body lolling with a serpent's grace upon the cushions. He felt the gaze of that eye go through him, searching out all the hidden places in his brain and flickering casually over the lifetime that lay behind him. The feathery crest quivered very gently above her head.

He met the gaze steadily. There was no expression upon that changeless face, for she could not smile, and the look in her single eye was meaningless to him. He had no way of guessing what emotions were stirring behind the alien mask. He had never realized before how essential is the mobility of the mouth in expressing moods, and hers was fixed, immobile, for ever stretched into its heart-shaped arch – like a lyre-frame, he thought, but irrevocably dumb, surely, for such a mouth as hers, in its immovable unhinged jaw, could never utter human speech.

And then she spoke. The shock of it made him blink, and it was a moment before he realized just how she was accomplishing the impossible. The fluted tissue within the arched opening of her mouth had begun to vibrate like harp-strings, and the humming he had heard before went thrilling through the air. Beside him he was aware of Apri shuddering uncontrollably as the humming strengthened and swelled, but he was listening too closely to realize her save subconsciously; for there was in that humming something that – that, yes, it was rounding into the most queerly uttered phrases, in a sort of high, unutterably sweet singing note, like the sound of a violin. With her moveless lips she could not articulate, and her only enunciation came from the varied intensities of that musical tone. Many languages could not be spoken so, but the High Venusian's lilt is largely that of pitch, every word-sound bearing as many meanings as it has degrees of intensity, so that the exquisitely modulated notes which came rippling from her harp-like mouth bore as clear a meaning as if she were enunciating separate words.

And it was more eloquent than speech. Somehow those singing phrases played upon other senses than the aural. From the first lilted note he recognized the danger of that voice. It vibrated, it thrilled, it caressed. It rippled up and down his answering nerves like fingers over harp-strings.

'Who are you, Earthman?' that lazy, nerve-strumming voice demanded.

He felt, as he answered, that she knew not only his name but much more about him than he himself knew. Knowledge was in her eye, serene and all-inclusive.

'Northwest Smith,' he said, a little sullenly. 'Why have you brought me here?'

'A dangerous man.' There was an undernote of mockery in the music. 'You were brought to feed the dwellers of Vonng with human blood, but I think – yes, I think I shall keep you for myself. You have known much of emotions that are alien to me, and I would share them fully, as one with your own strong, hot-blooded body, Northwest Smith. *Aie-e-e*' – the humming wailed along an ecstatic upward note that sent shivers down the man's spine – 'and how sweet and hot your blood will be, my Earthman! You shall share my ecstasy as I drink it! You shall – but wait. First you must understand. Listen, Earthman.'

The humming swelled to an inarticulate roaring in his ears, and somehow his mind relaxed under that sound, smoothed out, pliantly as wax for the recording of her voice. In that queer, submissive mood he heard her singing,

'Life dwells in so many overlapping planes, my Earthman, that even I can comprehend but a fraction of them. My plane is very closely akin to your own, and at some places they overlap in so intimate a way that it takes little effort to break through, if one can find a weak spot. This city of Vonng is one of the spots, a place which exists simultaneously in both planes. Can you understand that? It was laid out along certain obscure patterns in a way and for a purpose which are stories in themselves; so that in my own plane as well as here in yours Vonng's walls and streets and buildings are tangible. But time is different in our two worlds. It moves slower here. The strange alliance between your plane and mine, through two sorcerers of our alien worlds, was brought about very curiously. Vonng was built by men of your own plane, laboriously, stone by stone. But to us it seemed that through the magic of that sorcerer of ours a city suddenly appeared at his command, empty and complete. For your time moves so much faster than ours.

'And though through the magic of those strangely matched conspirators the stone which built Vonng existed in both planes at once, no power could make the men who dwelt in Vonng accessible to us. Two races simultaneously inhabited the city. To mankind it seemed haunted by nebulous, imponderable presences. That race was ourselves. To us you were tantalizingly perceptible in flashes, but we could not break through. And we wanted to very badly. Mentally, sometimes we could reach you, but physically never.

'And so it went on. But because time moved slower here, your Vonng fell into ruins and has been deserted for ages, while to our perceptions it is still a great and thronging city. I shall show you presently.'

'To understand why I am here you must understand something of our lives. The goal of your own race is the pursuit of happiness, is it not so? But our lives are spent wholly in the experiencing and enjoyment of sensation. To us that is food and drink and happiness. Without it we starve. To nourish our bodies we must drink the blood of living creatures, but that is a small matter beside the ravenous hunger we know for the sensations and the emotions of the flesh. We are infinitely more capable of experiencing them than you, both physically and mentally. Our range of sensation is vast beyond your comprehension, but to us it is an old story, and always we seek new sensations, other alien emotions. We have raided many worlds, many planes, many dimensions, in search of something new. It was only a short while ago that we succeeded in breaking into yours, through the help of Apri here.

'You must understand that we could not have come had there not been a doorway. Ever since the building of Vonng we have been mentally capable of entering, but to experience the emotions we crave we must have physical contact, a temporary physical union through the drinking of blood. And there has never been a way to enter until we found Apri. You see, we have long known that some are born with a wider range of perceptions than their comrades can understand. Sometimes they are called mad. Sometimes in their madness they are more dangerous than they realize. For Apri was born with the ability to gaze in upon our world, and though she did not know this, or understand what the light was which she could summon up at will, she unwittingly opened the door for us to enter here.

'It was through her aid that I came, and with her aid that I maintain myself here and bring others through in the dark of the night to feed upon the blood of mankind. Our position is precarious in your world, and we have not yet dared make ourselves known. So we have begun upon the lowest types of man, to accustom ourselves to the fare and to strengthen our hold upon humanity, so that when we are ready to go forth openly we shall have sufficient power to withstand your resistance. But soon now we shall come.'

The long, lovely, indescribable body upon the couch writhed round to front him more fully, the motion rippling along her limbs like a wavelet over water. The deep, steady gaze of the eye bored into his, the voice pulsed with intensity.

'Great things are waiting for you, Earthman – before you die. We shall become one, for a while. I shall savor all your perceptions, suck up the sensations you have known. I shall open new fields to you, and see them through your senses with a new flavor, and you shall share my delight in the taste of your newness. And as your blood flows you shall know all beauty, and all horror, and all delight and pain, and all the other emotions and sensations, nameless to you, that I have known.'

The humming music of her voice spun through Smith's brain soothingly. Somehow what she said held no urgency for him. It was like a legend of something which had happened long ago to another man. He waited gravely as the voice went on again, dreamily, gloatingly.

'You have known much of danger, O wanderer. You have looked upon strange things, and life has been full for you, and death an old comrade, and love – and love – those arms have held many women, is it not so? ... Is it not so?'

Unbearably sweet, the voice lingered murmurously over the vibrant query, something compelling and irresistible in the question, in the pitch and the queer, ringing tone of it. And quite involuntarily memories flashed back across the surface of his mind. He was quiet, remembering.

The milk-white girls of Venus are so lovely, with their sidelong eyes and their warm mouths and their voices pitched to the very tone of love. And the canal-women of Mars – coral pink, sweet as honey, murmurous under the moving moons. And Earth's girls are vibrant as swordblades, and heady with kisses and laughter. There were others, too. He remembered a sweet brown savage on a lost asteroid, and one brief, perfume-dizzied night under the reeling stars. And there had been a space-pirate's wench in stolen jewels, flame-gun belted, who came to him in a camptown on the edge of Martian civilization, where the drylands begin. There was that rosy Martian girl in the garden palace by the canal, where the moons went wheeling through the sky ... And once, very long ago, in a garden upon Earth – he closed his eyes and saw again the moonlight of home silvering a fair, high head, and level eyes looking into his and a mouth that quivered, saying—

He drew a long, unsteady breath and opened his eyes again. The pale steel stare of them was expressionless, but that last, deep-buried memory had burnt like a heat-ray, and he knew she had tasted the pain of it, and was exulting. The feathery crest that swept backward from her forehead was trembling rhythmically, and the colors blowing through it had deepened in intensity and were changing with bewildering swiftness. But her still face had not changed, although he thought there was a softening in the brilliance of her eye, as if she were remembering too.

When she spoke, the sustained, fluting note of her voice was breathless as a whisper, and he realized anew how infinitely more eloquent it was than a voice which spoke in words. She could infuse into the vibrant lilt blood-stirring intensities and soft, rich purrs that went sweeping along his nerves like velvet. His whole body was responding to the pitch of her voice. She was playing upon him as upon a harp, evoking chords of memory and sending burring thrills down his back and setting the blood athrob in his pulses by the very richness and deepness of her tone. And it strummed not only upon the responses of his body but also upon the chords of his very mind, waking thoughts to match her own, compelling him into the channels she desired. Her voice was purest magic, and he had not even the desire to resist it.

'They are sweet memories – sweet?' she purred caressingly. 'The women of the worlds you know – the women who have lain in those arms of yours – whose mouths have clung to yours – do you remember?'

There was the most flagrant mesmerism in her voice as it ran on vibrantly over him – again he thought of fingers upon harp-strings – evoking the melodies she desired, strumming at his memories with words like hot, sweet flames. The room misted before his eyes, and that singing voice was a lilt through timeless space, no longer speaking in phrases but in a throbbingly inarticulate purr, and his body was no more than a sounding-board for the melodies she played.

Presently the mesmerism of her tone took on a different pitch. The humming resolved itself into words again, thrilling through him now more clearly than spoken phrases.

'And in all these remembered women' – it sang – 'in all these you remember me … For it was I in each of them whom you remember – that little spark that was myself – and I am all women who love and are loved – my arms held you – do you not remember?'

In the midst of that hypnotic murmuring he did remember, and recognized dimly through the reeling tumult of his blood some great, veiled truth he could not understand.

The crest above her forehead trembled in slow, languorous rhythm, and rich colors flowed through it in tints that caressed the eyes – velvety purples, red like embers, flame colors and sunset shades. When she rose upon her couch with an unnamed gliding movement and held out her arms he had no recollection of moving forward, but somehow he was clasping her and the outstretched arms had coiled like serpents about him, and very briefly the heart-shaped orifice which was her mouth brushed against his lips.

Something icy happened then. The touch was light and fluttering, as if the membrane that lined that bowed and rigid opening had vibrated delicately against his mouth as swiftly and lightly as the brush of humming-birds' wings. It was not a shock, but somehow with the touch all the hammering tumult within him died. He was scarcely aware that he possessed a body. He was kneeling upon the edge of Julhi's couch, her arms like snakes about him, her weird, lovely face upturned to his. Some half-formed nucleus of rebellion in his mind dissipated in a breath, for her single eye was a magnet to draw his gaze, and once his pale stare was fixed upon it there was no possibility of escape.

And yet the eye did not seem to see him. It was fixed and glowing upon something immeasurably distant, far in the past, so intently that there was no consciousness in it of the walls about them, nor of himself so near, staring into the lucid depths wherein vague, cloudy reflections were stirring, queer shapes and shadows which were the images of nothing he had ever seen before.

He bent there, tense, his gaze riveted upon the moving shadows in her eye. A thin, high humming fluted from her mouth in a monotone which compelled all his consciousness into one straight channel, and that channel the clouded deeps of her remembering eye. Now the past was moving more clearly through it, and he could see the shapes of things he had no name for stirring sluggishly across a background of dimness veiling still deeper pasts.

Then all the shapes and shadows ran together in a blackness like a vacuum, and the eye was no longer clear and lucid, but darker than sunless space, and far deeper ... a dizzy deep that made his senses whirl. Vertigo came upon him overwhelmingly, and he reeled and somehow lost all hold upon reality, and was plunging, falling, whirling through the immeasurable, bottomless abysses of that dark.

Stars reeled all about him, streaks of light against a velvet black almost tangible in its utter dark. Slowly the lights steadied. His giddiness ceased, though the rush of his motion did not. He was being borne more swiftly than the wind through a dark ablaze with fixed points of brilliance, starry and unwinking. Gradually he became aware of himself, and knew without surprise that he was no longer of flesh and blood, a tangible human creature, but something nebulous and diffused and yet of definite dimensions, freer and lither than the human form and light as smoke.

He was riding through the starry dark a something all but invisible even to his keen new eyes. That dark did not muffle him as it would have blinded a human being. He could see quite clearly, his eyes utilizing something other than light in their perception. But this dim thing he rode was no more than a blur even to the keenness of his dark-defying gaze.

The vague outlines of it which were all he could catch as they flashed and faded and formed again, were now of one shape and now of another, but most often that of some fabulous monster with heaven-spanning wings and a sinuous body trailing out to incredible length. Yet somehow he knew that it was not in reality any such thing. Somehow he knew it for the half-visible manifestation of a force without name, a force which streamed through this starry dark in long, writhing waves and tides, taking fantastic shapes as it flowed. And those shapes were controlled in a measure by the brain of the observer, so that he saw what he expected to see in the nebulous outlines of the dark.

The force buoyed him up with a heady exhilaration more intoxicating than wine. In long arcs and plunges he swept on through the spangled night, finding that he could control his course in some dim way he managed without understanding. It was as if he had wings spread out upon conflicting currents, and by the poise and beat of them rode the air more easily than a bird – yet he knew that his strange new body bore no wings.

For a long while he swept and curved and volplaned upon those forces which flowed invisibly through the dark, giddy with the intoxicating joy of flight. He was aware of neither up nor down in this starry void. He was weightless, disembodied, a joyous ghost breasting the air-currents upon unreal wings. Those points of light which flecked the blackness lay strewn in clusters and long winnowed swaths and strange constellations. They were not distant, like real stars, for sometimes he plunged through a swarm of them and emerged with the breathless sensation of one who had dived into a smother of foaming seas and risen again, yet the lights were intangible to him. That refreshing sensation was not a physical one, nor were the starry points real. He could see them, but that was all. They were like the reflections of something far away in some distant dimension, and though he swung his course straight through a clustering galaxy he did not disarrange a single star. It was his own body which diffused itself through them like smoke, and passed on gasping and refreshed.

As he swept on through the dark he began to find a tantalizing familiarity in the arrangement of some of those starry groups. There were constellations he knew … surely that was Orion, striding across the sky. He saw Betelgeuse's redly glowing eye, and Rigel's cold blue blaze. And beyond, across gulfs of darkness, twin Sirius was spinning, blue-white against the black. The red glimmer in the midst of that wide swath of spangles must be Antares, and the great clustering galaxy that engulfed it – surely the Milky Way! He swerved upon the currents that bore him up, tilted wide, invisible pinions and plunged through its sparkling froth of stars, intoxicated with the space-devouring range of his flight. He spanned a billion light-years with one swoop, volplaned in a long steep curve across a universe. He looked for a tiny sun round which his native planets spun, and could not find it in the wilderness of splendor through which he was plunging. It was a giddy and joyous thing to know that his body dwelt upon some light-point too small to be seen, while here in the limitless dark he soared heedlessly through a welter of constellations, defying time and space and matter itself. He must be swooping through some airy plane where distance and size were not measured in the terms he knew, yet upon whose darkness the reflections of familiar galaxies fell.

Then in his soaring course he swept on beyond the familiar stars, across an intervening gulf of dark, and into another spangled universe whose constellations traced strange and shining patterns across the sky. Presently he became aware that he was not alone. Outlined like wraiths against the blackness, other forms went plunging down the spaceways, sweeping in long curves upon currents of flowing force, plunging into smothers of starry brilliance and bursting through a-sparkle with it to go swinging on again down swooping arcs of darkness.

And then reluctantly he felt the exhilaration begin to fade. He fought against the force that was drawing him backward, clinging stubbornly to this new and intoxicating pleasure, but despite himself the vision was paling, the constellations fading. The dark rolled suddenly away, curtain-wise, and with a jerk he was back again in Julhi's queerly walled room, solid and human once more, and Julhi's lovely and incredible body was pressing close to his, her magical voice humming again through his head.

It was a wordless humming she sang now, but it chose its pitch unerringly to play upon the nerves she sought, and his heart began to hammer and his breath came fast, and the noise of war was roaring in his ears. That singing was a Valkyrie battle-chant, and he heard the crash of conflict and the shouts of struggling men, smelled burnt flesh and felt the kick of the ray-gun's butt against his gripping hand. All the sensations of battle poured over him in unrelated disarray. He was aware of smoke and dust and the smell of blood, felt the pain of ray-burns and the bite of blades, tasted sweat and salt blood, knew again the feel of his fists crashing into alien faces, the heady surge of power through his long, strong body. The wild exhilaration of battle flamed through him in deepening waves to the sorcery of Julhi's song.

It grew stronger then, and more intense, until the physical sensation faded wholly and nothing was left but that soul-consuming ecstasy, and that in turn intensified until he no longer stood upon solid ground, but floated free through void again, pure emotion divorced from all hint of flesh. Then the void took nebulous shape around him, as he passed upward by the very intensity of his ecstasy into some higher land beyond the reach of any sense he possessed. For a while he floated through cloudy shapes of alien form and meaning. Little thrills of perception tingled through the calm of his exultation as he brushed by the misty things that peopled the cloudland to which he had penetrated. They came swifter, until that calm was rippled across and across with conflicting thrills and ecstasies that ran at crosscurrents and tossed up little wavelets, and clashed together, and—

Everything spun dizzily and with breath-taking abruptness he leaned once more in Julhi's embrace. Her voice lilted through his brain.

'That was new! I've never gone so high before, or even suspected that such a place existed. But you could not have endured that pitch of ecstasy longer, and I am not ready yet for you to die. Let us sing now of terror ...'

And as the tones that went humming over him shivered through his brain, dim horrors stirred in their sleep and lifted ghastly heads in the lowest depths of his consciousness to the awakening call of the music, and terror rippled along his nerves until the air dimmed about him again and he was fleeing unnamable things down endless vistas of insanity, with that humming to hound him along.

So it went. He ran the gamut of emotion over and over again. He shared the strange sensations of beings he had never dreamed existed. Some he recognized, but more he could not even guess at, nor from what far worlds their emotions had been pilfered, to lie hoarded in Julhi's mind until she evoked them again.

Faster they came, and faster. They blew over him in dizzy succession, unknown emotions, familiar ones, strange ones, freezingly alien ones, all hurrying through his brain in a blurred confusion, so that one merged into another and they two into a third before the first had done more than brush the surface of his consciousness. Faster still, until at last the whole insane tumult blended into a pitch of wild intensity which must have been too great for his human fiber to endure; for as the turmoil went on he felt himself losing all grasp upon reality, and catapulting upon the forces that ravaged him into a vast and soothing blankness which swallowed up all unrest in the nirvana of its dark.

After an immeasurable while he felt himself wakening, and fought against it weakly. No use. A light was broadening through that healing night which all his stubbornness could not resist. He had no sensation of physical awakening, but without opening his eyes he saw the room more clearly than he had ever seen it before, so that there were tiny rainbows of light around all the queer objects there, and Apri—

He had forgotten her until now, but with this strange awareness that was not of the eyes alone he saw her standing before the couch upon which he leaned in Julhi's arms. She stood rigid, rebellion making a hopeless mask of her face, and there was agony in her eyes. All about her like a bright nimbus the light rayed out. She was incandescent, a torch whose brilliance strengthened until the light radiating from her was almost palpable.

He sensed in Julhi's body, clinging to his, a deep-stirring exultation as the light swelled about her. She luxuriated in it, drank it in like wine. He felt that for her it was indeed tangible, and that he looked upon it now, in this queer new way, through senses that saw it as she did. Somehow he was sure that with normal eyes it would not have been visible.

Dimly he was remembering what had been said about the light which opened a door into Julhi's alien world. And he felt no surprise when it became clear to him that the couch no longer supported his body – that he had no body – that he was suspended weightlessly in midair, Julhi's arms still clasping him in a queer, unphysical grip, while the strangely banded walls moved downward all about him. He had no sensation of motion himself; yet the walls seemed to fall away below and he was floating freely past the mounting bands of mist that paled and brightened swiftly until he was bathed in the blinding light that ringed the top.

There was no ceiling. The light was a blaze of splendor all about him, and out of that blaze, very slowly, very nebulously, the streets of Vonng took shape; it was not that Vonng which had stood once upon the little Venusian island. The buildings were the same as those which must once have risen where their ruins now stood, but there was a subtle distortion of perspective which would have made it clear to him, even had he not known, that this city stood in another plane of existence than his own. Sometimes amidst the splendor he thought he caught glimpses of vine-tangled ruins. A wall would shimmer before his eyes for an instant and crumble into broken blocks, and the pavement would be debris-strewn and mossy. Then the vision faded and the wall stood up unbroken again. But he knew he was looking through the veil which parted the two worlds so narrowly, upon the ruins which were all that remained of Vonng in his own plane.

It was the Vonng which had been shaped for the needs of two worlds simultaneously. He could see, without really understanding, how some of the queerly angled buildings and twisted streets which could have no meaning to the eyes of a man were patterned for the use of these gliding people. He saw in the pavement the curious medallions set by the long-dead sorcerers to pin two planes together at this point of intersection.

In these shimmering unstable streets he saw for the first time in full light shapes which must be like that of the creature which had seized him in the dark. They were of Julhi's race, unmistakably, but he saw now that in her metamorphosis into a denizen of his own world she had perforce taken on a more human aspect than was normally her own. The beings that glided through Vonng's strangely altered streets could never have been mistaken, even at the first glance, as human. Yet they gave even more strongly than had Julhi the queer impression of being exquisitely fitted for some lofty purpose he could not guess at, their shapes of a perfect proportion toward which mankind might have aimed and missed. For the hint of humanity was there, as in man there is a hint of the beast. Julhi in her explanation had made them seem no more than sensation-eaters, intent only upon the gratification of hunger. But, looking upon their perfect, indescribable bodies, he could not believe that that goal for which they were so beautifully fashioned could be no more than that. He was never to know what that ultimate goal was, but he could not believe it only the satisfaction of the scenes.

The shining crowds poured past him down the streets, the whole scene so unstable that great rifts opened in it now and again to let the ruins of that other Vonng show through. And against this background of beauty and uncertainty he was sometimes aware of Apri, rigid and agonized, a living torch to light him on his way. She was not in the Vonng of the alien plane nor in that of the ruins, but somehow hung suspended between the two in a dimension of her own. And whether he moved or not, she was always there, dimly present, radiant and rebellious, the shadow of a queer, reluctant madness behind her tortured eyes.

In the strangeness of what lay before him he scarcely heeded her, and he found that when he was not thinking directly of the girl she appeared only as a vague blur somewhere in the back of his consciousness. It was a brain-twisting sensation, this awareness of overlapping planes. Sometimes in flashes his mind refused to encompass it and everything shimmered meaninglessly for an instant before he could get control again.

Julhi was beside him. He could see her without turning. He could see a great many strange things here in a great many queer, incomprehensible ways. And though he felt himself more unreal than a dream, she was firm and stable with a different sort of substance from that she had worn in the other Vonng. Her shape was changed too. Like those others she was less human, less describable, more beautiful even than before. Her clear, unfathomable eye turned to him limpidly. She said,

'This is my Vonng,' and it seemed to him that though her humming thrilled compellingly through the smoky immaterialism which was himself, her words, in some new way, had gone directly from brain to brain with no need of that pseudo-speech to convey them. He realized then that her voice was primarily not for communication, but for hypnosis – a weapon more potent than steel or flame.

She turned now and moved away over the tiled street, her gait a liquidity graceful gliding upon those amazing lower limbs. Smith found himself drawn after her with a power he could not resist. He was smokily impalpable and without any independent means of locomotion, and he followed her as helplessly as her shadow followed.

At a corner ahead of them a group of the nameless beings had paused in the onward sweep which was carrying so many of Vonng's denizens along toward some yet unseen goal. They turned as Julhi approached, their expressionless eyes fixed on the shadow-wraith behind her which was Smith. No sound passed between them, but he felt in his increasingly receptive brain faint echoes of thoughts that were flashing through the air. It puzzled him until he saw how they were communicating – by those exquisitely feathery crests which swept backward above their foreheads.

It was a speech of colors. The crests quivered unceasingly, and colors far beyond the spectrum his earthly eyes could see blew through them in bewildering sequence. There was a rhythm about it that he gradually perceived, though he could not follow it. By the vagrant echoes of their thoughts which he could catch he realized that the harmony of the colors reflected in a measure the harmony of the two minds which produced them. He saw Julhi's crest quiver with a flush of gold, and those of the rest were royally purple.

Green flowed through the gold, and a lusciously rosy tinge melted through the purple of the rest. But all this took place faster than he could follow, and before he was aware of what was happening a discord in the thoughts that sounded in his mind arose, and while Julhi's crest glowed orange those of the rest were angrily scarlet.

Violence had sprung up between them, whose origin he could not quite grasp though fragments of their quarrel flashed through his brain from each of the speakers, and wildly conflicting colors rippled through the plumes. Julhi's ran the gamut of a dozen spectra in tints that were eloquent of fury. The air quivered as she turned away, drawing him after her. He was at a loss to understand the suddenness of the rage which had swept over her so consumingly, but he could catch echoes of it vibrating through his mind from her own hot anger. She flashed on down the street with blurring swiftness, her crest trembling in swift, staccato shivers.

She must have been too furious to notice where she went, for she had plunged now straight into that streaming crowd which poured through the streets, and before she could win free again the force of it had swallowed her up. She had no desire to join the torrent, and Smith could feel her struggling violently against it, the fury rising as her efforts to be free were vain. Colors like curses raved through her trembling crest.

But the tide was too strong for her. They were carried along irresistibly past the strangely angled buildings, over the patterned pavements, toward an open space which Smith began to catch glimpses of through the houses ahead of them. When they reached the square it was already nearly filled. Ranks of crested, gliding creatures thronged it, their one-eyed faces, heart-mouths immobile, were lifted toward a figure on a dais in the center. He sensed in Julhi a quivering of hatred as he faced that figure, but in it he thought he saw a serenity and a majesty of bearing which even Julhi's indescribable and lovely presence did not have. The rest waited in packed hundreds, eyes fixed, crests vibrating.

When the square was filled he watched the being on the dais lift undulant arms for quiet, and over the crowd a rigid stillness swept. The feathery crests poised motionless above intent heads. Then the plume of the leader began to vibrate with a curious rhythm, and over all the crowd the antennae-like plumes quivered in unison. Every ripple of that fronded crest was echoed to the last shiver by the crowd. There was something infinitely stirring in the rhythm. Obscurely it was like the beat of marching feet, the perfect timing of a dance. They were moving faster now, and the colors that swept through the leader's crest were echoed in those of the crowd. There was no opposition of contrast or complement here; the ranks followed their leader's harmonies in perfect exactitude. His thoughts were theirs.

Smith watched an exquisitely tender rose shiver through that central crest, darken to crimson, sweep on through richness of deepening tones to infra-red and mount in an eloquence of sheer color that stirred his being, even though he could not understand. He realized the intense and rising emotion which swept the crowd as the eloquence of the leader went vibrating through their senses.

He could not have shared that emotion, or understood a fraction of what was taking place, but as he watched, something gradually became clear to him. There was a glory about them. These beings were not innately the sensation-hungry vampires Julhi had told him of. His instinct had been right. No one could watch them in their concerted harmony of emotion and miss wholly the lofty ardor which stirred them now. Julhi must be a degenerate among them. She and her followers might represent one side of these incomprehensible people, but it was a baser side, and not one that could gain strength among the majority. For he sensed sublimity among them. It thrilled through his dazzled brain from that intent, worshipping crowd about him.

And knowing this, rebellion suddenly surged up within him, and he strained in awakening anger at the mistress which held him impotent. Julhi felt the pull. He saw her turn, anger still blazing in her crest and her single eye glowing with a tinge of red. From her rigid lips came a furious hissing, and colors he could not name rippled through the plume in surges eloquent of an anger that burned like a heat-gun's blast. Something in the single-minded ardor of the crowd, the message of the orator, must have fanned the flame of her for at the first hint of rebellion in her captive she turned suddenly upon the crowd which hemmed her in and began to shudder her way free.

They did not seem to realize her presence or feel the force of her pushing them aside. Devoutly all eyes were riveted upon the leader, all the feathery crests vibrated in perfect unison with his own. They were welded into an oblivious whole by the power of his eloquence. Julhi made her way out of the thronged square without distracting a single eye.

Smith followed like a shadow behind her, rebellious but impotent. She swept down the angled streets like a wind of fury. He was at a loss to understand the consuming anger which blazed higher with every passing moment, through there were vague suspicions in his mind that he must have guessed rightly as he watched the crested orator's effect upon the throng – that she was indeed degenerate, at odds with the rest, and hated them the more fiercely for it.

She swept him on along deserted streets whose walls shimmered now and again into green-wreathed ruins, and took shape again. The ruins themselves seemed to flicker curiously with dark and light that swept over them in successive waves, and suddenly he realized that time was passing more slowly here than in his own plane. He was watching night and day go by over the ruins of that elder Vonng.

They were coming now into a courtyard of strange, angular shape. As they entered, the half-forgotten blur at the back of his mind which was Apri glowed into swift brilliance, and he saw that the light which streamed from her was bathing the court in radiance, stronger than the light outside. He could see her vaguely, hovering over the exact center of the courtyard in that curious dimension of her own, staring with mad, tortured eyes through the veils of the planes between. About the enclosure shapes like Julhi's moved sluggishly, the colors dull on their crests, their eyes filmed. And he saw, now that a suspicion of the truth had entered his mind, that Julhi herself did not have quite the clear and shining beauty of those who had thronged the square. There was an indescribable dullness over her.

When she and her shadowy captive entered the court those aimlessly moving creatures quickened into sudden life. A scarlet the color of fresh blood flowed through Julhi's crest, and the others echoed it with eager quiverings of their plumes which were somehow obscene and avid. And for the first time Smith's dulled consciousness awoke into fear, and he writhed helplessly in the recesses of his mind away from the hungry shapes around him. The crowd was rushing forward now with quivering plumes and fluttering, wide-arched mouths that had flushed a deeper crimson as if in anticipation. For all their strangeness, their writhing shapes and weird, alien faces, they were like wolves bearing down hungrily upon their quarry.

But before they reached him something happened. Somehow Julhi had moved with lightning swiftness, and vertigo seized Smith blindingly. The walls around them shimmered and vanished. Apri vanished, the light blazed into a dazzle and he felt the world shifting imponderably about him. Scenes he recognized flashed and faded – the black ruins he had awakened in, Julhi's cloud-walled room, the wilderness of pillars, this curiously shaped courtyard itself, all melted together and blurred and faded. In the instant before it vanished he felt, as from far away, the touch upon the mistiness of his bodiless self of hands that were not human, hands that stung with the shock of lightning.

Somehow in the timeless instant while this took place he realized that he had been snatched away from the pack for some obscure purpose. Somehow, too, he knew that what Apri had told him had been true, though he had thought her mad at the time. In some vague way all these scenes were the same. They occupied the same place, at the same time – ruined Vonng, the Vonng that Julhi knew, all those places he had known since he met Apri in the dark – they were overlapping planes through which, as through open doors, Julhi had drawn him.

He was aware of an unnamable sensation then, within himself, and the mistiness which had prisoned him gave way before the returning strength of his flesh-and-blood body. He opened his eyes. Something was clinging to him in heavy coils, and a pain gnawed at his heart, but he was too stunned at what surrounded him to heed it just then.

He stood among the ruins of a court which must once, long ago, have been the court he had just left – or had he? For he saw now that it too surrounded him, flickering through the ruins in glimpses of vanished splendor. He stared round wildly. Yes, shining through the crumbled walls and the standing walls that were one and the same, he could catch glimpses of that columned wilderness through which he had wandered. And rising above this, one with it, the misty-walled chamber where he had met Julhi. They were all here, occupying the same space, at the same time. The world was a chaos of conflicting planes all about him. There were other scenes too, intermingling with these, places he had never seen before. And Apri, incandescent and agonized, peered with mad eyes through the bewildering tangle of worlds. His brain lurched sickeningly with the incredible things it could not comprehend.

Around him through the chaotic jumbling of a score of planes prowled strange forms. They were like Julhi – yet unlike her. They were like those figures which had rushed upon him in that other Vonng – but not wholly. They had bestialized in the metamorphosis. The shining beauty was dulled. The incomparable grace of them had thickened into animal gropings. Their plumes burned with an ugly crimson and the clarity of their eyes was clouded now with a blind and avid hunger. They circled him with a baffled gliding.

All this he was aware of in the flashing instant when his eyes opened. Now he looked down, for the first time consciously aware of that pain which gnawed at his heart, of the clinging arms. And suddenly that pain stabbed like a heat-ray, and he went sick with the shock of what he saw. For Julhi clung to him, relaxed in avid coils. Her eyes were closed, and her mouth was fastened tightly against the flesh of his left breast, just over the heart. The plume above her head quivered from base to tip with long, voluptuous shudders, and all the shades of crimson and scarlet and bloody rose that any spectrum ever held went blowing through it.

Smith choked on a word halfway between oath and prayer, and with shaking hands ripped her arms away, thrust against her shoulders blindly to tear loose that clinging, agonizing mouth. The blood spurted as it came free. The great eye opened and looked up into his with a dull, glazed stare. Swiftly the glaze faded, the dullness brightened into a glare behind which hell-fires flamed scorchingly, to light up the nameless hells within. Her plume whipped erect and blazed into angry red. From the arched mouth, wet now, and crimson, a high, thin, nerve-twanging hum shrilled agonizingly.

That sound was like the flick of a wire whip on raw flesh. It bit into his brain-centers, sawed at his quivering nerves excruciatingly, unbearably. Under the lash of that voice Smith wrenched away from her clinging arms, stumbling over the stones, blundering anywhere away from the punishing shrill of that hum. The chaos spun about him, scenes shifting and melting together maddeningly. The blood ran down his breast.

Through his blind agony, as the world dissolved into shrilling pain, one thing alone was clear. That burning light. That steady flame. Apri. He was blundering unimpeded through solid walls and columns and buildings in their jumble of cross-angled planes, but when he came to her at last she was tangible, she was real. And with the feel of her firm flesh under his hands a fragment of sanity rose out of that piercing anguish which shivered along his nerves. Dully he knew that through Apri all this was possible. Apri the light-maker, the doorway between worlds ... His fingers closed on her throat.

Blessedly, blessedly that excruciating song was fading. He knew no more than that. He scarcely realized that his fingers were sunk yet in the softness of a woman's throat. The chaos was fading around him, the crazy planes righting themselves, paling, receding backward into infinity. Through their fragments the solid rocks of Vonng loomed up in crumbling ruins. The agony of Julhi's song was a faint shrilling from far away. And about him in the air he sensed a frenzied tugging, as if impalpable hands were clutching at his, ghostly arms pulling ineffectually upon him. He looked up, dazed and uncertain.

Where Julhi had stood among the tumbling planes an expanding cloudy image hovered now, bearing still the lovely outlines that had been hers, but foggy, spreading and dissipating like mist as the doorway closed between planes. She was scarcely more than a shadow, and fading with every breath, but she wrenched at him yet with futile, cloudy hands, striving to the last to preserve her gate into the world she hungered for. But as she clawed she was vanishing. Her outlines blurred and melted as smoke fades. She was no more than a darkening upon the air now, tenuous, indistinguishable. Then the fog that had been lovely Julhi had expanded into nothingness – the air was clear.

Smith looked down, shook his dulled head a little, bent to what he still gripped between his hands. It needed no more than a glance, but he made sure before he released his grasp. Pity clouded his eyes for an instant – Apri was free now, in the freedom she had longed for, the madness gone, the terrible danger that was herself banished. Never again through that gate would Julhi and her followers enter. The door was closed.

NYMPH OF DARKNESS

C. L. Moore and Forrest J. Ackerman

The thick Venusian dark of the Ednes waterfront in the hours before dawn is breathless and tense with a nameless awareness, a crouching danger. The shapes that move murkily through its blackness are not daylight shapes. Sun has never shone upon some of those misshapen figures, and what happens in the dark is better left untold. Not even the Patrol ventures there after the lights are out, and the hours between midnight and dawn are outside the law. If dark things happen there the Patrol never knows of them, or desires to know. Powers move through the darkness along the waterfront to which even the Patrol bows low.

Through that breathless blackness, along a street beneath which the breathing waters whispered, Northwest Smith strolled slowly. No prudent man ventures out after midnight along the waterfront of Ednes unless he has urgent business abroad, but from the leisurely gait that carried Smith soundlessly through the dark he might have been some casual sightseer. He was no stranger to the Ednes waterfront. He knew the danger through which he strolled so slowly, and under narrowed lids his colorless eyes were like keen steel probes that searched the dark. Now and then he passed a shapeless shadow that dodged aside to give him way. It might have been no more than a shadow. His no-colored eyes did not waver. He went on, alert and wary.

He was passing between two high warehouses that shut out even the faint reflection of light from the city beyond when he first heard that sound of bare, running feet which so surprised him. The patter of frantically fleeing steps is not uncommon along the waterfront, but these were – he listened closer – yes, certainly the feet of a woman or a young boy. Light and quick and desperate. His ears were keen enough to be sure of that. They were coming nearer swiftly. In the blackness even his pale eyes could see nothing, and he drew back against the wall, one hand dropping to the ray gun that hung low on his thigh. He had no desire to meet whatever it was which pursued this fugitive.

But his brows knit as the footsteps turned into the street that led between the warehouses. No woman, of whatever class or kind, ventures into this quarter by night. And he became certain as he listened that those feet were a woman's. There was a measured rhythm about them that suggested the Venusian woman's lovely, swaying gait. He pressed flat against the wall, holding his breath. He wanted no sound to indicate his own presence to the terror from which the woman fled. Ten years before he might have dashed out to her – but ten years along the spaceways teaches a man prudence. Gallantry can be foolhardy sometimes, particularly along the waterfront, where any of a score of things might be in close pursuit. At the thought of what some of those things might be the hair prickled faintly along his neck.

The frantic footsteps came storming down the dark street. He heard the rush of breath through unseen nostrils, the gasp of laboring lungs. Then those desperate feet stumbled a bit, faltered, turned aside. Out of the dark a hurtling figure plunged full-tilt against him. His startled arms closed about a woman – a girl – a young girl, beautifully made, muscular and firmly curved under his startled hands – and quite naked.

He released her rather quickly.

'Earthman!' she gasped in an agony of breathlessness. 'Oh, hide me, hide me! Quick!'

There was no time to wonder how she knew his origin or to ask from what she fled, for before the words had left her lips a queer, greenish glow appeared around the corner of the warehouse. It revealed a pile of barrels at Smith's elbow, and he shoved the exhausted girl behind them in one quick motion, drawing his gun and flattening himself still further against the wall.

Yet it was no nameless monster which appeared around the corner of the building. A man's dark shape came into view. A squat figure, broad and misshapen. The light radiated from a flash-tube in his hand, and it was an oddly diffused and indirect light, not like an ordinary flash's clear beam, for it lighted the man behind it as well as what lay before the tube, as if a greenish, luminous fog were spreading sluggishly from the lens.

The man came forward with a queer, shuffling gait. Something about him made Smith's flesh crawl unaccountably. What it was he could not be sure, for the green glow of the tube did not give a clear light, and the man was little more than a squat shadow moving unevenly behind the light-tube's luminance.

He must have seen Smith almost immediately, for he came straight across the street to where the Earthman stood against the wall, gun in hand. Behind the glowing tube-mouth Smith could make out a pale blur of face with two dark splotches for eyes. It was a fat face, unseemly in its putty palor, like some grub that has fed too long upon corruption. No expression crossed it at the sight of the tall spaceman in his leather garb, leaning against the wall and fingering a ready gun. Indeed, there was nothing to arouse surprise in the Earthman's attitude against the wall, or in his drawn gun. It was what any nightfarer along the waterfront would have done at the appearance of such a green, unearthly glow in the perilous dark.

Neither spoke. After a single long glance at the silent Smith, the newcomer began to switch his diffused light to and fro about the street in obvious search. Smith listened, but the girl had stilled her sobbing breath and no sound betrayed her hiding place. The sluggish searcher went on slowly down the street, casting his foggy light before him. Its luminance faded by degrees as he receded from view, a black, misshapen shadow haloed in unholy radiance.

When utter dark had descended once more Smith holstered his gun and called to the girl in a low voice. The all but soundless murmur of bare feet on the pavement heralded her approach, the hurrying of still unruly breath.

'Thank you,' she said softly. 'I – I hope you need never know what horror you have saved me from.'

'Who are you?' he demanded. 'How did you know me?'

'They call me Nyusa. I did not know you, save that I think you are of Earth, and perhaps – trustworthy. Great Shar must have guided my flight along the streets tonight, for I think your kind is rare by the sea edge, after dark.'

'But – can you see me?'

'No. But a Martian, or one of my own countrymen, would not so quickly have released a girl who dashed into his arms by night – as I am.'

In the dark Smith grinned. It has been purely reflexive, that release of her when his hand realized her nudity. But he might as well take credit for it.

'You had better go quickly now,' she went on, 'there is such danger here that—'

Abruptly the low voice broke off. Smith could hear nothing, but he sensed a tensing of the girl by his side, a strained listening. And presently he caught a far away sound, a curious muffled wheezing, as if something shortwinded and heavy were making laborious haste. It was growing nearer. The girl's caught breath was loud in the stillness at his elbow.

'Quick!' she gasped. 'Oh, hurry!'

Her hand on his arm tugged him on in the direction the squat black searcher had taken. 'Faster!' And her anxious hands pulled him into a run. Feeling a little ridiculous, he loped through the dark beside her with long, easy strides, hearing nothing but the soft fall of his own boots and the scurrying of the girl's bare feet, and far behind the distant wheezing breath, growing fainter.

Twice she turned him with a gentle push into some new byway. Then they paused while she tugged at an unseen door, and after that they ran down an alley so narrow that Smith's broad shoulders brushed its walls. The place smelled of fish and decayed wood and the salt of the seas. The pavement rose in broad, shallow steps, and they went through another door, and the girl pulled at his arm with a breathed, 'We're safe now. Wait.'

He heard the door close behind them, and light feet pattered on boards.

'Lift me,' she said after a moment. 'I can't reach the light.'

Cool, firm fingers touched his neck. Gingerly in the dark he found her waist and swung her aloft at arm's length. Between his hands that waist was supple and smoothly muscled and slim as a reed. He heard the fumble of uncertain fingers overhead. Then in an abrupt dazzle light sprang up about him.

He swore in a choked undertone and sprang back, dropping his hands. For he had looked to see a girl's body close to his face, and he saw nothing. His hands had gripped – nothing. He had been holding aloft a smooth and supple – nothingness.

He heard the fall of a material body on the floor, and a gasp and cry of pain, but still he could see nothing, and he fell back another step, lifting an uncertain hand to his eyes and muttering a dazed Martian oath. For look though he would, he could see no one but himself in the little bare room the light had revealed. Yet the girl's voice was speaking from empty air.

'What – why did – Oh, I see!' and a little ripple of laughter. 'You have never heard of Nyusa?'

The repetition of the name struck a chord of remote memory in the Earthman's mind. Somewhere lately he had heard that word spoken. Where and by whom he could not recall, but it aroused in his memory a nebulous chord of night peril and the unknown. He was suddenly glad of the gun at his side, and a keener awareness was in the pale gaze he sent around the tiny room.

'No,' he said. 'I have never heard the name before now.'

'I am Nyusa.'

'But – where are you?'

She laughed again, a soft ripple of mirth honey sweet with the Venusian woman's traditionally lovely voice.

'Here. I am not visible to men's eyes. I was born so. I was born—' Here the rippling voice sobered, and a tinge of solemnity crept in. '—I was born of a strange mating, Earthman. My mother was Venusian, but my father – my father was Darkness. I can't explain ... But because of that strain of Dark in me, I am invisible. And because of it I – I am not free.'

'Why? Who holds you captive? How could anyone imprison an invisibility?'

'The – Nov.' Her voice was the faintest breath of sound, and again, at the strange word, a prickle of nameless unease ran through Smith's memory. Somewhere he had heard that name before, and the remembrance it roused was too nebulous to put into words, but it was ominous. Nyusa's breathing whisper went on very softly at his shoulder. It was a queer, unreal feeling, that, to be standing alone in a bare room and a girl's sweet, muted murmur in his ears from empty air.

'The Nov – they dwell underground. They are the last remnant of a very old race. And they are the priests who worship That which was my father. The Darkness. They prison me for purposes of their own.

'You see, my heritage from the lady who bore me was her own lovely human shape, but the Thing which was my father bequeathed to his child stranger things than invisibility. I am of a color outside the range of human eyes. And I have entry into – into other lands than this. Strange lands, lovely and far – Oh, but so damnably near! If I could only pass by the bars the Nov have set to shut me away. For they need me in their dark worship, and here I must stay, prisoned in the hot, muddy world which is all they themselves can ever know. They have a light – you saw it, the green glow in the hands of the Nov who pursued me through the dark tonight – which makes me visible to human eyes. Something in its color combines with that strange color which is mine to produce a hue that falls within man's range of vision. If he had found me I would have been – punished – severely, because I fled tonight. And the Nov's punishments are – not nice.

'To make sure that I shall not escape them, they have set a guardian to dog my footsteps – the thing that wheezed on my track tonight – Dolf. He sprang from some frightful union of material and immaterial. He is partly elemental, partly animal. I can't tell you fully. And he is cloudy, nebulous – but very real, as you would have discovered had he caught us just now. He has a taste for human blood which makes him invaluable, though I am safe, for I am only half human, and the Nov – well, they are not wholly human either. They—'

She broke off suddenly. Outside the door Smith's keen ears had caught a shuffle of vague feet upon the ground, and through the cracks came very clearly the snuffle of wheezing breath. Nyusa's bare feet pattered swiftly across the boards, and from near the door came a series of low, sibilant hissings and whistlings in a clearer tone than the sounds the great Dolf made. The queer noise crescendoed to a sharp command, and he heard a subdued snuffling and shuffling outside and the sound of great, shapeless feet moving off over flagstones. At his shoulder Nyusa sighed.

'It worked that time,' she said. 'Sometimes I can command him, by virtue of my father's strength in me. The Nov do not know that. Queer, isn't it – they never seem to remember that I might have inherited more from their god than my invisibility and my access to other worlds. They punish me and prison me and command me to their service like some temple dancing girl – me, the half divine! I think – yes, I think that someday the doors will open at my own command, and I shall go out into those other worlds. I wonder – could I do it now?'

The voice faded to a murmurous undertone. Smith realized that she had all but forgotten his presence at the realization of her own potentialities. And again that prickle of unease went over him. She was half human, but half only. Who could say what strange qualities were rooted in her, springing from no human seed? Qualities that might someday blossom into – into – well, he had no words for what he was thinking of, but he hoped not to be there on the day the Nov tried her too far.

Hesitant footsteps beside him called back his attention sharply. She was moving away, a step at a time. He could hear the sound of her bare feet on the boards. They had almost reached the opposite wall now, one slow step after another. And then suddenly those hesitating footfalls were running, faster, faster, diminishing in distance. No door opened, no aperture in the walls, but Nyusa's bare feet pattered eagerly away. He was aware briefly of the vastnesses of dimensions beyond our paltry three, distances down which a girl's bare feet could go storming in scornful violation of the law that held him fast. From far away he heard those steps falter. He thought he heard the sound of fists beating against resistance, the very remote echo of a sob. Then slowly the patter of bare feet returned. Almost he could see a dragging head and hopelessly slumped shoulders as the reluctant footfalls drew nearer, nearer, entered the room again. At his shoulder she said in a subdued voice,

'Not yet. I have never gone so far before, but the way is still barred. The Nov are too strong – for a while. But I know, now. I know! I am a god's daughter, and strong too. Not again shall I flee before the Nov's pursuit, or fear because Dolf follows. I am the child of Darkness, and they shall know it! They—'

Sharply into her exultant voice broke a moment of blackness that cut off her words with the abruptness of a knife stroke. It was of an instant's duration only, and as the light came on again a queer wash of rosy luminance spread through the room and faded again, as if a ripple of color had flowed past. Nyusa sighed.

'That is what I fled,' she confided. 'I am not afraid now – but I do not like it. You had best go – or no, for Dolf still watches the door I entered by. Wait – let me think.'

Silence for a moment, while the last flush of rose faded from the air, to be followed by a ripple of fresh color that faded in turn. Three times Smith saw the tide of red flow through the room and die away before Nyusa's hand fell upon his arm and her voice murmured from emptiness,

'Come. I must hide you somewhere while I perform my ritual. That color is the signal that the rites are to begin – the Nov's command for my presence.

There is no escape for you until they call Dolf away, for I could not guide you to a door without having him sense my presence there and follow. No, you must hide – hide and watch me dance. Would you like that? A sight which no eyes that are wholly human have ever seen before! Come.'

Invisible hands pushed open the door in the opposite wall and pulled him thru. Stumbling a little at the newness of being guided by an unseen creature, Smith followed down a corridor through which waves of rosy light flowed and faded. The way twisted many times, but no doors opened from it nor did they meet anyone in the five minutes or so that elapsed as they went down the hallway through the pulsing color of the air.

At the end a great barred door blocked their passage. Nyusa released him for an instant, and he heard her feet whisper on the floor, her unseen hands fumble with something metallic. Then a section of the floor sank. He was looking down a shaft around which narrow stairs spiraled, very steeply. It was typically a Venusian structure, and very ancient. He has descended other spiraled shafts before now, to strange destinations. Wondering what lay in store for him at the foot of this, he yielded to the girl's clinging hands and went down slowly, gripping the rail.

He had gone a long way before the small, invisible hands plucked at his arm again and drew him through an opening in the rock through which the shaft sank. A short corridor led into darkness. At its end they paused, Smith blinking in the queer, pale darkness which veiled the great cavern that lay before them.

'Wait here,' whispered Nyusa. 'You should be safe enough in the dark. No one ever uses this passage but myself. I will return after the ceremony.'

Hands brushed his briefly, and she was gone. Smith pressed back against the wall and drew his gun, flicking the catch experimentally to be sure it would answer any sudden need. Then he settled back to watch.

Before him a vast domed chamber stretched. He could see only a little of it in the strange dark pallor of the place. The floor shone with the deep sheen of marble, black as quiet water underground. And as the minutes passed he became aware of motion and life in the pale dark. Voices murmured, feet shuffled softly, forms moved through the distance. The Nov were taking their places for the ceremony. He could see the dim outlines of their mass, far off in the dark.

After a while a deep, sonorous chanting began from nowhere and everywhere, swelling and filling the cavern and echoing from the doomed ceiling in reverberant monotones. There were other sounds whose meaning he could not fathom, queer pipings and whistlings like the voice in which Nyusa had commanded Dolf, but invested with a solemnity that gave them depth and power. He could feel fervor building up around the dome of the cavern, the queer, wild fervor and ecstasy of an unknown cult for a nameless god. He gripped his gun and waited.

Now, distantly and very vaguely, a luminance was forming in the center of the arched roof. It strengthened and deepened and began to rain downward toward the darkly shining floor in long streamers like webs of tangible light. In the mirrored floor replicas of light reached upward, mistily reflecting. It was a sight of such weird and enchanting loveliness that Smith held his breath, watching. And now green began to flush the streaming webs, a strange, foggy green like the light the Nov had flashed through the waterfront streets in pursuit of Nyusa. Recognizing the color, he was not surprised when a shape began to dawn in the midst of that raining light. A girl's shape, half transparent, slim and lovely and unreal.

In the dark pallor of the cavern, under the green luminance of the circling light, she lifted her arms in a long, slow, sweeping motion, lighter than smoke, and moved on tiptoe, very delicately. Then the light shimmered, and she was dancing. Smith leaned forward breathlessly, gun hanging forgotten in his hand, watching her dance. It was so lovely that afterward he could never be sure he had not dreamed.

She was so nebulous in the screaming radiance of the light, so utterly unreal, so fragile, so exquisitely colored in the strangest tints of violet and blue and frosty silver, and queerly translucent, like a moonstone. She was more unreal now, when she was visible, than she had ever seemed before his eyes beheld her. Then his hands had told him of her firm and slender roundness – now she was a wraith, transparent, dream-like, dancing soundlessly in a rain of lunar color.

She wove magic with her dancing body as she moved, and the dance was more intricate and symbolic and sinuous than any wholly human creature could have trod. She scarcely touched the floor, moving above her reflection in the polished stone like a lovely moonlight ghost floating in mid-darkness while green moon-fire rained all about her.

With difficultly Smith wrenched his eyes away from that nebulous creature treading her own reflection as she danced. He was searching for the sources of those voices he had heard, and in the green, revealing light he saw them ringing the cavern in numbers greater than he had dreamed. The Nov, intent as one man upon the shimmering figure before them. And at what he saw he was glad he could not see them clearly. He remembered Nyusa's words, '—the Nov are not wholly human either.' Veiled though they were in the misty radiance and the pallor of the dark, he could see that it was so. He had seen it, unrealizing, in the face of that squat pursuer who had passed him in the street.

They were all thick, shapeless, all darkly robed and white-faced as slugs are white. Their formless features, intent and emotionless, had a soft, unstable quality, not shaped with any human certainty. He did not stare too long at any one face, for fear he might make out its queer lack of contour, or understand the portent of that slug-white instability of feature.

Nyusa's dance ended in a long, floating whirl of unhuman lightness. She sank to the floor in deep obeisance, prostrate upon her own reflection. From the front ranks of the assembled Nov a dark figure stepped with upraised arms. Obediently Nyusa rose. From that dark form, from the slug-like, unfeatured face, a twittering whistle broke, and Nyusa's voice echoed the sounds unerringly, her voice blending with the other's in a chant without words.

Smith was so intent upon watching that he was not aware of the soft shuffling in the dark behind him until the wheeze of labored breath sounded almost upon his neck. The thing was all but on him before that sixth sense which had saved him so often before now shrieked a warning and he whirled with a choked oath of surprise and shock, swinging up his gun and confronting a dim, shapeless immensity out of which a dull glow of greenish light stared at him. His gun spat blue flame, and from the imponderable thing a whistling scream rang quaveringly, echoing across the cavern and cutting short that wordless chant between the Nov and the girl.

Then the dark bulk of Dolf lurched forward and fell smotheringly upon Smith. It bore him to the floor under an engulfing weight which was only half real, but chokingly thick in his nostrils. He seemed almost to be breathing Dolf's substance, like heavy mist. Blinded and gasping, he fought the curiously nebulous thing that was smothering him, knowing he must win free in a few seconds' time, for Dolf's scream must bring the Nov upon him at any moment now. But for all his efforts he could not break away, and something indescribable and nauseous was fumbling for his throat. When he felt its blind searching his struggles redoubled convulsively, and after a frantic moment he staggered free, gulping in clean air and staring into the dark with wide eyes, trying to make out what manner of horror he had grappled with. He could see nothing but that dull flare, as of a single eye, glowing upon him from an imponderable bulk which blended with the dark.

Dolf was coming at him again. He heard great feet shuffling, and the wheezing breath came fast. From behind the shouts of the Nov rose loud, and the noise of running men, and above all the high, clear call of Nyusa, screaming something in a language without words. Dolf was upon him. That revolting, unseen member fumbled again at his throat. He thrust hard against the yielding bulk and his gun flared again, blue-hot in the dark, full into the midst of Dolf s unstable blackness.

He felt the mass of the half-seen monster jerk convulsively. A high, whistling scream rang out, shrill and agonized, and the sucking organ dropped from his throat. The dim glow of vision dulled in the shape's cloudy midst. Then it flickered, went out. Somehow there was a puff of blackness that dissolved into misty nothing all about him, and the dark shape that had been Dolf was gone. Half elemental, he had gone back into nothingness as he died.

Smith drew a deep breath and swung round to front the first of the oncoming Nov. They were almost upon him, and their numbers were overwhelming, but his flame-gun swung its long arc of destruction as they swarmed in and almost a dozen of the squat, dark figures must have fallen to that deadly scythe before he went down under the weight of them. Pudgily soft fingers wrenched the gun from his hand, and he did not fight hard to retain it, for he remembered the blunt-nosed little flame-thrower in its holster under his arm and was not minded that they should discover it in any body-to-body fight.

Then he was jerked to his feet and thrust forward toward the pale radiance that still held Nyusa in its heart, like a translucent prisoner in a cage of light. A little dazed by the swiftness of events, Smith went on unsteadily in their midst. He towered head and shoulders above them, and his eyes were averted. He tried not to flinch from the soft, fish-white hands urging him forward, not to look too closely into the faces of the squat things swarming so near. No, they were not men. He knew that more surely than ever from this close sight of the puffy, featureless faces ringing him round.

At the brink of the raining light which housed Nyusa the Nov who had led the chanting stood apart, watching impassively as the tall prisoner came forward in his swarm of captors. There was command about this Nov, an air of regality and calm, and he was white as death, luminous as a corpse in the lunar reflections of the light.

They halted Smith before him. After one glance into that moveless, unfeatured face, slug pale, the Earthman did not look again. His eyes strayed to Nyusa, beyond the Nov who fronted him, and at what he saw took faint hope again. There was no trace of fear in her poise. She stood straight and quiet, watching, and he sensed a powerful reserve about her. She looked the god's daughter she was, standing there in the showering luminance, translucent as some immortal.

Said the leader Nov, in a voice that came deeply from somewhere within him, though his unfeatured face did not stir.

'How came you here?'

'I brought him,' Nyusa's voice sounded steadily across the space that parted them.

The Nov swung round, amazement in every line of his squatness.

'You?' he exclaimed. 'You brought an alien to witness the worship of the god I serve? How dared—'

'I brought one who had befriended me to witness my dance before my father,' said Nyusa in so ominously gentle a tone that the Nov did not realize for a moment the significance of her words. He spluttered Venusian blasphemy in a choked voice.

'You shall die!' he yelled thickly. 'Both of you shall die by such torment—'

'S-s-s-zt!'

Nyusa's whistling hiss was only a sibilance to Smith, but it cut the Nov's furious flow abruptly short. He went dead quiet, and Smith thought he saw a sicker pallor than before spreading over the slug face turned to Nyusa.

'Had you forgotten?' she queried gently. 'Forgotten that my father is That which you worship? Dare you raise your voice to threaten Its daughter? Dare you, little worm-man?'

A gasp ran over the throng behind Smith. Greenish anger suffused the pallid face of the priest. He spluttered wordlessly and surged forward, short arms clawing toward the taunting girl. Smith's hand, darting inside his coat, was quicker than the clutch of his captors. The blue flare of his flame-thrower leaped out in a tongue of dazzling heat to lick at the plunging Nov. He spun round dizzily and screamed once, high and shrill, and sank in a dark, puddly heap to the floor.

There was a moment of the deepest quiet. The shapeless faces of the Nov were turned in one stricken stare to that oddly fluid lump upon the floor which had been their leader. Then in the pack behind Smith a low rumble began to rise, the mutter of many voices. He had heard that sound before – the dawning roar of a fanatic mob. He knew that it meant death. Setting his teeth, he spun to face them, hand closing firmer about the butt of his flame-thrower.

The mutter grew deeper, louder. Someone yelled, 'Kill! Kill!' and a forward surge in the thick crowd of faces swayed the mass toward him. Then above that rising clamor Nyusa's voice rang clear.

'Stop!' she called. In sheer surprise the murderous mob paused, eyes turning toward the unreal figure in her cage of radiance. Even Smith darted a glance over his shoulder, flame gun poised in mid-air, his finger hesitating upon the catch. And at what they saw the crowd fell silent, the Earthman froze into stunned immobility as he watched what was happening under the rain of light.

Nyusa's translucent arms were lifted, her head thrown back. Like a figure of triumph carved out of moonstone she stood poised, while all about her in the misty, lunar colors of the light a darkness was forming like fog that clung to her outstretched arms and swathed her half-real body. And it was darkness not like any night that Smith had ever seen before. No words in any tongue could describe it, for it was not a darkness made for any vocal creature to see. It was a blasphemy and an outrage against the eyes, against all that man hopes and believes and is. The darkness of the incredible, the utterly alien and opposed.

Smith's gun fell from shaking fingers. He pressed both hands to his eyes to shut out that indescribably awful sight, and all about him heard a long, soft sighing as the Nov sank to their faces upon the shining floor. In that deathly hush Nyusa spoke again, vibrant with conscious godhood and underrun with a queer, tingling ripple of inhumanity. It was the voice of one to whom the unknown lies open, to whom that utterly alien and dreadful blackness is akin.

'By the Darkness I command you,' she said coldly. 'Let this man go free. I leave you now, and I shall never return. Give thanks that a worse punishment than this is not visited upon you who paid no homage to the daughter of Darkness.'

Then for a swift instant something indescribable happened. Remotely Smith was aware that the Blackness which had shrouded Nyusa was spreading through him, permeating him with the chill of that blasphemous dark, a hideous pervasion of his innermost being. For that instant he was drowned in a darkness which made his very atoms shudder to its touch. And if it was dreadful to him, the voiceless shriek that rose simultaneously from all about him gave evidence how much more dreadfully their god's touch fell upon the Nov. Not with his ears, but with some nameless sense quickened by that moment of alien blackness, he was aware of the scream of intolerable anguish, the writhing of extra-human torment which the Nov underwent in that one timeless moment.

Out of his tense awareness, out of the spreading black, he was roused by a touch that startled him into forgetfulness of that dreadful dark. The touch of a girl's mouth upon his, a tingling pressure of sweet parted lips that stirred delicately against his own. He stood tense, not moving a muscle, while Nyusa's mouth clung to his in a long, close kiss like no kiss he had ever taken before. There was a coldness in it, a chill as alien as the dark that had gathered about her translucency under the light, a shuddering cold that struck through him in one long, deep-rooted shock of frigid revulsion. And there was warmth in it, headily stirring the pulse which that cold had congealed.

In the instant while those clinging lips melted to his mouth, he was a battleground for emotions as alien as light and dark. The cold touch of Darkness, the hot touch of love. Alienity's shuddering, frozen stab, and humanity's blood-stirring throb of answer to the warm mouth's challenge. It was a mingling of such utter opposites that for an instant he was racked by forces that sent his senses reeling. There was danger in the conflict, the threat of madness in such irreconcilable forces that his brain blurred with the effort of compassing them.

Just in time the clinging lips dropped away. He stood alone in the reeling dark, that perilous kiss burning upon his memory as the world steadied about him. In that dizzy instant he heard what the rest, in their oblivious agony, could not have realized. He heard a girl's bare feet pattering softly along some incline, up and up, faster and faster. Now they were above his head. He did not look up. He knew he would have seen nothing. He knew Nyusa walked a way that no sense of his could perceive. He heard her feet break into an eager little run. He heard her laugh once, lightly, and the laugh cut off by the sound of a closing door. Then quiet.

Without warning, on the heels of that sound, he felt a tremendous release all about him. The darkness had lifted. He opened his eyes upon a dimly lighted cavern from which that rain of light had vanished. The Nov lay in quivering windrows, about his feet, their shapeless faces hidden. Otherwise the whole vast place was empty as far as his eyes could pierce the dark.

Smith bent and picked up his fallen gun. He kicked the nearest Nov ungently.

'Show me the way out of this place,' he ordered, sheathing the flame-thrower under his arm.

Obediently the sluggish creature stumbled to his feet.

THE COLD GRAY GOD

Snow fell over Righa, pole city of Mars. Bitter snow, whirling in ice-hard particles on the thin, keen wind that always seems to blow through Righa's streets. These cobblestoned ways were nearly empty today. Squat stone houses crouched low under the assaults of that storm-laden wind, and the dry snow eddied in long gusts down the reaches of the Lakklan, Righa's central street. The few pedestrians along the Lakklan huddled collars high about their ears and hurried over the cobbles.

But there was one figure in the street that did not hurry. It was a woman's figure, and by the swing of her gait and the high poise of her head one might guess that she was young, but it would be no more than a guess, for the fur cloak she clutched about her muffled every line of her body and the peaked hood of it hid her face. That fur was the sleek white hide of the almost extinct saltland snow-cat, so that one might presuppose her wealth. She walked with a swinging grace rarely encountered in Righa's streets. For Righa is an outlaw city, and young women, wealthy and beautiful and unattended, are seldom seen upon the Lakklan.

She strolled slowly down the broad, uneven way, her long hooded cloak making a white enigma of her. But she was somehow alien to this bleak, bitter scene. That almost dancing litheness which attended her motion, eloquent even through the concealing folds of rich snow-cat fur, was not a characteristic of Martian women, even the pink beauties of the canals. Indefinably she was foreign – exotically foreign.

From the shadow of her hood an eager gaze roved the street, avidly scanning the few faces she passed. They were hard-featured faces for the most part, bleak and cold as the gray city about them. And the eyes that met hers boldly or slyly, according to the type of passer-by, were curiously alike in their furtiveness, their shadow of alert and hunted watching. For men came to Righa quietly, by devious ways, and dwelt in seclusion and departed without ostentation. And their eyes were always wary.

The girl's gaze flicked by them and went on. If they stared after her down the street she did not seem to know, or greatly to care. She paced unhurriedly on over the cobbles.

Ahead of her a broad, low door opened to a burst of noise and music, and warm light streamed briefly out into the gray day as a man stepped over the sill and swung the door shut behind him. Sidelong she watched the man as he belted his heavy coat of brown pole-deer hide and stepped briskly out into the street. He was tall, brown as leather, hard-featured under the pole-deer cap pulled low over his eyes. They were startling, those eyes, cold and steady, icily calm. Indefinably he was of Earth. His scarred dark face had a faintly piratical look, and he was wolfishly lean in his spaceman's leather as he walked lightly down the Lakklan, turning up the deer-hide collar about his ears with one hand. The other, his right, was hidden in the pocket of his coat.

The woman swerved when she saw him. He watched her subtly swaying approach without a flicker of expression on his face. But when she laid a milkily white hand upon his arm he gave a queer little start, involuntarily, like a shiver quickly suppressed. A ripple of annoyance crossed his face briefly and was gone, as if the muscular start had embarrassed him. He turned upon her an absolutely expressionless stare and waited.

'Who are you?' cooed a throatily velvet voice from the depths of the hood.

'Northwest Smith.' He said it crisply, and his lips snapped shut again. He moved a little away from her, for her hand still lay upon his right arm, and his right hand was still hidden in the coat pocket. He moved far enough to free his arm, and stood waiting.

'Will you come with me?' Her voice throbbed like a pigeon's from the shadow of her hood.

For a quick instant his pale eyes appraised her, as caution and curiosity warred within him. Smith was a wary man, very wise in the dangers of the spaceways life. Not for a moment did he mistake her meaning. Here was no ordinary woman of the streets. A woman robed in snow-cat furs had no need to accost casual strangers along the Lakklan.

'What do you want?' he demanded. His voice was deep and harsh, and the words fairly clicked with a biting brevity.

'Come,' she cooed, moving nearer again and slipping one hand inside his arm. 'I will tell you that in my own house. It is so cold here.'

Smith allowed himself to be pulled along down the Lakklan, too puzzled and surprised to resist. That simple act of hers had amazed him out of all proportion to its simplicity. He was revising his judgment of her as he walked along over the snowdust cobbles at her side. For by that richly throaty voice that throbbed as colorfully as a dove's, and by the milky whiteness of her hand on his arm, and by the subtle swaying of her walk, he had been sure, quite sure, that she came from Venus. No other planet breeds such beauty, no other women are born with the instinct of seduction in their very bones. And he had thought, dimly, that he recognized her voice.

But no, if she were Venus-bred, and the woman he half suspected her of being, she would never have slid her arm through his with that little intimate gesture or striven to override his hesitation with the sheer strength of her own charm. His one small motion away from her hand on his arm would have warned a true Venusian not to attempt further intimacy. She would have known by the look in his still eyes, by the wolfish, scarred face, tight-mouthed, that his weakness did not lie along the lines she was mistress of. And if she were the woman he suspected, all this was doubly sure. No, she could no be Venus-bred, nor the woman her voice so recalled to him.

Because of this he allowed her to lead him down the Lakklan. Not often did he permit curiosity to override his native caution, or he would never have come unscathed through the stormy years that lay behind him. But there was something so subtly queer about this woman, so contradictory to his preconceived opinions. Very vital to Smith were his own quick appraisements, and when one went all awry from the lines he intuitively expected, he felt compelled to learn why. He went on at her side, shortening his strides to the gliding gait of the woman on his arm. He did not like the contact of her hand, although he could not have said why.

No further words passed between them until they had reached a low stone building ten minutes' walk on down the Lakklan. She rapped on the heavy door with a quick, measured beat, and it swung open upon dimness. Her bare white hand in the crook of Smith's arm pulled him inside.

A gliding servant took his coat and fur cap. Without ostentation, as he removed the coat he slipped out the gun which had lain in his right-hand pocket and upon which his hand had rested all the while he was in the street. He tucked it inside his leather jacket and followed the still cloaked woman down a short hallway and through a low arch under which he had to stoop his head. The room they entered was immemorially ancient, changelessly Martian. Upon the dark stone floor, polished by the feet of countless generations, lay the furs of saltland beasts and the thick-pelted animals of the pole. The stone walls were incised with those inevitable, mysterious symbols which have become nothing more than queer designs now, though a million years ago they bore deep significance. No Martian house, old or new, lacks them, and no living Martian knows their meaning.

Remotely they must be bound up with the queer, cold darkness of that strange religion which once ruled Mars and which dwells still in the heart of every true Martian, though its shrines are secret now and its priests discredited. Perhaps if one could read those symbols they would tell the name of the cold god whom Mars worships still, in its heart of hearts, yet whose name is never spoken.

The whole room was fragrant and a little mysterious with the aromatic fumes of the braziers set at intervals about the irregularly shaped room and the low ceiling pressed the perfume down so that it hung in smoky layers in the sweet, heavy air.

'Be seated,' murmured the woman from the depths of her hood.

Smith glanced about in distaste. The room was furnished in the luxuriant Martian style so at odds with the harsh characteristics of the Martian people. He selected the least voluptuous-looking of the couches and sat down, regarding the woman obliquely as he did so.

She had turned a little away from him now and was slowly unfastening her furs. Then in one slow, graceful motion she flung back the cloak.

Smith caught his breath involuntarily, and a little shiver rippled over him, like the queer shock which had shaken his usually iron poise in the street. He could not be certain whether it were admiration or distaste he felt more strongly. And this despite her breath-taking beauty. Frankly he stared.

Yes, she was Venusian. Nowhere save upon that sunless, mist-drenched planet are such milk-white women bred. Voluptuously slim she was, in the paradoxical Venusian way, and the sweet, firm curves of her under velvet were more eloquent than a love-song. Her deeply crimson robe swathed her close in the traditional Venusian way, leaving one arm and rose-white shoulder bare and slit so that at every other step her milky thigh gleamed through. Heavy lids veiled her eyes from him as she turned. Unmistakably, exquisitely, she was Venusian, and from head to foot so lovely that despite himself Smith's pulses quickened.

He bent forward, eyes eager upon her face. It was flawlessly lovely, the long eyes subtly tilted, the planes of her cheekbones and the set of her chin eloquent of the beauty which dwelt in the very bones beneath her sweet white flesh, so that even her skull must be lovely. And with an odd little catch in his breath, Smith admitted to himself that she was indeed the woman he had guessed. He had not mistaken the throbbing richness of her voice. But – he looked closer, and wondered if he really did catch some hint of – wrongness – in that delicately tinted face, in the oddly averted eyes. For a moment his mind ran backward, remembering.

Judai of Venus had been the toast of three planets a few years past. Her heart-twisting beauty, her voice that throbbed like a dove's, the glowing charm of her had captured the hearts of every audience that heard her song. Even the far outposts of civilization knew her. That colorful, throaty voice had sounded upon Jupiter's moons and sent the cadences of 'Starless Night' ringing over the bare rocks of asteroids and through the darkness of space.

And then she vanished. Men wondered awhile, and there were searches and considerable scandal, but no one saw her again. All that was long past now. No one sang 'Starless Night' any more, and it was the Earth-born Rose Robertson's voice which rang through the solar system in lilting praise of 'The Green Hills of Earth.' Judai was years forgotten.

Smith knew her in the first glimpse he had of that high-cheeked, rose-tinted face. He had felt before he saw her that surely no two women of the same generation could speak in a voice so richly colored, so throbbingly sweet. And yet there was a hint of something alien in those gorgeously rich tones; something indefinably wrong in her unforgettable face; something that sent a little shock of distaste through him in the first glimpse he had of her beauty.

Yes, his ears and his eyes told him that she was Judai, but that infallible animal instinct which had saved him so often in such subtly warning ways told him just as surely that she was not – could not be. Judai, of all women, to make such un-Venusian errors of intuition! Feeling a little dizzy, he sat back and waited.

She glided across the floor to his side. The subtly provocative sway of her body as she moved was innately Venusian but she moved to the couch beside him and allowed her body to touch his in a brushing contact that sent a little thrill through him involuntarily, though he moved away. No, Judai would never have done that. She would have known better.

'You know me – yes?' she queried, richly murmurous.

'We haven't met before,' he said non-committally.

'But you know Judai. You remember. I saw it in your eyes. You must keep my secret, Northwest Smith. Can I trust you?'

'That – depends.' His voice was dry.

'I left, that night in New York, because something called which was stronger than I. No, it was not love. It was stronger than love, Northwest Smith. I could not resist it.'

There was a subtle amusement in her voice, as if she told some secret jest that had meaning to none but her. Smith moved a little further from her on the couch.

'I have been searching a long while,' she went on in her low, rich voice, 'for such a man as you – a man who can be entrusted with a dangerous task.' She paused.

'What is it?'

'There is a man in Righa who has something I very much want. He lives on the Lakklan by that drinking-house they call The Spaceman's Rest.'

Again she paused. Smith knew the place well, a dark, low-roofed den where the shadier and more scrupulously wary transients in Righa gathered. For the Spaceman's Rest was owned by a grim-jawed, leathery old drylander named Mhici, who was rumored to have great influence with the powers in Righa; so that a drink in The Spaceman's Rest was safely taken, without danger of interruption. He knew old Mhici well. He turned a mildly inquiring eye upon Judai, waiting for her to go on.

Her own eyes were lowered, but she seemed to feel his gaze, for she took up her story again instantly, without lifting her lashes.

'The man's name I do not know, but he is of Mars, from the canal-countries, and his face is deeply scarred across both cheeks. He hides what

I want in a little ivory box of drylander carving. If you can bring that to me you may name your own reward.'

Smith's pale eyes turned again, reluctantly, to the woman beside him. He wondered briefly why he disliked even to look at her, for she seemed lovelier each time his gaze rested upon that exquisitely tinted face. He saw that her eyes were still lowered, the feather lashes brushing her cheeks. She nodded without looking up as he echoed,

'Any price I ask?'

'Money or jewels or – what you will.'

'Ten thousand gold dollars to my name in the Great Bank of Lakkjourna, confirmed by viziphone when I hand you the box.'

If he expected a flicker of displeasure to cross her face at his matter-of-factness, he was disappointed. She rose in one long gliding motion and stood quietly before him. Smoothly, without lifting her eyes, she said,

'It is agreed, then. I will see you here tomorrow at this hour.'

Her voice dropped with a note of finality and dismissal. Smith glanced up into her face, and at what he saw there started to his feet in an involuntary motion, staring undisguisedly. She was standing quite still, with downcast eyes, and all animation and allure were draining away from her face. Uncomprehending, he watched humanity fading as if some glowing inward tide ebbed away, leaving a husk of sweet, inanimate flesh where the radiant Judai had stood a moment before.

An unpleasant little coldness rippled down his back as he watched. Uncertainly he glanced toward the door, feeling more strongly than ever that inexplicable revulsion against some inner alienness he could not understand. As he hesitated, 'Go, go!' came in an impatient voice from between her scarcely moving lips. And in almost ludicrous haste he made for the door. His last glance as it swung to of its own weight behind him revealed Judai standing motionless where he had left her, a still figure silhouetted white and scarlet against the immemorial pattern of the wall beyond. And he had a curious impression that a thin gray fog veiled her body in a lowly spreading nimbus that was inexplicably unpleasant.

Dusk was falling as he came out into the street again. A shadowy servant had given him his coat, and Smith departed so quickly that he was still struggling into the sleeves as he stepped out under the low arch of the door and drew a deep breath of the keen, icy air in conscious relief. He could not have explained, even to himself, the odd revulsion which Judai and her house had roused in him, but he was very glad to be free of them both and out in the open street again.

He shrugged himself deep into the warm fur coat and set off with long strides down the Lakklan. He was headed for The Spaceman's Rest. Old Mhici, if Smith found him in the right mood and approached him through the proper devious channels, might have information to give about the lovely lost singer and her strange house – and her credit at the Great Bank of Lakkjourna. Smith had small reason to doubt her wealth, but he took no needless chances.

The Spaceman's Rest was crowded. Smith made his way through the maze of tables toward the long bar at the end of the room, threading the crowd of hard-faced men whose wide diversity of races seemed to make little difference in the curious similarity of expression which dwelt upon every face. They were quiet and watchful-eyed and wore the indefinable air of those who live by their wits and their guns. The low-roofed place was thick with a pungent haze from the *nuari* which nearly all were smoking, and that in itself was evidence that in Mhici's place they considered themselves secure, for *nuari* is mildly opiate.

Old Mhici himself came forward to the voiceless summoning in Smith's single pale-eyed glance as it met his in the crowd about the bar. The Earthman ordered red *segir*-whisky, but he did not drink it immediately.

'I know no one here,' he observed in the drylander idiom, which was a flagrant misstatement, but heavy with meaning. For the hospitable old salt-lands' custom demands that the proprietor share a drink with any stranger who comes into his bar. It is a relic from the days when strangers were rare in the salt-lands, and is very seldom recalled in populous cities like Righa, but Mhici understood. He said nothing, but he took the black Venusian bottle of *segir* by the neck and motioned Smith toward a corner table that stood empty.

When they were settled there and Mhici had poured himself a drink, Smith took one gulp of the red whisky and hummed the opening bars of 'Starless Night,' watching the old drylander's pointed, leathery features. One of Mhici's eyebrows went up, which was the equivalent of a start of surprise in another man.

'Starless Nights,' he observed, 'are full of danger, Smith.'

'And of pleasure sometimes, eh?'

'Ur-r! Not this one.'

'Oh?'

'No. And where I do not understand, I keep away.'

'You're puzzled too, eh?'

'Deeply. What happened?'

Smith told him briefly. He knew that it is proverbial never to trust a drylander, but he felt that old Mhici was the exception. And by the old man's willingness to come to the point with a minimum of fencing and circumlocution he knew that he must be very perturbed by Judai's presence in Righa. Old Mhici missed little, and if he was puzzled by her presence Smith felt that his own queer reactions to the Venusian beauty had not been unjustified.

'I know the box she means,' Mhici told him when he had finished. 'There's the man, over there by the wall. See?'

Under his brows Smith studied a lean, tall canal-dweller with a deeply scarred face and an air of restless uneasiness. He was drinking some poisonously green concoction and smoking *nuari* so heavily that the clouds of it veiled his face. Smith grunted contemptuously.

'If the box is valuable he's not putting himself into any shape to guard it,' he said. 'He'll be dead asleep in half an hour if he keeps that up.'

'Look again,' murmured Mhici. And Smith, wondering a little at the dryness of the old man's voice, turned his head and studied the canal-dweller more carefully.

This time he saw what had escaped him before. The man was frightened, so frightened that the *nuari* pouring in and out of his lungs was having little effect. His restless eyes were hot with anxiety, and he had maneuvered his back to the wall so that he could command the whole room as he drank. That in itself, here in Mhici's place, was flagrant. Mhici's iron fist and ready gun had established order in The Spaceman's Rest long ago, and no man in years had dared break it. Mhici commanded not only physical but also moral respect, for his influence with the powers of Righa was exerted not only to furnish immunity to his guests but also to punish peace-breakers. The Spaceman's Rest was sanctuary. No, for a man to sit with his back to the wall here bespoke terror of something more deadly than guns.

'They're following him, you know,' Mhici murmured over the rim of his glass. 'He stole that box somewhere along the canals, and now he's afraid of his shadow. I don't know what's in the box, but it's damn valuable to someone and they're out to get it at any cost. Do you still want to relieve him of it?'

Smith squinted at the drylander through narrowed eyes. How old Mhici learned the secrets he knew, no one could guess, but he had never been caught in error. And Smith had little desire to call down upon himself the enmity of whatever perils it was which kindled the fear of death in the canal-dweller's eyes. Yet curiosity rode him still. The puzzle of Judai was a tantalizing mystery which he felt he must solve.

'Yes,' he said slowly. 'I've got to know.'

'I'll get you the box,' said Mhici suddenly. 'I know where he hides it, and there's a way between here and the house next door that will let me at it in five minutes. Wait here.'

'No,' said Smith quickly. 'That's not fair to you. I'll get it.'

Mhici's wide mouth curved.

'I'm in little danger,' he said. 'Here in Righa no one would dare – and besides, that way is secret. Wait.'

Smith shrugged. After all, Mhici knew how to take care of himself. He sat there gulping down segir as he waited, and watching the canal-dweller across the room. Terror played in changing patterns across the scarred face.

When Mhici reappeared he carried a small wooden crate labeled conspicuously in Venusian characters. Smith translated,

'Six Pints Segir, Vanda Distilleries, Ednes, Venus.'

'It's in this,' murmured Mhici, setting down the box. 'You'd better stay here tonight. You know, the back room that opens on the alley.'

'Thanks,' said Smith in some embarrassment. He was wondering why the old drylander had taken such pains in his behalf. He had expected no more than a few words of warning. 'I'll split the money, you know.'

Mhici shook his head.

'I don't think you'll get it,' he said candidly. 'And I don't think she really wants the box. Not half so much as she wants you, anyhow. There were any number of men who could have got the box for her. And you remember how she said she'd been looking a long time for someone like yourself. No, it's the man she wants, I think. And I can't figure out why.'

Smith wrinkled his brows and traced a design on the tabletop in spilt *segir.*

'I've got to know,' he said stubbornly.

'I've passed her in the street. I've felt that same revulsion, and I don't know why. I don't like this, Smith. But if you feel you have to go through with it, that's your affair. I'll help if I can. Let's drop it, eh? What are you doing tonight? I hear there's a new dancer at the Lakktal now.'

Much later, in the shifting light of Mars' hurrying moons, Smith stumbled up the little alley behind The Spaceman's Rest and entered the door in the rear of the bar. His head was a bit light with much segir, and the music and the laughter and the sound of dancing feet in the Lakktal's halls made an echoing beat through his head. He undressed clumsily in the dark and stretched himself with a heavy sigh on the leather couch which is the Martian bed.

Just before sleep overtook him he found himself remembering Judai's queer little quirking smile when she said, 'I left New York because something called – stronger than love …' And he thought drowsily, 'What is stronger than love? …' The answer came to him just as he sank into oblivion. 'Death.'

Smith slept late the next day. The tri-time steel watch on his wrist pointed to Martian noon when old Mhici himself pushed open the door and carried in a tray of breakfast.

'There's been excitement this morning,' he observed as he set down his burden.

Smith sat up and stretched luxuriously.

'What?'

'The canal man shot himself.'

Smith's pale eyes sought out the case labeled 'Six Pints Segir' where it stood in the corner of the room. His brows went up in surprise.

'Is it so valuable as that?' he murmured. 'Let's look at it.'

Mhici shot the bolts on the two doors as Smith rose from the leather couch and dragged the box into the center of the floor. He pried up the thin board that Mhici had nailed down the night before over the twice-stolen box, and pulled out an object wrapped in brown canvas. With the old drylander bending over his shoulder he unwound the wrappings. For a full minute thereafter he squatted on his heels staring in perplexity at the thing in his hands. It was not large, this little ivory box, perhaps ten inches by four, and four deep. Its intricate drylander carving struck him as remotely familiar, but he had been staring at it for several seconds before it dawned upon him where he had seen those odd spirals and queer twisted characters before. Then he remembered. No wonder they looked familiar, for they had stared down upon him bafflingly from the walls of countless Martian dwellings. He lifted his eyes and saw a band of them circling the walls above him now. But they were large, and these on the box intricately tiny, so that at first glance they looked like the merest waving lines incised delicately all over the box's surface.

Not until then, following those crawling lines, did he see that the box had no opening. To all appearances it was not a box at all, but a block of carved ivory. He shook it, and something within shifted slightly, as if it were packed in loose wrappings. But there was no opening anywhere. He turned it over and over, peering and prying, but to no avail. Finally he shrugged and wrapped the canvas back about the enigma.

'What do you make of it?' he asked.

Mhici shook his head.

'Great Shar alone can tell,' he murmured half in derision, for Shar is the Venusian god, a friendly deity whose name rises constantly to the lips of the Hot Planet's dwellers. The god whom Mars worships, openly or in secret, is never named aloud.

They discussed the puzzle of it off and on the rest of the afternoon. Smith spent the hours restlessly, for he dared not smoke nuari nor drink much, with the interview so close ahead. When the shadows were lengthening along the Lakklan he got into his deerhide coat again and tucked the ivory box into an inner pocket. It was bulky, but not betrayingly so. And he made sure his flame-gun was charged and ready.

In the late afternoon sun that sparkled blindingly upon the snow crystals blowing along the wind, he went down the Lakklan again with his right hand in his pocket and his eyes raking the street warily under the shadow of his cap. Evidently the pursuers of that box had not traced it, for he was not followed.

Judai's house squatted dark and low at the edge of the Lakklan. Smith fought down a rising revulsion as he lifted his hand to knock, but the door swung open before his knuckles had touched the panel. That same shadowy servant beckoned him in. This time he did not put his gun away when he shifted it from his coat pocket. He took the canvas-wrapped box in one hand and the flame-pistol in the other, and the servant opened the door he had passed last night upon the room where Judai was waiting.

She stood exactly as he had left her in the center of the floor, white and scarlet against the queer traceries on the wall beyond. He had the curious notion that she had not stirred since he left her last night. She moved a little sluggishly as she turned her head and saw him, but it was a lethargy which she quickly overcame. She motioned him toward the divan, taking her seat at his side with the flowing, feline ease of every true Venusian. And as before, he shrank involuntarily from the contact of that fragrant, velvet-sheathed body, with an inner revulsion he could not understand.

She said nothing, but she held out her two hands cupped up in entreaty, and she did not lift her eyes to his face as she did so. He laid the box in her upturned palm. At that moment for the first time it occurred to him that not once had he met her eyes. She had never lifted those veiling lashes and looked into his. Wondering, he watched.

She was unwrapping the canvas with quick, delicate motions of her pink-stained fingers. When the box lay bare in her hands she sat quite motionless for a while, her lowered eyes fixed upon the carven block of the thing which had cost at least one life. And her quiet was unnatural, trance-like. He thought she must have ceased to breathe. Not a lash fluttered, not a pulse stirred in her round white wrists as she held the little symbol-traced box up. There was something indescribably horrid in her quiet as she sat and stared, all her being centered in one vast, still concentration upon the ivory box.

Then he heard such a deep breath rush out through her nostrils that it might have been life itself escaping, a breath that thinned into a high, shuddering hum like the whine of wind through wires. It was not a sound that any human creature could make.

Without realizing that he had moved, Smith leaped. Of their own volition his muscles tensed into a spring of animal terror away from that high-whining thing on the couch. He found himself half crouched a dozen paces away, his gun steady in a lifted hand and his hair stiffening at the roots as he faced her. For by the thin, high, shuddering noise he knew surely that she was not human.

For a long instant he crouched there, taut, feeling his scalp crawl with a prickling terror as his pale eyes searched for some reason in this madness which had come over them both. She still sat rigid, with lowered eyes, but though she had not stirred, something told him unerringly that his first instinct had been right, his first intuitive flinching from her hand on his arm – she was not human. Warm white flesh and fragrant hair and subtle, curving roundness of her under velvet, all this was camouflage to conceal – to conceal – he could not guess what, but he knew that loveliness for a lie, and all down his back the nerves tingled with man's involuntary shudder from the unknown.

She rose. Cradling the ivory box against the sweet high curve of her bosom, she moved slowly forward, her lashes making two dim crescents on her exquisitely tinted cheeks. He had never seen her lovelier, or more hideously repulsive. For in some obscure part of his brain he knew that the humanity which she had clutched like a cloak about her was being dropped. In another instant . . .

She paused before him, very near, so near that the muzzle of his half-forgotten gun was pressed against the velvet that sheathed her body, and the fragrance of her rose in a vague cloud to his nostrils. For one tense instant they stood so, she with lowered lashes, cradling her ivory box, he rigid with prickling revulsion, gun nosing her side, pale eyes set in a narrow-lidded stare as he waited shudderingly for what must come next. In the split second before her eyelids rose, he wanted overwhelmingly to fling up a hand and shut out the sight of what lay behind them, to run blindly out of the room and out of the house and never stop until the doors of The Spaceman's Rest closed shelteringly upon him. He could not stir. Caught in a frozen trance, he stared. The lashes fluttered. Slowly, very slowly, her lids rose.

The cold shock that jolted him into incredulity then made every detail of the picture so clear that he was never to forget, no matter how hard he tried, the vividness of that first glimpse into Judai's eyes. Yet for a full minute he did not realize what he saw. It was too incredible for the brain to grasp. With thickly beating heart he stood rigid, staring into the weird face turned to his.

From under those deep-curved lashes looked out no such luminous depths of darkness as he had expected. There were no eyes behind Judai's creamy lids. Instead he was looking into two lash-fringed, almond-shaped pits of gray smoke, smoke that seethed and shifted and boiled within itself, unresting as smoke from the fires of hell. He knew then that there dwelt in the curved and milk-white body which had been Judai's a thing more evil than any devil hell's fire ever spawned. How it came into that body he never knew, but he did know that the real Judai was gone. Looking into that restlessly seething smoky blindness, he was sure of that, and revulsion surged through him as he strained at his own body for the will to blast this hell-tenanted beauty into nothingness, and could not stir. Helpless in the frozen grip of his own horror, he watched.

She – it stood straight before him, staring blankly. And he was aware of a slow seepage from the gray pits of the eyes. Smoke was curling out into the room in delicate whirls and plumes. Sickness came over him as he realized it, and an extravagant terror, for it was not the sweet-smelling, clean smoke of fire. There was no physically perceptible odor to it, but from the unspeakably evil stench his very soul shuddered away. He could smell evil, taste it, perceive it with more senses than he knew he possessed, despite the intangibility of the swirling stuff that billowed now in deepening waves from under the lash-fringed lids that once had been Judai's. Once before he had been dimly aware of this, when he had looked back as he left, the night before, to see that vague gray veiling a woman's milk-whiteness in obscurity that was somehow – unpleasant. Even that remote hinting at what he saw now in full strength had been enough to send a warning shudder through him. But now – now it billowed about him in thickening deeps through which he could scarcely make out the pale shape of the figure before him, and the grayness was seeping through his body and mind and soul with a touch more dreadful than the touch of every ugly thing in creation. It was not tangible, but it was slimmer and more unclean than anything he could have named. Not upon his flesh but upon his soul that wet slime crawled.

Dimly through the swirl of it he saw the lips of Judai's body move. A ghost of a voice fluted into the grayness, a sweet, rich, throbbing thread of sound. So lovely had been Judai's voice that even the horror which stirred it now into speech could not evoke discords from a throat that had never uttered any sound but music.

'I am ready to take you now, Northwest Smith. The time has come to discard this body and these ways of seduction and put on a man's strength and straightforwardness, so that I may complete what I came to do. I shall not need it long, but your force and vitality I must have before I surrender them up to mighty —. And then I may go forth in my true form to bring the worlds under great —'s reign.'

Smith blinked. There had been a gap in her words where he should have heard a name, but it had not been a gap of silence. Her lips had moved, though no sound came forth, and the air shook with a wordless cadence so deeply stirring that he felt involuntary awe – if it were possible to feel awe at the utterance of a word without sound.

That sweetly murmurous voice was whispering through the fog that had thickened now until he could scarcely see the outlines of the figure before him.

'I have waited so long for you, Northwest Smith – for a man with a body and a brain like yours, to serve my needs. I take you now, in great —'s name. In that name, I bid you surrender your body. Go!'

The last word cracked through the mist, and abruptly blindness swept over him. His feet no longer pressed the floor. He was wallowing in a fog of such revolting horror that his very soul writhed within him for escape.

Slimily the gray stuff seeped through his being, crawling and sliding and oozing, and the touch of it upon his brain was a formless madness, so that the soul which shuddered from such indescribable dreadfulness would have fled into hell itself to escape.

Dimly he knew what was happening. His body was being made untenable to force his consciousness to leave it. And knowing this, realizing what its portent was, yet he found himself struggling desperately for release. The crawling ooze was a slime upon his very soul. There could be no alternative so frightful as this sickening reality. Madness was in the frightened writhing of self to escape the horror that enfolded him. Frantically he fought for release.

It came suddenly. He was aware of a distinct snapping, as of something tangible, and then freedom. On the instant those gray, crawling swaths of revulsion ceased to be. He floated free and light and impalpable in a void without light or dark, conscious of nothing but the blessed release from torment.

Gradually realization came back to him. He had no form or substance now, but he was aware. And he knew that he must seek his body again; how, he did not know, but the thought of it was a poignant longing, and his whole intangible being so concentrated upon that thought that in a moment or two the room he had left began to take shape about him, and his own tall figure swam hazily through the veiling fog. With a mighty effort he bent his thoughts upon that figure, and at last began to understand what was taking place.

He could see now with clear, unhampered vision around all points of the compass at once. Floating in nothingness, he watched the room. It was a little difficult at first to see any one thing, for he no longer had the focus of eyes to help him and the room was a wide panorama without center. But after a while he learned the trick of concentration, and saw clearly for the first time his own relinquished self, broad and tall and leather-brown, standing rigid in the midst of a sliding fog that curled about it in thick, slimy glidings which brought back memories of sickening vividness. At the feet of that brown, fog-veiled shape lay the body of Judai. Exquisitely graceful, it stretched in a glimmer of white and scarlet across the dark floor. He knew she was dead now. The breath of alien life which had been infused into her was withdrawn. Death's curious flatness was eloquent in the piteously lovely body rounding under the velvet robe. The Thing was done with her.

He turned his attention again to his own body. That horribly alive fog had thickened still more, into heavy, half-palpable robes of sliding slime that crawled unceasingly over and around the tall figure. But it was disappearing. It was seeping slowly, remorselessly, into the flesh he had vacated. Now it was more than half gone, and into that frozen body a semblance of life was stealing. He watched while the last of the gray stuff which was the Thing took possession of his lost self, waking it into a cold and alien life. He saw it seize upon the nerves and muscles he had trained, so that its first motion was the familiar quick gesture to slip the flame-gun into its holster under his arm. He saw his own broad shoulders shrug unconsciously to be sure the strap was in place. He watched himself crossing the room with the long, light steps that had once been his. He saw his own hands pick up the ivory box from the slim, pink-stained fingers of Judai.

Not until then did he realize that thoughts were open to his reading now, as clearly as words had been before. The only thoughts in the room had been the alien ones of the Thing, and until this moment they had not taken forms human enough to have meaning to him. But now he began to understand many things, and the strangeness of them whirled through his consciousness in half-incomprehensible patterns.

Then abruptly a name flashed through those thoughts, and the power of it struck him with such force that for an instant his hold upon the scene slipped and he whirled back into that void again where neither light nor darkness dwelt. As he fought his way back into the room his unbodied mind was struggling to put together the pieces of newly acquired knowledge, in which that name flamed like a beacon, the center and focus for all the patterns of the knowledge.

It was the name his ears had not been able to hear when Judai's lips spoke it. He knew now that though human lips could frame its syllables, no brain that was wholly human could send the impulses for that framing; so that it could never be spoken by a sane man, nor heard or understood by him. Even so, the wordless vibrations of it had eddied through his brain in waves of awe. And now, when its unveiled force struck full upon his unprotected consciousness, the mightiness of that name was enough to send him reeling all out of focus and control.

For it was the name of a Thing so powerful that even in his unreality he shuddered at the thought; a thing whose full might no flesh-veiled consciousness could grasp. Only in his disembodied awareness could he realize it, and he turned his mind away from that awful name even as he delved deeper into the alien thoughts that flashed before him from the creature which wore his semblance.

He knew now why the Thing had come. He knew the purpose of that which bore the name. And he knew why the men of Mars never spoke their cold god's title. They could not. It was not a name human brains could grasp or human lips utter without compulsion from Outside. Slowly the origins of that curious religion took shape in his mind.

The name had dwelt like some vast, brooding shadow among the earliest ancestors of Martian men, millions upon millions of years ago. It had come from its lair Outside, and dwelt dreadfully among mankind, sucking life from its worshippers and reigning with such awe and terror that even now, after countless eons had gone by, though its very existence was forgotten, that terror and awe lived yet in the minds of these remote descendants.

Nor was the name wholly gone, even now. It had withdrawn, for reasons too vast for comprehension. But it had left behind it shrines, and each of them was a little doorway into that presence, so that the priests who tended them furnished tribute. Sometimes they were possessed by the power of their god, and spoke the name which their devotees could not hear, yet whose awful cadences were a storm of power about them. And this was the origin of that strange, dark religion which upon Mars has been discredited for so long, though it has never died in the hearts of men.

Smith understood now that the Thing which dwelt in his body was a messenger from Outside, although he could never quite grasp in what capacity. It might have been a part of that vast composite power which bore the name. He never knew. Its thoughts when they wandered in that direction were too alien to carry any meaning into his mind. When it even turned those thoughts backward toward its origin, and the might of the name flashed through them, Smith quickly learned to shrink within himself, withdrawing his consciousness until that thought had passed. It was like gazing through an opened door into the furnaces of hell.

He watched himself turn the box slowly over between his hands, while his own pale eyes searched its surface. Or were they his eyes? Did there dwell now under his own lids the grayness of the Thing? He could not be sure, for he could not bring himself to concentrate directly upon that foggy dweller within his body. Its touch was so alien, so repulsive.

Now his hands had found some hidden opening. He could not tell exactly what happened, but suddenly he saw himself wrenching at the ivory box, with a queer, twisting motion, and the two halves of it fell apart along an uneven line of cleavage. Out of it a thick mist rose, a heavy, semitangible stuff in which the hands of his body groped as if through folds of cloth.

Sluggishly the mist spilled floorward, while from the box he saw himself drawing a thing which cleared away a little of the mystery that shrouded so much of what had happened. For he recognized the curious symbol that had lain in the mist-filled box. It was wrought from a substance which has no duplicate anywhere on the three worlds, a translucent metal through whose depths a smoky dimness was diffused in vague curls and plumes. And it shape was the duplicate of a symbol repeated often in the wall-carvings of every Martian house. Smith had heard whispers of this talisman passed from mouth to mouth in the secrecy of space-pirates' rendezvous. For its very existence was a secret to all save those rovers of the spaceways from whom nothing is wholly hidden.

The symbol, so those whispers said, was a talisman from the old religion, used in the worship of the nameless god in the ages before discredit had forced the worship into secrecy – a thing of terrible power had any living man known how to use it. It was said to be kept in inviolable hiding somewhere in one of the canal cities. He understood now in what terror the canal-dweller with the scarred face must have gone, knew why he had not dared face the consequences of his own theft. The priests of the name were held in the more terror for the darkness of their calling.

The story behind that theft he was never to know. It was enough that the Thing had the priceless talisman now. Through his own efforts that immemorial symbol had fallen into the only hands which would know how to wield it: paradoxically, the hands that had once been his. Helplessly he watched.

His own fingers lifted it up familiarly. It was not more than twelve inches long, a thing of subtle curves and arcs. Suddenly he knew what the symbol meant. From the cloudy alienness of the mind which dwelt where his mind had dwelt, he drew the certainty that the talisman had been wrought into the shape of the written name: that unspeakable word, crystallized into nameless metal. The Thing handled it with a sort of unhuman awe.

He watched himself turning slowly round as if in an effort to orient his body with some unknown point at a measureless distance. His hand, holding the symbol, rose high. The room was full of a tense solemnity, an unbreathing hush, as if some long-awaited moment of tremendous awe and portent had been reached at last. Slowly, with stiff steps, his lost body paced toward the eastern wall, the symbol held rigidly before it.

At that tracery-incised wall it stopped, and with a gesture full of ritualistic slowness lifted the talisman and set its curved apex against an identical symbol on the wall, the carven counterpart of the name. And from that point it drew the talisman down and crosswise as if it were painting an unseen curve on the wall. As he watched that moving apex Smith realized what was happening. Invisibly, with the metal-wrought talisman following lines in the symbols on the wall, it was tracing that name. And the ritual was invested with a depth of power and a nameless portent that sent sudden terror thrilling through him. What was the meaning of it?

Cold with a bodiless chill of foreboding, he watched the rite to its close. The talisman sketched the last lines of that pattern upon the wall, completely enclosing a space that covered perhaps six square feet of tracery. And then his own tall body flourished the metal symbol like one who welcomes a caller through an opened door, and dropped to its knees before the outlined pattern.

For a minute – for two minutes – nothing happened. Then, watching the wall, Smith thought he could discern the shape of the symbol that had been traced. Somehow it was becoming clear among the painted characters. Somehow a grayness was spreading within the outlines he had watched his own hands trace, a fogginess that strengthened and grew clearer and clearer, until he could no longer make out the traceries enclosed within its boundaries, and a great, misty symbol stood out vividly across the wall.

He did not understand for a moment. He watched the grayness take on density and grow stronger with each passing moment, but he did not understand until a long curl of fog drifted lazily out into the room, and the grayness began to spill over its own edges and eddy and billow as if that wall were afire. And from very far away, over measureless voids, he caught the first faint impact of a power so great that he knew in one flash the full horror of what he watched.

The name, traced upon that wall with its own metal counterpart, had opened a doorway for the Thing which bore the name to enter. It was coming back to the world it had left millions of years ago. It was oozing through the opened door, and nothing he could do would stop it.

He was a bodiless awareness drifting through voids that held neither light nor dark – he was a nothingness, and he must watch his own body bring down the destruction of the worlds he had dwelt in without any strength to oppose a feather's weight of resistance.

Despairingly he watched a long plume of the dawning terror brush his body's bent head. At the contact that body rose stiffly, as if in answer to a command, and backed slowly across the room to where the body of Judai lay sprawled upon the floor. It stooped like an automation and lifted her in its arms. It came forward again, walking mechanically, and laid her down under the billowing symbol that was a gateway into deeper depths than hell. The smoke wreathed downward hungrily, hiding the white and scarlet of her from view.

For an instant it writhed and boiled about the spot where she had been engulfed, and the impact of greater force struck in one mighty blow against Smith's consciousness. For across the measureless gulfs the power of the name was nearing. Whatever of energy it had absorbed from the body of Judai had brought it nearer with a long leap, so that now the might of it echoed round and round the symbol-walled room like the beat of drums. There was triumph in that beating. Remotely, in the recurrent waves of thunderous power, he understood at last the purpose of those symbols.

All this had been planned eons ago, when the Unnamable One departed from Mars. Perhaps the ages had been no more than a moment to its timeless might. But it had left with full meaning to return, and so had given more deeply than time could erase on the minds of its worshippers the need for those symbols upon their walls. Only the need; not the reason. They were to make full access into this world possible again. The remote touch which its priests kept through their shrines to the Nameless One were like tiny windows, but here, hidden among the traceries, opened a mighty gateway through which all that measureless power could sweep irresistibly when the hour came. And it had come.

Dimly he caught a vision of triumph from the mind of the Thing which stood rigid in his body before the billowing wall, a vision of other worlds wherever the symbols were graven opening like doors for the great gray surges to come flooding through, a vision of worlds engulfed and seething in one unbroken blanket of gray that writhed and eddied and sucked avidly at the bodies and souls of men.

Smith's consciousness shuddered in the void where it drifted, raged against its own helplessness, watched in horror-struck fascination the surges of billowing gray that rolled slowly into the room. The body of Judai had wholly vanished now. And the long fog-fingers were groping blindly as if in search for other food. In a swimming horror he watched his own tall body stumble forward and sink to its knees under the plumes of ravenous gray.

Somehow the vivid despair of that moment was strong enough to do something which nothing that preceded it had accomplished. The prospect of the world's destruction had made him sick with a hopeless dread; but the thought of his own body offered up as a sacrifice to the flooding gray, leaving him to drift for eternity through voids, cracked like a whiplash against his consciousness in one flash of hot rebellion that jerked him all out of focus to the scene he watched. Violent revolt surged up in him against the power of the Thing and the awful force of that which bore the name.

How it happened he did not know, but suddenly he was no longer floating disembodied through nothingness. Suddenly he was bursting the bonds that parted him from reality. Suddenly he was violently back again into the world from which he had been thrust, fighting desperately to gain access once more into his body, struggling in panic terror to force an entry against the thick grayness of what dwelt there now. It was a nauseous and revolting struggle, so close to the slimy presence of the Thing, but he scarcely heeded its nearness in his frenzy to save the body that was his.

For the moment he was not striving for full possession, but he pushed and raged and fought to seize his own muscles and drag his body back from the billows that were rolling hungrily toward it. It was a more desperate struggle than any hand-to-hand combat, the struggle of two entities for a single body.

The Thing that opposed him was strong, and firmly entrenched in the nerve-centers and brain-cells that had been his, but he was fighting the more hotly for the familiarity of the field he sought to win. And slowly he won entrance. Perhaps it was because he was not striving at first for full possession. In its struggles to cling fast to what it held, the Thing could not oppose his subtle sliding in among the centers that controlled motion, and by jerky degrees he dragged his own body to its feet and backward, step by hotly contested step, away from the seething pattern that oozed upon the wall. Sick to the very soul with the closeness of the Thing, he fought.

He was struggling now to force it wholly out, and if he was not driving it away, at least he held his own. It could not dislodge him from the foothold he had won. There were flashes when he saw the room through his own eyes again, and felt the strength of his body like a warm garment about the nakedness of the self which strove for its possession, yet a body through which crawled and slid the dreadfulness of that sickening fog-fluid which was a slime upon his innermost soul.

But the Thing was strong. It had rooted its tendrils deep in the body he fought for, and would not let go. And through the room in recurrent thunders beat the might of the coming name, impatient, insistent, demanding sustenance that it might pass wholly through the gateway. Its long fog-fingers stretched clutchingly out into the room. And in Smith a faint hope was growing that it must have his body before it could come farther. If he could prevent that, perhaps all was not yet lost. If he could prevent it – but the Thing he struggled with was strong …

Time had ceased to have meaning for him. In a dream of horror he wallowed amid the thick and sickening slime of his enemy, fighting for a more precious thing than his own life. He fought for Death. For if he could not win his body, yet he knew he must enter it long enough to die somehow, by his own hand, cleanly; else he would drift through eternity in the void where neither light nor darkness dwelt. How long it went on he never knew. But in one of those moments when he had won a place in his own body again, and perceived with its senses, he heard the sound of an opening door.

With infinite effort he twisted his head around. Old Mhici stood in the opening, flame-gun in hand, blinking bewilderedly into the fog-dim room. There was a dawning terror in his eyes as he stared, a terror deep-rooted and age-old, heritage from those immemorial ancestors upon whose minds the name had been graven too deeply for time to efface. Half comprehending, he stood in the presence of the god of his fathers, and Smith could see a paralyzing awe creeping slowly across the face. He could not have known from the sight of that fog-oozing wall what it was he looked upon, but an inner consciousness seemed to make clear to him that the thing which bore the name was a presence in the room. And it must have realized Mhici's presence, for about the walls in tremendous beats of command roared the thunderous echoes of that far-away might, ravenous to feed again upon man. Old Mhici's eyes glazed with obedience. He stumbled forward one mechanical step.

Something cracked in Smith's consciousness. If Mhici reached the wall,

all his struggles would be for nothing. With that nourishment the name might enter. Well, at any rate he could save himself – perhaps. He must die before that happened. And with all the strength that was in him summoned up in one last despairing surge he crowded the Thing that dwelt with him momentarily out of control, and fell upon Mhici with clawed hands clutching for his throat.

Whether the old drylander understood or not, whether he could see in the pale eyes that had been his friend's the slow writhing of the Thing, Smith could not guess. He saw the horror and incredulity upon the leathery features of the Martian as he lunged, and then, in blessed relief, felt wiry fingers at his own neck. Yet he knew that Mhici was striving not to injure him, and he struggled in desperation to lash the old drylander into self-defensive fury. He struck and gouged and tore, and felt in overwhelming relief the old man's strong grip tighten at last about his neck.

He relaxed then in the oncoming oblivion of those releasing fingers.

From very far away a hoarse voice calling his name dragged Smith up through layer upon layer of cloudy nothingness. He opened heavy eyes and stared. Gradually old Mhici's anxious face swam into focus above him. Segir was burning in his mouth. He swallowed automatically, and the pain of his bruised throat as the fiery liquid went down roused him into full consciousness. He struggled to a sitting position, pressing one hand to his reeling head and blinking dazedly about.

He lay upon the dark stone floor where oblivion had overtaken him. The patterned walls looked down. His heart suddenly leaped into thick beating. He twisted round, seeking that wall which had oozed grayness through a door that opened upon Outside. And with such relief that he sank back against Mhici's shoulder in sudden weakness, he saw that the Unnamable One no longer billowed out into the room. Instead, that wall was a cracked and charred ruin down which long streams of half-melted rock were congealing. The room was pungent and choking with the odor of a flame-gun's blast.

He turned questioning eyes to Mhici, croaking something inarticulate in the depths of his swollen throat.

'I – I burnt it,' said Mhici in a strange half-shame.

Smith jerked his head round again and stared at the ruined wall, a hot chagrin flooding over him. Of course, if the pattern were destroyed, that door would close through which the One which bore the name was entering. Somehow that had never occurred to him. Somehow he had wholly forgotten that a flame-gun was sheathed under his arm during all the long struggle he had held with the Thing co-dwelling in his body. He realized in a moment why. The awful power which in his bodiless state had thundered about him from that infinity of might which bore the name was so measureless that the very thought of a flame-gun seemed too futile to dwell upon. But Mhici had not known. He had never felt that vast furnace-blast of force beating about him. And quite simply, with one flash of his ray-gun, he had closed the door to Outside.

His voice was beating insistently in Smith's ears, shaking with emotion and reaction, and cracking a little now and then like the voice of an old man. For the first time old Mhici was showing his age.

'What happened? What in your own God's name – no, don't tell me now. Don't try to talk. I – I – you can tell me later.' And then rapidly, in disjointed sentences, as if he were talking to drown out the sound of his own thoughts, 'Perhaps I can guess – never mind. Hope I haven't hurt you. You must have been crazy, Smith. Better now? After you – you – when I saw you on the floor, there was a – well, a fog, I guess – thick as slime, that came rolling up from you like – I can't say what. And suddenly I was mad. That awful gray, rolling out of the wall – I don't know what happened. First I knew I was blazing away into the depths of it, and then the wall beyond cracked and melted, and the whole fog mass was fading out. Don't know why. Don't know what happened then. I must have been – out – a little while myself. It's gone now. I don't know why, but it's gone …

'Here, have some more *segir*.'

Smith stared up at him unseeingly. A vague wonder was circling in his mind as to why the Thing that had tenanted his body surrendered. Perhaps Mhici had choked life out of that body, so that the Thing had to flee and his own consciousness could enter unopposed. Perhaps – he gave it up. He was too tired to think at all. He sighed deeply and reached for the *segir* bottle.

YVALA

Northwest Smith leaned against a pile of hemp-wrapped bales from the Martian drylands and stared with expressionless eyes, paler than pale steel, over the confusion of the Lakkdarol spaceport before him. In the clear Martian day the tatters of his leather spaceman's garb were pitilessly plain, the ray-burns and the rents of a hundred casual brawls. It was evident at a glance that Smith had fallen upon evil days. One might have guessed by the shabbiness of his clothing that his pockets were empty, the charge in his ray-gun low.

Squatting on his heels beside the lounging Earthman, Yarol the Venusian bent his yellow head absently over the thin-bladed dagger which he was juggling in one of the queer, interminable Venusian games so pointless to outsiders. Upon him too the weight of ill fortune seemed to have pressed heavily. It was eloquent in his own shabby garments, his empty holster. But the insouciant face he lifted to Smith was as careless as ever, and no more of weariness and wisdom and pure cat-savagery looked out from his sidelong black eyes than Smith was accustomed to see there. Yarol's face was the face of a seraph, as so many Venusian faces are likely to be, but the set of his mouth told a tale of dissoluteness and reckless violence which belied his features' racial good looks.

'Another half-hour and we eat,' he grinned up at his tall companion.

Smith glanced at the tri-time watch on his wrist.

'If you haven't been having another dope dream,' he grunted. 'Luck's been against us so long I can't quite believe in a change now.'

'By Pharol I swear it,' smiled Yarol. 'The man came up to me in the New Chicago last night and told me in so many words how much money was waiting if we'd meet him here at noon.'

Smith grunted again and deliberately took up another notch in the belt that circled his lean waist. Yarol laughed softly, a murmur of true Venusian sweetness, as he bent again to the juggling of his knife. Above his bent blond head Smith looked out again across the busy port.

Lakkdarol is an Earthman's town upon Martian soil, blending all the more violent elements of both worlds in its lawless heart, and the scene he watched had under-currents that only a ranger of the spaceways could fully appreciate. A semblance of discipline is maintained there, but only the space-rangers know how superficial that likeness is. Smith grinned a little to himself, knowing that the bales being trundled down the gangplank from the Martian liner *Inghti* carried a core of that precious Martian 'lamb's-wool' on which the duties run so high. And a whisper had run through the New Chicago last night as they sat over their *segir*-whisky glasses that the shipment of grain from Denver expected in at noon on the *Friedland* would have a copious leavening of opium in its heart. By devious ways, in whispers running from mouth to mouth covertly through the spaceman's rendezvous, the outlaws of the spaceways glean more knowledge than the Patrol ever knows.

Smith watched a little air-freight vessel, scarcely a quarter the size of the monstrous ships of the Lines, rolling sluggishly out from the municipal hangar far across the square, and a little frown puckered his brows. The ship bore only the noncommercial numerals which all the freighters carry by way of identification, but that particular sequence was notorious among the initiate. The ship was a slaver.

This dealing in human freight had received a great impetus at the stimulation of space-travel, when the temptation presented by the savage tribes on alien planets was too great to be ignored by unscrupulous Earthmen who saw vast fields opening up before them. For even upon Earth slaving has never died entirely, and Mars and Venus knew a small and legitimate traffic in it before John Willard and his gang of outlaws made the very word 'slaving' anathema on three worlds. The Willards still ran their pirate convoys along the spaceways three generations later, and Smith knew he was looking at one now, smuggling a cargo of misery out of Lakkdarol for distribution among the secret markets of Mars.

Further meditations on the subject were cut short by Yarol's abrupt rise to his feet. Smith turned his head slowly and saw a little man at their elbow, his rotundity cloaked in a long mantle like those affected by the lower class of Martian shopkeepers in their walks abroad. But the face that peered up into his was frankly Celtic. Smith's expressionless features broke reluctantly into a grin as he met the irrepressible good-humor on that fat Irish face from home. He had not set foot upon Earth's soil for over a year now – the price on his liberty was too high in his native land – and curious pricks of homesickness came over him at the oddest moments. Even the toughest of space-rangers know them sometimes. The ties with the home planet are strong.

'You Smith?' demanded the little man in a rich Celtic voice.

Smith looked down at him a moment in cold-eyed silence. There was much more in that query than met the ear. Northwest Smith's name was one too well known in the annals of the Patrol for him to acknowledge it incautiously. The little Irishman's direct question implied what he had been expecting – if he acknowledged the name he met the man on the grounds of outlawry, which would mean that the employment in prospect was to be as illegal as he had thought it would be.

The merry blue eyes twinkled up at him. The man was laughing to himself at the Celtic subtlety with which he had introduced his subject. And again, involuntarily, Smith's straight mouth relaxed into a reluctant grin.

'I am,' he said.

'I've been looking for you. There's a job to be done that'll pay you well, if you want to risk it.'

Smith's pale eyes glanced about them warily. No one was within earshot. The place seemed as good as any other for the discussion of extra-legal bargains.

'What is it?' he demanded.

The little man glanced down at Yarol, who had dropped to one knee again and was flicking his knife tirelessly in the intricacies of his queer game. He had apparently lost interest in the whole proceeding.

'It'll take the both of you,' said the Irishman in his merry, rich voice. 'Do you see that air freighter loading over there?' and he nodded toward the slaver.

Smith's head jerked in mute acknowledgment.

'It's a Willard ship, as I suppose you know. But the business is running pretty low these days. Cargoes too hot to ship. The Patrol is shutting down hard, and receipts have slackened like the devil in the last year. I suppose you've heard that too.'

Smith nodded again without words. He had.

'Well, what we lose in quantity we have to make up in quality. Remember the prices Minga girls used to bring?'

Smith's face was expressionless. He remembered very well indeed, but he said nothing.

'Along toward the last, kings could hardly pay the price they were asking for those girls. That's really the best market, if you want to get into the "ivory" trade. Women. And there you come in. Did you ever hear of Cembre?'

Blank-eyed, Smith shook his head. For once he had run across a name whose rumors he had never encountered before in all the tavern gossip.

'Well, on one of Jupiter's moons – which one I'll tell you later, if you decide to accept – a Venusian named Cembre was wrecked years ago. By a miracle he survived and managed to escape; but the hardships he'd undergone unsettled his mind, and he couldn't do much but rave about the beautiful sirens he'd seen while he was wandering through the jungles there. Nobody paid any attention to him until the same thing happened again, this time only about a month ago. Another man came back half-cracked from struggling through the jungles, babbling about women so beautiful a man could go mad just looking at them.

'Well, the Willards heard of it. The whole thing may sound like a pipe-dream, but they've got the idea it's worth investigating. And they can afford to indulge their whims, you know. So they're outfitting a small expedition to see what basis there may be for the myth of Cembre's sirens. If you want to try it, you're hired.'

Smith slanted a non-committal glance downward into Yarol's uplifted black gaze. Neither spoke.

'You'll want to talk it over,' said the little Irishman comprehendingly. 'Suppose you meet me in the New Chicago at sundown and tell me what you've decided.'

'Good enough,' grunted Smith. The fat Celt grinned again and was gone in a swirl of black cloak and a flash of Irish merriment.

'Cold-blooded little devil,' murmured Smith, looking after the departing Earthman. 'It's a dirty business, Yarol.'

'Money's clean,' observed Yarol lightly. 'And I'm not a man to let my scruples stand in the way of my meals. I say take it. Someone'll go, and it might as well be us.'

Smith shrugged.

'We've got to eat,' he admitted.

'This,' murmured Yarol, staring downward on hands and knees at the edge of space-ship's floor-port, 'is the prettiest little hell I ever expect to see.'

The vessel was arching in a long curve around the Jovian moon as its pilot braked slowly for descent, and a panorama of ravening jungle slipped by in an unchanging wilderness below the floor-port.

Their presence here, skimming through the upper atmosphere of the wild little satellite, was the end of a long series of the smoothest journeying either had ever known. The Willard network was perfect over the three planets and the colonized satellites beyond, and over the ships that ply the space-ways. This neat little exploring vessel, with its crew of three coarse-faced, sullen slavers, had awaited them at the end of their journey outward from Lakkdarol, fully fitted with supplies and every accessory the most modern adventurer could desire. It even had a silken prison room for the hypothetical sirens whom they were to carry back for the Willard approval and the Willard markets if the journey proved successful.

'It's been easy so far,' observed Smith, squinting downward over the little Venusian's shoulder. 'Can't expect everything, you know. But that *is* a bad-looking place.'

The dull-faced pilot at the controls grunted in fervent agreement as he craned his neck to watch the little world spinning below them.

'Damn glad I'm not goin' out with you,' he articulated thickly over a mouthful of tobacco.

Yarol flung him a cheerful Venusian anathema in reply, but Smith did not speak. He had little liking and less trust in this sullen and silent crew. If he was not mistaken – and he rarely made mistakes in his appraisal of men – there was going to be trouble with the three before they completed their journey back into civilization. Now he turned his broad back to the pilot and stared downward.

From above, the moon seemed covered with the worst type of semi-animate, ravenous super-tropical jungle, reeking with fertility and sudden death, hot under lurid Jupiter's blaze. They saw no signs of human life anywhere below as their ship swept in its long curve over the jungle. The tree-tops spread in an unbroken blanket over the whole sphere of the satellite. Yarol, peering downward, murmured,

'No water. Somehow I always expect sirens to have fishtails.'

Out of his queer, heterogeneous past Smith dragged a fragment of ancient verse, '—gulfs enchanted, where the sirens sing …' and said aloud, 'They're supposed to sing, too. Oh, it'll probably turn out to be a pack of ugly savages, if there's anything but delirium behind the story.'

The ship was spiraling down now, and the jungle rushed up to meet them at express-train speed. Once again the little moon spun under their searching eyes, flower-garlanded, green with fertile life, massed solid in tangles of ravening growth. Then the pilot's hands closed hard on the controls and with a shriek of protesting atmosphere the little space-ship slid in a long dive toward the unbroken jungle below.

In a great crashing and crackling they sank groundward through smothers of foliage that masked the ports and plunged the interior of the ship into a green twilight. With scarcely an impact the jungle floor received them. The pilot leaned back in his seat and heaved a tobacco-redolent sigh. His work was done. Incuriously he glanced at the forward port.

Yarol was scrambling up from the floor-glass that now showed nothing but crushed vines and branches and the reeking mud of the moon's surface. He joined Smith and the pilot at the forward port.

They were submerged in jungle. Great serpentine branches and vines like cables looped downward in broken lengths from the shattered trees which had given way at their entrance. It was an animate jungle, full of hungry, reaching things that sprang in one wild, prolific tangle from the rich mud. Raw-colored flowers, yards across, turned sucking mouths blindly against the glass here and there, trickles of green juice slavering down the clear surface from their insensate hunger. A thorn-fanged vine lashed out as they stood staring and slid harmlessly along the glass, lashed again and again blindly until the prongs were dulled and green juice bled from its bruised surfaces.

'Well, we'll have blasting to do after all,' murmured Smith as he looked out into the ravenous jungle. 'No wonder those poor devils came back a little cracked. I don't see how they got through at all. It's—'

'Well – Pharol take me!' breathed Yarol in so reverent a whisper that Smith's voice broke off in mid-sentence and he spun around with a hand dropping to his gun to front the little Venusian, who had sought the stern port in his exploration.

'It's a road!' gasped Yarol. 'Black Pharol can have me for dinner if there isn't a road just outside here!'

The pilot reached for a noxious Martian cigarette and stretched luxuriously, quite uninterested. But Smith had reached the Venusian's side before he finished speaking, and in silence the two stared out upon the surprising scene the stern port framed. A broad roadway stretched arrowstraight into the dimness of the jungle. At its edges the hungry green things ceased abruptly, not encroaching by so much as a tendril or a leaf into the clearness of the path. Even overhead the branches had been forbidden to intrude, their vein-looped greenery forming an arch above the road. It was as if a destroying beam had played through the jungle, killing all life in its path. Even the oozing mud was firmed here into a smooth pavement. Empty, enigmatic, the clear way slanted across their line of vision and on into the writhing jungle.

'Well,' Yarol broke the silence at last, 'here's a good start. All we've got to do is follow the road. It's a safe bet there won't be any lovely ladies wandering around through this jungle. From the looks of the road there must be some civilized people on the moon after all.'

'I'd be happier if I knew what made it,' said Smith. 'There are some damned queer things on some of the moons and asteroids.'

Yarol's cat-eyes were shining.

'That's what I like about this life,' he grinned. 'You don't get bored. Well, what do the readings say?'

From his seat at the control panel the pilot glanced at the gauges which gave automatic report on air and gravity outside.

'OK,' he grunted. 'Better take blast-guns.'

Smith shrugged off his sudden uneasiness and turned to the weapon rack.

'Plenty of charges, too,' he said. 'No telling what we'll run into.'

The pilot rolled his poisonous cigarette between thick lips and said, 'Luck. You'll need it,' as the two turned to the outer lock. He had all the indifference of his class to anything but his own comfort and the completion of his allotted tasks with a minimum of effort, and he scarcely troubled to turn his head as the lock swung open upon an almost overwhelming gush of thick, hot air, redolent of green growing things and the stench of swift decay.

A vine-tip lashed violently into the opened door as Smith and Yarol stood staring. Yarol snapped a Venusian oath and dodged back, drawing his blast-gun. An instant later the eye-destroying blaze of it sheared a path of destruction through the lush vegetable carnivora straight toward the slanting roadway a dozen feet away. There was an immense hissing and sizzling of annihilated green stuff, and an empty path stretched before them across the little space which parted the ship's outer lock from the road. Yarol stepped down into reeking mud that bubbled up around his boots with a stench of fertility and decay. He swore again as he sank knee-deep into its blackness. Smith, grinning, joined him. Side by side they floundered through the ooze toward the road.

Short though the distance was, it took them all of ten minutes to cover it. Green things whipped out toward them from the walls of sheared forest where the blast-gun had burned, and both were bleeding from a dozen small scratches and thorn-flicks, breathless and angry and very muddy indeed before they reached their goal and dragged themselves onto the firmness of the roadway.

'Whew!' gasped Yarol, stamping the mud from his caked boots. 'Pharol can have me if I stir a step off this road after this. There isn't a siren alive who could lure me back into that hell again. Poor Cembre!'

'Come on,' said Smith. 'Which way?'

Yarol slatted sweat from his forehead and drew a deep breath, his nostrils wrinkling distastefully.

'Into the breeze, if you ask me. Did you ever smell such a stench? And hot! Gods! I'm soaked through already.'

Without words Smith nodded and turned to the right, from where a faint breeze stirred the heavy, moisture-laden air. His own lean body was impervious to a great variation in climate, but even Yarol, native of the Hot Planet, dripped with sweat already and Smith's own leather-tanned face glistened and his shirt clung in wet patches to his shoulders.

The cool breeze struck gratefully upon their faces as they turned into the wind. In a gasping silence they plodded muddily up the road, their wonder deepening as they advanced. What had made the roadway became more of a mystery at every step. No vehicle tracks marked the firm ground, no footprints. And nowhere by so much as a hair's breadth did the forest encroach upon the path.

On both sides, beyond the rigid limits of the road, the lush and cannibalistic life of the vegetation went on. Vines dangled great sucking disks and thorn-toothed creepers in the thick air, ready for a deadly cast at anything that wandered within reach. Small reptilian things scuttled through the reeking swamp mud, squeaking now and then in the toils of some thorny trap, and twice they heard the hollow bellowing of some invisible monster. It was raw primeval life booming and thrashing and devouring all about them, a planet in the first throes of animate life.

But here on the roadway that could have been made by nothing less than a well-advanced civilization that ravening jungle seemed very far away, like some unreal world enacting its primitive dramas upon a stage. Before they had gone far they were paying little heed to it, and the bellowing and the lashing, hungry vines and the ravenous forest growths faded into half-heard oblivion. Nothing out of that world entered upon the roadway.

As they advanced the sweltering heat abated in the steady breeze that was blowing down the road. There was a faint perfume upon it, sweet and light and utterly alien to the fetor of the reeking swamps which bordered their way. The scented gusts of it fanned their hot faces gently.

Smith was glancing over his shoulder at regular intervals, and a pucker of uneasiness drew his brows together.

'If we don't have trouble with that crew of ours before we're through,' he said, 'I'll buy you a case of *segir.*'

'It's a bet,' agreed Yarol cheerfully, turning up to Smith his sidelong cat-eyes as insouciantly savage as the ravening jungle around them. 'Though they were a pretty tough trio, at that.'

'They may have the idea they can leave us here and collect our share of the money back home,' said Smith. 'Or once we get the girls they may want to dump us and take them on alone. And if they haven't thought of anything yet, they will.'

'Up to no good, the whole bunch of 'em,' grinned Yarol. 'They – they—'

His voice faltered and faded into silence. There was a sound upon the breeze. Smith had stopped dead-still, his ears straining to recapture the echo of that murmur which had come blowing toward them on the breeze. Such a sound as that might have come drifting over the walls of Paradise.

In the silence as they stood with caught breath it came again – a lilt of the loveliest, most exquisitely elusive laughter. From very far away it came floating to their ears, the lovely ghost of a woman's laughing. There was in it a caress of kissing sweetness. It brushed over Smith's nerves like the brush of lingering fingers and died away into throbbing silence that seemed reluctant to let the exquisite sound of it fade into echoes and cease.

The two men faced each other in rapt bewilderment. Finally Yarol found his voice.

'Sirens!' he breathed. 'They don't have to sing if they can laugh like that! Come on!'

At a swifter pace they went on up the road. The breeze blew fragrantly against their faces. After a while its perfumed breath carried to their ears another faint, far-away echo of that heavenly laughter, sweeter than honey, drifting on the wind in fading cadences that died away by imperceptible degrees until they could no longer be sure if it was the lovely laughter they heard or the quickened beating of their own hearts.

Yet before them the road stretched emptily, very still in the green twilight under the low-arching trees. There seemed to be a sort of haze here, so that though the road ran straight the green dimness veiled what lay ahead and they walked in a queer silence along the roadway through ravening jungles whose sights and sounds might almost have been on another world for all the heed they paid them. Their ears were straining for a repetition of that low and lovely laughter, and the expectation of it gripped them in an unheeding spell which wiped out all other things but its own delicious echoes.

When they first became aware of a pale glimmer in the twilight greenness ahead, neither could have told. But somehow they were not surprised that a girl was pacing slowly down the roadway toward them, half veiled in the jungle dimness under the trees.

To Smith she was a figure walking straight out of a dream. Even at that distance her beauty had a still enchantment that swallowed up all his wondering in a strange and magical peace. Beauty flowed along the long, curved lines of her body, alternately cloaked and revealed by the drifting garment of her hair, and the slow, swinging grace of her as she walked was a potent enchantment that gripped him helpless in its spell.

Then another glimmer in the dimness caught his eyes away from the bewitchment that approached, and in bewilderment he saw that another girl was pacing forward under the low-hanging trees, her hair swinging about her in slow drifts that veiled and unveiled the loveliness of a body as exquisite as the first. That first was nearer now, so that he could see the enchantment of her face, pale golden and lovelier than a dream with its subtly molded smoothness and delicately tilted planes of cheekbone and cheek smoothing deliciously upward into a broad, low forehead when the richly colored hair sprang back in tendrils like licking flames. There was a subtly Slavic tilting to those honey-colored features, hinted in the breadth of the cheeks and the sweet straightness with which their planes slanted downward to a mouth colored like hot embers, curving now in a smile that promised – heaven.

She was very near. He could see the peach-like bloom upon her pale gold limbs and the very throb of the pulse beating in her round throat, and the veiled eyes sought his. But behind her that second girl was nearing, every whit as lovely as the first, and her beauty drew his gaze magnetlike to its own delicate flow and ripple of enchantment. And beyond her – yes, another was coming, and beyond her a fourth; and in the green twilight behind these first, pale blurs bespoke the presence of yet more.

And they were identical. Smith's bewildered eyes flew from face to face, seeking and finding what his brain could still not quite believe. Feature by feature, curve by curve, they were identical. Five, six, seven honey-colored bodies, half veiled in richly tinted hair, swayed toward him. Seven, eight, nine exquisite faces smiled their promise of ecstasy. Dizzy and incredulous, he felt a hand grip his shoulder. Yarol's voice, bemused, half whispered, murmured, 'Is this paradise – or are we both mad?'

The sound of it brought Smith out of his tranced bewitchment. He shook his head sharply, like a man half awake and striving for clarity, and said,

'Do they all look alike to you?'

'Every one. Exquisite – exquisite – did you ever see such satin-black hair?'

'Black – black?' Smith muttered that over stupidly, wondering what was so wrong with the word. When realization broke upon him at last, the shock of it was strong enough to jerk his eyes away from the enchantment before him and turn them sharply around to the little Venusian's rapt face.

Its stainless clarity was set in a mask of almost holy wonder. Even the wisdom and weariness and savagery of its black eyes was lost in the glamour of what they gazed on. His voice murmured, almost to itself.

'And white – so white – like lilies, aren't they? – blacker and whiter than—'

'Are you crazy?' Smith's voice broke harshly upon the Venusian's rapture. That trance-like mask broke before the impact of his exclamation. Like a man awaking from a dream, Yarol turned blinking to his friend.

'Crazy? Why – why – aren't we both? How else could we be seeing a sight like this?'

'One of us is,' said Smith grimly. 'I'm looking at red-haired girls colored like – peaches.'

Yarol blinked again. His eyes sought the bevy of bewildering loveliness in the roadway. He said,

'It's you, then. They've got black hair, every one of them, shiny and smooth and black as so many lengths of satin, and nothing in creation is whiter than their bodies.'

Smith's pale eyes turned again to the road. Again they met honey-pale curves and planes of velvet flesh half veiled in hair like drifting flames. He shook his head once more, dazedly.

The girls hovered before him in the green dimness, moving with little restive steps back and forth on the hardbeaten road, their feet like the drift of flower-petals for lightness, their hair rippled away from the smoothly swelling curves of their bodies and furling about them again in ceaseless motion. They turned lingering eyes to the two men, but they did not speak.

Then down the wind again came drifting the far echo of that exquisite, lilting laugh. The sweetness of it made the very breeze brush lighter against their faces. It was a caress and a promise and a summoning almost irresistible, floating past them and drifting away into the distance in low, far-off cadences that lingered in their ears long after its audible music had ceased.

The sound of it woke Smith out of his daze, and he turned to the nearest girl, blurting, 'Who are you?'

Among the fluttering throng a little shiver of excitement ran. Lovely, identical faces turned to him from all over the whole group, and the one addressed smiled bewilderingly.

'I am Yvala,' she said in a voice smoother than silk, pitched to caress the ear and ripple along the very nerve fibers with a slow and soothing sweetness. And she had spoken in English! It was long since Smith had heard his mother tongue. The sound of it plucked at some hidden heart-string with intolerable poignancy, the home language spoken in a voice of enchanted sweetness. For a moment he could not speak.

The silence broke to Yarol's low whistle of surprise.

'I know now we're crazy,' he murmured. 'No other way to explain her speaking in High Venusian. Why, she can't ever have—'

'High Venusian!' exclaimed Smith, startled out of his moment of silence. 'She spoke English!'

They stared at each other, wild suspicions rising in their eyes. In desperation Smith turned and hurled the question again at another of the lovely throng, waiting breathless for her answer to be sure his ears had not deceived him.

'Yvala – I am Yvala,' she answered in just that silken voice with which the first had answered. It was English unmistakably, and sweet with memories of home.

Behind her among the bevy of curved, peach-colored bodies and veils of richly tinted hair other full red lips moved and other velvety voices murmured, 'Yvala, Yvala, I am Yvala,' like dying echoes drifting from mouth to mouth until the last syllable of the strange and lovely name faded into silence.

Across the stunned quiet that fell as their murmurs died the breeze blew again, and once more that sweet, low laughter rang from far away in their ears, rising and falling on the wind until their pulses beat in answer, and falling, fading, dying away reluctantly on the fragrant breeze.

'What – who was that?' demanded Smith softly of the fluttering girls, as the last of it faded into silence.

'It was Yvala,' they chorused in caressing voices like multiple echoes of the same rich, lingering tones. 'Yvala laughs – Yvala calls … Come with us to Yvala …'

Yarol said in a sudden ripple of musical speech,

'*Geth norri a 'Yvali?*' at the same moment that Smith's query broke out,

'Who is Yvala, then?' in his own seldom-used mother tongue.

But they got no reply to that, only beckonings and murmurous repetitions of the name, 'Yvala, Yvala, Yvala—' and smiles that set their pulses beating faster. Yarol reached out a tentative hand toward the nearest, but she melted like smoke out of his grasp so that he no more than grazed the velvety flesh of her shoulder with a touch that left his fingers tingling delightfully.

She smiled over her shoulder ardently, and Yarol gripped Smith's arm.

'Come on,' he said urgently.

In a pleasant dream of low voices and lovely warm bodies circling just out of reach they went slowly on down the road in the midst of that hovering group, walking upwind whence that tantalizing laughter had rung, and all about them the golden girls circled on restless, drifting feet, their hair floating and furling about the loveliness of their half-seen bodies, the echoes of that single name rising and falling in cadences as rich and smooth as cream. Yvala – Yvala – Yvala – a magical spell to urge them on their way.

How long they walked they never knew. The changeless jungle slid away behind them unnoticed; the broad enigmatic pavement stretched ahead, a mysterious, green gloom shadowing the whole length of that laughter-haunted roadway. Nothing had any meaning to them outside the circle the murmurous girls were weaving with their swaying bodies and swinging hair and voices like the echoes of a dream. All the wonder and incredulity and bewilderment in the minds of the two men had sunk away into nothingness, drowned and swallowed up in the flagrant music of their enchantresses.

After a long, rapt while they came to the roadway's end. Smith lifted dreaming pale eyes and saw as if through a veil, so remotely that the scene had little meaning to him, the great park-like clearing stretching away before them as the jungle walls fell away on either side. Here the primeval swamplands and animate green life ceased abruptly to make way for a scene that might have been lifted straight over a million years. The clearing was columned with great patriarchal trees ages removed in evolution from the snaky things which grew in the hungry jungle. Their leaves roofed the place in swaying greenery through which the light sifted with twilight softness upon a carpet of flower-starred moss. With one step they spanned ages of evolution and entered into the lovely dim clearing that might have been lifted out of a world a million years older than the jungle that raved impotently around its borders.

The moss was velvety under their pacing feet. With eyes that but half comprehended what they saw, Smith gazed out across the twilight vistas through the green gloom brooding beneath the trees. It was a hushed place, mystical, very quiet. He thought sometimes he saw the flash of life through the leaves overhead, the stir of it among the trees as small wild things crossed their path and birds fluttered in the foliage, but he could not be sure. Once or twice it seemed to him that he had caught an echo of bird-song, somehow as if the melody had rung in his ears a moment before, and only now, when the sound was fading, did he realize it. But not once did he hear an actual song note or see any animate life, though the presence of it was rife in the green twilight beneath the leaves.

They went on slowly. Once he could have sworn he saw a dappled fawn staring at him with wide, unhappy eyes from a covert of branches, but when he looked closer there was nothing but leaves swaying emptily. And once upon his inner ear, as if with the echo of a just-past sound, he thought he heard a stallion's high whinny. But after all it did not greatly matter. The girls were shepherding them on over the flowery moss, circling like hollow-throated doves whose only music was 'Yvala – Yvala – Yvala ...' in unending harmony of rising and falling notes.

They paced on dreamily, the trees and mossy vistas of park sliding smoothly away behind them in unchanging quiet. And more and more strongly that impression of life among the trees nagged at Smith's mind. He wondered if he might not be developing hallucinations, for no arrangement of branches and shadows could explain the wild boar's head that he could have sworn thrust out among the leaves to stare at him for an instant with small, shamed eyes before it melted into patterned shadow under his direct gaze.

He blinked and rubbed his eyes in momentary terror lest his own brain was betraying him, and an instant later was peering uncertainly at the avenue between two low-hanging trees where from the corner of his eye he thought he had seen a magnificent white stallion hesitating with startled head upflung and the queerest, urgent look in its eyes, somehow warning and afraid – and ashamed. But it faded into mere leaf-cast shadows when he turned.

And once he started and stumbled over what was nothing more than a leafy branch lying across their path, yet which an instant before had looked bewilderingly like a low-slung cat-beast slinking across the moss with sullen, hot eyes upturned in hate and warning and distress to his.

There was something about these animals that roused a vague unrest in his mind when he looked at them – something in their eyes that was warning and agonized and more hotly aware than are the eyes of beasts – something queerly dreadful and hauntingly familiar about the set of their heads upon their shoulders – hinting horribly at another gait than the four-footed.

At last, just after a graceful doe had bounded out of the leaves, hesitated an instant and flashed away with a fleetness that did not look like the fleetness of a quadruped, turning upon him as she vanished a great-eyed agony that was warning as a cry, Smith halted in his tracks. Uneasiness too deep to be magicked away by the crooning girls urged him of danger. He paused and looked uncertainly around. The doe had melted into leaf-shadows flickering upon the moss, but he could not forget the haunting shame and the warning of her eyes.

He stared about the dim greenness of the tree-roofed clearing. Was all this a lotus-dream, an illusion of jungle fever, or a suddenly unstable mind?

Could he have imagined those beasts with their anguished eyes and their terribly familiar outlines of head and neck upon four-footed bodies? Was any of it real at all?

More for reassurance than for any other reason he reached out suddenly and seized the nearest honey-colored girl in a quick grip. Yes, she was tangible. His fingers closed about a firm and rounded arm, smoothly soft with the feel of peach-bloom velvet over its curving surface. The girl did not pull away. She stopped dead-still at his touch, slowly turning her head, lifting her face to his with a dream-like easiness, tilting her chin high until the long, full curve of her throat was arched taut and he could see the pulse beating hard under her velvet flesh. Her lips parted softly, her lips drooped low.

His other arm went out of its own accord, drawing her against him. Then her hands were in his hair, pulling his head down to hers, and all his uneasiness and distress and latent terror spun away at the kiss of her parted lips.

The next thing he realized was that he was strolling on under the trees, a girl's lithe body moving in the bend of his arm. Her very nearness was a delight that sent his senses reeling, so that the green woodland was vague as a dream and the only reality dwelt in the honey-colored loveliness in the circle of his arm.

Dimly he was aware that Yarol strolled parallel with them a little distance away through the leaves, a bright head on his shoulder, another golden girl leaning against his encircling arm. She was so perfectly the counterpart of his own lovely captive that she might have been a reflection in a mirror. Uneasily a remembrance swam up in Smith's mind. Did it seem to Yarol that a snow-white maiden walked with him, a black head leaned upon his shoulder? Was the little Venusian's mind yielding to the spell of the place, or was it his own? What tongue could it be that the girls spoke which fell upon his ears in English phrases and upon Yarol's in the musical lilt of High Venusian? Were they both mad?

Then in his arm the supple golden body stirred, the softly shadowed face turned to his. The woodland vanished like smoke from about him in the magic of her lips.

There were dim glades among the trees where piles of white ruins met Smith's unseeing eyes sometimes without leaving more than the merest trace of conscious remembrance. Vague wonders swam through his mind of what they might once have been, what vanished race had wrested this clearing from the jungle and died without leaving any trace save these. But he did not care. It had no significance. Even the half-seen beasts, who now turned eyes full of sorrow and despair rather than warning, had lost all meaning to his enchanted brain. In a lotus-dream he wandered on in the direction he was urged, unthinking, unalarmed. It was very sweet to stroll so through the dim green gloom, with purest magic in the bend of his arm. He was content.

They strolled past the white ruins of scattered buildings, past great bending trees that dappled them with shadow. The moss yielded underfoot as softly as thick-piled carpets. Unseen beasts slunk by them now and then, so that the tail of Smith's eyes was continually catching the – almost – hint of humanity in the lines of their bodies, the set of a head upon bestial shoulders, the clarity of urgent eyes. But he did not really see them.

Sweetly – intolerably sweetly and softly, laughter rang through the woods. Smith's head flung up like a startled stallion's. It was a stronger laughter now, from near, very near among the leaves. It seemed to him that the voice indeed must come from some lovely, ardent houri leaning over the wall of Paradise – that he had come a long way in search of her and now trembled on the very brink of his journey's end. The low and lovely sound echoed through the trees, ringing down the green twilight aisles, shivering the leaves together. It was everywhere at once, a little world of music superimposed upon the world of matter, enclosing everywhere within its scope in a magical spell that left no room for any other thing but its lovely presence. And its command rang through Smith's mind with the sharpness of a sword in his flesh, calling, calling unbearably through the woods.

Then they came out of the trees into a little space of mossy clearing in whose center a small white temple rose. Somehow Yarol was there too – and somehow they were alone. Those exquisite girls had melted like smoke into oblivion. The two men stood quite still, their eyes dazed as they stared. This building was the only one they had seen whose columns still stood upright, and only here could they tell that the architecture of those fallen walls whose ruins had dotted the wooded glades had been one at variance to anything on any world they knew. But upon the mystery of that they had no desire to dwell. For the woman those slim columns housed drove every other thought out of their dazzled minds.

She stood in the center of the tiny temple. She was pale golden, half veiled in the long cloak of her curls. And if the siren girls had been lovely, then here stood loveliness incarnate. Those girls had worn her form and face. Here was that same exquisitely molded body, colored like honey, half revealed among the drifts of hair that clung to it like tendrils of bright flames. But those bewildering girls had been mere echoes of the beauty that faced them now. Smith stared with a kindling of colorless eyes.

Here was Lilith – here was Helen – here was Circe – here before him stood all the beauty of all the legends of mankind; here on this marble floor, facing them gravely, with unsmiling eyes. For the first time he looked into the eyes that lighted that sweet, tilt-planed face, and his very soul gasped from the sudden plunge into their poignant blueness. It was not a vivid blue, not a blazing one, but its intensity far transcended anything he had words to name. In that blueness a man's soul could sink for ever, reaching no bottom, stirred by no tides, drowned and steeped through and through with an infinity of absolute light.

When the blue, blue gaze released him he gasped once, like a drowning man, and then stared with new amazement upon a reality whose truth had escaped him until this moment. That instant of submerged ecstasy in the blue deeps of her eyes must have opened a door in his brain to new knowledge, for he saw as he stared a very strange quality in the loveliness he faced.

Tangible beauty dwelt here, an indwelling thing that could root itself in human flesh and clothe a body in loveliness as with a garment. Here was more than fleshly beauty, more than symmetry of face and body. A quality like a flame glowed all but visibly – no, more than visibly – along the peach-bloomy lines and smoothly swelling curve of her, giving a glory to the high tilt of her bosom and the long, subtly curved thigh and the exquisite line of shoulder gliding down into fuller beauty half veiled in drifting hair.

In that dazed, revealing moment her loveliness shimmered before him, too intensely for his human senses to perceive save as a dazzle of intolerable beauty before his half-comprehending eyes. He flung up his hands to shut the glory out and stood for a moment with hidden eyes in a self-imposed darkness through which beauty blazed with an intensity that transcended the visible and beat unbearably on every fiber of his being until he stood bathed in light that permeated the ultimate atoms of his soul.

Then the blaze died. He lowered shaking hands and saw that lovely, pale-gold face melting slowly into a smile of such heavenly promise that for an instant his senses failed him again and the world spun dizzily around a focus of honey-pale features breaking into arcs and softly shadowed curves, as the velvety mouth curled slowly into a smile.

'All strangers are very welcome here,' crooned a voice like a vibration of sheerest silk, sweeter than honey, caressing as the brush of a kissing mouth. And she had spoken in the purest of earthly English. Smith found his voice.

'Who – who are you?' he asked in a queer gasp, as if his very breath were stopped by the magic he faced.

Before she could answer, Yarol's voice broke in, a little unsteady with sudden, savage anger.

'Can't you answer in the language you're addressed in?' he demanded in a violent undertone. 'The least you could do is ask her name in High Venusian. How do you know she speaks English?'

Quite speechless, Smith turned a blank gray gaze upon his companion. He saw the blaze of hot Venusian temper fade like mist from Yarol's black eyes as he turned to the glory in the temple. And in the lovely, liquid cadences of his native tongue, that brims so exquisitely with hyperbole and symbolism, he said.

'Oh, lovely and night-dark lady, what name is laid upon you to tell how whiter than sea-foam is your loveliness?'

For a moment, listening to the beauty of phrase and sound that dwells in the High Venusian tongue, Smith doubted his own ears. For though she had spoken in English, yet the loveliness of Yarol's speech seemed infinitely more suited to have fallen from the lyric curving of her velvet-red mouth. Such lips, he thought, could never utter less than pure music, and English is not a musical tongue.

But explain Yarol's visual illusion he could not, for his own steel-pale eyes were steadfast upon richly colored hair and pale gold flesh, and no stretch of imagination could transform them into the black and snow-whiteness his companion claimed to see.

A hint of mirth crept into the smile that curled up the softness of her mouth as Yarol spoke. She answered them both in one speech that to Smith was pure English, though he guessed that it fell upon Yarol's ears in the music of High Venusian cadence.

'I am beauty,' she told them serenely. 'I am incarnate Beauty. But Yvala is my name. Let there be no quarrel between you, for each man hears me in the tongue his heart speaks, and sees me in the image which spells beauty to his own soul. For I am all men's desire incarnate in one being, and there is no beauty but Me.'

'But – those others?'

'I am the only dweller here – but you have known the shadows of myself, leading you through devious ways into the presence of Yvala. Had you not gazed first upon these reflections of my beauty, its fullness which you see now would have blinded and destroyed you utterly. And later, perhaps, you shall see me even more clearly . . .

'But no, Yvala alone dwells here. Save for yourselves there is in this park of mine no living creature. Everything is illusion but myself. And am I not enough? Can you desire anything more of life or death than you gaze on now?'

The query trembled into a music-ridden silence, and they knew that they could not. The heaven-sweet murmur of that voice was speaking sheerest magic, and in the sound of it neither of them was capable of any emotion but worship of the loveliness they faced. It beat out in waves like heat from that incarnate perfection, wrapping them about so that nothing in the universe had existence but Yvala.

Before the glory that blazed in their faces Smith felt adoration pouring out of him as blood gushes from a severed artery. Like life-blood it poured, and like life-blood draining it left him queerly weaker and weaker, as if some essential part of him were gushing away in great floods of intensest worship.

But somewhere, down under the lowest depths of Smith's sub-consciousness, a faint disquiet was stirring. He fought it, for it broke the mirror surfaces of his tranced adoration, but he could not subdue it, and by degrees that unease struggled up through layer upon layer of rapt enchantment until it burst through into his conscious mind and the little quiver of it ran disturbingly through the exquisite calm of his trance. It was not an articulate disquiet, but it was somehow bound up with the scarcely seen beasts he had glimpsed – or had he glimpsed? – in the wood. That, and the memory of an old Earth legend of a lovely woman – and men turned into beasts ... He could not grasp it, but the elusive memory pricked at him with little pinpoint goads, crying danger so insistently that with infinite reluctance his mind took up the business of thinking once more.

Yvala sensed it. She sensed the lessening in that life-blood gush of rapt adoration poured out upon her loveliness. Her fathomless eyes turned upon his in a blaze of transcendent blueness, and the woods reeled about him at the impact of their light. But somewhere in Smith, under the ultimate layer of conscious thought, under the last quiver of instinct and reflex and animal cravings, lay a bed-rock of savage strength which no power he had ever met could wholly overcome, not even this – not even Yvala. Rooted deep in that immovable solidity the little uneasy murmur persisted. 'There is something wrong here. I mustn't let her swallow me up again – I must know what it is ...'

That much he was aware of. Then Yvala turned. With both velvety arms she swept back the curtain of her hair, and all about her in a glory of tangible loveliness blazed out the radiance that dwelt in such terrible intensity here. Smith's whole consciousness snuffed out before it like a blown candle-flame.

Remotely, after eons, it seemed, awareness overtook him again. It was not consciousness, but a sort of dumb, blind knowledge of processes going on around him, in him, through him. So an animal might be aware, without any hint of real self-consciousness. But hot above everything else the tranced adoration of sheer beauty was blazing now in the center of his universe, and it was devouring him as a flame devours fuel, sucking out his worship, draining him utterly. Helpless, unbodied, he poured forth adoration into the ravenous blaze that held him, and as he poured it out he felt himself fading, somehow sinking below the level of a human being. In his dumb awareness he made no attempt to understand, but he felt himself – degenerating.

It was as if the insatiable appetite for admiration which consumed Yvala and was consuming him sucked him dry of all humanity. Even his thoughts were sinking now as she drained him, so that he no longer fitted words to his sensations, and his mind ran into figures and pictures below the level of human minds …

He was not tangible. He was a dark, inarticulate memory, bodiless, mindless, full of queer, hungry sensations … He remembered running. He remembered the dark earth flowing backward under his flying feet, wind keen in his nostrils and rife with the odors of a thousand luscious things. He remembered the pack baying around him to the frosty stars, his own voice lifting in exultant, throat-filling clamor with the rest. He remembered the sweetness of flesh yielding under fangs, the hot gush of blood over a hungry tongue. Little more than this he remembered. The ravenous craving, the exultation of the chase, the satisfying reek of hot flesh under ripping fangs – all these circled through his memory round and round, leaving room for little else.

But gradually, in dim, disquieting echoes, another realization strengthened beyond the circle of hunger and feeding. It was an intangible thing, nothing but the faint knowledge that somehow, somewhere, in some remote existence, he had been – different. He was little more than a recollection now, a mind that circled memories of hunting and killing and feeding which some lost body in long-ago distances had performed. But even so – he had once been different. He had—

Sharply through that memory-circle broke the knowledge of presences. With no physical sense was he aware of them, for he possessed no physical senses at all. But his awareness, his dumb, numb mind, knew that they had come – knew what they were. In memory he smelled the rank, blood-stirring scent of man, felt a tongue lolling out over suddenly dripping fangs; remembered hunger gushed up through his sensations.

Now he was blind and formless in a formless void, recognizing those presences only as they impinged upon his. But from the man-presences realization reached out and touched him, knowing his presence, realizing his nearness. They sensed him, lurking hungrily so close. And because they sensed him so vividly, their minds receiving the ravenous impact of his, their brains must have translated that hungry nearness into sight for just an instant; for from somewhere outside the gray void where he existed a voice said clearly,

'Look! Look – no, it's gone now, but for a minute I though I saw a wolf …'

The words burst upon his consciousness with all the violence of a gun-blast; for in that instant, he *knew*. He understood the speech the man used, remembered that once it had been his speech – realized what he had become. He knew too that the men, whoever they were, walked into just such danger as had conquered him, and the urgency to warn them surged up in his dumbness. Not until then did he know clearly, with a man's word-thoughts, that he had no being. He was not real – he was only a wolf-memory drifting through the dark. He had been a man. Now he was pure wolf – beast – his soul shorn of its humanity down to the very core of savagery that dwells in every man. Shame flooded over him. He forgot the men, the speech they used, the remembered hunger. He dissolved into a nothingness of wolf-memory and man-shame.

Through the dizziness of that a stronger urge began to beat. Somewhere in the void sounded a call that reached out to him irresistibly. It called him so strongly that his whole dim being whirled headlong in response along currents that swept him helpless into the presence of the summoner.

A blaze was burning. In the midst of the universal emptiness it flamed, calling, commanding, luring him so sweetly that with all his entity he replied, for there was in that burning an element that wrenched at his innermost, deepest-rooted desire. He remembered food – the hot gush of blood, the crunch of teeth on bone, the satisfying solidity of flesh under his sinking fangs. Desire for it gushed out of him like life itself, draining him – draining him … He was sinking lower, past the wolf level, down and down …

Through the coming oblivion terror stabbed. It was a lightning-flash of realization from his long-lost humanity, one last throb that brightened the dark into which he sank. And out of that bed-rock of unshakable strength which was the core of his being, even below the wolf level, even below the oblivion into which he was being sucked – the spark of rebellion lashed.

Before now he had floundered helplessly with no firmness anywhere to give him foothold to fight; but now, in his uttermost extremity, while the last dregs of conscious life drained out of him, the bed-rock lay bare from which the well-springs of his strength and savagery sprang, and at that last stronghold of the *self* called Smith he leaped into instant rebellion, fighting with all the wolf-nature that had been the soil from which his man-soul rooted. Wolfishly he fought, with a beast's savagery and a man's strength, backed by the bed-rock firmness that was the base for both. Space whirled about him, flaming with hungry fires, black with flashes of oblivion, furious and ravenous in the hot presence of Yvala.

But he was winning. He knew it, and fought harder, and abruptly felt the snap of yielding opposition and was blindingly aware again, blindingly human. He lay on soft moss as a dead man lies, terribly relaxed in every limb and muscle. But life was flowing back into him, and humanity was gushing like a river in spate back into the drained hollows of his soul. For a while he lay quiet, gathering himself into one body again. His hold on it was so feeble that sometimes he thought he was floating clear and had to struggle hard to force re-entrance. Finally, with infinite effort, he tugged his eyelids open and lay there in a deathly quiet, watching.

Before him stood the white marble shrine which housed Beauty. But it was not Yvala's delirious loveliness he gazed on now. He had been through the fire of her deepest peril, and he saw her now as she really was – not in the form which spelled pure loveliness to him, and, as he guessed, to every being that gazed upon her, whether it be man or beast – not in any form at all, but as a blaze of avid light flaming inside the shrine. The light was alive, quivering and trembling and animate, but it bore no human form. It was not human. It was a life so alien that he wondered weakly how his eyes could ever have twisted it into the incarnate loveliness of Yvala. And even in the depths of his peril he found time to regret the passing of that beauty – that exquisite illusion which had never existed save in his own brain. He knew that as long as life burned in him he could never forget her smile.

It was a thing of some terribly remote origin that blazed here. He guessed that the power of it had fastened on his brain as soon as he came within its scope, commanding him to see it in that lovely form which meant heart's-desire to him alone. It must have done the same thing to countless other beings – he remembered the beast-wraiths that had brushed his brain in the forest with the faint, shamed contact of theirs. Well, he had been one of them – he knew now. He understood the warning and the anguish in their eyes. He remembered too the ruins he had seen in the woods. What race had dwelt here once, imposing its civilization and its stamp of quiet glades and trees upon the ravenous forest? A human race, perhaps, dwelling in seclusion under the leaves until Yvala the Destroyer came. Or perhaps not a human race, for he knew now that to every living creature she wore a different form, the incarnation of each individual's highest desire.

Then he heard voices, and after an infinity of effort twisted his head on the moss until he could see whence they came. At what he saw he would have risen if he could, but a deathly weariness lay like the weight of worlds upon him and he could not stir. Those man-presences he had felt in his beast-form stood here – the three slavers from the little ship. They must have followed them not far behind, with what dark motives would never be known now, for Yvala's magic had seized them and there would be no more of humanity for them after the next few moments were past. They stood in a row there before the shine with an ecstasy almost holy on their faces. Plainly he saw reflected there the incarnate glory of Yvala, though to his eyes the thing they faced was only a formless flame.

He knew then why Yvala had let him go so suddenly in that desperate struggle. Here was fresh fodder for her avidity, new worship to drink in. She had turned away from his outworn well-springs to drain new prey of its humanity. He watched them standing there, drunk with loveliness before what to them must be a beautiful woman veiled in drifting hair, glowing with more than mortal ardency where, to him, only a clear flame burned.

But he could see more. Cloudy about those three figures, rapt before the shrine, he could see – was it some queer reflection of themselves dancing upon the air? The misty outlines wavered as, with eyes that in the light of what he had just passed through had won momentarily a sight which penetrated beyond the flesh, he looked upon that dancing shimmer which clearly must be the reflection of some vital part of those three men, visible now in some strange way at the evocation of Yvala's calling.

They were man-shaped reflections. They strained toward Yvala from their anchorage in the bodies that housed them, yearning, pulling as if they would forsake their fleshly roots and merge with the incarnate beauty that called them so irresistibly. The three stood rigid, faces blank with rapture, unconscious of that perilous tugging at what must be in their very souls.

Then Smith saw the nearest man sag at the knees, quiver, topple to the moss. He lay still for a moment while from his fallen body that tenuous reflection of himself tugged and pulled and then in one last great effort jerked free and floated like a smoke-wreath into the white-hot intensity in the shrine. The blaze engulfed it, flaring brighter as if at the kindling of new fuel.

When that sudden brightness died again the smoke-wreath drifted out, trailing through the pillars in a form that even to Smith's dimmed eyes wore a strange distortion. It was no longer a man's soul. All of humanity had burned out from it to feed the blaze that was Yvala. And the beast foundation which lies so close under the veneer of civilization and humanity in every human creature was bared and free. Cold with understanding, Smith watched the core of beast instinct which was all that remained now that the layer of man-veneer had been stripped away, a core of animal memories rooted eons deep in that far-away past when all man's ancestors ran on four paws.

It was a cunning beast that remained, instinct with foxy slyness. He saw the misty thing slink away into the green gloom of the woods, and he realized afresh why it was he had seen fleeting glimpses of animals in the park as he came here, wearing that terrible familiarity in the set of their heads, the line of shoulder and neck that hinted at other gaits than the four-footed. They must have been just such wraiths as this, drifting through the woods, beast-wraiths that wore still the tatters and rags of their doffed humanity, brushing his mind with the impact of theirs until their vividness evoked actual sight of the reality of fur and flesh, just for a glimpse, just for a hint, before the wraith blew past. And he was cold with horror at the thought of how many men must have gone to feed the flame, stripping off humanity like a garment and running now in the nakedness of their beast natures through the enchanted woods.

Here was Circe. He realized it with a quiver of horror and awe. Circe the Enchantress, who turned the men of Greek legend into beasts. And what tremendous backgrounds of reality and myth loomed smokily behind what happened here before his very eyes! Circe the Enchantress – ancient Earthly legend incarnate now on a Jovian moon far away through the void. The awe of it shook him to the depths. Circe – Yvala – alien entity that must, then, rove through the universe and the ages, leaving dim whispers behind her down the centuries. Lovely Circe on her blue Aegean isle – Yvala on her haunted moon under Jupiter's blaze – past and present merged into a blazing whole.

The wonder of it held him so rapt that when the reality of the scene before him finally bore itself in upon his consciousness again, both of the remaining slavers lay prone upon the moss, forsaken bodies from which the vitality had been sucked like blood in Yvala's flame. That flame burned more rosily now, and out of its pulsing he saw the last dim wraith of the three who had fed her come hurrying, a swinish brute of a wraith whose grunts and snorts were almost audible, tusks and bristles all but visible as it scurried off into the wood.

Then the flame burned clear again, flushed with hot rose, pulsing with regular beats like the pulse of a heart, satiate and ecstatic in its shrine. And he was aware of a withdrawal, as if the consciousness of the entity that burned here were turned inward upon itself, leaving the world it dominated untouched as Yvala drowsed and digested the sustenance her vampire-craving for worship had devoured.

Smith stirred a little on the moss. Now, if ever, he must make some effort to escape, while the thing in the shrine was replete and uninterested in its surroundings. He lay there, shaken with exhaustion, forcing strength back into his body, willing himself to be strong, to rise, to find Yarol, to make his way somehow back to the deserted ship. And by slow degrees he succeeded. It took a long while, but in the end he had dragged himself up against a tree and stood swaying, his pale eyes alternately clouding with exhaustion and blinking aware again as he scanned the space under the trees for Yarol.

The little Venusian lay a few steps away, one cheek pressing the ground and his yellow curls gay against the moss. With closed eyes he looked like a seraph asleep, all the lines of hard living and hard fighting relaxed and the savageness of his dark gaze hidden. Even in his deadly peril Smith could not suppress a little grin of appreciation as he staggered the half-dozen steps that parted them and fell to his knees beside his friend's body.

The sudden motion dazed him, but in a moment his head cleared and he laid an urgent hand on Yarol's shoulder, shaking it hard. He dared not speak, but he shook the little Venusian heavily, and in his brain a silent call went out to whatever drifting wraith among the trees housed Yarol's naked soul. He bent over the quiet yellow head and called and called, turning the force of his determination in all its intensity to that summoning, while weakness washed over him in great slow waves.

After a long time he thought he felt a dim response, somewhere from far off. He called harder, eyes turned apprehensively toward the rosily pulsing flame in the shrine, wondering if this voiceless summoning might not impinge upon the entity there as tangibly as speech. But Yvala's satiety must have been deep, and there was no changing in the blaze.

The answer came clearer from the woods. He felt it pulling in toward him along the strong compulsion of his call as a fisherman feels a game fish yielding at last to the tug of his line. And presently among the leafy solitudes of the trees a little mist-wraith came gliding. It was slinking thing, feline, savage, fearless. He could have sworn that for the briefest instant he saw the outlines of a panther stealing across the moss, misty, low-slung, turning upon him the wise black gaze of Yarol – exactly his friend's black eyes, with no lessening in them of lost humanity. And something in that familiar gaze sent a little chill down his back. Could it be – could it possibly be that in Yarol the veneer of humanity was so thin over his savage cat-nature that even when it had been stripped away the look in his eyes was the same?

Then the smoke-beast was hovering over the prone Venusian figure. It curled round Yarol's shoulders for an instant; it faded and sank, and Yarol stirred on the moss. Smith turned him over with a shaking hand. The long Venusian lashes quivered, lifted. Black, sidelong eyes looked up into Smith's pale gaze. And Smith in a gush of chilly uncertainty did not know if humanity had returned into his friend's body or not, if it was a panther's gaze looking up into his or if that thin layer of man-soul veiled it, for Yarol's eyes had always looked like this.

'Are – are you all right?' he asked in a breathless whisper.

Yarol blinked dizzily once or twice, then grinned. A twinkle lighted up his black cat gaze. He nodded and made a little effort to rise. Smith helped him sit up. The Venusian was not a fraction so weak as the Earthman had been. After a little interval of hard breathing he struggled to his feet and helped Smith up, apprehension in his whole demeanor as he eyed the flame that pulsed in its white shrine. He jerked his head urgently.

'Let's get out of here!' his silent lips mouthed. And Smith in fervent agreement turned in the direction he indicated, hoping that Yarol knew where he was going. His own exhaustion was still too strong to permit him anything but acquiescence.

They made their way through the woods, Yarol heading unerringly in a direct course toward the roadway they had left such a long time ago. After a while, when the flamehousing shrine had vanished among the trees behind them, the Venusian's soft voice murmured, half to itself.

'—wish, almost, you hadn't called me back. Woods were so cool and still – remembering such splendid things – killing and killing – I wish—'

The voice fell quiet again. But Smith, stumbling on beside his friend, understood. He knew why the woods seemed familiar to Yarol, so that he could head for the roadway unerringly. He knew why Yvala in her satiety had not even wakened at the withdrawal of Yarol's humanity – it was so small a thing that the loss of it meant nothing. He gained a new insight in that moment into Venusian nature that he remembered until the day he died.

Then there was a gap in the trees ahead, and Yarol's shoulder was under his supportingly, and the road to safety shimmered in its tree-arched green gloom ahead.

LOST PARADISE

Across the table-top Yarol the Venusian reached a swift hand that closed on Northwest Smith's wrist heavily. 'Look!' he said in a low voice.

Smith's no-colored eyes turned leisurely in the direction of the little Venusian's almost imperceptible nod.

The panorama that stretched out under his causal gaze would have caught at a newcomer's breath with its very magnitude, but to Smith the sight was an old story. Their table was one of many ranged behind a rail along the edge of a parapet below which the dizzy gulf of New York's steel terraces dropped away in a thousand-foot sweep to the far earth. Lacing that swooning gulf of emptiness the steel spans of the traffic bridges arched from building to building, aswarm with New York's countless hordes. Men from the three planets, wanderers and space-rangers and queer, brutish things that were not wholly human mingled with the throngs of Earth as they streamed endlessly over the great steel bridges spanning the gulfs of New York. From the high parapet table where Smith and Yarol sat one could watch the solar system go by, world upon world, over the arches that descended by tiers and terraces into the perpetual darkness and twinkling, far-off lights of the deeps where solid earth lay hidden. In mighty swoops and arcs they latticed the void yawning below the parapet on which Yarol leaned a negligent elbow and stared.

Smith's pale eyes, following that stare, saw only the usual crowd of pedestrians swarming across the steel span of the bridge a story below.

'See?' murmured Yarol. 'That little fellow in the red leather coat. The white-haired one, walking slow at the edge of the rail. See?'

'Um-m.' Smith made a non-committal noise in his throat as he found the object of Yarol's interest. It was an odd-looking specimen of humanity that loitered slowly along in the outer edges of the crowd surging across the bridge. His red coat was belted about a body whose extreme fragility was apparent even at this elevation; though from what Smith could see of his foreshortened figure he did not seem like one in ill health. On his uncovered head the hair grew silky and silvery, and under one arm he clutched a squarish package which he was careful, Smith noticed, to keep on the railing side, away from the passing crowd.

'I'll bet you the next drinks,' murmured Yarol, his wise black eyes twinkling under long lashes, 'that you can't guess what race that little fellow's from, or where it originated.'

'The next drinks are on me anyway,' grinned Smith. 'No I can't guess. Does it matter?'

'Oh – curious, that's all. I've seen a member of that race only once before in my life, and I'll bet you never saw one. And yet it's an Earth race, perhaps the very oldest. Did you ever hear of the Seles?'

Smith shook his head silently, his eyes on the little figure below, which was slowly drawing out of sight beneath the overhang of the terrace on which they sat.

'They live somewhere in the remotest part of Asia, no one knows exactly where. But they're not Mongolian. It's a pure race, and one that has no counterpart anywhere in the solar system that I ever heard of. I think even among themselves their origin has been forgotten, though their legends go back so far it makes you dizzy to think of it. They're queer-looking, all white-haired and fragile as glass. Keep very much to themselves, of course. When one ventures out into the world you can be sure it's for some tremendously important reason. Wonder why that fellow – oh well, not that it matters. Only seeing him reminded me of the queer story that's told about them. They have a Secret. No, don't laugh; it's supposed to be something very strange and wonderful, which their race-life is dedicated to keeping quiet. I'd give a lot to know what it is, just for curiosity's sake.'

'None of your business, my boy,' said Smith sleepily. 'Like as not it's better for you that you don't know. These secrets have a way of being uncomfortable things to know.'

'No such luck,' Yarol shrugged. 'Let's have another drink – on you, remember – and forget it.'

He lifted a finger to summon the hurrying waiter.

But the summons was never given. For just then, around the corner of the railing which separated the little enclosure of tables from the street running along the edge of the terrace came a flash of red that caught Yarol's eye abruptly. It was the little white-haired man, hugging his squarish parcel and walking timorously, as if he were not accustomed to thronged streets and terraces a thousand feet high in steel-shimmering air.

And at the moment Yarol's eye caught him, something happened. A man in a dirty brown uniform, whose defaced insignia was indecipherable pushed forward and jostled the red-coated stroller roughly. The little man gave a squeak of alarm and clutched frantically at his parcel, but too late. The jostling had knocked it almost out from under his arm, and before he could recover his grip the burly assailant had seized it and shouldered quickly away through the crowd.

Stark terror was livid on the little man's face as he stared wildly around. And in the first desperate glance his eyes encountered the two men at the table watching him with absorbing interest. Across the rail his gaze met theirs in a passion of entreaty. There was something about the attitude of them, their worn spaceman's leather and faces stamped with the indefinable seal of lives lived dangerously, which must have told him in that desperate glimpse that perhaps help lay here. He gripped the rail, white-knuckled, and gasped across it,

'Follow him! Get it back – reward – oh, hurry!'

'How much of a reward?' demanded Yarol with sudden purpose in his voice.

'Anything – your own price – only hurry!'

The little man's face was suffusing with anguished scarlet. 'I swear it – of course I swear it! But hurry! Hurry, or you'll—'

'Do you swear it by—' Yarol hesitated and cast a curiously guilty glance over his shoulder at Smith. Then he rose and leaned across the rail, whispering something in the stranger's ear. Smith saw a look of intense terror sweep across the flushed face. In its wake the crimson drained slowly away, leaving the man's moon-white features blank with an emotion to which Smith could put no name. But he nodded frantically. In a voice that had strained itself to a hoarse and gasping whisper he said, 'Yes, I swear. Now go!'

With no further words Yarol vaulted the rail and plunged into the crowd in the wake of the vanishing thief. The little man stared after him for an instant, then came slowly around to the gate in the railing and threaded the empty tables to Smith's. He sank into the chair Yarol had left and buried his silkily silver head in hands that shook.

Smith regarded him impassively. He was somewhat surprised to see that it was not an old man who sat here opposite him. The mark of no more than middle years lay upon the anxiety-ravaged face, and the hands which were clenched above the bowed head were strong and firm, with a queerly fragile slenderness that somehow did not belie the sense of indwelling strength which he had noticed in his first glance. It was not, thought Smith, an individual slenderness, but, as Yarol had said, a racial trait that made the man look as if a blow would break him into fragments. And the race, had he not known better, he would have sworn dwelt upon some smaller planet than Earth, some world of lesser gravity where such delicate bone-structure as this would have purpose.

After a while the stranger's head rose slowly and he stared at Smith with haggard eyes. They were a queer color, those eyes – dark, soft, veiled in a sort of filmed translucency so that they seemed never to dwell directly upon anything. They gave the whole face a look of withdrawn, introspective peace wildly at odds now with the anguish of unrest upon the delicate features of the man.

He was scrutinizing Smith, the desperation in his eyes robbing the long stare of any impertinence. With averted eyes Smith let him look. Twice he was aware that the other's lips had parted and his breath caught as if for speech; but he must have seen something in that dark, impassive face across the table, scarred with the tale of many battles, cold-eyed, emotionless, which made him think better of attempting questions. So he sat there silently, hands twisting on the table, naked anguish in his eyes, waiting.

The minutes went by slowly. It must have been all of a quarter of an hour before Smith heard a step behind him and knew by the light which dazzled across the face of the man opposite that Yarol had returned. The little Venusian pulled up a chair and sank into it silently, grinning and laying on the table a flat, squarish package.

The stranger pounced upon it with a little, inarticulate cry, running anxious hands over the brown paper in which it was wrapped, testing the brown seals which splotched the side where the edges of the covering came together. Satisfied then, he turned to Yarol. The wild desperation had died upon his face now, magically allowing it to fall into lines of a vast tranquility. Smith thought he had never seen a face so suddenly and serenely at peace. And yet there was in its peacefulness a queer sort of resignation, as if something lay ahead of him which he accepted without a struggle; as if, perhaps, he was prepared to pay whatever tremendous price Yarol asked, and knew it would be high.

'What is it,' he asked Yarol in a gentle voice, 'that you wish as your reward?'

'Tell me the Secret,' said Yarol boldly. He was grinning as he said it. The rescue of the package had not been a task of any great difficulty for a man of his knowledge and character. How he had accomplished it not even Smith knew – the ways of Venusians are strange – but he had had no doubt that Yarol would succeed. He was not looking now at the Venusian's fair, cherubic face with its wise black eyes dancing. He was watching the stranger, and he saw no surprise upon the man's delicate features, only a little flash of quickly darkened brightness behind the veiled eyes, a little spasm of pain and acknowledgment twisting his face for a moment.

'I might have known that,' he said quietly, in his soft, low voice that held a taint of some alien inflection of speech beneath its careful English. 'Have you any conception of what it is you ask?'

'A little.' Yarol's voice was sobering under the graveness of the other's tones. 'I – I knew one of your race once – one of the Seles – and learned just enough to make me want very badly the whole Secret.'

'You learned – a name, too,' said the little man gently. 'And I swore by it to give you what you asked. I shall give it to you. But you must understand that

I would never have given that oath had even so vital a thing as my own life depended upon it. I, or any of the Seles, would die before swearing by that name in a cause less great than – than the one for which I swore. By that' – he smiled faintly – 'you may guess how precious a thing this package is. Are you sure, are you very sure you wish to know our secret?'

Smith recognized the stubbornness that was beginning to shadow Yarol's finely featured face.

'I am,' said the Venusian firmly. 'And you promised it to me in the name of—' he broke off, faintly mouthing syllables he did not utter. The little man smiled at him with a queer hint of pity on his face.

'You are invoking powers,' he said, 'which you very clearly know nothing of. A dangerous thing to do. But – yes, I have sworn, and I will tell you. I must tell you now, even if you did not wish to know; for a promise made in that name *must* be fulfilled, whatever it cost either promiser or promised. I am sorry – but now you *must* know.'

'Tell us, then,' urged Yarol, leaning forward across the table.

The little man turned to Smith, his face serene with a peace that vaguely roused unease in the Earthman's mind.

'Do you, too, wish to know?' he asked.

Smith hesitated for an instant, weighing that nameless unease against his own curiosity. Despite himself he felt curiously impelled to know the answer to Yarol's question, though he sensed more surely as he thought it over a queer, quiet threat behind the little stranger's calmness. He nodded shortly and scowled at Yarol.

Without further ado the man crossed his arms on the table over his precious parcel, leaned forward and began to speak in his soft, slow voice. And as he talked, it seemed to Smith that a greater serenity even than before was coming into his eyes, something as vast and calm as death itself. He seemed to be leaving life behind as he spoke, with every word sinking deeper and deeper into a peace that nothing in life could trouble. And Smith knew that the preciously guarded secret must not be thus on the verge of betrayal, and its betrayer so deathly calm, unless a peril as great as death itself lay behind the revelation. He caught his breath to check the disclosures, but a compulsion seemed to be on him now that he could not break. Almost apathetically he listened.

'You must imagine,' the little man was saying quietly, 'the analogy of – well, for example, of a race of people driven by necessity into pitch-black caverns where their children and grandchildren are reared without ever once having seen light or made any use of their eyes. As the generations passed a legend would grow up around the ineffable beauty and mystery of Sight. It would become a religion, perhaps, the tale of a greater glory than words could describe – for how can one describe sight to the blind? – which their forebears had known and which they still possessed the organs for perceiving, if conditions were such as to permit it.

'Our race has such a legend. There is a faculty – a sense – that we have lost through the countless eons since at our peak and origin we possessed it. With us "peak" and "origin" are synonymous; for, like no other race in existence, our most ancient legends begin in a golden age of the infinitely long past. Beyond that they do not go. We have no stories among us of any crude beginnings, like other races. Our origin is lost to us, though the legends of our people go farther back than I could make you believe. But so far as history tells us, we sprang full-fledged from some remote, unlegended birth into highly civilized, perfectly cultured being. And in that state of perfection we possessed the lost sense which exists only in veiled tradition today.

'In the wilderness of Tibet the remnants of our once mighty race dwell. Since Earth's beginnings we have dwelt there, while in the outside world mankind struggled slowly up out of savagery. And by infinite degrees we have declined, until to the majority of us the Secret is lost. Yet our past is too splendid to forget, and we disdain even now to mingle with the young civilizations that have risen. For our glorious Secret is not wholly gone. Our priests know it, and guard it with dreadful magics, and though it is not meet that even the whole of our own race should share the mystery, yet the meanest of us would scorn even so much as the crown of your greatest empire, because we, who inherited the Secret, are so far greater than kings.'

He paused, and the withdrawn look in his queer, translucent eyes deepened. Yarol said urgently, as if to call him back into the present again.

'Yes, but what is it? What is the Secret?'

The soft eyes turned to him compassionately.

'Yes – you must be told. There is no escape for you now. How you learned that name by which you invoked me I cannot guess, but I know that you did not learn much more, or you would never have used the power of it to ask me this question. It is – unfortunate – for us all that I can answer you – that I am one of the few who know. None but we priests ever venture outside our mountain retreat. So you have asked your question of one of the little number who could answer – and that is a misfortune for you as well as for me.'

Again he paused, and Smith saw that vast tranquility deepening upon his serene features. So might a man look who gazes, without protest, into the face of death.

'Go on,' urged Yarol impatiently. 'Tell us. Tell us the Secret.'

'I can't,' the little man's white head shook. He smiled faintly. 'There are no words. But I will show you. Look.'

He reached out one fragile hand and tilted the glass that stood at Smith's elbow so that the red dregs of the *segir*-whisky spilled in a tiny pool on the table.

'Look,' he said again.

Smith's eyes sought the shining redness of the spilled liquid. There was a darkness in it through which pale shadows moved so strangely that he bent closer to see, for nothing near them could possibly have cast such reflections. He was conscious that Yarol too was leaning to look but after that he was conscious of nothing but the red darkness of the pool stirred with pale flickerings, and his eyes were plunging so deeply into its secretness that he could not stir a muscle, and the table and the terrace and the whole great teeming city of steel about him was a mist that faded into oblivion.

From a great way off he heard that soft, slow voice, full of infinite resignation, infinite calm, and a vast, transcendent pity.

'Do not struggle,' it said gently. 'Surrender your minds to mine and I will show you, poor foolish children, what you ask. I must, by virtue of the name. And it may be that the knowledge you gain will be worth even the price it costs us all – for we three must die when the secret is revealed. You understand that, surely? Our whole race-life, from ages immemorial, is dedicated to the Secret's keeping, and any outside the circle of our priesthood who learn it must die that the knowledge be not betrayed. And I, who in my foolishness swore by the name, must tell you what you ask, and see that you die before I pay the price of my own weakness – with my own death.

'Well, this was ordained. Do not struggle against it – it is the pattern into which our lives are woven, and from our births we three moved forward to this moment around a table, together. Now watch, and listen – and learn.

'In the fourth dimension, which is time, man can travel only with the flow of its stream. In the other three he can move freely at will, but in time he must submit to the forward motion which is all he knows. Incidentally, only this dimension of the four affects him physically. As he moves along the fourth dimension he ages. Now once we knew the secret of moving as freely through time as through space, and in a way that did not affect our bodies any more than the motion of stepping forward or back up or down. That secret involved the use of a special sense which I believe all men possess, though through ages of disuse it has atrophied almost to non-existence. Only among the Seles does even a memory of it exist, and only among our priesthood have we those who possess that ancient sense in its full power.

'It is not physically that even we can move at will through time. Nor can we in any way affect what has gone before or is to come after, save in the knowledge of past and future which we gain in our journeyings. For our motion in time is confined strictly to what you may call memory. Through that all but lost sense we can look back into the lives of those who went before, or forward through the still unbodied but definitely existent "memories" of those who come after us. For as I have said, all life is woven into a finished pattern, in which future and past are irrevocably limned.'

'There is danger, even in this way of traveling. Just what it is no one knows, for none who meet the danger return. Perhaps the voyager chances into the memories of a man dying, and cannot escape. Or perhaps – I do not know. But sometimes the mind does not return – snaps out ...'

'Though there are no limits to any of these four dimensions so far as mankind is concerned, yet the distance which we may venture along any one of them is limited to the capacity of the mind that journeys. No mind, however powerful, could trace life back to its origin. For that reason we have no knowledge of our own beginnings, before that golden age I spoke of. But we do know that we are exiles from a place too lovely to have lasted, a land more exquisite than anything Earth can show. From a world like a jewel we came, and our cities were so fair that even now children sing songs of Baloise the Beautiful, and ivory-walled Ingala and Nial of the white roofs.'

'A catastrophe drove us out of that land – a catastrophe that no one understands. Legend says that our gods were angered and forsook us. What actually happened no one seems to know. But we mourn still for the lovely world of Seles where we were born. It was – but look, you shall see.'

The voice had been a low rising and falling of undernotes upon a sea of darkness; but now Smith, all his consciousness still centered upon the reflecting pool of hypnotic red, was aware of a stirring and subtle motion deep down in its darkness. Things were moving, rising, dizzily so that his head swam and the void trembled about him.

Out of that shaking darkness a light began to glow. Reality was taking shape about him, a new substance and a new scene, and as the light and the landscape formed out of darkness, so his own mind clothed itself in flesh again, taking on reality by slow degrees.

Presently he was standing on the slope of a low hill, velvet with dark grass in the twilight. Below him in that lovely half-translucency of dusk Baloise the Beautiful lay outspread, ivory-white, glimmering through the dimness like a pearl half drowned in dark wine. Somehow he knew the city for what it was, knew its name and loved every pale spire and dome and archway spread out in the dusk below him. Baloise the Beautiful, his lovely city.

He had not time to wonder at this sudden, aching familiarity; for beyond the ivory roofs a great moony shimmer was beginning to lighten the dim sky, such a vast and far-spreading glow that he caught his breath as he stood watching; for surely no moon that ever rose on Earth gave forth so mighty an illumination. It spread behind the stretch of Baloise's ivory roof-tops in a great halo that turned the whole night breathless with coming miracle. Then beyond the city he saw the crest of a vast silver circle glimmering through a wash of ground vapor, and suddenly he understood.

Slowly, slowly it rose. The ivory roof-tops of Baloise the Beautiful took that great soft glimmering light and turned it into pearly gleaming, and the whole night was miraculous with the wonder of rising Earth.

On the hillside Smith was motionless while the vast bright globe swung clear of the roofs and floated free at last in the pale light of the Moon. He had seen this sight before, from a dead and barren satellite, but never the exquisite luminance of Earth through the vapors of Moon-air that veiled the vast globe in a shimmer of enchantment as it swung mistily through the dusk, all its silvery continents faintly flushed with green, the translucent wonder of its seas shining jewel-clear, jewel-pale, colored like opals in the lucid tranquility of the Earth-bright dark.

It was almost too lovely a sight for man to gaze on unprepared. His mind was an ache of beauty too vivid for eyes to dwell on long as he found himself moving slowly down the hill. Not until then did he realize that this was not his own body through whose eyes he looked. He had no control over it; he had simply borrowed it to convey him through the moony dusk down the hillside, that he might perceive by its perceptions the immeasurably long-ago time which he was beholding now. This, then, was the 'sense' the little stranger had spoken of. In some eons-dead moon-dweller's memory the sight of rising Earth, marvelous over the spires of the forgotten city, had been graven so deeply that the wash of countless ages could not blot it away. He was seeing now, feeling now what this unknown man had known on a hillside on the Moon a million years ago.

Through the magic of that lost 'sense' he walked the Moon's verdant surface toward that exquisite city which was lost to everything but dreams so many eons ago. Well, he might have guessed from the little priest's extreme fragility alone that his race was not a native of Earth. The lesser gravity of the Moon would have bred a race of bird-like delicacy. Curious that they had moon-silver hair and eyes as translucent and remote as the light of the dead Moon. A queer, illogical link with their lost homeland.

But there was little time for wonder and speculation now. He was watching the loveliness of Baloise floating nearer and nearer through the dusk that seemed aswim with a radiance so softly real that it was like walking through darkly shining water. He was testing just how much latitude this new experience allowed him. He could see what his host saw, and he began to realize now that the man's other senses were open to his perception too. He could even share in his emotions, for he had known a moment of passionate longing for the whole white city of Baloise as he looked down from the hill, longing and love such as an exile might feel for his native city.

Gradually, too, he became aware that the man was afraid. A queer, dark, miasmic terror lurked just below the surface of his conscious thoughts, something whose origin he could not fathom. It gave the loveliness he looked on a poignancy almost as sharp as pain, etching every white spire and gleaming dome of Baloise deep into his remembering mind.

Slowly, moving in the shadow of his own dark terror, the man went down the hill. The ivory wall that circled Baloise rose over him, a low wall with a crest fretted into a band of lacy carving upon whose convolutions the lucent Earthlight lay like silver. Under a pointed arch he walked, still moving with that slow resolute step as if he approached something dreadful from which there was no escape. And strongly and more strongly Smith was aware of the fear that drowned the man's unformulated thoughts, washing in a dark tide beneath the consciousness of everything he did. And stronger still the poignant love for Baloise ached in him and his eyes lingered like slow caresses on the pale roofs and Earth-washed walls and the pearly dimness that lay shadowily between, where the light of rising Earth was only a reflection. He was memorizing the loveliness of Baloise, as an exile might do. He was lingering upon the sight of it with a yearning so deep that it seemed as if even unto death he must carry behind his eyes the Earth-lit loveliness on which he gazed.

Pale walls and translucent domes and arches rose about him as he walked slowly along a street paved in white seasand, so that his feet fell soundlessly upon its surface and he might have been walking in a translucent dream. Now Earth had swum higher above the reflecting roofs, and the great shining globe of it floated free overhead, veiled and opalescent with the rainbow seas of its atmosphere. Smith, looking up through the eyes of this unknown stranger, could scarcely recognize the configuration of the great green continents spread out beneath their veils of quivering air, and the shapes of the shining seas were strange to him. He looked into a past so remote that little upon his native planet was familiar to him.

Now his strange host was turning aside from the broad, sandy street. He went down a little paved alley, dim in the swimming light of Earth, and pushed open the gate of grille work that closed its end. Under the opened arch he walked into a garden, beyond whose Earth-bright loveliness a low white house rose pale as ivory against dark trees.

There was a pool in the garden's center, Earth swam like a great glimmering opal in its darkness, brimming the water with a greater glory than ever shone into earthly pool. And bending over that basin of spilled Earthlight was a woman.

The silvery cascade of her hair swung forward about a face paler than the pallor of rising Earth, and lovely with a delicacy more exquisite than ever shaped an Earthwoman's features into beauty. Her moon-born slimness as she bent above the pool was the slimness of some airy immortal; for no Earthly woman ever walked whose delicacy was half so sweet and fragile.

She lifted her head as the grille-gate opened, and swayed to her feet in a motion so unearthly light that she scarcely seemed to touch the grass as she moved forward, a creature of pale enchantment in an enchanted Moon-garden. The man crossed the grass to her reluctantly, and Smith was aware in him of a dread and a soul-deep aching that choked up in his throat until he could scarcely speak. The woman lifted her face, clear now in the Earthlight and so delicately modeled that it was more like some exquisite jewel-carving than a face of bone and Moon-white flesh. Her eyes were great and dark with an unnamed dread. She breathed in the lightest echo of voice.

'It has come?' … and the tongue she spoke rippled like running water, in strange, light, breathing cadences that Smith understood only through the mind of the man whose memory he shared.

His host said in a voice that was a little too loud in its resolution not to quiver.

'Yes – it has come.'

At that the woman's eyes closed involuntarily, her whole exquisite face crumpling into sudden, stricken grief so heavy that it seemed this fragile creature must be crushed under the weight of it, the whole delicate body sinking overburdened to the grass. But she did not fall. She stood swaying for an instant, and then the man's arms were about her, holding her close in a desperate embrace. And through the memory of the long-dead man who held her, Smith could feel the delicacy of the eons-dead woman, the warm softness of her flesh, the tiny bones, like a bird's. Again he felt futilely that she was too fragile a creature to know such sorrow as racked her now, and a helpless anger rose in him against whatever unnamed thing it was that kindled such terror and heartbreak in them both.

For a long moment the man held her close, feeling the soft fragility of her body warm against him, the rack of silent sobs, that must surely tear her bones apart, so delicate were they, so desperate her soundless agony. And in his own throat the tightness of sorrow was choking, and his own eyes burned with unshed tears. The dark miasma of terror had strengthened until the Earth-lit garden was blotted out behind it, and nothing remained but the black weight of his fear, the pain of his hopeless grief.

At last he loosed the girl in his arms a little and murmured against her silvery hair,

'Hush, hush, my darling. Do not sorrow so – we knew that this must come some day. It comes to everyone alive – it has come to us too. Do not weep so …'

She sobbed once more, a deep ache of pure pain, and then stood back in his arms and nodded, shaking back the silver hair.

'I know,' she said. 'I know.' She lifted her head and looked up toward Earth's great haloed mystery swimming through veils of colored enchantment above them. The light of it glistened in the tears on her face. 'Almost,' she said, 'I wish we two had gone – there.'

He shook her a little in his arms.

'No – life in the colonies, with only Seles' little glimmer of green light shining down on us to tear our hearts with memories of home – no, my dear. That would have been a lifetime of longing and yearning to return. We have lived in happiness here, knowing only this moment of pain at the end. It is better.'

She bent her head and laid her forehead against his shoulder, shutting out the sight of risen Earth.

'Is it?' she asked him thickly, her voice indistinct with tears. 'Is a lifetime of nostalgia and grieving, with you, not better than paradise without you? Well, the choice is made now. I am happy only in this – that you have been summoned first and need not know this – this dreadfulness – of facing life alone. You must go now – quickly, or I shall never let you. Yes – we knew it must end – that the summons must come. Good-bye – my very dear.'

She lifted her wet face and closed her eyes.

Smith would have looked away then if it had been possible for him. But he could not detach himself even in emotion from the host whose memory he shared, and the unbearable instant stabbed as deeply at his own heart as it did at the man whose memory he shared. He took her gently again into his arms and kissed the quivering mouth, salt with the taste of her tears. And then without a backward glance he turned toward the open gate and walked slowly out under its arch, moving as a man moves to his doom.

He went down the narrow way into the open street again, under the glory of risen Earth. The beauty of the eons-dead Baloise he walked through ached like a dull pain in his heart beneath the sharper anguish of that farewell. The salt of the girl's tears was still on his lips, and it seemed to him that not even the death he went to could give him ease from the pain of the moments he had just passed through. He went on resolutely.

Smith realized that they were turning now toward the center of Baloise the Beautiful. Great open squares here and there broke the ivory ranks of the buildings, and there were men and women moving infrequently through the streets, fragile as birds in their Moon-born delicacy, silvery pale under the immense pale disk of high-swinging Earth that dominated that scene until nothing seemed real but its vast marvel hanging overhead. The buildings were larger here, and though they lost none of their enchanted beauty they were more clearly places of industry then had been those domed and grille-fretted dwellings on the outskirts of the city.

Once they skirted a great square in whose center bulked a vast sphere of silvery sheen that reflected the brightness of the sky-filling Earth. It was a ship – a space-ship. Smith's eyes would have told him that even if the knowledge that floated through his mind from the mind of the Moon-dweller had not made it clear. It was a space-ship loaded with men and machinery and supplies for the colonies struggling against the ravening jungles upon steamy, prehistoric Earth.

They watched the last passengers filing up the ramps that led to orifices in its lower curve, Moon-white people moving silently as people in a dream under the vast pale glowing of the Moon-high Earth. It was queer how silent they were. The whole great square and the immense sphere that filled it and the throngs moving up and down the ramps might have been figures in a dream. It was hard to realize that they were not – that they had existed, flesh and blood, stone and steel, under the light of a vast, heaven-filling globe haloed in its rainbowy haze of atmosphere, once, millennia ago.

As they neared the farther side of the square, Smith saw through his host's scarcely observing eyes the ramps lower and the orifices close in the huge bubble-ship. The Moonman was too wrapped in his agony and heartbreak and despair to pay much heed to what was taking place there in the square, so that Smith caught only abstract glimpses of the great ship floating bubble-light up from the pavement, silently, effortlessly, with no such bursts of thunderous noise and great washes of flame as attend the launching of modern space-ships. Curiosity rode him hard, but he could do nothing. His only glimpses of this ages-past scene must be taken through the eyes of his host's memory. They went on out of the square.

A great dark building loomed up above the pale-roofed houses. It was the only dark thing he had seen in Baloise, and the sight of it woke into sudden life the terror that had been dwelling formlessly and deep in the mind of his host. But he went on unhesitatingly. The broad street led straight up to the archway that opened in the dark wall's façade, a portal as cavernous and blackly threatening as the portals of death itself.

Under the shadow of it the man paused. He looked back lingeringly upon the pearly pallor of Baloise. Over the domed and pinnacled roofs the great pale light of Earth brooded. Earth itself, swimming in seas of opalescent atmosphere, all its continents silver-green, all its seas colored like veiled jewels, glowed down upon him for the last time. The full tide of his love for Baloise, of his love for the lost girl in the garden, of his love for the whole green, sweet satellite he lived on came choking up in his throat, and his heart was near bursting with the sweet fullness of the life he must leave.

Then he turned resolutely and went in under the dark archway. Through his set eyes Smith could see nothing within but a gloom like moonlight shining through mist, so that the space inside was full of a grayness faintly translucent, faintly luminous. And the terror that clogged the man's mind was laying hold on his own as they went steadily forward, in sick fright, through the gloom.

The dimness brightened as they advanced. More and more inexplicable in Smith's mind grew the wonder that, though fear was turning the Moon-dweller's very brain icy with dread, yet he went unhesitatingly forward, no compulsion driving him but his own will. It was death he went to – there was no doubt about that now, from the glimpses he had of his host's mind – a death from which by instinct he shrank with every fiber of his being. But he went on.

Now walls were becoming visible through the dim fog of the darkness. They were smooth walls, black, unfeatured. The interior of this great dark building was appalling in its very simplicity. Nothing but a wide black corridor whose walls rose into invisibility overhead. Contrasting with the ornateness of every other manmade surface in Baloise, the stark severity of the building struck a note of added terror into the numbed brain of the man who walked here.

The darkness paled and brightened. The corridor was widening. Presently its walls had fallen back outside range of sight; and over a black, unflustered floor, through misty brightness the Moonman walked forward to his death.

The room into which the hall had widened was immense. Smith thought it must comprise the whole interior of the great dark building; for many minutes passed while his host paced steadily, slowly forward over the darkness of the floor.

Gradually through that queer bright dimness a flame began to glow. It danced in the mist like the light of a windblown fire, brightening, dimming, flaring up again so that the mist pulsed with its brilliance. There was the regularity of life in that pulsing.

It was a wall of pale flame, stretching through the misty dimness as far as the eye could reach on either side. The man paused before it, with bowed head, and he tried to speak. Terror thickened his voice so that it was only on the third attempt that he managed to articulate, very low, in a choked voice, 'Hear me, O Mighty. I am come.'

In the silence after his voice ceased, the wall of beating flame flickered once again, like a heart's beat, and then rolled back on both sides like curtains. Beyond the back-drawn flame a high-roofed hollow in the mist loomed dimly. It had no more tangibility than the mist itself, the inside of a sphere of dim clarity. And in that mist-walled hollow three gods sat. Sat? They crouched, dreadfully, hungrily, with such a bestial ravening in their poise that only gods could maintain the awful dignity which veiled them with terror despite the ugly humped hunger of their posture.

This one glimpse through glazing eyes Smith caught as the Moonman flung himself face down on the black floor, the breath stopping in his throat, choking against unbearable terror as a drowning man chokes against sea-water. But as the eyes through which he looked lost sight of the three ravenous figures, Smith had an instant's glimpse of the shadow behind them, monstrous on the curved mist-wall that hollowed them in, cast waveringly by the back-drawn flame. And it was a single shadow. These three were One.

And the One spoke. In a voice like the lick of flames, tenuous as the mist that reflected it, terrible as the voice of death itself, the One said:

'What mortal dares enter our immortal Presence?'

'One whose god-appointed cycle is complete,' gasped the prostrate man, his voice coming in little puffs as if he had been running hard. 'One who fulfills his share of his race's debt to the Three who are One.'

The voice of the One had been a voice full, complete, an individual speaking. Now out of the dim hollow where the three crouched a thin, flickering voice, like hot flame, less than full, less than complete, came quavering.

'Be it remembered,' said the thin, hot little voice, 'that all the world of Seles owes it existence to ourselves, who by our might hold fire and air and water around its globe. Be it remembered that only through ourselves does the flesh of life clothe this little world's bare bones. Be it remembered!'

The man on the floor shuddered in one long quiver of acquiescence. And Smith, his mind aware as that other mind was aware, knew that it was true. The Moon's gravity was too weak, even in this long-vanished era, to hold its cloak of life-supporting air without the aid of some other force than its own. Why these Three furnished that power he did not know, but he was beginning to guess.

A second little voice, hungry as flame, took up the ritual chant as the first died away.

'Be it remembered that only for a price do we wrap the robe of life about Seles' bones. Be that bargain remembered that the progenitors of the race of Seles made with the Three who are One, in the very long ago when even the gods were young. Let the price be not forgotten that every man must pay at the end of his appointed cycle. Be it remembered that only through our divine hunger can mankind reach us to pay his vow. All who live owe us the debt of their living, and by the age-old pact of their forefathers must return when we summon them into the shadow that gives their loved world life.'

Again the prostrate man shuddered, deep and coldly, acknowledging the ritual truth. And a third voice quavered out of that misty hollow with a flame's flickering hunger in its sound.

'Be it remembered that all who come to pay the race's debt and buy anew our favor that their world may live, must come to us willingly, with no resistance against our divine hunger – must surrender without struggle. And be it remembered that if so much as one man alone dares resist our will, then in that instant is our power withdrawn, and all our anger called down upon the world of Seles. Let one man struggle against our desire, and the world of Seles goes bare to the void, all life upon it ceasing in a breath. Be that remembered!'

On the floor the Moonman's body shivered again. Through his mind ran one last ache of love and longing for the beautiful world whose greenness and Earth-lit wonder his death was to preserve. Death was a little thing, if by it Seles lived.

In one full, round thunder the One said terribly,

'Come you willingly into our Presence?'

From the prone man's hidden face a voice choked,

'Willingly – that Seles may live.'

And the voice of the One pulsed through the flamewashed dimness so deeply that the ears did not hear, and only the beat of the Moonman's heart, the throbbing of his blood, caught the low thunder of the gods' command.

'Then come!'

He stirred. Very slowly he got to his feet. He faced the three. And for the first time Smith knew a quickened fear for his own safety. Heretofore the awe and terror he had shared with the Moon-host had been solely for the man himself. But now – was death not reaching out for him no less than for his host? For he knew of no way to dissociate his own spectator mind from the mind with which it was united that it might be aware of this fragment of the measureless past. And when the Moonman went forward into oblivion, must not oblivion engulf his own mind too? This, then, was what the little priest had meant when he told them that some, adventuring backward through the minds of their forebears, never returned. Death in one guise or another must have swallowed them up with the minds they looked through. Death yawned for himself, now, if he could not escape. For the first time he struggled, testing his independence. And it was futile. He could not break away.

With bowed head the Moonman stepped forward through the curtain of flame. It hissed hotly on either side, and then it was behind and he was close to that dim hell where the three gods sat, their shadow hovering terribly behind them on the mist. And it looked in that uncertain light, as if the three strained forward eagerly, hunger ravenous in every dreadful line of them, and the shadow behind spread itself like a waiting mouth.

Then with a swishing roar the flame-curtains swept to behind him, and darkness like the dark of death itself fell blindingly upon the hollow of the Three. Smith knew naked terror as he felt the mind he had ridden thus far falter as a horse falters beneath its rider – fail as a mount fails – and he was falling, falling into gulfs of vertiginous terror, emptier than the space between the worlds, a blind and empty hungriness that out-ravened vacuum itself.

He did not fight it. He could not. It was too tremendous. But he did not yield. One small conscious entity in an infinity of pure hunger, while sucking emptiness raved around him, he was stubborn and unwavering. The hunger of the Three must never before have known anything but acquiescence to the debt man owed them, and now fury roared through the vacuum of their hunger more terribly than any mortal mind could combat. In the midst of it, Smith clung stubbornly to his flicker of consciousness, incapable of doing anything more than resist feebly the ravenous desire that sucked at his life.

Dimly he realized what he was doing. It was the death of a world he compassed, if resistance to the hunger of the Three meant what they had threatened. It meant the death of every living thing on the satellite – of the girl in the Earth-bright garden, of all who walked Baloise's streets, of Baloise herself in the grinding eons, unprotected from the bombarding meteors that would turn this sweet green world into a pitted skull.

But the urge to live was blind in him. He could not have relinquished it if he would, so deeply rooted is the life-desire in us all, the raw, animal desperation against extinction. He would not die – he would not surrender, let the price be what it might. He could not fight that blind ravening that typhooned about him, but he would not submit. He was simply a passive stubbornness against the hunger of the Three, while eons swirled about him and time ceased and nothing had existence but himself, his living, desperate self, rebellious against death.

Others, adventuring through the past, must too have met this peril, must have succumbed to it in the weakness of their inborn love for the green Moon-world. But he had no such weakness. Nothing was so important as life – his own life, here and now. He would not surrender. Deep down under the veneer of his civilized self lay a bed-rock of pure savage power that nothing on any world he knew had ever tested beyond its strength. It supported him now against the anger of divinity, the unshakable foundation of his resolution not to yield.

And slowly, slowly the ravening hunger abated its fury about him. It could not absorb what refused to surrender, and all its fury could not terrorize him into acquiescence. This, then, was why the Three had demanded and reiterated the necessity for submission to their hunger. They had not the power to overcome that unshakable life-urge if it were not willingly put aside, and they dared not let the world they terrorized know this weakness in their strength. For a flashing moment he visioned the vampire Three, battening on a race that dared not defy them for love of the beautiful cities, the soft gold days and Earth-bright miracles of nights that counted more to mankind than its own life counted. But it was ended now.

One last furnace-blast of white-hot hunger raved around Smith's stubbornness. But whatever vampiric things they were, spawned in what unknown, eons-forgotten place, the Three who were One had not the power to break down that last rock-steady savagery in which all that was Smith rooted deep. And at last, in one final burst of typhoon-fury, which roared about him in tornado-blasts of hunger and defeat, the vacuum ceased to be.

For one blinding instant sight flashed unbearably through his brain. He saw sleeping Seles, the green Moon-world that time itself was to forget, pearl-pale under the glory of risen Earth, washed with the splendor of a brighter night than man was to know again, the mighty globe swimming through seas of floating atmosphere, veiled in it, glorious for one last brief instant in the wonder of its misty continents, its pearly seas. Baloise the Beautiful slept under the luminance of high-riding Earth. For one last radiant moment the exquisite Moon-world floated through its dreampale darkness that no world in space was ever to equal again, nor any descendant of the race that knew it ever wholly forget.

And then – disaster. In a stunned, remote way Smith was aware of a high, ear-splitting wail that grew louder, louder – intolerably louder until his very brain could no longer endure the agony of its sound. And over Baloise, over Seles and all who dwelt thereon, a darkness began to fall. High-swimming Earth shimmered through gathering dark, and from the rolling green hills and verdant meadows and silver sea of Seles the atmosphere ripped away. In long, opalescent streamers, bright under the light of Earth, the air of Seles was forsaking the world it cloaked. Not in gradual dissipation, but in abrupt angry destruction as if the invisible hands of the Three were tearing it in long bright ribbons from the globe of Seles – so the atmosphere fell away.

That was the last Smith saw of it as darkness closed him in – Seles, lovely even in its destruction, a little green jewel shimmering with color and brightness, unrolling from its cloak of life as the long, streaming ribbons of rainbowy translucency tore themselves away and trailed in the voice behind, slowly paling into the blackness of space.

Then darkness closed in about him, and oblivion rolled over him and nothing – nothing…

He opened his eyes, and startlingly, New York's steel towers were all about him, the hum of traffic in his ears. Irresistibly his eyes sought the sky, where a moment before, so it seemed to him, the great bright globe of pearly Earth hung luminous. And then, realization coming back slowly, he lowered his eyes and met across the table the wide, haunted stare of the little priest of the Moon-people. The face he saw shocked him. It had aged ten years in the incalculable interval of his journey back into the past. Anguish, deeper than any personal anguish could strike, had graven sharp lines into his unearthly pallor, and the great strange eyes were nightmare-haunted.

'It was through me, then,' he was whispering, as if to himself. 'Of all my race I was the one by whose hand Seles died. Oh, gods—'

'I did it!' Smith broke in harshly, driven out of his habit of silence in a blind effort to alleviate something of that unbearable anguish. 'I was the one!'

'No – you were the instrument, I the wielder. I sent you back. I am the destroyer of Baloise and Nial and ivory-white Ingala, and all the green loveliness of our lost world. How can I ever look up again by night upon the bare white skull of the world I slew? It was I – I!'

'What the devil are you two talking about?' demanded Yarol across the table. 'I didn't see a thing, except a lot of darkness and lights, and a sort of moon . . .'

'And yet' – that haunted whisper went on, obliviously – 'yet I have seen the Three in their temple. No other of all my race ever saw them before, for no living memory ever returned out of that temple save the memory that broke them. Of all my race only I know the secret of the Disaster. Our legends tell of what the exiles saw, looking up that night in terror through the thick air of Earth – but I *know*! And no man of flesh and blood can bear that knowledge long – who murdered a world by his blundering. Oh gods of Seles – help me!'

His Moon-white hands groped blindly over the table, found the square package that had cost him so dear a price. He stumbled to his feet. Smith rose too, actuated by some inarticulate emotion he could not have named. But the Moonpriest shook his head.

'No,' he said, as if in answer to some question of his own mind, 'you are not to blame for what happened so many eons ago – and yet in the last few minutes. This tangle of time and space, and the disaster that a living man can bring to something dead millennia ago – it is far beyond our narrow grasp of understanding. I was chosen to be the vessel of that disaster – yet not I alone am responsible, for this was ordained from time's beginning. I could not have changed it had I known at the beginning what the end must be. It is not for what you did, but for what you know now – that you must die!'

The words had not wholly left his lips before he was swinging up his square parcel like a deadly weapon. Close against Smith's face he held it, and the shadow of death was in his Moon-pale eyes and dark upon his anguished white face. For the flash of an instant it seemed to Smith that a blaze of intolerable light was bursting out all around the square of the package, though actually he could see nothing but the commonplace outlines of it in the priest's white hands.

For the breath of an instant almost too brief to register on his brain, death brushed him hungrily. But in that instant as the threatening hands swung up there was a burst of blue-white flame behind the priest's back, the familiar crackle of a gun. The little man's face turned livid with pain for an instant, and then peace in a great gush of calmness washed across it, blanking the anguished dark eyes. He slumped sidewise, the square box falling.

Across the huddle of his body on the floor Yarol's crouched figure loomed, slipping the heat-gun back into its holster as he glanced across his shoulder.

'Come on – come on!' he whispered urgently. 'Let's get out of here!'

There was a shout from behind Smith, the beat of running feet. He cast one covetous glance at the fallen square of that mysterious package, but it was a fleeting one as he cleared the body in a leap and on Yarol's flying heels made for the lower ramp to the crowded level beneath. He would never know.

THE TREE OF LIFE

Over time-ruined illar the searching planes swooped and circled. Northwest Smith, peering up at them with a steel-pale stare from the shelter of a half-collapsed temple, thought of vultures wheeling above carrion. All day long now they had been raking these ruins for him. Presently, he knew, thirst would begin to parch his throat and hunger to gnaw at him. There was neither food nor water in these ancient Martian ruins, and he knew that it could be only a matter of time before the urgencies of his own body would drive him out to signal those wheeling Patrol ships and trade his hard-won liberty for food and drink. He crouched lower under the shadow of the temple arch and cursed the accuracy of the Patrol gunner whose flame-blast had caught his dodging ship just at the edge of Illar's ruins.

Presently it occurred to him that in most Martian temples of the ancient days an ornamental well had stood in the outer court for the benefit of wayfarers. Of course all water in it would be a million years dry now, but for lack of anything better to do he rose from his seat at the edge of the collapsed central dome and made his cautious way by still-intact corridors toward the front of the temple. He paused in a tangle of wreckage at the courtyard's edge and looked out across the sun-drenched expanse of pavement toward that ornate well that once had served travelers who passed by here in the days when Mars was a green planet.

It was an unusually elaborate well, and amazingly well preserved. Its rim had been inlaid with a mosaic pattern whose symbolism must once have borne deep meaning, and above it in a great fan of time-defying bronze an elaborate grille-work portrayed the inevitable tree-of-life pattern which so often appears in the symbolism of the three worlds. Smith looked at it a bit incredulously from his shelter, it was so miraculously preserved amidst all this chaos of broken stone, casting a delicate tracery of shadow on the sunny pavement as perfectly as it must have done a million years ago when dusty travelers paused here to drink. He could picture them filing in at noontime through the great gates that—

The vision vanished abruptly as his questing eyes made the circle of the ruined walls. There had been no gate. He could not find a trace of it anywhere around the outer wall of the court. The only entrance here, as nearly as he could tell from the foundations that remained, had been the door in whose ruins he now stood. Queer. This must have been a private court, then, its great grille-crowned well reserved for the use of the priests. Or wait – had there not been a priest-king Illar after whom the city was named? A wizard-king, so legend said, who ruled temple as well as palace with an iron hand. This elaborately patterned well, of material royal enough to withstand the weight of ages, might well have been sacrosanct for the use of that long-dead monarch. It might—

Across the sun-bright pavement swept the shadow of a plane. Smith dodged back into deeper hiding while the ship circled low over the courtyard. And it was then, as he crouched against a crumbled wall and waited, motionless, for the danger to pass, that he became aware for the first time of a sound that startled him so he could scarcely credit his ears – a recurrent sound, choked and sorrowful – the sound of a woman sobbing.

The incongruity of it made him forgetful for a moment of the peril hovering overhead in the sun-hot outdoors. The dimness of the temple ruins became a living and vital place for that moment, throbbing with the sound of tears. He looked about half in incredulity, wondering if hunger and thirst were playing tricks on him already, or if these broken halls might be haunted by a million-year-old sorrow that wept along the corridors to drive its hearers mad. There were tales of such haunters in some of Mars' older ruins. The hair prickled faintly at the back of his neck as he laid a hand on the butt of his force-gun and commenced a cautious prowl toward the source of the muffled noise.

Presently he caught a flash of white, luminous in the gloom of these ruined walls, and went forward with soundless steps, eyes narrowed in the effort to make out what manner of creature this might be that wept alone in time-forgotten ruins. It was a woman. Or it had the dim outlines of a woman, huddled against an angle of fallen walls and veiled in a fabulous shower of long dark hair. But there was something uncannily odd about her. He could not focus his pale stare upon her outlines. She was scarcely more than a luminous blot of whiteness in the gloom, shimmering with a look of unreality which the sound of her sobs denied.

Before he could make up his mind just what to do, something must have warned the weeping girl that she was no longer alone, for the sound of her tears checked suddenly and she lifted her head, turning to him a face no more distinguishable than her body's outlines. He made no effort to resolve the blurred features into visibility, for out of that luminous mask burned two eyes that caught his with an almost perceptible impact and gripped them in a stare from which he could not have turned if he would.

They were the most amazing eyes he had ever met, colored like moonstone, milkily translucent, so that they looked almost blind. And that magnetic stare held him motionless. In the instant that she gripped him with that fixed, moonstone look he felt oddly as if a tangible bond were taut between them.

Then she spoke, and he wondered if his mind, after all, had begun to give way in the haunted loneliness of dead Illar; for though the words she spoke fell upon his ears in a gibberish of meaningless sounds, yet in his brain a message formed with a clarity that far transcended the halting communication of words. And her milkily colored eyes bored into his with a fierce intensity.

'I'm lost – I'm lost—' wailed the voice in his brain.

A rush of sudden tears brimmed the compelling eyes, veiling their brilliance. And he was free again with that clouding of the moonstone surfaces. Her voice wailed, but the words were meaningless and no knowledge formed in his brain to match them. Stiffly he stepped back a pace and looked down at her, a feeling of helpless incredulity rising within him. For he still could not focus directly upon the shining whiteness of her, and nothing save those moonstone eyes were clear to him.

The girl sprang to her feet and rose on tiptoe, gripping his shoulders with urgent hands. Again the blind intensity of her eyes took hold of his, with a force almost as tangible as the clutch of her hands; again that stream of intelligence poured into his brain, strongly, pleadingly.

'Please, please take me back! I'm so frightened – I can't find my way – oh, please!'

He blinked down at her, his dazed mind gradually realizing the basic facts of what was happening. Obviously her milky unseeing eyes held a magnetic power that carried her thoughts to him without the need of a common speech. And they were the eyes of a powerful mind, the outlets from which a stream of fierce energy poured into his brain. Yet the words they conveyed were the words of a terrified and helpless girl. A strong sense of wariness was rising in him as he considered the incongruity of speech and power, both of which were beating upon him more urgently with every breath. The mind of a forceful and strong-willed woman, carrying the sobs of a frightened girl. There was no sincerity in it.

'Please, please!' cried her impatience in his brain. 'Help me! Guide me back!'

'Back where?' he heard his own voice asking.

'The Tree!' wailed that queer speech in his brain, while gibberish was all his ears heard and the moonstone stare transfixed him strongly. 'The Tree of Life! Oh, take me back to the shadow of the Tree!'

A vision of the grille-ornamented well leaped into his memory. It was the only tree symbol he could think of just then. But what possible connection could there be between the well and the lost girl – if she was lost? Another wail in that unknown tongue, another anguished shake of his shoulders, brought a sudden resolution into his groping mind. There could be no harm in leading her back to the well, to whose grille she must surely be referring. And strong curiosity was growing in his mind. Much more than met the eye was concealed in this queer incident. And a wild guess had flashed through his mind that perhaps she might have come from some subterranean world into which the well descended. It would explain her luminous pallor, if not her blurriness; and, too, her eyes did not seem to function in the light. There was a much more incredible explanation of her presence, but he was not to know it for a few minutes yet.

'Come along,' he said, taking the clutching hands gently from his shoulders. 'I'll lead you to the well.'

She sighed in a deep gust of relief and dropped her compelling eyes from his, murmuring in that strange, gabbling tongue what must have been thanks. He took her by the hand and turned toward the ruined archway of the door.

Against his fingers her flesh was cool and firm. To the touch she was tangible, but even thus near, his eyes refused to focus upon the cloudy opacity of her body, the dark blur of her streaming hair. Nothing but those burning, blinded eyes were strong enough to pierce the veil that parted them.

She stumbled along at his side over the rough floor of the temple, saying nothing more, panting with eagerness to return to her incomprehensible 'tree.' How much of that eagerness was assumed Smith still could not be quite sure. When they reached the door he halted her for a moment, scanning the sky for danger. Apparently the ships had finished with this quarter of the city, for he could see two or three of them half a mile away, hovering low over Illar's northern section. He could risk it without much peril. He led the girl cautiously out into the sun-hot court.

She could not have known by sight that they neared the well, but when they were within twenty paces of it she flung up her blurred head suddenly and tugged at his hand. It was she who led him that last stretch which parted the two from the well. In the sun the shadow tracery of the grille's symbolic pattern lay vividly outlined on the ground. The girl gave a little gasp of delight. She dropped his hand and ran forward three short steps, and plunged into the very center of that shadowy pattern on the ground. And what happened then was too incredible to believe.

The pattern ran over her like garment, curving to the curve of her body in the way all shadows do. But as she stood there striped and laced with the darkness of it, there came a queer shifting in the lines of black tracery, a subtle, inexplicable movement to one side. And with that motion she vanished. It was exactly as if that shifting had moved her out of the one world into another. Stupidly Smith stared at the spot from which she had disappeared.

Then several things happened almost simultaneously. The zoom of a plane broke suddenly into the quiet, a black shadow dipped low over the rooftops, and Smith, too late, realized that he stood defenseless in full view of the searching ships. There was only one way out, and that was too fantastic to put faith in, but he had no time to hesitate. With one leap he plunged full into the midst of the shadow of the tree of life.

Its tracery flowed round him, molding its pattern to his body. And outside the boundaries everything executed a queer little sidewise dip and slipped in the most extraordinary manner, like an optical illusion, into quite another scene. There was no intervention of blankness. It was as if he looked through the bars of a grille upon a picture which without warning slipped sidewise, while between the bars appeared another scene, a curious, dim landscape, gray as if with the twilight of early evening. The air had an oddly thickened look, through which he saw the quiet trees and the flower-spangled grass of the place with a queer, unreal blending, like the landscape in a tapestry, all its outlines blurred.

In the midst of this tapestried twilight the burning whiteness of the girl he had followed blazed like a flame. She had paused a few steps away and stood waiting, apparently quite sure that he would come after. He grinned a little to himself as he realized it, knowing that curiosity must almost certainly have driven him in her wake even if the necessity for shelter had not compelled his following.

She was clearly visible now, in this thickened dimness – visible, and very lovely, and a little unreal. She shone with a burning clarity, the only vivid thing in the whole twilit world. Eyes upon that blazing whiteness, Smith stepped forward, scarcely realizing that he had moved.

Slowly he crossed the dark grass toward her. That grass was soft underfoot, and thick with small, low-blooming flowers of a shining pallor. Botticelli painted such spangled swards for the feet of his angels. Upon it the girl's bare feet gleamed whiter than the blossoms. She wore no garment but the royal mantle of her hair, sweeping about her in a cloak of shining darkness that had a queer, unreal tinge of purple in that low light. It brushed her ankles in it fabulous length. From the hood of it she watched Smith coming toward her, a smile on her pale mouth and a light blazing in the deeps of her moonstone eyes. She was not blind now, nor frightened. She stretched out her hand to him confidently.

'It is my turn now to lead you,' she smiled. As before, the words were gibberish, but the penetrating stare of those strange white eyes gave them a meaning in the depths of his brain.

Automatically his hand went out to hers. He was a little dazed, and her eyes were very compelling. Her fingers twined in his and she set off over the flowery grass, pulling him beside her. He did not ask where they were going. Lost in the dreamy spell of the still, gray, enchanted place, he felt no need for words. He was beginning to see more clearly in the odd, blurring twilight that ran the outlines of things together in that queer, tapestried manner. And he puzzled in a futile, muddled way as he went on over what sort of land he had come into. Overhead was darkness, paling into twilight near the ground, so that when he looked up he was staring into bottomless deeps of starless night.

Trees and flowering shrubs and the flower-starred grass stretched emptily about them in the thick, confusing gloom of the place. He could see only a little distance through that dim air. It was as if they walked a strip of tapestried twilight in some unlighted dream. And the girl, with her lovely, luminous body and richly colored robe of hair was like a woman in a tapestry too, unreal and magical.

After a while, when he had become a little adjusted to the queerness of the whole scene, he began to notice furtive movements in the shrubs and trees they passed. Things flickered too swiftly for him to catch their outlines, but from the tail of his eye he was aware of motion, and somehow of eyes that watched. That sensation was a familiar one to him, and he kept an uneasy gaze on those shiftings in the shrubbery as they went on. Presently he caught a watcher in full view between bush and tree, and saw that it was a man, a little, furtive, dark-skinned man who dodged hastily back into cover again before Smith's eyes could do more than take in the fact of his existence.

After that he knew what to expect and could make them out more easily: little, darting people with big eyes that shone with a queer, sorrowful darkness from their small, frightened faces as they scuttled through the bushes, dodging always just out of plain sight among the leaves. He could hear the soft rustle of their passage, and once or twice when they passed near a clump of shrubbery he thought he caught the echo of little whispering calls, gentle as the rustle of leaves and somehow full of a strange warning note so clear that he caught it even amid the murmur of their speech. Warning calls, and little furtive hiders in the leaves, and a landscape of tapestried blurring carpeted with a Botticelli flower-strewn sward. It was all a dream. He felt quite sure of that.

It was a long while before curiosity awakened in him sufficiently to make him break the stillness. But at last he asked dreamily, 'Where are we going?'

The girl seemed to understand that without the necessity of the bond her hypnotic eyes made, for she turned and caught his eyes in a white stare and answered.

'To Thag. Thag desires you.'

'What is Thag?'

In answer to that she launched without preliminary upon a little singsong monologue of explanation whose stereotyped formula made him faintly uneasy with the thoughts that it must have been made very often to attain the status of a set speech; made to many men, perhaps, whom Thag had desired. And what became of them afterward, he wondered. But the girl was speaking.

'Many ages ago there dwelt in Illar the great King Illar for whom the city was named. He was a magician of mighty power, but not mighty enough to fulfill all his ambitions. So by his arts he called up out of darkness the being known as Thag, and with him struck a bargain. By that bargain Thag was to give of his limitless power, serving Illar all the days of Illar's life, and in return the king was to create a land for Thag's dwelling-place and people it with slaves and furnish a priestess to tend Thag's needs. This is that land. I am that priestess, the latest of a long line of women born to serve Thag. The tree-people are his – his lesser servants.'

'I have spoken softly so that the tree-people do not hear, for to them Thag is the center and focus of creation, the end and beginning of all life. But to you I have told the truth.'

'But what does Thag want of me?'

'It is not for Thag's servants to question Thag.'

'Then what becomes, afterward, of the men Thag desires?' he pursued.

'You must ask Thag that.'

She turned her eyes away as she spoke, snapping the mental bond that had flowed between them with a suddenness that left Smith dizzy. He went on at her side more slowly, pulling back a little on the tug of her fingers. By degrees the sense of dreaminess was fading, and alarm began to stir in the deeps of his mind. After all, there was no reason why he need let this blank-eyed priestess lead him up to the very maw of her god. She had lured him into this land by what he knew now to have been a trick; might she not have worse tricks than that in store for him?

She held him, after all, by nothing stronger then the clasp of her fingers, if he could keep his eyes turned from hers. Therein lay her real power, but he could fight it if he chose. And he began to hear more clearly than ever the queer note of warning in the rustling whispers of the tree-folk who still fluttered in and out of sight among the leaves. The twilight place had taken on menace and evil.

Suddenly he made up his mind. He stopped, breaking the clasp of the girl's hand.

'I'm not going,' he said.

She swung round in a sweep of richly tinted hair, words jetting from her in a gush of incoherence. But he dared not meet her eyes, and they conveyed no meaning to him. Resolutely he turned away, ignoring her voice, and set out to retrace the way they had come. She called after him once, in a high, clear voice that somehow held a note as warning as that in the rustling voices of the tree-people, but he kept on doggedly, not looking back. She laughed then, sweetly and scornfully, a laugh that echoed uneasily in his mind long after the sound of it had died upon the twilight air.

After a while he glanced back over one shoulder, half expecting to see the luminous dazzle of her body still glowing in the dim glade where he had left her; but the blurred tapestry-landscape was quite empty.

He went on in the midst of a silence so deep it hurt his ears, and in a solitude unhaunted even by the shy presences of the tree-folk. They had vanished with the fire-bright girl, and the whole twilight land was empty save for himself. He plodded on across the dark grass, crushing the upturned flower-faces under his boots and asking himself wearily if he could be mad. There seemed little other explanation for this hushed and tapestried solitude that had swallowed him up. In that thunderous quiet, in that deathly solitude, he went on.

When he had walked for what seemed to him much longer than it should have taken to reach his starting point, and still no sign of an exit appeared, he began to wonder if there were any way out of the gray land of Thag. For the first time he realized that he had come through no tangible gateway. He had only stepped out of a shadow, and – now that he thought of it – there were no shadows here. The grayness swallowed everything up, leaving the landscape oddly flat, like a badly drawn picture. He looked about helplessly, quite lost now and not sure in what direction he should be facing, for there was nothing here by which to know directions. The trees and shrubs and the starry grass still stretched about him, uncertainly outlined in that changeless dusk. They seemed to go on for ever.

But he plodded ahead, unwilling to stop because of a queer tension in the air, somehow as if all the blurred trees and shrubs were waiting in breathless anticipation, centering upon his stumbling figure. But all trace of animate life had vanished with the disappearance of the priestess' white-glowing figure. Head down, paying little heed to where he was going, he went on over the flowery sward.

An odd sense of voids about him startled Smith at last out of his lethargic plodding. He lifted his head. He stood just at the edge of a line of trees, dim and indistinct in the unchanging twilight. Beyond them – he came to himself with a jerk and stared incredulously. Beyond them the grass ran down to nothingness, merging by imperceptible degrees into a streaked and arching void – not the sort of emptiness into which a material body could fall, but a solid *nothing*, curving up toward the dark zenith as the inside of sphere curves. No physical thing could have entered there. It was too utterly void, an inviolable emptiness which no force could invade.

He stared up along the inward arch of that curving, impassable wall. Here, then, was the edge of the queer land Illar had wrested out of space itself. This arch must be the curving of solid space which had been bent awry to enclose the magical land. There was no escape this way. He could not even bring himself to approach any nearer to that streaked and arching blank. He could not have said why, but it woke in him an inner disquiet so strong that after a moment's staring he turned his eyes away.

Presently he shrugged and set off along the inside of the line of trees which parted him from the space-wall. Perhaps there might be a break somewhere. It was a forlorn hope, but the best that offered. Wearily he stumbled on over the flowery grass.

How long he had gone on along that almost imperceptibly curving line of border he could not have said, but after a timeless interval of gray solitude he gradually became aware that a tiny rustling and whispering among the leaves had been growing louder by degrees for some time. He looked up. In and out among the trees which bordered that solid wall of nothingness little, indistinguishable figures were flitting. The tree-men had returned. Queerly grateful for their presence, he went on a bit more cheerfully, paying no heed to their timid dartings to and fro, for Smith was wise in the ways of wild life.

Presently, when they saw how little heed he paid them, they began to grow bolder, their whispers louder. And among those rustling voices he thought he was beginning to catch threads of familiarity. Now and again a word reached his ears that he seemed to recognize, lost amidst the gibberish of their speech. He kept his head down and his hands quiet, plodding along with a cunning stillness that began to bear results.

From the corner of his eye he could see that a little dark tree-man had darted out from cover and paused midway between bush and tree to inspect the queer, tall stranger. Nothing happened to this daring venturer, and soon another risked a pause in the open to stare at the quiet walker among the trees. In a little while a small crowd of the tree-people was moving slowly parallel with his course, staring with all the avid curiosity of wild things at Smith's plodding figure. And among them the rustling whispers grew louder.

Presently the ground dipped down into a little hollow ringed with trees. It was a bit darker here than it had been on the higher level, and as he went down the slope of its side he saw that among the underbrush which filled it were cunningly hidden huts twined together out of the living bushes. Obviously the hollow was a tiny village where the tree-folk dwelt.

He was surer of this when they began to grow bolder as he went down into the dimness of the place. The whispers shrilled a little, and the boldest among his watchers ran almost at his elbow, twittering their queer, broken speech in hushed syllables whose familiarity still bothered him with its haunting echo of words he knew. When he had reached the center of the hollow he became aware that the little folk had spread out in a ring to surround him. Wherever he looked their small, anxious faces and staring eyes confronted him. He grinned to himself and came to a halt, waiting gravely.

None of them seemed quite brave enough to constitute himself spokesman, but among several a hurried whispering broke out in which he caught the words 'Thag' and 'danger' and 'beware.' He recognized the meaning of these words without placing in his mind their origins in some tongue he knew. He knit his sun-bleached brows and concentrated harder, striving to wrest from that curious, murmuring whisper some hint of its original root. He had a smattering of more tongues than he could have counted offhand, and it was hard to place these scattered words among any one speech.

But the word 'Thag' had a sound like that of the very ancient dryland tongue, which upon Mars is considered at once the oldest and most uncouth of all the planet's languages. And with that clue to guide him he presently began to catch other syllables which were remotely like syllables from the dryland speech. They were almost unrecognizable, far, far more ancient than the very oldest versions of the tongue he had ever heard repeated, almost primitive in their crudity and simplicity. And for a moment the sheerest awe came over him, as he realized the significance of what he listened to.

The dryland race today is a handful of semi-brutes, degenerate from the ages of past time when they were a mighty people at the apex of an almost forgotten glory. That day is millions of years gone now, too far in the past to have record save in the vaguest folklore. Yet here was a people who spoke the rudiments of that race's tongue as it must have been spoken in the race's dim beginnings, perhaps, a million years earlier even than that immemorial time of their triumph. The reeling of millennia set Smith's mind awhirl with the effort at compassing their span.

There was another connotation in the speaking of that tongue by these timid bush-dwellers, too. It must mean that the forgotten wizard king, Illar, had peopled his sinister, twilight land with the ancestors of today's dryland dwellers. If they shared the same tongue they must share the same lineage. And humanity's remorseless adaptability had done the rest.

It had been no kinder here than in the outside world, where the ancient plainsmen who had roamed Mars' green prairies had dwindled with their dying plains, degenerating at last into a shrunken, leather-skinned bestiality. For here that same race root had declined into these tiny, slinking creatures with their dusky skins and great, staring eyes and their voices that never rose above a whisper. What tragedies must lie behind that gradual degeneration!

All about him the whispers still ran. He was beginning to suspect that through countless ages of hiding and murmuring those voices must have lost the ability to speak aloud. And he wondered with a little inward chill what terror it was which had transformed a free and fearless people into these tiny wild things whispering in the underbrush.

The little anxious voices had shrilled into vehemence now, all of them chattering together in their queer, soft, rustling whispers. Looking back later upon that timeless space he had passed in the hollow, Smith remembered it as some curious nightmare – dimness and tapestried blurring, and a hush like death over the whole twilight land, and the timid voices whispering, whispering, eloquent with terror and warning.

He groped back among his memories and brought forth a phrase or two remembered from long ago, an archaic rendering of the immemorial tongue they spoke. It was the simplest version he could remember of the complex speech now used, but he knew that to them it must sound fantastically strange. Instinctively he whispered as he spoke it, feeling like an actor in a play as he mouthed the ancient idiom,

'I – I cannot understand. Speak – more slowly—'

A torrent of words greeted this rendering of their tongue. Then there was a great deal of hushing and hissing, and presently two or three between them began laboriously to recite an involved speech, one syllable at a time. Always two or more shared the task. Never in his converse with them did he address anyone directly. Ages of terror had bred all directness out of them.

'Thag,' they said. 'Thag, the terrible – Thag, the omnipotent – Thag, the unescapable. Beware of Thag.'

For a moment Smith stood quiet, grinning down at them despite himself. There must not be too much of intelligence left among this branch of the race, either, for surely such a warning was superfluous. Yet they had mastered their agonies of timidity to give it. All virtue could not yet have been bred out of them, then. They still had kindness and a sort of desperate courage rooted deep in fear.

'What is Thag?' he managed to inquire, voicing the archaic syllables uncertainly. And they must have understood the meaning if not the phraseology, for another spate of whispered tumult burst from the clustering tribe. Then, as before, several took up the task of answering.

'Thag – Thag, the end and the beginning, the center of creation. When Thag breathes the world trembles. The earth was made for Thag's dwelling-place. All things are Thag's. Oh, beware! Beware!'

This much he pieced together out of their diffuse whisperings, catching up the fragments of words he knew and fitting them into the pattern.

'What – what is the danger?' he managed to ask.

'Thag – hungers. Thag must be fed. It is we who – feed – him, but there are times when he desires other food than us. It is then he sends his priestess forth to lure – food – in. Oh, beware of Thag!'

'You mean that the priestess brought me in for – food?'

A chorus of grave, murmuring affirmatives.

'Then why did she leave me?'

'There is no escape from Thag. Thag is the center of creation. All things are Thag's. When he calls, you must answer. When he hungers, he will have you. Beware of Thag!'

Smith considered that for a moment in silence. In the main he felt confident that he had understood their warning correctly, and he had little reason to doubt that they knew whereof they spoke. Thag might not be the center of the universe, but if they said he could call a victim from anywhere in the land, Smith was not disposed to doubt it. The priestess' willingness to let him leave her unhindered, yes, even her scornful laughter as he looked back, told the same story. Whatever Thag might be, his power in this land could not be doubted. He made up his mind suddenly what he must do, and turned to the breathlessly waiting little folk.

'Which way – lies Thag?' he asked.

A score of dark, thin arms pointed. Smith turned his head speculatively toward the spot they indicated. In this changeless twilight all sense of direction had long since left him, but he marked the line as well as he could by the formation of the trees, then turned to the little people with a ceremonious farewell rising to his lips.

'My thanks for—' he began, to be interrupted by a chorus of whispering cries of protest. They seemed to sense his intention, and their pleadings were frantic. A panic anxiety for him glowed upon every little terrified face turned up to his, and their eyes were wide with protest and terror. Helplessly he looked down.

'I – I must go,' he tried stumblingly to say. 'My only chance is to take Thag unawares, before he sends for me.'

He could not know if they understood. Their chattering went on undiminished, and they even went so far as to lay tiny hands on him, as if they would prevent him by force from seeking out the terror of their lives.

'No, no, no!' they wailed murmurously. 'You do not know what it is you seek! You do not know Thag! Stay here! Beware of Thag!'

A little prickling of unease went down Smith's back as he listened. Thag must be very terrible indeed if even half this alarm had foundation. And to be quite frank with himself, he would greatly have preferred to remain here in the hidden quiet of the hollow, with its illusion of shelter, for as long as he was allowed to stay. But he was not of the stuff that yields very easily to its own terrors, and hope burned strongly in him still. So he squared his broad shoulders and turned resolutely in the direction the tree-folk had indicated.

When they saw that he meant to go, their protests sank to a wail of bitter grieving. With that sound moaning behind him he went up out of the hollow, like a man setting forth to the music of his own dirge. A few of the bravest went with him a little way, flitting through the underbrush and darting from tree to tree in a timidity so deeply ingrained that even when no immediate peril threatened they dared not go openly through the twilight.

Their presence was comforting to Smith as he went on. A futile desire to help the little terror-ridden tribe was rising in him, a useless gratitude for their warning and their friendliness, their genuine grieving as his departure and their odd, paradoxical bravery even in the midst of hereditary terror. But he knew that he could do nothing for them, when he was not at all sure he could even save himself. Something of their panic had communicated itself to him, and he advanced with a sinking at the pit of his stomach. Fear of the unknown is so poignant a thing, feeding on its own terror, that he found his hands beginning to shake a little and his throat going dry as he went on.

The rustling and whispering among the bushes dwindled as his followers one by one dropped away, the bravest staying the longest, but even they failing in courage as Smith advanced steadily in that direction from which all their lives they had been taught to turn their faces. Presently he realized that he was alone once more. He went on more quickly, anxious to come face to face with this horror of the twilight and dispel at least the fearfulness of its mystery.

The silence was like death. Not a breeze stirred the leaves, and the only sound was his own breathing, the heavy thud of his own heart. Somehow he felt sure that he was coming nearer to his goal. The hush seemed to confirm it. He loosened the force-gun at his thigh.

In that changeless twilight the ground was sloping down once more into a broader hollow. He descended slowly, every sense alert for danger, not knowing if Thag was beast or human or elemental, visible or invisible. The trees were beginning to thin. He knew that he had almost reached his goal.

He paused at the edge of the last line of trees. A clearing spread out before him at the bottom of the hollow, quiet in the dim, translucent air. He could focus directly upon no outlines anywhere, for the tapestried blurring of the place. But when he saw what stood in the very center of the clearing he stopped dead-still, like one turned to stone, and a shock of utter cold went chilling through him. Yet he could not have said why.

For in the clearing's center stood the Tree of Life. He had met the symbol too often in patterns and designs not to recognize it, but here that fabulous thing was living, growing, actually springing up from a rooted firmness in the spangled grass as any tree might spring. Yet it could not be real. Its thin brown trunk, of no recognizable substance, smooth and gleaming, mounted in the traditional spiral; its twelve fantastically curving branches arched delicately outward from the central stem. It was bare of leaves. No foliage masked the serpentine brown spiral of the trunk. But at the tip of each symbolic branch flowered a blossom of bloody rose so vivid he could scarcely focus his dazzled eyes upon them.

This tree alone of all objects in the dim land was sharply distinct to the eye – terribly distinct, remorselessly clear. No words can describe the amazing menace that dwelt among its branches. Smith's flesh crept as he stared, yet he could not for all his staring make out why peril was so eloquent there. To all appearances here stood only a fabulous symbol miraculously come to life; yet danger breathed out from it so strongly that Smith felt the hair lifting on his neck as he stared.

It was no ordinary danger. A nameless, choking, paralyzed panic was swelling in his throat as he gazed upon the perilous beauty of the Tree. Somehow the arches and curves of its branches seemed to limn a pattern so dreadful that his heart beat faster as he gazed upon it. But he could not guess why, though somehow the answer was hovering just out of reach of his conscious mind. From that first glimpse of it his instincts shuddered like a shying stallion, yet reason still looked in vain for an answer.

Nor was the Tree merely a vegetable growth. It was alive, terribly, ominously alive. He could not have said how he knew that, for it stood motionless in its empty clearing, not a branch trembling, yet in its immobility more awfully vital than any animate thing. The very sight of it woke in Smith an insane urging to flight, to put worlds between himself and this inexplicably dreadful thing.

Crazy impulses stirred in his brain, coming to insane birth at the calling of the Tree's peril – the desperate need to shut out the sight of that thing that was blasphemy, to put out his own sight rather than gaze longer upon the perilous grace of its branches, to slit his own throat that he might not need to dwell in the same world which housed so frightful a sight as the Tree.

All this was a mad battering in his brain. The strength of him was enough to isolate it in a far corner of his consciousness, where it seethed and shrieked half heeded while he turned the cool control which the spaceways life had taught him to the solution of this urgent question. But even so his hand was moist and shaking on his gun-butt, and the breath rasped in his dry throat.

Why – he asked himself in a determined groping after steadiness – should the mere sight of a tree, even so fabulous a one as this, rouse that insane panic in the gazer? What peril could dwell invisibly in a tree so frightful that the living horror of it could drive a man mad with the very fact of its unseen presence? He clenched his teeth hard and stared resolutely at that terrible beauty in the clearing, fighting down the sick panic that rose in his throat as his eyes forced themselves to dwell upon the Tree.

Gradually the revulsion subsided. After a nightmare of striving he mustered the strength to force it down far enough to allow reason's entry once more. Sternly holding down that frantic terror under the surface of consciousness, he stared resolutely at the Tree. And he knew that this was Thag.

It could be nothing else, for surely two such dreadful things could not dwell in one land. It must be Thag, and he could understand now the immemorial terror in which the tree-folk held it, but he did not yet grasp in what way it threatened them physically. The inexplicable dreadfulness of it was a menace to the mind's very existence, but surely a rooted tree, however terrible to look at, could wield little actual danger.

As he reasoned, his eyes were seeking restlessly among the branches, searching for the answer to their dreadfulness. After all, this thing wore the aspect of an old pattern, and in that pattern there was nothing dreadful. The tree of life had made up the design upon that well-top in Illar through whose shadow he had entered here, and nothing in that bronze grille-work had roused terror. Then why – ? What living menace dwelt invisibly among these branches to twist them into curves of horror?

A fragment of old verse drifted through his mind as he stared in perplexity:

What immortal hand or eye
Could frame thy fearful symmetry?

And for the first time the true significance of a 'fearful symmetry' broke upon him. Truly a more than human agency must have arched these subtle curves so delicately into dreadfulness, into such an awful beauty that the very sight of it made those atavistic terrors he was so sternly holding down leap in a gibbering terror.

A tremor rippled over the Tree. Smith froze rigid, staring with startled eyes. No breath of wind had stirred through the clearing, but the Tree was moving with a slow, serpentine grace, writhing its branches leisurely in a horrible travesty of voluptuous enjoyment. And upon their tips the blood-red flowers were spreading like cobras' hoods, swelling and stretching their petals out and glowing with a hue so eye-piercingly vivid that it transcended the bounds of color and blazed forth like pure light.

But it was not toward Smith that they stirred. They were arching out from the central trunk toward the far side of the clearing. After a moment Smith tore his eyes away from the indescribably dreadful flexibility of those branches and looked to see the cause of their writhing.

Ablaze of luminous white had appeared among the trees across the clearing. The priestess had returned. He watched her pacing slowly toward the Tree, walking with a precise and delicate grace as liquidly lovely as the motion of the Tree. Her fabulous hair swung down about her in a swaying robe that rippled at every step away from the moon-white beauty of her body. Straight toward the Tree she paced, and all the blossoms glowed more vividly at her nearness, the branches stretching toward her, rippling with eagerness.

Priestess though she was, he could not believe that she was going to come within touch of that Tree the very sight of which roused such a panic instinct of revulsion in every fiber of him. But she did not swerve or slow in her advance. Walking delicately over the flowery grass, arrogantly luminous in the twilight, so that her body was the center and focus of any landscape she walked in, she neared her horribly eager god.

Now she was under the Tree, and its trunk had writhed down over her and she was lifting her arms like a girl to her lover. With a gliding slowness the flame-tipped branches slid round her. In that incredible embrace she stood immobile for a long moment, the Tree arching down with all its curling limbs, the girl straining upward, her head thrown back and the mantle of her hair swinging free of her body as she lifted her face to the quivering blossoms. The branches gathered her closer in their embrace. Now the blossoms arched near, curving down all about her, touching her very gently, twisting their blazing faces toward the focus of her moon-white body. One poised directly above her face, trembled, brushed her mouth lightly. And the Tree's tremor ran unbroken through the body of the girl it clasped.

The incredible dreadfulness of that embrace was suddenly more than Smith could bear. All his terrors, crushed down with so stern a self-control, without warning burst all bounds and rushed over him in a flood of blind revulsion. A whimper choked up in his throat and quite involuntarily he swung round and plunged into the shielding trees, hands to his eyes in a futile effort to blot out the sight of lovely horror behind him whose vividness was burnt upon his very brain.

Heedlessly he blundered through the trees, no thought in his terror-blank mind save the necessity to run, run, run until he could run no more. He had given up all attempt at reason and rationality; he no longer cared why the beauty of the Tree was so dreadful. He only knew that until all space lay between him and its symmetry he must run and run and run.

What brought that frenzied madness to an end he never knew. When sanity returned to him he was lying face down on the flower-spangled sward in a silence so deep that his ears ached with its heaviness. The grass was cool against his cheek. For a moment he fought the back-flow of knowledge into his emptied mind. When it came, the memory of that horror he had fled from, he started up with a wild thing's swiftness and glared around pale-eyed into the unchanging dusk. He was alone. Not even a rustle in the leaves spoke of the tree-folk's presence.

For a moment he stood there alert, wondering what had roused him, wondering what would come next. He was not left long in doubt. The answer was shrilling very, very faintly through that aching quiet, an infinitesimally tiny, unthinkably faraway murmur which yet pierced his eardrums with sharpness of tiny needles. Breathless, he strained in listening. Swiftly the sound grew louder. It deepened upon the silence, sharpened and shrilled until the thin blade of it was vibrating in the center of his innermost brain.

And still it grew, swelling louder and louder through the twilight world in cadences that were rounding into a queer sort of music and taking on such an unbearable sweetness that Smith pressed his hands over his ears in a futile attempt to shut the sound away. He could not. It rang in steadily deepening intensities through every fiber of his being, piercing him with thousands of tiny music-blades that quivered in his very soul with intolerable beauty. And he thought he sensed in the piercing strength of it a vibration of queer, unnamable power far mightier than anything ever generated by man, the dim echo of some cosmic dynamo's hum.

The sound grew sweeter as it strengthened, with a queer, inexplicable sweetness unlike any music he had ever heard before, rounder and fuller and more complete than any melody made up of separate notes. Stronger and stronger he felt the certainty that it was the song of some mighty power, humming and throbbing and deepening through the twilight until the whole dim land was one trembling reservoir of sound that filled his entire consciousness with its throbbing, driving out all other thoughts and realizations, until he was no more than a shell that vibrated in answer to the calling.

For it was a calling. No one could listen to that intolerable sweetness without knowing the necessity to seek its source. Remotely in the back of his mind Smith remembered the tree-folk's warning, 'When Thag calls, you must answer.' Not consciously did he recall it, for all his consciousness was answering the siren humming in the air, and, scarcely realizing that he moved, he had turned toward the source of that calling, stumbling blindly over the flowery sward with no thought in his music-brimmed mind but the need to answer that lovely, power-vibrant summoning.

Past him as he went on moved other shapes, little and dark-skinned and ecstatic, gripped like himself in the hypnotic melody. The tree-folk had forgotten even their inbred fear at Thag's calling, and walked boldly through the open twilight, lost in the wonder of the song.

Smith went on with the rest, deaf and blind to the land around him, alive to one thing only, that summons from the siren tune. Unrealizingly, he retraced the course of his frenzied flight, past the trees and bushes he had blundered through, down the slope that led to the Tree's hollow, through the thinning of the underbrush to the very edge of the last line of foliage which marked the valley's rim.

By now the calling was so unbearably intense, so intolerably sweet that somehow in its very strength it set free a part of his dazed mind as it passed the limits of audible things and soared into ecstasies which no senses bound. And though it gripped him ever closer in its magic, a sane part of his brain was waking into realization. For the first time alarm came back into his mind, and by slow degrees the world returned about him. He stared stupidly at the grass moving by under his pacing feet. He lifted a dragging head and saw that the trees no longer rose about him, that a twilit clearing stretched away on all sides toward the forest rim which circled it, that the music was singing from some source so near that – that –

The Tree! Terror leaped within him like a wild thing. The Tree, quivering with unbearable clarity in the thick, dim air, writhed above him, blossoms blazing with bloody radiance and every branch vibrant and undulant to the tune of that unholy song. Then he was aware of the lovely, luminous whiteness of the priestess swaying forward under the swaying limbs, her hair rippling back from the loveliness of her as she moved.

Choked and frenzied with unreasoning terror, he mustered every effort that was in him to turn, to run again like a madman out of that dreadful hollow, to hide himself under the weight of all space from the menace of the Tree. And all the while he fought, all the while panic drummed like mad in his brain, his relentless body plodded on straight toward the hideous loveliness of that siren singer towering above him. From the first he had felt subconsciously that it was Thag who called, and now, in the very center of that ocean of vibrant power, he knew. Gripped in the music's magic, he went on.

All over the clearing other hypnotized victims were advancing slowly, with mechanical steps and wide, frantic eyes as the tree-folk came helplessly to their god's calling. He watched a group of little, dusky sacrifices pace step by step nearer to the Tree's vibrant branches. The priestess came forward to meet them with outstretched arms. He saw her take the foremost gently by the hands. Unbelieving, hypnotized with horrified incredulity, he watched her lead the rigid little creature forward under the fabulous Tree whose limbs yearned downward like hungry snakes: the great flowers glowing with avid color.

He saw the branches twist out and lengthen toward the sacrifice, quivering with eagerness. Then with a tiger's leap they darted, and the victim was swept out of the priestess' guiding hands up into the branches that darted round like tangled snakes in a clot that hid him for an instant from view. Smith heard a high, shuddering wail ripple out from that knot of struggling branches, a dreadful cry that held such an infinity of purest horror and understanding that he could not but believe that Thag's victims in the moment of their doom must learn the secret of his horror. After that one frightful cry came silence. In an instant the limbs fell apart again from emptiness. The little savage had melted like smoke among their writhing, too quickly to have been devoured, more as if he had been snatched into another dimension in the instant the hungry limbs hid him. Flame-tipped, avid, they were dipping now toward another victim as the priestess paced serenely forward.

And still Smith's rebellious feet were carrying him on, nearer and nearer the writhing peril that towered over his head. The music shrilled like pain. Now he was so close that he could see the hungry flower-mouths in terrible detail as they faced round toward him. The limbs quivered and poised like cobras, reached out with a snakish lengthening, down inexorably toward his shuddering helplessness. The priestess was turning her calm white face toward his.

Those arcs and changing curves of the branches as they neared were sketching lines of pure horror whose meaning he still could not understand, save that they deepened in dreadfulness as he neared. For the last time that urgent wonder burned up in his mind why – *why* so simple a thing as this fabulous Tree should be infused with an indwelling terror strong enough to send his innermost soul frantic with revulsion. For the last time – because in that trembling instant as he waited for their touch, as the music brimmed up with unbearable, brain-wrenching intensity, in that one last moment before the flower-mouths seized him – he saw. He understood.

With eyes opened at last by the instant's ultimate horror, he saw the real Thag. Dimly he knew that until now the thing had been so frightful that his eyes had refused to register its existence, his brain to acknowledge the possibility of such dreadfulness. It had literally been too terrible to see, though his instinct knew the presence of infinite horror. But now, in the grip of that mad, hypnotic song, in the instant before unbearable terror enfolded him, his eyes opened to full sight, and he saw.

That Tree was only Thag's outline, sketched three-dimensionally upon the twilight. Its dreadfully curving branches had been no more than Thag's barest contours, yet even they had made his very soul sick with intuitive revulsion. But now, seeing the true horror, his mind was too numb to do more than register its presence: Thag, hovering monstrously between earth and heaven, billowing and surging up there in the translucent twilight, tethered to the ground by the Tree's bending stem and reaching ravenously after the hypnotized fodder that his calling brought helpless into his clutches. One by one he snatched them up, one by one absorbed them into the great, unseeable horror of his being. That, then, was the reason why they vanished so instantaneously, sucked into the concealing folds of a thing too dreadful for normal eyes to see.

The priestess was pacing forward. Above her the branches arched and leaned. Caught in a timeless paralysis of horror, Smith stared upward into the enormous bulk of Thag while the music hummed intolerably in his shrinking brain – Thag, the monstrous thing from darkness, called up by

Illar in those long-forgotten times when Mars was a green planet. Foolishly his brain wandered among the ramifications of what had happened so long ago that time itself had forgotten, refusing to recognize the fate that was upon himself. He knew a tingle of respect for the ages-dead wizard who had dared command a being like this to his services – this vast, blind, hovering thing, ravenous for human flesh, indistinguishable even now save in those terrible outlines that sent panic leaping through him with every motion of the Tree's fearful symmetry.

All this flashed through his dazed mind in the one blinding instant of understanding. Then the priestess' luminous whiteness swam up before his hypnotized stare. Her hands were upon him, gently guiding his mechanical footsteps, very gently leading him forward into – into—

The writhing branches struck downward, straight for his face. And in one flashing leap the moment's infinite horror galvanized him out of his paralysis. Why, he could not have said. It is not given to many men to know the ultimate essentials of all horror, concentrated into one fundamental unit. To most men it would have had that same paralyzing effect up to the very instant of destruction. But in Smith there must have been a bed-rock of subtle violence, an unyielding, inflexible vehemence upon which the structure of his whole life was reared. Few men have it. And when that ultimate intensity of terror struck the basic flint of him, reaching down through mind and soul into the deepest depths of his being, it struck a spark from that inflexible barbarian buried at the roots of him which had force enough to shock him out of his stupor.

In the instant of release his hand swept like an unloosed spring, of its own volition, straight for the butt of his power-gun. He was dragging it free as the Tree's branches snatched him from its priestess' hands. The fire-colored blossoms burned his flesh as they closed round him, the hot branches gripping like the touch of ravenous fingers. The whole Tree was hot and throbbing with a dreadful travesty of fleshly life as it whipped him aloft into the hovering bulk of incarnate horror above.

In the instantaneous upward leap of the flower-tipped limbs Smith fought like a demon to free his gun-hand from the gripping coils. For the first time Thag knew rebellion in his very clutches, and the ecstasy of that music which had dinned in Smith's ears so strongly that by now it seemed almost silence was swooping down a long arc into wrath, and the branches tightened with hot insistency, lifting the rebellious offering into Thag's monstrous, indescribable bulk.

But even as they rose, Smith was twisting in their clutch to maneuver his hand into a position from which he could blast that undulant tree trunk into nothingness. He knew intuitively the futility of firing up into Thag's imponderable mass. Thag was not of the world he knew; the flame blast might well be harmless to that mighty hoverer in the twilight. But at the Tree's root, where Thag's essential being merged from the imponderable to the material, rooting in earthly soil, he should be vulnerable if he were vulnerable at all. Struggling in the tight, hot coils, breathing the nameless essence of horror, Smith fought to free his hand.

The music that had rung so long in his ears was changing as the branches lifted him higher, losing its melody and merging by swift degrees into a hum of vast and vibrant power that deepened in intensity as the limbs drew him upward into Thag's monstrous bulk, the singing force of a thing mightier than any dynamo ever built. Blinded and dazed by the force thundering through every atom of his body, he twisted his hand in one last, convulsive effort, and fired.

He saw the flame leap in a dazzling gush straight for the trunk below. It struck. He heard the sizzle of annihilated matter. He saw the trunk quiver convulsively from the very roots and the whole fabulous Tree shook once with an ominous tremor. But before that tremor could shiver up the branches to him the hum of the living dynamo which was closing round his body shrilled up arcs of pure intensity into a thundering silence.

Then without a moment's warning the world exploded. So instantaneously did all this happen that the gun-blast's roar had not yet echoed into silence before a mightier sound than the brain could bear exploded outward from the very center of his own being. Before the awful power of it everything reeled into a shaken oblivion. He felt himself falling …

A queer, penetrating light shining upon his closed eyes roused Smith by degrees into wakefulness again. He lifted heavy lids and stared upward into the unwinking eye of Mars' racing nearer moon. He lay there blinking dazedly for a while before enough of memory returned to rouse him. Then he sat up painfully, for every fiber of him ached, and stared round on a scene of the wildest destruction. He lay in the midst of a wide, rough circle which held nothing but powdered stone. About it, rising raggedly in the moving moonlight, the blocks of time-forgotten Illar loomed.

But they were no longer piled one upon another in a rough travesty of the city they once had shaped. Some force mightier than any of man's explosives seemed to have hurled them with such violence from their beds that their very atoms had been disrupted by the force of it, crumbling them into dust. And in the very center of the havoc lay Smith, unhurt.

He stared in bewilderment about the moonlight ruins. In the silence it seemed to him that the very air still quivered in shocked vibrations. And as he stared he realized that no force save one could have wrought such destruction upon the ancient stones. Nor was there any explosive known to man which would have wrought this strange, pulverizing havoc upon the blocks of Illar. That force had hummed unbearably through the living dynamo of Thag, a force so powerful that space itself had bent to enclose it. Suddenly he realized what must have happened.

Not Illar, but Thag himself had warped the walls of space to enfold the twilit world, and nothing but Thag's living power could have held it so bent to segregate the little, terror-ridden land inviolate.

Then when the Tree's roots parted, Thag's anchorage in the material world failed and in one great gust of unthinkable energy the warped space-walls had ceased to bend. Those arches of solid space had snapped back into their original pattern, hurling the land and all its dwellers into – into – his mind balked in the effort to picture what must have happened, into what ultimate dimension those denizens must have vanished.

Only himself, enfolded deep in Thag's very essence, the intolerable power of the explosion had not touched. So when the warped space-curve ceased to be, and Thag's hold upon reality failed, he must have been dropped back out of the dissolving folds upon the spot where the Tree had stood in the space-circled world, through that vanished world-floor into the spot he had been snatched from in the instant of the dim land's dissolution. It must have happened after the terrible force of the explosion had spent itself, before Thag dared move even himself through the walls of changing energy into his own far land again.

Smith sighed and lifted a hand to his throbbing head, rising slowly to his feet. What time had elapsed he could not guess, but he must assume that the Patrol still searched for him. Wearily he set out across the circle of havoc toward the nearest shelter which Illar offered. The dust rose in ghostly, moonlit clouds under his feet.

WEREWOMAN

With the noise of battle fading behind him down the wind, Northwest Smith staggered into the west and the twilight, stumbling at he went. Blood spattered brightly behind him on the rocks, leaving a clear trail to track him by, but he knew he would not be followed far. He was headed into the salt wastelands to the westward, and they would not follow him there.

He urged his reluctant feet faster, for he knew that he must be out of sight in the gray waste before the first of the scavengers came to loot the dead. They would follow – that trail of blood and staggering footsteps would draw them like wolves on his track, hot in the hope of further spoils – but they would not come far. He grinned a little wryly at the thought, for he was going into no safety here, though he left certain death behind. He was stumbling, slow step by step, into almost as certain a death, of fever and thirst and hunger in the wastelands, if no worse death caught him first. They told tales of this gray salt desert . . .

He had never before come even this far into the cold waste during all the weeks of their encampment. He was too old an adventurer not to know that when people shun a place completely and talk of it in whispers and tell little half-finished, fearful stories of it over campfires, that place is better left alone. Some might have been spurred by that very reticence into investigation, but Northwest Smith had seen too many strange things in his checkered career to doubt the basis of fact behind folktales or care to rush in heedlessly where others had learned by experience not to tread.

The sound of battle had dwindled to a faint murmur on the evening breeze. He lifted his head painfully and stared into the gathering dark ahead with narrowed eyes the no-color of pale steel. The wind touched his keen, scarred face with a breath of utter loneliness and desolation. No man-smell of smoke or byre or farmstead tainted it, blowing clear across miles beyond miles of wastelands. Smith's nostrils quivered to that scent of unhumanity. He saw the grayness stretching before him, flat and featureless, melting into the dark. There was a sparse grass growing, and low shrub and a few stunted trees, and brackish water in deep, still pools dotted the place at far intervals. He found himself listening . . .

Once in very long-ago ages, so campfire whispers had told him, a forgotten city stood here. Who dwelt in it, or what, no man knew. It was a great city spreading over miles of land, rich and powerful enough to wake enmity, for a mighty foe had come at last out of the lowlands and in a series of tremendous battles razed it to the ground. What grievance they had against the dwellers in the city no one will ever know now, but it must have been dreadful, for when the last tower was laid to earth and the last stone toppled from its foundation they had sown the land with salt, so that for generations no living thing grew in all the miles of desolation. And not content with this, they had laid a curse upon the very earth wherein the city had its roots, so that even today men shun the place without understanding why.

It was very long past, that battle, and history forgot the very name of the city, and victor and vanquished alike sank together into the limbo of the forgotten. In time the salt-sown lands gained a measure of life again and the sparse vegetation that now clothed it struggled up through the barren soil. But men still shunned the place.

They said, in whispers, that there were dwellers yet in the salt-lands. Wolves came out by night sometimes and carried off children straying late; sometimes a new-made grave was found open and empty in the morning, and people breathed of ghouls … Late travelers had heard voices wailing from the wastes by night, and those daring hunters who ventured in search of the wild game that ran through the underbrush spoke fearfully of naked werewomen that howled in the distances. No one knew what became of the adventurous souls who traveled too far alone into the desolation of the place. It was accursed for human feet to travel, and those who dwelt there, said the legends, must be less than human.

Smith discounted much of this when he turned from the bloody shambles of that battle into the wastelands beyond. Legends grow, he knew. But a basis for the tales he did not doubt, and he glanced ruefully down at the empty holsters hanging low on his legs. He was completely unarmed, perhaps for the first time in more years than he liked to remember; for his path had run for the most part well outside the law, and such men do not go unarmed anywhere – even to bed.

Well, no help for it now. He shrugged a little, and then grimaced and caught his breath painfully, for that slash in the shoulder was deep, and blood still dripped to the ground, though not so freely as before. The wound was closing. He had lost much blood – the whole side of his leather garments was stiff with it, and the bright stain spattering behind him told of still greater losses. The pain of his shoulder stabbed at him yet, but it was being swallowed up now in a vast, heaving grayness …

He drove his feet on stubbornly over the uneven ground, though the whole dimming landscape was wavering before him like a sea – swelling monstrously – receding into vague distances … The ground floated up to meet him with surprising gentleness.

He opened his eyes presently to a gray twilight, and after a while staggered up and went on. No more blood flowed, but the shoulder was stiff and throbbing, and the wasteland heaved still like a rolling sea about him. The singing in his ears grew loud, and he was not sure whether the faint echoes of sound he heard came over gray distances or rang in his own head – long, faint howls like wolves wailing their hunger to the stars. When he fell the second time he did not know it, and was surprised to open his eyes upon full dark with stars looking down on him and the grass tickling his cheek.

He went on. There was no great need of it now – he was well beyond pursuit, but the dim urge to keep moving dinned in his weary brain. He was sure now that the long howls were coming to him over the waste stretches; coming nearer. By instinct his hand dropped to clutch futilely at the empty holster.

There were queer little voices going by overhead in the wind. Then, shrill. With immense effort he slanted a glance upward and thought he could see, with the clarity of exhaustion, the long, clean lines of the wind streaming across the sky. He saw no more than that, but the small voices shrilled thinly in his ears. Presently he was aware of motion beside him – life of some nebulous sort moving parallel to his course, invisible in the starlight. He was aware of it through the thrill of evil that prickled at the roots of his hair, pulsing from the dimness at his side – though he could see nothing. But with that clarity of inner vision he felt the vast and shadowy shape lurching, formlessly through the grass at his side. He did not turn his head again, but the hackles of his neck bristled. The howls were nearing, too. He set his teeth and drove on, unevenly.

He fell for the third time by a clump of stunted trees, and lay for a while breathing heavily while long, slow waves of oblivion washed over him and receded like waves over sand. In the intervals of lucidity he knew that those howls were coming closer and closer over the grayness of the salt-lands.

He went on. The illusion of that formless walker-in-the-dark still haunted him through the grass, but he was scarcely heeding it now. The howls had changed to short, sharp yaps, crisp in the starlight, and he knew that the wolves had struck his trail. Again, instinctively, his hand flashed downward toward his gun, and a spasm of pain crossed his face. Death he did not mind – he had kept pace with it too many years to fear that familiar visage – but death under fangs, unarmed … He staggered on a little faster, and the breath whistled through his clenched teeth.

Dark forms were circling his, slipping shadowily through the grass. They were wary, these beasts of the outlands. They did not draw near enough for him to see them save as shadows gliding among the shadows, patient and watching. He cursed them futilely with his failing breath, for he knew now that he dared not fall again. The gray waves washed upward, and he shouted something hoarse in his throat and called upon a last reservoir of strength to bear him up. The dark forms started at his voice.

So he went on, wading through oblivion that rose waist-high, shoulder-high, chin-high – and receded again before the indomitable onward drive that dared not let him rest. Something was wrong with his eyes now – the pale-steel eyes that had never failed him before – for among the dark forms he was thinking he saw white ones, slipping and gliding wraithlike in the shadow …

For an endless while he stumbled on under the chilly stars while the earth heaved gently beneath his feet and the grayness was a sea that rose and fell in blind waves, and white figures weaved about his through the hollow dark.

Quite suddenly he knew that the end of his strength had come. He knew it surely, and in the last moment of lucidity left to him he saw a low tree outlined against the stars and staggered to it – setting his broad back against the trunk, fronting the dark watchers with lowered head and pale eyes that glared defiance. For that one moment he faced them resolutely – then the tree-trunk was sliding upward past him – the ground was rising – He gripped the sparse grass with both hands, and swore as he fell.

When he opened his eyes again he stared into a face straight out of hell. A woman's face, twisted into a diabolical smile, stooped over him – glare-eyed in the dark. White fangs slavered as she bent to his throat.

Smith choked back a strangled sound that was half-oath, half-prayer, and struggled to his feet. She started back with a soundless leap that set her wild hair flying, and stood staring him in the face with wide slant eyes that glared greenly from the pallor of her face. Through the dark her body was white as a sickle moon half-veiled in the long, wild hair.

She glared with hungry fangs a-drip. Beyond her he sensed other forms, dark and white, circling restlessly through the shadows – and he began to understand dimly, and knew that there was no hope in life for him, but he spread his long legs wide and gave back glare for glare, pale-eyed and savage.

The pack circled him, dim blurs in the dark, the green glare of eyes shining alike from white shapes and black. And to his dizzied eyes it seemed that the forms were not stable; shifting from dark to light and back again with only the green-glowing eyes holding the same glare through all the changing. They were closing in now, the soft snarls rising and sharp yaps impatiently breaking through the guttural undernotes, and he saw the gleam of teeth, white under the stars.

He had no weapon, and the wasteland reeled about him and the earth heaved underfoot, but he squared his shoulders savagely and fronted them in hopeless defiance, waiting for the wave of darkness and hunger to come breaking over him in an overwhelming tide. He met the green desire of the woman's wild eyes as she stooped forward, gathering herself for the lunge, and suddenly something about the fierceness of her struck a savage chord within him, and – facing death as he was – he barked a short, wild laugh at her, and yelled into the rising wind. 'Come on, werewoman! Call your pack!'

She stared for the briefest instant, half poised for leaping – while something like a spark seemed to flash between them, savageness calling to savageness across the barriers of everything alive – and suddenly she flung up her arms, the black hair whirling, and tossed back her head and bayed to the stars; a wild, long, ululating yell that held nothing of humanity, a triumphant bay of fierce delight echoing down the wind. All about her in the dark, hoarse throats caught up the yell and tossed it from voice to voice across the salt-lands until the very stars shivered at the wild, exultant baying.

And as the long yell trembled into silence something inexplicable happened to Smith. Something quivered in answer within him, agonizingly, the gray oblivion he had been fighting so long swallowed him up at a gulp – and then he leaped within himself in a sudden, ecstatic rush; and while one part of him slumped to its knees and then to its face in the grass, the living vital being that was Smith sprang free into the cold air that stung like sharp wine.

The wolf-pack rushed clamorously about him, the wild, high yells shivering delightfully along every nerve of his suddenly awakened body. And it was as if a muffling darkness has lifted from his senses, for the night opened up in all directions to his new eyes, and his nostrils caught fresh, exciting odors on the streaming wind, and in his ears a thousand tiny sounds took on sudden new clarity and meaning.

The pack that had surged so clamorously about him was a swirl of dark bodies for an instant – then in a blur and a flash they were dark no longer – rose on hind legs and cast off the darkness as they rose – and slim, white, naked werewomen swirled around him in a tangle of flashing limbs and streaming hair.

He stood half dazed at the transition, for even the wide salt moor was no longer dark and empty, but pale gray under the stars and peopled with nebulous, unstable beings that wavered away from the white wolf-pack which ringed him, and above the clamour of wild voices that thin, shrill chattering went streaming down the wind overhead.

Out of the circling pack a white figure broke suddenly, and he felt cold arms about his neck and a cold, thin body pressing his. Then the white whirl parted violently and another figure thrust through – the fierce-eyed woman who had called him across the barriers of flesh into this half-land of her own. Her green-glaring eyes stabbed at the sister wolf whose arms twined Smith's neck, and the growl that broke from her lips was a wolf's guttural. The woman fell away from Smith's embrace, crouching at bay, as the other, with a toss of wild hair, bared her fangs and launched herself straight at the throat of the interloper. They went down in a tangle of white and tossing dark, and the pack fell still so that the only sound was the heavy breathing of the fighters and the low, choked snarls that rippled from their throats. Then over the struggle of white and black burst a sudden torrent of scarlet. Smith's nostrils flared to the odor that had a new, fascinating sweetness now – and the werewoman rose, bloody-mouthed, from the body of her rival. The green-glowing eyes met his, and a savage exultation flowing from them met as savage a delight wakening in him, and her keen, moon-white face broke into a smile of hellish joy.

She flung up her head again and bayed a long, triumphant cry to the stars, and the pack about her took up the yell, and Smith found his own face turned to the sky and his own throat shouting a fierce challenge to the dark.

Then they were running – jostling one another in savage play, flying over the coarse grass on feet that scarcely brushed the ground. It was like the rush of the wind, that effortless racing, as the earth flowed backward under their spurning feet and the wind streamed in their nostrils with a thousand tingling odors. The white werewoman raced at his side, her long hair flying behind her like a banner, her shoulder brushing his.

They ran through strange places. The trees and the grass had taken on new shapes and meanings, and in a vague, half-realized way he was aware of curious forms looming round him – buildings, towers, walls, high turrets shining in the starlight, yet so nebulous that they did not impede their flight. He could see these shadows of a city very clearly sometimes – sometimes he ran down marble streets, and it seemed to him that his feet rang in golden sandals on the pavement and rich garments whipped behind him in the wind of his speed, and a sword clanked at his side. He thought the woman beside him fled in bright-colored sandals too, and her long skirts rippled away from her flying limbs and the streaming hair was twined with jewels – yet he knew he ran naked beside a moon-bare wolf-woman over coarse grass that rustled to his tread.

And sometimes, too, it seemed to him that he fled on four legs, not two – fleetly as the wind, thrusting a pointed muzzle into the breeze and lolling a red tongue over dripping fangs …

Dim shapes fled from their sweeping onward rush – great, blurred, formless things; dark beings with eyes; thin wraiths wavering backward from their path. The great moor teemed with these half-seen monstrosities; fierce-eyed, some of them, breathing out menace, and evil, angry shapes that gave way reluctantly before the were-pack's sweep. But they gave way. There were terrible things in that wasteland, but the most terrible of all were the werewomen, and all the dreadful, unreal beings made way at the bay of those savage voices. All this he knew intuitively. Only the thin chattering that streamed down the wind did not hush when the were-voices howled.

There were many odors on the wind that night, sharp and sweet and acrid, wild odors of wild, desolate lands and the dwellers therein. And then, quite suddenly on a vagrant breeze, lashing their nostrils like a whip – the harsh, rich blood-tingling scent of man. Smith flung up his head to the cold stars and bayed long and shudderingly, and the wild wolf-yell rang from throat to throat through the pack until the whole band of them was shaking the very air to that savage chorus. They loped down the wind-stream, nostrils flaring to that full, rich scent.

Smith ran at the forefront, shoulder to shoulder with the wild white creature who had fought for him. The man-smell was sweet in his nostrils, and hunger wrenched at him as the smell grew stronger and faint atavistic stirrings of anticipation rose in his memory ... Then they saw them.

A little band of hunters was crossing the moorland, crashing through the underbrush, guns on their shoulders. Blindly they walked, stumbling over hummocks that were clear to Smith's new eyes. And all about them the vague denizens of the place were gathering unseen. Great, nebulous, cloudy shapes dogged their footsteps through the grass, lurching along formlessly. Dark things with eyes flitted by, turning a hungry glare unseen upon the hunters. White shapes wavered from their path and closed in behind. The men did not see them. They must have sensed the presence of inimical beings, for now and then one would glance over his shoulder nervously, or hitch a gun forward as if he had almost seen – then lower it sheepishly and go on.

The very sight of them fired that strange hunger in Smith's new being, and again he flung back his head and yelled fiercely the long wolf-cry toward the frosty stars. At the sound of it a ripple of alarm went through the unclean, nebulous crowd that dogged the hunters' footsteps. Eyes turned toward the approaching pack, glaring angrily from bodies as unreal as smoke. But as they drew nearer the press began to melt away, the misty shapes wavering off reluctantly into the pallor of the night before the sweep of the wolves.

They skimmed over the grass, flying feet spurning the ground, and with a rush and a shout they swooped down around the hunters, yelling their hunger. The men had huddled into a little knot, backs together and guns bristling outward as the were-pack eddied round them. Three or four men fired at random into the circling pack, the flash and sound of it sending a wavering shudder through the pale things that had drawn back to a safe distance, watching. But the wolf-women paid no heed.

Then the leader – a tall man in a white fur cap – shouted suddenly in a voice of panic terror. 'No use to fire! No use – don't you see? These aren't real wolves ...'

Smith had a fleeting realization that to human eyes they must, then, seem wolf-formed, though all about him in the pale night he saw clearly only white, naked women with flying hair circling the hunters and baying hungrily with wolf-voices as they ran.

The dark hunger was ravaging him as he paced the narrowing circle with short, nervous steps – the human bodies so near, smelling so richly of blood and flesh. Vaguely memories of that blood running sweetly eddied through his mind, and the feel of teeth meeting solidly in flesh; and beyond that a deeper hunger, inexplicably, for something he could not name. Only he felt he would never have peace again until he had sank his teeth into the throat of that man in the white fur cap; felt blood gushing over his face …

'Look!' shouted the man, pointing as his eyes met Smith's ravenous glare. 'See – the big one with white eyes, running with the she-wolf…' He fumbled for something inside his coat. 'The Devil himself – all the rest are green-eyed, but – white eyes – see?'

Something in the sound of his voice lashed that hunger in Smith to the breaking point. It was unbearable. A snarl choked up in his throat and he gathered himself to spring. The man must have seen the flare of it in the pale eyes meeting his, for he gasped, 'God in Heaven! …' and clawed desperately at his collar. And just as Smith's feet left the ground in a great, steel-muscled spring straight for that tempting throat the man ripped out what he had been groping for and the starlight caught the glint of it upraised – a silver cross dangling from a broken chain.

Something blinding exploded in Smith's innermost brain. Something compounded of thunder and lightning smote him in midair. An agonized howl ripped itself from his throat as he fell back, blinded and deafened and dazed, while his brain rocked to its foundations and long shivers of dazzling force shuddered through the air about him.

Dimly, from a great distance, he heard the agonized howls of the were-women, the shouts of men, the trample of shod feet on the ground. Behind his closed eyes he could still see that cross upheld, a blinding symbol from which streamers of forked lightning blazed away and the air crackled all around.

When the tumult had faded in his ears and the blaze died away and the shocked air shuddered into stillness again, he felt the touch of cold, gentle hands upon him and opened his eyes to the green glare of other eyes bending over him. He pushed her away and struggled to his feet, swaying a little as he stared round the plain. All the white werewoman were gone save the one at his side. The huntsmen were gone. Even the misty denizens of the place were gone. Empty in the gray dimness the wasteland stretched away. Even the thin piping overhead had fallen into shocked silence. All about them the plain lay still, shuddering a little and gathering its forces again after the ordeal.

The werewoman had trotted off a little way and was beckoning to him impatiently over her shoulder. He followed, instinctively anxious to leave the spot of the disaster. Presently they were running again, shoulder to shoulder across the grass, the plain spinning away under their flying feet. The scene of that conflict fell behind them, and strength was flowing again through Smith's light-footed body, and overhead, faintly, the thin, shrill chattering began anew.

With renewed strength the old hunger flooded again through him, compellingly. He tossed up his head to test the wind, and a little whimper of eagerness rippled from his throat. An answering whine from the running woman replied to it. She tossed back her hair and sniffed the wind, hunger flaming in her eyes. So they ran through the pale night, hunter and huntress, while dim shapes wavered from their path and the earth reeled backward under their spurning feet.

It was pleasant to run so, in perfect unison, striding effortlessly with the speed of the wind, arrogantly in the knowledge of their strength, as the dreadful dwellers of the aeon-cursed moor fled from their approach and the very air shuddering when they bayed.

Again the illusion of misty towers and walls wavered in the dimness before Smith's eyes. He seemed to run down marble-paved streets, and felt again the clank of a belted sword and the ripple of rich garments, and saw the skirts of the woman beside him moulded to her limbs as she fled along with streaming, jewel-twined hair. He thought that the buildings rising so nebulously all around were growing higher as they advanced. He caught vague glimpses of arches and columns and great domed temples, and began, somehow uneasily, to sense presences in the streets, unseen but thronging.

Then simultaneously his feet seemed to strike a yielding resistance, as if he had plunged at a stride knee-deep into heavy water, and the woman beside him threw up her arms wildly in a swirl of hair and tossed back her head and screamed hideously, humanly, despairingly – the first human sound he had heard from her lips – and stumbled to her knees on the grass that was somehow a marble pavement.

Smith bent to catch her as she fell, plunging his arms into unseen resistance as he did so. He felt it suck at her as he wrenched the limp body out of those amazing, invisible wavelets that were lapping higher and higher up his legs with incredible swiftness. He swung her up clear of them, feeling the uncontrollable terror that rippled out from her body course in unbroken wavelets through his own, so he shook with nameless panic, not understanding why. The thick tide had risen mufflingly about his thighs when he turned back the way he had come and began to fight his way out of the clinging horror he could not see, the woman a weight of terror in his arms.

It seemed to be a sort of thickness in the air, indescribable, flowing about him in deepening waves that lapped up and up as if some half-solidified jelly were swiftly and relentlessly engulfing him. Yet he could see nothing but the grass underfoot, the dim, dreamlike marble pavement, the night about, the cold stars overhead. He struggled forward, dragging his legs by main force through the invisible thickness. It was worse than trying to run through water, with the retarded motion of nightmares. It sucked at him, draggingly, as he struggled forward through the deeps of it, stumbling, not daring to fall, the woman a dead weight in his arms.

And very slowly he won free. Very slowly he forced his way out of the clinging horror. The little lapping waves of it ceased to mount. He felt the thickness receding downward, past his knees, down about his ankles, until only his feet sucked and stumbled in invisibility, the nameless mass shuddering and quaking. And at long last he broke again, and as his feet touched the clear ground he leaped forward wildly, like an arrow from a bow, into the delightful freedom of the open air. It felt like pure flying after that dreadful struggle through the unseen. Muscles exulting at the release, he fled over the grass like a winged thing while the dim buildings reeled away behind him and the woman stirred a little in his arms, an inconsidered weight in the joy of freedom.

Presently she whimpered a little, and he paused by a stunted tree to set her down again. She glanced round wildly. He saw from the look on her bone-white face that the danger was not yet past, and glanced round himself, seeing nothing but the dim moor with wraith-like figures wavering here and there and the stars shining down coldly. Overhead the thin shrilling went by changelessly in the wind. All this was familiar. Yet the were-woman stood poised for instant flight, seeming unsure in just what direction danger lay, and her eyes glared panic into the dimness. He knew then that dreadful though the were-pack was, a more terrible thing haunted the wasteland – invisibly, frightfully indeed to wake in the wolf-woman's eyes that staring horror. Then something touched his foot.

He leaped like the wild thing he was, for he knew that feel – even in so short a time he knew that feel. It was flowing round his foot, sucking at his ankle even as he poised for flight. He seized the woman's wrist and twisted round, wrenching his foot from the invisible grip, leaping forward arrow-swift into the pale darkness. He heard her catch her breath in a sobbing gasp, eloquent of terror, as she fell into stride beside him.

So they fled, invisibility ravening at their heels. He knew, somehow, that it followed. The thick, clutching waves of it were lapping faster and faster just short of his flying feet, and he strained to the utmost, skimming over the grass like something winged and terror-stricken, the sobbing breath of the woman keeping time to his stride. What he fled he could not even guess. It had no form in any image he could conjure up. Yet he felt dimly that it was nothing alien, but rather something too horribly akin to him ... and the deadly danger he did not understand spurred on his flying feet.

The plain whirled by blurrily in their speed. Dim things with eyes fluttered away in panic as they neared, clearing a terror-stricken way for the dreadful were-people who fled in such blind horror of something more dreadful yet.

For eternities they ran. Misty towers and walls fell away behind them. In his terror-dimmed mind it seemed to him in flashes that he was that other runner clad in rich garments and belted with the sword, running beside that other fleeing woman from another horror whose nature he did not know. He scarcely felt the ground underfoot. He ran blindly, knowing only that he must run and run until he dropped, that something far more dreadful than any death he could die was lapping hungrily at his heels, threatening him with an unnameable, incomprehensible horror – that he must run and run and run ...

And so, very slowly, the panic cleared. Very gradually sanity returned to him. He ran still, not daring to stop, for he knew the invisible hunger lapped yet not far behind – knew it surely without understanding how – but his mind had cleared enough for him to think, and his thoughts told curious things, half-realized things that formed images in his brain unbidden, drawn from some far source beyond his understanding. He knew, for instance, that the thing at their heels was unescapable. He knew that it would never cease its relentless pursuit, silent, invisible, remorseless, until the thick waves of it had swallowed up its quarry, and what followed that – what unimaginable horror – he somehow knew, but could not form even into thought-pictures. It was something too far outside any experience for the mind to grasp it.

The horror he felt instinctively was entirely within himself. He could see nothing pursuing him, feel nothing, hear nothing. No tremor of menace reached toward him from the following nothingness. But within him horror swelled and swelled balloon-like, a curious horror akin to something that was part of him, so it was as if he fled in terror of himself, and with no more hope of ever escaping than if indeed he fled his own shadow.

The panic had passed. He no longer ran blindly, but he knew now that he must run and run forever, hopelessly ... but his mind refused to picture the end. He thought the woman's panic had abated, too. Her breathing was evener, not the frantic gasping of that first frenzy, and he no longer felt the shaking waves of pure terror beating out from her against the ephemeral substance that was himself.

And now, as the gray landscape slid past changelessly and the thin shapes still wavered from their path and the piping went by overhead, he became conscious as he ran of a changing in the revulsion that spurred him on. There were little moments when the horror behind drew him curiously, tightening its hold on that part of his being so strangely akin to it. As a man might stare over a precipice-edge and feel the mounting urge to fling himself over, even in the face of his horror of falling, so Smith felt the strong pull of the thing that followed, if thing it might be called. Without abatement in his horror the curious desire grew to turn and face it, let it come lapping over him, steep himself in the thick invisibility – even though his whole being shuddered violently from the very thought.

Without realizing it, his pace slackened. But the woman knew, and gripped his hand fiercely, a frantic appeal rippling through him from the contact. At her touch the pull abated for a while and he ran on in an access of revulsion, very conscious of the invisibility lapping at their heels.

While the access was at its height he felt the grip of her hand loosen a little and knew that the strange tugging at something within was reaching out for her. His hand tightened over hers and he felt the little shake she gave to free herself of that blind pull.

So they fled, the strength in each bearing the other up. Behind them relentlessly the Something followed. Twice a forward lapping wave of it brushed Smith's heel. And stronger and stronger grew the blind urge within him to turn, to plunge into the heavy flow of what followed, to steep himself in invisibility until – until – He could form no picture of that ultimate, but each time he reached the point of picturing it a shudder went over him and blankness clouded his mind.

And ever within him that thing akin to the Follower strengthened and grew, a blind urge from his innermost being. It grew so strong that only the grip of the werewoman's hand held him from turning, and the plain faded from about him like a gray dream and he ran through a curving void – a void that he somehow knew was bending back upon itself so that he must eventually, if he ran on, come round behind his pursuer and overtake it, wade head-on into the thick deeps of invisibility . . . yet he dared not slacken his running, for then it would catch him from behind. So he spun in the treadmill, terror ahead, terror behind, with no choice but to run and no hope for all his running.

When he saw the plain at all it was in dim flashes, unaccountably blurred and not always at the correct angles. It tilted without reason. Once he saw a dark pool of water slanting before him like a door, and once a whole section of landscape hung mirage-like above his head. Sometimes he panted up steep inclines, sometimes he skimmed fleetly down steeper slopes – yet he knew the plain in reality lay flat and featureless from edge to edge.

And now, though he had long ago left those misty towers and walls far behind, he began to be aware that his flight had somehow twisted and they loomed once more, shadowily; overhead. With a sickening sense of futility he fled again down the dream-vague marble pavements between rows of cloudy palaces.

Through all these dizzy metamorphoses the pursuer flowed relentlessly behind, lapping at his heels when he slowed. He began to realize, very dimly, that it might have overtaken him with ease, but that he was being spurred on thus for some vast, cloudy purpose – perhaps so that he might complete the circle he was so vaguely aware of and plunge of his own effort headlong into the very thing from which he fled. But he was not fleeing now, he was being driven.

The dim shapes of buildings reeled past. The woman running at his side had become something cloudy and vague too, a panting presence flying from the same peril – into the same peril – but unreal as a dream. He felt himself unreal too, a phantom fleeing hand in hand with another phantom through the streets of a phantom city. And all reality was melting away save the unreal, invisible thing that pursued him, and only it had reality while everything else faded to shapes of nothingness. Like driven ghosts they fled.

And as reality melted about them, the shadowy city took firmer shape. In the reversal everything real became cloudy, grass and trees and pools dimming like some forgotten dream, while the unstable outlines of the towers loomed up more and more clearly in the pale dark, colors flushing them as if reviving blood ran through the stones. Now the city stood firm and actual around them, and vague trees thrust themselves mistily through unbroken masonry, shadows of grass waved over firm marble pavements. Superimposed upon the unreal, the real world seemed vague as a mirage.

It was a curious architecture that rose around them now, so old and so forgotten that the very shapes of it were fantastic to Smith's eyes. Men in silk and steel moved down the streets, wading to their greave-clad knees in shadowy grass they did not seem to see. Women, too, brushed by in mail as fine-linked and shining as gowns of silver tissue, belted with swords like the men. Their faces were set in a strained stare, and though they hurried they gave an impression of aimlessness, as if moved by some outer compulsion they did not understand.

And through the hurrying crowd, past the strange colored towers, over the grass-shadowed streets, were-woman and wolf-man fled like the shadows they had become, pale wraiths blowing through the crowds unseen, the invisible follower lapping at their feet when they faltered. That force within which had urged them to turn and meet the pursuer now commanded them irresistibly to flee – to flee toward that same ending, for they knew now that they ran toward what they fled, roundaboutly; yet dared not stop running for deadly fear of what flowed along behind.

Yet in the end they did turn. The werewoman ran now in blind submission, all the strength dissolved that at first had carried her on. She was like a ghost blowing along on a gale, unresisting, unquestioning, hopeless. But in Smith a stouter spirit dwelt. And something strong and insistent was urging him to turn – an insistence that had no relation to the other urge to wait. It may have been a very human revolt against being driven, it may have been a deeply ingrained dislike of running from anything, or of allowing death to overtake him from behind. It had been bred in him to face danger when he could not escape it, and the old urge that every fighting thing knows – even a cornered rat will turn – drove him at last to face what followed him and die resisting – not in flight. For he felt that the end must be very near now. Some instinct stronger than the force that harried them told him that.

And so, ignoring the armored crowd that eddied round them, he gripped the werewoman's wrist hard and slackened his speed, fighting against the urge that would have driven him on, choking down the panic that rose involuntarily as he waited for the thick waves to begin their surging round his feet. Presently he saw the shadow of a tree leaning through the smooth stone of a building, and instinctively he chose that misty thing he knew to be real for a bulwark to set his back against, rather than the unreal wall that looked so solid to his eyes. He braced his shoulders, holding a firm grip on the woman's wrist as she struggled and whimpered and moaned in her wolf-voice, straining to break the hold and run on. About, the mail-clad crowd hurried by heedlessly.

And very soon he felt it – the lapping wavelets touching his toes. He shuddered through all his unreal body at the feel, but he stood steady, gripping the struggling wolf-woman in a resolute hold, feeling the thick waves flowing around his feet, creeping up to his ankles, lapping higher and higher round his legs.

For a while he stood at bay, feeling terror choke up and up in his throat as the waves rose round him, scarcely heeding the woman's struggles to be free. And then a further rebellion began to stir. If die he must, let it be neither in headlong flight nor in dazed and terrified quiescence, but violently, fighting against it, taking some toll, if he could, to pay for the life he was to lose. He gasped a deep breath and plunged forward into the quaking, unseen mass that had risen almost to his waist. Behind him at arm's length the werewoman stumbled unwillingly.

He lurched forward. Very swiftly the unseen rose about him, until arms and shoulders were muffled in thickness, until the heavy invisibility brushed his chin, his closed mouth, sealed his nostrils … closed over his head.

Through the clear deeps he forged on, moving like a man in a nightmare of retarded motion. Every step was an immense effort against that flow, dragged through resisting depths of jelly-like nothingness. He had all but forgotten the woman he dragged along behind. He had wholly forgotten the colored city and the shining, armored people hurrying past. Blinded to everything but the deep-rooted instinct to keep moving, he forced his slow way onward against the flow. And indescribably he felt it begin to permeate him, seeping in slowly through the atoms of his ephemeral being. He felt it, and felt a curious change coming over him by degrees, yet could not define it or understand what was happening. Something urged him fiercely to go on, to struggle ahead, not to surrender – and so he fought, his mind whirling and the strange stuff of the thing that engulfed him soaking slowly through his being.

Presently the invisibility took on a faint body, a sort of clear opaqueness, so that the things outside were streaked and blurred a little and the splendid dream city with its steel-robed throngs wavered through the walls of what had swallowed him up. Everything was shaking and blurring and somehow changing. Even his body no longer obeyed him completely, as if it trembled on the verge of transition into something different and unknown. Only the driving instinct to fight on held clear in his dazed mind. He struggled forward.

And now the towered city was fading again, its mailed people losing their outlines and melting into the grayness. But the fading was not a reversal – the shadow-grass and trees grew more shadowy still. It was as if by successive steps he was leaving all matter behind. Reality had faded almost to nothing, even the cloudy unreality of the city was going now, and nothing but a gray blankness remained, a blankness through which he forged stubbornly against the all-engulfing flow that steeped him in nothingness.

Sometimes in flashes he ceased to exist – joined the gray nothing as part of it. The sensation was not that of unconsciousness. Somehow utter nirvana swallowed him up and freed him again, and between the moments of blank he fought on, feeling the transition of his body taking place very slowly, very surely, into something that even now he could not understand.

For gray eternities he struggled ahead through the clogging resistance, through darkness of non-existence, through flashes of near-normality, feeling somehow that the path led in wild loops and whorls through spaces without name. His time-sense had stopped. He could hear and see nothing, he could feel nothing but the immense effort of dragging his limbs through the stuff that enfolded him, and the effort was so great that he welcomed those spaces of blankness when he did not exist even as an unconsciousness. Yet stubbornly, unceasingly, the blind instinct drove him on.

There was a while when the flashes of non-existence crowded closer and closer, and the metamorphosis of his body was all but complete, and only during brief winks of consciousness did he realize himself as an independent being. Then in some unaccountable way the tension slackened. For a long moment without interludes he knew himself a real being struggling upstream through invisibility and dragging a half-fainting woman by the wrist. The clarity of it startled him. For a while he could not understand – then it dawned upon him that his head and shoulders were free – free! What had happened he could not imagine, but he was free of it.

The hideous gray nothingness had gone – he looked out over a plain dotted with low trees and low, white, columned villas like no architecture he had ever seen before. A little way ahead a stone slab no higher than himself leaned against a great boulder in a hollow fringed with trees. Upon the slab an indescribable symbol was incised. It was like no symbol of any writing he had ever seen before. It was like no symbol of any writing at all, nor traced by any human hand. Yet there was a curious familiarity about it that did not even puzzle him. He accepted it without question. He was somehow akin to it.

And between him and the engraved slab the air writhed and undulated. Streamers of invisibility flowed toward him, mounting as they flowed. He struggled forward, exultation surging within him, for – he knew, now. And as he advanced the thick resistance fell away from him, sliding down his shoulders, ebbing lower and lower about his struggling body. He knew that whatever the invisibility was, its origin lay in that symbol on the stone. From that it flowed. Half-visibly, he could see it. And toward that stone he made his way, a dim purpose forming in his brain.

He heard a little gasp and quickened breathing behind him, and turned his head to see the werewoman, moon-white in the undulating, almost-visible flow, staring about with wakened eyes and incomprehension clouding her face. He saw that she did not remember anything of what had happened. Her green-glowing eyes were empty at if they had just opened from deep slumber.

He forged on swiftly now through the waves that lapped futilely around his waist. He had won. Against what he did not yet know, nor from what cloudy terror he had saved himself and her, but he was not afraid now. He knew what he must do, and he struggled on eagerly toward the slab.

He was still waist-deep in the resisting flow when he reached it, and for a dizzy instant he thought he could not stop; that he must wade on into the very substance of that unnameable carving out of which came the engulfing nothingness. But with an effort he wrenched round and waded cross-stream, and after a while of desperate struggle he broke free into the open air.

It was like a cessation of gravity. In the release from that dragging weight he felt he must scarcely be touching the ground, but there was no time now to exult in his freedom. He turned purposefully toward the slab.

The werewoman was just floundering clear of the stream when she saw what he intended, and she flung up her hands with a shriek of protest that startled Smith into a sidewise leap, as if some new terror were coming upon him. Then he saw what it was, and gave her an amazed stare as he turned again to the stone, lifting his arms to grapple with it. She reeled forward and seized him in a cold, desperate embrace, dragging backward with all her might. Smith glared at her and shook his shoulders impatiently. He had felt the rock give a little. But when she saw that, she screamed again piercingly, and her arms twined like snakes as she struggled to drag him away.

She was very strong. He paused to unwind the fierce clasp, and she fought savagely to prevent it. He needed all his strength to break her grip, and he pushed her from him then with a heavy shove that sent her reeling. The pale eyes followed her, puzzling why, though she had fled in such a frenzy of terror from what flowed out of the stone, she still strove to prevent him from destroying it. For he was quite sure, without understanding why, that if the slab were broken and the symbol destroyed that stream would cease to flow. He could not understand her. He shook his shoulders impatiently and turned again to the stone.

This time she was on him with an animal spring, snarling low in her throat and clawing with frantic hands. Her fangs snapped just clear of his throat. Smith wrenched free with a great effort, for she was steel-strong and very desperate, and gripped her by the shoulder, swinging her away. Then he set his teeth and drove a heavy fist into her face, smashing against the fangs. She yelped, short and sharply, and collapsed under his hand, sinking to the grass in a huddle of whiteness and wild black hair.

He turned to the stone again. This time he got a firm grip on it, braced his legs wide, heaved. And he felt it give. He heaved again. And very slowly, very painfully, he uprooted its base from the bed where for ages it must have lain. Rock ground protestingly against rock. One edge rose a little, then settled. And the slab tilted. He heaved again, and very deliberately he felt it slipping from his hands. He stood back, breathing heavily, and watched.

Majestically the great slab tottered. The stream flowing invisibly from its incised symbol twisted in a streaked path through the air, long whorls of opacity blurring the landscape beyond. Smith thought he felt a stirring in the air, a shiver, as of warning. All the white villas dimly seen through the dark wavered a little before his eyes, and something hummed through the air like a thin, high wailing too sharp to be heard save as a pain to the ears. The chattering overhead quickened suddenly. All this in the slow instant while the slab tottered.

Then it fell. Deliberately slow, it leaned outward and down. It struck the ground with a rush and a splintering crash. He saw the long cracks appear miraculously upon its surface as the great, fantastic symbol broke into fragments. The opacity that had flowed outward from it writhed like a dragon in pain, flung itself high-arching into the shivering air – and ceased. In that moment of cessation the world collapsed around him. A mighty wind swooped down in a deafening roar, blurring the landscape. He thought he saw the white villas melting like dreams, and he knew the werewoman on the grass must have recovered consciousness, for he heard a wolf-yell of utter agony from behind him. Then the great wind blotted out all other things, and he was whirling through space in a dizzy flight.

In that flight understanding overtook him. In a burst of illumination he knew quite suddenly what had happened and what would happen now – realized without surprise, as if he had always known it, that the denizens of this wasteland had dwelt here under the protection of that mighty curse laid upon the land in the long-past century when the city fell. And he realized that it must have been a very powerful curse, laid down by skill and knowledge that had long since vanished even from the legends of man, for in all the ages since, this accursed moor had been safe haven for all the half-real beings that haunt mankind, akin to the evil that lay like a blanket over the moor.

And he knew that the curse had its origin in the nameless symbol which some sorcerer of forgotten times had inscribed upon the stone, a writing from some language which can have no faintest kinship with man. He knew that the force flowing out from it was a force of utter evil, spreading like a river over the whole salt waste. The stream of it lapped to and fro in changing courses over the land, and when it neared some dweller of the place, the evil that burnt for a life-force in that dweller acted as a magnet to the pure evil which was the stream. So, evil answering to evil, the two fused into one, the unfortunate dweller swallowed up into a nirvana of nonexistence in the heart of that slow-flowing stream.

It must have worked strange changes in them. That city whose shapes of shadow still haunted the place assumed reality, taking on substance and becoming more and more actual as the reality of the captive waned and melted into the power of the stream.

He thought, remembering those hurrying throngs with their strained, pale faces, that the spirits of the people who had died in the lost city must be bound tenuously to the spot of their death. He remembered that young, richly garmented warrior he had been one with in fleeting moments, running golden-sandaled through the streets of the forgotten city in a panic of terror from something too long past to be remembered – the jeweled woman in her colored sandals and rippling robes running at his side – and wondered in the space of a second what their story had been so many ages ago. He thought that curse must somehow have included the dwellers in the city, chaining them in earth-bound misery for centuries. But of this he was not sure.

Much of all this was not clear to him, and more he realized without understanding, but he knew that the instinct which guided him to turn upstream had not been a false one – that something human and alien in him had been a talisman to lead his staggering feet back toward the source of his destroyer. And he knew that with the breaking up of the symbol that was a curse, the curse ceased to be, and the warm, sweet, life-giving air that humanity breathes swept in a flood across the barrens, blowing away all the shadowy, unclean creatures to whom it had been haven for so long. He knew – he knew …

Grayness swooped round him, and all knowledge faded from his mind and the wind roared mightily in his ears. Somewhere in that roaring flight oblivion overtook him.

When he opened his eyes he could not for an instant imagine where he lay or what had happened. Weight pressed upon his entire body suffocatingly, pain shot through it as jagged flashes. His shoulder ached deeply. And the night was dark, dark about him. Something muffling and heavy had closed over his senses, for no longer could he hear the tiny, sharp sounds of the plain or scent those tingling odors that once blew along the wind. Even the chattering overhead had fallen still. The place did not even smell the same. He thought he could catch from afar the odor of smoke, and somehow the air, as nearly as he could tell with his deadened senses, no longer breathed of desolation and loneliness. The smell of life was in the wind, very faintly. Little pleasant odors of flower-scent and kitchen smoke seemed to tinge it.

'—wolves must have gone,' someone was saying above him. 'They stopped howling a few minutes ago – notice? – first time since we came into this damned place. Listen.'

With a painful effort Smith rolled his head sidewise and stared. A little group of men was gathered around him, their eyes lifted just now to the dark horizon. In the new density of the night he could not see them clearly, and he blinked in irritation, striving to regain that old, keen, clarity he had lost. But they looked familiar. One wore a white fur cap on his head. Someone said, indicating something beyond Smith's limited range of vision,

'Fellow here must have had quite a tussle. See the dead she-wolf with her throat torn out? And look – all the wolf-tracks everywhere in the dust. Hundreds of them. I wonder …'

'Bad luck to talk about them,' broke in the fur-capped leader. 'Werewolves, I tell you – I've been in this place before, and I know. But I never saw or heard tell of a thing like what we saw tonight – that big white-eyed one running with the she-wolves. God! I'll never forget those eyes.'

Smith moved his head and groaned. The men turned quickly.

'Look, he's coming to,' said someone, and Smith was vaguely conscious of an arm under his head and some liquid, hot and strong, forced between his lips. He opened his eyes and looked up. The fur-capped man was bending over him. Their eyes met. In the starlight Smith's were colorless as pale steel.

The man choked something inarticulate and leaped back so suddenly that the flask spilled its contents half over Smith's chest. He crossed himself frankly with a hand that shook.

'Who – who are you?' he demanded unsteadily.

Smith grinned wearily and closed his eyes.

SONG IN A MINOR KEY

Beneath him the clovered hill-slope was warm in the sun. Northwest Smith moved his shoulders against the earth and closed his eyes, breathing so deeply that the gun holstered upon his chest drew tight against its strap as he drank the fragrance of Earth and clover warm in the sun. Here in the hollow of the hills, willow-shaded, pillowed upon clover and the lap of Earth, he let his breath run out in a long sigh and drew one palm across the grass in a caress like a lover's.

He had been promising himself this moment for how long – how many months and years on alien worlds? He would not think of it now. He would not remember the dark spaceways or the red slag of Martian drylands or the pearlgray days on Venus when he had dreamed of the Earth that had outlawed him. So he lay, with his eyes closed and the sunlight drenching him through, no sound in his ears but the passage of a breeze through the grass and a creaking of some insect near by – the violent, blood-smelling years behind him might never have been. Except for the gun pressed into his ribs between his chest and the clovered earth, he might be a boy again, years upon years ago, long before he had broken his first law or killed his first man.

No one else alive now knew who that boy had been. Not even the all-knowing Patrol. Not even Venusian Yarol, who had been his closest friend for so many riotous years. No one would ever know – now. Not his name (which had not always been Smith) or his native land or the home that had bred him, or the first violent deed that had sent him down the devious paths which led here – here to the clover hollow in the hills of an Earth that had forbidden him ever to set foot again upon her soil.

He unclasped the hands behind his head and rolled over to lay a scarred cheek on his arm, smiling to himself. Well, here was Earth beneath him. No longer a green star high in alien skies, but warm soil, new clover so near his face he could see all the little stems and trefoil leaves, moist earth granular at their roots. An ant ran by with waving antennae close beside his cheek. He closed his eyes and drew another deep breath. Better not even look; better to lie here like an animal, absorbing the sun and the feel of Earth blindly, wordlessly.

Now he was not Northwest Smith, scarred outlaw of the spaceways. Now he was a boy again with all his life before him. There would be a white-columned house just over the hill, with shaded porches and white curtains blowing in the breeze and the sound of sweet, familiar voices indoors. There would be a girl with hair like poured honey hesitating just inside the door, lifting her eyes to him. Tears in the eyes. He lay very still, remembering.

Curious how vividly it all came back, though the house had been ashes for nearly twenty years, and the girl – the girl …

He rolled over violently, opening his eyes. No use remembering her. There had been that fatal flaw in him from the very first, he knew now. If he were the boy again knowing all he knew today, still the flaw would be there and sooner or later the same thing must have happened that had happened twenty years ago. He had been born for a wilder age, when men took what they wanted and held what they could without respect for law. Obedience was not in him, and so—

As vividly as on that day it happened he felt the same old surge of anger and despair twenty years old now, felt the ray-gun bucking hard against his unaccustomed fist, heard the hiss of its deadly charge ravening into a face he hated. He could not be sorry, even now, for that first man he had killed. But in the smoke of that killing had gone up the columned house and the future he might have had, the boy himself – lost as Atlantis now – and the girl with the honey-colored hair and much, much else besides. It had to happen, he knew. He being the boy he was, it had to happen. Even if he could go back and start all over, the tale would be the same.

And it was all long past now, anyhow; and nobody remembered any more at all, except himself. A man would be a fool to lie here thinking about it any longer.

Smith grunted and sat up, shrugging the gun into place against his ribs.

Acknowledgements

JUDGMENT NIGHT: A SELECTION OF SCIENCE FICTION

JUDGMENT NIGHT

Here in the flickering darkness of the temple, a questioner stood silent before the Ancients, waiting an answer he knew he could not trust.

Outside were the soft green hills and the misty skies of Ericon, but not even a breath of that sweet rainy air blew through the portals of the House of the Ancients. Nothing temporal ever touched them now. They were beyond all time and change. They had lived here since the first silver ships came swarming through the Galaxy; they would never die.

From this world of Ericon the pulse of empire beat out through interstellar space, tides waxing and ebbing and breaking in distant thunder upon the shores of the planets. For the race that held Ericon held the Galaxy.

Kings and emperors beyond counting had stood as this questioner stood now, silent before the Ancients in their star-shot dark. And the questioners were always answered – but only the Ancients knew if the answer meant its hearer's doom.

For the Ancients were stern in their own strange code. No human minds could fathom it. No human ever knew if his race had met their rigid tests and passed them, or if the oracle he received was a mercy-blow that led by the quickest road to destruction.

Voiceless, unseen behind their high altar, the Ancients answered a question now. And small in the tremendous shaking darkness of the temple, he who had come to satisfy a doubt stood listening.

'Let them fight,' the unspeaking oracle said. 'Be patient a little longer. Your hour is almost here. They must have their chance in the final conflict that is nearly upon them now – but you know how blind they are. Be patient. Be silent. Watch all they say and do, but keep your secret—'

The hundred emperors of Ericon looked down gravely out of their hundred pasts upon Juille, striding with a ring of spurs through the colored twilight of their sanctum.

'If I were a man,' said Juille, not turning her head, 'maybe you'd listen to me.'

No answer.

'You used to want a son,' reminded Juille, and heard her own voice echo and re-echo high up among the arches where sunlight came pouring through plastics the color of jewels.

'I know, I know,' the old emperor said from the platform behind her. 'When I was your age, I was a fool, too.'

Juille flashed him a sudden grin over her shoulder. Once in a while even now, she thought, you could catch a glimpse of the great and terrible man her father had once been.

Out of their crystal-walled niches his predecessors and hers looked down as she strode past them. Here were men who had conquered the Galaxy world by reluctant world, great warriors who had led their armies like devouring flame over alien planets and alien seas and the passionless seas of space. Here were emperors who knew the dangerous ways of peace and politics, who had watched civilization mount tier upon shining tier throughout the Galaxy.

She turned at the end and came back slowly along the rows of later rulers, to whom peace and the Galaxy and a rich heritage of luxury had been an old story. Pride of race was strong upon all these faces. People on outworld planets had worshiped them as gods. All of them had been godlike in the scope of their tremendous powers, and the knowledge of it was vivid upon their faces. Not many men have looked up by night with a whole planet for a throne, to watch the stars that are their empire parading in slow review across the heavens. Such knowledge would give even a weak face an appalling pride and dignity, and none of the emperors of Ericon had been weak. Men like that would not live very long upon the throne of the Galaxy of Lyonese.

The last three faces in the row had known humiliation almost as vast in its scope as the great scope of their pride. For now there were rebellious stars in the nightly array across the sky. And that fierce trouble showed in the eyes and the grimly lined faces of the emperors who had been defied.

The last portrait of all was the portrait of Juille's father.

She stood in silence, looking up at the young emperor in the niche, and the old emperor, arms folded on the platform rail, leaned and looked down across a gulf of many years and much hard-won experience, into the face of a stranger.

'Yes,' the emperor said gravely, 'I was a fool too, then.'

'It was a fool's work to let them live,' Juille told him hotly. 'You were a great warrior in those days, father. Maybe the greatest the Galaxy ever had. I wish I'd known you then. But you weren't great enough. It takes a great man to be ruthless.'

The emperor looked at her under the shadow of his brows. 'I had a hard problem then,' he said, '—the same problm you're facing now. If I'd chosen the solution you're choosing, you probably wouldn't be here today. As a matter of fact, you might be sitting in a cave somewhere, gnawing a half-cooked bone.'

Juille gave him a bright violet glare. 'I'd have wiped them out,' she declared furiously, 'if it meant the end of the empire. I'd have killed every creature with a drop of H'vani blood, and razed every building on every world they had, and sown the rocks with radium! I'd have left their whole dead system hanging in the sky as a warning for all time to come. I'll do it yet – by the Hundred Emperors, I will!'

'The Ancients permitting, maybe you will, child.' The old emperor stared down into his own young face in the niche. 'And maybe you won't. The time may come when you're old enough to realize what warfare on that scale would mean, even to the victors. And there'd be no victors after a fight like that.'

'But father, we'll have to fight. Any day – any hour—'

'Not yet awhile, I think. The balance is still too even. They have the outer fringes with all their resources, but we … well, we have Ericon and that counts for a lot. More than the men and machines we have. More than all the loyal worlds. Nobody knows how many dynasties there were before ours, but everyone knows that the race on Ericon rules the Galaxy.'

'As long as they hold Ericon. But sooner or later the balance is going to tip and they'll attack us. We'll have to fight.'

'We'll have to compromise.'

'We could cut our throats and be done with it.'

'That's what I'm trying to prevent. How much of civilization do you think would survive any such holocaust as that? It would mean our ruin even if we won. Come up here, child.'

Juille gave him a searching, sidewise glance and then turned slowly, hooking her thumbs into her sword belt, and mounted the shallow steps to the dais. Here in orderly array were the worlds of her father's empire, stretching in a long row left and right along the platform. She watched a little sulkily as the emperor laid a possessive hand upon the great green globe of Ericon in the center of the row and set it whirling beneath his fingers. The jewels that marked its cities flashed and blurred.

'This is the empire, Juille,' he said. 'This one world. And the empire means a great deal more than – well, a row of conquered planets. It means mercy and justice and peace.' He shook his head unhappily. 'I can't administer all that any more to every world in the Galaxy. But I won't throw the loyal worlds after the ones we've lost if any word of mine can prevent it.' He let his hand fall from the spinning globe. Its turning slowed, and the jeweled cities flashed and faded and twinkled over the curved surface. 'After all,' the old man said, 'isn't peace as we've known it worth—'

'No,' said Juille flatly. Her father looked at her in heavy silence. 'I can do *that* to Ericon,' she told him, and with a slap of her hand set the big globe spinning again, until all the glittering cities blurred upon its sides. 'As long as I can, the empire is ours. I won't share it with those hairy savages!'

The emperor was silent, looking at her from under his brows.

After a slightly uncomfortable pause, the girl turned away.

'I'm leaving,' she said briefly.

'Where?'

'Off-world.'

'Juille—'

'Nothing rash, father, I promise. I'll be back in time for the council. And I'll have a majority vote, too. You'll see the worlds agree with me.' Her voice softened. 'We've got to fight, father. Everyone says so but you. Nothing anyone can do will prevent it now.'

Looking down, her father saw on the girl's face a look he knew very well – the terrible pride of a human who has tasted the attributes of divinity, who rules the turning worlds and the very stars in their courses. He knew she would not relent. He knew she could not. There were dark days ahead that he could not alter.

And he wondered with sudden self-doubt if after all, in her frightening certainty, she might be right.

Juille strode down the hallway that led to her living quarters, her spurs ringing with faint rhythmic music and the scabbard of her fire sword slapping against her thigh.

There had been many tremendous changes in the Lyonese culture even in her own lifetime, but perhaps none greater than the one which made it possible for her to take the part a son might have taken, had the emperor produced a son. Women for the past several generations had been turning more and more to men's professions, but Juille did not think of herself as filling a prince's shoes, playing a substitute role because no man of the proper heritage was available. In her the cool, unswerving principles of the amazon had fallen upon fertile ground, and she knew herself better fitted and better trained for the part she played than any man was likely to be.

Juille had earned her military dress as a man might have earned it, through lifelong training in warfare. To her mind, indeed, a woman was much more suited to uniform than a man, so easily can she throw off all hampering civilian ideas once she gives her full loyalty to a cause. She can discard virtues as well as vices and live faithfully by a new set of laws in which ruthless devotion to duty leads all the rest.

For those women who still clung to the old standards, Juille felt a sort of tolerant contempt. But they made her uneasy, too. They lived their own lives, full of subtle nuances she had never let herself recognize until lately. Particularly, their relationship with men. More and more often of late, she had been wondering about certain aspects of life that her training had made her miss. The sureness and the subtlety with which other women behaved in matters not associated with war or politics both annoyed and fascinated Juille. She was, after all, a woman, and the uniform can be discarded as well as donned. Whether the state of mind can be discarded, too – what lay beneath that – was a matter that had been goading her for a long while. And now it had goaded her to action.

In her own rooms she gave an abstracted glance to the several women who hurried forward at her entrance, said briefly, 'Out. And send me Helia,' and then leaned to the mirror and stood there peering with solemn intentness at her own face under the shining helmet. It was a sexless face, arrogant and intolerant, handsome as her fluted helmet was handsome, with the same delicately fine details and well-turned curves. The face and the helmet belonged together.

She saw a figure move shadowily in the doorway reflected beyond her shoulder, and said without moving, 'Helia – how will I look in dresses? Would you say I'm pretty?'

'You certainly aren't ugly, highness,' Helia told her gruffly. It was as much of a compliment as she had ever extracted from the amazon ex-warrior who had been Juille's childhood nurse and girlhood tutor in the arts of war. She had a seamed face, scarred from combat in the revolution zones, and the twinkling narrow eyes of a race so old that Juille's by comparison seemed to lack a history. Helia was an Andarean. The tide of conquest had swept over the Galaxy and ebbed again since the day of Helia's race and its forgotten glory. Perhaps somewhere under the foundations of the Lyonese cities today lay rubble-filled courses the Andareans had once built upon the ruins of cities yet older. No one remembered now, except perhaps the Ancients.

Juille sighed.

'I'll never find out from you,' she said.

'You'll get an answer on Cyrille, highness, and you may not like it.'

Juille squared her shoulders. 'I hope you've kept your mouth shut about all this. Is the ship ready?'

'It is. And I haven't told a soul. But what your father would say, highness, if he knew you were going to a notorious resort like Cyrille—'

'Perfectly respectable people go there, and you know it. Anyhow, I'm going incognito. And if I hear another word about it I'll have you whipped.'

Helia's lipless mouth compressed in disapproval.

'Incognitos don't always work, highness. You should know how secrets leak out around a palace.' She caught a dangerous violet glance and subsided, muttering. She knew that stubborn look upon Juille's fine, hard features. But she knew the dangers upon Cyrille, too. She said, 'You're taking me with you, I hope?'

'One more word and I won't,' Juille warned her. 'One more word!' She straightened from the mirror, after one last curiously appraising glance. 'Come along, if you want to. I'm leaving.'

At the door a small, smoothly furred creature rippled past Juille's ankles with an ingratiating murmur and looked up out of enormous eyes. Juille stooped to let it climb upon her shoulder, where it sat balancing easily and staring about it with the grave animal dignity and the look of completely spurious benignity and wisdom that distinguishes all *llar.* Very few on Ericon own such pets. They were perhaps the true aborigines of Ericon themselves, for they had lived here, and upon no other world, from time immemorial, reserved little creatures of fastidious habits and touchy, aloof ways.

'I'll take both of you,' Juille said. 'And I expect you'll be just about equally in the way. Come on.'

Their ship spiraled up through the rainy gray air of Ericon, leaving the green mountains farther and farther below with each wide circle, until the surface of the planet looked like undulating green fur, soft with Ericon's eternal summer. Presently they were above the high clouds, and rain ceased to beat softly against the glass.

The little ship was riding a strictly prescribed course. The sternest of the Ancients' few restrictions upon human life on Ericon was the restriction on air traffic. All passage was forbidden over the great forests in which the living gods dwelt. The Galaxy's vast space liners had of their own weight to establish an orbit and transact all direct business through tenders, but tenders and private ships plying Ericon's forbidden airways complied with rigid rules about height and course. Because of them, Ericon was a world of surface traffic except in the rarest instances.

Juille sent her vessel flying along an invisible airway of strict boundaries. Presently they overtook twilight and plunged into the evening air that was darkening over the night side of the world. A great luminous bubble floated in the dark ahead, too large for a star, too small for a moon, rolling along its course around Ericon. Helia scowled at it.

This little pleasure world swinging opalescent upon its orbit housed the tangible distillation of all pleasure which a hundred emperors had made possible in the Galaxy. No human desire, however fantastic, went unfulfilled upon Cyrille so long as the client paid for his fantasy. It is an unhappy commentary upon human desires that the reputation of such a place must inevitably be bad.

Juille's ship hovered up below the shining curve of the bubble and a dark square opened in the curve. Then luxury reached out in the form of a tractor beam to take all navigation out of her hands. They rose with smooth speed through a shaft of darkness.

Because privacy and anonymity were prerequisites of many patrons here, they saw no one and were seen by none. The ship came to a velvety stop; Juille opened its door and stepped out straight into a cubicle of a room whose walls glowed in a rosy bath of indirect sunlight. Low couches made a deeply upholstered ledge all around the room. There was a luminous panel beside a closed door. Otherwise – nothing.

Helia climbed out disapprovingly. 'I hope you know what you're doing, highness,' she said. For answer,

Juille stepped to the luminous panel and let her shadow fall across it. Instantly a voice of inhuman sweetness said dulcetly:

'Your pleasure?'

'I will have,' Juille said in a musing tone, 'a lounge with sunlight and an ocean view – no particular planet – and a bedroom that – Oh, something restful and ingenious. Use your own ideas on that. A water bath with the emphasis on coolness and refreshment. Now let me see the public rooms for today.'

'Immediately,' the dulcet voice cooed. 'The suite will be ready in five minutes. Refreshment?'

'No food yet. What have you?'

A breath as soft and cool as a mountain breeze at dawn sighed instantly through the room. It smelled faintly of pine. Gravity lessened almost imperceptibly underfoot, so that they seemed to be blowing with the breeze, though they did not move.

'Very nice,' Juille told the panel. 'Now, the public rooms?'

'The central hall will be a spring twilight on Egillir for the next twelve hours,' the inhuman voice announced, and in the panel, in miniature, appeared a vast sphere of a room, the inside of a luminous bubble whose walls were the green translucence of an evening in spring, just dim enough to cloud the vision. Up through the center of the bubble sprang an enormous tree, its great trunk gnarled and twisted. Around the trunk wound a crystal staircase entwined with flowers. Men and women moved leisurely up and down the steps around the vast trunk.

Spraying out exquisitely through the hollow of the sphere were the tree's branches, feathery with leaves of pastel confetti. And floating here and there through the green twilight of the bubble, or nested among the limbs, or drifting idly about through the flowers and the leaves of the vast tree, were crystal platforms upon which diners sat embowered in little arbors of confetti leaves like the tree's.

A soft breeze blew delicately through the twilight, stirring the leaves, and the softest possible music swelled and sank upon the air.

'There is also,' the disembodied voice went on as the vision faded, 'dancing upon the royal lake of the Dullai satellite—' And in the panel Juille saw couples gliding to stronger music across what appeared to be the mirror-smooth waters of a lake that reflected a moving array of stars. She recognized the lake and the lighted tiers of a city around it, which she had visited on a political mission once several years ago, on a world far away across the Galaxy. The panel blurred again.

'We have also,' continued the sugary voice, 'several interesting variations of motion available for public use just now. A new swimming medium—' Pause. 'An adaptation of musical riding—' Pause. 'A concert in color and motion which is highly recommended as—'

'Never mind just now,' Juille interrupted. 'Send me your best dresser, and let me have some of the Dullai mountain music. I'll try your flower scents, too – something delicate. Keep it just subsensual. I don't want to be conscious of the separate odors.'

Helia gave her mistress a piercing look as the panel went blank. Juille laughed.

'I did it well, didn't I? For one who never visited the place before, anyhow. I've been reading everything I could find about it for a month. There – nice music, isn't it?'

The distinctive plaintive vibration of Dullai music sheets began to shiver softly through the room. On a world far away in space, from a period three generations ago, the sad, wailing echoes rang. No living musicians could play the flexible metal sheets now, but upon Cyrille all things were available, at a price.

'The rooms seem to be ready, highness,' Helia remarked dryly.

Juille turned. A broad doorway had opened in the wall, and beyond it was a long, low room through which sunlight poured softly. The floor gave underfoot, firm and resilient. Furniture held out upholstered arms in invitation to its series of upholstered laps. Beyond a row of circular windows which filled one wall an ocean of incredible greenness broke in foam upon colored rocks.

The bedroom was a limbo of dim, mysterious blue twilight beyond a circular doorway veiled in what looked like floating gauze. When Juille stepped through she found it was a sort of captive fog instead, offering no resistance to the touch.

The nameless designers of Cyrille had outdone themselves upon the bedroom. For one thing, it appeared to have no floor. A film of very faintly dim-blue sparkles overlying a black void seemed to be all that upheld the tread. A bed like a cloud confined in ebony palings floated apparently clear of the nonexistent floor. Overhead in a night sky other clouds moved slowly and soporifically over the faces of dim stars. A few exquisitely soft and firm chairs and a chaise longue or two had a curious tendency to drift slowly about the room unless captured and sat upon.

There was a fog-veiled alcove that glittered with mirrors, and beyond it a bathroom through which a fountain of perfumed water played musically and continuously.

Helia's astringent expression was eloquent of distaste as she followed her mistress through the rooms. The pet *llar*, clinging to her shoulder, turned wide eyes about the apartment and murmured now and then in meaningless whispered syllables.

'Just what are your plans, highness?' Helia demanded when they had finished the tour. Juille glanced at her crossly.

'Very simple. I'm going to spend a few days enjoying myself. Is there anything wrong with that? I'll have some new clothes and visit the public rooms and see what it's like to be an ordinary woman meeting ordinary people.'

'If you were an ordinary woman, there might still be something very wrong with it, highness. But you aren't. You have enemies—'

'No one knows I'm here. And don't look so grim. I didn't come to experiment with exotic drugs! Besides, I can take care of myself. And it's none of your business, anyhow.'

'Everything you do is my business, highness,' Helia said gruffly. 'I have no other.'

Elsewhere in Cyrille a young man in a startling cloak sat at breakfast beside broad windows that opened upon a fairyland of falling snow. The hushed, whispering rush of it sounded through opened casements, and now and then a breath of chilly wind blew like a stimulant through the warm room. The young man was rubbing the curls of the short, yellow beard that just clouded the outlines of his jaw, and grinning rather maliciously at his companion.

'I work too hard,' he said. 'It may be Juille of Ericon, and again, it may not. All the same, I'm going to have my vacation.'

'It's time to stop playing, Egide,' said the man across the table. He had a tremendous voice, so deep and strong that it boomed through the hush of the falling snow and the glasses vibrated on the table to its pitch. It was a voice that seemed always held in check; if he were to let it out to full volume the walls might come down, shaken to ruins by those deep vibrations.

The man matched his voice. He wore plain mail forged to turn a fire-sword's flame, and his hair and his short beard, his brows and the angry eyes beneath were all a ruddy bright color on the very verge of red. Red hair grew like a heat haze over the rolling interlace of muscles along his heavy forearms folded upon the table, and like a heat haze vitality seemed to radiate from his bull bulk and blaze from his scarred, belligerent face.

'I didn't ... acquire ... you to be my conscience, Jair,' the young man said coldly. He hesitated a little over the verb. Then, 'Oh, well – maybe I did.' He pushed back his chair and stood up, the outrageous cloak swirling about him. 'I don't really like this job.'

'You don't?' The big red man sounded puzzled. Egide gave him an odd glance.

'Stop worrying about it. I'll go. What will she be like? Hatchet face, nose like a sword – will I have to kiss her feet?'

Jair said seriously, 'No, she's incognito.' The glasses rang again to the depth in his voice.

Egide paused before the mirror, admiring the sweep of cloak from his fine breadth of shoulder. Alone he would have seemed a big man himself; beside Jair he looked like a stripling. But no one, seeing them together here, could fail to sense a coldness and a curious lack of assurance behind all Jair's dominant, deep-voiced masculinity. He watched Egide with expressionless eyes.

The younger man hunched his shoulders together. '*Br-r-r!* What a man will go through to change the fate of the Galaxy. Well, if I live through it I'll be back. Wait for me.'

'Will you kill her?'

'If I can.'

'It must be done. Would you rather I did, later?'

Egide gave him a dispassionate glance. For a moment he said nothing. Then—

'No ... no, she doesn't deserve that. We'll see what she's like. Unless it's very bad, I'll spare her that and kill her myself – gently.'

He turned to the door, his amazing cloak swinging wide behind him. Jair sat perfectly motionless, watching him go.

Helia said, 'This will be the dresser.' A sustained musical note from the entry preceded the amplified sweetness of the familiar inhuman voice, and Juille turned to the door with considerable interest to see what came next.

The best dress designer upon Cyrille seemed to be a soft-voiced, willowy woman with the pink skin and narrow, bright eyes of a race that occupied three planets circling a sun far across the outskirts of the Galaxy. She exuded impersonal deftness. One felt that she saw no faces here, was aware of no personalities. She came into the room with smooth, silent aloofness, her eyes lowered.

But she was not servile. In her own way the woman was a great artist, and commanded her due of respect.

The composition of the new gown took place before the mirrored alcove that opened from the bedroom. Helia, her jaw set like a rock, stripped off the smart military uniform which her mistress was wearing, the spurred boots, the weapons, the shining helmet. From beneath it a shower of dark-gold hair descended. Juille stood impassive under the measuring eyes of the newcomer, her hair clouding upon her shoulders.

Now she was no longer the sexless princeling of Lyonese. The steely delicacy was about her still, and the arrogance. But the long, fine limbs and the disciplined curves of her body had a look of waxen lifelessness as she stood waiting between the new personality and the old. She was aware of a certain embarrassed resentment, suddenly, at the step she was about to take. It was humiliating to admit by that very step that the despised femininity she had repudiated all her life should be important enough to capture now.

The quality of impassivity seemed to puzzle the artist, who stood looking at her thoughtfully.

'Is there any definite effect to be achieved?' she asked after a moment, speaking in the faintly awkward third person through which all employees upon Cyrille address all patrons.

Juille swallowed a desire to answer angrily that there was not. Her state of mind confused even herself. This was her first excursion into incognito, her first conscious attempt to be – not feminine; she disdained that term. She had embraced the amazon cult too wholeheartedly to admit even to herself just what she wanted or hoped from this experience. She could not answer the dresser's questions. She turned a smoothly muscular shoulder to the woman and said with resentfulness she tried to conceal even from herself:

'Nothing … nothing. Use your own ingenuity.'

The dresser mentally shot a keen glance upward. She was far too well-trained actually to look a patron in the face, but she had seen the uniform this one had discarded, she saw the hard, smooth symmetry of her body and from it understood enough of the unknown's background to guess what she wanted and would not request. She would not have worked her way up a long and difficult career from an outlying planet to the position of head designer on Cyrille if she had lacked extremely sensitive perception. She narrowed her already narrow eyes and pursed speculative lips. This patron would need careful handling to persuade her to accept what she really wanted.

'A thought came to me yesterday,' she murmured in her soft, drawling voice – she cultivated the slurred accent of her native land – 'while I watched the dancers on the Dullai Lake. A dark gown, full of shadows and stars. I need a perfect body to compose it on, for even the elastic paint of undergarments might spoil my effect.' This was not strictly true, but it served the purpose. Juille could accept the gown now not as romance personified, but as a tribute to her own fine body.

'With permission, I shall compose that gown,' the soft voice drawled, and Juille nodded coldly.

The dresser laid both hands on a section of wall near the alcove and slid back a long panel to disclose her working apparatus. Juille stared in frank enchantment and even Helia's feminine instincts, smothered behind a military lifetime, made her eyes gleam as she looked. The dresser's equipment had evidently been moved into place behind the sliding panel just before her entrance, for the tall rack at one end of the opening still presented what must have been the color-section of the last patron. Through a series of level slits the ends of almost countless fabrics in every conceivable shade of pink showed untidily. Shelves and drawers spilled more untidiness. Obviously this artist was great enough to indulge her whims even at the expense of neatness.

She pressed a button now and the pink rainbow slid sidewise and vanished. Into its place snapped a panel exuding ends of blackness in level parallels – satin that gleamed like dark water, the black smoke of gauzes, velvet so soft it looked charred, like black ash.

The dresser moved so swiftly and deftly that her work looked like child's play, or magic. She chose an end of dull silk and reeled out yard after billowing yard through the slot, slashed it off recklessly with a razor-sharp blade, and like a sculptor modeling in clay, molded the soft, thick stuff directly upon Juille's body, fitting it with quick, nervous snips of her scissors and sealing the edges into one another. In less than a minute Juille was sheathed from shoulder to ankle in a gown that fitted perfectly and elastically as her skin, outlining every curve of her body and falling in soft, rich folds about her feet.

The dresser kicked away the fragments of discarded silk and was pulling out now such clouds and billows of pure shadow as seemed to engulf her in fog. Juille almost gasped as the cloud descended upon herself. It was something too sheer for cloth, certainly not a woven fabric. The dresser's deft hands touched lightly here and there, sealing the folds of cloud in place. In a moment or two she stepped back and gestured toward the mirror.

Juille turned. This tall unknown was certainly not herself. The hard, impersonal, perfect body had suddenly taken on soft, velvety curves beneath the thick soft fabric. All about her, floating out when she moved, the shadowy billows of dimness smoked away in drapery so adroitly composed that it seemed an arrogance in itself.

'And now, one thing more,' smiled the dresser, pulling open an untidy drawer. 'This—' She brought out a double handful of sequins like flashing silver dust and strewed them lavishly in the folds of floating gauze. 'Turn,' she said, and Juille was enchanted to see the tiny star points cling magnetically to the cloth except for a thin, fine film of them that floated out behind her and twinkled away to nothing in midair whenever she moved.

Juille turned back to the mirror. For a moment more this was a stranger whose face looked back at her out of shining violet eyes, a face with the strength and delicacy of something finely made of steel. It was arrogant, intolerant, handsome as before, but the arrogance seemed to spring now from the knowledge of beauty.

And then she knew herself in the mirror. Only the gown was strange, and her familiar features looked incongruous above it. For the first time in her life Juille felt supremely unsure of herself. Not even the knowledge that the very stars in the Galaxy were subject to her whim could help that feeling now. She drew a long breath and faced herself in the glass resolutely.

The tiny elevator's door slid back and Juille stepped out alone upon a curve of the crystal stairs which wound upward around that enormous tree trunk in the central room. For a moment she stood still, clutching at the old arrogance to sustain her here in this green spring twilight through which perfume and music and soft breezes blew in twisting currents. In that moment all her unsureness came back with a rush – she had no business here in these despised feminine garments; she belonged in helmet and uniform. If she walked, she would stride as if in boots and rip these delicate skirts. Everyone would look up presently and recognize her standing here, the warrior leader of the Lyonese masquerading like a fool.

But no one seemed to be looking at all, and that in itself was a humiliation. Perhaps it was true that she was not really pretty. That she did not belong in soft silken gowns. That no man would ever look at her except as a warrior and an heiress.

Juille squared her shoulders under the cloud of mist and turned toward her waiter, who had snapped the switch of a cylinder fastened to the back of his wrist and focused the invisible beam of it upon an empty floating platform across the great hollow. It drifted toward them slowly, circling on repellor rays around intervening objects. Then it was brushing through the leaves of a mighty bough above them, and Juille took the waiter's arm and stepped out over green twilit space into the tiny leafy arbor of the platform. She had expected it to tilt a little underfoot, but it held as steady as if based upon a rock.

She sank into the elastic firmness of a crystal chair, leaned both elbows upon the crystal table and moodily ordered a strong and treacherous drink. It came almost instantly, sealed in an apricot tinted sphere of glass on a slender pedestal, a glass drinking tube rising in a curve from the upper surface. The whole sphere was lightly silvered with frost.

'Shove me off,' she told the waiter, and sipped the first heady draft of her drink in mild defiance as the arbored platform went drifting off among the leaves. A vagrant current caught it there and carried her slowly along in a wide circle in and out of the branches, past other platforms where couples sat with heads close together with exotic drinks. Juille felt very lonely and very self-conscious.

*

On the curving stairs a young man in a startling cloak looked after her thoughtfully.

There were times, he told himself, when even the most trustworthy of secret informants made mistakes. He thought this must be one of the times. He had been waiting here for some while, watching the crystal stairs patiently. But now – the amazonian princess of Ericon was a familiar figure to him from her newsscreen appearances, and it was impossible to identify that striding military creature with this woman swathed in shadows, her garments breathing out Stardust that drifted and twinkled and faded behind her like wafts of faint perfume as she moved.

The young man knew very well what magic the dress designers of Cyrille could work, but he could not believe their magic wholly responsible for this. He grinned a little and lifted his shoulders imperceptibly under the remarkable cloak. It would be amusing to find out.

He kept an eye upon the drifting platform and mounted the stairway slowly, keeping level with it.

Juille watched her drink go down in the frosted sphere and was somewhat ironically aware that her spirits were rising to match it. The rigid self-consciousness of her first few minutes had relaxed; the drink made her mind at once cloudy and sparkling, a little like the shadowy draperies she wore. This was a delicious sensation, floating free upon drifts of perfumed breeze while music breathed and ebbed around her in the green twilight.

She watched the other patrons drifting by, half-seen among the confetti-like leaves of their bowers. Many of the faces she thought she recognized. Cyrille was not a world for the rank and file of the Galaxy to enjoy. One had to present stiff credentials to make reservations here, and by no means all of the patrons came incognito. It was a place to enjoy forbidden pleasures secretly, of course, but equally a place to see and be seen in. The wealthy and the noble of all the Galaxy's worlds took considerable pride in showing off their elaborate costumes and the beauty of their companions here, for the very fact of their presence was as good as a published statement of wealth and ancestry.

Presently a flash of scarlet seen through the leaves of a passing platform caught her eye. She remembered then that she had noticed that same shocking cloak upon a young man on the stairs. It was a garment so startling that she felt more than a passing wonder about the personality of the man who would wear it. The garment had been deliberately designed to look like a waterfall of gushing blood, bright arterial scarlet that rippled from the shoulders in a cascading deluge, its colors constantly moving and changing so that one instinctively looked downward to see the scarlet stream go pouring away behind its wearer down the stairs.

Now the blood-red deluge moved fitfully between the branches of a passing arbor. The platform turned so that she could see through the arch of the entrance, and for a long moment as they moved lazily by one another she looked into the interested face of a young man with yellow curls and a short blond beard. His eyes followed her all during the leisurely passing of their platforms, and Juille suddenly sparkled behind the delicious languorous spell her drink had laid upon her. This was it! This was what she had hoped for, and not quite admitted even to herself.

A panel glowed into opaque life in the center of the table she leaned upon. The ubiquitous, inhumanly sweet voice of Cyrille murmured:

'A young man in a red cloak has just asked the privilege of speaking to the occupant of this platform. His identity is not revealed, but the occupant is assured from our records that he is of noble family and good reputation except for a casual tendency toward philandering of which the occupant is warned. He is skilled in the military arts, knows most forms of music well, enjoys athletic games, has done some composing of considerable merit. If the occupant wishes further acquaintance, press the left chair arm which will cut front repellors.'

Juille almost giggled at the curious blend of chaperonage, social report and conversational guide with which the honeyed voice prefaced an informal meeting. She wondered if her own anonymous record had been presented to the man, and then decided that it would not be, without her permission.

She wondered, too, just how another woman in her place, with the background she had usurped, would probably act. After a moment of almost panicky hesitation she laid a hand upon the chair arm and leaned on it.

The other platform had evidently made a wide circle around her while the introduction was in progress. Now it swung about in front of her arbor and she could see that the red-cloaked man was leaning on his own chair in a similar position. Across the clear green gulf he called in a pleasant voice:

'May I?'

Juille inclined her dark-gold head, carefully coifed under the hooding veil. The platforms drifted closer, touched with the slightest possible jar. The young man ducked under the arbor, darkening the entrance with the swoop of his bloody cloak. It billowed out behind him extravagantly in the little wind upon which the platforms drifted.

Juille was glowing with sudden confidence. Now she had achieved part of what she had set out to do. Surely this proved her capable of competing with other women on their own unstable, mysterious ground. The magic of the shadowy gown she wore had a part in it, and the drink she had almost finished added its dangerous warmth.

After all, humanity was a strange role to Juille, not one to maintain long. The subservient planets had wheeled across the heavens for her imperial family too long. That look of intolerable pride was coming back subtly into her delicate, steely face beneath the veil that drew its shadow across her eyes.

She nodded the newcomer to a crystal chair across from her, studying him coolly from under the cobwebby veil. He was smiling at her out of very blue eyes, his teeth flashing in the short curly beard. He looked foppish, but he was a big young man, and she noticed that the cloak of running blood swung from very fine shoulders indeed. She felt a faint contempt for him – music, composing, when the man had shoulders like that! Lolling here in that outrageous cape, his beard combed to the last careful curl, oblivious to the holocaust that was rising all through the Galaxy.

She had a moment's vision of that holocaust breaking upon Cyrille, as it was sure to break very soon even this close to the sacred world of Ericon. She thought of H'vani bombs crashing through this twilight sphere in which she floated. She saw the vast tree trunk crumbling on its foundation, crashing down in ruins, its great arms combing all these drifting crystal bowers out of the green perfumed air. She thought of the power failing, the lights going out, the cries of the suddenly stricken echoing among the shattered Edens. She saw the darkness of outer space with cold stars twinkling, and the vast luminous bulk of Ericon looming up outside through the riven walls of Cyrille.

The young man did not appear to share any such premonitions of disaster. He sank into the chair she had indicated and stretched his long legs out comfortably. He had set down on the table a crystal inhaler shaped like a long flattened pitcher with its lip closed except for a tiny slit. Blue-green liquid inside swung gently to the motion of the platform.

He smiled at Juille very charmingly. In spite of herself she warmed to him a little. The charm was potent; though she disparaged it, she could not wholly resist returning the smile.

'This is Cyrille at its best,' he said, and gestured toward the twilit hush through which their transparent islet was floating in a long, ascending spiral. The gesture came back to include the bower's intimacy. 'Maybe,' he said reflectively, 'the best I've ever known.'

Juille gave him a remote glance under the veil.

'The best dream,' he explained seriously. 'That's what we come for, isn't it? Except that what we get here is much nicer than most dreams. You, for instance.' The charming smile again, both repelling and attracting her. 'If this were a dream, I might wake up any moment. But as it is—'

He stared at her for an instant in silence, while a little breeze rustled the leaves about them and green space swam underfoot below the transparent floor.

'You might be a princess,' he went on in a voice of deliberate musing. 'Or something made up out of synthetics by some magic or other – I've heard of such things on Cyrille. Maybe you have no voice. Maybe you're just made to sit there and smile and look beautiful. Is it too much to hope you're alive, too – not an android?'

Juille said to herself, 'This young man is much too glib, and he certainly enjoys the sound of his own voice. But then, I enjoy it, too—'

Aloud she said nothing, but she smiled and inclined her head a little, so that from the disturbed veil a mist of frosty lights floated out and twinkled into nothingness in the bowery gloom.

The young man stared at her, half enchanted by his own fancy, half convinced in spite of himself that she might after all be one of the fabulous androids of Cyrille, endowed with a compelling charm stronger than the charm of humans.

'If you were,' he went on, 'if you were born yesterday out of a matrix just to sit there and be beautiful, I wonder what we'd talk about?'

Juille decided it was time to speak. She made her voice remote and low, and said through the sparkling shadows of her veil:

'We'd talk about the worlds you know ... you would tell me what it's like outside Cyrille.'

He smiled at her delightedly. 'They gave you a beautiful voice! But I'd rather show you the worlds than talk about them. What would you like to see?'

'Which do you like best?'

Egide lifted his crystal inhaler and put its slitted lip to his mouth, tilting out a few drops of the blue-green liquid within. Then he closed his eyes and let the liquor volatize upon his tongue and go expanding and rising all through his head in dizzying sweetness. He was wondering if he would have to kill this beautiful, low-voiced creature, and if so, whether he would strangle her or use a knife, or whether the little gun tucked inside his belt would be safest. He said:

'I've never been sure of that. You'll have to help me decide. If we find one beautiful enough, I'll take you there tonight.' He leaned forward above the panel in the table top and spoke into it briefly. 'Now watch,' he said.

Juille leaned across the table, folding her arms upon its cool surface. The veil settled about her in slow, cloudy shadows, little lights sparkling among them. With their heads close together they watched pictures form and hover briefly and fade in the panel.

Their islet floated out in a long arc over the abysses of spring evening, and followed a vagrant air current back through the branches again, while they reviewed world after changing world.

'Do you know,' said Egide, 'that we're doing what only the emperor of Ericon could do?' He watched Juille's dim reflection in the table top, and saw her expression change sharply. He smiled. Yes, she was probably – herself. He went on. 'We're making the worlds parade for our amusement. I'll be emperor and give you the one you choose. Which shall it be?'

Juille was hesitating between laughter and outraged divinity. Did the lesser races really talk like this among themselves, with disrespect even for the emperor of the Galaxy? She did not know. She had no way of guessing. She could only swallow the unintended sacrilege and pretend to play his impious little game.

'There,' she said in a moment, pointing a tapered forefinger, 'give me that city.'

'Yorgana is yours,' he told her, with a regal gesture that made his cloak sweep out in a sudden gush of blood. And he spoke again into the panel. The great swinging branches began to drift more swiftly by them as their platform picked up motion toward the giant tree trunk and the stairs.

Juille was accustomed to a certain amount of informality from her officers and advisers. She had never insisted upon the full rendition of her imperial rights, which in some cases bordered almost upon semidivinity. But she knew now for the first time that no one had ever been really at ease in her presence before.

Half a dozen times as they went up the stairs and entered a fancifully drop-shaped elevator she was on the verge of laughter or outraged dignity, or both together, at the young man's attitude toward her. No one before had ever pretended even in jest to bestow largesse upon her; no one had ever assumed the initiative as a matter of course and told her what she was expected to do next. For the moment Juille was amused, but only, she thought, for the moment.

The real Yorgana had been in ruins a thousand years. Here in Cyrille, under the light of its three moons, it lay magically restored once more, a lovely city of canals and glimmering waterways in a night made bright as some strange-colored day by its circling moons.

They walked along the sand-paved streets, strolled over the bridges, dropped pebbles into the rippling reflections of the canals. And they talked with a certain stiffness of reserve which began to wear off imperceptibly after a while. Their range of subject matter was limited, for her companion appeared as determined to preserve his incognito as Juille was herself. So they talked of Cyrille instead, and of the many strange things it housed. They talked of the libraries of Cyrille, where the music of all recorded times lay stored, and of the strange pastime of musical levitation which was currently popular here. They speculated about the nationalities, the world origins, the rank of their fellow strollers through the oddly ghostlike city of Yorgana. They talked of the dark places of Cyrille, where beauty and terror were blended for the delectation of those who loved nightmares. But they did not talk of one another except guardedly, and any speculation on either side was never spoken aloud.

Juille was surprised at her own rather breathless enjoyment of this evening. They shared a little table on a terrace that overhung the spangled heights of the city, arid they drank pungent deep-red wine, and Juille sat silently, watching the three moons of Yorgana reflecting in tiny focus in her glass while Egide said outrageously flattering things to her.

They drifted in a boat shaped like a new moon along the winding canals under balconies hung with dark flowers, and Egide sang cloyingly sweet ballads, and the night was theatrically lovely. Once he leaned toward her, making the boat rock a little, and hesitated for what seemed a very long moment, while Juille tensed herself to repel whatever advances he was about to make. She knew so little of matters like this, but she knew by instinct that this was too soon. She was both relieved and sorry when he sank back with a deep sigh, saying nothing.

Except for that one incident, insignificant as it was, Juille had no reason at all to distrust the man. But as the evening went on she found that she did distrust him. There was no logic about it. His ingratiating charm struck responsive chords in her against her own desire, but the distrust went deeper still. It was not any telepathic awareness of his surface thoughts, but an awareness of the man himself as his casual opinions revealed him. He was, she thought, too soft. His height and his easy muscular poise had nothing to do with it. She had felt gun callouses on his palm when he helped her into the boat, and she knew he was not wholly the careless fop he pretended, but too many of his casual words tonight had betrayed him. He reminded her more than once of all she disliked most in her father's attitude. She thought, before the evening ended, that she knew this young man better than he suspected, and she did not trust him. But she found his facile charm curiously disturbing.

The disturbance reached its height at the end of the evening, when they danced upon the starry black mirror of the Dullai Lake, where lessened gravity let them move with lovely long gliding steps to the strains of music which seemed to swoon extravagantly from chord to lingering chord. Juille was delightfully conscious of her gown's effect here, in the very scene that had inspired the designer to create it. She was part of the dark, drifting shadows; the clouds of dim gauze billowed out behind her, astream with vanishing stars. And the dance itself was perfection. They were both surprised at the intoxicating rhythm with which their bodies moved together; it was like dancing in a dream of weightless flight, buoyed up on the rise and flow of music.

In this one thing they lost themselves. Neither was on guard against the other while the music carried them along, swirling them around and around in slow, lovely spirals over the starry floor. They said nothing. They did not even think. Time had suspended itself, and space was a starry void through which they moved in perfect, responsive rhythm to music that was an intoxicant more potent than wine. They had known one another forever. In this light embrace a single mind controlled them and they moved to a single rhythm. Apart, their thoughts were antagonists, but in this moment all thoughts had ceased and their bodies seemed one flesh. When the music circled intricately to its close, they danced out the last lingering echoes and came reluctantly to a halt, looking at one another in a stilled, mindless enchantment, all barriers let down, like people awakening from a dream and drenched still with the dream's impossible sweetness.

They stood in a little tree-shadowed cove on the lake shore, dark water rippling in illusion beneath their feet. They were quite alone here. The music seemed to have lifted from the surface of the lake and breathed above their heads through the stirring leaves. And Juille was suddenly aware that Egide had tensed all over and was looking down at her with a queer intentness. Light through the trees caught in his eyes and gave them an alarming brightness. He reached for her in the darkness, and there was something so grimly purposeful about the gesture that she took a step backward, wary and poised. If he had intended a kiss, there was still something frightening in his face and the brilliance of his eyes.

Perhaps even Egide had not been sure just what he intended. But after a moment of intense silence while they stood in arrested motion, staring at one another, he let his arms fall and stepped back, sighing again with a deep, exhaling breath as he had sighed in the boat.

Juille knew then that it was time to leave.

When she came out into her own quiet apartments, sunlight still gleamed changelessly upon the sea beyond her windows. It was not really night, of course. Arbitrary day and night are not observed upon Cyrille, so that though individuals come and go the crowd remains fairly constant in the public rooms. Helia looked up and gave Juille a quick, keen stare as she went through the sunny room without a word.

She stepped through blue mist into the shadowy bedroom, walking upon a mist of twinkling lights through its dimness. A delicious weariness was expanding along her limbs, and her mind felt cloudy like the cloudy, inviting bed. Deep under the lassitude a reasonless unease about that last moment on the lake stirred in her mind, but she would not follow the thought through.

She was looking back with lazy amusement upon the incredible romance of their hours together, and seeing now, without annoyance, how deftly her companion had induced the mood which drowned her now, against her own will and judgment, submerging even the strange, chilly remembrance of the moment after the dance.

Deliberately he had led her through scene after scene of the most forthright and outrageous romanticism, moonlight and starlight, flowers and rippling streams, songs of incredibly honeyed import. She felt vaguely that if the romance had been stressed a little less blatantly it might have been laughable, but the sheer cumulative weight of it had bludgeoned her senses into accepting at its full, false value all the cloying sweetness of the scenes. Toward the end, she thought, he had overreached himself. Whatever his original intention had been, whatever hers, in that one timeless, intoxicating dance they had been caught in the same honeyed trap.

And afterward, when he reached for her with that frightening purpose and the frightening brilliance in his eyes – well, what was so alarming about a kiss? Surely it had been foolish to read anything more menacing into the gesture. She would see him again, and she would know then.

Juille realized suddenly that she had been standing quite still in the middle of the room for a long while, staring blindly at the slowly drifting chairs, reviewing the dance over and over, and the dissolving sweetness of the music and the rhythms of their motion.

She said, 'Damn the man!' in a clear voice, and yawned extravagantly, and stepped through another veil of fog into the showering bath. The shadowy gown she had worn all evening melted upon her and went sluicing away under the flashing water. She was both glad and sorry to see it go.

Her dreams in the cloudy bed were lovely and disturbing.

'We've known one another three days,' Juille said, 'and I may as well tell you I don't like you. Wouldn't trust you out of my sight, either. Why I stay on here—'

'It's my entertainment value,' Egide told her, and then rubbed the cropped curls of his beard in a thoughtful way. 'Trust I don't expect. But liking, now – you surprise me. Is it the short time we've known each other?'

'Hand me a sandwich,' Juille said. He pushed the picnic basket toward her over a billowing surface of clouds – curious, she thought, how the cloud motif had haunted her days here – and remarked:

'I can manage the time angle if that's all that bothers you. Wait.' He took up a luminous disk lying beside him and murmured into it. After a moment the clear sunlight that bathed them began to mellow to an afternoon richness.

They were lunching in shameless, childlike fantasy upon a cloud that drifted across the face of a nameless planet. Any pleasure that the mind can devise the body may enjoy in Cyrille. Its arts can expand the walls of a room so that sunlit space seems to reach out toward infinity all around. From the cumulus billows they rode upon today they could lean to watch the shadow of their cloud moving over the soft-green contours of the turning world below, very far down. For the present all gravity and all logic had released them, and in this simple fulfillment of the dream every child knows, Juille let all her past float away. And she had sensed in her companion a similar release. He had been almost irresistibly charming in these careless days, as if, like her, he had deliberately shed all responsibilities and all remembrance of past duties, and had interests now only in being charming and being with her. The three days had affected them both. Juille found she could sit here now and listen to her companion's nonsense with very little recollection that she had been and must be again the princess of Ericon. There was no shadow over the present. She would not look beyond it.

She could even accept without much disbelief the fantastic thing Egide was accomplishing now, and when he said, 'Look – not even the emperor could do this!' no shadow crossed her face. He was not watching for such signals now. He had no need to.

Over the world below them evening had begun to move. The air dimmed, and the great soft billows of their cloud flushed pink above the darkening land below. A star broke out in the sky, and another. It was night, full of flaming constellations in the velvet dark. And then dawn began to glow beyond a distant mountain range. The air sparkled; dew was bright upon the face of the turning world.

'See?' said Egide. 'Tomorrow!'

Juille smiled at him indulgently, watching the morning move swiftly across the planet. He made no move to halt its progress and the shadows lengthened fast below them as the day declined once more. A fabulous sunset enveloped them in purple and pink and gold, and the sky was green, and violet, and then velvet black. The cycle repeated itself, faster and faster. Evening and night and dawn, noon, evening again.

When a week of evanescent days had flashed over them, Egide spoke into the disk and the circling progress slowed down to normal. He grinned at her.

'Now you've known me about ten days,' he said. 'Don't I improve with acquaintance? Do you feel you know me any better?'

'I've aged too fast to tell.' She smiled. 'What fun it is, being a god.' She rose on an elbow and looked down over the edge of the cloud. 'Let there be cities down there,' she said, and waved a careless arm along which bright blue water appeared to ripple, breaking into a foam of bubbles about the wrist.

'Cities there are.' Egide snapped his fingers and over the horizon a twinkle of lights began to lift. 'Shall we have evening, to watch them shine?' Juille nodded, and the air dimmed about them once more. She held up a blue-sheathed arm to watch the light fading along the liquid surfaces of her sleeve.

They had sailed yesterday under leaning white canvas over a windy sea, and Egide had sent the dress designer to Juille this morning with a new idea. So today she wore a gown of changing blues and greens that flowed like sea water as his cloak had once flowed like blood. An immaculate foam of bubbles rippled about her feet.

Almost every waking hour of the past three days they had spent together. And Juille had almost forgotten that once, on their first meeting, some look about him had frightened her. In her sight the look was not repeated. Behind her back – perhaps. But the three days had been unshadowed, full of laughter and light talk and the entertainment Cyrille alone knew how to provide. They still had no names for one another, but restraint had long gone from their conversation. Juille had even let her first mistrust of him sink into temporary abeyance, so that only occasionally some passing word of his evoked it again.

Just now something else evoked it. At any other place and time there would probably have been real annoyance in her voice, but she spoke today with gentle lassitude.

'You have a decadent mind,' she told him. 'I've often noticed that. Look – even your clothes show it.'

Egide glanced down with a certain complacence. To all appearance he was cloaked today in long blond hair that rippled rather horribly from his shoulders. Beneath it his fine muscular body was sheathed in wetly shining blue satin the exact color of his eyes, and of the same translucent texture.

'Oh, there's a lot I haven't tried yet,' he assured her. 'Rain, fire – By the way, how would you like a rainstorm over your cities?'

Juille dismissed her shadow of distaste and leaned upon one elbow, peering down.

'Not now. Look. How pretty they are!'

Dusk was purpling over the world below, and the cities twinkled in great spangled clusters of light that shook enchantingly all over the face of the darkening planet as the air quivered and danced between them.

'Look up,' murmured Egide, his voice hushed a little in the growing hush of their synthetic night. 'I wonder if the stars really look like that, anywhere in the Galaxy.'

There were great shining rosettes of light, shimmering from red to blue to white again in patternless rhythms against a sky of thick black velvet. And as they leaned back upon the cloud to watch, a very distant music began to breathe above them among the stars.

It made Juille think of the music upon the lake to which they had danced so beautifully, and in a moment she knew she must sit up and say something to break the gathering magic in the air. She did not trust that magic. She had been careful not to let another moment like the moment of the dance engulf them. She mistrusted it both for its own sake and for the sake of what barriers it might let down in her. The thought of Egide's embrace was frightening, in some obscure, illogical way she did not try to fathom. In just a moment she would break the gathering spell.

The music sank slowly toward them in intangible festoons of sweetness. The stars blazed like great fiery roses against the dark. They were floating through space upon that most lulling and deeply remembered of all motions – the gentle swing of the cradle. Their cloud rocked them above the turning world and the stars poured down enchantment. And now it was too late to speak.

The same dissolving magic was upon them as their cloud went drifting slowly among the stars. All reality was draining away. Juille heard the long breath her companion drew, and saw the stars blotted out by the silhouette of his curly head and broad cloaked shoulders leaning above her. And suddenly something about their tensed outline roused Juille from her lovely lassitude. She sat up abruptly, terror flashing over her. In this swimming darkness his face and the brilliance of his eyes was veiled, but she could see his arms reach out for her and all the latent fear came back with a rush.

But before she could move he had her. His strength was surprising. He held her struggles quiet in one arm, and she felt the calloused palm of the other hand fitting itself gently around her throat. For one unreasoning moment, in the face of all logic, she knew what he intended. In her mind she could already feel that hand tightening with its terrible gentleness until the night swam red around her as she strangled. If this was murder, she must forestall it, and her body knew the way. What she did was pure instinct, unguided by reason. She relaxed in his arms with a little sigh, letting her eyes close softly. When she felt his grip begin to loosen just a bit she got one arm free and laid it about his neck.

What happened then must have amazed them both if their minds had been capable of surprise. But their minds were not functioning now. As in the moment of the dance, all antagonisms of thought had ceased without warning, and it was the flesh instead that governed and responded. Juille felt one dim warning stir far back in her brain, drowned beneath the immediate and urgent delight of his expert kisses, but she would not think of it now. She could not. Later, perhaps, she would remember. Much later. Not now.

The burning stars had paled a little when she noticed them again. Some warm, light fabric covered her – that cloak of rippling yellow hair. Her head was pillowed upon the cumulous couch and dawn was beginning to freshen the air, though no light yet glowed above the horizon. She could see her companion darkly silhouetted against the stars as he sat upon a billow of cloud a little distance away, resting his chin on his fist and staring downward.

Juille pushed the clouds into a support behind her and leaned upon it, watching him, formless thoughts swirling in her mind. Presently his head turned toward her. In this warm darkness his face was barely visible, lighted by the dimming stars. She could see starlight reflecting in the mirrory surfaces of his tunic and glancing down, she caught the same reflections broken among the water ripples of her own skirt.

They looked at one another in silence, for a long while.

Juille woke in the dimness of her apartment, upon her bed of cloud, and lay for a few moments letting the fog of her dreams clear slowly away, like mist dispelling. Then she sat up abruptly, knowing that after all it had been no dream. But when she looked back upon the bewildering complexity of what had happened on the cloud, she saw no rhyme or reason to it. The dimness was suddenly smothering about her.

'Light, light!' she called pettishly, brushing at the room's darkness with both hands, as if she could clear it away like a curtain. And someone waiting beyond the call panel of the bed must have heard – it was strange to wonder how much those listeners heard and watched and knew – for the darkness paled and a rosy glow of morning flooded the room.

Helia stood in the doorway, the little *llar* preening itself upon her shoulder. Her weathered face showed no emotion, but there was a certain gentleness in the look she bent upon her mistress.

'Did I sleep long?' Juille asked.

Helia nodded. The *llar* unclasped its flexible pads and plucked at her dark hair, beginning very swiftly and deftly to braid it between quick, multiple fingers like the fingers of sea-anemones. Helia stroked the little animal and it snapped sidewise with razory teeth and sprang to the floor with one fluid motion of grace like flight.

'Any calls?'

'Not yet, highness.' Helia's grave stare was almost disconcerting.

Juille said, 'Go away,' and then sat clasping her knees and frowning. In the mirrors of the dressing alcove she could see herself, the fine, hard delicacy of her face looking chill even in this rosy light. She felt chill.

What had happened last night was too complex to understand. Would his hand have tightened about her throat if she had not taken the one way to prevent it? Or was the heavy touch a caress? What possible reason, she wondered, could the man have for wanting to strangle her? But if he had meant to, and if he had let her seduce him from his purpose – why, that was no more than she might have expected from him. The old mistrust, the old dislike, came back in a flood. His decadent clothes betrayed him, she thought, and his sensitive, sensuous mouth betrayed him, and the careless opinions he had expressed too often. He was a man who would always make exceptions; he would always be pulled two ways between sentiment and duty. If it had not really happened last night, then it would happen when the first test came. No, she did not respect him at all – but a dangerous weakness loosened all her muscles as she leaned here remembering that stunning of the sense which Cyrille's false glamour could work upon her.

Everything about her was an illusion, she realized with sudden cold insight that no Cyrillian art could dispell. But it was an illusion so dangerous that the very integrity of the mind could be enchanted by it, the keen edge of reason dulled. And she felt frightened as no possible physical threat could frighten her. When the amazon discards a woman's gentleness of body and mind she is almost certain to make the discard complete. Juille thought she was not asking too much of an intellectual equal when she expected from him the same cold, unswerving devotion to a principle that was the foundation of her own life. Egide would never have it.

But she knew she had better not see that disarming face of his any more. Not even to solve for herself the perplexing question of his intention last night. Better to let it slide. Better to go now and forget everything that had happened upon the drifting cloud, beneath those burning stars. Now she knew the shifting, unstable ground upon which women walk; she would not tread it again. She sat up.

'Helia,' she called through the fog-veiled doorway. 'Helia, send for our ship. We're starting back to Ericon – now.'

Egide sat clasping one knee, leaning his head back on the window frame and looking out over a field of pale flowers that nodded in the rays of tricolored suns. He did not look at Jair. His cloak today was a mantle of licking flame.

'Well?' said Jair, the boom in his voice under close control. No answer. Jair looked down reflectively at his own clasped hands. He tightened them, watching the great muscles writhe along his forearms under the red-heat haze of hair. 'Has she recognized you?' he asked.

Egide picked up the glass beside him and spun it thoughtfully. Rainbows flickered across the floor as sunlight struck it. He did not answer for a moment. Then he said in a detached voice, 'That. It's a false alarm, Jair.'

'A false alarm!' Jair's voice made the glass shiver in Egide's hand. The muscles crawled spectacularly along his arms as his great fists clenched. 'She *isn't* the emperor's daughter?'

Egide flashed him a clear, blue glance, and grinned.

'Never mind,' he said. 'You don't have to impress me.'

There was a certain blankness in Jair's reddish gaze that Egide recognized with an odd, illogical shiver. He said, 'Sometimes I forget how good you are at your job, Jair. And sometimes it surprises me—'

'You mean,' Jair said, and even in restraint his voice made the glass vibrate, 'we've wasted all this time and money—'

'Well, no, I wouldn't call it wasted. I've had a very pleasant time. But we'd better leave today. It wasn't the emperor's daughter.'

Rain danced from the high curve of the crystal wall and went streaming in long, irregular freshets down the sides of the glass room, veiling Ericon's soft-green hills outside. Within, firelight wavered beneath a great white mantelpiece carved with the mythological loves of gods and goddesses worshiped a long time ago by another race.

The rain and the firelight and the silence of the people in the room should have made it a peaceful hour here under the high glass curve of the walls. But over the mantelpiece was a communicator panel that was like an open window upon death and disaster. Every man in the room leaned forward tensely in his chair, eyes upon the haggard, blood-streaked face that spoke to them hoarsely through the panel.

The voice carried over long-lapsed time and the unfathomable dark distances that stretch between worlds. The man who called was probably dead now; he spoke from another planet that circled far outside the orbit of Ericon.

'Dunnar has just surrendered to the H'vani,' he was telling them in a tired, emotionless voice that sounded as if it had been shouting a little while ago, though it was not shouting now. 'We hadn't a chance. They came down in one wave after another all around the planet, bombing everything that moved. They landed troops on the night side and kept raining them down all around the world as the dark belt moved on. The day side got the bombing heaviest, beginning in the dawn belt and moving on around with the planet. They had their own men planted everywhere, ready to rise. Smothered our antiaircraft from the ground. Much of it must have been manned by their spies. Some of our interceptor craft were shot down deliberately from below. Watch out for H'vani men planted—'

Behind the speaker a flaming rafter fell into the range of the communicator screen and crashed somewhere near, out of sight. The man glanced back at it, then leaned to the screen and spoke on in a voice of quickened urgency. Above the crackling of the flames, other voices shouted in the background, coming nearer. There was the noise of what might be gunfire, and another sliding crash as more beams fell. The speaker was shouting now, his voice almost drowned out in the rising uproar of Dunnar's destruction.

'The weapon—' he called above the crashing. 'No chance for us … came too fast – We've smuggled out one man … fast ship … bringing a model to you. Watch for him. They'll follow—' A blazing beam came down between his face and the screen. Through a thin curtain of fire he mouthed at them some last urgent message of which only a word or two came through. 'Weapon … might save the Galaxy … give them a blast for Dunnar—' And then the fire blazed up to blot out face and voice alike, and Dunnar's ruined image faded from the screen.

For a moment after it was gone, the warm firelight flickering through the room seemed horrible, a parody of the flames that had engulfed the spokesman in the panel. The crash of burning Dunnar still echoed through the quiet, and the hoarse, despairing voice of the last man. Then the emperor said in a flattened tone:

'I wanted you all to hear it a second time, before we go out to meet the ship.'

Juille uncrossed her long bare legs and leaned forward, scowling under the crown of dark-gold braids.

'We're ready for them,' she said grimly. 'That weapon wasn't quite finished, though.'

'That's why they struck when they did,' murmured an amazon officer beside her. 'Beautiful timing – beautiful! Almost a split-second attack, between the finish of the weapon and the mounting of it.'

There was silence in the room. The opening blow had been struck of a battle that must engulf every world in the Galaxy before it ended. No one spoke for a while, but the air was heavy with unvoiced thoughts and most of them were grim.

The emperor put out a hand to the game set up on a table before him and moved a bead along a curve of colored wire. It was a game of interplanetary warfare, played like chess, though the men moved both vertically and horizontally on wires like an abacus. Firelight glinted on the colored beads carved like ships and worlds.

'You'll lose your master planet unless you bring up the blues,' Juille told him absently.

'This is a solitaire game,' said the emperor. 'Mind your own business.'

The rain blew pattering against the glass and the fire crackled softly. Juille's *llar* came out from beneath her chair, stretching elaborately, yawning to show a curved pink tongue. The crackling of the logs was a whisper of the terrible roaring crackle they had heard across the void from Dunnar's collapsing cities. They would hear it again from other worlds before the holocaust ended that had begun almost before their eyes here. Perhaps they might listen to it in this very room, on the sacred soil of Ericon itself. Other dynasties had crumbled upon Ericon before theirs.

'Why don't they report again on that ship?' the emperor said irritably, flipping a carved bead around a curve with too much force, Juille, seeing its course, automatically opened her mouth to object, and closed it again without saying anything. The *llar* swung itself up on the emperor's table with soundless ease and put out its webby-fingered paw to move two beads precisely along the notched wire.

'Ah, so you know Thori's Gambit, little friend?' The emperor's tired face creased in a smile as the *llar's* round-eyed stare met his through the maze of painted wires. He moved a translucent red bead between the two the *llar* had shifted. 'I wish I could be sure that was an accident. How much does a *llar* really know?'

The little animal put its head down, rolled up its strange, shining eyes and wriggled all over, like a playful kitten. But when the emperor stretched out a hand to stroke it, the *llar* turned deftly away and flowed down over the table edge onto the floor with a grace that was almost frightening in its boneless ease.

The screen glowed above the fireplace. Everyone looked up, even the *llar.* An expressionless face announced in expressionless tones:

'Escaping Dunnar ship approaching landing field from space. Three enemy pursuit ships have succeeded in passing the Ericon space guard and still survive.'

The emperor got up stiffly. 'Come along,' he said. 'We'll watch.'

They came out in a window-walled room above the landing field. A fine mist blew in through the openings, sweet with the fragrance of the wet green hills beyond. The clean smell of wet concrete rose from the broad, brown expanse below, where the small figures of attendants dashed about excitedly in preparation for the landing.

One inner wall of the room was a screen upon which they could all see now what had been taking place overhead, above the layers of rain cloud. The emperor sat down without taking his eyes from the screen. Juille crossed her arms on the high back of his chair and watched, too, ringing one spur in a half-unconscious, continuing jingle. Everyone else was silent, standing respectfully back, and the sound of breathing was loud in the quiet.

On the screen they could see how the tiny black ship from Dunnar had cut its rockets and hurled itself headlong into the gravitational embrace of Ericon, swinging around the planet to subdue the speed it had not dared slacken in space. Behind it, still in suicidal pursuit, the three H'vani ships flamed on. They had escaped the space guard only because of their smallness and mobility, which meant that the range of their weapons was too limited to do much damage at a distance. But they were cutting down the space between them and their quarry, and the race was close.

'They'll have to turn back now,' breathed Juille, gripping the chair-back. 'They won't dare … look, there go our interceptors.'

The screen divided itself in half with an oddly amoebalike motion, one section showing the swift rise of Ericon's interceptors while the other mirrored the orbit of the newcomer as it swung around the Control Planet still at dangerous speed. It was curious to think of the plunge into circumscribed space-time which that ship was just now making as it emerged from deep space where neither time nor distance have real meaning. The fugitive had flashed through morning and noon and night, and come around the world into dawn again, and so into the misty forenoon above the watchers.

Now they saw it put out wings upon the thin upper air, like a diver suddenly stretching out his arms, and come coasting down upon their sustaining surfaces in a great sweeping spiral above the field.

'There goes one of 'em,' the emperor said in a satisfied voice. Juille glanced back at the upper screen and saw one of the pursuers from space twisting downward, its black sides beginning to glow already from the friction of that thin high air. It dropped incandescently out of the picture, which was following the other two ships in their headlong flight. Their own sheer speed gave them an advantage. They were drawing away from the interceptors, taking full and suicidal advantage of the fact that upon Ericon immutable law forbids any aircraft to fly at will over the surface of the sacred planet.

'They won't dare—' Juille told herself under her breath, leaning forward. Behind her a rustle and an indrawn breath all through the room spoke the same thought. For the enemy ships, winged now and swinging down through the heavier air in pursuit of their escaping prey, were being driven farther and farther off the prescribed course beyond which all air traffic is forbidden.

The interceptor ships were sheering away. Juille could picture the frantic indecision of their commanders, torn between the necessity to destroy the invaders and the still more urgent necessity not to transgress an immemorial law laid down by powers even higher than the Galactic emperor's.

In the lower half of the screen, the single-winged ship had leveled off for a landing. Someone outside shouted, and for a moment all eyes turned to the windows and the broad concrete field outside.

Down out of the misty clouds came a duplicate of the shape upon the screen. In silence, the black-winged ship came swooping through the rain, lower and lower over the heads of running attendants. It hovered to a halt and sank down gently upon its own reflection in the wet concrete. And upon the screen behind them, the same scene took place in faithful duplicate.

Indeed, the image was more faithful than the reality, for at this distance the naked eye could see only a swarming of tiny figures around the newly arrived ship. The emperor called, 'Closer,' and turned back to the screen.

The scene below rushed into a close-up upon the wall, swooping toward them with dizzy speed. Now they could watch the opening slide into view upon the ship's side, and the man who ducked out and stepped down upon the brown concrete in the drizzle of misting rain. It beaded his shoulders with moisture in the first few moments. He blinked the rain out of his eyes and looked about calmly, not in the least hurried or alarmed.

The envoy from Dunnar was an astonishing figure, so tall and so very thin that at first glance he looked like a scarecrow shape beside his vessel. But when he turned to face the crowding attendants and the screen, he moved with a grace and sureness that had something unmistakably regal about it. He wore his plain black overall with a remarkable sort of elegance, and his own quiet sureness seemed to throw everyone else on the field out of focus. The muscular attendants looked squat and brutish by contrast with his scarecrow height; the well-dressed officials moving forward to receive him were vulgar beside his overalled simplicity.

He looked up into the featureless clouds where his pursuers and his defenders still waged an invisible battle. All around him the crowding men looked up, too, futilely. Only in the control room, where the emperor and his staff sat, did the eyes that followed that lifted gaze see what was happening overhead.

And now, as their gaze went back to the neglected drama above, a horrified fascination seized upon every watcher in the room. Even Juille's unconsciously jingling spur was silent. She felt the sudden clutch of small fingery paws, but she did not glance down as the *llar* came swarming up her leg to a vantage point upon her shoulder. She felt its tiny, quick breathing against her cheek as it, too, stared.

Not within the memory of any living man had the law of the Ancients been violated which forbade air traffic over Ericon. Obedience to those laws had been rooted as deeply as obedience to the law of gravity. There were violations, of course; tradition said all such violators died instantly.

Juille watched the first such episode in modern times with a catch in her breath and her throat closed from tremendous excitement. She wondered if everyone else in the room felt the same half-guilty anticipation, the impious wonder.

For there was a wide gap now between the enemy ships and the Ericon interceptors. It had been a suicide pursuit anyhow, for the H'vani. They were certainly doomed. And they were taking one last headlong chance in the hope of destroying their quarry before they were themselves destroyed. The interceptors had forced them by now far out of the narrow traffic lane whose invisible boundaries should have been so rigid. For the first time in living memory, ships spread their wings upon the forbidden air of Ericon.

They were swooping down in a long dive now, coming fast through the clouds toward the landing field where the newcomer stood unconcernedly staring up into the mists that hid them.

'They're going to make it – they are!' Juille whispered to herself, gripping the chair-back with aching fingers.

Out of the landing field, crews were manning the antiaircraft guns in frantic haste, sheer incredulity numbing their fingers as they worked. No one had ever quite believed that these guns could be needed. They were meant for defense against ships attacking from directly overhead, in the prescribed landing lane from space. Even that possibility had seemed absurd. But now—

'Get that fool off the field!' the emperor roared suddenly, making everyone jump. 'Get him off! They'll be here in a minute. Look at them come!'

Down through the mist the two surviving ships came driving through air that shrieked away from their wings. Men were scattering wildly from the field. Loudspeakers roared at the Dunnarian to take shelter. He stood imperturbably, tall and thin and quiet, looking up into the clouds.

And for a timeless moment a faith rooted millenniums deep in human minds shook terribly as the Ancients were defied – and stayed their hand. No peril to the defenseless envoy on the field – though he carried a secret that might save their race – moved the watchers half so deeply as what they were seeing now. The ships dived on through the screaming air, and behind them clouds boiled furiously in the vortex of their passage.

Did the Ancients really exist at all? Or had all those legends been legends only? The breath of every watcher paused in his throat as he waited the answer.

But no one saw the vengeance the Ancients took. All over the planet shaken watchers followed the action upon their screens – but no human eye saw the blow fall.

One moment, the black ships were screaming down through grayness; the next instant, without warning, there came a soundless flash like the flash of sunlight glancing from some colossal mirror, blinding every eye that watched.

There was no sound. The riven air screamed itself quiet. When those who stared could see again out of dazzled eyes, nothing remained but the vortex of clouds split by the plunging ships. And even the vortex was quieting now. Of the ships, nothing remained. For the first time in living memory, the Ancients had struck, invisibly, before a world of watchers, in the deadly dignity of silence.

And all over Ericon, a world-wide sigh of relief went up wordlessly.

*

In the utter quiet, the envoy moved forward at last across the wet concrete. Overhead, that vast boiling of clouds had cleared a space for the rare blue sky to shine. The reflecting pavement turned suddenly blue and glorious as he stalked across it with his long scarecrow stride. Awed eyes watched him come, a black figure moving with strange, smooth elegance over the blinding blueness of the sky's reflection.

'Stop that jingling and come along, Juille,' the emperor said at last in the silence, rising as stiffly as he had sat down. 'We'll see him in my library, alone. Wake up, girl! Come along.'

'—And the weapon?' said the emperor eagerly, leaning forward between the arms of a great carved chair before his library fire.

No one could have guessed from the look of the man before him that he had come straight from a desperate flight and an awesome rescue, or that he carried a cargo so precious a whole Galaxy's fate might depend on it. He was the last Dunnarian left to speak for his ruined world, but no emotion at all showed upon his cool, impassive face.

'I'll want my men to look over the weapon at once,' the emperor went on. 'It's in your ship?'

'Highness, I brought no weapon.'

'No weapon!'

Juille watched a familiar thunderous look gather upon her father's face, but the storm did not quite break and Juille smiled to herself, understanding why. It was difficult to treat this man like an ordinary person. His appearance was extraordinary enough, without that recollection of an hour ago which had struck a whole world into reverent silence.

This was the man who had stood unafraid beneath the plunge of the enemy ships, unprotected, so confident in the power of the Ancients that he had not wavered even when death seemed certain. This was the man above whom the Ancients had for the first time in living memory put out their hands and wrought a miracle. He had, of course, been only the occasion, certainly not the cause. But he was haloed still in the reflected glory of that moment which was already taking its place in legend.

'I have no weapon,' he said again, meeting the emperor's glare with an imperturbable gaze from his great, luminous eyes that never winked. 'We dared not risk letting a model fall into H'vani hands, highness. I will have to make one for you.'

Juille saw her father settle back, mollified, perhaps a bit relieved that he need not thunder at this remarkable and disconcerting man. Perhaps it had occurred to the emperor, as it had to Juille, that immortality which might outlast their own had already descended upon the envoy's smooth, narrow-skulled head. Unborn generations would repeat in awe the story of his experience today.

She stared frankly at the man, wondering very much from what ancient line he sprang and what knowledge lay behind the strange, thin face with its falcon nose and its large, transparent gray eyes and the mouth that looked at once cruel and oversensitive. Seen this near, he seemed even taller and thinner and more oddly scarecrowlike than on the screen, yet the extraordinary fastidious precision of his motion made every other man alive seem crude and clumsy. He had an ageless face, and a poise that seemed bred into the very genes of his ancestors. Juille had a glancing, vivid recollection of Cyrille – for a moment she was drifting on a cloud again, and a young man cloaked in flowing yellow curls bending above her – and she thought wryly how much he would have envied this Dunnarian's unstudied elegance. Even the stained overall, thus worn, looked like some fashion a Galactic prince had just set for the capitals of the worlds to copy.

'You'll have to get to work immediately,' the emperor's voice recalled her to the urgent present. 'We must have a model of the weapon at once. Too bad the H'vani timed their attack so well. In a few days more you might have fought them off with it, eh?'

The Dunnarian shook his narrow, bird-shaped head gravely.

'Our men never succeeded in expanding the scope of the weapon that much, highness. It remains a weapon for the individual, against the individual, but within that scope I believe it's the most effective thing ever made.'

'A delayed-action killing, isn't it?' Juille said.

The luminous eyes turned to her. There was an infinite quietness in their stare, curiously at odds with the man's words.

'It is, highness. That gives it a strong psychological threat value, as well as a physical one. With every other comparable weapon, its operator has to sight and fire while the enemy is exposed to view. With the new one, a man may be killed not only at any distance, but at any time, once its sight has been fixed upon him. A quasi-photograph of the victim's brain pattern is snapped, and he is doomed from that moment, though you may not choose to pull the trigger for many days. Then, irrevocably, the weapon remains focused upon him, figuratively speaking, until it is discharged. He will be unable to travel far enough to escape it, and no hiding place can save him.'

'Like a fuse,' Juille murmured. 'An invisible fuse, long enough to follow him wherever he goes, and you can light it when you wish. Oh, very nice! It's easily portable, I suppose?'

'The weapon itself is a bulky machine which must be set up in some impregnable position, perhaps sealed in against possible bombardment. But the focusing instrument is a small double lens in a frame. It has a slightly telescopic property. Once a man is centered in the cross hairs and a trigger sprung, he's your victim whenever you spring the second trigger on the lens and thus touch off his particular pattern in the central machine.'

The emperor put his fingertips together and stared at them, shaking his head.

'It's a treacherous thing,' he said. 'The ultimate refinement of a stab in the back, eh? I suppose the victim can't tell if he's been spotted?'

'Probably the victim never does know, highness. Death is almost instantaneous.'

The emperor shook his head again. 'Personally,' he said, 'I don't like it. But I can see why the H'vani wiped out a world trying to get it away from us. As you say, the psychological value of the thing is tremendous, once they know what they're up against.'

Juille laughed, a short, triumphant sound. '*I* like it,' she said. 'I'm not squeamish. Think of it, father! We can send armed spies into their bases to snap their leaders, and wait until the height of battle to pick them off. Imagine the effect during some complicated maneuver if all the leaders fell dead simultaneously! And that's saying nothing of how the leaders themselves will feel, knowing they're walking dead men, doomed the moment they step into a responsible position and start giving orders. Oh, I do like it!'

Her father nodded, frowning. 'Once it's known,' he said, 'once it's actually proved in combat, I should think every H'vani officer with any responsibility would become either a reckless fatalist or a nervous wreck. It isn't so bad to be killed outright – every soldier knows that can happen, and there's an end of it. But to know the assassin will strike inevitably at the high point of your responsibility, when thousands of lives depend on yours and the whole outcome of a battle may hinge on what you do – this ought to cause the most profound psychological reactions all along the line in any army the weapon's used against.'

Juille took a short turn about the room, spurs tinkling, and came back with shining violet eyes.

'Do you know what we've got here?' she demanded. 'It's something so new it almost frightens me. Not just the weapon – but the principle behind it. It's the only new thing, really, since cavemen led off the procession of warfare with the bow and arrow. From that time forward, weapons have been increasing in range and scope and volume. The whole story of military warfare's been a seesaw between defense and offense – new method of attack, new defense against it, stalemate, then a newer weapon that kills more people quicker. But now—' She laughed exultantly. 'Don't you see? This is a complete rightabout-face. Ever since the beginning of time, all martial invention's been forging ahead in one direction only, toward bigger and bigger weapons with greater range and scope. Men's minds are trained to think in those terms only. But with this new thing, we're flashing back in the other direction entirely, turning their flank, smashing them in a vulnerable spot left absolutely unprotected all this while. Their minds won't even be able to cope with it or devise a defense. People just don't think in terms like that.'

The emperor looked at her thoughtfully, stroking his beard. The envoy's great, translucent eyes dwelt upon her animated face with an impersonal remoteness.

'See it?' Juille demanded. 'Now we can strike them where they least expect it. We're back at the very beginning, even before the sword or the club. It's the individual we attack now. This is a weapon as terrible as anything that wipes out cities, but aimed at the other end of the scale of offense – the individual himself. Each man alone, in personal danger of a doom that's picked him out from all the rest and will follow him wherever he goes. This attacks the mind as well as the body. It's like a germ of terror that can eat a man's morale out and leave his body intact. He won't trust himself or his leader. And do you know the only possible defense?'

She struck her hands together and her voice almost crowed with triumph.

'Individual responsibility. The breakup of an integrated war machine. No one can depend on anyone else for anything, once our weapon's in action. They'll have to throw out all their elaborate maneuvers and all their training and start again from scratch. Each man for himself. An army of guerrillas. Utterly reckless, of course, fatalistic to the last degree. But I don't see how they can hope to conduct space warfare with every man in the army independent of every other man. It'll win the war for us, father!'

The emperor drummed his fingers on the table. 'You may be right,' he conceded. 'If we can keep it for ourselves, that is. But if anyone stole it—'

'Who else knows how to build the machine?' Juille demanded of the Dunnarian.

'No one, highness. There were few of us at the beginning, and I saw all my co-workers die. The knowledge is quite safe so far, with us.'

Juille bent upon him a curiously cold, violet stare. The grave, gray eyes met it without a flicker, though he must have known what passed through her mind. Artisans who create the unique for jealous emperors are notoriously shortlived, and in this case the need for uniqueness went far beyond petty jealousy.

'You'll want a constant guard,' Juille told the man thoughtfully. 'And you'll have to work fast.'

The Dunnarian bowed silently as the emperor waved a dismissing hand. He looked more than ever falconlike for a moment, and as he turned his head and Juille saw the narrow skull and the beaked nose outlined, she wondered how he could seem so birdlike and yet so smoothly poised, for birds are creatures of small, nervous motions.

Then she remembered that before the bird came the snake. It was the snake behind the falcon that epitomized this man's smooth gestures, his elegance, his quiet, lidless stare.

In another part of the palace a figure slipped quietly and unseen out of a curtained window. He dropped to the dark grass of a garden and, moving with the sureness of one who has come this way many times before, went out through an unguarded postern and through a band of trees dripping with rain that flashed in the lights behind him.

Quickly and silently through the rustling silence of the night he moved away, leaving the turmoil of the palace behind him, where the news of the ruin of world after world flamed across the luminous screens that pictured their destruction.

He went disdainfully through the dark, picking his way with delicate steps. He knew the path so well that no one challenged him, no one saw the dark figure slipping from shadow to shadow. He had a long way to go, but he knew every step of it, even in the dark.

He was tired when he came to the far end of the journey, for it had been a long way to come on foot. In the end it was intricate, too, because he had to enter by a hidden way.

But the end was reward enough for all his weariness and secrecy, as he had known it would be. Indeed, he knew and loved each step of the path because it brought him nearer this goal. He stood in a dark archway at the end of the journey, and looked out over the low rooftops of the city of his people, glittering with warm, soft lights through curtained windows. No two curtains were of quite the same shade, nor were the windows shaped alike at all, so that the city glowed with myraid flowery shapes, like a lighted garden. His heart swelled with the knowledge that he was at home again, that the city was his and he the city's. He no longer moved stealthily as he went down the slope of sand toward the sandy streets before him.

There were few abroad at this hour, but those he passed knew him and exchanged with him the reserved formula of greeting behind which lay a deep, sure affection between individuals for the sake of the group itself – a feeling almost indescribable to anyone unfamiliar with such a community as this.

He went along the sand-padded street silently, straight for the house where his friends awaited him. Reserve was strongly rooted in them all, and their meeting betrayed no emotional unbalance, but common purpose and common danger had welded them into a group so close and strong that words were scarcely necessary among them.

Still, when he was refreshed and relaxed, he could not help voicing the dominant emotion which had harried him all the way here.

'I wish it were over!' he sighed. 'I left them listening to the news of their own destruction, and making noises about it. Ericon will be a better world when the last of them dies.'

'A better place for us, I hope,' one of the others said. 'Will it be soon?'

'I think so, don't you? I think they're finished now, if they only knew it.'

'They stand at a very definite crisis,' said someone else, and glanced around the group with grave, affectionate eyes. 'They can still save themselves – perhaps. There's time for it, if they only knew the way. Such a simple way, too. Some of them see it, but I don't think they'll have the chance to try.'

'They're doomed,' the newcomer declared in his soft voice. 'I know them too well. Poor ignorant, blundering creatures.' He hesitated. 'I almost feel pity sometimes, watching them. But they've had their turn, and the sooner they finish the better. We've waited so long—'

'Would you help them if you could?' asked someone.

'If it weren't for us – perhaps. At heart they mean well. But they're muddled beyond all hope now, and I can't believe anything could straighten them out. Think how long we've waited—'

'Think of *Their* promise,' murmured a voice.

'It wasn't a flat promise, remember,' someone else warned cautiously. 'It was contingent, you know. They haven't failed yet. If this war turns in the right direction, they still have their chance, and we may have to begin our waiting all over again.'

'They'll miss the chance,' the newcomer said, half exultantly and half in reluctant pity. 'I know them too well.'

The officers' lounge in one of the tower tops was roofed and walled in glass, against which gusts of storming rain beat fitfully now, out of a purple sky. Ericon is so much a world of rain that all its architecture is designed to take advantage of rain's beauty, much like solariums on other worlds.

Today the lounge was crowded, and there was a murmur of grave undertones beneath the voice of the news screen that filled one wall. It rolled out the toll of ruined cities and silenced worlds. All over the Galaxy, insurrection was spreading inward toward Ericon like a plague from the rotting fringes of the empire. The imperial cities were going down like ninepins on world after crashing world.

'They're slowing up a bit, though,' Juille said thoughtfully. 'You know, I believe they had to strike sooner than they meant to, because of that weapon from Dunnar.' She nodded at the envoy from that now voiceless planet, who sat in a deep chair beside her, long legs crossed, long fingertips interlaced, his lidless stare upon the screen that covered one wall of the room. Unobtrusively his bodyguard leaned upon the wall behind him.

Around them sat Juille's staff of officers, most of them young, many of them women, who among them divided most of the power of the empire today. Helia leaned across the back of her chair, the *llar* on her shoulder preening its sleek sides with hands like fingery starfish.

'You're right about that, highness,' remarked a grim-faced woman in a plumed helmet. 'They're definitely slowing down. But the best we can hope for now, I think, is the striking of some balance. We can fall into a deadlock – beyond that we can't hope to pass just now.'

'There are worse things than deadlocks,' Juille told her. 'Wait till the weapon's finished! But if my father's conference this afternoon comes to anything—' She slapped the chair arms angrily. 'If it should, I think the whole Galaxy's lost.'

'The emperor, highness, would call it lost if the conference fails.' The man from Dunnar turned his grave, luminous eyes upon her.

'I won't sit down to a peace conference with those bloody savages,' Juille declared fiercely. 'Why they ever agreed to a conference I can't understand, but there's something behind it we won't like. As for me, I wouldn't offer them peace if they held a knife at my throat, and now – when we really hold a knife to theirs, if they only knew it—' She gave an angry shrug and did not finish.

'Do you feel there's any hope of their accepting the emperor's terms?'

Juille scowled. 'It depends on how intelligent they are. I'd have called them utter savages, unable to see beyond the next battle, if they hadn't planned this invasion of the inner systems so well. And just now, of course, they do have the upper hand. They took us by surprise. But we're finding our balance and beginning to strike back. They may realize they've struck a little too soon. Maybe they can see ahead to the time when we'll reach that deadlock – and then the new weapon may very well turn the balance to our side.' She shook her head fretfully, so that the windows gleamed in reflection upon her shining helmet. 'I don't know. It worries me that they came at all. Since they did, it's just possible they might agree to a treaty. Yes, I might almost say I think there's some danger of their agreeing to peace.'

'You consider it a danger, highness?'

'The greatest the empire has to face. I say crush them utterly, whatever it costs us. I'd rather inherit a bankrupt empire, when my turn comes, than live on side by side with those murderous savages, giving them our arts and sciences, letting them think themselves our equals. No. No, I feel so strongly about this that I've had to discard a luxury no empire can afford to keep when it threatens the common good.' Juille glanced around the room, gathering the eyes of her staff. She nodded.

'We've all agreed to this,' she went on. 'We make no secret of it. I'm so afraid of even the remote chance of peace at this stage that I've given orders to prevent it.' She paused a moment. 'I've given orders that the H'vani ambassadors be assassinated before they reach the conference table.'

There was silence for a moment. The Dunnarian regarded Juille with expressionless eyes. 'They're under truce,' he said at last, matter-of-factly. Juille's lips thinned.

'I know. But I intend to be merciless in victory, and I may as well start now. In this case I believe that the end more than justifies any means necessary to achieve it.'

'You feel there is that much danger that the H'vani will agree to peace at this stage, when they're winning on all fronts?'

'Why else would they consent to come?' Juille shrugged. 'I don't mean to waste any more thought on the matter. If they don't agree now, my father will offer it again and again, to prevent a long war. Sooner or later, as we gain more of the balance of power, they'll accept if they have the chance. If we kill their envoys under a flag of truce now – well, there'll be no more conferences.'

The Dunnarian nodded quietly. 'A very interesting decision, highness. I assure you I wouldn't interfere even if' – he glanced up at the clock – 'even if you'd given me time to.'

Juille followed his gaze, 'Ah,' she said. 'You're right – they should be landing. Helia, get us the scene.'

Helia, moving with the forthright clumping tread of an old soldier, crossed to the screen where an animated map of an embattled world was tracing the course of insurrection. As she passed the Dunnarian the *llar* on her shoulder gave itself a last preening stroke, gathered its sleek limbs and leaped without a jar onto the envoy's shoulder. He put up a hand to stroke it, and the little creature bent its head to the caress, rolling up its great round eyes with solemn pleasure.

Juille stared. 'I've never' – she stammered with surprise – 'never in my life … why, he'll hardly let me touch him! I'll swear I haven't stroked him like that twice in my life. And he never even saw you before!'

The envoy's delicate, lean features creased in the first smile she had seen upon them. 'I feel the honor keenly,' he said to the *llar*. It butted its round forehead against his palm like a cat.

A blast of music from the screen interrupted them. Swimming into focus as Helia turned the controls, the scene of the H'vani envoy's landing sharpened into colorful view. Juille curled her lip at it.

'All that ceremony,' she murmured, 'when we ought to be cutting their throats! Well, they'll soon see what the empire really thinks of them. My men ought to show up very soon now.'

She took off her helmet and leaned forward to watch, chin on fist, her dark-gold braids catching the red reflections of banners from the screen and shining as if in firelight. The braids were pinned like a coronet across her head to cushion the heavy helmet which she held now upon her knee. In its surface the red reflections moved too, blurrily, as if – in obvious simile – she cradled the momentous event in her very lap.

The H'vani newcomers were small, brightly clothed figures moving in a press of soldiers. Because the emperor had insisted that their representatives be the highest officials of the enemy race – its hereditary leader and its commander in chief – there had been tremendous haggling over the terms of safe conduct. In the end, they had been assigned a camp outside the city, near enough the boundaries of the Ancients' forbidden territory to remind them of the fate their ships had suffered. And now in the midst of a bodyguard of imperial soldiers they rode toward the city on horseback, amid much flurry of trumpets and streaming of red imperial banners.

Juille was not much interested in the dignitaries as individuals. Her eyes were sweeping the crowd in quick, impatient glances, picturing the flash of her assassins' guns. And the same thought, the same picture, was in every mind in the room with her. No one moved, waiting for that instant. If the power of thought had tangibility, their common concentration of purpose should have been enough in itself to strike the H'vani down.

With intolerable slowness, on the backs of tall, mincing horses, the procession drew near the city. It was a long, colorful ride. The people of Ericon, at the heart of the Galaxy's culture, paradoxically ride horseback when they travel. Except for the straight, paved roads which link city to city, there is little power-driven traffic, and that chiefly the transportation of supplies. Radio-television is so superlatively developed that almost no occasion ever arises for travel upon Ericon itself. Sightseeing is not encouraged upon the sacred control planet, and so much of its surface is forbidden by the Ancients for their own mysterious ends, and by the emperor for his imperial prerogatives, that as a rule only legitimate business traffic, with its prescribed roadways, moves upon the face of Ericon.

As a result, horseback riding is highly fashionable, pleasant enough and sufficiently picturesque to satisfy those of that world who go abroad for amusement. Actually, the terrene of other planets is much more familiar, and more easily reached, because of these restrictions, than the surface of Ericon itself.

The party had been riding a long time, and the tension in the room where the watchers sat was growing unbearable, when a nagging familiarity about one of the mounted figures she watched struggled up past the level of awareness into Juille's conscious mind.

'Focus it down, Helia,' she said sharply. 'I want to see those men.'

The picture swooped dizzily as the vision seemed to hover downward above the slowly moving procession. Then the two H'vani were large upon the screen in bright, three-dimensional life, the rustle of their cloaks audible in the room, the creak of harness, the clink of fire sword against belt.

Juille struggled against a moment of sheer suffocation. She was horrified to feel a tide of prickling warmth sweep up within her, clear to the roots of the dark-gold braids. Too many emotions were striving for dominance in her mind – the effect made her reel. For she knew this blond and bearded young man with a harp slung across his shoulder, riding a tall horse toward the city. She knew him very well, indeed.

Then their meeting on Cyrille had been no accident. And – that half-forgotten grip upon her throat had been no caress. For a moment, her mind and her gaze turned inward, calling back the brief, puzzling idyl which the urgency of recent events had so nearly eclipsed even from memory now. It came back vividly enough, with that picture moving on the screen to remind her.

She sat quite still, sorting out the memories of those three careless, oddly disturbing days on Cyrille. Egide – that was his name, then, Egide the H'vani – must surely have come there because of certain knowledge of her presence. And he must have come with a purpose that was not hard to guess. Especially not hard now, when she looked back to those few strange, tense interludes when she had been frightened without understanding why.

But he had never fulfilled his mission. He had come to kill her and he had let her live. She felt a sudden triumphant flush of vindication – she had guessed his weakness even before she knew his name. It was all there to see in that sensitive and sensuous mouth of his, and she had forestalled him through sheer instinct in the moment of his greatest resolution. A wave of scorn for him washed over her. A man like that was no fit leader for revolutionaries to follow. She had forestalled him in his most urgent duty – but how had she done it? Juille felt the deep blush returning, and bent her head futilely to hide it as her mind went back to that strange, frightening, delightful interlude upon the cloud.

Whatever her motive, she knew it had been herself, not he, who made that first inviting gesture. He had meant to kill her. Every calculating compliment he paid, every scene of elaborate romance he lead her through, had been meant only to lull her to unguarded ease. He must have had no other purpose. But she … she took it all at face value and had seemed in the end to beg for his kisses. The deepest depths of humiliation closed over her head as she sat there motionless, burning to the hairline with a red blush of rage.

When her swimming gaze focused again, she met Helia's warning eyes and fought for self-control. And because Helia had bred discipline into her from infancy, after a moment she gained it. But the turmoil of her thoughts went on. No wonder, she thought bitterly, he had agreed to this conference. He had every right to think that she knew him now – had recognized him in some portrait or news screen if she did not recognize him on Cyrille – and he must believe that she herself had insisted upon the meeting, that the terms of peace were hers. He might preen himself now with the thought that his amorous work upon Cyrille had borne fruit already in her betrayal of her own people into compromise with the enemy. She thought hotly that he would judge her by himself and think her as ready as he to toss principles away for the weakness of a personal desire. She had to fight down another surge of blinding humiliation that she had made herself vulnerable to the patronizing scorn of such a man as this. And for an instant she hated, too, the amazonian upbringing that had left her unarmed against him.

Well, there was one good thing in the ugly situation. She would never have to face him again. Her assassins had delayed unpardonably already, but they surely would not delay much longer. He would die without seeing her, without knowing – without knowing she was not deceived! Still thinking the peace plans were hers, because of love for him! No, if he died now she thought she would die, too, of sheer anger and shame.

She sat forward in her chair, watching the two H'vani, reading insolent swagger into every motion they made. To her eyes they rode like conquerors already, coming to accept the peace they thought her ready to hand them on a platter. And she knew she must kill Egide herself or never know self-respect again.

They were at the city gates now. She watched feverishly, on a sword-edge of impatience for the assassins to fail after all. Trumpets echoed from the high white walls and the procession wound along broad streets toward the palace. Juille, waiting on tenterhooks for the flash of the gun that would rob her of her last hope for self-respect, began to realize as the procession moved on, that somehow her hope was to be granted. Somehow the assassins had failed. It was too late already for any efficient job of killing to be done, here in the crowded streets. She leaned to the screen, breathless, seeing nothing else.

She did not know that Helia was watching her anxiously, or that the Dunnarian's great luminous eyes dwelt upon her face with a fathomless sort of speculation.

She paused outside the arch of the conference hall, balancing the *llar* upon her shoulder, drawing a deep breath. Behind her Helia whispered, 'All right, all right. Come along now.' The familiar voice was marvelously bracing. Juille smiled a grim smile, tossed her cloak back over one shoulder and strode in under the archway, hearing the trumpets blare for her coming.

They rose from their chairs around the white table in the center of the room. She would not look at individual faces as she swung down the room with a clank of empty scabbards – externally she must keep the truce. She felt very sure of herself now. She held her bright-helmed head arrogantly, making the cloak ripple with every long stride, hearing her spurs jingle as she came. The trumpet notes shivered and echoed among the arches of the ceiling.

Above them rose the soaring transept of a vast hall. Its purple walls paled to violet and then to white as they rose toward an intricate interlacing of arches through whose translucent heights pale sunlight came pouring. It was a very old hall. The emperors of Ericon had reared it upon the ruins of the race they had displaced. And that race had built here upon the ruins of other emperors, ages before.

The present emperor stood white and tall at the head of the table. Juille bowed to him formally, but she flicked over and past the other two men a glance so icy that it barely acknowledged their presence.

In one glance, though, she saw all that she needed to see. It *was* Egide. The same handsome, rash, blue-eyed young face with the curly short beard, the curly hair. He had hung his harp over the chair arm where he sat, and Juille thought it the ultimate touch of decadent foppishness, incongruous in a barbarian prince. He wore today not an extravagantly designed cloak of blood or hair, but black velvet that looked spectacular against the silvery gleam of his mesh mail. There was a fire-sword scar half-healed across his cheek and temple, and he looked a little more tired and wary than the careless lover of Cyrille. But the blue eyes were as confident as ever on her face.

All this in one cold, flashing glance that ignored him. She folded her fingers lovingly over a tiny palm gun hidden in her hand, its metal warm from that close hiding place. Her glance flicked over the other man and went on.

Big, bull-chested, with reddish hair and beard and eyes. Huge forearms crossed over his chest. A barbarian, typical of the savage H'vani. And yet so openly savage, with such a direct, fighting glare on his scarred face, that she felt a reluctant flash of kinship with him. Such a man, she thought, her own remote forefathers must have been who conquered the Galaxy by brute force and left it for her heritage. Beside him Egide looked the fop he was, and her father the senile idealist.

She nodded distantly as the emperor introduced the two. Egide, hereditary leader of the H'vani, Jair, his commander in chief. Her only thought was a murderous one. 'If I can kill them both, what a blow to the H'vani! And what fools they were to come!'

Her father was speaking. She scarcely listened to the sonorous voice whose echoes went whispering among the arches in confused murmurs high overhead.

'We sit today,' the old man declared, 'over the graves of a score of races who made the same mistake we are on the verge of making here, and who died because they did.'

She could feel Egide's blue stare upon her face. It was intolerable. All the ages of imperial pride rose behind her, the pride of a hundred generations that had commanded the stars in their courses. This one bearded barbarian sitting here staring at her unashamedly, as if he were her equal, as if he thought she, too, must be remembering a fantastic night-time ride upon a cloud, under stars like burning roses in constellations without a name.

She turned full upon him one bright, furious glare that flashed like a violet fire sword beneath the helmet brim. 'You ought to be dead,' the burning glance implied. 'When I find who failed me, and why they failed, they'll be dead, too. You're living on borrowed time. You ought to be dead and you will be soon – you will be soon!' She made a chant of it in her throat, letting her eyes half-close to slits of bright fire-blade violet.

The emperor talked on. 'We are too evenly matched. Neither can win without such destruction as will cast the whole Galaxy back a thousand years. On all the worlds of that Galaxy – many new worlds that have not yet known war – our forces stand poised in armed, precarious truce, watching what happens here today. If we join in battle—'

Juille made an impatient gesture and recrossed her legs. The little palm gun was warm in her hand. She wished passionately that the platitudes were over. And then a treacherous spasm of pity went over her as she listened to the deep old voice roll on. He had been a great warrior once, her father. This meant so much to him, and it was so hopelessly futile – But there was no room for pity in the new Galaxy of today. Her lips thinned as she fondled the trigger of her gun. Soon, now.

'The H'vani are a young race,' the old man went on. 'A crude race, unlettered in any science but warfare. Let us give you the incalculable wealth we have to spare, that you could never take by force. We can teach you all our science has learned in the rich millenniums of our history. In one stride you can advance a thousand years.

'If you refuse – there is no hope for you. At the very best, we can and will destroy you, if only after such struggles as will cost us all we have. At worst – well, other races have met in deadly conflict on Ericon. Where are they now?' He pointed toward the marble floor. 'Down there, in the dark. Under the foundations of this hall lie the building stones of all who fought here before us. Have you ever been down there in the catacombs, any of you? Do you know the old kings who once ruled Ericon? Does anyone alive? And will anyone remember us, if we fail to learn by their example?'

Juille's hand came down roughly on the sleek-furred little animal that had slid down upon her knee, and then all her scornful inattention vanished as the small body twisted snake-like under her hand. She snatched it back with lightning quickness, just in time to avoid the slash of her pet's teeth. It stared up at her, nervously poised, clutching her knee with flexible fingery pads, a look of completely spurious benignity and wisdom in its round eyes even now.

A new voice, so deeply resonant that the air shuddered in response to it, was saying powerfully, 'When peace terms are proposed, it'll be the H'vani who dictate them!'

Juille looked up sharply. The emperor had paused. He stood beside her now with his head sunk a little, watching the two envoys from under his bristling brows. She felt a fresh spasm of pity. But the new voice was making strong echoes rumble among the arches of the ceiling, and she knew it was time to pay attention.

Jair was on his feet, his great fists planted like mallets upon the table edge. 'We'll talk peace with the Lyonese,' he boomed triumphantly, 'but we'll talk it from the throne. Time enough for—'

Juille shoved back her chair with a sudden furious motion and leaped to her feet, her eyes blazing across the table. The *llar* had sprung sidewise and caught the emperor's arm, where it hung staring over its shoulder at her with enormous benignant eyes.

But before she could speak, Egide's chair scraped leisurely across the floor, the harp strings ringing faintly with the motion. He stood up almost lazily, but his words preceded hers.

'We ask the emperor's pardon,' he said in a calm voice. 'Jair, let me talk.'

Jair gave him a strangely blank look and sat down. Egide went on:

'What my general means to say is that peace terms must come from us if they're to come at all. What the emperor says is true and we realize it, but we believe it to be only part of the truth. A divided victory isn't enough for the H'vani, no matter how many secrets you offer as a bribe. My people are not to be bought with promises for the future.' He smiled whitely in the impeccable flaxen curls of his beard. 'My people, I am afraid, are a very literal race. Not too ready to trust an enemy's promises. Now if you had some specific benefit to offer us here and now – something that might reassure the H'vani about your sincerity' – he glanced from Juille to the emperor and went on with an impulsive persuasion in his voice that Juille remembered well – 'I think we might have a better chance of convincing my people that you mean what you say.'

Juille met his guileless blue gaze with a steely look. She knew quite well what he was hinting. So that was why they'd come, was it? To wheedle the Dunnarian weapon out of the emperor's senile, peace-bemused hands, and taking full advantage of their supposed immunity because of what had happened upon Cyrille, because they must think that she herself was equally bemused at the memory of it. Obvious strategy, and yet – Juille glanced at her father. No expression showed upon his thoughtful face, but she felt a sudden cold uncertainty about what he might decide to do. Surely he could not believe that the H'vani meant what they said. Surely he must see that once they had a share in the new and subtle weapon from Dunnar there'd be no stopping them this side of the imperial throne. No, he was certainly not yet mad.

But this was only the beginning. Talk would go on and on, endless circlings around the proposal Egide had just voiced. Endless counterproposals from the emperor. Days and days of it, while Egide still went on believing that she was the reason why he had been invited here, still exchanged with her these sudden blue glances that recalled their days upon Cyrille – the crystal platform drifting through flowery branches and the green evening light of spring. The starry lake beneath their feet as they danced, and the long smooth rhythms when they moved together to enchanting music. The landscapes unreeling beneath their couch of cloud, the great stars blazing overhead.

No, she would not endure it. She would end it here and now.

'Egide—' she said in a clear, high voice.

He turned to her with a quick eagerness she had not seen before. This was the first word she had addressed to him upon Ericon, the first time she had ever spoken his name. He was searching her face with a look of eagerness she did not understand. She didn't want to.

She walked slowly around the table toward him. They were all on their feet now, looking at her in surprise. All speech had ceased and the hall was very still. The emperor said, 'Juille?' in a voice not yet very much alarmed, but she did not glance at him. She rounded the end of the table and saw Egide push his chair out of the way with a careless thrust that knocked the harp from its back. In the silence, the jarred strings wailed a thin, shrill, plaintive discord through the hall, and Egide caught the falling instrument and smiled uneasily at her.

She came toward him without a flicker of returning smile. 'Egide—' she said again. She was quite near him now. Near enough to see the crinkling edges of the scar that furrowed his cheek, the separate curling hairs of his shining beard, his thick golden lashes. Behind him she was aware that Jair had drawn an uneasy step or two nearer. She was looking straight into Egide's blue eyes, large and unfathomable at this nearness. She came forward one last step, bringing her gun hand up.

'I want you to know,' she said distinctly, 'that I had no part in asking you here. I hate your race and all it stands for. I mean to do everything I can to prevent any truce between us. Everything. Do you understand me?'

The emperor did. He knew his child. He took one long stride toward her around the table, crying, 'Juille, Juille! Remember the truce—'

But he was too far away. Juille fixed Egide's fascinated stare with a hot, exultant stare of her own, and her lips drew back in a tight grin over her teeth. With her face very near his, and her gaze plumbing his gaze, she smiled and pulled the trigger.

Then time stopped. A dozen things happening at once, jumbled themselves together bewilderingly, prefaced and veiled by a great fan of violet heat that sprang up terribly between her face and Egide's. Juille heard Jair's roar and her father's cry, and the crash of overturning chairs. But her brain was numbed by the shock of that violet heat where there should have been no heat – only a thin needle beam of force boring through Egide's corselet.

She and Egide reeled apart with singed lashes and cheeks burning from that sudden glare as the instantaneous fan of light died away. Her dazzled eyes saw dimly that he was gasping like a man who had taken a sudden sharp blow in the stomach, but he was not dead. He should be dead, and he only stood there gasping at her, blinking singed golden lashes.

For a split second her mind could not grasp it. She saw the silver mail burned away across his chest where that fierce needle beam should have bored through flesh and bone. She saw beneath it not charred white skin and spurting blood, but a smooth shining surface which the beam had not even blackened. Everything was ringed with rainbows, and when she closed her smarting eyes she saw the outline of burned mail and gleaming surface beneath in reversed colors bright against the darkness of her lids.

Then time caught up with her. Things began to happen again with furious speed. The explanation flashed into her mind as she saw Egide reaching for her. He wore some sort of protection even under his mail, then – some substance that deflected the needle beam into a blast of thin, scorching heat diffused into harmlessness. And she had an instant of foolish and incongruous rage that he had come thus protected, doubting the validity of their truce.

Then Egide's arm slammed her hard against the unyielding surface of whatever armor he wore beneath his mail. She felt a small, reluctant admiration of the strength in that arm – an unexpected strength, remembered from Cyrille – and of his almost instantaneous action even when she knew he must be sick and breathless from a severe blow in the pit of the stomach. The gun's beam would have bruised him heavily even through the armor, before its force fanned out into sheer heat.

It all happened too quickly to rationalize. She did not even have time to wonder why he seized her, or why Jair, bellowing with a sound of exultation, was dragging them both across the floor toward the far wall. She had a confused glimpse of her father's bewildered and outraged face. She saw the guards leaning out of their hidden stations in the wall across from her, guns leveled. But she knew she herself was a shield for the two H'vani, though what they planned, she could not even guess.

Other guards were tumbling from their posts, running toward them across the hall. Juille suddenly began to fight hard against the restraining clasp that held her. She bruised her fists upon the armor beneath Egide's mail. Jair roared inexplicably:

'Open up! You hear me? Open!'

Egide crushed her ribs painfully against his corselet and swung her feet off the ground. For a dizzy instant the violet walls and the sunlit white arches of the ceiling spun in reverse around her. She was hanging head-down over Egide's shoulder, seething with intolerable rage at this first rough handling she had ever known in her life. But she was bewildered, too, and off-balance and incredulous that such things could happen. She was briefly aware of cries from the hall, her father's voice shouting commands, the guards yelling. And then came sudden darkness and a smooth, swishing noise that cut off all sounds behind them.

The dark smelled of dust and age-old decay. Juille's mind told her what her reason refused to accept – that somehow, incredibly, these barbarians had come forearmed with knowledge about some panel in the walls of the imperial council hall which a hundred generations of ruling emperors had never guessed.

She was still upside down over Egide's shoulder, acutely uncomfortable, her cheek pressed against something cold and hard, her eyes stinging from the heat of her own gun. Voices whispered around them. Someone said, 'Hurry!' and there was the muffled sound of feet through dust that rose in stifling clouds. And then a long, sliding crash that filled the darkness deafeningly and made the eardrums ache from its sudden pressure in this confined space. Someone said after a stunned moment, 'There, that does it.' Someone else – Jair? – said, 'How?' and the first voice, familiar but unplaceable:

'When they break through the wall, they'll find this rock-fall, and a false tunnel that leads outside the city walls. They'll think you went that way. We laid a trail of footprints through it yesterday. Safe now.'

But who ... who was it?

'Put me down!' Juille demanded in a fierce, muffled voice. That someone whose tones sounded very familiar indeed, said:

'Better not yet. Come along. Can you manage her?'

And the nightmare went on. Someone ahead carried a light that cast great wavering shadows along the rough walls. Juille was joggling up and down across Egide's shoulder through the musty dark, sick with fury and outrage and bewilderment. Her eyes streamed with involuntary tears as an aftermath of that heat flash; her burning cheek was pressed hard against the corner of something cold and unyielding – Egide's harp? – and the dust rose chokingly all around.

After smothered ages, the familiar voice said:

'You can put her down now.'

There came one last upheaval and Juille was on her feet again, automatically smoothing down her tunic, glaring through the dimness in a speechless seizure of rage. She saw Egide looking down at her with expressionless eyes, saw Jair's savage face dark in the torchlight, his eyes gleaming. Between them she saw the familiar, comforting, tough-featured face of Helia.

For an instant her relief was greater than she would have thought possible. All her life that face had meant comfort, protection, gruff encouragement against disappointment. In the midst of this bewilderment and indignity, the one familiar sight made everything all right again. Even in the face of reason—

Egide still held her arms.

'Turn her around,' Helia told him, in the familiar voice, with the familiar homely gesture of command Juille had known all her life, from nursery days. She found herself spun around, her arms held behind her, while Helia reached under the mail tunic and took away the little dagger that no one else knew about, the dagger that Helia herself had taught Juille to hide there and use unexpectedly as a last resort.

Juille closed her eyes.

'The others will be waiting,' Helia's capable voice remarked calmly. 'First, though – highness, I had better tie your hands.'

Juille wondered madly whether that violet flash of heat had really killed her. Perhaps it had only stunned her – that must be it – and all this was an irrational dream.

Helia's familiar hands that had bathed her from babyhood, dressed her hurts, taught her sword play and target practice – were binding her wrists behind her now with sure, gentle swiftness. The well-known voice said as the binding went on:

'You must understand, highness, before you meet the rest. I don't want you to face them without understanding.' She drew the soft cords tighter. 'I am an Andarean, highness. Your race conquered ours a hundred generations ago. But we never forget. Here under the city, in the catacombs that were once our own imperial halls, we've met to pass along from father to son the tradition of our heritage. We've planned all these centuries for a day like this. There.' She gave the cords a final pat. 'Now, keep your head up and don't let them see it if you're confused. Wait a minute.' She came around in front of Juille, clucked disapprovingly, and took out a handkerchief to wipe the dust from Juille's hot face where the tears had streaked it. Then she straightened the helmet that had fallen by its chin strap over one ear.

'Keep your head up,' she said again. 'Remember what I've taught you. We may have to kill you later, my dear – but while you live, you're still my girl and I want to be proud of you. Now – march!'

*

And so, bewildered to the point of madness, still choked by the dust in her nostrils, her eyes burning and her hands tied behind her, but with her head up because Helia, insanely, wanted to be proud of her, Juille let herself be marched forward, up shallow steps and into a big low cavern lighted by square windows through which light streamed from some outside source.

There were people here, sitting along the walls on benches. Not many. Juille knew some of the faces – servants and small courtiers about the palace. A few of them held responsible positions with the defense forces.

From among them a man stepped forward. Juille did not know him, except that his features were Andarean. He wore a purple tunic and cloak, and he bowed to the two H'vani.

'We are making history here,' he said in a soft, low-pitched voice. 'This is the turning point in the war for Galactic domination. We of Andarea welcome you and the future you will control.'

Jair drew a deep breath and started to say something. Juille was aware that Egide's elbow jammed into his ribs. Egide, still breathing a little unevenly from the gun bolt in the stomach, spoke instead in his most courtly voice:

'We H'vani will owe you a great deal. You've managed things perfectly so far. But we haven't much time now. The weapons—'

The Andarean's long eyes slid around to Juille. It was at once a query and a murderous suggestion, without words. Juille felt a sudden shudder of goose flesh. New experiences had crowded one another in these last few minutes until she was dizzy with trying to adjust to them – she had never been man-handled before, she had never been treated like an object instead of a person, and she hotly resented the fact that Egide had not directly addressed a word to her since the moment in the hall when she had tried to kill him.

Behind her dimly she saw Helia step forward to lay a hand on Egide's arm. Suddenly she knew how Egide had learned of her presence on Cyrille – perhaps, too, why her assassins had failed to reach the H'vani during their ride into the city. But when Egide spoke his voice was firm, as if he had not needed prompting.

'Juille is our hostage,' he told the Andarean. 'There, I think, we've improved on your plan. If anything goes wrong, we still have something to bargain with.'

The Andarean nodded dubiously, his narrow, impassive eyes lingering on her face as if in reluctance. 'Perhaps. Well, we'd better get started. We—'

'Wait.' Egide glanced around the cavern, dim in the light that so oddly came through from outside. 'Are these all of you?'

'Almost all.' The Andarean said it carelessly. 'Our numbers have dwindled very much in the last few generations.'

Juille narrowed her eyes at him. That was a lie. The Andareans were few, but certainly not this few. Grateful for some problem she could take a real hold upon, she cast her mind back searchingly over the past history of this race, making a mental note to have the heads off certain of her espionage officials if she ever got out of this alive.

Long ago the earlier emperors had kept close spies upon their overthrown predecessors, but the watch had relaxed as generations passed and the Andarean numbers grew less. They were too few, really, to matter except in some such accident as this, when chance assembled just the right factors to make their treachery dangerous.

So the two H'vani had come – why? Exactly why? Groping back among the tangled skeins of plot and counterplot Juille lost her grip again upon clear thinking. They were here because they thought in her weakness she had asked them to talk peace terms – because they hoped to trick possession of the Dunnarian weapon out of the Lyonese hands – because of some treacherous promises from these skulkers in the underground. And those skulkers themselves were lying out of the depths of further schemes of their own.

She got a cold sort of comfort out of that. If the H'vani had deceived her and her father, they in turn were being deceived. For there were far more Andareans upon Ericon than she saw here. Their leader would not have lied just now if he were not playing some desperate game with his new allies.

Weapons. Egide had asked about weapons. Were the Andareans offering him some new offensive measure to use against the Lyonese? And why? The Andareans were a subtle race; surely they had cherished the memories of their great lost heritage too long, if Helia told the truth, to give up their future to H'vani rule, supposing the H'vani won. And surely they were too wise in the ways of deceit to trust H'vani promises even should they win.

Juille gave up the problem as Helia took her arm again and drew her after the others. They were moving out of the low cavern with its strange outside lighting. Helia padded along softly at Juille's side, her eyes downcast. Juille looked at her in the dim light, finding no words with which to reproach her. She was still too stunned by this sudden failure of the solidest assurance in her life to look at it with any rational clarity.

Nor was Helia a woman to offer apologies.

'Look around you,' she said brusquely as they filed out of the cavern. 'You may never see a sight like this again.'

The cavern, seen from outside in clearer light, was obviously the collapsed remnants of a much higher room. What might once have been a hallway ran around it outside, the walls patterned with luminous blocks that shed a glow which must be three thousand years old.

The walls showed scars of age-old battle. Juille's first imperial ancestors might very well have commanded the guns that made them. For this uppermost level of the tunnels which lay beneath the city must once have comprised the lower stories of the palace the Andareans had built in the days of their glory.

The ruins had been leveled off and sealed when the modern palace was built. Everyone knew of the honeycombing layers which went down and down in unknown depths of level under level. Some of them had been explored, cursorily. But they were much too unsafe for any systematic examination, and far too deep to be cleared out or filled up to give the city a firm foundation.

The confusion of interlacing passages, level blending with level, was so complex that explorers had been known to vanish here and never reappear. And immemorial traps, laid down millenniums ago by retreating defenders in forgotten wars, sometimes caught the innocent blundering along dusty tunnels. Walls and floors collapsed from time to time under the weight of exploring footsteps. No, it was not a safe place for the casual adventurer to visit.

But perhaps in each dynasty the survivors of the defeated race had lurked here in the cellars of their lost and ruined city, remembering their heritage and plotting to regain it. Perhaps – Juille thought of it grimly – her own people one day might creep in darkness through the shattered remnants of her purple plastic halls and jeweled arches, buried beneath the mounting stories of a new city, whispering the traditions of the Lyonese and plotting the downfall of triumphant H'vani. And perhaps they, too, might explore downward, as the Andareans had obviously done, searching the dangerous lower levels for some weapon to turn against the victors.

From the murmurs that drifted back to her along the tunnels she knew that something valuable lay hidden here, unless the Andareans were lying again. It was hard to believe that any such weapon actually existed, unknown after so many generations of curious explorers. And yet the Andareans sounded very sure. Egide and Jair would certainly not have risked their necks on such a mission unless the promise had been soundly based on evidence.

Indeed, it seemed incredible that these two foremost leaders of the revolt would have dared to endanger their lives and their whole campaign on such a gamble as this, had they not been very sure of escape.

Someone ahead was carrying a radiant globe of translucent plastic on the end of a tall handle. She could see Egide's confident yellow head haloed with light from it, and Jair's great bulk outlined against the glow. The light sliding along the walls showed scenes of forgotten Andarean legends, winged animals and eagle-headed men in low relief upon which dust had gathered like drifts of snow. They passed windows of colored glass that no longer opened upon anything but darkness. They passed rooms which the soft light briefly revealed in amorphous detail under mounds of smothering dust.

And once they came out on a balcony over a scene that took Juille's breath away. The vast hall below them was built on a scale so tremendous that it seemed incredible that human minds had conceived it. Its vast oval was proportioned so perfectly that only the giddy depths below them made the room seem as large as it was. A muted blue radiance lighted it from incredible heights of windows lifting columns of blue unbroken glass from floor to ceiling, all around the walls.

Helia said with a sort of gruff pride, 'This was one of our temples once, highness. No one's ever built such a temple since. See that glass? The secret of it's lost now. The light's in the glass itself, not from outside.' She was silent for a moment, looking down. Then she said in a softer voice, 'Andarea was a great nation, highness. You feel the same about yours. Remember what you said today, about breaking the truce? The end justifies any means you have to take. I think so, too.'

It was as near as she could come to apology or explanation. And Juille, after a moment of blinking dismay at this application of her own theories turned against her, was conscious of sudden respect for this inflexible woman at her side. Here was the true amazon, she thought, more ruthless than any man in the naked simplicity of her cast-off femininity. This was the one quality Juille could respect above all others. She glanced ahead at Egide's broad back, despising him for the lack of it. Unswerving faithfulness to a principle, whatever that principle might be.

Juille wondered what Egide was thinking, how he interpreted to himself her attempt at murder. Well, if she had failed it was not for weakness like his. And there might come another chance. Her mind had begun to awaken again after the stunning shocks of the past half hour. Already she was making plans. Helia she thought she understood. Helia would protect her while she could. She would see to her comfort and save her face whenever possible, but when the time came, Helia might kill her with a steady hand. And Juille would have despised her if the hand shook.

They went down a sweep of tremendous stairs and filed, a pigmy row, across the floor of that vast hall under the shining blue columns of the windows. And from there they went down sharply, and down again.

There was tension in the air of these lower levels. Once an Andarean went ahead to a curtain of spider webs that veiled the passage and lifted it aside on the point of a staff, with exaggerated care, while the party passed beneath. And once they balanced carefully in single file along a bridge of planks laid upon perfectly solid flooring.

They had come so far now, by such devious ways, that she had no idea where she was, or at what level. She was sure the H'vani were equally at a loss. And it occurred to her briefly that they were at the mercy of their guides now – that the Andareans could come very close to putting an end to the Galaxy-wide warfare here and now in the dusty dark. For robbed of their leaders, the armies would certainly falter. But Juille felt quite sure that whatever the Andareans wanted, it was not peace.

They had, perhaps, taken steps even surer than her own to make certain that the emperor's peace conference came to nothing. The H'vani, primed with promises of mysterious weapons, would be in no mood to make a truce with any idea of keeping it.

She demanded suddenly of Helia, still walking at her elbow in the old accustomed place, 'Why haven't the Andareans used these weapons themselves?' And she saw Egide's broad back tense a little, the harp slung across his shoulder – where she had hung ignobly a little while before – shifting place at the motion of muscles beneath. She knew that he must have been wondering the same thing. And she knew he was listening.

'As we told the H'vani,' Helia said, 'we aren't a nation of fighters any more, highness. And there are too few of us. We couldn't risk losing the weapons in any tentative uprising.'

So they'd told the H'vani that already, had they? And it hadn't satisfied Egide any more than it did herself. Helia was a magnificent fighter. She had taught Juille all she knew. A determined, secret band of men and women armed with an unexpected weapon could have seized key positions on planets enough to swing the balance of power to themselves if they chose, and if they were gifted with the subtle minds the Andareans had already shown themselves to possess. Juille would not have hesitated, in such a case. And she didn't think Helia would either, if there were no alternative.

Obviously, there was an alternative. They were using the H'vani against the imperial forces – why?

Suddenly, Juille saw the answer. It was the simplest strategy in the world, and the safest. You could risk an uprising, your own neck and ultimate failure by acting yourself, or you could pit the two forces of greatest power against one another, preventing any truce between them by devious methods, arming one against the other to maintain a perfect balance – until they had wiped each other out. When both sides had struggled to exhaustion, then let the Andareans step in and take over the control they had been prepared to take for so many centuries. It was so easy.

'Here it is,' the Andarean in the purple tunic said.

They all crowded forward to stare. And it was a sight worth staring at. The shadows hid most of the long room, shadows heavy as velvet curtains, as if their own age had thickened them into tangible things. But they could not wholly hide the weapons racked shining upon the walls, shining and defiant of dust and rust and the aeons. Cobwebs had formed upon them like festoons, gathering dust until their own weight tore them. There were many layers of such cobwebs, woven and thickened and torn anew over these untarnished swords and pistols and nameless things. Wherever the velvety dust of the webs revealed them, they were brilliant in the light. Some other lost race had known and buried with itself the secret of such metal.

The Andarean dismissed that array with a gesture.

'Unimportant things there, on the walls. Only variations of weapons already in use. Out of all this arsenal there are only three important weapons that haven't been paralleled in later ages. We want to give you those three.'

He padded silently forward through the dust, lifting his feet like a man who walks in snow, and took up from a clean-swept stand a little pistol not much bigger than the palm gun Juille had dropped in the council hall.

'This,' he said, hefting its shining smallness on his hand, 'discharges a miniature lightning bolt that feeds on metal. It leaps from armed man to armed man, or from girder to girder, feeding and growing as it goes, until the gap becomes too wide to jump.'

Juille stared at the little gun, a confused realization taking shape in her mind that this war was to be unlike any war before in Lyonese history – unless she could escape somehow in time to prevent the use of these weapons. It would be as if the gods took part, so strange and new would the weapons be on both sides.

The Andarean leader was looking at her uneasily. 'Is it wise to let the princess hear about all this?' he asked Egide.

The H'vani turned and for the first time since that moment in the council hall, looked straight into Juille's eyes. She met the look almost happily, with a defiance he could not mistake. She was eager to bring into the open all her hatred of him, all her scorn. She wanted it put it into words, but before she could have spoken, he said in his faintly malicious drawl that she remembered very well, 'You'd better stay here. Helia will keep you company.' It was a patronizing tone. Half turned away, he added over one shoulder, 'I'll be back—' and gave her a long look.

Speechless with fury, Juille watched him plowing away through the dust with the others. Everything he had said might have been deliberately calculated to enrage her. She twisted her wrists futilely against the cords.

Helia was looking at her with narrow, speculative eyes. Juille gave her a quelling glance and turned her back, looking up at the dust-swathed weapons with an angry, unseeing stare. Voices receded down the room. And as Juille's anger ebbed a little, she found that the rack of weapons made a very interesting sight. Just possibly some of those guns might still be loaded. If their look of shining, immortal efficiency could be trusted, she might, with luck, find one that had been left in working order.

And there had, she thought, been something a little false about the Andarean's casual dismissal of the guns. She would have been willing to bet that six months from now, if the H'vani, with their gift of weapons, were gaining the upper hand too quickly over the imperial forces, there would be Andarean patriots from the tunnels to make a gift of other weapons to the Lyonese. These Andareans were much too subtle to give away their whole stock to the first comer. And if they were really holding back weapons to offer the Lyonese should the H'vani seem to win too easily, might not some of these devices on the wall be worth taking? If she could – if she only could—

This rack before her presented a display of curiously shaped weapons half shrouded in velvet-thick webs of dust. Some of them looked vaguely familiar. She didn't want those. Probably the Andarean had told at least a half-truth when he said many of them were simply variations of known things. But this odd, slim, flexible pistol, with a bell-shaped mouth and a coil of silver tubing twined about its length—

Juille turned her back on the wall and glanced down the room. Helia was watching the group at the far end, where men appeared to be handling what looked like a big folded net of loose meshes with nodes that sparkled opalescent in the light. She could not hear what they said.

Juille took three steps backward, soundless in the deep dust, hitched her cloak painstakingly out of the way and groped blindly with her bound hands through layers of velvety dust. She thought shudderingly of the spiders that had spun these webs, and it occurred to her that she would probably never like the touch of velvet again as she tore the clinging, thick softness from the gun she wanted. It was not easy, with her hands bound. She prayed for Helia to watch the other end of the room a moment longer—

There. Cool and slick against her palms, enigmatic, potentially very dangerous – the slender gun was hers. What might happen when she pulled its trigger no one could guess. Probably nothing at all. But the feel of it was heartening. She thrust it down inside the back of her belt and let her cloak swing over it. And when Helia turned again to glance at her, she was looking up at a rack of daggers with bored, aloof eyes.

'Those won't help you, highness,' Helia said. 'That cord I used on you is a woven plastic. Knives can't touch it.'

'I know,' Juille told her, not turning.

Voices drew nearer along the big, dim hall. Juille glanced around. She could see that Egide wore the lightning gun thrust through his belt, and Jair's bull-bulk was padded even further by the heavy net folded and looped through his own belt. She could see no third weapon. She could not even guess what the net was for. But she had her own secret now, and her feeling of utter helplessness was mitigated a little.

She watched them come slogging back through the dust, their voices rumbling between the walls. Now and then, curiously, a weapon's delicate blade rang with a thin sound when some chance note of the voices struck it to response, as if the immeasurable past protested in futile, tongueless, inhuman speech against this violation.

There was a new and triumphant assurance in the very carriage of the two H'vani as they neared her. Jair's eyes and teeth gleamed from his ruddy dark face, and Egide glowed with a sort of shining exhilaration.

At the door of the room he paused to look back along the shadowy depths, and his bright, careless face lighted. Then he grinned and unslung his harp. The others stared. Egide's calloused fingers swept the strings into a sudden, wild, wailing chord, and another, and then a third. The underground room rang with it, and on the wall a quiver of life leaped into shining motion as here and there a thin blade shrilled response. Egide laughed, a deep, full-throated sound, and shouted out what must have been a line or two of some old H'vani battle song. His voice was startlingly sweet and strong and true.

The arsenal boomed with the deep, rolling echoes of it. Somewhere hidden under tons of dust, a forgotten drum boomed back, distant and softly muffled. Some metal cylinder of forgotten purpose took up the echo and replied with a clear, metallic reverberation, and down the hall an æons-dead warrior's helmet rang with its hollow mouth like a clapperless bell, and fell clanging to the floor and the silencing dust.

Egide laughed again, with a timbre of sudden intoxication, and smote his harp to a last wild, shrilling wail, sent one more phrase of the song booming down the room. And all the room replied. The muffled drum boomed back, and the clear ringing twang of the hidden cylinder, and the little blades shrilled like tongues upon the wall, shivering and twinkling with tiny motion.

Echoes rolled and rolled again. Egide's voice sang on for a moment or two without him, diminishing against the walls. And this was no longer a thin, hopeless protest of the voiceless past against intrusion as the arsenal replied. Egide's was a warrior's voice, promising battle again, strong and savage with the savagery of a barbarous young race. These weapons had rung before, in the unfathomable past, to the voices of such men. Arsenal and weapons roared an answer to that promise of blood again, and the echoes died slowly among the blades and the drums and the hollow, hanging shields that might never echo any more to the sounds they were made to echo.

Juille, meeting the unashamed melodrama of his blue eyes and his laughter as he turned away, was appalled by a surge of genuine warmth and feeling. This was naked sentiment again, like the deliberate romance of Cyrille, but to her amazement she found herself responding, and with an unexpected, overwhelming response she did not understand. Egide, laughing, had reslung his harp. He said:

'Come on – now the danger starts. You have a ship for us, Andarean?'

'Ready and waiting. You'd better not try to leave, though, until dark.'

'The real danger comes then,' Jair rumbled.

Egide bent a shining smile upon Juille. 'That's where you come in, my dear. We couldn't have a better hostage.'

Juille gave him her stoniest glance and looked away. She was profoundly troubled by that moment of sympathy with his unashamed romanticism. It made her think of the warm, resistless mood which had engulfed them both on the dance floor, and that hour on the starry cloud – swift, irresistible, and vanishing to leave nothing but humiliation behind, and a stronger dislike and distrust of the man who could evoke such weakness.

They went back along winding, upward tunnels, past the carving of forgotten history upon the walls, past level above level of successive cultures whose dust mingled now under the feet of new rival cultures, one of which must pass so soon. Several times they edged past danger points again, and the leading Andarean twice closed and locked metal grilles after them across their path. The implication was ominous, though no one referred to it aloud.

Egide's intoxicated assurance began to ebb perceptibly and he grew more thoughtful as they neared the upper levels. Juille, watching his broad back and thinking with a sort of detached passion how pleasant it would be to set the bell-muzzle of her new weapon against it, began to wonder presently at his preoccupation.

She saw him murmur to Jair, and saw the big red beard turn in the lamplit dimness to stare almost incredulously at his leader. Then Egide went ahead to murmur further with the purple-robed Andarean. Juille began to feel a bit cold. Were they talking about herself? Had the time come already to dispose of her? Surely not yet, before they were safely away—

When they came out onto a lighted level that showed signs of Andarean traffic, Egide halted. Helia and Juille exchanged an involuntary glance of mutual query. Egide came back through the column to them. There was a strange, stilled look upon his face, as if he had come to some momentous decision in the grip of which he seemed to want human nearness, for he put out both hands and laid them upon Juille's shoulders. Automatic reaction against the lese majesty made her tense to shake him off, but something about the look in his eyes halted her.

'I'm going – out,' he said, in a quiet voice not at all like the melodious roar that had shaken the arsenal below.

'They'll catch you.' She had meant it for a threat, but his look subdued her and the words came out a warning.

He shook his yellow head. 'I think not. They tell me there's a tunnel into the forest from here.'

'But the forest—' Julie broke off and stared up at him, a sinking in the pit of her stomach. For the forest marked the edge of that forbidden ground surrounding the temple of the Ancients. They looked at one another briefly, antagonisms forgotten for a moment. Egide was nodding.

'I think I need advice. None of us ever had this chance before. Now I'm here – well, I'm going to take it.'

Juille stared up at him with real awe. Even the emperors of the Galaxy, with the stars of heaven for an empire, dared not think too deeply or too often of the living gods of Ericon. Long ago, she knew, there had been emperors who went to consult the Ancients in their temple. So far as she knew, none had done so for a long while now. Upon this one world of all the Galaxy, men lived side by side with the gods, and they had learned not to presume upon their nearness. The very aloofness of the Ancients, striking only to punish, never to reward, did not encourage familiarity. She looked up at Egide with eyes emptied of all thought but reluctant awe.

His own eyes were very still. He had not quite her feeling of the god's remoteness because, paradoxically, he had not lived so near them. But everyone tended to fall silent at the thought of the Ancients.

He looked down at her thoughtfully, and for a moment Juille knew, with a sort of angry certainty, that he was about to kiss her. Her pride and her scorn of him made that thought intolerable, but a dissolving warmth was running through her treacherous body as she met his look, and the most humiliating gladness that her arms were tied so that she could not resist. Then the humiliation drowned everything else as he let his hands fall and turned away.

'Tie her up somewhere until I get back,' he said briefly to Helia. 'Jair, come with me as far as the tunnel—'

Juille sat angrily on a floor deeply cushioned with dust, leaning upon a dusty wall. Profound dimness all around her was feebly diluted by the light of a distant lamp. Helia had left it, after a short disagreement with her companions. Juille realized that the Andareans probably distrusted the depths of Helia's loyalty to themselves where Juille was concerned, and oddly, she rather resented their distrust. The cult of the amazon was still too new not to resent man's misunderstanding of its principles. Juille was conscious of a sort of fierce pride in Helia's betrayal of her lifelong trust, for the bleak ideal of Andarean loyalty. The Andareans' doubt of it was a slap in the face to all amazons.

But she was not thinking of that now. She was mentally following Egide through the dripping green forest toward the temple which she had never seen. She knew it would be dark and broad and tall among the trees. She pictured Egide in his black velvet and charred silver mail, striding up to the portal and – but her mind balked at following him farther.

And that, too, humiliated her. It seemed to her that she had been wallowing in enforced humilities for the past several hours, each of them more irritating than the last. This was particularly so, because it involved the moral courage she prided herself on possessing. She did not like to think of Egide walking boldly up to a doorway so awesome that she herself scarcely dared visit it in thoughts. Even the knowledge that he was a barbarian and an outworlder, with the courage of ignorance, was not too comforting. And presently, in the dimness, she began to wonder whether she could do as he was doing, supposing herself free again. Step in under that great shadowy, unimaginable portal and ask for guidance? Intrude her small human presence upon the living gods, whose millenniums of aloofness showed so clearly that they did not welcome human interference?

Even if she were free, would she dare?

Suddenly, hideously, there were tiny cold hands fumbling at hers.

The darkness reeled about her. Mad thoughts went racing through her mind – denizens of the lower levels, creeping up in the dark to seize her? Unseen things against which the Andareans locked their great grilles in vain? Tiny, clammy-fingered demons from some lost race's hell – gammy-fingered – many-fingered—

Juille sank back against the wall and laughed hysterically in the dark, weak with relief, feeling a sleek, furry side brushing her wrist as the little hands tugged at her bonds. The *llar*, of course, but how ... how could it possibly have followed or found her here? No *llar* had ever done such a thing before. They had none of the canine's fawning faithfulness. No, there must be rescuers close behind it, though how anyone could have followed her here unseen by the Andareans, she could not imagine.

She called softly into the dimness. No answer, but the *llar* hissed at her gently, rather like a man whistling in preoccupation as he works. A moment later, she was amazed to feel the cord slackening at her wrists. Knowing how efficiently Helia had tied it, she could not believe the little animal could have loosened the knots. Nor could its teeth have parted the strands no knife could touch. But her hands were free, and already prickling with the pins and needles of returning circulation.

She rubbed them together, luxuriating in the pleasure of relaxed arm muscles again, and then felt the *llar*'s lithe, boneless weight on her knees. Something was thrust into her hands. Her fingers closed stiffly on a packet – a little leather bag. With fingers clumsy as thumbs, she expored it.

A tiny cylinder fell out, and something like a mirror on a chain, and what felt like a card. She knew the shape of the cylinder. It was a needle-beam flashlight that was weapon and torch in one. Cautiously, awkwardly, she switched on the flash to its weakest power. In the little blue-white circle of its light she could make out writing on the card.

It was a message of almost incredible impersonality:

> I am sending you the first completed focusing agent for our weapon. Center your target in the cross-hairs, then press the white stud. Target will register in the machine here; can be destroyed at will by pressing the black stud. Sorry this is a model, good for one shot only. Choose well.
>
> DUNNAR.

Juille reread the note slowly, puzzled by its laconic detachment. This might be a problem in ethics instead of the desperate reality it was. She saw in her mind's eye the strange, avian face of the envoy as it had so often regarded her with an impersonal, lidless gaze. She could not imagine emotion showing in it. Not even his own danger, she remembered now, had moved him at all when he came in from space with the weapon. Certainly no peril of hers moved him. She sensed some unfathomable purpose of his own working out, calmly and unhurried, behind all that had just been happening. Was he an Andarean? Certainly there was something behind those great, unwinking eyes, something locked secretly in the narrow skull, that evoked awe and distrust together.

Well, at any rate, now she had a weapon. Two weapons, for the flashlight would serve, too. She turned the thing like a mirror over in her hand. A double lens on a chain, she saw now, each lens threaded with a cross-hair and manipulated by studs in the tiny frame. A white stud, a black one. Such a simple thing to carry that deadly power. She tossed it up and caught it in her palm, grinning with sudden, fierce confidence. The tables were turning a little. Egide had left her bound and helpless; he would come back to her free and armed with a weapon of such surpassing treachery as no race had owned before, a weapon that struck out of empty air, in solitude, at the striker's will. But since this was a model, it would strike only once. She cursed that restriction in a whisper. Would it be Egide, then? Her feeling for him was too much a jumble of passionate contradictions now, to be sure. Although—

The *llar* squeaked impatiently at her knee. She glanced down in the faint blue light. 'Well, little friend?'

It was hard sometimes to know just where to place the limitations of that tiny animal brain. The *llars* were like cats in their fastidious withdrawal from any human attempt to probe their small minds or catalogue them according to human standards. She thought her own pet understood a limited vocabulary very well. She said, 'What is it now? Where *did* you come from? Is there danger?'

The great benign eyes stared up at her; the furry body twisted away and then back as if in an urgent plea to follow. Juille said, 'All right,' and stood up, brushing off the thick dry dust. The *llar* scuttled to the door and peered out. Then it scuttled back and looked up expectantly. 'Run along,' Juille told it. 'I'll follow.'

She slipped the lens chains over her head and dropped the circular instrument down inside her tunic. It would look like some innocent ornament if anyone caught her now. But she felt, without knowing why, a curious faith in the *llar's* ability to guide her out of this place in safety. She even experienced an illogical flicker of gratification that the impersonal little beast had troubled itself so much in her behalf. The entire performance was one no naturalist would have believed possible, certainly no owner of the proud, fastidious animals.

She went swiftly along the tunnel, over the cushioning dust, lighting her way with the dimmest blue radiance of her torch. It could be changed to a weapon of needle-beam force by a twist of the handle if anyone came out to intercept her, but her unreasoning faith in the *llar* was justified more deeply with every passing moment, for it led her along tunnels that seemed to have been uninhabited since the last Andarean emperor died at the hands of the first Lyonese.

Watching the sleek, lithe body flowing through the dimness, Juille wondered at its unerring certainty of the path. Some homing instinct, or actual knowledge of these passages? No one knew enough about the *llar* species to answer that.

The chain of small, flower-shaped footprints in the dust led her on and on. Up level, down level. Over crumbled ruins, through chambers of resounding echoes and caverns muffled in age-old dust.

They must be nearing the end of the journey now. She could smell fresh air blowing along the tunnels and smiled as she pictured the excitement in the palace when she came out. Her deep uneasiness about the unknown weapons of the Andareans would be appeased soon; those weapons would never now be turned against her. And she thanked her imperial ancestors that Egide had thought he must consult the Ancients, for it gave her the time she needed. The H'vani and their smuggled weapons would never leave Ericon now.

Her own emotional reactions to the immediate past and the immediate future were too tangled to sort out She didn't want to. That would come later. At any moment she would be coming out into the bustling exhilaration of the palace, and her long inactivity and helplessness would be ended. She smiled into the dark.

At her feet the *llar* scurried, rippling, on ahead.

The end came suddenly. They turned a corner and an unbarred door hung half open before them. The *llar* gave one small, whispering cry and then drew aside into the shadows of the tunnel. Cautiously, but with a beating pulse of triumph in her throat, Juille pushed the door open. Words were on her lips – urgent commands, reassurances, all the details of the plans she had been working out to put into practice the moment she reached her destination.

But she stood open-mouthed in the doorway and said nothing. There was no one to say it to. A gust of sweet, rainy air blew past her, the smell of green things and fragrant wet earth. The freshness was delightful after so long underground, but this was no palace scene. It was not even a city garden, but an empty, dripping forest stretched out as far as the eye could see. Nothing stirred anywhere but the patter of rain on leaves.

Juille glanced wildly around for her little guide. It had vanished. She shot a blue beam around the corridor behind her, finding only a confusing array of fingery footprints that vanished into the dark. She cursed the evasive little beast in a voice that was close to tears. To come so near victory and then find only this!

For she knew what this forest must be. Indeed, when she cast her blue light down she saw what must be the footprints Egide had left when he came out this very tunnel into the woods where the Ancients lived. Forbidden woods, uncharted, unknown, kept sacrosanct by countless generations of human life on Ericon.

She glanced about uneasily. Jair and the Andareans could not be far away. But what she could do next she had no idea. Where or how far the city lay was impossible to guess. Certainly she could not return through the pathless honeycomb of the caverns, and if she tried the forbidden woods she might wander for days in the wrong directions. If the *llar* had been visible now, she might have blasted it with a needle beam for bringing her so far astray. But there was no help for it. She would have to get back to the city, hit or miss, perhaps too late to do anything but warn them of impending blows from nameless weapons.

The memory of Egide's glowing confidence when he came back to her armed with the Andarean gifts gave her a feeling of sinking dismay. The impending conflict had taken on too many prospects of unguessable proportions. The effect of the new weapons might be overwhelming, unless she could find some way to prevent it.

Unless – Juille stared out speculatively through the trees. If she could delay Egide – but how could she, short of killing him? And did she want that? Her mind flashed off on a tangent – he had stayed his hand, too, when killing her might have meant a great deal in the outcome of the revolt. Her scorn for that weakness had gone deep. Yet she was hesitating now in the face of the same problem. She set her chin.

This was the way he had come, down this narrow glade into the forest. For all the woods seemed to slope downward as if toward a sunken path that wound between the hills. She could trace his tracks, perhaps, in the sodden ground.

If she hunted a way out of the forest, she might wander for days, while Egide and Jair escaped unhindered with their loot. But if she followed Egide now, if she used her needle beam upon him, or the lens of the Dunnarian weapon – would Jair leave Ericon without him? Could she gain time enough to find her way back to the city, leaving Egide dead here in the rainy forest?

It was too confusing – she did not know what she wanted. But this alternative seemed best of all the impossible choices she had. Follow Egide – let the rest take care of itself.

It was very quiet here in the woods. Juille could not remember ever having been quite so alone before. She walked through a drowned green gloom beneath the dripping trees, making no sound. Egide had gone this way before her; she found his prints now and then in bare places along the valley. She strained her ears and eyes for him returning, but nothing moved except the leaves, nothing made any sound except the drip-drip of rain and the occasional liquid bubbling voice of a tree frog enjoying the wet.

And presently, in spite of herself, the silence and the solitude began to lull her senses. This was the holy place, and the old awe began to oppress her as she walked. Through this quivering gloom the gods had moved upon their own unfathomable errands; perhaps they were moving now. She looked about uneasily. She had seen the power of the Ancients manifested tangibly, terribly, overhead in the open sky so brief a time ago that the memory was still appalling.

And then sudden anger washed over her. Egide had come this way. He was a fool, blundering in ignorance through the sacred woods, but wherever he dared to go surely she dared follow. Even into the temple itself.

Her mind went back to those troubled thoughts in the solitary caverns, before the *llar* had come. Could she go? Could she not, when Egide had ventured there and perhaps learned celestial wisdom that might turn the tide of battle? For the Ancients *did* give advice, so legend said. If human supplicants dared make the pilgrimage, they sometimes brought back knowledge that could make them great.

Well, it would be humiliating to come second into their presence, but if Egide had come and gone, Juille began to realize that she must, too. Indeed, in this rainy solitude she realized even more. Her mind was clarifying itself of shock and confusion, and now as she walked alone, it began to grope back toward that firm bedrock of principle and duty upon which she had prided herself so long. In her mind she had faltered at the thought of killing him.

Far back, deep down, the roots of weakness were there when she thought of Egide. Even to herself, she could not admit that yet. But subconsciously, perhaps, she knew herself as weak as he in this one thing, and subconsciously she sought to justify herself by surpassing him. It took less courage from Egide than from her to face the Ancients in their temple, because he knew less about them. She knew this much clearly – that she would never be at peace again with herself if she let him outface her here. Impatiently, she shrugged the tangled thoughts away. Time enough for introspection if she lived through the next hour.

Before she left the tunnel, Juille had taken the belated precaution of removing her bell-mouthed pistol from its uncomfortable hiding place and pushing it up into the lining of her helmet, where its flexible barrel adjusted to the curve. Should Egide by any mischance see her first here in the woods, he might not think of searching there for this last reserve, unpredictable as the weapon was. But she did not mean him to surprise her. She was better prepared than he for the meeting before them, and she knew very well that if they met unexpectedly only one was likely to return.

All the strange undertones of their relationship, confused, twisting together, not clear to either, were unimportant in the basic motive behind their final reckoning. She must not forget that. She must let nothing swerve her. If she died before Egide, the H'vani would most likely sit next upon the throne of Ericon. Egide knew that as well as she, and she thought that this time he would not forget it.

How did a traveler through this trackless wood know the way to the temple? Juille could not guess, but she did know the way. It was a part of the magic of the Ancients which she could feel thickening about her in the fragrant green silence as she went on. And how did one know what the temple would look like, when no human creature had ever brought back word of it? She could not guess that, either – but she knew.

She knew without surprise how the great black walls would lean inward above the trees that hid their foundations. She stood almost without breathing, gazing up between the branches at that towering, massive darkness which housed the living gods.

It was a little while before she could bring herself to come nearer. Only the thought of Egide made her do it. He must still be in there, in the unthinkable sanctum of the Ancients, hearing the voices that no living man had ever told of. At the back of her mind, a craven alternative stirred briefly – why not wait until he came out, and do then whatever impulse moved her to do? With a mental squaring of the shoulders she dismissed that idea. No, if he were in there still, she would confront him before the very altar of the gods.

Her heart was beating heavily as she went up the slope toward those great dark leaning walls that breathed out silence. She saw no door. The grassy furrow she had been following led up between the trees to a clear space against the solid black wall, and ended there. She was not breathing as she took the last step forward and put out hesitant hands toward that blackness.

She could tell then, of course, that it was not there at all. The walls were black and the dark inside was black, and the entrance made no difference between them to the eye. Light from outside did not penetrate over the threshold. Juille took a long, deliberate breath and stepped forward.

She walked three paces through utter darkness. Then light began to show faintly underfoot. Glancing back now, she could see the outlines of the portal, and the woods beyond looking indescribably changed and enchanted, like the woods of another dimension. Beneath her feet the light grew slowly stronger as she went on.

Above rose only the fathomless heights of the dark. And there was no one here but herself. She felt that with unreasoning certainty. The terrible, oppressive presences of the gods, which she had expected must paralyze her with their very awesomeness, she did not feel at all. And she thought Egide was not here, either. The dark around her had that vast, impersonal emptiness she had known before only during flights through the emptiness of space – cold, measureless, still beyond all human compass.

The light from below was strengthening, with an oddly vertiginous effect. She could see nothing down there, not even the substance of the floor. If she walked on pavement, it was pavement of the clearest crystal without flaws or jointure. She was like one walking above a void on invisible supports that might vanish before the next step. When she thought of that she slowed automatically, unable to control the fear that each next step would overreach the edge of the flooring and plunge her into the lighted infinities below. By contrast, the dark overhead was almost a solid, unrelieved in the least by any reflection of light. The impression grew so strong that she began to imagine the blood was pounding in her ears and temples from reversed gravity, as she walked upside down like a fly across a ceiling of glass.

She took a few more dizzy steps and then halted, too confused and frightened to go on. She had forgotten Egide. For the moment, she had even ceased to expect the Ancients. There was nothing anywhere but herself standing upon a crystal ceiling looking down into the sky, frozen with awe and terror.

Nothing happened for what seemed a very long time. No sound, no motion. Juille stood alone in the darkness upon the light, not conscious of any presence but her own. She was never conscious of any other presence, from first to last. But after a long interval, something began to happen.

Far, far away through the crystal on which she stood, a lazy motion stirred. Too far to make out clearly. It moved like smoke, but she did not think it was smoke. In a leisurely, expanding column it moved toward her, whether swiftly or slowly she did not even think, for awareness of time had ceased. And she could not tell if it were rising from fathoms underfoot or coiling down out of the sky toward her as she stood upside down on a crystal ceiling.

Nearer and nearer it came twisting, intangible as smoke and moving with the beautiful, lazy billowing of smoke – but it was not smoke at all.

When it had come almost to her feet it expanded into a great, slow ring and came drifting toward her and around her and up past her through the solid substance on which she stood. And as the ring like a wide, hazy, yawning mouth swept upward a voice that she thought she knew, said quietly in her ears:

'You may speak.'

The shock of that voice, when she had felt no presence near, was nothing compared with the deeper shock of the voice's familiarity. 'I can't stand it!' Juille told herself in sudden hysteria. 'I can't!' Was there no one at all to be trusted? Did everyone she knew have a second self waiting behind veils of intrigue to speak enigmatically when she least expected it? First Helia – now – whose was the voice? It might be her father's. It might be her own. It might not be familiar at all until this terrible enchantment made it seem so.

A second intangible yawning ring swallowed her and passed by.

'You may speak,' it said with infinite patience, in exactly the same inflection as before. And this time she decided wildly that it must indeed be her own voice.

'I … I—' What did she want to say? Was she really standing here upon a ceiling of glass, speaking in the gods' voices and answering herself with her own? It could not be the gods who spoke. They were not here. No one was here but herself. She knew that. She had an unalterable conviction of aloneness, and it must be herself who spoke with the yawning smoke-mouths and answering herself in the same stifled voice.

'You may speak,' the third mouth said, and drifted on past her into the solid darkness above. (Or was it really below?)

'I … my name is—' She paused. It was ridiculous to stand here telling her own voice who she was. She tried again.

'I came for guidance about the … about what to do next. So many lives depend on me – tell me how to save my people from the H'vani.'

The smoke shifted lazily as if in a little breeze. Then a series of widening rings floated up – or down – around her in quick succession, and as each went by, a voice spoke in her ears. One of them was familiar. It might still be hers. The others she had not heard before, and this multiplicity of voices coming just in time to shatter her theory that she had been talking to herself, was intolerably bewildering. The voices spoke to one another impersonally, as if she were not there.

'She says she came for guidance.'

'She came out of jealousy.'

'She cares very little for her people. It was for herself she came.'

'Is her race worth saving?'

'They must have their chance, remember.' (This was the voice she knew.) 'The game is almost played, but not quite finished yet. Give her the guidance she asks, and then – watch.'

'But this is so wearying. We have seen it all before. Is there any good in her at all?'

'Little. Little enough. But let the game play out.'

And with that last ring the dizzying swirl of them past her face came to a pause. Juille's head was reeling. For a while, nothing happened except that the column which was not smoke swayed gracefully like a hazy snake. Then it widened to another mouth that came gaping up through the floor to swallow her.

'You will have your chance to save the race that bred you,' the voice she knew so well said leisurely. 'Think well before you take it, for your instinct will be wrong. Upon you and the next few hours the fate of your race depends. What you are yourself will decide it.'

The lazy cloud floated past and faded into the darkness beyond her.

And then a vertigo came upon Juille, so terrible that every cell in her body seemed struggling against every other cell to right itself – to separate and right itself even at the expense of partition from the rest. Up was down, and down was up. In the dreadful, wrenching confusion, she thought she had one glimpse below her of rolling clouds and rain that came lancing straight upward toward her feet, while she saw despairingly that treetops, head downward, were blowing in a strong breeze above her. For an instant she stood reversed in space, like an image which the retina reverses upon the brain.

And then she was stumbling through darkness again, with the universe right side up.

She was stumbling through a darkness all clouded with swimming colors. Would the gods appear at all? Was the audience over without a glimpse of them? Or would they rise presently through this swimming dark, vast, inscrutable, wearing no human shapes?

Grass was slippery beneath her feet.

Someone seized her by the shoulders and a man's voice said, 'Open your eyes! Open your eyes! You're all right now.'

'Egide!'

Her eyes flew open. There was no darkness. The temple – She looked around wildly. Egide's hard grip bruised her shoulders. Automatically she felt for the needle flash that was her only immediate weapon, Nothing. Her relaxing fingers must have let it fall somewhere in that bewildering darkness. She was still too dazed to understand what had happened, but reflexive animal reactions made her whip into motion, squirming away from his grip.

'No you don't.' Egide's hands slid down her arms to clench like iron about her wrists. Memory of Helia's training came back now and she arched all her whipcord strength to pivot him off balance. But he knew that maneuver as well as she, and it resolved after a moment into a blind, furious hand-to-hand struggle. And since he was much stronger than she, with the sheer, solid bulk of muscular weight, in a short while she hung gasping with rage against his chest, both arms twisted agonizingly behind her.

'This,' said Egide with a breathless grin, 'is luck!'

'Luck!' Juille's blind and frantic brain cleared a little at the word. Luck? Perhaps it was. At any rate, now she had found him. What she would do next she had no idea. Somehow she had to gain the upper hand, keep him from Jair, delay the H'vani flight until she had power enough to stop it. And the Ancients had promised her a chance—

She made herself relax. 'Well?' she said coolly.

Egide frowned down at her, taken aback. 'Not angry?'

No, she could not afford to be angry. Somehow she must find some lever to control him, and she must control herself until she had. She must control more than her temper – it was infuriating that this nearness to him made her heart quicken and sent a treacherous weakness sliding through her limbs. Hanging helpless against his shoulder, her wrists fixed immovably in his grasp, Juille looked up at him with forced detachment. She was an amazon. She must remember it. Her heart and mind were trained to a discipline as stringent as her body's, and they must not falter.

She made herself study his face with critical calm, looking for the flaws of character she had marked there before. Coolly she regarded him. The fine-grained texture of his weathered skin. The sweat upon his forehead from their sharp struggle, and the drops of blowing rain. Rain beading his hair and the fair curls of his short, careful beard, and his curling yellow lashes. The blue eyes narrowed as he returned her scrutiny.

Yes, it was a weak face. Too sensitive a mouth. She knew she would never trust an amazon with that look about the mouth and eyes. Sentiment and self-indulgence showed there plainly. And other qualities that might pass as virtues in a peacetime world. But she remembered the code of the amazon that demanded a sacrifice of virtues as well as vices to serve the common good. Pity, mercy, compassion – she saw them all here and she despised them all as they looked down out of Egide's face.

But by the simple, unfair advantage of weight and muscle, he had the upper hand. She must alter that before she could afford to despise him. She made her voice impersonal and asked quietly, 'How did you catch me?' And between the question and his answer, she knew suddenly what she must do. One sure weapon remained to her. Somehow she must trick him into freeing her long enough to use that lens the *llar* had brought. Afterward – well, then she would have him on a leash, with death at the far end of it. The threat would be a whip to make him obey whatever commands she chose to give. After that, there would be time enough to consider these tangled personal feelings that were undermining all her amazonian resolve. First of all, she must get away.

'Catch you?' he was saying. 'Don't you know? You came out of the temple with your eyes shut and walked down the slope. I was sitting by the ... the door there, under the trees. I was – thinking.'

Juille glanced around. Trees everywhere. No great walls leaning inward above their swaying tops. She said:

'Where are we? The temple – it's gone.'

'Yes. I followed you away from the door. Not very far – but it's gone now.'

They looked up together, searching for those leaning walls. But the gods had withdrawn with a finality that seemed to deny they had ever been. Juille had a sudden, desperate feeling of loneliness and rebuff. The human mind needs so ardently to lean upon its gods. Even upon terrifying gods, cold and impersonal and aloof as these. But the Ancients had heard their pleas, tolerated their uninvited presence, sent them forth with comfortless, enigmatic words, careless whether humanity lived or died. As if they had tired of human doings altogether. The forest seemed very remote about them just now. It, too, would go on unchanging, whether man lived or vanished from the face of Ericon.

Well – Juille squared her shoulders mentally again – she was far better prepared to face such a universe than Egide would ever be. As to what the gods had told him, it wouldn't matter once she centered him in her lens. What *had* they told him? Overpowering curiosity suddenly filled her.

'What ... what happened in the temple?' she asked him a little diffidently. He looked down at her, his eyes going unfocused as he remembered. She was pleased to notice that his grip on her wrists had slackened perceptibly, too. A little more conversation and perhaps – 'Tell me what happened,' she persisted. 'Did they speak to you? Egide, was it really upside down?'

He glanced at her briefly. 'You must be crazy,' he said.

Juille stiffened. Another count against him. But curiosity was still strong. She tested his loosening grip very subtly and said again:

'Do tell me about it. You saw the light, and the … the smoke rings—'

'I saw a light, yes.' His eyes came into focus again and he scowled at her. 'Smoke rings? You're out of your head. There was a high altar like a wall, with the … the figures … above it. What did they tell you?'

Juille opened her mouth to protest, and then closed it again, trying to remember what it was they had said. They? Had there really been more voices than one? Voices – voices. For a tantalizing instant, she poised on the very verge of remembering whose that familiar tone had been. But when she reached for the memory, it slipped away.

What was it they had told her? They'd said unpleasant things, certainly. Something about a game that was almost played. Some assurance that she would have her chance – what chance? When? And her instinct would be wrong.

'Never mind,' she said. 'But I'm not concerned about the H'vani any more. Not now.' And she smiled secretly. After all, it was nearly true. For she thought she understood what her chance would be. Egide's grip was slack. In a minute or two she would wrench loose, spin away from him into the forest, hide somewhere just long enough to center his figure in her lens as he blundered after in pursuit.

And then – well, she might not need to kill him. The threat might be enough. With luck, she might even find her way back to the city before Jair gave up waiting and tried for open space. Night was hours away still.

He looked down at her strangely. 'You're lying,' he said. 'Unless—' He hesitated. 'You know the legend, don't you? Is there any truth in it?'

'That they'll give you bad advice if they've decided against your side? I don't know.' Juille exchanged a grave, long look with him. 'I don't know. Do you believe it?'

He hesitated a moment longer, and then his eyes crinkled with laughter.

'No, I don't. Whatever they told you, I know how to win now.'

She gave him a speculative glance. 'Then they lied to one of us. Because I know, too.'

Egide threw back his head and laughed. The confident, full-throated sound of it rang through the forest, silencing the tree frogs' bubbling songs. His grip upon her wrists was the merest touch now. Juille raked the woods for the nearest refuge, set her teeth and wrenched away. And she knew even as she wrenched that she had moved too soon. Sick dismay flooded her as he whipped out a long arm and grazed her shoulder with clutching fingers – grazed – gripped – held.

Her momentum spun them both around and it was touch and go for a moment. Then his big hands locked upon her shoulders and her jerked her toward him so that she smashed breathlessly against the hard armor of his chest and was pinned there in a heavy embrace that had no tenderness in it.

Not then.

They stood together in that close interlocked intimacy which only lovers or struggling enemies ever share.

'They gave you the wrong advice, then,' Egide told her, as if the scuffle had never happened. Only his shortened breath testified that it had. 'They mean your side to lose.'

'How can you be sure?' Juille asked him, straining hard away against his arms.

And he sobered as he met her eyes. He could not be sure. Neither of them could ever be sure, until the last battle ran to its bloody close. There was silence between them for a moment. The dripping forest rustled all around, full of the whisper of fine rain upon leaves, the throaty, dovelike throbbing of tree-frog voices, the murmur of the wet, soft breeze. And there was a feeling of sorcery in the air. Perhaps the vanished temple still lifted its great inward-leaning walls above them, filled with the watching eyes of gods and the gods' humorless, dispassionate patience that waited to see their doomed supplicant take the first step toward his own ruin.

Each of them was suddenly very thankful for human companionship. For an instant they were no longer antagonists, and the struggle in which they were locked resolved itself imperceptibly, with the old treachery their bodies knew, into an embrace neither intended. In the back of their minds, neither of them forgot that they were enemies. Each remembered that only one of the two might leave these woods alive. But for the moment, another memory came back to engulf them both, blotting away the forest and the rain and even the aloof presence of the gods.

They did not speak for a while. They looked at one another with remembering eyes, and Egide's embrace held no more of its savage coercion, and Juille was not straining against it. Presently, he said in a low voice:

'Juille – did you know me on Cyrille?'

She shook her head in silence, not sure that she wanted to recognize this mood with speech. Before, it had been a thing of the senses, to let slip when the senses released it, and with no words to pin the remembrance inescapably in their minds.

But Egide went on. 'I knew you,' he said. 'I meant to kill you. Did you guess that?'

She nodded, her eyes on his face watchfully.

'But no one else ever knew about it,' Egide told her. 'Not even Jair. No one knows at all but you and me.'

Juille stared up at him. She knew the truth when she heard it, and she thought this was the truth. If she accepted it, a great many preconceived ideas would begin to turn themselves over in her mind. So many implications lay behind that simple speech – but just now she could not pause to think. Just now Egide was about to kiss her—

It was a long kiss. Their first since Cyrille, and perhaps their last. While it endured, all sound blanked out around them and a dissolving intoxication loosened all Juille's muscles, and even her mind ceased to be wary and afraid.

Then Egide's unsmiling face was looking down at her from very near, an eagerness and a humility upon it she had never seen there before. And suddenly she knew how treacherous this was. Egide had surrendered without reservation to it. In this moment she knew she could bend him to whatever purpose she chose. Even compromise with the Lyonese. Even peace, if it were peace she wanted.

Abruptly she was frightened. This strong emotion between them was a drug and a drunkenness more dangerous than wine, the most treacherous thing that ever happened to an amazon. Because he might be able to sway her, too – and she desperately feared her own surrender. Like drunkenness, this emotion distorted the focus of reality, dulled reason's keen edge, reduced the mind to a maudlin softness that denied all values but its own. It was no more to be trusted than drunkenness. It was as false as the illusions of Cyrille. As false, and as irresistibly lovely, and as dangerous as death.

If she ever gave up to it, the moment was not now. Later, when she had him under tangible control – he was weak now, but the weakness might not last. She needed the leash of the Dunnarian weapon, and the whip of the threat it held. She lifted her eyes to Egide's.

He was holding her like a lover, waiting with an eagerness he made no attempt to conceal. This was the moment the Ancients must have meant. Now, in his weakness – now!

Juille lowered her head and struck him a heavy blow beneath the chin with her helmet. In the same moment, she leaped backward out of his embrace and whirled toward the nearest trees.

Egide dropped – dropped to hands and knees and thrust one leg out to its full, long length. Juille saw just too late what was coming. Futile rage flared up consumingly in the timeless instant while she struggled to avoid him. She could not let Egide frustrate her again – she could not! But momentum was too much for her. She felt her own foot catch against the outthrust leg, and she felt herself plunging face down into the underbrush beneath the trees.

Hard hands dragged her upright before she could move. She had a glimpse of blue eyes blazing with anger. She had one flash of a big square fist, startlingly foreshortened, hurtling toward her face.

Then moons and stars exploded between her and the green woods.

With no consciousness whatever of elapsed time, Juille found herself lying on a bank of soft blue grass at the edge of a lapping sea. Her mind was as blank as the mind of Adam first wakening in Eden. It took her a perceptible while to remember who she was. That returned after a little uneasy groping, but where she was—

She sat up with difficulty. Her hands appeared to be tied behind her. And then memory rushed back in a flood. Egide, the sacred forest – her chin felt sore and swollen – that moment of warmth and treachery – and humiliation.

How much time had passed? And where in the Galaxy was she now? Egide must have left her here, securely tied, while he went about some private business – the weapons? Had the Ancients given him some special knowledge? It was painful to think. Too many questions spun through her mind. She looked confusedly around.

Low blue hillock, blue lapping water out to the hazy horizon. Behind her, a high wall of colored stones, with an iron-hinged gate in it. And to left and right, willows that trailed their yellow-green streamers down across the grass.

Blue grass – grass on Ericon was green. She listened. A faint breeze was moving among the willows, and upon the beach scalloping wavelets whispered. No other sound. No craft at sea. No Egide. Nothing even remotely familiar anywhere she looked. She had a moment of serious wonder whether she could possibly have switched personalities with some unknown woman, under the power of the all-powerful Ancients.

With some vague idea of looking beyond the willows, she walked awkwardly across the beach, off-balance because of her bound hands. The yellow-green leaves streamed across her shoulders like extravagantly flowing hair as she pushed through their swaying lengths. A roadway curved down toward the water a little distance away, and she could see people strolling along it, laughing and talking. As she watched, a young couple came toward her, swinging hands, murmuring together. She called.

The strolling lovers did not turn their heads. Juille called again, more loudly. They did not even glance around. Juille shouted in a parade-ground voice that made the willows shiver. No response. The girl looked up to smile at the young man, and her face was turned so that she must see Juille, but she gave no sign.

Not sure whether to be more angry or alarmed – was she invisible? – Juille pushed forward toward them through the leaves. And suddenly something moved in the air before her – someone materialized in her very face, ghostlike, blocking her path. Juille started back. The ghost did, too. It was a ghost in cloak and helmet, with its arms behind it—

Juille stood perfectly still before the faint reflection of herself. Presently she pushed out one knee and felt a transparent wall between her and the road. Shouldering up to it, she traced the unseen barrier from the willow grove up to the stone wall. By the time she reached it, she had an idea where she was.

The strolling lovers went obliviously past, laughing to one another, and vanished around another clump of trees. Along the road a boy with a donkey came whistling, but Juille made no attempt to signal him. He did not, she thought, exist. Or if he ever had lived, most likely he had been dead for some while. There was almost certainly war upon the world he lived on. There was war upon most worlds now.

Juille went up the slope toward the wall, her lips set thinly. She thought she knew what she would find there, and in a moment or two she did – a rectangle of cloudy glass set into the stones. That settled it. Egide, for some unfathomable reason of his own, had brought her back to the pleasure world where their brief idyl had run its course. This was Cyrille.

Why was she here? She had a brief, wild idea that Egide might have imagined the revisiting of old scenes would win her anew to the evanescent mood that had once enchanted them both. But in the urgency of current happenings, she knew not even Egide would attempt anything so fantastic. No, if he were here – and he must be – then Jair and the Andarean weapons would be here, too. Obviously they had come this far at least without interference from the imperial forces. Was this, then, a stopover on their way to the H'vani base, or had they a reason for visiting Cyrille? Or – might they have dropped her here and gone on alone? No – because the real danger from the Lyonese space guards lay beyond Cyrille's orbit, not inside it. If they needed her at all, they needed her as a hostage to pass them by the guards.

Well, they must be here, then. Somewhere on Cyrille, with their nameless weapons, and perhaps armed also with advice from the Ancients that could certainly mean no good for Ericon. She could not even count very much on interference from the skeleton staff of attendants left on Cyrille. The H'vani were armed and ruthless. She could imagine Jair making very short work of anyone who crossed his path. Her very presence, bound and helpless in this room, testified that no staff member had lived long enough to spread an alarm.

She stood before the gate, looking around what must be a moderately small room, though her gaze reached out unhindered toward distant horizons. The grass, the foremost willows, the wall were real. Perhaps some of the lapping water. But the rest was all illusion reflecting upon mirrored walls. Somewhere beyond them, Egide and Jair would be at work – on what? And alone? Probably, unless some of the Andareans had come on with them. Their own ship and men would have been impounded from the very first.

Well – she twisted at her tied hands hopefully. The bonds felt softer, like cloth instead of the knifeproof cord Helia had used. How could she test it? There were no sharp stones; the glass walls would not break, she knew. There was nothing that—

Juille laughed suddenly and fell to her knees. She had her spurs. It seemed interminably long ago that Helia had put them on her heels for a morning ride. In the crowded lifetime since so much had happened that she knew she might never ride a horse again, perhaps might never live to see these spurs removed. But they could do her one last service now, if her cords were made of cloth. She strained backward, sawing precariously.

The rowels bit satisfyingly into her bonds. It was back-breaking and tedious, but it was working. After a long while she felt the cords let go, and for the second time began to rub the prickles of returning circulation from her hands.

And now – what? To all appearances, Juille still sat upon an open beach with blue water breaking at her feet. It was difficult to believe that the walls of a small room were really close about her. The door itself probably lay beyond the gateway in the wall, but she knew it would be locked – it was. Her only contact with the outside was the communication panel, which might be dead. Still, since the illusion of this beach with its strolling ghosts persisted, the communications might be open, too. It was difficult to guess what effect the death of Cyrille's operators would have on the persistence of Cyrille's illusions. Perhaps none at all.

Rubbing her wrists, she walked up the blue grassy slope and pressed the buttons for sight and sound beneath the panel. In the brief moment while it glowed into life, she heard a distant murmur of laughter and saw the young lovers strolling again beyond the trees. The sight of them was oddly dreadful, and somehow oddly pathetic. They were so perfect an illusion of a perfect, idyllic past which might never come again, a peacetime when lovers could walk unheedingly over open beaches. Somewhere, the originals of this living reproduction had once walked hand in hand. They might have grown old many years ago; they might have died yesterday or last week on some other world under the bombardment of H'vani guns. Or they might be cowering at this moment in some underground shelter shaken with the detonation of bombs. But they walked here in an eternal moment of laughter and murmuring, beside a bright blue sea, and they turned indifferent, blind faces to Juille's predicament. Their detachment partook, in a way, almost of the Ancients' divine disinterest, or of the cold, still, passionless reaches of space.

Juille looked away.

The panel was lighting up. She looked through it into a corner of some office, with a black glass desk below a wall board on which lights winked busily. Across the desk, a dead man sprawled. Juille looked at him stonily and pressed the buttons again. She did not know the proper combination, but she thought that eventually she must find a room where the men she sought were working. Probably the control room. Because, until she knew better, she must assume that the H'vani had come to Cyrille for a purpose, and she knew the only purpose in their minds would be destruction. The control room, she had heard, was the only one here with a visual screen that looked down upon the great green world of Ericon. She hunted on and on.

And she found other dead men. She found offices wrecked and charred. She found empty rooms. But she found no living creatures until at last, by a lucky accident, she finally hit upon the combination that opened a little window upon the men she was hunting. And her guess had been right. They were in the control room.

Its vast space was crowded with the machinery that kept Cyrille upon its course and filled with the living illusions of its fantasies. One wall was glass, like a telescopic lens focused upon the world beneath. And though that world was directly below, in the window it stood at right angles to the floor like a looming green wall.

Before it, two men were laboring busily. Juille, watching as if from a small opening high up on the side of the great room, saw Jair's red head and beard, and Egide's yellow curls. No other figures moved in the room. They had come on alone, then. And they worked with utter absorption before the glass wall.

The object of their interest was a great searchlight, far larger than themselves. They had maneuvered it before the window on its rolling frame and were centering its focus now upon something outside, with much reference to a chart engraved upon the wall. Over the face of the light, a metal net with rainbow nodes had been spread.

Juille remembered that net. Watching, she felt a cold sinking in the pit of her stomach. She had no idea how the arrangement would function, but its implication was very plain. The Ancients had betrayed her, then, and Helia's people had betrayed her, and unless she could get out into that room very soon, the Lyonese Empire would be betrayed, too.

For Egide had found a substitute for his invading fleet. Here inside the defenses of Ericon, was a ship so cunningly disguised that it could swing a path of destruction all around the planet. He was making Cyrille itself that ship. And Juille thought to herself that if this were the advice the Ancients had given him, then they must have lied to her and the Lyonese. For, unless she could put a stop to it quickly, the world below them was certainly doomed.

Until now, no weapons had ever existed strong enough to bridge the airless gap between Ericon and its satellite, but the confidence showing in every gesture of the men she watched must mean that such a weapon existed now. This searchlight, netted with shining, colored bulbs. It was hard to believe that the light could be cast so far, or that the simple addition of the net would charge it with destroying violence. But the H'vani worked like men who knew what they were doing. Obviously they meant to let the little pleasure-world circle on around Ericon until it floated above the target they had marked. That target would almost certainly be the Imperial City itself. And before avenging ships could blast Cyrille from its course, the city and half the countryside could be wiped out if this weapon had any real power.

Could she stop the destroyers first? It looked hopeless. From this angle she could see only a great panoramic curve of hill and forest below, partly obscured by a rolling thunderstorm. That dim light might be morning or evening; they could be ten minutes from the city or a full turn of the planet. And she had no idea which way the control room lay from here. Even if she knew, the door that shut her in was locked.

Wait, though. She had one weapon, if Egide had not found it. Hopefully Juille groped in her helmet lining. A hard handle met her fingers, and her spirits rose on a swift curve to something almost like hope. She laughed aloud and pulled out the little gun. There it lay, fitting her hand as it once had fitted the hands of a race whose very name no longer had meaning in the Galaxy they once had ruled. It might yet save the race that ruled today, if luck was with Juille.

Slim, flexible barrel with its spiral of silver tubing, bell-shaped muzzle, trigger curved like a tiny sickle – what would happen when she pulled it? Most likely – nothing, unless just possibly the Andareans had made use of the weapons on that rack within recent years. Lightning might come blasting out when she touched the trigger, or the gun might explode in her hand, on—

Juille set her finger on the trigger, clenched her teeth and turned the bell-muzzle toward the lapping sea. Slowly she tightened her finger.

She pressed it back to the guard, and nothing happened Nothing? She had time for one wave of sickening disappointment, and then thought she felt life against her palm. The gun was quivering. The quiver ran up the coil of tubing and shook against her fist, and a tiny glow seemed to be forming about the bell-shaped orifice. A glow that spun and spun. Juille stood holding the gun out at arm's length, while the glow grew brighter and faster, and the spinning increased.

Then a globe of luminous fire drifted from the bell-muzzle. It spun brilliantly like a tiny sun, moving away from her at leisurely speed and expanding as it moved. Straight out to sea it went, and the ripples mirrored its broken reflection on their surface. Juille held her breath.

There was a moment more of silence, while the waves lapped softly on the beach and the willows whispered and distant voices laughed. Then the spinning sun in midair flared out in one expanding flash and one tremendous hissing roar, like fire in water. The flash was golden.

When Juille could see again what she saw looked unbelievable even in the face of knowledge. Hanging in what seemed like open air above the still-rippling ocean was a circle of twisted girders, black and peacock blue from the heat of their destruction. Through the wall she could see a stretch of dim corridor. Plaster fell crumbling between the beams. And all around the edge of the opening a strange little dazzle of dancing colored motes faded slowly. The revolving sun had vanished.

Except for that hole in the air, everything remained unchanged about her. And though that hole was the only touch of reality in all this small world, it was fantastic as it hung there over the serene ocean rolling in from illusory distances.

She waded out through the warm blue ripples. Even when the shattered wall was within arm's length and she could see the transparent glimmer of her own reflection swimming above the wavelets in the reflecting wall, she had a feeling of instability as she set one knee upon a girder that hung unsupported on the air.

Beyond the opening lay a narrow corridor running left and right, lighted only by a dim thread of luminous paint down the center of the floor. Which way? What next? She had no idea even of how many charges remained in her weapon. Perhaps none. Perhaps only two or three. What she must do was find Egide as soon as possible and somehow manage to see him first, just long enough to focus him in the cross-hairs of the lenses which still hung about her neck.

She thought she had shut her mind to Egide now. He must remain only an enemy to kill if necessary, to capture if possible on the invisible leash of her strange lensed weapon. Until she held his life a forfeit in the lens all else must wait. And Jair – well, she must deal with him as opportunity arose. Without quite understanding it, she had a feeling that Jair was less of a danger than Egide.

She turned at random to the right, following the luminous line warily. At the end of the corridor she came out into the office with the black glass desk which she had first seen in the communicator panel. The dead man still sprawled across the glass. Juille, struck by a sudden hopeful thought, began jerking open drawers of translucent opal plastic. Papers – files of colored cards – a bottle of green brandy. A manicure kit. And – ah! A little palm gun with an extra clip of charges!

Juille laughed exultantly. This was for Jair! The bell-mouthed pistol might never fire again; the lens at her throat was a one-shot weapon. But this find put her on an equal footing with the two H'vani.

There was a large communicator panel on the wall behind the dead man. One of the labeled buttons below it said, 'Control Room.' Juille thought to herself, 'I'm not afraid of you now,' and pushed the button, watching the panel glow and the great central room take shape beyond it.

Egide and Jair had finished their work. The searchlight was like a long-legged bird with its big eye craning downward through the window that opened upon Ericon. The trap was set. The Imperial City somewhere on the face of the globe below was rolling slowly upward toward its doom.

Egide at the moment was talking into a tiny portable communicator which he certainly had not worn when he landed upon Ericon that day. Reporting – success? – to some H'vani base. Perhaps summoning some armada of invading ships to follow the path of destruction he was about to launch upon the Imperial City. Juille wasted no fruitless speculation on that. She put her face close to the communicator and called:

'Egide! Egide, look up!'

She could hear her own voice echoing hollowly from the walls of the huge room beyond the panel. Egide stared about for several seconds before he located the connected panel. At that distance, though she could see his face change, she was not sure what emotions showed there for a moment. He shouted, 'Where are you?' and the echoes rolled back from the high walls.

'Come and find me,' she called derisively, and waved her unbound hands at the panel to show that she was free. Before he could answer she pressed the disconnector. Then she counted to ten and pushed the same button again, looking down with a grin into the big room. A struggle of sorts was taking place there. Egide, dropping his private communicator, had evidently made a lunge toward the master control panel to locate the screen she had just used. Jair held him by the cloak and they were disputing fiercely. Juille scowled. Evidently the big red man did not trust his prince with this dangerous captive. But it was no part of her plan to have Jair come hunting her. She listened to the indistinguishable deep murmur of their argument. Then Egide gave a savage shrug and turned back to the window. Jair's white grin split the dark-red beard, visible even from here. She saw him give his belt a hitch, draw his gun and lumber purposefully away, his enormous shoulders swaggering a little.

Juille made an insulting noise into the panel. The two men glanced up, startled. She waved again, even more insultingly, and disconnected the panel. Well, no help for it now. She must find the Control Room herself, and do it quickly, and she must play hide and seek with Jair through the strange interior of Cyrille while she hunted it. Luck decidedly was not with her. But she was well armed now, and the element of surprise was in her favor.

The first thing to do was to get as far as possible from this room before

Jair arrived. And since he might come by some swift intramural means she did not know of, she had better go quickly. It was eminently satisfying to feel the weight of a gun in each hand as she turned to the opposite wall – even though one gun might be empty, or very nearly empty. The very feel of it sent her spirits soaring. The odds were fairly even after all, for she did not think Jair could know much more about Cyrille's inner workings than she did, nor could he guess that his quarry was as well armed as he. She had no illusions about Jair's purpose. He would certainly shoot on sight. No need any longer to hold her for a hostage, with that deadly mechanism in the Control Room already trained upon Ericon. Jair would shoot without warning, but he would not know that she could, and that gave her a little advantage.

Outside the office a wide, shallow, moving ramp carried Juille down to a hall and an empty foyer with arched doors all around its wall. She glanced about nervously. This was no place for her. Her spurs rang faintly as she ran across the floor and dodged under the nearest arch. Another hallway, curving to the left. For all she knew she might be running straight into Jair's arms. She opened the first door she came to, glanced inside, and then sprinted through a field of waving lilies, knee-high, leaped a chuckling stream, tore open the door of a thatched cottage and found herself in another dim hall lighted by a luminous floorstrip.

The next random door led her into an arcade above a frozen twilight sea, with gusts of snow blowing through the open arches. Her breath went pluming frostily over one shoulder as she ran. Another hallway. An orchard that showered pink-scented blossoms upon her and housed one startled rabbit. It lolloped ahead in a frenzy, dodging off to the side just before she came to a gate in the orchard wall that let out onto the usual hallway.

She lost all sense of direction and ran as haphazardly as the rabbit had done, through a confusion of smallish rooms filled with every conceivable scene and climate. In several that she passed time had stopped. Clouds hung motionless in illusory skies, scenes reflected upon the wall were motionless, too, and lost all power to deceive. No water stirred and the air was windless. But most of the rooms she ran through were functioning still, and she passed a medley of mornings and noons and nights dwelling upon a wide variety of tiny worlds.

So closely is the human mind bound by the revolutions of its planet that after a while she found she had lost her time-sense as well, and could not help feeling that the hours had telescoped together in a dream as she ran, that this should be tomorrow, or even the day after that. Egide's playful device upon the cloud for making the days go by had turned to convincing reality here. She had been through too many nights and mornings for the present to remain today. She had even passed too many winters and blossomy springs for her own mental comfort, and though her reasoning consciousness derided the feeling, it lurked uneasily just below the surface and darkened her subconscious thoughts as she ran on.

But the time came when she tired of running. She must have come far enough by now that Jair would not be likely to trace her from the office where she had called. As a matter of fact, Cyrille was so large and so intricately honeycombed with rooms that it would be quite possible for them to wander about for hours, or even days, without meeting. And Juille was of no mind for such a flight as that. She had little time to waste. Every moment that passed now carried Cyrille closer to its target.

The Control Room, then, was her real goal. Jair might or might not find her soon, but if she failed to find Egide and the controls and the enigmatic weapon angling downward toward Ericon, it would not matter much what came after. And she might wander for hours through these circling rooms without reaching Egide.

Juille scowled thoughtfully and hefted the bell-muzzled pistol in her hand. There might be one more charge in it, or a limitless number, or none at all. But this was no time for indecision, not when the very minutes of life left to the Imperial City might be ticking off to nothing.

She was standing in a corridor at the moment. After a second's hesitation she pointed the bell toward the light-striped floor and pulled the trigger. The gun shivered. A glow gathered again within the bell mouth, gathered and spun and grew. The tiny sun came whirling from its socket, drifted floorward, struck with the hiss of fire in water. When Juille's sight came back after that golden glare, she saw blued girders again, and again the little storm of dancing colored notes which marked the edges of the gap. They flew up in her face this time as she leaned over the hole, stung her briefly and went out.

Below was a dim-green twilight forest of wavering weeds. Not too far below. Juille took a tight grip on both her guns and jumped. She was in midair before she saw the terrible pale face peering up at her through the reeds, its dark mouth squared in a perfectly silent scream.

It was a madman's face.

Juille's throat closed up and her heart contracted to a cold stop as she met that mindless glare. She was falling as if in a nightmare, with leisurely slowness, through air like green water that darkened as she sank. And the face swam upward toward her among the swaying weeds, its mouth opening and closing with voiceless cries.

The floor was much farther than it had seemed, but her slow fall discounted the height. And the creature came toward her as slowly, undulating with boneless ease among the weeds. Juille sank helpless through wavering green currents, struggling in vain to push against the empty air and lever herself away. The room was a submarine illusion of retarded motion and subdued gravity, and the dweller in it, swimming forward with practiced ease against the leverage of the tangled weeds, had a mad underwater face whose human attributes were curiously overlaid with the attributes of the reptile.

Juille's reason told her that she had stumbled into one of the darker levels of Cyrille, where perversions as exotic as the mind can conceive are bought and practiced to the point of dementia and beyond. This undulating reptilian horror must be one of the hopeless addicts, wealthy enough to indulge his madness even when civilization was crumbling outside the walls of Cyrille.

There was no sound here. Juille's feet came down noiselessly upon the sand, scarcely printing it with her weightless contact. The thing with the mouthing inhuman face came writhing toward her through the blue-green shadows and the swaying of the reeds. She felt her own throat stretching with a scream, but the silence of underwater rippled unbroken around her. For one sickening moment she stood there swaying on tiptoe, scarcely touching the sandy floor, staring at the oncoming madman while her lips opened and closed like his and no sounds came forth. The illusion of fishes in a submarine cavern was complete.

Then she saw a door between two marble pillars that wavered as if behind veils of shifting sea water, and wheeled unsteadily toward it, moving with nightmare slowness over the ripple-patterned sand unmarked by footprints. Behind her the thing came gliding.

As Juille struggled forward she had to force herself against every instinct to draw each breath. The illusion was so perfect that she could not help expecting strangling floods of bitter water to fill her lungs. Her garments wavered up around her and the helmet tugged at its chin strap.

The door was locked. Automatically she burned out the bolt with her palm gun, too sick with utter revulsion to notice, except dimly, that its characteristic thin shriek of riven air was silent here, too. But when the jolt of the gun against her hand responded and the door swung open, reason returned to her. She was armed. She need not fear this hideous writhing thing that swam after her with clutching webby hands outstretched.

She gave one last strong lurch against the weightless gravity of the room and stumbled out into the corridor, where normal gravity for a moment seemed to jerk her down against the floor. Stumbling, she regained her balance and then swung up the gun and sent a thinly screaming bolt back into the green dimness of the submarine room where the creature that mouthed its soundless screams was floating after her. The gun bolt struck him in the chest and its impact sent him wavering backward through the watery air. She saw him double with the strong, convulsive arc of a fighting fish. He began to sink slowly floorward through the reeds, but like the reptile he aped, he was slow to die.

Holding her gun ready for a second shot, Juille backed away. And slowly the madman swam toward her, one clawed hand pressing to its chest where the bolt had gone through. He moved with hideous, inhuman grace until he reached the threshold. Then gravity slammed him flat upon the floor and he lay there gasping and heaving himself up like a fish out of water. The normal pull of Cyrille was more than he could fight against. Juille pressed against the wall and watched him die.

She was badly shaken. Common danger was an old story to her, but the dark, contaminating psychic horrors which she thought she stood among now were a menace she had no armor against. She glanced about the corridor, reluctant to move lest she intrude upon another of the small private hells which, she knew now, fully justified the evil reputation of Cyrille's hidden levels.

And yet she must move. There was no time to waste now. She set her teeth resolutely and leveled her bell-mouthed gun at random toward an angle of the wall and floor. With luck it should open up to avenues of escape, and if one proved untenable, the other might do.

The gun quivered in her hand; its spinning sun gathered and floated free. And she was not sure if her imagination alone made the glow of it look duller than before. Was the precious charge running low? She wondered for one panic-stricken moment if she would have to defend herself now with the little palm gun alone, and then the sun bullet struck with its golden flare and hissing, and she had no more time for wonder.

Low in the wall a broken opening showed when the glare died away. Through it Juille had an incredulous glimpse of a city spread out in sprawling avenues and parks between the ridges of rolling hills. She saw people moving like tiny animated dots through the streets – all of it either in incredibly perfect miniature or incredibly far away. Then a cloud of saffron smoke came rolling through the gap and billowed up into her face. She caught one whiff of its exotic, spicy fragrance and then pulled her short cloak over her face and dived precipitously through the other gap in the flooring, without looking where she dived. For she knew that smoke. She had no desire to go mad in any of the delirious ways its spicy odor offered.

She struck the floor below and rolled for a moment in a bank of pale-pink snow that tingled instead of chilling. More snow drifted from low clouds, blinding her when she looked up. Veils of it, dancing rosily about her, hid the rest of the room. A wind blew, and the veils spun and writhed together in serpentine columns, through which she saw just a glimpse of motion before the wind died again. All the room was pink and dancing with warm snow, and through it a hideous low laughter quietly shook the air.

Juille scrambled to her feet, her heart thudding madly. Snow blinded her, but her ears gave the warning her eyes could not, and she was sure she heard footsteps shuffling nearer through the silence and the blowing veils. The laughter came again, low, satisfied, evil as she had never imagined laughter could be.

Until she felt the quiver of the bell-mouthed gun in her hand she did not know she had pulled its trigger. There was a paralyzing quality about that voice. The whirling sun drifted from the muzzle, vanished briefly through clouds of pink snow, then struck somewhere invisibly with its hiss and its golden flash. The voice chuckled, fell almost silent, then chuckled again, nearer. And Juille plunged wildly away from it, her feet slipping upon the snow.

Light pouring through a gap in the wall made the dancing flakes glitter with all their rainbow facets. But it was a very thin beam. When Juille had groped her way to the source of it, watching across one shoulder and holding her breath as she listened for the laughter in the snow to follow, she found a breach barely large enough to squirm through. The gun was certainly losing its strength.

It took all Juille's courage to force herself through the gap. Only her glimpse of a calm, sunlit meadow beyond made her try; that and the sound of a low, evil chuckle somewhere beyond the swirling veils. For to squeeze through the wall meant rendering herself helpless during the passage, and what might happen while she struggled there she could not and dared not think aloud.

But, somehow, she made the meadow unharmed. And then stood gripping her two guns and looking back sheepishly at the ragged gap through which pink snow whirled now and again. She heard no further echo of the terrible, soft, satisfied mirth. But her self-confidence was very seriously disturbed now. It annoyed her to find her hands shaking and the thumping of her heart refusing to slow even though she stood alone in an empty, static meadow in some little world whose functions had ceased.

Turning over rather panicky thoughts in her mind, she crossed to a gate at the far side, keeping her attention alert for any following thing from the broken wall. She had hoped to blast her way somehow through to the Control Room and destroy the great searchlight there with the aid of the bell-muzzled gun. But she knew now that would be impossible. Each charge might be the last, and each lessened in effectiveness. She wished passionately for the lightning gun Jair might be carrying. She wished even more passionately for human company, even Jair's. And she began rather shakily to fit the two desires together.

Supposing she lured Jair within range of her palm gun. Could she force him to give up the lightning-caster or to guide her back with him to the Control Room? Certainly she could try. Even if the plan failed, she would be no worse off than now, for at very worst she could surely kill him before he killed her. And incongruously she found herself longing for the presence of his impressive human bulk, the vibration of his voice. Even though he meant to kill her, and she him. He was so reassuringly human, after these horrible inhuman travesties in their madhouses.

So she went out the gate and into a corridor, and she followed the corridor to the office at its end. And closed and locked the door after her, between herself and any sound of laughter that might follow from the room of the pink storming snow.

This office was almost a duplicate of the other. A desk of deep-blue glass this time, and with no dead man behind it. But the wall behind the desk had the same array of communicator panels. She went straight across to it and pressed the universal broadcast button.

'Jair,' she said clearly. 'Jair, do you hear me? I'm in' – she glanced at the board – 'Office No. 20 on the Fifth Level. I'll wait here until you come. Please hurry.'

The thought of her own voice echoing among all the corridors and the strange myriad worlds of Cyrille made her shiver a little. Even Egide would hear it, where he worked out Ericon's destruction in the Control Room. And somewhere in the homeycomb of apartments and corridors Jair would hear it, too. He might already be very near. He would put his own interpretation on the appeal, for he must think her unarmed.

There was not much hope for an ambush here. Cyrille was not a world that offered materials for building gun-proof barricades. She pulled a screen patterned in swimming colours across one corner of the room and waited behind it, watching the two doorways that opened in the far wall. She had her guns ready. The whole world was silent about her, and the moments dragged interminably.

She heard Jair approaching before he entered the room. He made no attempt to come quietly, and his heavy boots woke echoes along the corridor. Very obviously he thought her unarmed.

He paused in the doorway, big and red-bearded, his red-brown eyes frankly murderous in a cold, dispassionate sort of way as he glared about the room, gun lifted and ready. Juille saw that it was the lightning gun, and her heart jumped. She had to have it. But she saw in her first glance that he had no intention of speaking a single word before he killed her. She might not have been of the same species as he at all, so matter-of-factly did he scan the room for his quarry.

Juille had not expected quite this workmanlike preparedness. She had imagined some interval in which she could address him from behind her shelter and offer a bargain. But she felt that her first word now would serve only as the target for his shot. Still, it had to be done. Perhaps if he knew she was armed—

She said in a clear, firm voice, 'I have a gun—'

Jair's lightning thrower leaped up. His fierce eyes raked the room, not quite sure where the voice had come from. He did not believe what she had said, or he did not care. Obviously he hesitated only long enough to know where to fire.

Sighing, Juille fired at him around the edge of the screen, her needle beam making the air shriek as it passed. She had meant to pierce him through the shoulder, but he was inhumanly quick. He must have jumped even before she pressed the stud, because the screaming beam only seared him across the arm and died away in a thin, high wail and a splatter of blue heat against the wall behind him.

Jair laughed, a cold, satisfied sound that partook a little of the terrible laughter in the snow room, and seemed to throw his gun and a thunderbolt at her in one incredibly quick overhand motion. But the shock of his burn must have confused him, spoiling his judgment if not his aim. The bolt went rocketing over Juille's head where she crouched as nearly flat upon the floor as she could in a poise for flight.

The painted screen disintegrated in a rain of colored flinders around her. Those that touched her burned, but she scarcely felt it. Both she and Jair were stunned by the violence of the bolt as it crashed through the wall in a blinding, blue-white glare, leaving behind it a moderate thunderclap and a smell of ozone.

After a second, Juille's mind cleared and she heard Jair's bull-like roar deep in his throat, saw his finger tighten again on the trigger. She faced him over the ruins of the screen, not daring to wait for another shot at him. He was too quick, and a second thunderbolt might strike her squarely.

She was whirling as the room still shook with thunder. Of its own accord her hand closed on a fragment of weighted plastic from the screen and she flung it at Jair, seeing it splinter against his forehead. Then she had spun away toward the shattered wall, moving more quickly than she had ever moved in her life before.

She cleared the wall with one flying leap, grateful in a flash of remembrance to Helia's relentless training over years and years, that had built muscles and reflexes to hair-trigger response. How very strange it was that Helia had trained her thus, so that she might escape the weapon which Helia herself had put into the hands of her enemies.

The thunderbolt had made havoc through a series of rooms before it came to a gap too wide to leap. If Cyrille's materials had not been almost uniformly fireproof, she might never have lived to run even as far as this. But she knew she must dodge behind some other ambush and shoot Jair from behind where he could not be forewarned by the sight of her motion. His reflexes were even quicker than her own. Luckily the bolt had leaped haphazardly, not in one straight path, or Juille's flight must have been halted before she finished her second stride.

Arch upon shattered, tottering arch opened up before her through rooms of sunlit fields whose light spilled over into rooms of twilight. At the far end she could see an angle of a room full of branches and terrified birds. She ran smoothly, dodging, taking advantage of every broken wall. If Jair was behind her, he came silently. She dared not glance back to see.

When Juille came to the room of branches it seemed to have no floor, only leaves and vines and more branches below at various levels leading down to sunny, bottomless space. But some of the birds lay dead in midair, and she guessed the presence of a glass floor and went skating precariously over nothingness toward the gap in the far wall. Birds beat hysterically about her head, screaming protest and alarm.

In the last room, but one which the bolt had wrecked, she dropped behind a ledge of green ice, on a floor of strange green moss, and waited with steady gun. This time she did not hear Jair coming. He went silently past her a dozen feet away, moving with smooth, deadly speed. Juille took careful aim and her finger tightened upon the stud.

Jair's quickness was inhuman. His senses must have risen to razor-keenness under such stress as this, for something warned him in the instant before Juille fired. Some tension in the air, some awareness of her breathing or sight of the motion she made vaguely reflected in the crystal walls of the room. He flung himself flat upon the moss and the needle beam shrieked over his head and flattened to blue heat in midair upon some invisible wall. He fired from the floor, grinning up at Juille with a singular cold detachment that fascinated her. Then the leaping bolt dazzled her eyes. Fantastic luck was still with her.

Because he fired from such an angle, he missed by a very brief margin. Juille felt the searing heat of its passage and heard it go crashing through walls again, somewhere behind her. The concussion shook them heavily again, and low thunder rolled and echoed through the opened rooms.

Juille spun around. Beyond the broken wall was dimness. Dimness to shoot from – an ambush at last. She reached the opening in three flying strides, a split second before Jair could scramble to his feet. She knew vaguely that he was lunging after her, almost upon her heels, as she vaulted the gap into dimness. But she knew very little else with any degree of clarity for some seconds.

For she landed not upon a level floor, but on a rubbery, cushioned surface that swooped into life as she touched it. Inertia flattened her to the cushions as it rocketed toward the ceiling in a long, smooth glide. Behind her she heard Jair's startled bellow trailing out and away as something unexpected happened to him. For a few moments she could see nothing.

Then violet light dawned slowly about her and she was gliding swiftly down a long mirrored slope between trees like great nodding plumes, white in the purple dimness. The slopes were deep-violet and all the pale trees stood upon their own reflections.

Juille was sitting in a cushioned boat with a harp-shaped prow. And it was sliding faster and faster, down and down, while the plumy trees blurred together and a great crashing chord of music paralleled her flight. Far off through the trees she saw motion – red beard, a streaming cloak. Too dazed to realize what had happened, she was not yet too dazed to recognize Jair, and she sent a random beam screaming at him through the trees. He bellowed a distant, echoing challenge.

By the time its resounding chords had died away a little, and her boat carried her around a wide swinging curve under the trees, she thought she knew what was happening. They had stumbled, somehow, into one of the game rooms of Cyrille. Jair's last lightning bolt must have opened a wall directly above a waiting line of cars, and the two of them were swooping now, very fast, through the opening measures of some one of the elaborate competitive entertainments of Cyrille.

Unexpectedly the familiar despairing wail of a needle beam screamed overhead and spattered blue-violet in the dimness upon an unseen wall behind her. Juille ducked instinctively and heard Jair's diminishing shout as he was carried past along a curve beyond the nodding trees. Obviously he was afraid to use the lightning bolts here. If he wrecked the invisible track, he might come to grief himself before he could escape from his flying boat.

Juille craned about her in the sleepy twilight. The trees nodded with soporific soothing motion; the cushioned boat swept on up a swift incline to the music of an invisible orchestra. Again the screams of a gun beam split the music, searing the cushions before her. Scorched rubber tainted the air. She twisted in time to see the other boat go swooping away through the trees in a long, smooth dive, and hurled a whining beam in pursuit. Jair yelled derisively.

The music swelled and sank. The boats swung gracefully around tree-shadowed curves, under feathery plumes that brushed the cheek. The mirrored slopes reflected everything in violet distances underfoot, like still water. And above and below the music Jair and Juille exchanged random shots that missed in blue-spattering fountains or seared the cushions of one boat or the other, but because of their speed, somehow never quite struck the occupants. Several times severed tree trunks came down in avalanches of white plumes.

But presently the light began to glow with a rosy brightening, and Juille realized that a second phase of the entertainment was about to begin. What it would be she did not know, but since this was very likely a competitive game, it would no doubt involve a clearer light and a more open field for some kind of maneuvers in the gliding boats. She imagined the music that kept pace with the speed of her flight had some connection with the harp on the prow of each boat. Was it some sort of musical competition as well? She remembered Egide in the underground arsenal, shouting until the weapons all replied, and for an unexpected moment she was appalled by a melting warmth at the memory. She had an irresistible vision of the young H'vani riding in a boat like this with his yellow hair streaming, leaning forward to strike music from the harp and shouting out the stanzas of some ballad in reply to the distant, shouting song from other boats, and the wild chords of the harps.

She turned her mind grimly away from that, wondering if anyone who had ridden this track before could have imagined the deadly stakes for which she played today. And she knew she dared not play it through. In the light and the open, Jair would have the advantage. Those lightning bolts would probably not miss a third time.

But one advantage she did have. She had entered the game first. She remembered enough of the contests to know that they usually involved an elaborate crossing and recrossing of paths, woven in and out like a Maypole dance. It was not impossible that Jair's boat, while not following exactly the path of her own, did cross it now and then in her wake. If she could wreck the track—

Leaning over the back of the swiftly gliding boat, she pointed her bell-mouthed gun at the floor and pulled the trigger. While she waited for the whirling sun to form she speculated as to what would happen if she herself were carried over the resulting chasm first.

Something was wrong. The gun was shivering in her hand like some living creature forced beyond its strength. But no glow gathered. Juille shook it in some faint hope of utilizing the last of whatever charge it used. But the shivering itself began to slacken in a moment or two, and then the little weapon from the nameless past lay dead in her hand. She looked at it regretfully. Well, now she would have to take the lightning gun from Jair or give up all hope of reaching the Control Room even in time to take vengeance. After an instant's hesitation she gripped her palm gun tightly and slipped over the side of the boat.

This was a slow place, mounting the rise of a mirrored hill. She skidded a moment or two on the uncertain flooring and then caught herself and watched the boat go sliding on down a slope to waves of diminishing music. Juille dived into the shelter of a great feathery tree that overhung the path. Violet twilight closed about her. She stood in a bower of shivering white plumes, exquisitively delicate, wavering upon the air so that her very breath stirred them into slight motion all around. She could trace the departure of her boat by the quivering plumes in its wake.

The music sank and swelled again. She spent an interminable five minutes thinking she had guessed wrong, and wondering wildly how she could ever hope to escape now, without her bell gun to blast a way through the floor. And then upon a rising tide of music she saw a boat come gliding by, parting the trailing plumes. Jair leaned forward over the prow, his red-brown eyes raking the twilight with quick, comprehensive glances. He was almost machine-like in the cold efficiency that lay like a hard foundation beneath the warmth and the dominant, overwhelming masculinity of him.

But he did not see Juille. This time she was hidden. This time she could not fail.

She raised her gun, took steady aim, and shot him through the stomach.

The beam's high wail still shook the scorched and plumy branches around her as she leaped for the stern of the sliding boat. It was picking up speed again. Jair had doubled forward without a sound, both big hands clutching at the wound. His lightning gun thudded softly to the car's cushioned floor. The air smelled of burned flesh and burned feathers. He did not move as she leaned over the moving side and snatched up the gun. It was all over in the flash of a moment.

Then she dropped off the padded gunwale as the boat gathered more speed. She stood watching it go, sliding faster and faster to the beat of rising music, swooping away over the violent reflections of the floor while the white trees foamed in its wake.

The gun was still warm from Jair's hand. After a moment of quiet staring as the boat and the dying man vanished, Juille drew a long breath and pointing the lightning gun at random, pulled its trigger.

Thunder and lightning – the crash of the bolt against some hidden wall, then booming echoes that rolled and rolled again. Plumed trees convulsed violently away from that path of destruction, delicate fronds tearing free so that the air was filled with a storm of feathery snow. Through their drifting, Juille could see only confusedly what had happened. In the wake of the thunderclap, and tinkling between its echoes, she heard shattered crystal showering from some ruined wall.

Setting her lips, she turned the gun in the opposite direction and loosed a second bolt. There was a curious intoxication in the feeling of sheer destruction as she heard the lightning smash and another wall come sliding down in musically tinkling fragments. Echo piled upon echo through the boiling snow of feather fronds. Again and again and again, in diminishing distances, she heard the bolt strike and leap and strike again, wall beyond wall, until it found a gap too wide to bridge. The thunder rolled away and rolled again long after the crashes ceased, and the air was heady with ozone. The whole forest was lashing itself to fragments now, and the storm of feathery snow had become almost too thick to breathe.

Holding her cloak over her face, Juille tilted the gun down and loosed a bolt at the floor some distance ahead. Destruction was her only goal now. Jair had fired recklessly, in the hope of killing her, but he had not shared this utter recklessness of Juille's. She knew she could not find the Control Room except by chance, but the lightning bolts she was loosing must sooner or later crash through the floors into the room where Egide stood waiting by the window that looked down upon Ericon.

Whether the Imperial City still stood she could not guess. Perhaps not. She did not know how much time had passed since her escape from the first room, or how near Cyrille had been then to the city. At best she might still save it; at worst she would have revenge. For if she missed the Control Room, she must eventually pierce the outer walls of Cyrille and let free the air that kept them both alive. And she would do it if she had to demolish the whole pleasure world, room by room.

A fan of bright sunlight glowed upward through the wrecked floor. Like the pink snow in that room of terrible laughter, the feathery snow of this one turned and twisted like great motes in its beam. Juille skipped back in alarm as the floor before her collapsed with a great sliding crash into the gap. Dust billowed up into the sun rays.

When the sliding had ceased, Juille saw a network of beams that looked fairly steady, and made a precarious descent to the floor below through the choking dust and the swirls of feathers. The air still shook to thunderous echoes and the distant crashes as her lightning bolt went leaping on, far away.

Here was another jumble of ruined rooms opening upon one another, mingling the components of their worlds into one insane potpourri of incongruities. Strong sunlight from a wrecked daisy field stretched fingers of illumination into the fragments of a spring night sparkling with stars. A burst of feather snow from above blew past on some sudden draft and swirled over the daisies and through the broken wall above them into a stretch of desert that lifted blue peaks against the sky miles upon miles away.

Juille looked about upon the chaos she had wrought and laughed aloud with something of a god's intoxication in the sound. She felt like a god indeed, hurling the thunderbolts, wrecking the helpless worlds about her. She drilled a fresh path of destruction through the nearest wall, reeling a little with the concussion of the blow, and then breathed the ozone deeply and felt her head spin with its stimulation.

Through the wrecked wall in the wake of the lightning and thunder a gust of sudden rain came beating, and the sound of distant surf breaking upon rocks, and a swirl of leaves from some exotic purple tree. Juille climbed through the gap and watched her bolt leaping three rooms away across a jungle glade to crash with redoubled violence into a twilight scene where pink boats drifted. Beyond it some scarcely visible new world opened up, a place of darkness and blazing orange suns whirling in a black sky.

Something cold lapped about Juille's ankles. She looked down at a stream that appeared to have sprung to sudden existence from empty air between the columns of a golden autumn wood. It gushed harder as she looked, broke away more of the wall upon which the autumn trees were reflected, and became a minor torrent in the course of a few seconds.

Remembering the many water scenes of Cyrille, Juille took alarm. There must be great reservoirs of it somewhere here. She had no wish to release it all at once, to overwhelm her before her work was done. She cast another lightning bolt at the floor in the torrent's path, staggered from the concussions and watched the broadening stream plunge downward in the wake of thunderous echoes to create new havoc beneath.

Then she clambered over ruins and hurled a new bolt before her to blast a path through the worlds. Where was Egide? Which way did the Control Room lie? Echoes piled upon echoes as she blazed her way along. Ozone mingled with the heavy fragrances of tropic flowers and autumn leaves burning, and nameless, unknown odors from the opening rooms.

There was something truly godlike about such destruction as she was wreaking. This was more than human havoc. As she went striding and destroying from room to room she left ruin in her wake that could not have been paralleled since God first created the Galaxy out of similar chaos. All the ingredients of creation were here, tossed together in utter confusion. And if her race was doomed, if it never ruled the stars again, then she was creating here in miniature all the havoc her race would leave behind it when it fell. World by tiny world she returned them to the original anarchy from which God had assembled them, but there would be no gods to come after her and build them up again.

She was glad that she came upon none of the scenes she might have remembered from her few days here with Egide, in the lost times of peace. Subconsciously she kept watch for that vast central room of the floating platforms and the great tree, where they had met. And once she came to an opening that might once have been that room, and stood on the brink of its great space, looking out. Lightning bolts had been here before her, and nothing coherent remained. The whole enormous space had evidently once been veiled with vast swinging curtains of gossamer, but they were in ribbons now and held startling bits of flotsam in their nets, as if some giant had been seining chaos for the relics of ruined worlds.

Methodically she went on with her labor of hurling the thunderbolts.

Cyrille was builded well. The little worlds collapsed into one another and the walls and floors collapsed, but the small planet itself held surprisingly long. But eventually, as Juille paused to look down a long newly-opened vista – like someone gazing godlike from the shore of the river of time, looking across the eras into many parallel worlds – she saw something amazing happen.

Far away, tiny in the distance at the end of the lightning-riven chain, trees and walls and shattered buildings began with stately precision to collapse. An invisible hand seemed to be sweeping toward her along the newly created corridor of the worlds, crushing them to the floor in leisurely successions. Juille had a moment's insane impression that by the hurling of the thunderbolts she had made herself a god – that the world bowed down before her.

She stood amazed, watching the long sets fold slowly to the ground, nearing and nearing, until – a giant palm smashed her to the floor. She was no god now, but a puppet in the grip of a monstrous gravity that was making the very floor sag beneath her incredible weight.

It passed on and she got up shakily, full of a grim exultance even in the face of this terrible threat. Cyrille was breaking up. The gravity machines had been damaged. And that – she laughed aloud – must mean that one of her random bolts had reached the Control Room at last. From now on, anything might happen. She thought with chilly amusement of Egide's surprise. He must think Jair was being very careless indeed with the Andarean lightning. Perhaps he might come to investigate. Perhaps he might! She warmed at the thought. She had no idea along which of the many corridors that her bolts had opened the Control Room lay, but Egide might follow the path that had broken in its wall and so find her. She began to watch for a human figure among the vistas.

But Cyrille was collapsing faster than she had thought. The faraway, hissing howl of air through punctured space walls had not yet begun to drain the planet of life, but some other force of destruction was loose among the worlds now. She felt the roar before she heard it, a thunderous shaking of the air that swelled and swelled into a stunning juggernaut of sound. The floor tilted, sending her reeling against a wall through whose breach bright-scaled branches hung. They clutched at her feebly, with a malignant reptilian life. But she scarcely noticed. The roaring grew so vast that its own weight seemed to turn Cyrille off balance as it neared. She heard a series of tremendous avalanching crashes beyond the walls.

Then a solid stream of green water burst through the wall she leaned on, and crashed against the opposite barrier, brimming the room waist high in a split second. Juille went whirling helplessly into the vortex boiling at its center. But before she had gulped more than a searing lungful of the water a screaming uproar filled the room as it dropped away again around her. She leaned gasping against the wall while the sudden torrent drained away through a hole in the flooring. The last of it vanished with a gurgling, shrieking scream that sounded nearly human.

Gravity shifted madly while the sound still echoed. Juille found herself shooting up diagonally toward a corner of the ceiling which had suddenly become the floor. An utter hodgepodge of her self-created chaos fell with her. Before she could adjust her balance on the angular floor, it tipped anew and amid floating debris she drifted down again. Far off the roaring of the released torrent diminished among the echoing rooms, but the floor still vibrated from its thunder. Obviously the water supplies had burst their reservoirs at last and were crashing through Cyrille, flattening everything in their path.

If she had created chaos before, there was no word to describe this.

Gravity tilted again, to send her reeling down a steep incline of inter-opening rooms. Warm rain beat in her face, snow stung it. Air currents went screaming by, mingling the odors of a dozen ruined worlds. Then the floor retilted, so that the bottom of the slope she stumbled along was suddenly the top of a high hill, and she went scrambling and spinning away sidewise through a cold ice cavern that opened upon a swamp.

When Juille found herself looking up into Egide's face, she was not at all surprised. Creation had flown apart all around her; nothing would be surprising now. Everything in her brain was as hopelessly confused as the external confusion all about, and with the letting go of gravity, all sense of responsibility seemed to have let go, too. Far away, long ago, she knew she had been desperately worried about something. It was all right now. Nothing mattered. Nothing remained intact to matter. When natural laws suspend and reverse themselves, the mind tends to accept suspension as natural in itself.

Egide seemed to be carrying her. Everything bobbed curiously around them. He was carrying her doggedly through a snowstorm that changed to a gust of tiny frightened birds, white and pink and yellow, rushing by them shoulder high in a great beat of wings. And now they were flying, too, twisting over and over around each other in the midst of a twisting tornado of colored debris. Juille laughed weakly at the ludicrous feeling of weightlessness.

'Glad it amuses you,' Egide told her savagely, trying in vain to right himself. 'If this is your idea of suicide, go ahead. I'm leaving.' He shoved her violently away and struck off awkwardly through midair, pushing a way ahead through the floating jetsam of the worlds, and holding on to the ceiling for leverage.

'Wait! Come back!' Juille floundered after him, knowing vaguely in the back of her mind that there had once been some urgent reason why he should not leave her. Nothing mattered now that had mattered before, but there was still that nagging remembrance.

'Stop following me!' Egide barked angrily, pushing a drifting boulder aside.

'Wait! Wait!' Juille wailed, and brushed the boulder from her way.

If they had been tensely staking their lives a few minutes before on the hope of killing each other, all memory of that had relaxed and floated away with the floating worlds. There was nothing ludicrous to either of them now in the futile anger of their voices. And if, in this utter suspension of all they had been thinking and believing, Egide fled from Juille as a danger and a menace, and if Juille struggled after him calling him to return, it may have meant nothing at all.

Juille had little recollection of what happened between that time and the time she found herself helping Egide, who resisted her irritably, to lever open a door in a slanting ceiling. They hoisted themselves through it with difficulty. Then Juille turned suddenly very sick as gravity reversed itself in midair and whirled the floor around underfoot, jerking the door handle from her grasp.

After a moment, everything righted itself. Juille found herself leaning on a cold, smooth wall of plastic, looking over a familiar room. Machinery filled it, and from the walls, hundreds of paneled screens looked down in serried rows. Many of them still functioned, mirroring insane pictures as world tumbled through world. Sounds howled down from their windows, hodgepodging together into a continuous ululating roar. And before her, a vast glass wall opened upon the red glow of fire.

That was Ericon down there.

Remembrance avalanched back upon her. And for a stunned moment, the sight she saw below meant nothing. She had looked too long upon ruin to be shocked by it now. Ericon stood up like a great green wall before her in the telescopic glass, its surface crisscrossed with a path of destruction. The Imperial City, like a toy relief map spread upright on the wall, sent great rolling plumes of smoke upward from its shattered buildings. She could see the wreckage of the Imperial patrol ships lying where they had fallen among the ruins. The futile flashes of gunfire from far below sparkled like fireflies in the dusk of the consuming smoke. But she could not quite force her mind to believe any of it. She had seen too much miniature destruction in the past few hours to accept this destruction, so far away, as real, full-sized, disastrous.

No. What sent a cold flooding of despair through her now was the sight of the great black shapes which were forging silently past the window in perfect formation, silhouettes against the pulsing red glow of Ericon beneath.

The great armada of the H'vani was driving in from space through the breaches of the devastated space defenses. They were coming in now – now, as she stood watching. This was something real. There was no parallel for this in the make-believe destruction she had just wrought. She leaned against the wall and let her wide eyes absorb the sight of Ericon's ultimate ruin, unable to make her mind take hold upon anything but that.

So her futile adventures among the little worlds of Cyrille had been for nothing, then. Sometime while she had gone striding among them dealing thunderbolts, Cyrille had swung at last over the target Egide awaited. And he had loosed a real thunderbolt upon a real world. She could see the ravaged surface of it interlaced with broad molten tracks of ruin. Cyrille's traitorous work was done. Juille thought sickly of what must have happened down there when the unsuspected moon, which had circled Ericon for countless ages, suddenly began to pour death upon the city.

That silent armada could take over now. It would take over, against whatever resistance might be left in the stunned and ruined city below. Her father might be dead already. And without either of them to organize the shattered remnants of the empire, what hope did the Lyonese have? She tried to turn over in her mind the names of those who might succeed her, she tried to think how quickly the forces on the outlying planets of this system might be summoned in, but with the very heart of the empire lying in burning ruins down there, it was hard to think at all.

Then her hand at her throat touched the outlines of that small lensed weapon which had been Dunnar's last gift to the Lyonese, and a faint hope began to struggle in her mind. If the Lyonese had lost their Imperial City and the services of herself as a leader, had not the H'vani lost their leaders, too? Jair, dead somewhere out in the raving chaos of Cyrille, and Egide here – Egide leaning against the window and looking down at the great armada that was pouring in upon Ericon.

Egide had crossed the still-intact floor of the Control Room while Juille stood stricken against the wall, gazing upon the ruin of her empire. Now he lifted his head and watched her without moving as she pulled out her lens upon its chain. She must have seemed to be looking in a mirror as she lifted the lens and tried vainly to steady it enough for her purpose. Certainly there was no overt threat in the action. He stared, not interfering, as she braced her elbows on a projecting bar and centered him in the thin cross-hairs of the weapon.

Then Juille drew a deep breath and pressed the white stud. Nothing happened. Nothing, of course, would happen until the other stud was pressed. But Juille felt oddly disappointed that her supreme purpose had been accomplished in this moment, with so little fanfare. It surprised her a bit that she had no emotional reaction now. Neither triumph nor regret, although Egide's life hung upon the pressure of a stud. No feeling seemed left in her at all.

She looked around vaguely, wondering just what to do next. Egide still stood before the window where the great black shapes of his armada passed in stately formation, silent, limned against the light of the burning city. All around them the howling from the ruined worlds of Cyrille still poured down from their screens upon the wall. Through the one ragged gap where Juille's lightning bolt had crashed came more confused roars and thunderings as the tides of water and the shifting gravities put a last touch of havoc on the work she had done. But here in the Control Room, gravity still prevailed, and so far the ruinous tides had not rolled this way. Very likely they soon would. And then there would be no survivors at all upon Cyrille.

Juille shook herself awake. One last faint hope remained with her, but even that must be fulfilled quickly. She held the lens up, her thumb upon the black stud that meant death.

'Egide,' she called. 'Egide, look here. Remember the weapon from Dunnar?'

He blinked. He had not recovered quite as quickly as she from that curious relaxing of all human values which the shifting gravities induced. He had not had reason to recover so soon, as Juille did, at the shock of what lay below the window. He said:

'What do you mean? Dunnar?'

She flashed the lens impatiently at him. 'This is the weapon. This, here! Do you understand me?' She saw that he did, for he reached abortively toward his holster. 'No, don't move!' She cried it sharply above the noise from the walls. 'I can press this stud before you shoot, and then—' She made a grim little gesture.

Egide hesitated. 'That's not the weapon there.'

'It's enough to kill you.'

He furrowed his brow at her. 'The real weapon – that must be down below, on Ericon.' He glanced over his shoulder at the gliding armada and the flames of the burning city, and his hand moved a little nearer his gun.

'Don't do it!' Juille's voice was confident and commanding. 'The real weapon's safe, even now. In a bombproof vault outside the city. We thought of everything, you see. Even this. I wouldn't risk it, Egide.' She held the lens higher, so the red light from below caught brightly in it, and showed him her thumb already on the lethal stud. He hesitated a little even now.

Juille held her breath. She did not want to kill him yet. She was not sure she wanted to kill him at all, and certainly he would be no use to her dead at this stage. But she might have to press the stud. This harmless-looking adjunct of a distant machine lacked the compelling power of a gun muzzle aimed between a man's eyes. Her own confidence might be a more effective psychological threat than the very real danger of the lens in her hand.

She said in a brisk, decisive voice, 'You're coming with me to Ericon, Egide – if we can find a way to get there. The Ancients promised me my chance, too, you know – and mine comes last. You can come back with me to be our hostage – or stay here dead. We haven't lost yet. With Jair gone and you captive, and with this new weapon of ours, I think we've still a good chance. The weapon's going to work its very best under circumstances like . . . don't touch that gun!'

He stood there staring at her, fingers hovering over his holster, decision still tilting in the balance. What would have happened had nothing interrupted them, Juille had no way of guessing. But as they faced one another in tense silence, a voice suddenly boomed from the wall above.

'So that's the Dunnar weapon!' Jair's bull-throated bellow roared above the roar of smashing worlds.

Juille started violently. But even in her amazement, she kept her thumb upon the stud and her eyes upon Egide's gun, though insane thoughts whirled frantically through her mind. Jair? Jair alive, with a needle beam through his stomach? Jair, talking in that full, confident bellow of his, when she'd left him dead and drifting through the violet twilight? It was some trick. She had seen illusions enough here to know that it *must* be some trick.

She risked one lightning glance away from Egide. The unmistakable figure of Jair himself leaned forward into the communicator screen of some yet undamaged world, grinning a bold white grin through the red beard. His red eyes twinkled with triumph, and the burn of her needle beam still marred his tunic to show that the shot had gone home. It *must* have gone home. There had been no heat flare to prove the presence of armor such as Egide had worn when she turned her gun on him.

She dared not look long at him, but her bewilderment had registered upon the screen as she flashed her gaze back to Egide, and she heard the familiar, rolling vibrations of Jair's laughter ring through the room.

'You shot me straight enough,' he announced. 'But you'll never kill me with a gun. Tell her, Egide.'

Egide was looking up at the laughing giant with a strange expression on his face.

'Jair is an android,' he said. 'You can't kill him.'

Juille gave him a blank stare. She heard herself repeating stupidly, 'An android?'

But she did not believe it. That was against all reason. Jair, the very essence of all warm, human masculinity – the frankly barbarous, the laughing Jair, with his voice that shook the walls to its deep timbre. She knew, of course, that androids existed. Cyrille had been making robot humans for a long while now, in such perfect simulacra of reality that only the very closest association could prove the difference. To all intents and purposes, they were real anthroids – manufactured humans with all the external attributes of flesh. But Jair—

'I had him made ten years ago,' Egide told her in a bemused sort of voice, his eyes upon the window where the counterfeit H'vani looked down. 'The perfect H'vani type – for a figurehead, you know. I'd got so used to him I seldom think of his not being – human. Sure you're all right, Jair?'

A bellow of mirth shook the walls above the roaring of Cyrille's worlds.

'All right?' Jair doubled a mallet-like fist and struck himself heavily upon the needle char where Juille's shot had gone home. The two humans winced involuntarily. 'Just doubled me up for a minute,' the android said. 'That was enough, though. You did a fine job of wreckage, girl. Now we'll do a better – down below.'

Juille got her breath back with a rush.

'Oh, no, you won't,' she told him confidently. 'Not now.' And she caught the red firelight again in her lens.

Jair's laughter was curiously cold. And Juille realized that it had always been cold. The laugh itself should have proved him inhuman. And a flurry of small recollections came back to convince her – his incredible quickness in gun-fighting, his speed, his silence, his machine-smooth efficiency of motion. Even the fact that he had not worn needleproof armor beneath his tunic. Then the bull-voice with its deeply vibrant pitch that should have been warm and human, and was instead cold to her ears now with the chill of machinery beneath the flesh said:

'Go ahead, girl. Kill him.'

Egide's face did not change. Juille thought she understood then his oddly bemused look of a few minutes before. He had remembered that Jair was what he was. He had known this moment was coming, and it did not surprise him now. The android could have no human emotions; loyalty was not in him.

And there went Juille's new hope of forcing Jair into captivity, too, with the threat upon Egide. Her shoulders sagged a little. But even in this fresh disappointment she kept her pressure firm upon the lens stud, and her eyes upon Egide.

'I'd save you if I could,' the android's deep voice told the man who had ordered his creation. 'It can't be done now. You aren't necessary any more. We've got Ericon, or will have. Too bad, Egide.'

Egide nodded, no emotion on his face.

'The barons can carry on now,' Jair told him carelessly. 'Malon can take over, or Edka. They'll need me.'

Egide looked up at the grinning, red-bearded face in the screen.

'They don't even know you're an android,' he said emotionlessly.

Jair bent down upon them one last brilliantly warm smile. His eyes glinted with a sudden look of the pure machine.

'I know,' he said.

Then he swung away and they watched his broad back receding into the depths of the panel. Beyond him Juille could see the shapes of tiny space boats racked as if in hangars, and untouched as yet by the destruction that was raging through Cyrille. That was the room she must get to, then.

Juille turned back to Egide, realizing for the first time that she had forgotten to keep her eyes on him. But he had not moved. He stared up at the screen, and his shoulders had the little sag her own had assumed a few minutes ago. When he met her eyes he grinned a bit.

'Am I still worth killing?' he asked.

Juille jerked her head toward the empty screen. 'What do you think he's planning?'

'He wasn't built to plan. I don't know.'

'What was he built for?'

Egide looked at her speculatively. 'You don't understand the H'vani very well, do you? Savagery isn't always a vice, you know. There's got to be an influx of it every so often or civilization would bog down in its own rut. It always has happened – it probably always will. Right now my people are on the first rung of the ladder – they're emotional and childish and they need a figurehead. Well' – he nodded toward the wall – 'that's Jair.'

'Why not you?'

'They don't quite trust me. I'm not typical. Too much veneer for a true H'vani. Maybe too many brains. I had to have some perfectly trustworthy bully who could outfight and outyell the people. Someone with his own brand of charm, too. But anyone with those gifts would be too dangerous to use. He might want to take over, and I couldn't have stopped him. So' – Egide grinned ruefully – 'I had the Cyrillians make Jair. It seemed like a wonderful idea. And it worked, too. Jair did a magnificent job. He never had to think, but he certainly could lead. I suppose even now he's done the right thing. From a perfectly cold-blooded viewpoint, the H'vani need a rallying point worse than they need me as a leader. Jair's much better for the job.'

'But if none of your men knows he's an android—'

'I'm not so sure it matters now. I kept it a secret because I couldn't trust anyone at all not to let it slip, and my people – well, they wouldn't like that.

But Jair's done his job well up to now. No reason why anyone needs to know.'

'He certainly doesn't mean to tell them.'

'I wonder. Hard to understand what was in his mind. No android ever had an opportunity just like this before. He never showed any more ambition, until now, than you'd expect from a machine. He may never show any.'

'He won't.' Juille said it confidently. Egide gave her an inquiring look. 'The H'vani are going to find out their leader's not human. You're going to tell them.' Her voice took on warmth as the new idea grew. 'I haven't lost yet! You're still a hostage. You're going to broadcast to your people just what Jair is. Maybe we'll suggest that some of the other leaders are androids, too. If Jair's what they've been worshiping and following, that ought to shake all their confidence – or else nothing would!'

Egide stared at her almost with a reluctant admiration. She gave him no time to speak. 'Drop your guns,' she said. 'And then go over there and try to get Ericon on the communicators. I don't think you can, but it's worth trying.'

Egide gave her one long, searching look, as if not yet quite convinced of the validity of her weapon. But a change in the timbre of the noise that still poured in distantly through the breached wall reminded them both of the imminent danger, and after a moment, he obeyed.

Juille watched the guns clatter to the floor. Her mind was spinning with wary plans now – how to reach the room of the ships, how to keep Egide from overpowering her on the tumultuous way there, what to do first if they ever reached Ericon alive.

Egide turned from the unresponsive screens after ten minutes of futile effort.

'Cyrille's dead,' he shrugged. 'Now what?'

Juille looked down at the lens in her hand. 'We'll have to suspend hostilities for a while,' she told him. 'I can't keep my thumb on this stud forever. And I don't want to kill you now. I'll have to, though, unless you promise to keep a truce until we get back to Ericon. I'll even have to trust your word—'

He looked down at her with a smile. 'I seem to fall somewhere between H'vani and Lyonese,' he said dryly. 'I'm civilized enough to make a promise and – well, savage enough to keep it. You can trust my word, Juille.'

Juille's lips thinned; she dropped the lens back on its chain inside her tunic. All she said was, 'We'll have to trace the hangar room from the screen up there. Do you know how?'

Egide pointed to a chart engraved on the wall beneath the panels. 'If anything like halls are left outside here, we'll find it,' he declared.

There were halls. Not many and not much of them, but enough to help materially. They opened the door and stood staring out at a crazily angled ceiling on which a tangle of debris clung as if to a floor. And Juille glanced up to find Egide looking at her gravely, without words. It was not difficult to guess his thoughts. Perhaps anger was the dominant emotion that made her flush so hotly. She could not be sure herself. After a moment, she said in a voice that sounded a little unsteady, 'Let's go.'

The fragments of hallways that remained were small, lucid stretches between lengths of howling chaos. Nothing in those lengths had any resemblance now to any normally balanced world. Juille found time to be thankful anew that most of Cyrille's materials were fireproof. Earth and air and water were churning insanely through the broken walls; if the fourth and most ravenous element were loose here too, not she or Egide or Jair would ever have left alive.

As it was, they were nearly swept away time and again as they made frantic dashes from shelter to shelter through the hurricane. Curiously, only the very small and delicate relics remained intact now. Trees, buildings, furniture that had made up the illusions were battered almost unrecognizably, but a swarm of gorgeously colored autumn leaves, for instance, had ridden with the storm and brushed stinging past.

Gravity shifted imponderably. They ran slowly, like people in a leaden-footed nightmare; they changed with unexpected suddenness to long, swooping strides that covered ten feet at a step. They sailed through the clogged air; they were smashed crushingly to the ground amid a rain of fragments made suddenly heavy.

The air was in strong motion now, and twice as they staggered along they heard the distant shriek of it rushing furiously through punctured space walls, dragging great winds behind it. But each time the tortured pleasure-world healed itself and they heard the suck and slam of locks automatically closing off the broken rooms. It might be a matter of minutes or hours before some stray lightning bolt, still ravening through the walls, pierced some bulkhead with broken locks, and Cyrille was sucked empty in one vast, sudden gust.

The avalanching water thundered somewhere not far off as they came at last to the hangar room, buffeted, breathless, very sore from the bounding of the tornado. But they had no time to rest. This apartment, like the Control Room, seemed to have a gravity machine of its own and the ships remained intact in their cradles, waiting to be launched each through its separate door. But a bolt might come smashing through the walls at any moment. The two refugees never remembered afterward just how they managed their escape. Neither of them had really expected to leave Cyrille alive.

*

The emperor looked up from his map. The cluster of officers looked up, too, but no one said anything as Juille came quickly into the room, saying, 'Father—'

'Glad you got back,' the emperor told her in a voice she did not know. She found she scarcely knew the man himself – this helmeted warrior with the fierce blue blaze in his eyes and the look of stunned bewilderment still a shadow upon his lined face. They all had that stunned look. Ericon had been invincible so long – only the emperor seemed to know exactly what he was about. Even with this disaster upon him, even with the bewilderment still in his eyes, he knew what he was doing now, what he must do next. This was the man who had been so great and terrible a leader in the days of his youth; he was great and terrible again. No trace remained of the patriarch in white robes, pleading for peace. No trace remained either, Juille thought, of the indulgent father she had left.

He said again, 'Glad you're back—' and for a moment stared at her with eyes that really saw what they looked at. But it was a curiously blind stare still. He knew vaguely that something more than that phrase might be expected of him, that in normal times, his only child's return from death would have been a signal for tremendous emotional release. Not any more. He was no longer a father or a man, but an emperor with the weight of imminent disaster on his shoulders. His mind was not functioning now except in terms of empire. He was a machine at this moment as Jair was a machine, all his faculties bent toward one consuming purpose.

'We're evacuating the city,' he told Juille without preamble, and a cold, bright intensity burned in his voice and his lined face. It was not his daughter he spoke to, but a tried officer whose advice might be helpful. He was not questioning her presence or her past experiences, only her usefulness at this terribly urgent moment. 'Through this pass here—' His steady finger traced a course across the map. 'Up into the mountains where the forbidden woods make a pocket, the H'vani can't attack by air. Enough troops are left to make a stand until reinforcements start coming in from the planets. That Dunnar weapon ought to prove useful, too. Now—'

'It's still working?' Juille had seen too much of the city and the surrounding countryside ravaged by those dreadful broad swathes of molten ruin to have much confidence in anything material now.

'It's working. With any luck, it always will work.' The emperor gave a ghost of a chuckle. 'The H'vani sealed it in so tightly I don't believe anyone could ever dig it up again. That's once they've overreached themselves.'

Juille received that and dismissed it with a nod. 'Good luck for us. Father – so much has happened. You've got to listen to me. Haven't you even a minute to spare alone?'

The emperor gave her a keen look under his brows, then nodded to the little group of men and women around the table. 'All right – one minute.' Juille waited while they fell back out of earshot, down the length of the big shattered room through whose walls the smoke of the burning palace blew now and then in pungent, strangling gusts. She spoke fast.

'The Andareans – you don't know about that yet? They've been holding revolutionist meetings in the tunnels. And there's Egide – they told you I've brought him in as a hostage? I—'

'Hostage be damned,' the emperor said abstractedly. 'Only one thing matters right now – getting my troops out. You can't bargain with madmen like the H'vani when they're looting a city. Later – maybe. A wonder you ever got through their fleet—'

'I didn't come through. I thought I'd better circle—'

The emperor wasn't listening. 'We have half an hour to clear the city. If you have anything important to say, say it and let me get back to work.' He gave her a sudden cold glance across the map. 'I haven't forgotten what you did in the council hall, Juille. That was treason. You'll have to stand trial for it later. You may be responsible for the loss of the city.'

'Your peace wouldn't have gone through, father. The H'vani came in conspiracy with Helia and her people. They got their new weapons from them. They never meant to keep the truce themselves.'

The emperor's fierce blue eyes fixed her sharply. 'You're not lying about that, are you? It's true?' His voice deepened with a note of anger she knew well. 'All of you were playing me for a fool, eh? Using my truce to work your own lying schemes in. All of you! By the Ancients—' There was a thunder as vibrant as Jair's in the old man's voice. 'By the Ancients, you all deserve to die together! I ought to let you! I had the possibility of peace in my very hands, and I let you destroy it among you—' But the brief anger passed, and the deep old voice diminished to a rumbling echo. 'No, it wasn't your fault or mine. I saw the way out, but I couldn't show it to you. The race isn't worth saving.' His big shoulders slumped. Then he saw the map and his head came up with a familiar blue glare in the eyes. 'But I will save it! By the gods, I will. Get out of here and let us work, will you?'

'But father—' Juille groped in bewilderment for the reins of government that seemed so abruptly to have dropped from her hands. 'I want to broadcast to the H'vani. If they find out we have Egide – and about Jair being an android, they—'

He scowled at her, his face bright with alert intensity. 'Android?'

Juille explained it in a few jumbled phrases, and saw a shadow dim the brilliance of his eyes as he followed that knowledge to its conclusion.

'Stop babbling,' the emperor snapped. 'You can't broadcast, you little fool. Didn't you see what's happened to the city? About that android—'

*

Juille gaped at him, not listening. She had seen ruin indeed, all the way here. Whole city blocks melted into slag, fire pouring from the public buildings, half the palace itself battered into a shambles. But the thought of a blinded and silenced communicator system had somehow never occurred to her.

'None … none of it works any more?' she stammered.

'None.' The emperor's voice was definite. 'About the android – I don't like it. I don't like it at all.' He brooded a moment. 'Well – we'll climb that wall when we come to it. Now by the gods, will you get out and let me work?'

Juille looked up at the shattered walls of the room, with rain blowing through them, pungent with the smoke of nearing fires. She could see a stretch of purple thunderclouds, and her mind seized almost eagerly upon the sight – was it the same storm she had glimpsed from Cyrille, moving majestically over the face of Ericon? She knew she was grasping at straws, anything to avoid facing the truth. She had not yet realized the full extent of what had happened here, she did not really want to. Ericon was lost, but her mind would not face that yet. Automatically she looked about for the nearest communicator screen, so that she might convince herself with the grimness of the actual sight.

And there were no communicators. She could see no farther now than her unaided eyes could look. The knowledge was suddenly smothering. All her life she had had the wonderful windows of those screens to open at a touch upon any view she wanted, anywhere in the Galaxy. No walls had ever really shut her in before. No limits of eye or voice seemed narrow, for the sight and sound of worlds light-millenniums away had always been available at the touch of a stud. But now—

Juille looked frantically about the broken room, feeling for the first time in her life the full, crushing weight of a claustrophobia such as no race could ever have felt before now. Not a fear of confining walls, but of confining worlds – of solar systems too small to be endured. This was a blindness and a deafness beyond all previous experience – a god's scope cut abruptly down to the scope of a human. For a moment she fought an insane desire to batter against the intangible prisoning limits of her own senses. Their terrible pigmy boundaries struck her dumb. For the first time she knew what it was to be one small human creature in a galaxy of worlds, unaided by all her race had achieved on its way to the powers of godhood.

This was what the loss of civilization really meant. For the first time the full import of the Galaxy's great loss overwhelmed her. So long as she could see those lost worlds she might hope to win them back, but to be struck blind like this was to lose them forever. She knew a sudden agony of homesickness for all the planets she might never see again, a sudden terrible nostalgia for the lost, familiar worlds, for the fathomless seas of space between them.

Ericon's eternal greenness was hateful, strangling in its tiny limitations.

And this was what her father had so desperately feared to lose that he had been willing to compromise even with the H'vani, so long as both races might maintain it. In this shattering revelation of what barbarism might really mean, she knew that her father had been right, indeed, and herself terribly wrong. But it was far too late to do anything at all about it now.

Through the green folds of the hills veiled by slanting rain, the emperor watched the remnants of his army wind slowly upward. He sat his fretting horse easily, looking down from this hilltop with much the same look upon his face that his portrait had worn in the Hall of the Hundred Emperors. Eager and fierce and proud. Around his neck over the armor he wore a chain and the small lens of the Dunnarian weapon. It was ironically pleasant to know that the heart of that weapon lay safe forever beneath the very halls the H'vani were tramping now.

Juille knew he was thinking of that by the shadow of a grim smile that crossed his bearded face as he glanced back toward the tower of smoke above the city. Once, it seemed very long ago, she had wished aloud that she might have known the young warrior her father used to be. She knew him now. The emperor was magnificently that man again, with all the years of his experience added to give a depth the young man never knew. Age seemed not to have touched him today. He sat at the front of a little group of officers, watching the armies that were to avenge the Lyonese go streaming up the pass.

From this elevation they all could see the distant, undulating mass far down the valley that was the pursuing H'vani. Juille smiled a tight, triumphant smile. They were fighting on their home planet now, under conditions they knew by heart. They would beat the H'vani yet. On any other planet, planes could have bombed their infantry out of existence in a few minutes. But here, in this long arm of mountain land that lay between two forbidden territories, the Ancients permitted no aircraft to fly. The H'vani – Juille's smile deepened – had learned that to their awe-struck cost a little while before. They would send up no more ships over the lightning-guarded territory of the Ancients.

She looked sidewise at Egide. He sat with bound hands before him, his two guards near, his eyes on the following H'vani horde. They had spoken very little to one another since that long, silent flight through the H'vani fleet, with Ericon turning on its axis far below. Juille was a little startled to hear Egide speak now.

'Jair'll be leading them,' he said, nodding down the valley. She gave him a keen glance, not at all sure even yet just how she felt about the H'vani's captive leader. She said in a noncommittal voice:

'He won't be leading long. We'll get our broadcasters in order again—'

'Maybe,' said Egide, and was silent.

Juille glanced down at the small animal balancing on her knee. The *llar* had a curious way of turning up at most of the crises in her life. It was here now at one of the highest. She put out a tentative hand to caress it, and to her surprise, the little creature permitted the gesture. She wondered if its recollection of that episode in the tunnels had reconciled it to her touch at last. The great eyes stared up into hers with owlish intentness as it pushed its smooth head against her hand.

Someone said, 'I see we have something in common, highness,' and she looked up into the gray gaze of the man from Dunnar. He was smiling and nodding toward the *llar* as it bent its head to her caress. Juille smiled.

'It's my turn to be flattered now. The two of you did me a great service. I may not have thanked you properly yet.'

The envoy shook his head. 'Your pet deserves the thanks, highness.'

'It was amazing,' Juille began eagerly. 'How did you manage it? I'd never have believed such a thing could happen.'

The man smiled his remote, enigmatic smile. 'I will tell you that soon, highness,' he said. 'Not quite yet, but soon.' He flung one corner of his dark cloak over his shoulder and turned away. Juille watched him thoughtfully, a tall thin figure of regal elegance in that cloak.

Egide's voice recalled her.

'I think I can see Jair from here,' he said, leaning forward over his bound hands on the saddlehorn. 'They've got that third weapon, Juille. See it – the glint of light there at the front?'

Juille caught her breath sharply. The third gift of the Andareans! She had forgotten that. She had let her father plan his campaign without considering it.

'What is it?' she asked Egide fearfully, wondering if he would tell. He looked at her with an expression difficult to analyze.

'A paralyzer,' he said simply.

'But we've got those. That's nothing new.'

'This works on a bigger scale than anything we've ever had. You've got small hand-paralyzers. This is an attachment that transforms a standard heat-beam caster into a machine to throw a long cone of force. It can whittle your army down by battalions. Once that goes into operation—' He shook his head, lips tightened.

Juille gave Egide a curious glance. Then, without speaking, she shook her reins and rode forward to her father's side. They spoke briefly. In a few minutes, several men with lenses hanging at their necks, slipped down the hillside and vanished into the underbrush bordering the valley. Juille rode back looking confident.

'All right,' she said. 'They won't find it so easy now. We have our weapons, too, you know. You might have guessed I'd stop that cannon if I could.'

'Of course I guessed.'

Juille looked at him in bewilderment. He was smiling.

'I'd like to talk to you alone,' he said. She hesitated. Then she nodded to his guards and turned her horse aside, leading the way a little distance off toward the brow of the hill. They sat there side by side, watching the two armies winding up the valley. Rain had almost ceased now. A cold wind blew in their faces, and overhead the purple thunderclouds came rolling up faster than the H'vani hordes.

Egide said, 'Juille—' and stopped. After a moment, he tried again. 'Juille – do you think the H'vani will defeat you?'

'They have a chance,' she admitted. 'But no, they won't.'

'You're sure?'

'How can anyone be sure? I don't believe they will.'

'But they have the edge now.'

'What of it?' She twisted to face him angrily. 'You don't have to boast about your people.'

He smiled at her. 'They aren't my people now.' Juille looked at him with bewildered eyes. He went on, 'I'm through with the H'vani. I couldn't say so before – you'd have thought I was afraid and trying to join the winning side. But you can't think that now.'

Juille struggled for words. 'But – why? *Why?* You organized the attack! You—'

'Oh, I had a great many plans,' he said, smiling rather wryly. 'I liked working out ideas and watching them succeed. But lately – I've changed.' He looked at her as if uncertain whether to follow that idea any further just now. She was still staring at him in puzzled confusion. He said, 'Don't look at me like that. I've been thinking this over for quite a while. It isn't as if I were deserting them when they need me. And I've never had much in common with them. Remember, it took Jair to win their hearts.'

'But you can't change over like that, without any reason,' Juille insisted uncomprehendingly. 'You don't—'

'I have my reasons. You're thinking it's a trick, aren't you? Well, it isn't. Why should I trick you now, when it's your side that's losing? When you've got my life there around your neck on a chain?'

Juille's hand went up automatically to her breast where the lenses hung. She thought she was beginning to understand what Egide meant. Her mind went back over the confusion of disastrous things that had happened so swiftly, and paused at the episode in the forbidden woods of the Ancients, when she had stood in Egide's arms and tentatively made herself a promise. When she had him where she wanted him, she remembered now, she had told herself she might not fear the treacherous weakness of emotion. She had thought then that even love might be safe – later. And it was – later – now.

Egide was watching her, a smile beginning to quirk his mouth. She watched his face warm and soften, finding that she knew just how each line and plane would alter with the changing mood. He was very attractive when he smiled. The rain had made his yellow curls darken and tighten to almost sculptured flatness, and the rain on his lashes and his beard twinkled as he shook his head, still smiling.

'You'll never trust me, will you?' he said. 'You'll never trust anyone. Even yourself. Least of all yourself—'

'I might,' Juille told him softly, hardly knowing her own voice. Her fingers were on the chain about her neck, and almost unconsciously she found herself pulling out the deadly little ornament that held Egide's life. When she realized what she was doing she glanced down, and then sat perfectly still for a long moment, her eyes growing wider and wider. Very slowly she pulled the chain all the way out of her tunic. The color had drained from her face; and as Egide looked, his own color faded. They sat in silence, looking at the broken chain.

The lens was gone.

Juille stared down at the break, too stunned for thought. Somewhere, somehow, in the turmoil of evacuation, she had lost it. Anywhere. In the city. Along the road. In these pathless hills. Somewhere – anywhere. At this moment some curious person might be stooping to pick it up and toy with the black stud. It might lie lost forever, untouched, here in the woods. Or at this moment, or any moment hereafter, Egide might slump over dead in his saddle.

There were many disastrous implications behind the loss, but her thoughts had room for only one just now. All the emotions that had churned in her mind so long about him – all the distrust, the contempt, the reluctant warmth – suddenly crystallized. Her defenses went down with a rush and she knew that of all things in life, what she wanted least was Egide's death.

They sat looking at one another in the midst of a tremendous silence. For this small interval, there was nothing at all to stand between them, neither H'vani nor Lyonese, nor could ideals nor mistrust, nor any of the hours of their enmity. During all the time they had known one another, only a few moments had validity. The interval on the cloud beneath the stars; the interval of their dance, the moment of their kiss in the green, forbidden woods. All other meetings had been meetings of strangers, not themselves.

For Juille it was a moment of almost intolerable poignancy. And perhaps her barriers were down so utterly in this one destroying moment because she knew in her heart that the hours of this surrender were numbered. Traitor she might be to all her amazon principles – but she could not be traitor long.

Wordlessly Juille leaned forward and untied the cords that held Egide's hands together. While she touched him, for an instant longer, the stars and the shadows of the wood still hung about them. But before either could speak, or wanted to, the emperor's voice broke in.

'Juille, I'm going down,' he called. 'Wait here, child. I'll signal when I want you. The H'vani are catching up with our rear guard.'

She came out of the bemusing quiet slowly, too distracted to realize how completely now the reins of control had been taken from her hands. The emperor and most of his men were riding down the hillside before the import of his words came to her clearly. She watched them hurrying down, cloaks billowing, and the rain slanting in long gusts between.

Farther down, half hidden by the hills, she could see that the vanguard of the H'vani was almost upon the last of the escaping Lyonese. There was a turmoil about the length of the shining cannon whose secret the Andareans had betrayed, and Juille knew the new weapon of the Lyonese had taken its first toll among the enemy. There would be more.

She turned to Egide. He was watching her gravely, hands clasped on his saddlehorn. There seemed very little to say just now. Perhaps the time had not yet come for speech. Juille urged her horse nearer his and they sat side by side, knees touching, and watched the emperor riding down the hill.

In the valley the two forces had begun their meeting. From here they could see a big figure at the H'vani's front, red beard and red head a beacon for the invaders to follow. Now and again an echo of Jair's tremendous resonant roar floated up to them above the rising clamor of battle, but for the most part, they heard little. The wind was strengthening; it screamed in their ears and carried the shouts of the fighters away up the valley.

They could see turmoil growing among the H'vani. Far back in the ranks where no men should yet be falling, men fell. The Dunnarian weapon was reaping its first casualties. But Jair's great voice and his irresistible, compelling presence were keeping order among the frightened men.

And suddenly Juille knew that the Dunnarian weapon must fail. Its intrinsic purpose was the slaughter of the leaders at their peak of importance. And Jair would never die by that weapon. He was immortal, not heir to any weakness of human flesh. So long as he remained on his feet the H'vani would not break even in the face of this mysterious silent death that had begun to strike among them.

Jair would become a legend. He might even become a god for his awe-struck followers. And the last hope of demoralizing the barbarians was gone now. If Juille could have proclaimed Jair's origin before this battle, the H'vani might have been shaken. But now nothing could shake them. Even if they believed her story, the very belief might deify Jair still further.

A familiar voice at Juille's side echoed the thought.

'How strange,' said the man from Dunnar, 'that they found no human creature to personify for them half the courage and warmth and power they see in this man of metal!'

Something about the pitch of his voice made Juille turn sharply, almost unseating the *llar* that still clung to her knee. The Envoy was looking down the valley, his strange, narrow-skulled head in outline against the piling storm clouds. The cold wind whipped his cloak backward, but his great translucent eyes did not narrow to the blast. Juille was searching his face with a new fascination. The beaked nose, the controlled, cruel mouth. The air of intolerable elegance and fastidious, aloof poise. Juille swallowed hard. For she had heard his voice before, under strange circumstances. She groped after the memory, almost caught it. That calm, clear, familiar tone, saying—

Suddenly she knew. She had heard it in the temple of the Ancients.

He turned his head slowly, and the enormous, clear eyes met hers. He smiled.

'Yes,' he said.

Afterward, looking back, the interlude seemed like a hallucination, an unconvincing stage-set painted upon gauze, drawn briefly between Juille and the woods, while the thunderstorm rolled above them in the purple sky. But in the first moment after she had recognized that voice, realities stood out sharp and clear all around her, intensified because she could not speak or think coherently. Everything else was drowned in the overwhelming knowledge of who this man must be. And that he was no man at all. And what unimaginable shape he must really wear behind that illusion of humanity. And—

'Yes,' said the Envoy, smiling his thin smile across her at Egide. 'You, too.'

Juille never knew how long they sat there in silence, while the cold wind whistled about them and in the strange yellow light of storm, the two armies locked in battle down below. She thought she would never speak again. She could not even turn her head to face Egide for comfort in this bleak and overwhelming moment.

The Envoy said, 'Each of you came to us for help. And each of you was answered. But you and your people had gone too far already along the road all humans go. There was still one brief moment when you could have saved yourselves. But your instincts were wrong. That time is gone now.

'Every race has come to this end, since the first men conquered the Galaxy. Each of them sows the seed of its own destruction. Always a few see the way toward salvation, and always the many shout them down. But each race has its chance—'

He looked down sternly over the struggling masses in the valley. Mists were beginning to drift between them now. The Envoy was a tall silhouette against the purple clouds of the storm. As he spoke again, the thunder rolled in his voice and in the darkening sky.

'Every nation digs its own grave,' he said. 'And we are weary of mankind, forever thwarting his highest dreams and trapping himself in the end to a ruin like' – he nodded – 'that down there.'

Silence for a long moment, while the noises of battle came up faintly, Jair's great rich, carrying shout above all the rest, bellowed from his throat of brass. Juille sat very still on her horse, glad of the pressure of Egide's warm knee, all thought and speech frozen in her as she saw the Envoy's head turning her way. He looked thoughtfully into her face.

'You have set in motion already the forces that must destroy the Lyonese. You were the spokesman for your race, chosen fairly, typical of your kind. And of your own free choice you did it. Nothing can change that now.' Then the narrow skull turned farther and he looked across her at Egide. His great eyes were the color of the spattering rain, as cool and translucent and inhuman. 'You,' he went on, 'gave your people a man of iron to worship, and nothing you can do now would swerve them from following it. It will lead them to destruction. How very strange—' The Envoy paused a moment and looked at the two with a sort of puzzled wonder. 'How very strange you humans are! How unerringly you unleash upon yourselves the instruments of your own destruction. How long ago the two of you here took the turnings that led you to this hilltop, and your people to their ruin down there. Perhaps the turnings were taken long before your births.' He smiled impersonally in the vivid yellowish light. 'I know they were. Your first forefathers took them, and you had no choice but to follow, being of human flesh.' He sighed. 'But the end comes just the same. It's very near now.

'You wonder which will win down there.' He glanced toward the struggling armies, almost hidden in the mist. 'Neither.

'Neither will win,' he told them. 'Man has run his last course in our Galaxy. There were those before him who ran theirs, too, and failed to profit from it, and died. Now we weary of man. Oh, he may live out his failing days on the other worlds. We plan no pogrom against mankind.' His voice quivered for an instant with aloof amusement. 'Man himself attends to that. But here on Ericon, our own peculiar world, we are weary of man and we want no more of him.'

He sent one cool downward glance toward the sounds of battle in the fog, the shouts, the muffled roar of guns, the flashes of fire-sword and pistol and artillery. Then he shook his reins gently and his horse turned toward the woods, where rain was beginning to rustle again among the leaves.

'We have great hopes,' he said, 'for our new race to come.' And he held out his hand.

Something stirred upon Juille's knee. She looked down dumbly. The *llar* flashed up at her one fathomless glance, all the sadness and wisdom and benignity of its race luminous in the great grave eyes so startlingly like the Envoy's. Then it flowed down from her lap to the ground with its alarming, boneless ease, and went rippling over the wet grass toward the Envoy.

Juille looked up. She had no idea why. But she was not surprised to see again the heights of great inward-leaning walls looming dark above the trees. When she lowered her eyes the Envoy and the *llar* had gone.

'I suppose we'd better go down now,' Juille said, and put out her hand. Egide turned a quiet blue gaze upon her. The faintest flicker of a smile touched his face and his warm, gun-calloused fingers closed about the hand.

'Yes, I suppose so,' he said.

Juille had an extraordinary conviction of hiatus in her life for the past ten minutes. She knew quite well what had been happening while she sat there stricken voiceless and all but mindless in the presence of the gods. She knew she would never quite forget it – or ever speak of it to Egide. But it seemed singularly unreal. The human mind is not constructed to accept defeat even in the the face of finality. She could not now bring hers to accept that memory. What had happened seemed of a different time and texture from the period before or since – an interval of flimsy unreality, a gauze incident, to be dismissed and forgotten.

And yet, she thought, if it were true – if she herself had set into motion the juggernaut that would destroy all her hopes – a part of it was still good. Egide's life was forfeit to pure chance now, through her doing alone. But if she had not imperiled it, she might never have valued the life or the man. Meeting that faint softening of a smile that touched his face, she knew he was sharing a thought like hers. Thanks to that one terrible error, they would at least live each measured moment that remained to them with a vividness that should pack a lifetime's awareness into every hour.

Still clasping hands, they rode down the hill slowly, Mists were thick now, and they could see almost nothing of the turmoil below, but Jair's great brazen voice, rich with the vibrating warmth of his spurious humanity, came rolling up to them in brief snatches. A juggernaut of brass. Egide's juggernaut. Perhaps mankind's last and coldest and most ardently worshiped god.

In the temple of the Ancients a small figure stood before the high, dark altar like a wall, too high for it to see the gods. It clasped and unclasped the facile, fingery paws, like a sea-anemone's tendrils – so many-fingered, so dexterous, so nervously eager to be about the great task of testing the limits of their skill.

Its mind was not here in the temple. It was seeing the warm, sand-floored caverns of its people, lit by a garden of colored windows, multi-shaped in the twilight of the cave. It was not alone, though it sat here nervously twisting those eager, impatient fingers. No llar is ever alone. The warm awareness of its unity with its city lies behind that poise and quiet pride. It looks out of the strange round eyes with a wisdom and benignity which is of the race, not the individual. This race alone, of all thinking species, finds deity in itself, in the warm closed circle of its own unity. Once it gains the little foothold it needs on which to found its soaring possibilities, this race alone need not depend upon the gods.

Serene in its own confidence, in its own warm knowledge of identity with its race, the llar sat clasping and unclasping those eager fingers and listening to the oracle it knew it could not trust.

PARADISE STREET

Loki planet rolled its wild ranges and untrodden valleys up out of darkness toward morning under Morgan's thundering ship. Morgan was in a hurry. His jets roared out ice-plumes in the thin, high air, writing the scroll of his passage enormously in vapor across half Loki's pale sky. There was no other visible trace of man anywhere in the world.

Behind Morgan in the cargo bin there were three kegs with *sehft* washing about oilily inside them. They made the tiny cabin smell of cinnamon, and Morgan liked the smell. He liked it for itself, and for the pleasant memories it evoked of valley canebrakes and hillside forests where he had gathered his cargo in discomfort, danger and perfect freedom. He also liked it because it was going to be worth fifty thousand credits at Ancibel Key.

Either fifty thousand, or nothing.

That depended on how soon he reached Ancibel Key. He had caught a microwave message back there in the predawn over Great Swamp, and he had been pushing his ship to top speed ever since. He had been muttering angrily, kicking the ship along her course, cursing her and Loki planet and mankind in general, after the fashion of men who are much alone and talk to themselves for company.

Radar patterns pulsed noiselessly across the screen before him, and ahead under a blanket of morning fog he knew Ancibel Key lay sprawled. Around the edges of the fog he could see the telltale marks of civilization spread out upon the soil of Loki – carbon-blacked fields with neat straight roads between them, racks of orchards checkering the sides of the valleys he remembered wild and lonely. He thought of old days not very long ago when he had hunted the bearded Harvester bulls across these meadows and trapped *sehft*-rats where the orchards grew.

The sky was a little soiled already, above Ancibel Settlement. Morgan wrinkled his lean, leather face and spat.

'People!' he said with fierce contempt to the pulse of the radar pattern. 'Settlers! Scum!'

Behind him in the clear morning the vapor-trail of his journey swept in one enormous plume clear back to the horizon, back over Wild Valley, over Lookout Peak and Nancy Lake and the Harvester Range. He decelerated above the invisible landing field, and the soft gray fog closed over him. The plume of the passage he had scrawled over half a planet dissipated slowly above the peaks and the lakes that had been his alone for a long time now, grew dim and broad, and vanished.

Morgan stamped into the assay office with a carboy of *sehft* swashing on his shoulder. He moved in a haze of cinnamon. The assay office was also general store now. Morgan scowled around the too-neat shelves, the laden bins and labeled barrels. Toward the back a redheaded youngster with the dark tan of Mars on his freckled face was waiting on – yes, Morgan looked twice to make sure – a parson. A parson on Loki!

The Mars-tanned boy was belted into a slick silver apron. So was the storekeeper himself. Suppressing a snort of contempt, Morgan gazed past the heavy, bent shoulders of a settler in brown knitted orlon and met the keen and faded blue eyes of Warburg, assay agent turned storekeep.

Morgan's eyes flicked the silver apron. And then he grinned thinly. The settler straightened his heavy shoulders and glanced from the list in his hand up along the shelves. He was a youngster in his twenties, thick-muscled, tall, fair as a Ganymedan, with flat, red-flushed cheeks.

'Need some more of that hormone spray, Warburg,' he said. 'Same as last time. And what about this new fungus? My potatoes aren't doing so good. Think actidione might do the trick?'

'It did with Laany'i,' Warburg said, evading Morgan's gaze. 'And his fields are right next to yours. Actidione's a good antibiotic. O.K., Eddie. Had any trouble with rats lately?'

'Just a little. Not enough to mention.'

'Stop it right there,' Warburg advised. 'I got some compound forty-two just in – the dicoumarol stuff. It fixes rats better than squill. Those critters breed too fast to take chances.'

'Not as fast as settlers,' Morgan said.

The young settler looked up sharply. He had mild brown eyes under sun-bleached brows that drew together with suspicion as he regarded the lean newcomer. Morgan ignored him. Shouldering forward, he thumped the carboy on the counter.

'Forty gallons, Joe,' he said.

'In a minute,' Warburg said.

'I haven't got a minute. I'm in a hurry.'

'It's late for that, Jaime,' Warburg said, looking at him.

Morgan's hand tightened on the neck of the carboy. His eyes drew up narrowly. He swung his gaze to the young settler and jerked his head doorward.

'Take a walk,' he said.

The settler straightened to his full height and looked down on the slighter man. The red deepened in his flat cheeks.

'Who's this, Warburg?' he demanded. 'One of the fast-money boys?'

'Easy,' Warburg said. 'Easy, now.' His hand moved toward the gun on the counter. It was a Barker ultrasonic – it barked before it bit, uttering loud threats before its frequency slid up into the killing range. Morgan sneered at it.

'Up till lately, before the rats moved in,' he said, 'when a man pulled a gun he used it. I guess people scare easy around here these days.'

'Who is he?' the settler demanded again. 'Gunman?'

'I carry one,' Morgan said.

Warburg came to a decision. Smoothing down his silver apron, he said, 'I'll send Tim over with your stuff, Eddie. Do me a favor and—' He nodded toward the door. 'Here,' he added, shoving a cellobag into the settler's big hand. 'For the kids. Go on now, git.'

But the settler, scowling at Morgan, didn't move.

'You're wrong,' he said. 'The rats didn't come till the settlers were here already. Your kind isn't wanted in Ancibel, mister. We don't need any more hoodlums or gambling houses or—'

Morgan's whole lean body, moving very slightly, tightened forward in a barely perceptible crouch. Perhaps the settler didn't know what that meant, but Warburg was an old Loki frontiersman himself. He knew. His hand closed on the butt of the Barker gun.

Feet grated on the dusty black floor. From the back of the store the parson came forward, nodding casually at Morgan, moving equally casually between the two men. Behind old-fashioned lenses his mild eyes regarded them. He took the cellobag out of the settler's hand.

'What's this?' he asked. 'Candy? Well, we'd better make sure your kids get it, Eddie. Be a pity if a bullet went through the bag. Might mash the candy.'

Warburg said quickly, 'I've got some news for you, Jaime. The—'

'Shut up,' Morgan said. He looked from the parson to the settler, shrugged, spat on the black floor and turned away. He was ready to let the quarrel drop. He knew he'd have to talk to Warburg alone. Behind him he heard retreating footsteps and a door thudded shut.

Warburg bent and lifted a roped carton from under the counter. Lettering on its side in three languages said, 'Micrografting Kits.'

'Tim,' Warburg called. 'Get this over to Eddie's. And don't hurry back, either.'

The boy came forward, unbelting his slick apron. His eyes regarded Morgan with a sort of grave wariness. His freckles scarcely showed under the deep Martian tan. Morgan grinned at him a little and said in hissing Middle-Martian, 'What do you hear from the cockeyed giant, young one?'

The boy's sudden smile dazzled in the dark face, showing missing teeth. He was about eighteen, but he made a child's gesture, holding up both hands, making a wide circle in front of one eye and a narrow one in front of the other. It was the old, childhood legend of the watching giant with Deimos and Phobos for eyes.

'All right, Tim,' Warburg said. 'Get at it.'

The boy hoisted the carton to his shoulders and staggered out with it. Morgan's grin faded. The store was silent when the door had closed.

Morgan slapped the carboy on the counter.

'Forty gallons of *sehft*,' he said. 'Fifty thousand credits. Right?'

Warburg shook his head.

Morgan snarled soundlessly to himself. So he was too late, after all. Well, that just made it harder. Not impossible, he thought, but harder. Surely Warburg couldn't refuse him. Not even the Warburg who faced him now, plump and soft in a storekeeper's apron. Warburg had been here almost as long as Morgan himself, from the days when Loki was as wild as the men who trapped and hunted here. And it was wild still, of course. He told himself that fiercely. Most of Loki was still untrodden. Only here at Ancibel Key the spreading disease called civilization fouled the planet. So long as Morgan could find a market for *sehft*, so long as he could buy the few things he needed from that disease-source, it wouldn't matter how many settlers swarmed like flies around Ancibel.

'How much?' he asked grimly.

Warburg snapped open a transparent sack, set it on the little scale at his side, and began weighing sugar with a rustling noise. He pinched the top of the first sack tight to seal it before he spoke.

'Five hundred for the lot, Jaime,' he said, not looking up.

Morgan didn't move a muscle. The store was very still except for the hiss of sugar into the cellobag. Softly Morgan said:

'Sure your authorization on the price-cut came in before I did, Joe?'

'It came in,' Warburg said, 'a couple of hours ago. Sorry, Jaime.'

'Don't be,' Morgan said. '*I* came in four hours ago. Remember? It's four hours ago now. That means you can still pay me fifty thousand.'

'Sorry, Jaime. I had to turn in a spot-check inventory.'

'All right! You overlooked this—'

'Nobody overlooks forty gallons of *sehft*,' Warburg said, shaking his head regretfully. 'I've got a license to worry about, Jaime. I can't do a thing. You should have got here faster.'

'Look, Joe – I need the money. I owe Sun-Atomic nearly ten thousand on my last fuel grubstake. I can't get more until I—'

'Jaime, I can't do it. I don't dare. I guess you caught the broadcast about the price-cut, but you didn't go on listening or you'd know who's here to enforce it.'

'Who?'

'Old friend of yours. Major Dodd.'

'Rufus Dodd?' Morgan asked incredulously. 'Here?'

'That's right.' Warburg snapped open a fresh sack noisily and shoved it under the sugar spout. The glittering white torrent hissed into the bag, expanding it to plump solidity. The two men regarded it in silence.

Morgan was thinking fast. Coincidence has a long, long arm. Dodd and he had grown up together in a little town on Mars. Dodd went into the Jetborne Patrol and Morgan had hit for the empty places as soon as he was big enough to work his way aboard a freighter, but the two ran into each other now and then in spite of the vastnesses of space. It wasn't too unlikely. Space is wide and deep, but men tend to congregate in big centers of civilization on central worlds, and those with like interests inevitably seek out like spots.

'Funny thing, isn't it?' Morgan said reminiscently. 'Last time I saw Rufus I was running furs on Llap over in the Sirius range. A bunch of Redfeet ganged up on the Jetborne and I helped Rufus hold 'em off till relief came. A long time ago, that was. So now he's here on Loki. What for, Joe? He didn't come in just to play nursemaid to a new set of export rules. What's up?'

Warburg nodded at the big Barker on the counter.

'You ought to guess. Happens often enough. That's why young Eddie wouldn't back down when you tried to start something. He took you for one of the easy-money boys. Town's swarming with 'em. They follow the settlers. Grab a ripe world and squeeze it dry, quick, before the law moves in. *You* know. The town's wide open and there's been a lot of trouble already, killings, stores looted, crops damaged if the settlers won't pay protection. The usual thing. Some of us sent in a petition, and we got Major Dodd and his boys by return ship. He'll clean the place up – I suppose. Sooner or later.' Warburg looked obscurely troubled.

'What do you mean?' Morgan demanded. 'Rufe's honest, isn't he? You couldn't buy Rufe with all the credits Sun-Atomic ever issued.'

'No, not him, I guess.' Warburg looked dubious. 'But his higher-ups, maybe. All I know is, there's been too much delay. Pay-offs to political bosses have happened before now, you know. My guess is there's some routine dirty work going on, and Major Dodd's hands are tied. Or maybe he's taking a cut direct. Who knows?' Warburg slapped the Barker lightly. 'One of these days we'll take things into our own hands.'

'What's this "we", Joe?' Morgan asked sharply.

Warburg shrugged. 'I have a living to make.'

Morgan snorted noisily. 'You're soft, Joe. I never thought I'd see you with a potbelly and an apron around it. Old before your time.'

'I show it,' Warburg said. 'You don't. I know when it's time to slow down.

You're not much younger than I am, Jaime. Remember what happened to Sheml'li-hhan?'

'He got careless.'

'He got old. Just once, he was too slow, and the stagbison got him. Oh no – I like it here. Times change, Jaime. We change, too. Can't help it. I'm glad of a little store like this to keep me going now. Maybe some day you'll—'

'Not me!' Morgan snorted again, an angry sound. 'I'm a free man. I depend on nobody but Jaime Morgan! And a good thing, too. If I tried to depend on my friends I'd starve. Look at you – scared out of your senses by the Trade Control. I'll go on forever, getting tougher and tougher as the years go by. Just like old leather.' He grinned and slapped his chest. But the grin faded.

'What's the matter with the Trade Control, Joe?' he demanded, tapping his carboy of *sehft*. 'Why did they cut the price? *Why?* If the bottom's out of the *sehft* market you might as well plow up the whole planet and plant it with wheat so far as I'm concerned. *I* can't live here.'

'They've synthesized *sehft*,' Warburg said stolidly.

Morgan whistled a low, angry note. Then he said, 'All right, they've synthesized it. But there'll always be a market for the natural oil, won't there?'

'Maybe. But the Settlers' Council asked for an extermination order, Jaime.' Warburg spoke reluctantly. 'I'm sorry, but that's the way it is. You see, the *sehft*-rats are pests. They destroy crops. They've got to be wiped out, not milked of their throat-sac secretions and let go to secrete more *sehft*.'

Morgan's face went deep red under the leathery tan. He showed his teeth and swore in the hissing Martian vocables of his boyhood. A tall crate beside the counter caught his angry eye and he brought his fist down hard on its lid. The wood splintered, releasing a pungent fragrance and showing glints of bright golden fruit inside.

'Settlers!' Morgan said savagely. 'So the *sehft*-rats spoil their orchards! Who was it got here first, Joe? You and me, that's who! And now you're siding with them.' He kicked the crate. 'Fruit orchards! Fruit orchards on Loki! Mooing livestock! Settlers stink up every world they land on!'

'I know, I know,' Warburg said. 'Careful of the goldenberries, Jaime. I paid hard cash for those.'

'Sure you did! You'll be out there grubbing in the dirt, too, next thing you know. Joe, I don't understand it.' Morgan's voice grew gentler. 'Have you forgotten Deadjet Range and the time the wild Harvester bulls stampeded? Remember when young Dain and I came in with our first load of *sehft*? Joe, I passed over Chocolate Hill today, where we left Dain. The moss grows fast there, Joe, but you can still see the Martian Circle we cut for him, to mark the place.'

Warburg snapped another sack open.

'I know, Jaime. I remember Dain. I land there now and then myself and cut the Circle clean again. I remember Wild Bill Hennessy, and old Jacques, and Sheml'li-hhan as well as if they were alive today. Wild Bill's tree where he fought the red bear is standing in the middle of a cornfield now, Jaime. The farmer left it when I told him what the gouges on the trunk were. These people mean well. You've got to play along if you have a living to make. Can't turn back the clock, Jaime. You just can't do it.' Sugar ran glittering into the sack.

'Settlers!' Morgan growled. 'Scum! They don't belong here. This is our world, not theirs! We opened it up. We ought to run them off Loki! But I forgot. Not you – not Joe Warburg. You tie an apron around your belly and sell 'em carbon-black to warm up the soil and micrograft kits to make the goldenberries grow! Wild Bill must be turning in his grave!'

Morgan slapped the counter, making the sugar-sacks dance. The oily liquid in the carboy shivered thickly. 'Fifty thousand credits!' Morgan said bitterly. 'Two hours ago! Not worth the fuel to bring it in, now. That's piracy for you, Joe. I tell you, I've got more respect for those hoodlums and gamblers you're so scared of. They rob a man at gun point. They don't sneak behind his back and cry on the shoulder of the Trade Control while they pick his pockets. I think I'll find me somebody who'll pay a better price for my *sehft*. Price-juggling doesn't hurt the real value of the stuff and you know it, Joe. There must be somebody—'

'Don't you do it!' Warburg urged with sudden earnestness. 'I know just what's on your mind, Jaime, and you can't get away with it. Sure, the woods are full of contraband runners, now. You go out and whistle and you'll have to comb the smugglers out of your hair. But it's dangerous business, Jaime.'

Morgan laughed contemptuously. '*I* don't wear an apron,' he said. 'You think I'm afraid?'

'If you've got good sense, you will be. These are tough boys. And they're organized. Times have changed on Loki since you were here last, Jaime. I don't keep a Barker on the counter for nothing. You're a good man in the hills and you know the wild country inside out, but the city boys are smarter than you are, Jaime, and a whole lot trickier.'

'You're a fool,' Morgan said savagely. 'I've got to have money, and I'll get it where I can. Nobody's tougher than Jaime Morgan. Who do I see, Joe? You know the hoods around here. Or are you too scared to tell me?'

'You think I'd do it?' Warburg asked wryly. 'Even if it weren't for the danger of it, I haven't forgotten Major Dodd. He won't stand for any funny business, and he knows everything that goes on at Ancibel. He'd deport you, Jaime.'

Morgan reached for the carboy.

'Somebody'll tell me,' he said. 'You or somebody.' Cunningly he added, 'If I go to the wrong dealer, I may lose my scalp. But you're too busy weighing sugar. Forget it. I'll find out.'

'Jaime, if Dodd hears of this—'

Morgan hefted the carboy. 'I'll ask around,' he said.

Warburg sighed. 'All right. Go into the Feather Road and ask for a fellow named Valley. He comes from Venus and he's smarter than you are, Jaime. Don't say I sent you.'

'Thanks for nothing,' Morgan snapped. He hefted the carboy to his shoulder and turned away.

'You owe me fifty credits,' Warburg said stolidly. 'You've spoiled half a crate of goldenberries.'

Morgan said with a furious grin, 'Make it an even hundred,' and swung his boot. Wood crackled and a bright torrent of fruit gushed out over the smooth black floor. Morgan stamped, making the clear juice gush. His angry glare met Warburg's.

'Send me a bill to Chocolate Hill,' he said. 'Leave it in Dain's Circle. Or pin it on Wild Bill's tree. You'll get your money – settler!'

He went out with a heavy stride.

The fresh, cold air of morning over Ancibel Settlement was fragrant with breezes blowing over miles of orchards, rank after rank of them on the patterned hills around Ancibel.

To Morgan, it stank.

He spat in the dust of the rubberized street, took a plug of *nicca* from his belt, and bit off a chew, thinking as he did of New Moon, beyond Sirius, and the way it used to be when New Moon was a frontier world, years ago, before he came to Loki. Now settlers grew *nicca* on that dim, pearl-gray world. Waterbound Galvez II was settled in, too, now, all the mystery gone from the sliding seas. They were dotted with control islands where men grew food-crops of algae and seaweed in the watery fields.

Now they were overrunning Loki. He scowled about the single main street of Ancibel Settlement, feeling a little uneasy at the nearness of so many people. A buxom young woman in pink-striped orlon balanced a grocery-flat on her head and craned after him curiously as he passed. A man in the brown, tight uniform of the Jetborne went by, a sergeant with a weathered face, and the crowd fell silent and watched him resentfully, muttering a little, until he turned the corner and vanished.

There were three lemon-haired men from Venus lounging in the morning sun at the doorway to the Feather Road, and the townspeople gave them a wide berth. They wore Barkers conspicuously belted on over their long, fringed coats and most of their conversation was carried on in a series of rapid, fingery gestures which their opaque eyes never seemed to watch. They smelled faintly of fish.

Morgan nodded and strode between them into the big, arched, echoing room inside. It had been blown over an inflated form, like all the quickly built houses in Ancibel Settlement, and somebody had over-estimated the space the Feather Road would be needing. Or maybe they hadn't. Maybe it just hadn't got under way yet. Also, of course, this was still an early hour.

The bar looked as though it needed artificial respiration. There weren't enough customers for the Road's size and setup.

Rustling plastic curtain partitions made the room much smaller than normal – you could tell by the angles of the roof – but it still wasn't cut down enough to avoid that fatal air of desolation an interplanetary bar must shun at any cost. The customers, striking new roots, feeling lost enough as it is on an alien world. A good bar must be a convincing artificial home.

Morgan grinned sourly. A thermo roll was all the home he needed. He had taproots. All worlds were home to Morgan.

The bartender was a hawk-nosed Red Amerindian. He fixed Morgan with bright, expressionless black eyes and said, 'Morning. Have one on the house, stranger.'

Morgan thumped his carboy on the bar, rubbed his shoulder and said, 'Sure.'

The Amerindian tore the top off a fresh bottle of brandy and left it invitingly in front of Morgan, who poured himself one sparing shot and then firmly pressed the bottle's neck together, sealing it with a practiced zip of the thumbnail.

An old man with a red, bleary face hunched over the bar ten feet away, cradling a smoky glass in his hand. Beyond him were two young surveyors in swamp boots, having a quick one before they set out for the day's wet, exhausting labor. Beyond them a black-haired girl in tight, crimson orlon leaned her elbow on the bar and her chin in her hand. Her eyes were shut and she whistled a soft, dreary tune to herself.

Most of the noise in the room came from a table of heavy-shouldered young men who were playing some Ganymedan game with counters that clicked on the table top. Their voices were loud and blurred. Clearly they had been here all night. They looked to Morgan like a group of ranch hands, and he despised them.

'I'm looking for a man named Valley,' he said to the bartender.

The man's black eyes appeared to grow smaller and brighter in the dark face as Morgan regarded him, waiting. The girl at the end of the bar opened her eyes briefly and stared at him, her whistle drawing out to a low note of surprise. Then she shut her eyes again and the mournful tune continued.

'Who sent you?' the bartender asked.

Morgan looked deliberately away. There was a button in front of each bar stool on the counter, and he pressed a slow forefinger upon the one beside his elbow. A section of the bar rolled aside and the hot, salty, pungent smells of a lavish free-lunch smoked up in his face. A moving belt below carried the leisurely array of thirst-making foods past.

He let a bowl of popped and buttered moss-buds go by, and a rack of pretzels, and a broad round platter of Martian soul-seeds crackling with the heat of the plate they lay on. His hand moved finally. He took up a pin-wheel of blue-streaked paste, dipped it into a bowl of sullenly smoldering oil, and spinning it on its silver stick, popped the appetizer deftly into his mouth toward the back of the tongue, where the right taste buds would work on it.

When he could speak again, he said with an impatient glance at the silent and waiting bartender, 'What about that man Valley?'

'I asked you a question,' the Indian said.

Morgan shrugged. He slipped his hand inside the strap of the carboy on the counter and went through the motions of rising.

'I can always go somewhere else,' he said.

The Indian measured him with a long, expressionless look. Neither of them spoke. Finally the Indian shrugged in turn.

'I just work here,' he said. 'Wait.'

He ducked under the bar-flap and vanished between plastic curtains on the other side of the room. Morgan ate three mockbeaks and sat quietly on his stool, watching the illuminated mural that circled the backbar with a series of videoed dryland scenes – the Mohave on Earth, the sun-side of Mercury with every shadow etched in acid, a long shimmer of Martian desert with dustdevils dancing and the air a thin violet clearer than crystal. He allowed a certain not unpleasant quiver of nostalgia to stir in his mind at the sight.

But he caught the first shimmer of motion behind him reflected in the surface of the mural screen, and turned to face a thin, very pale Venusian in a long fawn-colored coat who was walking toward him with meticulous placement of his feet beneath fluttering fringes. The man's skin was white as dough. He had very sleek, lemon-colored hair and his eyes were round and flat and opaque.

The man bowed gravely.

'You Valley?' Morgan demanded.

'My name is Shining Valley,' the pale man said. 'May I buy you a drink? Bill—' He gestured toward the Amerindian, who had ducked back under the bar and was resuming his position.

Morgan said quickly, 'No.' He slid a hand into his pocket, fingered the few coins there in the cubical, nested currency of Loki, and pulled out one of the cubes. He shook three of the inner and smallest out onto the bar and reached for the Ferrad brandy bottle, tore off its top and poured himself another sparing shot. His thumbnail sealed the neck again.

'You talk business here, Valley?' he asked.

The flat eyes flickered at the *sehft*. 'Certainly,' the Venusian said, and glided forward with a flutter of fringes. He sat down on the stool next to Morgan and said crisply to the bartender, 'Bill, give us a curtain.'

The Indian's expression did not change, but he nodded and jerked a rope in a cluster of cords behind the bar. Morgan dodged a little, involuntarily, as something came swooping and rustling down upon them from overhead. It was another of the plastic curtains, unfurling like a sail from a semicircular rod overhead. It closed the two men neatly in, cutting off most of the noises from behind them. Morgan glanced back nervously. The curtain was moderately transparent, and he felt a little better. He looked questioningly at the Venusian.

'No one can see us from the other side,' Valley said. 'Nor hear. Bill, give me a gin.'

Morgan wrinkled his nose as the Venusian dropped a red pill into the glass the Indian set before him. An aromatic camphor odor arose to blend with the elusive but definite fish-smell of the man from Venus.

Sipping, Valley said, 'You came to the right place, Jaime Morgan. You see, I know your name. I've been hoping to make a deal with a man like—'

'Cut it, Valley,' Morgan said. 'Let's not be polite. I don't like Venusians. I don't like their smell.'

'Then try the smell of this,' Valley said, and laid a thousand-credit note on the bar's edge. Morgan lifted his eyebrows. The liquor was beginning to hit him a little; it had been months since he'd taken a drink. He realized he was going to get thirstier and thirstier from now on. As usual, it was cumulative. He ignored the note.

Valley spread out ten of his fingers in a quick, flickering gesture.

'When I flew in here today,' Morgan said, 'my cargo was worth fifty thousand. Do you think I'll sell it for ten?'

'The ten is only a starter. I need a man like you.'

'I'm not for sale. My cargo is.'

There was silence for a while. Valley sipped his camphor-smelling gin. Presently he said in a soft voice, 'I think you are for sale, Morgan. You may not know it yet, but you'll learn.'

'How much for the *sehft?*' Morgan demanded.

Valley exhaled softly. He made a meditative sound in his throat, like the waters of Venus lapping with a gentle noise against his palate.

'You have forty gallons in all,' he said. 'Warburg won't go over five hundred for it. Major Dodd will impound your cargo and you'll get legal price – no more. I offer you more. I'm gambling, you see.'

'I'm not,' Morgan growled. 'Make me an offer.'

'Ten thousand credits.'

Morgan laughed unpleasantly.

'I told you I'm gambling,' Valley said in his soft, patient voice. He exhaled a smell of fish and camphor at Morgan. 'The stuff's been synthesized. But one of my markets is on a planet that's passing through an H-K spectra matter cloud. They haven't got the spacecast about the price-drop. Ultra-short waves won't penetrate. A ship, of course, will. Maybe one has already. If so, the news has gone ahead of me. If not, I clean up a tidy profit by buying at a cut price and selling at the old one. That's what I mean by a gamble.'

'I don't like the odds,' Morgan said. 'You could pay me better and still—'

'It's my price. You won't get any better offer. I'll pay you ten thousand for forty gallons.' The surf-sounds of Venusian seas beat in his throat briefly. He added, '*Skalla*,' and made a rolling, interlacing gesture with his fingers, so Morgan knew that would be the top figure. When a Venusian said *skalla*, poker-bluff wouldn't work.

Still, with ten thousand – there were gambling joints in Ancibel Key now. Like most men who gamble with life and know the odds well enough to win, Morgan erroneously thought he could call the odds on other games of chance. Besides, the brandy was beginning to burn enticingly in his stomach, calling irresistibly for more of the same brand. And he couldn't buy any, not with the few coin-nest cubes in his pocket.

He reached over and took the notes from the Venusian's boneless fingers, riffling the edges to count.

There were ten. He took a key out of his pocket and dropped it on the bar.

'A locker key?' Valley inquired. 'Very wise of you.'

'The other two are lockered,' Morgan said. 'It's a deal.'

'Not yet,' Valley said gently, his round, flat eyes on Morgan's. 'We want you to work with us. We can offer you a very good bargain on that, my friend.'

Morgan got off the bar stool with a quick, smooth motion, struck impatiently at the curtain behind him. 'Let me out of here,' he said. 'I'm no friend of yours, Valley.'

'You will be,' Valley murmured, gesturing. The curtain slid up with a hiss and rustle, and the noises of the bar flowed back around them.

It was newsier than it had been before. The ranch hands were stumbling up from their table, staggering a little, blinking at an angry middle-aged homesteader in the doorway.

'I'd fire you all,' he was shouting as the curtain rose. 'If I could, I'd do it! Outside, you loafers! Get out, before I break your necks!' His furious glare flashed around the room. 'We'll clean you out yet,' he roared at the bartender, who shrugged impassively. 'We don't want your kind here!'

One of the ranch hands stopped quickly to drain a shot-glass on the table before he joined the rest. The homesteader crossed the floor with quick, angry strides, snatched the glass from the man's hand, pivoted and hurled it against the glass of the skylight that illumined the curtain-cubicled bar. A shower of tinkling fragments rained down upon the emptied table. The man turned and stalked noisily out, driving his reluctant help before him.

Morgan laughed shortly.

'Compared to me,' he said, 'he *likes* you.'

'Come back when you're ready,' Shining Valley said with a round, impassive look. 'You'll come, Jaime Morgan. You're ready—'

Morgan spat on the floor, turned his back on Valley, and stamped out of the bar.

He needed another drink.

Painfully Morgan opened his eyes, wincing at the impact of light. For a perceptible interval he had no idea who he was, or where. Then a familiar face leaned over him and for a moment he was ten years old again, looking into the face of the ten-year-old Rufus Dodd. Rufe had been playing soldier. He was dressed up incongruously in a tight brown uniform with the Solar Ring emblem at his collar, and gold leaves on his shoulders. But outside, in the thin violet air of the Martian morning the dead sea-bottoms must be stretching, purple-shadowed under the level rays of sunrise, and in a few minutes now their mothers would be calling them both away to breakfast.

Dust-motes danced in the beam of light that struck between curtains in his eyes. He turned his head far enough to see that he lay in an unfamiliar little shack with dust thick on everything. The metal uprights of a bunk rose left and right before him. Plastic curtains discolored at the folds shut him partially in.

Bitter fumes were in his head and dead, unpleasant air was in his lungs. He squinted painfully against his headache and he saw a small black scuttling object move across the wall – man's ancient supercargo, the cockroach. He shut his eyes and grimaced. He knew now who he was.

'Hello, Rufe,' he said thickly.

'Get up, Jaime,' the familiar, crisp voice snapped. 'You're under arrest.'

Morgan sighed heavily. He rubbed his palms down the sides of his face; the harsh scratch of stubble rasped his nerves. He hated the cockroach and the discolored curtains and this whole filthy, stinking town the settlers had built upon his world, his clean, wild, lonely Loki.

'What for, Rufe?' he asked. The motion of face-rubbing had brought his wrists into view and there was a fresh knife-scratch along the edge of his forearm. He looked at it thoughtfully.

'It might be for a lot of things,' Dodd said. He stepped back a pace and hooked his thumbs into his uniform belt. His face looked many times ten years old now. Time must have acted as filter between them in that first moment of waking, a filter that screened out the firm, harsh set of Rufe's jaw and the lines incised lengthwise from nose to chin, and the cool, disciplined narrowing of the eye. Rufe had never spared himself. It wasn't likely that he'd spare others.

'It might be for drunkenness, assault and battery or conduct unbecoming a human being,' he told Morgan, his voice crisp. 'It might be for trying to wreck a gambling joint when you lost your last credit there. But it isn't. What I'm arresting you for is selling *sehft* to a contraband runner called Shining Valley. You're a fool, Jaime.'

'Sure I'm a fool.' Morgan wriggled his toes in muddy socks. 'Only I didn't do it, Rufe.'

'Too late for lies now. You always did talk too much when you're drunk. You shoot off your mouth before a dozen settlers, Jaime, and then you hole up here like a sitting duck. Jaime, I've got orders to arrest any violators of the new *sehft*-law. I can't help myself. I don't make the laws.'

'I do,' Morgan said. 'I make my own. You're trespassing, Rufe. Loki's *my* world.'

'Sure, I know. You and a few others opened it up. But it belongs to the Trade Control now, and you've got to abide by their rules. Get up, Jaime. Put your shoes on. You're under arrest.'

Morgan rose on one elbow. 'What'll they do to me?'

'Deport you, probably.'

'Oh no!' Morgan said. 'Not me.' He raised a wild and savage gaze to his old friend. 'Loki's mine.'

Dodd shrugged. 'You should have thought of that sooner, Jaime. You've got to ride with the times.'

'Nobody's going to put me off Loki,' Morgan said stubbornly. 'Nobody!'

'Be sensible, Jaime. There's always plenty of room – out there.' He looked up; so did Morgan. 'Out there' was always up, no matter how far toward the Galaxy's rim you stood. 'One of the big outfits would finance you if you needed grubstaking—'

'And they'd tie me hand and foot, too,' Morgan said. 'When I open up a new world I do it my way, not the way of Inter-Power or Sun-Atomic. When I take a walk down Paradise Street, I go under my own power.'

They were both silent for an instant, thinking of that trackless path among the stars, that road exactly as wide and exactly as narrow as a ship's bow, pointing wherever a ship's bow points and always bordered by the stars. The course on the charts is mapped by decimals and degrees, but all courses run along Paradise Street.

The explorers and the drifters and the spacehands are misfits mostly, and, therefore, men of imagination. The contrast between the rigid functionalism inside a spaceship and the immeasurable glories outside is too great not to have a name. So whenever you stand in a ship's control room and look out into the bottomless dark where the blinding planets turn and the stars swim motionless in space, you are taking a walk down Paradise Street.

'There'll always be jackpot planets left, Jaime,' Dodd said, making his voice persuasive.

'I won't go,' Morgan told him.

'What are your plans, Jaime?' Dodd asked ironically. 'Have you looked in your pockets?'

Morgan paused halfway through a gesture to search his rumpled clothing, his inquiring gaze on Dodd. 'I didn't—' he began.

'Oh yes you did. Everything. Even your guns are gone now. Those gambling joints don't let a man get away as long as there's anything negotiable on him. Go on, search your pockets if you don't believe me. You're broke, Jaime.'

'Not the whole ten thousand credits!' Morgan said with anguish, beginning frantically to turn his jacket inside out.

'Ten thousand credits?' Dodd echoed. 'Is that all Valley gave you? For forty gallons of the drug?'

'Drug?' Morgan said abstractedly, still searching. 'What drug? I sold him *sehft*.'

'*Sehft's* a drug. Didn't you know?'

Morgan lifted a blank gaze.

'It's been kept quiet, of course,' Dodd went on. 'But I thought you knew. A narcotic can be synthesized from the natural raw *sehft*. Not from the synthetic stuff. It hasn't got the proteins.'

Morgan looked up in bewilderment that slowly gave way to a dawning fury. 'Then the stuff's worth … why, it'll be priceless!' he said. 'If the *sehft*-rats are exterminated, what I sold Valley's worth a hundred times the penny-ante price he paid me!'

'That's what you get when you play around with city boys, Jaime,' Dodd told him unsympathetically.

Morgan stared straight ahead of him at the discolored curtains and the moted sun. A vast and boiling rage was beginning to bubble up inside him. All down the line, Shining Valley had outwitted him, then. And Dodd had stepped in to take over where the Venusian left off. And Warburg sat back smugly to watch while the Trade Control put a roof over Loki and Loki's rightful dwellers. He thought for one weak and flashing moment, with a sort of bitter envy, of young Dain safe on Chocolate Hill under his Martian Circle, and of Wild Bill dead before Loki's downfall, and of Sheml'li-hhan with no more problems to deal with. They'd been the lucky ones, after all.

But Morgan was no defeatist at heart. He'd think of something. Jaime Morgan would last forever, and Loki was still his world and nobody else's. He choked the fury down and turned to face Dodd.

'I can take care of myself,' he said. 'Kick my boot over this way, Rufe.'

The major scuffled with one foot in the dust. Morgan swung his feet over the bunk's edge and stooped, grunting, to snap the clasps of his boots.

'You're wasting your time, Rufe,' he said, looking up under his brows. 'Why don't you get on out there and round up a few of the local hoods, if you feel so law-abiding? They're the real criminals, not me.'

Dodd's face tightened. 'I obey orders.'

'From what I hear, the settlers are going to take things into their own hands one of these fine days,' he said. 'Oh well, forget it.' He stretched for the farthest buckles, grunting. Then he slanted a grin up at the watching major.

'What do you hear from the cockeyed giant, Rufe?'

Dodd's stern mouth relaxed slightly. The smile was reluctant, but it came. Encouraged, Morgan made his voice warm and went on, still struggling laboriously with the boot.

'I can't reach the last snaps, Rufe,' he said. 'Remember that crease from a spear I got on Llap, when we stood off the Redfeet together for three days? Makes it hard for me to bend this far. Guess you don't outgrow these things once you start getting old. Damned if you're not starting to show gray yourself, Rufe.'

'Maybe you aren't,' Dodd said. 'But your hands are shaky, Jaime.'

'If you had a night like mine,' Morgan grinned, 'you'd be resonating ultrasonics. I'll get over it. I—' He grunted piteously, stretching in vain for the last clasp.

'I'll get it,' Dodd said, and stooped.

'Thanks,' Morgan said, watching his moment. When Dodd's jaw was within range Morgan narrowed his eyes, braced himself in the bunk, and let the heavy boot fly forward and upward with all his lean weight behind it.

The kick caught Dodd on the side of the jaw and lifted him a good six inches before he shot backward and struck the dusty floor, his head making a hollow thump on the rubberized plastic.

Morgan followed his foot without a second's delay. Dodd had no more than hit the dust before Morgan's knees thudded upon the floor on each side of him and Morgan's hands slapped down hard upon his throat.

It wasn't necessary. Dodd lay motionless.

'Sorry, Rufe,' Morgan grinned. 'Hope I didn't—' His hands explored the unconscious skull before him. 'Nope, you're all right. Now I'll just borrow your gun, Rufe, and we'll see about a little unfinished business here in town. Deport me, eh? Let me give you a little good advice, Rufe. Never underestimate an old friend.'

He got up, grinning tightly, slipping the stolen gun in his belt.

The hangover thudded inside his head, but he showed no outward sign of it. Moving cautiously, light and easy, he slid out of town, through the new orchards toward the woods about a mile away. Wild woods, circling down upon Ancibel Settlement in ranks unbroken for countless miles upon miles far over the curve of Loki planet.

There was a fresh-water brook coming down out of the foothills in the edge of the woods. Morgan stripped and bathed in the icy water until his head cleared and he began to feel better. Afterward he went back toward Ancibel, the gun heavy in his shirt, looking for a man named Shining Valley.

'I was waiting for you,' Shining Valley said dreamily, blinking up through a rising mist of bubbles that flowed in a slow fountain from the pewter mug in his hand. He leaned his elbows on the table, moving the mug from side to side and swaying his head to and fro with it in a smooth, reptilian motion. The spray of rising bubbles bent like an airy tree in the wind. 'I was waiting,' he said again, only this time he sang it. All Venusians sing among themselves, but not to outsiders unless they are euphoric.

Morgan's nostrils stung with the sharp, almost painfully clear aroma of the high-C *pouilla* Valley was inhaling. He knew better than to rely on the hope that the man was drunk.

Valley made a gesture in the air, and again out of the ceiling a descending swoop and rustle sounded and a curtain closed the two of them in, this time a circle of it around the table toward the rear of the Feather Road.

Valley's opaque stare was candid and curiously limpid through the rising spray. 'Now you will work with us,' he sang.

'Now I'll take the rest of my credits,' Morgan corrected him.

Valley's fingers caressed the pewter mug with a faintly unpleasant tangling motion.

'I paid you ten thousand. *Skalla.*'

'That was a first installment. I want the rest.'

'I told you—'

Morgan inhaled, wrinkling his nose. 'You told me a fish story. The stuff I sold you will be priceless as soon as Trade Control clears out the *sehft*-rats. There isn't any planet with an H-K spectra matter cloud. You'll process the *sehft* for narcotics and ask your own price. Get it, too. I want mine. Will you pay up now, or shall I blow your head off?'

Valley made the familiar sea-wave sound in his throat meditatively. Suddenly he bent his head and nuzzled his face into the spray of pin-point bubbles.

'Give me the ten thousand back,' he said, 'and I'll return your *sehft*. Things have been happening. Forty gallons isn't worth running a risk for, and forty's all I have.'

'You're lying,' Morgan told him flatly.

Shining Valley smiled through the spray. 'No. I had more, yesterday. Much more. I've been collecting it for weeks now, from everyone I could buy from. But last night Major Dodd confiscated the lot. Now I have nothing but the forty gallons you sold me. You want it back?'

Morgan struck fiercely at the empty air in front of him, as if he brushed away invisible gnats. He hated this quicksand shifting underfoot. What was true? What was false? What devious double-dealing lay behind the Venusian's dreamy smile? He wasn't used to this kind of byplay. There was always one way to end it, of course. He slid his hand inside his shirt and closed it on Dodd's gun.

'I'll make you an offer, though,' Shining Valley said.

Morgan tightened a little in every muscle. Here it came, he thought. They'd been maneuvering him toward some untenable spot he could yet only dimly glimpse. In a moment or two, perhaps he'd know.

'Go on,' he said.

'You're in a bad position, Jaime Morgan,' the man from Venus said softly. 'Very bad indeed. You drunkenly squandered your money away and now you can't leave Ancibel Key. No one will sell you a liter of fuel until you pay up your old debts. I know how frontiersmen work, always one trip behind themselves, operating on credit, using this year's cargo to pay last year's bills. Without the price of the *sehft* you can't re-establish your credit. Am I right?'

Morgan bent forward, resting his chin on his hand, his elbow on the table. In this position his shirt front was covered, and he slipped Dodd's gun out and laid it on his knee, muzzle facing Shining Valley's middle under the table.

'Go on,' was all he said.

'You'll be deported from Loki planet as soon as the Jetborne catch up with you,' Valley went on in the same dreamy singsong. 'You want to stay. But you can't stay unless you co-operate with me.'

'I can work out my own problems,' Morgan said. 'Pay me what you owe and forget about me.'

'That deal is finished. I have said *skalla* and it can't be reopened. If you offered me a ton of *sehft* now, I wouldn't give you a link for it. You have only one thing for sale I'll buy from you, Morgan – your co-operation. I'll pay you forty thousand credits if you'll do a little job for us.'

Morgan moved the gun muzzle forward on his knee a little, felt the trigger with a sensitive forefinger.

'What's the job?' he asked.

'Ah.' Shining Valley smiled mistily through the spray. 'That *you* must tell *me*. I can only give you my problem and hope you have the answer – because you know Loki planet so well.' He made a disagreeably fingery gesture toward the far end of town. 'Out there stand the big ships, pointing into space,' he said. 'One of them is ours. We are very well organized here at Ancibel Key. Much money is behind us. But Major Dodd has grounded all the ships in port. Also, he has confiscated our treasure. What we wish to do is regain the *sehft* he stole from us, load it aboard our ship and send it off. How can we do this, Jaime Morgan?'

'You've got some idea,' Morgan said impassively. 'Go on.'

Valley shrugged. 'An idea only. Perhaps it will work. Are you afraid of the wild Harvesters, Morgan?'

'Sure I am,' Morgan said. 'Be a fool not to be.'

'No, no, I mean, could you handle a herd of them? Guide such a herd, perhaps?'

Morgan squinted at him, letting his finger slip off the trigger a little. 'You crazy?' he demanded.

'I had heard it can be done. Perhaps some frontiersman more expert than yourself—'

'It can be done, all right,' Morgan interrupted. 'But why should it? Where would it get you?'

'To the ship, with my cargo, if we're lucky,' Valley said. 'I would like you to stampede such a herd straight through Ancibel Settlement. What would happen then?'

'Blue ruin,' Morgan said. 'Half the population wiped out and every building in their way trampled flat. That what you want?'

Shining Valley shrugged.

'That doesn't concern me. What I want is to draw the Jetborne and the settlers away from the building where the *sehft* has been stored. I want enough confusion in Ancibel to clear the spacefield. I think what you describe would do the job nicely, don't you?'

'Yes,' Morgan said dubiously. 'Maybe it would.'

'So you will?'

'There must be easier ways,' Morgan said.

'How? Fire the town? It won't burn. Only the church and a few of the older stores are made of wood. Of course some other way might be devised, in time, but I have no time to waste. I thought of the Harvesters because one of my men reports a herd of them grazing down a valley only a few miles from here.'

'The town must be protected automatically somehow,' Morgan objected. 'Harvesters are dangerous. There must be—'

'I believe some sort of devices have been set up. Seismographic pickups catch the vibrations of their approach and cut in automatic noisemaking devices. Harvesters I believe are very sensitive to sound? Very well. They won't react to these, because the noisemakers won't operate. My men will see to that, if you can take care of guiding the herd.'

'It's too dangerous,' Morgan said.

'Nobody earns forty thousand credits easily, my friend. Will you do it, or must I search for a man with less timidity for the job?'

'There isn't a man on Loki any less scared of Harvesters than I am,' Morgan said practically. 'I'm thinking of afterward. Do you know the only way a herd of stampeding Harvesters can be guided? Somebody's got to ride the lead bull. All right, I could do it. But I'd be pretty conspicuous up there, wouldn't I? And a lot of the settlers are bound to get hurt.'

'Do you owe them anything, my friend?'

'Not a thing. I hate the sight of 'em. I'd like to throw the lot of 'em clear off Loki planet, and you and your crowd right after. Every man, woman and child in Ancibel Settlement can die for all I care, the way I feel now. But I'm not going to run my neck in a noose killing 'em. I'll be up there in plain sight, and there's bound to be survivors. If I earn that forty thousand credits, Valley, I want to live to enjoy it. I don't want a crowd of vigilantes stringing me up to a tree the minute I drop off the Harvester bull. So that's out.'

'Perhaps,' Valley sighed. 'Perhaps. A pity, isn't it? I have the forty thousand right here.'

He groped inside the sleeve of his fawn-colored robe and laid a packet of credit notes on the table. It was thick and crisp, smelling of the mint.

'This is yours,' he said. 'For the taking. *If* you earn it. Isn't it worth a little risk, Jaime Morgan?'

'Maybe,' Morgan said. He gazed hungrily at the money. He thought of his ship lying portbound beyond Ancibel, fuelless and immobile – like himself. What did he owe the settlers, anyhow? Had they spared *him*, when they had the chance? Like most men who travel the lonely worlds, Morgan had great respect for life. He killed only by necessity, and only as much as he had to.

Still – with this much money he could get clear away. Loki was a big world, after all. He moved his fingertip caressingly on the trigger of the hidden gun.

Suddenly he grinned and his right arm moved with startling speed. The table jerked, the shining tree of spray bowed sidewise between Valley and him. When it righted again the muzzle of Morgan's gun rested on the table edge and its unwinking eye was fixed steady upon the Venusian. Valley met that round black stare, going a little cross-eyed through the bubbles. He lifted a flat, waiting gaze to Morgan.

'Well?' he said.

'I'll take the money. Now.'

Valley held the flat stare for an interminable moment. Then slowly he pushed the packet of credits across the table, not shifting his eyes from Morgan's. Morgan did not look down, but his free hand found and pocketed the sheaf with a sure gesture.

The Venusian made a very small motion. Morgan gave him no time to complete it, whatever it was.

'Don't!' he advised sharply.

'You can't get away with this, Morgan,' the man from Venus said. 'My boys will—'

'No they won't.' Morgan sounded confident. 'Why should they? I'm going to earn the money.'

Valley's pale brows rose. 'How?'

'I'll stampede the Harvesters, all right. But not through the town. That's murder, and I won't stick my neck out that far for anybody. The Jetborne won't tolerate murder.'

'What's your plan, then?'

'You know that stretch of orchards east of town? And the farmland between them and Ancibel? I could lead the Harvesters through that valley. Trample their stinking crops right back into the ground. Break their fruit trees down. Ruin a good half-year's work. It might even drive 'em clear off Loki.' Morgan smacked his lips. 'That ought to do the trick.'

Shining Valley frowned. 'I'm not so sure.'

'Did you ever hear a herd of Harvesters stampeding?' Morgan demanded. 'The ground shakes like a quake. Windows break for half a mile around. When the settlers feel and hear and see what's happening, they'll swarm out like wasps out of a hive. Give you all the free time you need in Ancibel. Besides, that's what I'm going to do. Nothing else. You want me to earn this money or just take it and go away?'

Shining Valley looked down at his long, boneless fingers clasping the pewter mug. He moved them intricately over and under one another, as if he were weaving a complex Venusian finger-sentence of advice to himself. After a moment he nodded and looked up, his eyes veiled by the rising spray.

'Very well,' he said. 'I can count on you?'

Morgan stood up, pushed back his chair.

'Sure I'll do it,' he said. 'My way, not yours.'

Shining Valley nuzzled again among the rising bubbles. He made in his throat the noise of a Venusian sea lapping a pebbled shore.

'Your way, not mine,' he agreed in the smoothest of smooth voices.

Harvesters are mindless angels of destruction. They look like kerubs, the magnificent bearded kerubs of Assyrian legend, bull-bodied, tremendous, with great lion-faces and thick, streaming Assyrian beards. Bosses of sound-sensitive antennae stud their brows and they have hair-trigger neural reactions as comprehensive as radar-sonar. Any variation from the rhythmic patterns of normality send them into terrible, annihilating flight.

A good explorer never has a dangerous adventure, Morgan remembered the old saying, and qualified it: *barring the unexpected*. New worlds have a way of being unexpected. The first water he drank on Loki registered pure by every chemical test, but gave him a fortnight's fever because of a new virus that science was able to classify – later, after he had discovered it. A virus that went through porcelain filters, withstood boiling and resisted every standard disinfectant was so far outside the normal frame of reference that extrapolation hadn't helped – not unless you extrapolated to infinity, and then you'd never dare try anything new.

Like the Harvesters. There was a way to handle them. Not many men knew the way, and fewer still had the split-second synaptic reactions that made it possible.

Morgan, waiting perfectly motionless in his ambush, scarcely breathed. He was almost as immobile as a stone. Not quite; that would have been a mistake, for he wasn't a stone, and without natural hereditary camouflage, he couldn't hope to imitate immobility. But he could perceive, with all his senses, the natural rhythm and pattern of the dark forest around him, the stars overhead, the sleeping rhythms and the waking rhythms of Loki's nighttime pattern, and slowly, gradually, sink into an absolute, dynamic emptiness in perfect time with the world around him.

He emptied his mind. He was not even waiting. The ultrasonic gun was planted and due to go off at the right moment. He had charted the position of the grazing Harvester herd, the wind-drift, the rhythms of movement that flowed through and above this forest. The herd dozed, grazed, shifted gently down the dark forested valley toward him. Now they were motionless, drowsing perhaps under the stars. Morgan squatted in the humming quiet, letting his fingertips touch the moss and send soft vibrations toward his brain.

Once he stirred, drifting with a little scatter of dry leaves like confetti, toward a spot where the filtered starlight blended better with his own pattern. He had not realized this second spot was better until he caught the rhythm of Loki.

How many worlds he had exchanged this psychic blood-brotherhood with, this beating pulse of planetary life that opened the way for a transfusion between a living world and a living man. All Loki, it seemed to him now, slept and was unaware. Only he crouched here in perfect co-ordination with the turning world. He scarcely needed to glance at the shaded oscilloscope he had rigged to check upon his co-ordination. He knew with a deeper sense than sight how attuned he was. A shaking green line on the face of the oscilloscope translated Loki's night sounds into sight. A second line trembled across it – his own. No man could ever make those two lines completely merge, of course. At least, not while he lived.

Morgan's mind, emptied of circulating memories, let old eidetic ones swim up unbidden. *And wears the turning globe*, he remembered out of some forgotten book. A dead man, clad in the turning world. He wore Loki now, but not as the poet meant. That would come later. Some day, somewhere on some world whose name he might not even know yet, he would make that last and completest marriage with some turning globe, and then the green lines would tremble and blend.

But now he wore Loki, his world, fought for and earned. He meant to keep it. And he could. There was room. The villages would grow, and the webs of steel spin farther, but there would still be the forests and the mountains. It would be a long, long while before settlers dared explore Deadjet Range, or Great Swamp Valley, or Fever Hills.

The ground shivered. The green line on the oscilloscope wavered into a jagged dance. The Harvesters were moving.

More and more wildly the green line danced. In the moss under his fingertips Morgan felt vibrations grow strong. Scores of mighty hoofs bearing tons of tremendous bodies moved leisurely down the steep canyon valley toward him. He waited. There was no feeling of stress at all.

They were not yet in sight when the sense of movement all around him first began. Leaves rustled, tree trunks vibrated. The herd was coming near. Morgan relaxed utterly, letting the pulse of Loki carry him on its restless current.

High up among the leaves, seen dimly by starlight at a sharp angle from his crouch on the ground, Morgan was aware of a tremble of vines, a crackle and tearing, and suddenly a great, black, bearded face wreathed in torn leaves thrust forward. Vines snapped over a mighty chest and the herd leader burst majestically into sight, black and sleek and shining with blue highlights, his tight-curled mane merging with his curly beard. The antennae writhed slowly and restlessly above his round eyes, warily blinking. The breath snorted and soughed in his nostrils. The ground shook when he set his mighty hoofs upon it.

Morgan did not move, but every muscle inside him drew taut as springs, and the internal balances of his wiry body shifted for a leap. He waited his moment, and then his right hand closed hard upon the firing device that linked him with the hidden gun.

The gun was a Barker, set for its highest decibel-count of sheer noise. Morgan heard the first forerunning sound-wave of that tremendous mechanical roar, and opened his own mouth wide and shouted as loud as he could. His voice would be drowned in the noisy blast of the Barker, but he was not concerned with that. He had to balance the vibrations on both sides of his eardrums; the shout saved him from being deafened.

Upon the Harvesters the full impact of the roar fell shatteringly. All through the forest one concerted tremble and gather of mighty muscles seemed to ripple as the herd drew itself in for the spring into full stampede. Morgan had timed himself to a split second. His reactions would have to be exactly right.

It took just two fifths of a second for the Harvesters' sense-organs to drop to maximum loss of sensitivity after exposure. Very briefly indeed, the herd was deaf. It would not react with its normal supersensitivity. But in that two fifths of a second pure reflex would hurl them into headlong flight.

In that fraction of a second, Morgan sprang.

It was a tricky stunt. He timed himself to strike the bulge of the herd-leader's off foreleg with his knee in the instant before the bull surged forward. His hands seized two fists-full of curly mane and he clawed himself desperately upward in the same moment that the foreleg drove backward like a pistol, great muscles bunching to hurl Morgan upward within reach of the great black column of the neck.

He was ready and waiting when the lift came. He flung his knee over the sleek withers and fell forward flat and hard against the neck, both hands darting forward in a quick grab that had to be absolutely precise, to gather in each fist the bases of the thick antennae-clumps sprouting like horns from their twin bosses above the animal's eyes.

He felt the cool, smooth sheaf of tendrils against his left palm, and closed his fist hard. His right hand groped – slipped—

Missed.

Missed!

It couldn't be happening. He had never missed before. He was as sure as the stars in their turning. His own body was a mechanism as faithful as the rising of the sun over Loki planet. Jaime Morgan would go on forever. How could age weaken him? It must never happen—

But he missed the right-hand boss. His own momentum carried him helplessly forward, and the fatal toss of the bull's head hurled him on over the side of the gigantic neck. He felt the strong, hard column of its throat slide by under him. He felt the sickening vibrations of the herd's thousand hoofs striking the ground in earth-quaking unison. He saw the forest floor sweep by with blurring speed as he slid sidewise toward it. He remembered how a man looked after a Harvester herd had passed over him—

As he shook like a falling leaf that slid sidewise through air, his mind closed and gripped and clung furiously to one single thing – his own name.

Jaime Morgan, his mind cried frantically, tightening on that awareness and that identity which looked so close to forsaking him forever. The ground shuddered with rhythmic thunder, the Harvester's great neck pumped and tossed, the moss of the forest floor blurred by under his straining eyes.

Mixed up with Jaime Morgan was the memory of Sheml'li-hhan. *He got old. He got careless. Just once he was too slow, and the stag bison got him.* Was this how it had looked and felt to Sheml'li-hhan, in the instant before death? Morgan had never failed before – would he have a chance to fail again, ever again in this life?

Oh yes, he would.

Afterward, trying to remember exactly how he had done it, what crazy contortion had locked him into place on the bull's neck again, he found he could not remember. One instant he was swinging almost free, sliding down toward the shaking ground. The next, his knees were locked hard on both sides of that great muscular column again, and his hands frozen in the familiar grip on both the antennae-bosses, gripping and deadening the proprioceptors of the bull.

Nobody else could have saved himself, he thought, dizzy with fright and triumph. *Nobody but me.* But the words wouldn't stop there. *I missed, though. I missed. Like Sheml'il-hhan, a man gets old—*

He looked back. Behind him the Harvester herd came pouring in the strong starlight, one black, tossing waterfall of annihilation. They were magnificent, mindless angels of destruction, a host of heaven thundering down upon Ancibel Key. Tightening his fists, Morgan swung the herd leader imperceptibly toward the right side in a wide arc whose end would be the fields outside Ancibel. The leader obeyed—

Suddenly Morgan found himself roaring with laughter. Tears burned in his eyes from the wind of their passage and the pressures of his mirth. He didn't know why he laughed. He only knew that some deep, ancient fear inside him relaxed and quieted as the breath beat in his throat. Old? Not yet – not yet! Somewhere, some day – but not yet!

Lying close along the tremendous, pumping neck, his hands locked on the antennae bosses and his knees tireless in their grip upon the Harvester's withers, Morgan led the herd. Exultation boiled up in him like strong liquor, a wild intoxication of the mind. The power of the beast he rode burned through him and the rhythmic thunder of the running herd made his blood beat with the same strong rhythm. It was Loki planet itself which he was turning against the sleeping settlers, Loki rising in its anger to cast the intruders off.

Leaves whipped his face. The chill rush of wind made his eyes water. The hot, strong smell of the running bull stung in his nostrils. Then the leaves thinned suddenly and the thunder of the running beasts behind him changed in its sound as the forest fell away and open country lay before them. Morgan tightened his right hand on the bull's antennae-boss. Its perceptions dulled by the grip, it swung toward the left, toward the hillside of vines and orchards and the broad tilled fields above the town. Swinging after them came the herd, and the ground roared and trembled under their pounding hoofs.

The stars seemed to tremble, too. In the black sky nameless constellations shivered, new, foreshortened images seen from the far edge of the Galaxy and unnamed until men like Morgan came to watch by night and call them by familiar titles. He saw the Jetship sprawling its long oval above the town and the Stag-bison hurtling without motion toward the horizon. All the stars were watching along Paradise Street.

But the settlement slept. A few lights burned where saloons and gambling houses clustered at the far side of town, and out beyond, over the shielding hills, five spaceships towered against the stars. Lights from below shimmered upon their tapered sides, and stars shimmered upon their peaks. The Jetborne would be camped out there, guarding the spaceport. Morgan grinned savagely. Rufe Dodd was in for a surprise.

He leaned forward upon the tremendous neck, looking for the network of guarding wires which would warn the villagers if intruders came too close. He saw cut ends glitter and a tangle of torn netting piled aside, and he gripped the bosses harder, swinging the herd through the gap.

Now the trees loomed before them, heavy-laden with forming fruit. The orderly rows stretched downhill in ranks like soldiers. The lead bull tossed its bearded head as the strong scent of man rose before it like invisible fountains in the air. But the pressure of the herd behind it was strong, and it thundered forward among the trees.

Great shoulders crackled among the branches. The orchard's resistance seemed to madden the Harvesters. They plunged and snorted among the trees, roaring, pawing, crashing down through laden boughs. In an irresistible surging wedge driven by sheer momentum, they poured forward.

Morgan leaned forward upon the great maned neck and howled above the crashing of the herd.

'Smash 'em down!' he roared to his unhearing mount. 'Smash 'em under! Flatten the last rotten, stinking fruit-tree on Loki!' He loosed his grip a little on the antennae-bosses and screamed a wild Indian falsetto to madden the bull to its utmost, as if the few weak decibels of any human voice could be heard above the bellowing and the thunder of the herd.

He was half wild himself with the drunkenness of destruction and every new row of trees that went crashing under fanned him to new heights of furious joy. It was intoxicating to think of the long labors and the endless months of effort that had gone into the planting of this orchard. He drank in the scent of crushed fruit and ruined trees, and it was like the scent of strong whiskey in his nostrils. A man could be drunk on the very thought of the destruction he was wreaking now upon his enemies.

He howled louder and drummed with his knees upon the mighty, oblivious neck.

'Smash 'em down, you juggernauts! Roll 'em under!'

Ahead of him, beyond the ruined orchards, lay the fields. Clinging tight to his terrible mount, Morgan began to measure his course. Eventually he would have to dismount. That was going to be tricky.

He couldn't go down. Not into that thundering charge. He would have to swing off the lead bull's back, and that meant something he could swing to, something higher than the Harvester.

The herd crashed through the last line of trees and the cornfields stretched before them, silvery under the stars. Shouting, Morgan lay forward on the great neck and urged the Harvesters on. Soft ground churned under their hoofs and they plowed forward floundering and roaring until their gait adjusted to this new element of destruction. Morgan yelled with a drunken joy. He was the mightiest man alive. He wielded the thunderbolts like Jove himself, hurling his great herd down the fields.

To his right, in the town parallel with the galloping Harvesters, he saw lights begin to go on, heard shouts of alarm and presently the rhythmic clang of a bell swing wildly in the church steeple. He roared with furious laughter. Drive him off Loki, would they? Let them try! He bellowed a wordless challenge to the clanging bell.

Far ahead of him he saw a row of *serith* trees at the end of the fields. He would swing off upon one of those strong curved boughs when he reached them, for they marked the end of his journey. When the herd passed those trees, his job would be finished.

He looked back, clenching his hands hard upon the bosses he held. After him thundered the Harvesters, a terrifying melee of tossing heads, streaming beards, rippling, sleek flanks in the strong starlight. He could see the ruined orchards they had charged through, and behind them now a widening stretch of ruined fields, every blade and grain trampled into the carbon-blacked soil in a swath of total destruction. He laughed exultantly. Plow up

Loki planet, would they? Plant his wild and lonely valleys with corn? Tonight he was beating those alien crops back into the soil they had invaded. The very planet shuddered under the thunder of the charge he led. He knew how the centaurs must have felt, who were half gods—

There was a furtive motion back there along the edges of the broken trees. He turned his head and saw more of it bordering the fields parallel with his course. He was leading his herd along the outskirts of the town now, and the row of *serith* trees swept closer and closer. He had no time left to concern himself with that furtive motion, because the end of the ride was almost upon him, but he didn't like it. He didn't understand it. Something was afoot he had not allowed for—

The *serith* trees, distinct in the starlight, were rushing toward him, expanding with a startling illusion of rapid growth as the herd swept nearer. He gathered his muscles taut, gauged his leap—

Between him and the trees lightning and thunder exploded with blinding suddenness. Dazed, half-stunned by it, Morgan could only clutch the antennae-bosses in a paralyzing grip and cling like death itself to the plunging neck he rode.

Under him he felt the whole enormous bulk of the bull shudder in a violent convulsion, shudder and leap and seem to turn in midair. When it struck the ground again the whole valley must have shaken with the impact. Morgan gripped hard with knees and hands, dulling the bull's perceptions as much as he could, but not enough, not enough.

The world was reeling around him, standing up edgewise upon the horizon like the world below a turning plane. It whirled upon the pivot of the Harvester's drumming hoofs, and the herd whirled with it. There was more stunning, tremendous noise, but behind them now, bursting out in crazy roarings along the edge of the trampled fields.

Barkers. Ultrasonic guns bellowing at full sonic range.

So that was it, Morgan thought, shaking his dazed head. There hadn't been lightning in the thunder at all. It was merely his shocked senses that filled the lightning in. Gripping the lead bull hard, he looked back and saw what he had half-known, all along – a row of lemon-colored heads edging the field, long pale robes flickering in the starlight, dull metal shining as the Barkers roared.

They were driving the herd, and Morgan with it. But where?

He knew before he turned. The whole simple plan was perfectly clear to him, so clear he realized what a fool he must have been not to see it all along.

Low houses flashed by the Harvester's shoulders. Morgan turned in time to see the sprawling buildings of Ancibel Key fanning out on both sides as he led the herd between them straight toward the main street of Ancibel Key.

Crazily he roared at them to halt. But his own voice was drowned in his throat by the bellow of the Barkers to their rear and the deafening thunder of hoofbeats as Harvesters and rider together swept forward into Ancibel Key in one terrible, annihilating tide.

The murderous rage of utter impotence rose strangling in Morgan's throat, rage with everything that existed. He hated the bull beneath him, and the Harvester herd they led. He hated the running settlers he could glimpse between buildings ahead. He hated the clangor of the churchbell shouting out its alarm. His mind ached with a fury of hatred for the man from Venus who had tricked him into this, and for all the men who lined the fields outside the town, lashing on the herd with roaring Barkers.

But most of all he hated Jaime Morgan, the blundering fool who rode headlong to his own destruction, and Ancibel Key's.

In the crash and crackle of ruined buildings the Harvester herd poured through Ancibel. Dust swirled blindingly as the plastic walls buckled in and the arched roofs thundered down. It was a nightmare of disaster in the dark, with rainbows of rising dust around every street-light, so that Morgan could scarcely see or breathe.

He had incoherent glimpses of running men, shouting and beckoning to one another and vanishing again into darkness. Directly before him, in a rift in the dust and the dark, he saw a settler drop to one knee, throw a rifle to his shoulder, and squint upward at the man who rode the leading bull—

Something like a red-hot wire laid itself along Morgan's shoulder. He swung himself sidewise upon the gigantic neck he rode, and the kneeling man and the alley he knelt in swept backward and away like a fragment in a dream.

When Morgan righted himself again, his knees were trembling. His grip on the antennae-bosses felt less sure. A new terror flooded through him. He could not cling to this desperately precarious perch forever, and he knew it. But his chance of swinging off the bull lay far behind, and distance lengthened between with every stride of the Harvesters.

He remembered Sheml'li-hhan again.

And still the dust swirled and the buildings along both sides of the ruined street crackled and crashed anew before the shoulders of the stampeding herd. Men's shouts and the thin, high screams of women, and deep-throated clangor of the churchbell echoed above the planet-shaking thunder of drumming hoofs.

Harvesters had been known to run for days, once the hypnotic compulsion of a stampede gripped them. They might run until they dropped. Long before that happened, Morgan's grip would slack upon the beast he rode. Thinking of it, he felt his sinews shiver anew with the effort at holding firm.

He had to swing off somehow, and he had to do it soon.

That was nonsense, of course. What was the use of prolonging by a few minutes the death that was bound to take him when the infuriated settlers reached the man who was flattening their town? Too many must have recognized him already, up here in the rider's seat upon Juggernaut. How many men and woman had gone down already under this rolling avalanche, and how many lay smashed under the ruined houses?

He took cold comfort from the thought that it was mostly business houses and gambling dens along this main street, not residences. Some had died already. Some must have died. And if one life was lost, the Jetborne would hang him whether the settlers did or not.

Stunned with the noise and the vibration that pounded through him, dazed with his own anger and dismay, blinded with the swirling dust, he looked up at last and saw rising before him above the dust and the film of reflecting lights the five tall shining towers of spaceships at the port ahead. He was near enough now to see the ladder dangling from the nearest, and a flicker of faint hope stirred anew in his mind.

The ships were one manmade thing that could withstand even a charge of maddened Harvesters. He even grinned faintly, thinking how the Jetborne would scurry in ignominious flight when this tossing avalanche pounded through the field.

The five ships poised like the fingers of a steel-gloved hand above the town, as if some gigantic figure leaned with one negligent hand upon Loki, watching a small human drama play itself out to its insignificant climax.

Up, up the hill beyond the town the Harvester herd went thundering. Now the last buildings had fallen behind, and the shouts grew thin and the lights of Ancibel fell away. Up and over the hill-crest swept Morgan's mount. He drew himself together for a final desperate effort as the ground dropped away again and the galloping bull plunged forward down the slope toward the ships.

Small figures in uniform drew up at the edge of the field, firelight flashing on leveled guns. Ultrasonics whined into the herd briefly, but it was only a gesture and Morgan knew it as well as the others did. The tremendous vitality of the Harvesters, plus their terrible momentum, made any hope of killing the beasts preposterous. Even dying, the herd would still overwhelm the Jetborne at the edge of the field.

An invisible broom seemed to catch them as the foremost bulls plowed forward. Still firing futilely, they scattered and vanished.

Now the tall ships swept toward Morgan with nightmare speed. He saw starlight glimmer on their lifted heads and firelight on the long, smooth swelling of their flanks. He saw the rope-ladder dangling from the nearest, and as the herd surged onward, dividing among the gigantic columns of steel and closing again like black water around their fins, he drew himself together, waited his moment—

And leaped.

In midair for one timeless instant his faith shook. He could not be *sure* he would make it. Sheml'li-hhan's face swam before him, every feature vivid in his mind's eye. Then his hands closed on the rope and its hard burning as it jerked through his fingers dispelled the doubt and the illusion instantly.

He held on with all his strength, feeling his arms drag at the sockets of his shoulders. At the same moment he let go with his gripping knees and felt the mighty neck of the Harvester drop away below him, felt the thunder of the herd shake the very air as he hung swaying and turning above that trampling torrent.

The weakness of exhaustion was waiting to pour like water along his muscles the instant he let them go slack. He didn't dare relax. He locked both hands on the rope, pawed the air with his feet, found a rung at last and hung there blind and deaf and shivering, while the river of the stampede surged by under him forever. He shut his eyes and held his breath and clung for dear life, never dearer than now in spite of the perils still ahead of him. A long, long lifetime went by.

The thunder was in his head, and would probably never stop again. Time took on a bewildering fluidity. He couldn't tell if it was his own blood pounding in his ears, or the pounding of the herd. It seemed to him that he heard men shouting very near by, just under him perhaps, in that twenty feet of space separating him from the galloping herd. But how could there be men down there? All initiative seemed to have drained out of him and he could only hang tight to the ropes and wait for his head to clear.

Under his hands the rope jerked violently, almost hurling him loose. Painfully he clung. Again it snapped. This time he opened his eyes and peered down stupidly past his own shoulder.

A ring of pale, upturned faces regarded him from below. It seemed to him that he still heard the Harvesters thundering by, but the beating was in his own ears, for the herd had gone. After it, upon the very heels of the last, the men from Venus came.

Starlight made their sleek, pale hair look white below him. He saw firelight glint upon the heavy carboys they carried, and on the length of rifle barrels.

Then the rope he clung to jerked violently again, and he lost one handgrip and swung in perilous midair, staring down without comprehension. What was happening? Why?

He saw two of the pale-haired men gripping the ladder's dangling ends. He saw them give the ropes another vicious shake.

They were trying to throw him off the ladder.

*

Morgan shook his head in a trite and futile effort to get the fog out of it. Some things, at least, were clear. Shining Valley hadn't lost a moment. In the very wake of the stampede he and his men must have looted the settlement of their treasure. Before Ancibel could pull itself together after this shattering blow, the crew from Venus would be loaded and aspace with their loot. It had all worked with machinelike precision. And they were winding up one unimportant detail now—

The ladder snapped again and the rung Morgan stood on flew out from under his groping feet. He hung by his hands, cursing helplessly. They had cheated him all down the line, then. From the very first, when they swindled him out of his precious cargo, to this moment when they seemed about to cheat him of his very life, they'd had the upper hand. It wasn't enough to drive him through Ancibel and use him as an instrument of outright murder – for he knew men had died under that juggernaut of Harvesters. Now they were going to loot him of the money he had taken and probably shut his mouth forever. Bitterly he remembered Warburg's warning. It had been true, of course. Jaime Morgan was no match for these wily and devious men.

His hands on the rope went numb. He swung dizzily. He couldn't let go to reach his gun. It took both hands to cling. Suddenly he knew without any doubt that he was old. Civilization had been too much for Jaime Morgan.

The rope jerked under his grip again and his failing hands let go. For a long moment he hurtled outward through dark air. The stars turned remotely above him, Sirius a diamond glitter in the Jetship constellation and the Stag-bison picked out in white fire upon infinity.

The ground was a good twenty feet down. He struck it hard.

He knew how to fall, of course. He'd taken worse falls than this and bounced up again ready for anything. He'd had to learn that. But this time he hit the ground stunningly and lay dazed for an interval he could not gauge at all.

Rough hands rolled him over, tore at his pockets. He felt his gun rasp out of its holster and heard the crackle of credit-notes ripped free.

'Is he dead?' somebody asked in the fluting foreign speech he understood only imperfectly.

Morgan heard his own voice say, 'No!' suddenly and harshly. He levered himself to a sitting position with painful effort. He still could hear the thundering echoes in his head, and the spacefield tilted before him. He looked up into a ring of incurious faces. Behind them the hurried activity of loading went on half-heeded. He knew one face.

Shining Valley smiled down at him, pale as paper in the starlight. Morgan glowered savagely, full of fury and entirely without hope. Never before had his mind and his body failed him together in a crisis. If he couldn't outguess an opponent, he could outfight him. Now he was helpless. He swore at Valley uselessly in middle-Martian.

'You're a hard man to kill, Jaime Morgan,' Shining Valley said. 'You've had good luck – until now.'

Morgan cursed the man in lilting Venusian, knowing futilely that he was getting the inflections so wrong the phrases were probably innocuous.

Valley smiled. 'You helped me to my goal, Morgan. I'll reward you for it. There are dead men back in Ancibel, and you'd swing for that unless I save you.' He lifted a boneless hand toward the collar of his robe, where the men of his race carry their thin, straight throwing-knives. His own subtlety made him smile wider. 'You shall not hang for murder,' he promised.

'You will!' Morgan snarled. 'The Jetborne'll get you, Valley. They'll—'

'They'll do nothing,' Valley assured him. 'They can't.' His glance swerved to the hurried loading that went on beyond the ring that circled Morgan. 'Thanks to you,' he said, 'their hands will be tied. We'll load the cargo you helped us get, and ship it because you cleared the field for us. The sale of it will pay our protection on Loki for as long as we choose to stay here. Your Jetborne take their orders from authority like the hirelings they are. This, however, is no concern of yours, my friend. Very little is, any longer.' He gave Morgan a sweet, cold smile and touched the knife-hilt.

'Rufe Dodd will get you,' Morgan promised him, hearing his own voice crack with anger that bordered on despair. 'Nobody's orders will stop *him* when he finds out what—'

Shining Valley laughed abruptly. 'You think not, Morgan? Then wait a moment! Perhaps you'd like a word with Dodd – while you can still speak.'

Morgan regarded him fixedly, paying little attention to what the man from Venus said. It made no difference. He was wishing without hope that there was some way he could kill Valley. He formed a shapeless and not very practical plan. In the last moment before the throwing-knife was drawn, he thought he would launch himself at Valley's knees and drag him down within reach.

His own legs might not hold him, and his arms still quivered from the long strain of the ride, but with any luck at all he ought to be able to wreak some dirty work on Valley's smooth face before they killed him. He thought with reminiscent pleasure of the technique of eye-gouging, and his right thumb suddenly twisted in the dust, a small motion that meant nothing to anyone here but himself. He was grinning thinly in anticipation when Valley's shout startled him.

'Major Dodd!' the man from Venus was calling. 'Major Dodd, step over here!'

Morgan went rigid on the dusty ground, not daring to turn his head. He remembered the scattering of the Jetborne before the Harvesters' charge, and knew that Rufe Dodd would not have run far – relief for an instant made him weak. Then he knew it made no real difference whether Valley killed him with a knife or the Jetborne hanged him for murder. He was technically guilty of it and he had no defense the law would accept. Rufe wouldn't have any choice. But still—

Footsteps made the ground vibrate a little under him. Morgan did not turn, even when a familiar voice spoke just above him.

'Morgan,' Rufe said with formality and in anger, 'you're under arrest. Lieutenant, have him taken in charge.'

Morgan regarded his own knees steadily, not looking up even when he saw brown-uniformed legs step up on both sides and felt a stranger's firm grip touch his shoulder. At the last moment Shining Valley spoke.

'Just a minute, major! You have no jurisdiction here. Stand back, you men! Morgan belongs to us.'

'I'm arresting him for murder,' Dodd's crisp voice said. 'Lieutenant—'

'You're exceeding your authority, major,' Valley interrupted smoothly. 'I didn't call you over here to violate orders. You've had your instructions from headquarters, haven't you?'

Dodd's breathing was noisy in the quiet for a moment. Without looking up Morgan knew his jaw was set and his breath whistled through his nostrils. After a long pause, he spoke.

'I have, Valley.'

'And what are they?'

Silence again. After another long pause Dodd said tightly, 'I am not to interfere in local matters between you and civilians.'

'Very well, then. I called you over chiefly to set Morgan's mind at rest.' Valley smiled down at Morgan's set and averted face. 'He was under the impression you might … ah … cause a disturbance if he should die as a result of an armed robbery he committed against me earlier today. He was mistaken, wasn't he, major? You couldn't interfere, could you?'

There was dead silence for a long time.

'You couldn't interfere,' Valley repeated, 'between me and civilians, could you, Dodd? Those are your orders? And you never violate orders, do you, major?'

Still Dodd did not speak.

Morgan, without looking up, was the one who finally broke the silence.

'Forget it, Rufe,' he said. 'Nothing you can do. I asked for it. Just like you to know they tricked me into that Harvester stampede. I never meant to ride 'em through the town. You heard their Barkers, didn't you? That was what—'

'All right, Morgan.' Valley's voice was suddenly cold. 'I haven't much time to waste here. Major, you can go now. This is a matter between me and the civilian population. You've had your orders.' He lifted a tentative hand toward his knife-hilt again. Morgan gathered himself taut, one palm flat on the ground for the leap. His thumb made a small, anticipatory circle in the dust.

'Get out, Rufe,' he said, not looking up. 'Go on – git!'

'Be quiet, Morgan,' Shining Valley said. 'I give the orders on Loki now. Dodd, take your men and go.' He smiled. 'You might prepare to leave Loki while you're about it,' he added. 'Your orders will come through from headquarters as soon as this shipment gets there. Money in the right places gives very persuasive advice, major, and this is heading for the rightest possible place. In the meantime you may as well get used to taking my orders. Get out, Dodd. Get out of my sight.'

Still Rufus Dodd did not speak or move. It struck Morgan suddenly how strange that was. Not like Rufe Dodd. Was something funny up? He was almost impelled to turn and look, though he had no wish to meet Rufe's eyes. He was not forgetting that he'd kicked Rufe in the face the last time they met, and he was perfectly content to look at the ground now. Rufe wouldn't have taken that too kindly.

But something about Rufe's motionless silence warned him not to turn. He had a curious notion that Rufe was listening to something he himself couldn't hear. It didn't seem likely, but he caught a faint hint of command from somewhere and wondered if Rufe had some plan in mind he wouldn't want interrupted. When you have known a man as long as Morgan had known Rufe Dodd, and shared with him spots as tight as this often before now, you can catch the vibration of a silent command when there is one in the air. Morgan sat motionless, ready for anything.

Valley's opaque eyes watched Dodd. Presently the man from Venus shrugged. 'Stay if you like,' he said. 'I would have spared you. The impulse to meddle may be very strong, major, but you're outnumbered even if you were rash enough to disobey orders. By all means, watch if it amuses you. Morgan—' His gaze dropped. '*Skalla!*' he said.

His hand swept upward in a swift, dipping arc and flashed high with the blade in his hand already glinting red with firelight. Morgan gathered himself together against the hard ground, threw his weight forward on one knee, gauged his timing, and—

A thin, high shrilling wailed like a banshee out of the dark, and Valley's lifted hand jerked convulsively. The boneless fingers spread and the red-glinting knife fell flashing out of it. A round crimson spot the size of a quarter-credit appeared by sheer magic upon the center of the lifted wrist.

Nobody moved. Nobody breathed.

Slowly Valley turned his head to stare at his own hand. It took that long for the blood to begin pumping from his pierced wrist. The first sight of it broke the spell and everything dissolved into sudden, intensely rapid motion, most of it without purpose.

Valley snapped his wrist forward and seized it hard with his other hand, his face going gray as all color drained out of it. He chattered in incoherent Venusian to his men. There was tremendous scurry and confusion, in the midst of which Major Dodd's calm voice spoke. He had not stirred an inch, and he did not now except to say quietly:

'They're coming, Valley. Over the hill. Listen. I've been hearing them for about five minutes now. If you'll look, you'll see what I mean.'

Everyone turned, as if on a single pivot. The brow of the hill between the spaceport and the town was outlined suddenly in a crown of winking lights. As they stared, the lights poured forward downhill, merged and blended and were a spreading river that jogged onward at the pace of striding men.

Under the torches light burned bright upon the dust-whitened heads and the angry, determined faces of the men from ruined Ancibel.

Shining Valley took the situation in with a quick, incredulous glance. He shouted orders in rapidly cadenced speech and the men from Venus redoubled their swarming pace around the ship they were loading. The last carboys went rapidly up the ladders and the rest of the workers began to deploy cautiously around the ship, unslinging their weapons.

Again the banshee wailed out of the darkness just beyond the reach of the firelight, and one of the riflemen under the ship reeled in a circle and fell heavily across his gun. A voice called from the darkness.

'I'll nail the next man who moves! We mean business.'

Morgan breathed softly, 'Joe! Joe Warburg.' He knew that shooting as well as he knew the voice.

The merging river of lights streamed forward at a rapid stride. Now you could see the separate faces and the dusty, disheveled clothing of the mob. Not all of them were armed. Some carried Barkers, and some had old-fashioned projectile-rifles, and some carried the immemorial weapons of the embattled farmer on every world where farmers have been called upon to fight. Morgan saw pitchforks gleam and here and there a flash of light down the blade of an ancient, outmoded scythe, which was a wicked weapon at Flodden and Poictiers, and has not grown kindlier since.

Morgan knew some of the faces. The young settler he had quarreled with in Warburg's store strode in the front rank, his ultrasonic balanced across his heavy forearm and his flat Ganymedan face crimson with anger and firelight. A white-haired farmer walked beside him, pitchfork in hand, and on his other side the parson's eyeglass lenses caught red light. The parson's palms were raw from pulling the bellrope in the church tower, and he carried a coil of orlon rope across his arm.

When they came to the place where the banshee had wailed and the voice spoken out of darkness, a figure stood up and took familiar shape in the light. Warburg stepped out and fell into stride beside the parson, his Barker balanced lightly in his big hands, set for a killing beam.

Shining Valley spoke very rapidly in a soft, slurring voice to his men, who put their loads down and then straightened up with carefully slow motions, facing the oncoming mob. At the back, under the shadow of the ships, a few of them sank into crouches, lifting their guns and moving carefully into deeper shelter.

'Speak to them, major,' Valley said. He was clutching his wrist tightly, and blood spattered the dust with light, splashing sounds. 'Tell them the stampede was Morgan's fault. You saw him lead it. Speak to them – quick!'

Rufe Dodd laughed, a quick, harsh bark of sound.

'How can I interfere,' Dodd asked, 'between you and civilians on Loki? I have my orders. Valley!'

Shining Valley swung round toward the mob.

'Stop right there!' he shouted. 'I've got men deployed around you under the ships. Stand still and nobody else will get hurt. Start something, and—'

'It's no use, Valley,' Warburg said. 'There's eight dead men back there in Ancibel, and two dead women. Our boys aren't in any bargaining mood. We know what happened. We saw who started this. Now get ready to finish it.'

'I call on the Jetborne!' Shining Valley shouted. 'We had nothing to do with that stampede! This is mob rule!'

'These are vigilantes,' the young settler with the ultrasonic said. 'The Jetborne's out of it. Stand by, major, if you don't want to get your men killed. We're going to string up the killers who did this, and we won't take interference.' His red cheeks flushed a deeper color and his flat Ganymedan face hardened as his eyes met Morgan's.

'We'll start,' the settler said in a hard voice, 'with the fellow who led the herd. Stand up, mister! You rode over ten people in Ancibel tonight. If the law won't deal with you, the vigilantes will!'

Morgan got up slowly and stiffly. He did not speak a word, but his gaze sought Warburg's with a silent inquiry. Warburg shook his gray head.

'We all saw you, Jaime,' he said. 'We know what happened. You didn't do it alone – but you rode the herd. There's ten people dead. And the crops are ruined. There isn't a man in Ancibel who isn't ruined right along with 'em. They sank a year's work and all the money they could borrow in those crops, Jaime. The lucky guys are the dead ones – anyhow, that's the way we feel tonight. We can't bring the dead back to life, but we can sure take care of the men who killed them. You're in bad company, Jaime.' His dust-streaked face was grim. 'I wouldn't do a thing to stop the boys,' he said, 'even if I could.'

Morgan nodded briefly.

'I figured you might feel that way, Joe,' he said. 'All right, boys. Let's go.'

He stepped forward. The young settler reached for the rope the parson carried, making a long forward stride toward Morgan. Morgan braced himself, not sure what he would do next.

That was when the first shots wailed out from the shadow of the ships where Valley's men were hidden. The red-cheeked Ganymedan halted in the middle of a stride, dropped his gun, spun halfway around and grabbed futilely with both hands at his chest.

A boy jumped forward past him out of the crowd behind. It was the Mars-tanned Tim, Warburg's clerk. He seized the falling gun and went down with it, reaching expertly for the controls, his body braced and ready for the jar of his fall. The gun began to whine toward the ships in a flicker of violet fire three seconds after he hit the ground.

There was a great deal of confusion after that.

It could have but one ending, of course. The men from Venus were far outnumbered. Morgan didn't take much interest. That was because of the stunning burn across the side of the head which one faction or the other succeeded in placing on him before he prudently hit the ground a very short instant after Tim did.

He lay there curled tight against the surging of the struggle above him, dizzy and knowing he hadn't a chance no matter who won. He was too tired to run and too dazed to fight.

He was too old.

He had some idea that the battlefield roar of Rufe Dodd's voice bellowed for a while above the tumult, demanding Jaime Morgan as his prisoner. But Rufe didn't get very far. The settlers had little patience with the Jetborne just now. Rufe's shouting grew muffled and farther and farther away.

Somebody kicked Morgan in the head after that and he saw a burst of the stars that line Paradise Street, and relaxed into total darkness.

The next thing Morgan remembered was the reek of trampled ground and trampled growing things. Rough, moist soil was soft under him and he heard a great deal of uneasy motion and the low, purposeful rumbling sounds of determined men around him in the night. His hands seemed to be tied behind him, and he opened his eyes to discover that he was leaning against a tree. He looked up.

The tree was a *serith* and the stars regarded him through its leaves. Head-downward over the horizon the Stag-bison lurched, and blue-white

Sirius at the Jet-ship's nose pointed toward Loki's pole-star. In their light he could see the ruined fields east of Ancibel, the jagged fragments of orchards black against the stars. So the men of Ancibel had brought him back to the scene of his crime to die. He whistled soundlessly through his teeth and sat up straighter to see what was going on.

This was the row of *seriths* that marked the far end of the field. It was even a little funny, he thought, that a few short hours ago he'd actually been *trying* to swing onto one of these trees.

Ten feet to the right he saw a pale figure lying bound against the bole of the nearest *serith*. Ten feet to the left lay another. Each assigned to his own gallows, Morgan thought. Was that Shining Valley at his right, fawn-colored fringes fluttering in the night breeze? He craned futilely. He thought it was, but he couldn't be sure.

Farther down the line the grim business of the vigilantes was already under way. Morgan wondered what Warburg really thought about it. It wasn't like Joe. Still, Joe had changed. Taken on settlers' ways. They were dirty ways, Morgan thought. This was no proper sort of death to inflict even on proved killers. Maybe settlers had to do it, though. No understanding how their cloddish minds worked. After all, you could hardly blame them. He'd taken his chance and lost, and when you play a stranger's game you abide by the stranger's rules. Still, it was no way to die.

They were working up the line toward him, grim, businesslike men performing their job resolutely. Somebody dropped a rope over a limb and a muttering rose like low thunder from the crowd as the loop fell over the neck of the man below.

Morgan watched critically.

He felt tired and not particularly unhappy, after all, now that the moment had almost come which he had faced and escaped so often before, on so many worlds. He whistled gently to himself and was glad he wasn't wearing a long fringed robe like the Venusian's. It fluttered so ludicrously, when a man was swinging by the neck under a *serith* tree.

The prisoner beneath the neighboring tree turned his head, catching Morgan's eye.

'*Skalla*' Morgan said. It *was* Shining Valley. Morgan grinned.

But then he looked away. He didn't particularly care for the thought of the company he had to keep on this final journey. It probably didn't matter. He whistled quietly to himself.

Something rustled very gently in the dark behind him. He tightened all over, listening. Then a cold touch slid like metal against his wrist and the rope that tied him gave slightly.

'Hold still, you fool,' Joe Warburg's voice muttered.

*

Morgan picked his way carefully along the backs of Ancibel's houses, keeping to the darkest shadows. There were more people in town than he would have thought, considering the crowd out there in the fields.

He didn't feel very good. His head still buzzed from the beating he had taken, and he wasn't sure in his own mind that he'd really held that quick, muttered talk with Warburg in the shadows behind the *serith* tree while the vigilantes worked their way grimly nearer and nearer. It seemed now more like a dream a man might have, waking after a knockout blow.

'Hit for town,' Warburg had urged him in the dream. 'Make for the alley behind the last saloon facing the spaceport. Keep under cover. You old fool, did you really think I'd let you hang?'

Maybe it had really happened. Maybe it hadn't. Anyhow, here was the alley. Morgan flattened himself against its wall, darting quick glances up and down the street beyond. Ruined buildings, ruined pavement, a huge dead Harvester bull lying on its side, a nervous settler or two picking his way along toward the center of town. Why was Morgan here? What had Joe had in mind?

'Maybe my ship's at the port?' Morgan wondered. 'Maybe old Joe filled her up? I wish I knew what—'

Then he heard the beat of marching feet, and flattened himself harder into the shadows as a detachment of the Jetborne went by, brown legs moving in unison, brown arms swinging. Morgan stood motionless, letting them pass perilously near.

Last of the Jetborne came two officers, walking side by side. One of them was Rufe Dodd.

Rufe passed just beyond the mouth of the alley. Morgan could see his shadow on the trampled street, hear his crisp voice speaking.

'You can start searching from the east edge of town,' he said. 'Spread out fast. He escaped only ten minutes ago. He hasn't had time to get far yet. On the double!'

The footsteps of the Jetborne went on, double-time down the street. Dodd said, more quietly, 'What are you waiting for, lieutenant?'

'Your orders, sir. You said – take him alive?' The other voice was puzzled.

'Certainly. I want Morgan. He's got charges facing him.'

'But he's dangerous, major. He's tasted blood now. Should I risk my men unnecess—'

'You questioning my command, lieutenant?'

There was a little silence. Dodd's shadow on the street got out a shadow-cigar and lit it leisurely, puffed smoke toward the stars. Morgan could smell the fragrance of Mars-bred tobacco. He couldn't see the other man at all. He wondered if his own heartbeats were not making very audible thunder in this narrow alley. When Dodd spoke, his voice was calm.

'Jaime Morgan won't kill anybody else tonight, lieutenant,' he said. 'It isn't a matter of tasting blood. It's a matter of touching pitch. Morgan got too close to civilization and he got himself fouled with it. But it'll wash off. Maybe he's learned the lesson he was bound to learn, sometime.'

There was a pause.

'Sir—'

Dodd paid no attention. 'Yes,' he said, 'when a man's young, he's always on the move. He can't stop too long on any one world. But he gets habits, and they slow him down. One day he finds he isn't ready to leave when the time comes. But he can't stop civilization moving in, the good and the bad of it. What can he do? A world gets civilized; nothing can stop it once it gets opened up. So a man like Morgan gets sucked in before he knows it. He's got to follow the rules of civilization, even when he thinks he's fighting it. You can't be neutral. Morgan didn't know that.'

The shadow puffed smoke fragrantly. 'Loki isn't Morgan's any more. It belongs to the settlers. But the sky's still full of stars, lieutenant. You heard about that new planet they've opened up, over by Rehoboam IV?'

The lieutenant's voice said, 'That's another thing, sir. We're not guarding that freighter. If Morgan should hear about it – if he should stow away—'

'He doesn't know the *Nineveh's* taking off at dawn,' Dodd said, enunciating his words with great distinctness. 'He doesn't even known I've lifted the grounding orders. There's no need for a guard around the *Nineveh*. A man follows his habit patterns. Morgan will take to the woods.' He chuckled. 'Morgan's too old to change,' he said with a certain sardonic inflection in his voice. It sounded like a challenge. 'He's forgotten what other worlds are like. He doesn't remember the cockeyed giant.'

'Sir?'

'Never mind, lieutenant. Get along now. Better join your men before you lose them.'

'Yes, sir,' the voice said, not quite convinced.

'Let's go,' Dodd's voice insisted, and two pairs of footsteps moved away. Dodd's voice floated back, clear and thoughtful.

'There'll always be worlds to open, you know, and there'll always be men like Morgan to find them. There always has been. There always will be. One of the old poets wrote about Jaime. He said a man like that would always know there was—' The voice paused, then strengthened into firm command. '"*—Something lost beyond the ranges lost and waiting for you … Go.*"' Heavy boots rang loud on the dark street, and less loud, and then mingled with the other night sounds.

Morgan stood quite still until the last rhythmic beat of footfalls was silent. Then he tipped his head back and looked westward toward the port. He saw five tall ships and the shining sky behind them.

He was feeling very sad, but much better, and hardly old at all. He stooped quickly once, and touched the ground. Good-by, Loki, he thought. Good-by, world.

Then he turned in the dark and ran soundlessly toward the west and the towering ships and the endless reaches of Paradise Street.

PROMISED LAND

People got out of Fenton's way as he walked scowling through the palace, heading for the great steel doors that only half a dozen men in the Unit knew how to open. Fenton was one of the half dozen. The pale scar that made a zigzag like lightning across his dark cheek pulled his face awry a little as he snapped an angry command into the intercom.

A voice murmured apologetically out of it:

'Sorry, he's busy right now. If you'll—'

Fenton slapped his palm with ringing fury against the metal beside the intercom. The echoing metallic boom rang like thunder down the hall behind him, where courtiers, diplomats and politicians waited their chance for an audience with the Protector of Ganymede.

'Open these doors!'

There was another pause. Then the voice murmured something again, and the great steel doors slid softly apart a few feet. Fenton stalked through, hearing them thud together behind him, shutting off the sound of whispering, angry and curious, that had begun to fill the hall.

He went through an antechamber and into a tall-columned room shaped like a well, with a dome of starry sky very far overhead. (It was day outside, on Ganymede, and thick, eternal clouds shut out the sky, but if a man is wealthy enough he can arrange to have the stars reflected into his palace if he wants them.)

In the center of the room, under the sky dome, stood the Protector's water bed where his five-hundred-pound bulk wallowed luxuriantly. Like truth, the monstrous man floated at the bottom of his well and watched the stars.

He was not looking at them now. Great billows of lax flesh stirred on his cheeks as he grinned cavernously at the newcomer.

'Patience, Ben, patience,' he said in his deep rumble. 'You'll inherit Ganymede in due time – when it's habitable. Be patient, even—'

Fenton's angry glance dropped to the man sitting on the raised chair beside the water bed.

'Get out,' he said.

The man stood up, smiling. He stooped a little, standing or sitting, as though his big-boned frame found even the scanty weight of flesh it carried burdensome. Or maybe it was the responsibilities he carried. He had a gaunt face and his eyes, like his hair, were pale.

'Wait,' the monster in the tank said. 'Byrne's not finished with me yet, Ben. Sit down. Patience, son, patience!'

Fenton's right hand jerked doorward. He gave Bryne a cold glance.

'Get out,' he said again.

'I'm no fool,' Bryne remarked, turning away from the water bed. 'Apologies, Protector, and so on. But I'd rather not be in the middle. Ben seems upset about something. Call me when it's safe.' He shambled off, was lost behind the pillars. The sound of his footsteps died.

Fenton drew a deep breath to speak, his dark face flushing. Then he shrugged, sighed and said flatly: 'I'm through, Torren. I'm leaving.'

The Protector wallowed as he raised an enormous hand. Gasping with the effort, he let it fall back into the dense, oily liquid of his bath.

'Wait,' he said, panting. 'Wait.'

The edge of the bath was studded with colored buttons just under the water level. Torren's gross fingers moved beneath the surface, touching buttons deftly. On a tilted screen above the tank snow fields flickered into view, a road threading them, cars sliding flatly along the road.

'You've just come from the village,' Torren said. 'You've talked to Kristin, I suppose. You know I lied to you. Surprised, Ben?'

Fenton shook his head impatiently.

'I'm leaving,' he said. 'Find yourself another heir, Torren.' He turned away. 'That's all.'

'It isn't all.' The Protector's deep voice had command in it. 'Come back here, Ben. Patience is what you want, my boy. Patience. Spend thirty years in a water bed and you learn patience. So you want to walk out, do you? Nobody walks out on Torren, son. You ought to know that. Not even my inheritor walks out. I'm surprised at you. After I've taken so much trouble to change a whole world to suit your convenience.' The vast cheeks wrinkled in a smile. 'It isn't thoughtful of you, Ben. After all I've done for you, too.'

'You've done nothing for me,' Fenton told him, still in the flat voice. 'You picked me out of an orphanage when I was too young to protect myself. There's nothing you can give me I want, Torren.'

'Getting dainty, aren't you?' the man in the water demanded with what sounded like perfect good humor. 'I'm surprised at you, Ben. So you don't want the Torren empire, eh? Ganymede wouldn't be good enough for you, even when I make it habitable, eh? Oh, Ben, come to your senses. I never thought you'd go soft on me. Not after what you've been through.'

'You put me through plenty,' Fenton said. 'I grew up the hard way. It wasn't worth it, Torren. You wasted your time. I tell you I'm finished.'

'I suppose the light of a good woman's eyes has reformed you,' Torren mocked. 'Pretty little Kristin changed your mind, I suppose. A charming creature, Kristin. Only a foot taller than you, too, my boy. Only a hundred pounds heavier, I expect. But then she's young. She'll grow. Ah, what a pity I never met a really good woman when I was your age. Still, she'd have had to weigh five hundred pounds, to understand me, and such women never really appealed to my aesthetic tastes. You should have seen the charming little things in the Centrifuge, Ben. They're still there, you know – the ones who haven't died. I'm the only Centrifuge baby who got out and stayed out. I made good. I earned enough to stay out.'

The monstrous head fell back and Torren opened his vast mouth and roared with laughter. The oily liquid in the bath heaved in rhythmic tides and echoes of his mirth rolled along the pillars and up the well toward the stars, rolled up the walls that had imprisoned Torren since his birth. They were walls he himself had burst apart against odds no man had ever before encountered.

'*You* grew up in a hard school,' Torren laughed. '*You!*'

Fenton stood silent, looking at the monstrous being in the bath, and the anger in his eyes softened a little in spite of himself. The old respect for Torren stirred in his mind. Tyrant the man might be, ruthless autocrat – but had ever man such reason to be pitiless before? Perhaps in very ancient times when, for profit, skilled practitioners warped and broke the bodies of children to make them valuable freaks and monsters for the entertainment of royalty. Perhaps then, but not again, until the planets were opened for colonization three hundred years ago.

Fenton had seen the Threshold Planetaria, back on Earth, the fantastic conditioning units where eugenics, working through generation after generation of selected stock, bred humans who could sustain themselves in the ecology of other worlds. He knew little about these remarkable experiments in living flesh. But he did know that some of them had failed, and one such Planetarium had held Torren – thirty years ago.

'Thirteen generations,' Torren said deliberately, drawing the familiar picture for him again, relentlessly as always. 'Thirteen generations one after another, living and dying in a Centrifuge that increased its rotation year after year. All those treatments, all those operations, all that time under altered radiations, breathing altered air, moving against altered gravity – until they found out they simply couldn't breed men who could live on Jupiter, if they took a thousand generations. There was a point beyond which they couldn't mutate the body and keep intelligence. So they apologized.' He laughed again, briefly, the water surging around him in the tank.

'They said they were sorry. And we could leave the Centrifuge any time we wanted – they'd even give us a pension. Five hundred a month. It takes a thousand a day to keep me alive outside the Centrifuge!'

He lay back, spent, the laughter dying. He moved one vast arm slowly in the fluid.

'All right,' he said. 'Hand me a cigarette, Ben. Thanks. Light—'

Holding the igniter for him, Fenton realized too late that Torren could have got his own cigarette. There was every possible convenience, every luxury, available to the water bed. Angrily Fenton swung away, paced to and fro beneath the screen upon which the snow fields were reflected. His fingers beat a tattoo on his thigh. Torren waited, watching him.

At the far end of the screen, without turning, Fenton said quietly: 'So it was bad in the Centrifuge, Torren? How bad?'

'Not bad at first. We had something to work toward. As long as we thought our descendants could colonize Jupiter we could stand a lot. It was only after we knew the experiment had failed that the Centrifuge was bad – a prison, just as our bodies were a prison.'

'But you'd shut the Ganymedans up in place like that.'

'Certainly,' Torren told him. 'Of course I would. I'd shut you up, or anyone else who stood in my way. I owe the Ganymedans nothing whatever. If there's any debt involved, the human race owes *me* a debt that can never be repaid. Look at me, Ben. Look!'

Fenton turned. Torren was raising his gigantic arm out of the water. It should have been an immensely powerful arm. It had the potential muscle. It had the strong, bowed bone and the muscles springing out low down along the forearm, as the Neanderthaler and the gorilla's did. And Torren had a gorilla's grip – when he did not have to fight gravity.

He fought it now. The effort of simply lifting the weight of his own arm made his breath come heavily. His face darkened. With tremendous struggle he got the arm out of the water as far as the elbow before strength failed him. The uselessly powerful arm crashed back, splashing water high. Torren lay back, panting, watching his sodden cigarette wash about, disintegrating in the tank.

Fenton stepped forward and plucked it out of the water, tossed it aside, wiped his fingers on his sleeve. His face was impassive.

'I don't know,' he said. 'I don't know if that debt ever can be discharged. But, by God, you're trying hard.'

Torren laughed. 'I need the money. I always need money. There aren't enough Ganymedans to develop the planet. That's all there is to it. With the ecology changed, normal humans can live here within ten years.'

'They'll be able to live here in another hundred and fifty years anyhow, if plantings and atmospherics follow the program. By then the Ganymedans will adapt – or at least, their great-grandchildren will. That was the original plan.'

'Before I got control, yes. But now *I* give the orders on Ganymede. Since

Jensen isolated Jensenite out there,' and he nodded toward the snowy screen, 'everything's changed. We can speed up the plantings a hundred percent and the air ought to be breathable in—'

'Jensen's a Ganymedan,' Fenton broke in. 'Without Jensen you'd never have been able to break the original agreement about changing over. You owe the Ganymedans that much for Jensen's sake alone.'

'Jensen will get paid. I'll finance him to an ambulatory asylum on any world he chooses. I owe the others nothing.'

'But they're all in it together!' Fenton slapped the edge of the tank angrily. 'Don't you see? Without the whole Ganymede Threshold experiment you'd never have had Jensenite. You can't scrap every Ganymedan except Jensen now! You—'

'I can do as I please,' Torren declared heavily. 'I intend to. Ganymede is an unimportant little satellite which happens to belong to me. I hate to mention it, son, but I might say the same thing about you. Benjamin Fenton is an unimportant young man who happens to belong to me. Without my influence you're nothing but a cipher in a very large solar system. I've invested a lot of money and effort in it and I don't intend to throw it away. Just what do you think you'd do if you left me, Ben?'

'I'm a good organizer,' Fenton said carefully. 'I know how to handle people. I've got fast reflexes and dependable judgment. You toughened me. You gave me some bad years. You arranged for me to kill a few people – in line of duty, naturally – and I've done your dirty jobs until I know all the ropes. I can take care of myself.'

'Only as long as I let you,' Torren told him with a faintly ominous ring in the deep voice. 'Maybe it was a whim that made me pick you out of the asylum. But I've invested too much in you, Ben, to let you walk out on me now. What you need is work-hardening, my boy.' He cupped water in his hand and let it drain out. 'Who was it,' he inquired, 'that said no man is an island? You're looking at an island, Ben. *I'm* an island. A floating island. No one alive has any claim on me. Not even you. Don't try me too far, Ben.'

'Have you ever thought I might kill you some time, Torren?' Fenton asked gently.

The colossus in the tank laughed heavily.

'I ran a risk, making you my heir,' he admitted. 'But you won't kill me to inherit. I made sure. I tried you. You were given chances, you know ... no, I don't think you did know. I hardened you and toughened you and gave you some bad years, and some men might want to kill me for that. But not you. You don't hate me, Ben. And you're not afraid of me. Maybe you ought to be. Ever think of that, Ben?'

Fenton turned and walked toward the door. Between two pillars he paused and glanced back.

'I nearly killed you thirteen years ago,' he said.

Torren slapped his palm downward, sending a splash of liquid high.

'You nearly killed me!' he said with sudden, furious scorn. 'Do you think I'm afraid of death? When I wasn't afraid to *live*? Ben, come back here.'

Fenton gave him a level look and said, 'No.'

'Ben, that's an order.'

Fenton said, 'Sorry.'

'Ben, if you walk out of this room now you'll never come back. Alive or dead, Ben, you'll never come back.'

Fenton turned his back and went out, through the anteroom and the great steel doors that opened at his coming.

Stooping above the open suitcase on his bed, both hands full, Fenton saw the slightest possible shadow stirring in reflection on the window before him and knew he was not alone in the room. No buzzer had warned him, though the full spy-beam system was on and it should have been impossible for anyone to pass unheralded.

He lifted his head slowly. Beyond the broad window the snowy hills of Ganymede lay undulating to the steep horizon. The clouds that blanketed the world were blue-tinged with Jupiter-light, reflecting from Jupiter's vast bright-blue seas of liquid ammonia. Between two hilltops he could see one of the planting-valleys veiled in mist, dull turquoise warm by contrast with the snow. The reflection swam between him and the hills.

Without turning he said: 'Well, Bryne?'

Behind him Bryne laughed.

'How did you know?'

Fenton straightened and turned. Bryne leaned in the open doorway, arms folded, sandy brows lifted quizzically.

'You and I,' Fenton said in a deliberate voice, 'are the only men who know most of the rabbit-warren secrets in this Unit. Torren knows them all. But it had to be you or Torren, obviously. You know how I knew, Bryne. Are you trying to flatter me? Isn't it a waste of time, now?'

'That depends on you,' Bryne said, adding thoughtfully a moment later, '—and me, of course.'

'Go on,' Fenton said.

Bryne shifted his gaunt body awkwardly against the door.

'Do you know what orders Torren gave me an hour ago? No, of course you don't. I'll tell you. You're not to be admitted to him again even if you ask, which I told him you wouldn't. You're not to take anything out of the Unit except the clothes you wear, so you can stop packing. Your accounts have been stopped. All the money you're to have is what's in your pocket. This suite is out of bounds as soon as you leave it.' He glanced at his wrist. 'In half an hour I'm to come up here and escort you to Level Two. You eat with the repair crew and sleep in the crew dormitory until Thursday, when a frighter is due in at the spaceport. You'll sign on with the crew and work your way back to Earth.' Bryne grinned. 'After that, you're on your own.'

Fenton touched his scarred cheek meditatively, gave Bryne a cold glance.

'I'll expect you in half an hour, then,' he said. 'Good-by.'

Bryne stood up straighter. The grin faded.

'You don't like me,' he said, on a note of sadness. 'All the same, you'd better trust me. Half an hour's all we have now. After that I pass over into my official capacity as the Protector's representative, and I'll have to carry Torren's orders out. *He* thinks you need work-hardening. I may find myself finagling you into a slave-contract in the underlands.'

'What do you suggest?' Fenton asked, folding another shirt.

'That's better.' Bryne dropped a hand into his pocket, stepped forward, and tossed a thick packet of money onto the bed. Beside it he dropped a key and a folded ticket, bright pink for first-class.

'A ship leaves six hours from now for Earth,' Bryne said. 'There's a tractor car waiting in the gully at the foot of G-Corridor. That's its key. Torren keeps a close watch on all the Corridors, but the system's complex. Now and then by accident one of the wiring devices gets out of order. G-Corridor's out of order right now – not by accident. How do you like it, Fenton?'

Fenton laid the folded shirt into place, glanced at the money without expression. He was thinking rapidly, but his face showed nothing.

'What do you stand to gain, Bryne?' he asked. 'Or is this one of Torren's subtler schemes?'

'It's all mine,' the gaunt man assured him. 'I'm looking toward the future. I'm a very honest man, Fenton. Not direct – no. You can afford to be direct. I can't. I'm only an administrator. Torren's the boss. Some day you'll be boss. I'd like to go on being an administrator then, too.'

'Then this is by way of a bribe, is it?' Fenton inquired. 'Waste of time, Bryne. I'm stepping out. Torren's probably rewriting his will already. When I leave Ganymede I leave for good. As if you didn't know.'

'I know, all right. Naturally. I've already been notified to get out the old will. But I'll tell you, Fenton – I like administering Ganymede. I like being cupbearer to the gods. It suits me. I'm good at it. I want to go on.' He paused, giving Fenton a keen glance under the sandy lashes. 'How much longer do you think Torren has to live?' he inquired.

Fenton paused in his methodic packing. He looked at Bryne.

'Maybe a year,' Bryne answered his own question. 'Maybe less. In *his* condition he ought to be glad of it. I'm thinking about afterward. You and I understand each other, Fenton. I don't want to see the Torren holdings broken up. Suppose I keep the will that names you inheritor and tear up the new one Torren's going to make today? Would that be worth anything to you?'

Fenton looked out over the snow toward the turquoise valley where Kristin would be scattering yellow seeds into the furrows of the ploughed Ganymedan soil. He sighed. Then he stooped and picked up the money, the ticket and the key.

'You'll have to take my word for it,' he said, 'that it would be. But I wish I understood why you're really doing this. I thought you and Torren got along better than that.'

'Oh, we do. We get along fine. But – Fenton, he scares me. I don't know what makes him tick. Funny things are happening to the human race these days, Fenton.' Unexpected sincerity showed on the gaunt face in the doorway. 'Torren … Torren isn't human. A lot of people aren't human any more. The important people aren't.'

He swung a long arm toward the turquoise valley. 'The Threshold people are getting the upper hand, Fenton. I don't mean here. I don't mean literally. But *they're* the inheritors of the future, not us. I guess I'm jealous.' He grinned wryly. 'Jealous, and a little scared. I want to feel important. You and I are human. We may not like each other much, but we understand each other. We can work together.' He drew his shoulders together with a small shiver. 'Torren's a monster, not a man. You know it, now. I know why you quarreled. I'm glad of it.'

'I'll bet you are,' Fenton said.

When it was safe, he drove the tractor car down the gorge between high banks of snow, rolling as fast as he dared toward the turquoise valley. The Ganymedan landscape framed in the square window openings all around him looked like so many television images on square screens. Probably some of it really was framed upon screens', back there in the Unit whose mile-square walls fell farther and farther behind as the tractor treads ground on.

Proabably Torren's screen, tilted above the water bath, reflected some such landscape as this. But there were often tractor cars trundling along the snowy roads. Unless Torren had reason to suspect, he was not likely to focus too sharply upon this one. Still, Fenton knew he would feel more comfortable after he had passed beyond the range of the 'visor. Not that Torren couldn't summon up a picture of any Ganymedan area he happened to feel curious about. The thing was to keep his curiosity asleep, until the time came to rouse it.

The cold hills swung by. The heavy air swirled a little as the car spun along, making eddies like paradoxic heat waves between Fenton and the road. No man could live without an insulated suit and breathing-apparatus on the surface of Ganymede – yet. But the specially bred Ganymedans from the Threshold Planetarium could.

When men first reached the planets they found their thresholds fatally different from Earth. They began to alter the planets, and to alter the men. This after one whole wasted generation in which they tried to establish colonies that could be supported from Earth and could operate from artificial shelters. It didn't work. It never worked, even on Earth, when men tried to create permanent colonies in alien lands without subsisting on the land itself.

There is more to it than the lack of bread alone. Man must establish himself as a self-sustaining unit on the land he works, or he will not work it long. Neither humans nor animals can subsist or function efficiently on alien territory. Their metabolism is geared to a different ecology, their digestive organs demand a different food, melancholia and lassitude overcome them eventually. None of the great bonanza ventures on the mineral-rich planets ever came to a successful production because agriculture could not keep up with them and they collapsed of their own weight. It had been proved true time and again on Earth, and now on the planets the old truism repeated itself.

So the Threshold Planetaria were set up and the vast experiment got under way. And they altered the planets as well as the stock that was to possess them.

Ganymede was cold. The atmosphere of heavy gases could not sustain human life. So with atomic power and technological weapons man began to alter the ecology of Ganymede. Through the years the temperature crept gradually up from the deadly level of a hundred degrees below centigrade zero. Wastefully, desperately, the frozen water was released, until a cloud-blanket began to form over Ganymede to hold in the heat.

There were many failures. There were long periods of inactivity, when the insulated domes were deserted. But as new methods, new alloys, new isotopes were developed, the process became more and more practical. When the final generation of Ganymede-slanted stock was bred, Ganymede was ready for them.

Since then, three generations had become self-sustaining on the satellite. They could breathe the air – though men could not. They could endure the cold – though men could not. They were taller than men, solider and stronger. There were several thousand of them now.

As they had driven along a genetic parabola to meet the rising parabola of an altered planetary balance, so now the Ganymedans and Ganymede together followed a new curve. In a few more generations it would circle back to meet normal humanity. By that time, Ganymede should be habitable for Earthmen, and by then Ganymedans should have altered once more, back toward the norm.

Perhaps the plan was not the best possible plan. Humanity is not perfect. They made many errors, many false guesses, when the Age of Technology began. Balance of power among the nations of Earth influenced the development of the Threshold Planetaria. Social conflicts changed and shifted as civilization found new processes and methods and power-sources.

Fenton thought of Torren. Yes, there had been many errors of judgment. The children of Torren should have walked like giants upon a free planet. Centrifuge-bred colossi. But that experiment had failed. Not even upon tiny Ganymede could Torren use the tremendous strength inherent in his helpless body to stand upright.

It was easier to work eugenically with animals. In the new Ganymedan seas, still growing, and on the frigid Ganymedan continents, were creatures bred to breathe the atmosphere – arctic and subarctic creatures, walrus and fish, snow-rabbit and moose. Trees grew on Ganymede now, mutated tundra spread across the barrens, supplemented by the photosynthesis laboratories. A world was being born.

And across the world marched the heat-giving, life-giving towers built over a hundred-year period by the Earth government, still owned by Earth, not to be touched even by Torren, who owned Ganymede. Fenton swung the tractor over the brow of the hill and paused for an instant to look west. A new tower was rising there, one of hundreds, to supplement the old towers with a new method of speeding up changes. Within ten years these snowy hills might ripple with wheat—

The road forked here. One way led toward the valley. The other lay like a long blue ribbon across the hilltops, dipping suddenly as the horizon dipped toward the spaceport and the ship that was headed for home.

Fenton touched the scar on his cheek and looked at the spaceport road. Earth, he thought. And then? He thought of Bryne's wise, gaunt face, and of Torren wallowing in his water bed that was linked like the center of a spider's web with every quarter of the mile-square Unit and every section of the little globe it stood on. No, not a spider web – an island. A floating island with no link that bound him to humanity.

Fenton spoke one furious word and wrenched violently at the wheel. The car churned up snow in a blinding haze and then leaped forward along the right-hand road, down toward the turquoise mist that hid the valley.

An hour later he came to the village called Providence.

The houses were of local stone, with moss-thatched roofs. Early experiments with buildings of metal, plastics and imported wood had been discarded, as might be expected, in favor of indigenous materials. For life on Ganymede no houses proved quite so satisfying as houses built of Ganymede stone.

The people came mostly of hardy Norse stock, with Inuit and other strains mingled for the desirable traits. The Ganymedans who came out into the snow-powdered street when Fenton stopped his car were an entirely new race. An unexpectedly handsome race, since they had certainly not been bred for beauty. Perhaps much of their good looks sprang from their excellent health, their adjustment to their lives and their world, the knowledge that the world and the work they did upon it were both good and necessary. Until now.

A big yellow-haired man in furs bent to the window of the car, his breath clouding the heavy air which no normal human could breathe.

'Any luck, Ben?' he asked, his voice vibrating through the diaphragm set in the side of the car. It was only thus that a Ganymedan could speak to an Earth-born human. Their voices had to filter to each other through carbon dioxide air and metal and rubber plates. It meant nothing. There are higher barriers than these between human minds.

'About what you expected,' Fenton told him, watching the diaphragm vibrate when sound struck it. He wondered how his own voice sounded, out there in the cold air heavy-laden with gases.

Yellow heads and brown nodded recognition of what he meant. The tall people around the car seemed to sag a little, though two or three of them laughed shortly, and one big woman in a fur hood said:

'Torren's fond of you, Ben. He must be, after all. Maybe—'

'No,' Fenton told her positively. 'He's projected himself in my image, that's all. I can walk around. But I'm simply an extension, like an arm or a leg. Or an eye. And if Torren's eye offends him—'

He broke off abruptly, slapped the steering wheel a couple of times and looked ahead of him down the wide, clean street lined with clean, wide-windowed houses that seemed to spring from the rock they stood on. They were strong houses, built low to defy the blizzard winds of Ganymede. The clear, wide, snowy hills rolled away beyond the rooftops. It was a good world – for the Ganymedans. He tried to think of these big, long-striding people shut up in asylums while their world slowly changed outside the windows until they could no longer breathe its air.

'But, Ben,' the woman said, 'it isn't as if people *needed* Ganymede. I wish I could talk to him. I wish I understood—'

'Have you any idea,' Fenton asked, 'how much Torren spends in a year? People don't need living room on Ganymede, but Torren needs the money he could get if… oh, forget it. Never mind, Marta.'

'We'll fight,' Marta said. 'Does he know we'll fight?'

Fenton shook his head. He glanced around the little crowd.

'I'd like to talk to Kristin,' he said.

Marta gestured toward the slope that led down into the farmland valley.

'We'll fight,' she said again, uncertainly, as the car started. Fenton heard her and lifted a hand in salute, grinning without mirth or cheerfulness. He heard the man beside her speak as the car drew away.

'Sure,' the man said. 'Sure. What with?'

*

He knew Kristin as far as he could see her. He picked her figure out of the fur-clad group dark against the snow as they stepped out of the road to let the car go by. She waved as soon as she recognized him behind the glass. He drew the car to a halt, snapped on the heating units of the insulated suit he wore, closed the mask across his face and then swung the car door open. Even inside the mask his voice sounded loud as he called across the white stillness.

'Kristin,' he said. 'Come over here. The rest of you, go on ahead.'

They gave him curious glances, but they nodded and trudged on down the hill toward the valley. It seemed odd to watch them carrying hoes and garden baskets in the snow, but the valley was much warmer below the mist.

Kristin came toward him, very tall, moving with a swift, smooth ease that made every motion a pleasure to watch. She had warm yellow hair braided in a crown across her head. Her eyes were very blue, and her skin milk-white below the flush the cold had given it.

'Sit in here with me,' Fenton said. 'I'll turn off the atmosphere unit and leave the door open so you can breathe.'

She stooped under the low door and got in, folding herself into the too-small seat. Fenton always felt out of proportion beside these big, friendly, quiet people. It was their world, not his. If anyone were abnormal in size here, then it was he, not the Ganymedans.

'Well, Ben?' she said, her voice coming with a faint vibration through the diaphragm in his helmet. He smiled back at her and shook his head. He did not think he was in love with Kristin. It would be preposterous. They could not speak except through metal or touch except through glass and cloth. They could not even breathe the same air. But he faced the possibility of love, and grinned ironically at it.

He told her what had happened, exactly as it took place, and his mind began to clarify a little as he talked.

'I suppose I should have waited,' he said. 'I can see that, now. I should have kept my mouth shut until I'd been back on Ganymede at least a month, sounding things out. I guess I lost my temper, Kristin. If I'd only known, while I was still back on Earth ... if you could only have written—'

'Through the spaceport mail?' she asked him bitterly. 'Even the incoming letters are censored now.'

He nodded.

'So the planets will go on thinking we *asked* for the changeover,' she said. 'Thinking we failed on Ganymede and *asked* to be shut up in asylums. Oh, Ben, that's what we all hate worst of all. We're doing so wonderfully well here ... or we were, until—' She broke off.

Fenton touched the button that started his motor and turned the car around so they could look out across the broad plain below. They faced away from the Unit, and except for blurs of turquoise mist here and there where other warm valleys breathed out moisture and the exhalation of growing things there was no break in the broad sweep of snowy hills – the towers marching in a long row across the planet.

'Does he knew we'd die in the asylums?' Kristin asked.

'Would you?'

'I think we would. Many of us would. And I think we'd never have any more children. Not even the idea of having great-great-grandchildren who might be able to walk on Ganymede again would keep the race alive. We wouldn't kill ourselves, of course. We wouldn't even commit race-suicide. We won't want to die – but we won't want to live, either – in asylums.'

She twisted on the smooth car seat and looked anxiously at Fenton through the glass of his respirator.

'Ben, if the planets knew – if we could get word outside somehow – do you think they'd help? Would anyone care? I think some might. Not the Earth-bred, probably. They wouldn't really *know*. But the Thresholders would know. For their own safety, Ben, I think they might *have* to help us – if they knew. This could happen to any Threshold group on any world. Ben—'

A blue shadow gliding across the snow caught her eye and she turned her head to watch it.

Then concussion heeled the car over.

Dimly Fenton heard metal rip around him against rocks hidden under the snow they plowed through. In the echoing immobility while the vehicle hung poised, before it settled back, he tasted blood in his mouth and felt Kristin's weight heavy against his shoulder, saw the black outlines of his own hands with fingers spread, pressing the glass against the whiteness of snow.

The car smashed over the edge, jolting downward on its treads, down faster and more roughly with each jolt. The winged blue shadow wheeled back and sailed over them again.

The silhouetted hands moved fast. Fenton was aware of them turning, pulling, gripping numbly at levers they scarcely felt. The idling motor exploded into a roar and the car sprang forward, straight down the unbroken slope.

Then the second blast came.

The rear of the vehicle lifted, hurling Fenton and the girl against the cushioned panel and the thick, shatterproof windshield, which released its safeties under the impact and vanished in a whirl of brightness somewhere outside. The treads screamed as the car ground across the bare rock and snow boiled up in a whirlwind around them. The car shot forward again to the very edge of the slope and hung tottering over a hundred-foot drop beyond.

There was a timeless interval of what felt like free fall. Fenton had time to decide that his instinct had been right. The fall was the safer choice. The car's interior was braced and shock-absorbent, and they would survive a drop better than another bomb-hit.

Then they struck the ground, whirled out, struck again, in an increasing avalanche of ice and rock and snow. The shocks changed to the thunder of bombs, and then absolute darkness and silence without echo.

Neither of them could have survived alone. It took Kristin's Ganymedan strength and vitality and the resilience that had kept her from serious injury, plus Fenton's knowledge of mechanics and his fierce, devouring anger.

Buried thirty feet under a solid, freezing mass of debris, Fenton whipped the girl with words when even her hardiness began to fail. With one arm broken, he drove himself harder still, ignoring the shattered bone, working furiously against time. Enough air was trapped in the loose snow to supply Kristin, and Fenton's respirator and suit were tough enough to survive even such treatment as this.

The mercury-vapor turbine that generated the car's power had to be repaired and started anew. It took a long time. But it was done. What Fenton wanted was the tremendous thermal energy the exhaust would give them. Very slowly, very carefully, using a part of the turbine sheath as a shield, they burned their way to the open air.

Twice settling rock nearly crushed them. Once Kristin was pinned helpless by the edge of the shield, and only Fenton's rage got them through that. But they did get through. When only a crust remained, Fenton carefully opened small view-cracks in the shadow, and waited until he was sure no hovering helicopter still waited. Then they climbed free.

There were signs in the snow where a copter had landed and men had walked to the edge of the abyss, even climbed part of the way down.

'Who was it, Ben?' Kristin asked, looking down at the footprints. When he did not answer, 'Ben – your arm. How bad—'

He said abruptly, not listening to her: 'Kristin, I've got to get back to the Unit. Fast.'

'You think it was Torren?' she asked fearfully. 'But, Ben, what could you do?'

'Torren? Maybe. Maybe Byrne. I'm not sure. I've got to *be* sure. Help me, Kristin. Let's go.'

'To the village first, then,' she said firmly, setting her marble-hard forearm beneath his elbow to steady him. 'You'll never make it unless we patch you up first. Would Torren really do a thing like that to you, Ben?

The nearest thing to a son he'll ever have? I can't believe it.'

The dry snow squeaked underfoot as they climbed the hill.

'You don't know Torren,' Fenton said. He was breathing unevenly, in deep gasps, partly from pain, partly from weariness, mostly because the air in the respirator was not coming fully enough to supply his increased need. But the outer air was pure poison. After awhile he went on, the words laboring a little.

'You don't know what Torren did to me, thirteen years ago,' he said. 'Back on Earth. I was sixteen, and I wandered out one night in one of the old Dead Ends – the ruined cities, you know – and I got myself shanghaied. At least, that's what I thought for three years. One of the gangs who worked the ruins got me. I kept thinking Torren's men would find me and get me out. I was young and naive in those days. Well, they didn't find me. I worked with the gang. For three years I worked with them. I learned a lot. Things that came in handy afterward, on some of the jobs Torren had for me—

'When I was tough enough, I finally broke away. Killed three men and escaped. Went back to Torren. You should have heard him laugh.'

Kristin looked down at him, doubtfully. 'Should you be talking, Ben? You need your breath—'

'I want to talk, Kristin. Let me finish. Torren laughed. He'd engineered the whole thing. He wanted me to learn pro-survival methods right at the source. Things he couldn't teach me. So he arranged for me to learn from – experts. He felt that if I was capable I'd survive. When I knew enough, I'd escape. Then I'd be a tool he could really use. Work-hardening, he called it.'

Fenton was silent, breathing hard, until he got enough breath to finish. 'After that,' he said, 'I was Torren's right hand. His legs. His eyes. I was Torren. He'd put me into an invisible Planetarium, you see – a Centrifuge like the thing he grew up in, the thing that made him into a monster. That's why I understand him so well.' He paused for a moment, swiped vainly at the face-plate as if to wipe away the sweat that ran down his forehead. 'That's why I've got to get back,' he said. 'Fast.'

Only Torren knew all the secrets of the Unit. But Fenton knew many. Enough for his purpose now.

When the rising floor inside the column of the round shaft ceased its pressure against his feet, he stood quiet for a moment, facing the curved wall, drawing a deep breath. He grimaced a little as the breath disturbed his arm, splinted and strapped across his chest under his shirt. With his right hand he drew the loaded pistol from its holster and, swinging it from the trigger guard, used his thumb to find the spring hidden in the curved wall.

The spring moved. Instantly he swung the pistol up, the grip smacking into his receiving palm, his finger touching the trigger. The hollow pillar in which he stood slid half apart, and Fenton looked straight at Torren in his water bed.

He stood still then, staring.

The colossus had managed to heave himself up to a sitting position. The huge hands gripped the edge of the tank and, as Fenton watched, the great fingers curved with desperate fury on the padded rim. Torren's eyes were squeezed shut, his teeth bared and set, and the room was full of the sound of his harsh, wheezing breath.

The blind, gargoyle face hung motionless for an instant. Then Torren exhaled with a gasp and let go. There was a tremendous wallowing splash as the Protector of Ganymede plunged back into the water bed.

Fenton's gaze lowered to the long strip of floor beside the bath where a row of tiles had been lifted to expose the intricate complex of wires leading into the banked controls by which Torren ruled his palace and his planet. The wires lay severed on the floor, tangled fringes of them ripped and cut and torn out. It was almost as much a mutilation as if Torren's actual nerve-fibres had been torn. He was as helpless as if they had been.

There was a table set up a little distance from the bath. The key wires in the flooring snaked across the tiles toward the table. Upon it a control box had been set up, and the audio and video devices which were Torren's ganglia.

At the table, his profile to Fenton, Bryne sat, his long, thin body humped forward intently, the pale eyes fixed upon his work. He had a privacy-mute on the microphone he held to his mouth and as he murmured his fingers played lightly with a vernier. He watched the green line ripple and convulse across the face of an oscilloscope. He nodded. His hand struck down quickly at a switch, closed it, opened another.

'Bryne!' The breathless bellow from the tank echoed among the pillars, but Bryne did not even glance up. He must have heard that cry a good many times already, since this phase of his work began.

'Bryne!'

The shouted name mounted in a roar of sound up the well to the star-reflections far above and reverberated to a diminishing whisper that blended with Torren's heavy breathing. Again the huge hands slid futilely over the rim of the tank.

'Answer me, Bryne!' he roared. *'Answer me!'*

Bryne did not look up. Fenton took a step forward, onto the open floor. His eyes were hard and narrow. The blood had gone out of his face until the pale scar along his jaw was almost invisible. Torren, seeing him, gasped and was silent in the midst of another shout. The small eyes sunk in fat stared and then shut tight for an instant over a leap of strange, glancing lights.

'Why don't you answer him, Bryne?' Fenton asked in an even voice.

Bryne's hands opened with a sudden, convulsive gesture, letting the microphone fall. After a long moment he turned an expressionless face to Fenton. The pale eyes regarded the gun muzzle and returned to Fenton's face. His voice was expressionless, too.

'Glad to see you, Fenton,' he said. 'I can use your help.'

'Ben!' Torren cried, a thick gasp of sound. 'Ben, he's trying ... that ... that scum is trying to take over! He—'

'I suppose you realize,' Bryne said in a quiet voice, 'Torren sent a helicopter to bomb you when he found you were getting away from him. I'm glad he failed, Fenton. We're going to need each other.'

'Ben, I didn't!' Torren shouted. 'It was Bryne—'

Bryne picked up the microphone again, smiling thinly.

'It's going to be perfectly simple, with your help, Fenton,' he said, ignoring the heavy, panting gasps of the Protector in the tank. 'I see now I might have taken you into my confidence even more than I did. This was what I meant when I told you Torren hadn't very much longer to rule. The chance came sooner than I expected, that's all.'

'Ben!' Torren was breathing hard, but his voice was under more control now. He swallowed heavily and said: 'Ben, don't listen to him. Don't trust him. He ... he wouldn't even *answer* me! He wouldn't even pay any attention ... as though I were a ... a—' He gulped and did not finish. He was not willing to put any name to himself that came to his mind.

But Fenton knew what he meant. 'As though I were a ... monster. A puppet. A dead man.' It was the horror of utter helplessness that had disarmed Torren before Bryne. For thirty years he had sought and claimed power by every means at his command, driven himself and others ruthlessly to combat the deepest horror he knew – the horror of helplessness. It was that which frightened him – not the fear of death.

'Don't waste your sympathy, Fenton,' Bryne said, watching him. 'You know Torren better than I do. You know what he planned for you. You know how he's always treated you. When he saw you escaping, he sent the 'copter to make sure you wouldn't get away. He isn't human, Fenton. He hates human beings. He hates you and me. Even now he'll play on your sympathy until he gets you to do what he wants. After that ... well, you know what to expect.'

Torren shut his eyes again, not quite soon enough to hide the little glitter of confidence, perhaps of triumph, in them. In an almost calm voice he said: 'Ben, you'd better shoot him now. He's a plausible devil.'

'Just what are your plans, Bryne?' Fenton asked in a level voice.

'What you see.' Bryne's gaunt shoulders moved in a shrug. 'I'll pretend he's ill, at first. Too ill to see anyone but me. This is a Maskelyne vodor I've got here. I'm working out a duplicate of his voice. It's a *coup d'etat*, Fenton, nothing new. I've got everything planned thoroughly. I've done nine-tenths of the management of Ganymede for years now, anyhow. Nobody's going to wonder much. With your help, I can get the rest of the empire for us, too.'

'And what about me?' Torren demanded thickly.

'You?' The pale eyes flickered toward him and away. 'As long as you behave, I suppose you can go on living.' It was a lie. No falser statement of intent was ever spoken. You could tell it by the flat tone of his voice.

'And the Ganymedans?' Fenton asked.

'They're yours,' Bryne said, still flatly. 'You're the boss.'

'Torren?' Fenton turned his head. 'What do *you* say about the Ganymedans?'

'No,' Torren breathed. 'My way stands, Ben.' His voice was an organ whisper. 'My way or nothing. Make your choice.'

The slightest possible flicker of a smile twitched the corner of Fenton's lip. He swung his pistol higher and sent a bullet exploding straight into Bryne's face.

The gaunt man moved like lightning.

He must have had his farther hand on a gun for some seconds now, because the two explosions came almost as one. In the same instant he sent his chair clattering backward as he sprang to his feet.

He moved too fast. His aim was faulty because of his speed. The bullet whined past Fenton's ear and smacked into the pillar behind him. Fenton's shot struck Bryne an invisible blow in the shoulder that spun him half around, knocked him three-quarters off his feet. He scrambled desperately backward to regain his balance. His foot caught in a tangle of ripped-up wiring beside the water bath, and he went over backward in slow motion, his pale stare fixed with a strange illusion of calmness on Fenton's face as he fell.

For an instant he tottered on the brink of the bath. Then Torren chuckled a vast, deep, terrible chuckle and with tremendous effort lifted a hand far enough to seize Bryne by the wrist.

Still expressionless, still with that pale, intent stare fixed upon Fenton, Bryne went backward into the tank. There was a surge of heaving water. Bryne's suddenly convulsed limbs splashed a blinding spray and his hand groped out of nowhere for Torren's throat.

Fenton found himself running, without intending to or – he knew – needing to run. It was pure impulse to finish a job that needed finishing, though it was in better hands than his, now. He put his good hand on the rim of the huge tank, the revolver still gripped in it, leaning forward.

Bryne vanished under the oily, opaque surface. The incalculable weight of Torren's arm was like a millstone pressing him down, merciless, insensate as stone. After a while the thick, slow bubbles began to rise.

*

Fenton did not even see the motion Torren made. But when he tried to spring backward, it was too late. A vast, cold, slippery hand closed like iron over his. They wrestled unequally for several slow seconds. Then Torren's grip relaxed and Fenton stumbled back, swinging his half-crushed fingers, seeing his revolver all but swallowed up in Torren's enormous grasp.

Torren grinned at him.

Slowly, reluctantly, Fenton grinned back.

'You knew he was lying,' Torren said. 'About the bombs.'

'Yes, I knew.'

'So it's all settled, then,' Torren said. 'No more quarreling, eh, son? You've come back.' But he still held the revolver watchfully, his eyes alert.

Fenton shook his head.

'Oh, no. I came back, yes. I don't know why. I don't owe you a thing. But when the bombs fell I knew you were in trouble. I knew he'd never dare bomb me in sight of the 'visor screens as long as you had any power on Ganymede. I had to find out what was happening. I'll go, now.'

Torren hefted the revolver thoughtfully. 'Back to your Ganymedans?' he asked. 'Ben, my boy, I brought you up a fool. Be reasonable! What can you do for them? How can you fight me?' He rumbled with a sudden deep chuckle. 'Bryne thought I was helpless! Step over there, Ben. Switch on the 'visor.'

Watching him carefully, Fenton obeyed. The snowy hills outside sprang into view. Far off above them, tiny specks upon the blue-lit clouds, a formation of planes was just visible, humming nearer.

'About ten minutes more at the outside, I'd say,' Torren estimated. 'There are a lot of things about this set-up nobody even guesses except me. I wonder if Bryne really imagined I hadn't thought of every possibility. I allowed for this years and years ago. When my regular signals stopped going out an alarm went off – out there.' The huge head nodded. 'My guards would have got here in another ten minutes whether you came or not. Still, son, I'm obliged. You spared me that much time of feeling – helpless. You know how I hate it. Bryne could have killed me, but he could never have held me helpless very long. I owe you something, Ben. I don't like being obligated. Within reason, I'm willing to give you—'

'Nothing I want,' Fenton cut in. 'Only freedom for the Ganymedans, and that I'll have to take. You won't give it. I can take it, Torren. I think I know the way, now. I'm going back to them, Torren.'

The huge hand floating at the surface of the water turned the pistol toward Fenton.

'Maybe you are, son. Maybe not. I haven't decided yet. Want to tell me just how you plan to stop me on Ganymede?'

'There's only one way.' Fenton regarded the pistol with a grim smile. 'I can't fight you. I haven't any money or any influence. Nobody on Ganymede has except you. But the Ganymedans can fight you, Torren. I'll teach them. I learned guerrilla warfare in a hard school. I know all there is to know about fighting against odds. Go on and put your new towers up, Torren. But – try and keep them up! We'll blow them apart as fast as you can put them together. You can bomb us, but you can't kill us all – not soon enough, you can't.'

'Not soon enough – for what?' Torren demanded, the small eyes burning upon Fenton's. 'Who's going to stop me, son? I've got all the time there is. Ganymede belongs to *me!*'

Fenton laughed, almost lightly.

'Oh, no it doesn't. You lease it. But Ganymede belongs to the solar system. It belongs to the worlds and the people of the worlds. It belongs to your own people, Torren – the Thresholders who are going to inherit the planets. You can't keep the news of what's happening quiet here on Ganymede. The Earth government owns the towers. When we blow them over the government will step in to find out what goes on. The scandal will get out, Torren. You can't keep it quiet!'

'Nobody will care,' Torren grunted. But there was a new, strange, almost hopeful glint in his eyes. 'Nobody's going to war over a little satellite like Ganymede. Nobody has any stake here but me. Don't be childish, Ben. People don't start wars over an ideal.'

'It's more than an ideal with the Thresholders,' Fenton said. 'It's their lives. It's their future. And *they're* the people with power, Torren – not the Earth-bred men like me. The Thresholders are the future of the human race, and they know it, and Earth knows it. The new race on Mars with the three-yard chest expansions, and the new people on Venus with gills and fins may not look much like the Ganymedans, but they're the same species, Torren. *They'll* go to war for the Ganymedans if they have to. It's their own hides at stake. Ideals don't come into it. It's survival, for the Thresholders. Attack one world and you attack all worlds where Thresholders live. No man's an island, Torren – not even you.'

Torren's breath came heavily in his tremendous chest.

'Not even me, Ben?'

Fenton laughed and stepped backward toward the open pillar. On the screen the planes were larger now, nearer and louder.

'Do you know why I was so sure you hadn't ordered those bombs to kill me?' he asked, reaching with his good hand for the open door. 'For the same reason you won't shoot me now. You're crazy, Torren. You know you're crazy. You're two men, not one. And the other man is me. You hate society because of the debt it owes you. Half of you hates all men, and the Ganymedans most of all, because they're big like you, but they can walk like men. Their experiment worked and yours failed. So you hate them. You'll destroy them if you can.'

He found the door, pushed it open wide. On the threshold he said:

'You didn't adopt me on a whim, Torren. Part of your mind knew exactly what it was doing. You brought me up the hard way. My life was spent in a symbolic Centrifuge, just like yours. I *am* you. I'm the half that doesn't hate the Ganymedans at all. I'm the half that knows they're *your* people, the children you might have had, walking a free world as yours would have walked if your experiment had come out right, like theirs. I'll fight for them, Torren. In a respirator and mask, but I'll fight. That's why you'll never kill me.'

Sighing, Torren tilted the pistol. His thick finger squeezed itself inside the guard, began slowly to tighten upon the trigger. Slowly.

'Sorry, son,' he said, 'but I can't let you get away with it.'

Fenton smiled. 'I said you were crazy. You won't kill me, Torren. There's been a fight going on inside you ever since you left the Centrifuge – until now. Now it's going on outside, in the open. That's a better place. As long as I'm alive, I'm your enemy and yourself. Keep it on the outside, Torren, or you *will* go mad. As long as I'm alive I'll fight you. But as long as I'm alive, you're not an island. It's *your* battle I'm fighting. You'll do your best to defeat me, Torren, but you won't kill me. You won't dare.'

He stepped back into the pillar, groping for the spring to close the door. His eyes met Torren's confidently.

Torren's teeth showed under grimacing lips.

'You know how I hate you, Ben,' he said in a thick, fierce voice. 'You've always known!'

'I know,' Fenton said, and touched the spring. The door slid shut before him. He was gone.

Torren emptied the revolver with a sort of wild deliberation at the unmarred surface of the pillar, watching the bullets strike and richochet off it one by one until the hall was full of their whining and the loud explosions of the gun. The pillar stood blank and impervious where Fenton's face had been.

When the last echo struck the ceiling Torren dropped the gun and fell back into his enormous tank, caught his breath and laughed, tentatively at first and then with increasing volume until great billows of sound rolled up the walls and poured between the pillars toward the stars. Enormous hands flailed the water, sending spray high. The vast bulk wallowed monstrously, convulsed and helpless with its laughter.

On the screen the roar of the coming planes grew until their noise swallowed up even Torren's roaring mirth.

THE CODE

Through the parlor windows Dr. Bill Westerfield could see the village street, with laden branches hanging low above the blue-shadowed snow. The double tracks of tires diminished in the distance. Peter Morgan's sleek sedan was parked by the curb, and Morgan himself sat opposite Bill, scowling into his coffee cup.

Bill Westerfield watched a few flakes of snow making erratic pseudo-Brownian movements in the winter twilight. He said under his breath, *'Now is the winter of our discontent—'*

Morgan moved his heavy shoulders impatiently and drew his heavy black brows closer together. 'Yours?'

'His.' Both men looked up, as though their vision could pierce wood and plaster. But no sound came from upstairs, where old Rufus Westerfield lay in the big walnut bed carved with grapes and pineapples. He had slept and wakened in that same bed for seventy years, and he had expected to die in it. But it was not death that hovered above him now.

'I keep expecting Mephistopheles to pop up through a star trap and demand somebody's soul,' Bill said. '*His* discontent ... *my* discontent ... I don't know. It's going too smoothly.'

'You'd feel better if there were a price tag hanging on the bedpost, would you? "One Soul, Prepaid."'

Bill laughed. 'Logic implies somebody has to pay. Energy must be expended to do work. That's the traditional price, isn't it? Youth restored at the cost of Faustus' soul.'

'So it's really thaumaturgy after all?' Pete Morgan inquired, pulling down the corners of his heavy mouth until the lines standing deep made his face look a little Mephistophelian after all. 'I've been thinking all along I was an endocrinologist.'

'O.K., O.K. Maybe that was how Mephisto did it too. Anyhow, it works.'

Upstairs the nurse's heels sounded briefly on bare boards, and there was a murmur of voices, one light, one flat with age but echoing now with an undertone of depth and vibration that Bill Westerfield remembered only vaguely, from his boyhood.

'It works,' agreed Pete Morgan, and rattled the coffee cup in its saucer. 'You don't sound too happy. Why?'

Bill got up and walked down the room without answering. At the far end he hesitated, then swung around and came back with a scowl on his thin face to match Morgan's black-browed saturninity.

'There's nothing wrong about reversing the biological time-flow – if you can,' he declared. 'Father hasn't got his eye on a Marguerite somewhere. He isn't doing it for selfish reasons. We aren't tampering with the Fountain of Youth because we want glory out of it, are we?'

Morgan looked at him under a thicket of black brows. 'Rufus is a guinea pig,' he said. 'Guinea pigs are notoriously selfless. We're working for posterity ourselves, and a halo after we're dead. Is that what you want me to say? Is there something the matter with you, Bill? You've never been squeamish before.'

Bill went down the room again, walking quickly as if he wanted to get to the far end before his mind changed. When he came back he was holding a framed photograph.

'All right, look here.' He thrust it out roughly. Morgan put down his cup and held the frame up to the light, squinting at the pictured face. 'That was Father ten years ago,' Bill said. 'When he was sixty.'

In silence Morgan looked long and steadily at the photograph. Upstairs they could hear faintly in the stillness how the carved bed creaked as Rufus Westerfield moved upon it. He moved more easily now than he had done a month ago, in the depth of his seventy years. Time was flowing backward for old Rufus. He was nearing sixty again.

Morgan lowered the photograph and looked up at Bill.

'I see what you mean,' he said deliberately. 'It isn't the same man.'

Biological time is a curious, delusive thing. It is no quirk of imagination that makes a year seem endless to the child and brief to the grandfather. To a child of five a year *is* long, a fifth of his whole life. To a man of fifty, it represents only a fiftieth. And the thing is not wholly a matter of the imagination. It links inescapably into the physical make-up of a man, in a sort of reverse ratio. In youth the bodily processes are demonstrably as much faster as the time-sense is slower. The fetus, during gestation, races through a million years of evolution; the adolescent in ten years' time covers an aging process that will take him another fifty years of slowing change to equal. The young heal rapidly; the old sometimes never heal. Dr. du Nouy in his *Biological Time* plunges even deeper than this into the mysteries of youth and age, speculating on the private time universe in which each of us lives alone.

Rufus Westerfield was groping his way slowly backward through his.

Another experimenter, a Dr. Francois this time, had given the clue which he was following, as Theseus followed another sort of clue through the labyrinthine ways where the Minotaur lurked in hiding. Dr. Francois trained subjects to tap a telegraph key three hundred times a minute in their normal state. Then he applied heat and cold, gently, not to distract his subjects. And heat shortened their appreciation of time. The key tapped faster. Academically speaking they were older when warmth surrounded them. In the cold, time ran slower, like the long days of youth.

It had not, of course, been as simple as all that. The cardiac and vascular systems of the human machine needed powerful stimulus; the liver had almost ceased to build red cells. For these time could not turn backward without help. And there had been hypnosis, too. Seventy years of habit-patterns took a lot of erasing, and more esoteric matters than these had to be dealt with. The awareness of time itself, flowing soundlessly past in a stream that moved faster and faster as it neared the brink.

'It isn't the same man,' Morgan repeated without emotion, his eyes on Bill's face. Bill jerked his shoulders irritably.

'Of course it's the same man. It's Father at sixty, isn't it? Who else could it be?'

'Then why did you show it to me?'

Silence.

'The eyes,' Bill said carefully after awhile. 'They're ... a little different. And the slope of the forehead. And the angle of the cheek isn't ... well, not quite the same. But you can't say it isn't Rufus Westerfield.'

'I'd like to compare them,' Morgan said practically. 'Shall we go up?'

The nurse was closing the bedroom door behind her as they reached the stair head.

'He's asleep,' she mouthed silently, her glasses glittering at them. Bill nodded, stepping past her to push the door soundlessly open.

The room inside was big and bare with an almost monastic simplicity that made the ornately carved bed incongruous. A night light glowing on a table near the door cast long humped shadows upward on walls and ceilings, like shadows cast by a fire that has burned low. The man in the bed lay quiet, his eyes closed, his thin, lined face and thin nose austere in the dimness.

They crossed the floor silently and stood looking down. Shadows softened the face upon the pillow, giving it an illusion of the youth to come. Morgan held the photograph up to catch what light there was, his lips pursed under the black mustache as he studied it. This was, of course, the same man. There could be no possibility of error. And superficially the two faces were identical. But basically—

Morgan bent his knees a little and stooped to catch the angle of forehead and cheek as the photograph showed it. He stood stooping for a full minute, looking from face to photograph. Bill watched anxiously.

Then Morgan straightened, and as he rose the old man's eyelids rose too. Rufus Westerfield lay there looking up at them without moving. The night light caught in his eyes, making them very black and very bright. They looked sardonic, all that was alive in the weary face, but young and wise and amused.

For a moment no one spoke; then the eyes crinkled in slanting enjoyment, and Rufus laughed, a thin, high laugh that was older than his years. Senility sounded in the laugh, and a man of sixty should not be senile. But after the first cracked cackle the sound deepened slightly and was no longer old. His voice was liable, at this stage, to break into senility as an adolescent's breaks into maturity. The adolescent break is normal, and perhaps Rufus' break was normal too, in a process that created its own norm because it was as yet unique in human history.

'You boys want something?' inquired Rufus.

'Feel all right?' Morgan asked.

'I feel ten years younger,' Rufus grinned. 'Anything wrong, son? You look—'

'No, not a thing.' Bill smoothed the frown off his face. 'Almost forgot your shots. Pete and I were talking—'

'Well, hurry up. I'm sleepy. I'm growing fast, you know. Need sleep.' And he laughed again, no cackle in the sound this time.

Bill went out hastily. Morgan said, 'You're growing, all right. And it does take energy. Have a good day?'

'Fine. You going to unlearn me any this evening?'

Morgan grinned. 'Not exactly. I want you to' do a little … thinking … though. After Bill's finished.'

Rufus nodded. 'What's that under your arm? The frame looks familiar. Anyone I know?'

Morgan glanced down automatically at the photograph he was holding, the face hidden. Bill, coming in at that moment with the nurse behind him, saw the old man's brilliant, quizzical stare, and Morgan's eyes shift away from it.

'No,' said Morgan. 'Nobody you'd know.'

Bill's hand shook a little. The hypodermic he was carrying, point up, trembled so that the drop upon its needle spilled over and ran down the side.

'Steady,' Rufus said. 'You nervous about something, son?'

Carefully Bill did not meet Morgan's gaze. 'Not a thing. Let's have your arm, Father.'

After the nurse had gone Morgan pulled a stump of candle from his pocket and set it upon Rufus' bedside table. 'Put out the night light, will you?' he said to Bill as he held a match to the wick. Yellow flame bloomed slowly in the dimness.

'Hypnosis,' Rufus said, squinting at the flicker.

'Not yet, no. I'm going to talk. Look at the flame, that's all.'

'That's hypnosis,' Rufus insisted in an argumentative voice.

'It makes you more receptive to suggestion. Your mind has to be liberated enough so you can … see … time.'

'Mm-m.'

'All right – not see it, then. Sense it, feel it. Realize it as a tangible thing.'

'Which it isn't,' Rufus said.

'The Mad Hatter managed.'

'Sure. And look what happened to him.'

Morgan chuckled. 'I remember. It was always teatime. You don't need to worry about that. We've done this before, you know.'

'I know you say we have. I'm not supposed to remember.' Rufus' voice imperceptibly had begun to soften. His gaze was on the flame, and its reflection wavered in miniature in his eyes.

'No. You never remember. You'll forget all about this, too. I'm talking to a level of your mind that lies beneath the surface. The work goes on down there, in the quiet, just as the shots you're getting work in secret inside your body. You're listening, Rufus?'

'Go ahead,' Rufus said drowsily.

'We must shatter the temporal idols in your mind that stand between you and youth. Mental energy is powerful. The whole fabric of the universe is energy. You've been conditioned to think you grow old because of time, and this is a false philosophy. You must learn to discount it. Your belief acts upon your body, as the adrenals react to fear or anger. It's possible to set up a conditioned reflex so that the adrenals will respond under a different stimulus. And you must be conditioned to reverse time. The body and the mind react inseparably, one upon the other. Metabolism controls the mind, and the mind governs the metabolism. These are the two faces of a single coin.'

Morgan's voice slowed. He was watching the flicker of the reflected light shining beneath the old man's lids. The lids were heavy.

'A single coin—' echoed Rufus' voice, very low.

'The life processes of the body,' said Morgan in a monotone, 'are like a river that flows very swiftly at its source. But it slows. It runs slower and slower into age. There's another river, though, the awareness of time, and that stream runs with an opposite tempo. In youth it's so slow you don't even guess it's moving. In age, it's a Niagara. That is the stream, Rufus, that's going to carry you back. It's rushing by you now, deep and swift. But you've got to be aware of it, Rufus. Once you recognize it, nothing can stop you. You must learn to know time.'

The monotone droned on.

Fifteen minutes later, downstairs, Morgan set the photograph of Rufus at sixty upon the mantelpiece and regarded it with a heavy scowl.

'All right,' he said. 'Let's have it.'

Bill fidgeted. 'What is there to say? We're doing something so new we have no precedent. Father's changing, Pete – he's changing in ways we didn't expect. It worries me. I wish we hadn't had to use him for a guinea pig.'

'There was no choice, and you know it. If we'd used up ten years of testing and experiment—'

'I know. He couldn't have lasted six months when we started. He knew it was risky. He was willing to chance it. I know all that. But I wish—'

'Now be reasonable, Bill. How the devil could we experiment except on a human subject, and a man with a high I.Q. at that? You know I tried it with chimps. But we'd have had to evolve them into humans first. After all, in the last analysis it's the intelligence factor that makes the trick possible. It's lucky your father's breakdown was purely physical.' He paused, looking again at the photograph. 'About this, though—'

Bill spread his hands with a distracted motion. 'I'd thought of every possible chance of error – except this one.' He laughed wryly. 'It's crazy. It isn't happening.'

'The whole thing's crazy as a bedbug. I still don't believe it's working. If Rufus is really back to sixty already, then anything can happen. It wouldn't surprise me if the sun came up from California tomorrow.' Morgan fished in his pocket and brought out a cigarette. 'All right, then,' he said, fumbling for a match, 'so he doesn't look exactly as he did ten years ago. Does he act the way he did then?'

Bill shrugged. 'I don't know. I wasn't taking notes in those days. How was I to guess what you and I'd be up to now?' He paused. 'No, I think he doesn't,' he said.

Morgan squinted at him through smoke. 'What's wrong?'

'Little things. That look in his eyes when he woke awhile ago, for instance. Did you notice? A sort of sardonic brightness. He takes things less seriously. He ... just doesn't match his face any more. That austere look ... it used to suit him. Now when he wakes suddenly and looks at you, he's ... well, looking out of a mask. The mask's changing ... some. I know it's changing. The photograph proves that. But it isn't changing as fast as his mind.'

Deliberately Morgan blew smoke out in a long, swirling plume. 'I wouldn't worry too much,' he said soothingly. 'He'll never be the same man he was ten years ago, you know. We aren't erasing his memory. Maybe he mellowed more than you realize in the decade he's just retracted. At forty, at thirty, he'll still be a man who's lived seventy-odd years. It won't be the same mind or the same man that existed in the Eighties. You're just getting a case of the jitters, my boy.'

'I'm not. His face has changed! His forehead angle's different!' His nose is beginning to arch up a little. His cheekbones are higher than they ever were in his life. I'm not imagining that, am I?'

Morgan blew a leisurely ring.

'Don't get excited. We'll check the shots. Maybe he's getting an overdose of something. You know how that can affect the bony structure. There's no harm done, anyhow. His physical condition is good and getting better. His mind's keen. I'm more worried about you than him right now, Bill.'

'About me?'

'Yeah. Something you said before we went upstairs. Something about Faust. Remember? Now, just what did you have in mind?'

Bill looked guilty. 'I don't remember.'

'You were talking morals. You seemed to think there might be some punishment from on high hanging over us if our motives weren't pure. How about that?'

Bill's tone was defensive, if his words were not. 'You know better than to sneer at tradition just because it's smart to. You were the one who convinced me that the old boys knew more than they ever passed on. Remember how the alchemists wrote their formulas in code to sound like magical spells? "Dragon's Blood," for instance, meant something like sulphur. Translated, they often made very good sense. And the Fountain of Youth wasn't water by accident. That was purely symbolic. Life rose from the water—' He hesitated. 'Well, the moral code may have had just as solid a basis. What I said was that energy has to be expended to accomplish anything. Mephistopheles didn't do any work; a demon has power at his birthright. Faust had to expand the energy. In the code of the formula – his soul. It all makes sense except in the terms they used.'

Morgan's heavy brows met above his eyes. 'Then you think someone's got to pay. Who and what?'

'How do I know? There wasn't any glossary in the back of the book to show what Marlowe meant when he put down "soul." All I can say is we're repeating, in effect, the same experiment Faust went through. And Faust had to pay, somehow, in some coin or other that we'll never know. Or' – he looked up suddenly with a startled face – 'will we?'

Morgan showed his teeth and said something rude.

'All right, all right. Just the same, we're doing a thing without any precedent but one, unless—' He hesitated. 'Wait a minute. Maybe there was more than one. Or was it just a coincidence?'

Morgan watched him mouthing soundless phrases, and said after a moment, '*Are* you crazy?'

'Full fathoms five thy father lies,' Bill recited. 'How about that?

'Of his bones are coral made,
  These are pearls that were his eyes,

Nothing of him that doth fade
  But doth suffer a sea change
  Into something rich and strange—'

Morgan snorted. 'Forget that and go on. What about precedent?'

'Well, say there's only been one, then. But there was that. And it won't hurt us to take as much advantage as we can of what our predecessors learned. We can't take very much. It's all hidden in legend and code. But we do know that whoever Mephistopheles and Faust really were, and whatever means they used to get where we are now, they had trouble. The experiment seemed to succeed, up to a point – and then it blew up in their faces. Legend says Faust lost his soul. What that really means I don't know. But I say our own experiment is showing the first faint symptoms of getting out of hand, and *I* say we may find out some day what that code really means. I don't want to learn at Father's expense.'

'I'm sorry.' Morgan ground out his half-finished cigarette. 'Is it any good my saying I think you're letting your imagination run away with you? Or have you got me cast as Mephistopheles?'

Bill grinned. 'I doubt if you want his soul. But you know, in the old days you'd have got into trouble. There's something a little too ... too thaumaturgical about hypnotism. Especially about the kind of thing you put Rufus through.' He sobered. 'You have to send his mind out – somewhere. What does he find there, anyhow? What does time look like? How does it feel to stand face to face with it?'

'Oh, cut it out, Bill. Worry about your own mind, not Rufus'. He's all right.'

'Is he, Mephisto? Are you sure? Do *you* know where his mind goes when you send it out like that?'

'How could I? Nobody knows. I doubt if Rufus knows himself, even in his dreams. But it works. That's all that matters. There's no such thing as time, except as we manufacture it.'

'I know. It doesn't exist. But Rufus has seen it. Rufus knows it well. Rufus – and Faust.' Bill looked up at the picture on the mantelpiece.

Spring came early that year. Rains sluiced away the last of the snow, and the long curved street outside the Westerfield windows began to vanish behind frothing green leaves. In the familiar cycle winter gave way to spring, and for the first time in recorded history a man's wintertime of life came round again to his own improbable spring.

Bill could not think of him any more as *father*. He was Rufus Westerfield now, a pleasant stranger to look at, though memory had kept pace with his retrogression and no lapse of awareness made him a stranger to talk to.

He was a healthy, vigorous, handsome stranger to the eye, though. Flesh returned solidly to fill out the aesthetic, fine-drawn body that Bill remembered. It did not seem to him that his father had been so physically solid a man in his earlier youth, but he was, of course, receiving medical care now far in advance of what had been available to him then. And as Morgan pointed out, the intention had not been to recapture a facsimile of the Rufus of an earlier day, but simply to restore the old Rufus' lost strength.

The facial changes were what mystified them most. Bodily a man may change through perfectly normal causes, but the features, the angles of forehead and nose and chin, ought to remain constant. With Rufus they had not.

'We're getting a changeling in reverse,' Morgan admitted.

'A few months ago,' Bill pointed out, 'you were denying it.'

'Not at all. I was denying the interpretation you put on it. I still deny that. There are good reasons behind the changes, good solid reasons that haven't got a thing to do with thaumaturgy or adventures in hypnosis, or pacts with the devil, either. We just haven't found out yet what causes the changes.'

Bill shrugged. 'The strangest thing is that he doesn't seem to know.'

'There's a great deal, my friend, that he doesn't seem to know.'

Bill looked at him thoughtfully. 'That's got to wait.' He hesitated. 'We can't afford to tamper much with … with discrepancies of the mind, when we aren't sure about the body yet. We don't want to bring anybody else in on this unless we have to. It wouldn't be easy to explain to a psychiatrist what's behind these aberrations of his.'

'There are times,' Morgan said, 'when I wish we hadn't decided to keep quiet about all this. But I suppose we hadn't any choice. Not until we can put down Q.E.D., anyhow.'

'There's plenty to be done before that. If we ever can. If the stream isn't too strong for us, Pete.'

'Cold feet again? He'll stop at thirty-five, don't worry. One more series of shots, then say another month to strike a glandular balance, and he'll start back to age with the rest of us. If he weren't your father, you wouldn't jitter about the whole thing this way.'

'Maybe not. Maybe I wouldn't.' Bill's voice was doubtful.

They were in the living room again, on a morning in May. And as Morgan looked up to speak, the door opened and Rufus Westerfield, aged forty, came into the room.

He was handsome in the solid, sleek manner of early middle age. His hair had returned to rich dark-red, growing peaked above tilting brows. The black eyes tilted too, in shallow sockets, and there was a look in them entirely strange to any Westerfield who had ever borne the name before. The face and the thoughts behind it were equally alien to the Westerfields. But it was a subtle change. He had not noticed it himself.

He was whistling as he came into the room.

'Beautiful morning,' he said happily. 'Beautiful world. You youngsters can't appreciate it. Takes a man who's been old to enjoy youth again.' And he put the curtains aside to look out on the new leaves and the freshness of May.

'Rufus,' said Morgan abruptly, 'what's that tune?'

'What tune?' Rufus slanted a surprised black glance over his shoulder.

'You're whistling it. You tell me.'

Rufus frowned thoughtfully. 'I dunno. An old one.' He whistled another bar or two, strange, almost breathless swoops of sound. 'You ought to know it – very popular in its day. The words—' He paused again, the black eyes narrow, looking into infinity as he searched his memory. 'On the tip of my tongue. But I can't quite – Foreign words, though. Some light opera or other. Oh well – catchy thing.' He whistled the refrain again.

'I don't think it's catchy,' Bill declared flatly. 'No melody. I can't follow the tune at all, if it's got one.' Then he caught Morgan's eye, and was silent.

'What does it make you think of?' Morgan pursued. 'I'm curious.'

Rufus put his hands in his pockets and regarded the ceiling. 'My young days,' he said. 'That what you mean? Theater parties, lights and music. A couple of other young fellows I used to see a lot. There was a girl, too. Wonder whatever became of her – probably an old woman now. Her name was—' He hesitated. 'Her name was—' He shaped the name with lips, or tried to. Then an extraordinary expression crossed his face and he said, 'You know, I can't remember at all. It was something outlandish, like—' He tried again to shape with his lips a word that refused to come. 'I *know* the name, but I can't say it,' he declared fretfully. 'Is that a psychic block or something, Pete? Well, I daresay it doesn't matter. Funny, though.'

'I wouldn't worry. It'll come to you. Was she pretty?'

A slightly muzzy look crossed Rufus' face. 'She was lovely, lovely. All … spangles. I wish I could remember her name. She was the first girl I ever asked to … to—' He paused again, then said, '—to marry me?' in a thin, bewildered voice. 'No, that's not right. That's not right at all.'

'It sounds terrible,' Morgan remarked dryly. Rufus shook his head violently.

'Wait. I'm all mixed up. I can't quite remember what they … what was—' His voice faltered and died away. He stared out the window in an agony of concentration, his lips moving again as he struggled for some reluctant memory. Morgan heard him murmur, 'Neither marriage nor giving in marriage … no, that's not it—'

In a moment he turned back again, looking bewildered and shaking his head. There was a fine beading of sweat on his forehead, and his eyes for the first time had lost their look of sardonic confidence. 'There's something wrong,' he said simply.

Morgan stood up. 'I wouldn't worry,' he soothed. 'You're still going through some important changes, remember. You'll get straightened out after awhile. When you, do remember, let me know. It sounds interesting.'

Rufus wiped his forehead. 'That's a funny feeling – getting your memories twisted. I don't like it. The girl ... it's all confused—'

Bill, from a far corner of the room, said:

'I thought mother was your first love, Rufus. That's the story we always heard.'

Rufus gave him a dazzled look. 'Mother? Mother? Oh, you mean Lydia. Why, yes, she was, I think—' He paused for a moment then shook his head again. 'Thought I had it that time. Something you said about – mother, that's it. I was thinking of mine. Are those pictures you've got there, Bill? Maybe I could remember whatever it is that's bothering me if I saw—'

'Grandma's picture? It's just what I was hunting. I suddenly had an idea that you might ... uh ... be getting more like her side of the family as you grow younger. Don't know why I never thought of that before. Here she is.' He held up a yellowed metal rectangle, a tintype framed in plush. He scowled at it. 'No. She's nothing like you at all. I hoped—'

'Let me see it.' Rufus held out his hand. Something very strange happened then. Bill laid the tintype in his father's palm, and Rufus lifted it and looked into the shadowy features of the picture. And almost in the same motion he cried violently, 'No! No, that's ridiculous!' and hurled the thing to the floor. It bounced once, with a tinny sound, and lay face down on the bare boards.

Nobody spoke. The silence was tense for half a minute. Then Rufus said in a perfectly reasonable voice, 'Now what made me do that?'

The other two relaxed just perceptibly, and Morgan said, 'You tell us. What did?'

Rufus looked at him, the tilted black eyes puzzled. 'It was just ... wrong, somehow. Not what I expected. Not at *all* what I expected. But what I did expect I couldn't tell you now.' He sent a distracted glance about the room. The window caught his eye and he looked out at the pattern of leaves and branches beyond the porch. 'That looks wrong to me,' he added helplessly. 'Out there. I don't know why, but when I see it suddenly I know it isn't right. It's the first glance that does it. Afterward, I can tell it's just the way it's always been. But just for a minute—' He drew his shoulders together in a shrug of discomfort, and grimaced at the two men appealingly. 'What's wrong with me, boys?'

Neither of them answered for a moment, then both spoke together.

'Nothing to worry about,' Bill said, and Morgan declared in the same breath:

'Your memory hasn't caught up with your body yet, that's all. It's nothing that won't straighten out in a little while. Forget it as much as you can.'

'I'll try.' Rufus sent a bewildered look about the room again. For a moment he seemed not only a stranger to the house and the street outside, but a stranger to his own body. He looked so sleek and handsome, so solidly assured of his place in the world. But there was nothing but bewilderment behind the facade.

'I think I'll take a walk,' he said, and turned toward the door. On the way he stooped and picked up the tintype of his mother's face, pausing for an instant to look again at the unfamiliar picture. He shook his head doubtfully and laid the tintype down again. 'I don't know,' he said. 'I just don't know.'

When the door had closed behind him, Morgan looked at Bill and whistled a long, soft note.

'Well, you'd better get the record book,' he said. 'We ought to put it all down before we forget it.'

Bill glanced at him unhappily and went out of the room without a word. When he came back, carrying the big flat notebook in which they had been keeping, detail by detail, the record of their work, he was scowling.

'Do you realize how impossible all that was?' he asked. 'Rufus wasn't remembering *his* past. He never had a past like that. Forgetting all the other aberrations, the thing isn't possible. He grew up in a Methodist minister's household. He believed theaters were houses of sin. He's often told me he never set his foot inside one until long after he was married. He couldn't have known a girl who was – all spangles. He never had any affairs – Mother was his first and last love. He's told me that often. And he was telling the truth. I'm sure he was.'

'Maybe he led a double life,' Morgan suggested doubtfully. 'You know the proverbs about preachers' sons.'

'Anybody but Rufus. It just isn't in character.'

'Do you *know?*'

Bill looked at him. 'Well, I've always understood that Rufus was—'

'Do you know? Or is it hearsay evidence? You weren't there, were you?'

'Naturally,' Bill said with heavy irony, 'I wasn't around before I was born. It's just possible that up to that time Rufus was a black magician or Jack the Ripper or Peter Pan. If you want to go nuts, you can build up a beautiful theory that the world didn't exist until I was born, and you can make it stick because nobody can disprove it. But we're not dealing with blind faith. We're dealing with logic.'

'What kind of logic?' Morgan wanted to know. He looked gloomy and disturbed.

'My kind. Our kind. *Homo sapiens* logic. Or are you implying that Rufus—' He let the thought die.

Morgan picked it up. 'I'm willing to imply. Suppose Rufus *was* different when he was young.'

'Two heads?' Bill said flippantly. And after a pause, in a soberer voice, 'No, you've got the wrong pig by the tail. I see your point. That there might be … some biological difference, some mutation in Rufus that ironed itself out as he grew older. But your theory breaks down. Rufus lived in this town most of his life. People would remember if he'd … had two heads.'

'Oh. Yeah, of course. Well, then … it could have been subtler. Something not even Rufus knew about. Successful minor mutations aren't noticed, because they *are* successful. I mean … a different, more efficient metabolic rate, or better optical adjustment. A guy with slightly super vision wouldn't be apt to realize it, because he'd take it for granted everybody else had the same kind of eyes. And, naturally, he wouldn't ever need to go to an optometrist, because his eyes would be *good*.'

'But Rufus has had eye tests,' Bill said. 'And every other kind. We gave him a complete check-up. He was normal.'

Morgan sampled his lower lip and apparently didn't like it. 'He was when we ran the tests, yes. But back in the Nineties? All I'm saying is, it's not inconceivable that he started out with some slight variations from the norm which may have been adjusted even by the time he reached adolescence. But the potentialities were there, like disease germs walled off behind healthy tissue, waiting for a lowering of resistance to break out again. Maybe that happens oftener than we know. Maybe it happens to nearly everybody. We do know that for every child that's born there've been many conceptions that would have produced nonviable fetuses if they'd gone to full term. These are discarded too early to be recognized. Maybe even in normal children adjustments have to be made sometimes before the adolescent perfectly fits into our pattern. And when something as revolutionary as what we did to Rufus takes place, the weak spots in the structure – the places where adjustments were made – break down again. Or say the disease germs are turned loose and rebuild the old disease. I'm mixing my metaphors. There isn't any perfect analogy. Am I making sense at all?'

'I wish you weren't,' Bill said uncomfortably. 'I don't like it.'

'All we can do is guess, at this stage. Guess – and wait. We can't tell without a control, and we haven't got any control. There's only Rufus. And—'

'And Rufus is changing,' Bill finished for him. 'He's changing into someone else.'

'Don't talk like a fool,' Morgan said sharply. 'He's changing into Rufus, that's all. A Rufus we never knew, but perfectly genuine. My guess is that most of the adjustments took place in adolescence, and he isn't going back that far. I'm only suggesting that the stories you heard about his young days may have been – well, not entirely true. He's confused now. We'll have to wait until the changes stop and his mind clears up to find out what really happened.'

'He's changing,' Bill said stubbornly, as if he had not been listening. 'He's going back, and we don't know where it will end.'

'It's ended already. He's on his last series of shots now. You haven't any reason to think he won't stop at thirty-five, when we wind up the treatments, have you?'

Bill laid down the book and looked at it thoughtfully. 'No reason,' he said. 'Only – the current's so strong. Biological time flows so fast when you reach the midpoint. Like the river flowing toward Niagara. I wonder if you can go too far. Maybe there's a point beyond which you can't stop. I'm an alarmist, Pete. I have a feeling we've saddled a tiger.'

'Now *you're* mixing metaphors,' Morgan said dryly.

In June Bill said, 'He won't let me in his room any more.'

Morgan sighed. 'What now?'

'The decorators finished two days ago. Dark-purple hangings all around the walls. I'm sure they thought he was a little crazy, but they didn't argue. Now he's got an old clock up there he's been tinkering with, and he found a table somewhere with a chessboard top, and he's making the strangest calculations on it.'

'What kind of calculations?'

Bill shrugged irritably. 'How do I know? I'd thought he was getting better. Those spells of ... of false memory haven't seemed to bother him so much lately. Or if they do, he doesn't talk about it.'

'When was the last?'

Bill opened his desk drawer and flipped the notebook cover. 'Ten days ago he said the view from his windows wasn't right. Also that his room was ugly and he didn't know how he'd stood it all these years. It was about then that he began to complain of these pains, too.'

'Oh, the "growing pains." And they began to localize – when?'

'A week ago.' Bill scowled. 'I don't like 'em. I thought it was gastric – I still think it is. But he shouldn't be having any trouble at all. He's perfect, inside and out. Those last X-rays—'

'Taken a week ago,' Morgan reminded him.

'Yes, but—'

'If he keeps having a bellyache after meals, something may have gone wrong only a few days ago. Remember, Rufus is unique.'

'He's that, all right. Well, I'll start all over, if I can catch him. He's getting very skittish these days. I can't keep up with him any more.'

'Is he out now? I'd like to have a look at his room.'

Bill nodded. 'You won't find out anything. But come on up.'

Purple curtains inside clogged the door for a moment as if the room itself were trying to hold them out. Then the door came open, and a draft from the hall made the four walls billow and shiver with rich, dark-purple folds, as if things had run to hiding everywhere an instant before the two men entered. The only light come in a purple glow through curtains across the windows, until Bill crossed the room and put back the draperies that covered them. Then they could see more clearly the big carved bed, the chest of drawers, the few chairs.

At the bed's foot stood the chessboard table, chalk marks scrawled across the squares. At the back of the table stood the clock, an old-fashioned mantelpiece ornament that filled the room with a curious sort of hiccupping tick. They listened a moment, then Morgan said, 'That's funny. Wonder if it's accidental. Do you hear a … a halfbeat between the ticks?' They listened again. *Tick-ti-tock* went the clock.

'It's old,' Bill said. 'Probably something wrong with it. What I want you to look at is the second hand. See?'

A long sweep-hand was moving very slowly around the broad face. It did not match the other two. The presumption was that Rugus had found it elsewhere and added it very inefficiently, for as they watched it leaped about three seconds and resumed its slow crawl. A little farther on it leaped again. Then it made almost a complete circuit, and jumped five seconds.

'I hope Rufus isn't keeping any dates by this thing,' Morgan murmured. 'Lucky for him he doesn't repair clocks for a living. What's the idea?'

'I wish I knew. I asked, of course, and he said he was just tinkering. It looks like it, too, in a way. But here's something funny.' Bill stooped and opened the glass. 'Look. It's very small. Here, and over here, see?'

Bending, Morgan made out upon the face of the clock, irregularly spaced between the numerals, a series of very tiny colored markings painted upon the dial. Red and green and brown, tiny and intricate, with curled lines like Persian writing. All around the face they went, varicolored and enigmatic. Morgan pulled his mustache and watched the erratic second-hand twitch around its path. Whenever it jumped it came to rest somewhere upon a twist of colored lines.

'That can't be accidental,' he said after a moment. 'But what's the idea? What does it record? Did you ask him?'

Bill gave him a long look. 'No,' he said finally, 'I didn't.'

Morgan regarded him narrowly. 'Why not?'

'I'm not sure. Maybe … maybe I didn't want to know.' He closed the glass face. 'It looks crazy. But when it comes to machinery that measures time

– Well, I wonder if Rufus doesn't know more than we do.' He paused. '*You* turned his mind loose to explore time,' he said almost accusingly.

Morgan shook his head. 'You're losing your perspective, Bill.'

'Maybe. Well – what do you make of the chessboard?'

They looked at it blankly. Careful scrawls had been traced almost at random within the squares, though it seemed evident that to the mind which directed that scrawling, purpose had been clear.

'He could just be working out some chess problem, couldn't he?' suggested Morgan.

'I thought of that. I asked him if he'd like to play, and he said he didn't know how and didn't want to be bothered. That was when he threw me out. I think it's got something to do with the clock, myself. You know what I think, Pete? If the clock measures hours, maybe the squares measure days. Like a calendar.'

'But why?'

'I don't know. I'm not a psychiatrist. I've got one idea, though. Suppose during the hypnosis he imagined he did see something that – disturbed him. Say he *did* see something. Posthypnotic command stopped him from remembering it consciously, but his subconscious is still worried. Couldn't that emerge into a conscious, purposeless tinkering with things that have to do with time? And if it could, do you think maybe he may suddenly remember, some day, what's behind it all?'

Morgan faced him squarely across the table and the hiccupping clock.

'Listen, Bill. Listen to me. You're losing your perspective badly over this. You won't do Rufus any good if you let yourself get lost in a morass of mysticism.'

Bill said abruptly, 'Pete, do you know much about Faust?'

If he had expected a protest, he was surprised. Morgan grimaced, the heavy lines deepening around his mouth.

'Yeah. I looked him up. Interesting.'

'Suppose for a minute that the legend's got a basis of fact. Suppose that somewhere back three hundred years there really were two men who tried this same experiment and made a record of it in code. Does that give you any ideas?'

Morgan scowled. 'Nothing applicable. The legend's basis is the old medieval idea that knowledge is essentially evil. "thou shalt not eat of the fruit of the Tree." Faust, like Adam, was tempted and tasted the fruit, and got punished. The moral's simply that to know too much is to disobey God and nature, and God and nature will exact a penalty.'

'That's just it. Faust paid with his soul. But the point is that the experiment didn't run smoothly up to the end, and then suddenly collapse. Mephistopheles didn't really present a bill and carry off his reward. Their experiment went wrong almost from the start – like ours. Faust was an intelligent man. He wouldn't have bartered his immortal soul for a short fling on earth. It wouldn't have been worth while. The whole point was that Faust never took Mephisto seriously until it was too late. He deliberately let Mephistopheles spread out his trumpery pleasures, perfectly sure that they wouldn't give him enjoyment enough to matter any. And of course if they didn't the bargain was void. It was when he actually began to enjoy what Mephistopheles had to offer that he lost his soul, not at the end, when the bill was paid.' Bill thumped the chess table emphatically. 'Could a code tell you any plainer that the thing got out of hand almost at the beginning?' He looked at Morgan with narrowed eyes. 'All we've got to do now is find out what the code for "soul" means.'

'Got any ideas?' Morgan inquired sardonically. 'I'm worried more about you, Bill, than I am about Rufus. I'm beginning to wonder if we haven't made a mistake in our subject. You're too close to Rufus.'

He was surprised at the look that came over Bill's face. He watched him frown a little, thump the table again, and then walk to the window and back without saying anything. Morgan waited. Presently:

'I'm not, really,' Bill said. 'Father and I never were very close emotionally. He wasn't the type. Rufus, I think, could be. Rufus has all the warmth that Father lacked. I like him. But it's more than that, Pete. There's something in the relationship between us that affects me as Rufus is affected. It's a physical thing. Rufus is my closest living relative, though he's a stranger now even in appearance. Half my chromosomes are his. If I hated him, I'd still be linked to him by that much heritage. Things are happening to him now that never happened to a human being before, so far as we know. It's as if, when you pull him out of the straight course of human behavior, you pull me too. I can't look at the thing abstractly any more.' He laughed almost apologetically. 'I keep dreaming about rivers. Deep, swift waters running faster and faster, with the abyss just ahead and no way on earth to escape it.'

'Dream-symbolism—' began Morgan.

'Oh, I know, of course. But the river itself is a symbol. Sometimes it's Rufus on the raft, sometimes it's me. But the riptide has always caught us. We've gone too far to turn back. I wonder if—'

'Stop wondering. You've worked too hard. What you need is a rest from Rufus and everything connected with him. After you get those X-rays and figure out what's wrong with him, suppose you get away for awhile. When you come back Rufus will be thirty-five going-on-forty again and you can forget about the river and start dreaming about snakes or teeth or something like that. O.K.?'

Bill nodded doubtfully. 'O.K. I'll try.'

*

Three days later, in the Westerfield stydy, Morgan held an X-ray plate against the light and squinted at the shadowy maze of outlines. He looked a long time, and his hand was shaking when he laid the plate down carefully, scowling at Bill under brows so heavy they almost hid the expression of his eyes. It was an expression of bewilderment that verged on fear.

'You faked these!'

Bill made a futile gesture. 'I wish I had.'

Morgan gave him another piercing glance and turned back to the light for a second look. His hand was still shaking. He steadied it with the other and stared. Then he took up another plate and looked at that.

'It's impossible,' he said. 'It never happened. It couldn't.'

'The ... the simplification—' began Bill in an uncertain voice.

'The wonder is he can digest *anything*, with this setup. Not that I believe it for a minute, of course.'

'Everything's simplifying,' Bill went on, as if he had not heard. 'Even his bones. Even his ribs. They give like a child's ribs, half cartilage. I got to thinking, you know, after I saw that. I gave him a basal, just on a hunch, and he's plus forty. His thyroid is burning him up. But Pete, it doesn't seem to hurt him! No loss of weight, no increased appetite, sleeps like a baby – why, my nerves are twice as jumpy as his.'

'But – that's impossible.'

'I know.'

Silence. Then, 'Anything else wrong?'

Bill shrugged helplessly. 'I don't know. I was afraid to run any more tests on him after that. It's the truth, Pete – I was afraid to.'

Morgan put the last plate down very gently, and turned his back on the table. For the first time there was uncertainty in his motions. He was no longer a man supremely sure of himself. He said, in an indecisive voice, 'Yeah. Well, we'll start tomorrow and give him a thorough going over. I ... I think maybe we can find what's—'

'It's no use, Pete. You see that. We've started something we can't stop. He's gone too far along the river, and the current's got him. All the basic life processes that move so fast in youth are moving in him now faster than we can move. God knows where he's going – not back along any path a man ever heard of before – but he's into the current and we can't do a thing about it.'

And after a moment Morgan nodded. 'You were right,' he said. 'You've been right all along, and I've been wrong. Now what?'

Bill made a gesture of futility. 'I can't tell you. This is still your party, Pete. I'm just along for the ride. I saw the dangers first because ... well, maybe because Rufus is my own kin and the pull was ... tangible ... between us. When he went off the beam I could feel it psychically. Could that explain anything?'

Morgan sat down with sudden limpness, like a man whose muscles have abruptly gone weak. But his voice, after a moment's bewilderment, began to grow firm again.

'It's up to us to find out. Let's see.' He shut his eyes and rubbed the closed lids with unsteady fingers. There was another silence. Presently he looked up again and said, 'He's been changing from the very first. I suppose I've been assuming that something in our treatment had shuffled his chromosomes and genes around into a new pattern of heredity, and he was beginning to throwback to some ancestor we never knew about. But now I wonder if—' He paused, and a startled look crossed his face. He stared at Bill with eyes that widened enormously. 'Now I wonder—' he echoed tonelessly, as if his lips repeated something meaningless, while his mind raced ahead too fast for utterance.

After that he got up with a sudden, abrupt motion and began to pace the floor, his steps rapid. 'No,' he murmured, 'that's crazy. But—'

Bill watched him for a moment or two longer. Then he said in a quiet voice, 'I had the same idea quite awhile ago. I was afraid to say anything, though.'

Morgan's head jerked up and he stared. Their eyes held in a long look, awe in Morgan's. 'That they were shuffled – too much? The chromosomes could have fallen into a pattern – too different?'

'You saw the X-rays,' Bill said gently.

'Let's have a drink,' was all Morgan answered to that.

When they were settled again, and there was something very soothing and matter-of-fact about the tinkle of ice in their glasses, Morgan began in a voice that strained a little for the prosaic.

'There *may* be a race that looks like Rufus. Or there may once have been. No use jumping at the impossible before we exhaust normal possibilities. I've been trying to think of any race at all with just this facial characteristics, and there isn't one on earth today, but that's not saying there never has been. No race sprang full-blown into the world, you know. You and I must have had remote ancestors who lived on Atlantis, or were contemporaries of the Atlanteans anyhow. And who knows what *they* looked like?'

'You keep forgetting,' Bill reminded him, still gently. 'The X-rays. And this may be only the beginning. He'll move faster and faster now. Physiological time is fast – terribly fast – as it nears the source. Do you think there was ever a race like Rufus – inside?'

Morgan looked at him over the glass rim. He caught his breath to say something forcefully, then let it out in a sigh. 'No. I don't think there ever was. Not here.'

'All right,' Bill said. 'You take it from there.'

'How can I?'

'Try. I'm afraid to. My ideas are too ... too credulous. I'm curious to see if your mind follows the same track. Go on – take over.'

'He's a ... a changeling,' Morgan began, groping. 'There've been stories about changelings for a long time. Older than the Faustus legend. I wonder, was Faust a changeling too? Did he have the same potential trace of heredity that a time-reversal could make dominant? Changeling ... fairy's child ... fairies? Fragile people, invisible at will, built to another scale than ours – another dimension? Other dimensions, Bill?'

Bill shrugged. 'He can't eat what we eat. If these changes go on, there won't be a food on earth he can digest. Maybe, somewhere, there is.'

Morgan said abruptly, 'Maybe the changes won't go on, either. We don't know they will. Are we making fools of ourselves, groping around in fairy stories for an answer we may not need?'

'I think we'll need it, Pete. Anyhow, let's go on and see what we get. Another dimension, you were saying.'

'O.K., suppose there *were* changelings,' Morgan said violently. 'Suppose there *are* goblins and things that go bump in the night—'

'"Good Lord, deliver us,"' Bill finished the quotation with a grin. 'Use a little logic, Pete. I don't expect you to believe the pumpkin turned into a coach. But if we apply the alchemist's formula to the changeling idea, or the Faust legend, do we get anything at all?'

'Oh, that isn't so new. It's been suggested before that the supernatural beings of legend might be distorted memories of some other-dimensional visitors. But Rufus—'

'All right, Pete, say it.'

With an air of deliberate sacrifice, Morgan lifted his black-mustached lip in a snarl and said, 'Rufus may be – he appears to be – an hereditary throwback to some inhabitant of another world. Is that what you want?'

'It'll do.'

'It explains—' Morgan suddenly glowed with an idea that justified his sacrifice. 'It explains his reaction to the picture of his mother. It explains why things look wrong to him here. It even explains his impossible memories, in part.'

Bill looked doubtful. 'Yes – in part. There's something more, Pete. I'm not sure what – I just know this isn't all. It's not quite so easy. The clock, and the calender, if that's what the chessboard is – yes, you could say he senses a different time-scheme from ours and he's groping to recapture something familiar from some other life-experience he can't quite remember yet. But there's something more. We'll know before we're through, Pete. He's on his way back now. I'm scared. I don't want to know about it. My mind panics when I think of it. It's too close to me. But we'll know. We'll find out. We haven't got to the root of the thing yet, but when we do we'll see it isn't as easy as all this.'

'The root? I wonder. There's one thing, Bill. Rufus wasn't like this during his normal growth-period. You remember what we were discussing once about the possibility of aberrations at birth that smoothed out in adolescence? He *could* be experiencing now the results of disturbing that adjustment. But you can't mutate backward. It simply isn't remotely conceivable, by any application of logic, on this or any other world. You can say he's inherited a potentiality of Martian or other-dimensional chromosomes, but that still won't explain it. Mutation is a ... spreading out, a flowering, not a drawing in. And that *must* hold good anywhere in this—' He stopped, his heavy brows drawing together. After a while, he began again, gropingly.

'I'm wrong on that. It ... let's see. It holds good only as long as there's the same temporal constant. And that's just what doesn't apply to Rufus.'

Bill scowled. 'He's going back in time, but it's all subjective, isn't it?'

'It started out that way. Could be the subjective's affecting the objective.'

'That Rufus is warping *time?*'

Morgan was not listening. He had found pencil and paper in his pocket and was absorbing himself in meaningless squiggles. The heavy moments moved past. The pencil point stopped.

Morgan looked up, his eyes still puzzled. 'Maybe I've got it,' he said. 'Maybe. Listen, Bill—'

In a railroad yard there are many tracks. Each track carries a train, moving forward relentlessly in space – and parallel.

According to the theory of parallel time, each train is a spatial universe, and the tracks are laid on the dark roadbed of time itself. Far, far back, in the black beginning, there may have been one track only, before it branched.

As it branched and branched again, the parallel roads spread out, forming in little groups – the New York Central, the Pennsylvania, the Southern Pacific and the Santa Fe. The trains – the universes – of each are roughly similar. The Penn has many cars rushing headlong through the dim mistiness of time, but they all contain recognizable variations of *homo sapiens.* The tracks branched, but the system is still a unit.

There are other units.

One thing they have in common – no, two things. They are parallel in time, and originally they came from the same unthinkable source, hidden in the mind-staggering, vast mysteries of the womb of space and time. *In the beginning—*

But you can't go back to the beginning. You can't even go back along your timetrack. Because the train is moving on, it isn't where it was twenty, fifty, eighty years before, and if you try to retrace your steps, you're walking along a strange road. It isn't quite spatial or temporal, really. It may involve – well, call it a dimension – that's so remarkably alien to us that we can't even conceive of it except as a – *difference.*

But it may be a bridge, a shortcut, this strange road the traveler finds when he tries to retrace time. It may be a tightrope stretched precariously between parallel time-tracks. The letter N expresses it. The vertical lines are the timetracks where the trains go by. The angled line is the shortcut – from the Penn to the New York Central.

Different companies. Different lines. Different – *groups.*

So you can't recapture *your* youth; you can't go home again; that home isn't there any more. It's away back along the track, lost in the dusk where the dead ashes of Tyre and Nineveh have smoldered out.

And it isn't just merely a matter of chromosomes. Not merely subjective. But going back, at an angle, into one of the parallel times where a certain equivalent of Rufus Westerfield existed.

Parallels do not imply similarity – not when the cosmic equations are involved. The basic matrix may not vary, but only a god can recognize such an ultimate basic. The mammal matrix, for example. Whales and guinea pigs are each mammalian.

So there were, perhaps, many equivalents of Rufus Westerfield, in the infinity of trains along the infinity of tracks – but he was not retracing his course along the Pennsylvania line.

The New York Central line was – parallel – but only on the Penn road were tickets sold to *homo sapiens.*

Rufus Westerfield was twenty-five. He lay at full length in the porch swing, somnolent in the hot July afternoon. One arm was behind his head and he tugged at the support-chain now and then to keep himself in lazy motion.

Laziness, indeed, was his keynote at this stage. Which seemed odd in contrast with the keen, humorous face so subtly unlike his face of forty-odd years ago, when he had once before been twenty-five. You would still have known at a glance that Rufus and Bill were closely related; the change was too subtle to alter that. But there was a sharpening of all the features now, a more than physical sharpening. And the contradictory indolence of him made Rufus look arrogant.

It was, given this outrageous setup, a normal indolence, but it went curiously with the youth of the man. At twenty-five a mind as keen and a face and body as forceful as Rufus' should have had no indolence about them. But at twenty-five the normal man is just entering upon the most productive period of his life. All through adolescence he has been building impatiently toward this fulfillment of his maturity.

But there had been nothing immature about Rufus Westerfield's immediate past. And life was not before him. The swift temporal current flowed away past him and out of sight. He moved toward the helplessness of infancy, not to the activity of his prime. And each day that went by was longer and more pellucid to him than the last. As the physical processes of his body moved faster and faster, nearing adolescence, so the temporal processes of his mind went slower. The thoughts of youth, wrote Longfellow, are long, long thoughts.

Rufus put out his free hand and deftly took up a glass from the porch floor as the swing lifted him toward it. Ice tinkled pleasantly; it was a rum Collins, his fifth today. He watched the flicker of leaf-shadows on the porch roof and smiled comfortably as he sipped the sweet, strong liquid, rolling it upon his tongue. Taste was developing more and more keenly in him as the years retrogressed. The infant's whole mouth is lined with taste buds, and in Rufus' mouth, little by little, those taste buds were returning.

He had drunk a good deal in the past two months. Partly because he liked to drink, partly because alcohol was one of the few things his changing digestion could tolerate. And it helped to blur that nagging sense in him which he could not put a name to, the feeling that much he saw about him was indescribably wrong.

Rufus was an intelligent young man. Also he was tolerant. He saw no point in letting the sense of wrongness color his life unduly. He dismissed it when he could. In part this was simply an admirable adjustment to environment. It was a great pity that the man through whose changing phases Rufus moved so rapidly must remain only half known. He would have been a fascinating man, with his memories and mature wisdom accumulated over seventy years, his vigorous mind and body, and the sardonic keenness, the warmth and humor developing in him now. And with all these the enthralling subtleties of change from no source a man ever drew upon before. He was a blend, perhaps, of human and extra-human, and perhaps the best of each, but no one would ever know him wholly. The man he might have been was moving too swiftly for more than a glimpse at the life he might have lived. The stream that bore him along could not run slowly.

In part, then, it was a tolerant adjustment to life that let him accept what was happening so calmly. But it was also a form of precociousness in reverse. Because he was keenly intelligent, he would normally – at twenty-five going on twenty-six – have been in advance of his years. His brain would have fitted him to cope successfully with men many years his senior. And now, at twenty-five going on twenty-four he was still in advance of his age. But in reverse. In Rufus, it was efficiency that his mind was slowing leisurely toward the long thoughts of youth. It spared him a great deal.

The pleasant blur of drunkenness had another effect, too. It released the surface tension of his mind and let strange flotsam drift upward. Memories and fragments which he knew had no place in the past he had already lived. Knowing it, he made no effort to reconcile the paradox. More and more as time went by he approached that period when the individual questions only the superficial aspects of his world. Basically, he accepts it, turning trustfully to the protection of those around him. And in Rufus, his very intelligence forced him backward prematurely into that state of mind which belongs to childhood, because it was in that state that he could find the greatest protection from a peril his subconscious must have sensed and would not let the surface of his mind suspect.

On the surface, memories from two pasts floated and merged and sank away again, lazily, evoked by alcohol. In the beginning, memories of that other past had been thin as smokewreaths drifting transparently across the face of his clearer remembrance, indistinguishable from realities. It was a long time before he became consciously aware that two sets of memories, many of them mutually exclusive, were moving at once through his mind. By the time he was sure, he had passed beyond the stage of caring. Things beyond his control were happening with inexorable rhythms that carried him smoothly toward a goal he did not try to glimpse yet; it would come in good time, he could not miss it, he was ready.

Now the memories from that other past were superimposed over nearly all his Westerfield memories. He looked back upon Westerfield years more dimly, through a haze of obscuring events that did not seem in the least strange to him, and no more alien than his remembrances of Bill's youth, and of his long-dead wife. He could no longer distinguish at a mental glance which memory belonged to the Westerfield period and which to the other. But they had been different. Very different indeed. Individuals moved past and through his memories of Bill and Lydia, individuals whose names he knew but could not yet pronounce, beings who had played tremendous roles, perhaps, in that other past, in that other place.

But they too were veiled in this all-encompassing indifference which was his protection and his precociousness. Like the Westerfields, they belonged to an era that was moving too fast to be savored much. He had not time to spare for leisurely evocations of the past.

So he remembered, pleasantly, not questioning anything, letting the liquor release the double stream of memories and letting the memories glide by and go. Faces, colors, sensations he did not try to name, songs – like the song he was singing under his breath, now, to the slow rhythm of the swing.

Bill, coming up the steps, heard the song and tightened his lips. It was no tune at all. It was one of the nagging, impossible harmonies Rufus hummed so constantly, not really knowing that he did it. The words were not English, when he sang them in absent-minded snatches, and the melody was more alien than the cacophonies of oriental music. Bill had given up trying to understand. He had given up a great deal in the past month, since it became obvious that Rufus was going on beyond the thirty-five which was to have been his stopping point. Bill had met failure halfway and acknowledged the meeting with what equanimity he could summon. There was nothing to salvage now but sufficient grace to confess defeat.

Rufus in the swing seemed half asleep. The lids were lowered above the tilted black eyes, and the face had no expression beyond indolence. It worried Bill that although this was not a Westerfield face any more, it remained akin to his own. Again and again of late he felt with unreasoning discomfort that as Rufus changed in feature, he pulled Bill's own features awry to conform. It was not true, of course, the change was indescribably outside the mere matter of facial angles, but the effect remained disconcertingly the same.

Rufus did not open his eyes as his son's step sounded on the porch, but he said lazily, 'Want a date tonight, Bill?'

'No thanks, not with one of your girls. I know when I'm well off.'

Rufus laughed without lifting his lids, blind, indolent laughter that showed his white teeth. Then he stirred a little and looked up at his son, and Bill felt sudden helpless horror congealing in him. It was too abruptly inhuman a thing to face with no warning at all.

For though the lids had lifted, Rufus was not looking directly up with the black gaze that had once been sardonic and was now only lazy and amused. Something thin and blind stretched over his eyes, something that drew back slowly, with the deliberation of a cat's gaze, or an owl's. Rufus sometime in the immediate past had developed a nictitating membrane, a third eyelid.

If he knew it, he gave no evidence. He was grinning in amusement. The lid slipped back and vanished, and might never have been there. Rufus stretched and got up with a long, slow litheness, and Bill found it possible to forget for the moment what it was he had just seen.

Rufus' body had a beautiful muscular co-ordination which was in its own way tragic just now. And within it, the mechanism must differ impossibly from the norm. Bill had not checked upon the changes in the past two weeks, changes which he knew must be taking place almost while one watched. He should be fascinated, from a purely clinical viewpoint, in what took place. But he was not. He could accept the knowledge of failure, because he must, but he had in this case no urge to probe the reasons for failure. It was more than an unsolved problem. It was a matter intimately involving his own flesh and blood. As a man with an incurable disease might shun the sight of his infirmity, so Bill would not investigate any further the impossible things that were changing in this body which was half his own.

Rufus was looking at him and smiling.

'How you've aged,' he murmured. 'You and Pete both. I can remember when you were just youngsters, two or three months ago.' He yawned.

'Have you got a date?' Bill asked. The young Rufus nodded, and for a moment his black eyes almost closed and the third lid slid drowsily forward, half veiling the irises. He looked like an aloof, contented cat. Bill could not watch him. He had become calloused enough by now to these changing paradoxes and he was not shocked out of self-possession, but he still could not look straight at this latest evidence of abnormality. He only said, 'Don't look so smug,' and went into the house abruptly, letting the screen slam behind him.

Rufus' eyes opened a little and the extra lid slid back, not all the way. He gazed after his son, but calmly, as incurious as a man might feel who watches a cat withdraw, disinterest in an alien species clouding his eyes.

He came in that night very late, and very drunk. Morgan had been waiting with Bill in the parlor, and they went out in silence to the taxi to bring Rufus in. His limp body was graceful even in this extremity. The driver was nearly in hysterics. He would not touch his passenger. It was impossible to make out exactly why – something that Rufus had done, or had not done, or perhaps had only said, on the way home.

'What was he *drinking*?' the driver kept demanding in a voice that broke on the last word. 'What could he have been *drinking*?'

They could not answer that, and could get no coherent reason from the man why they should. He went away as soon as Bill had paid him – he refused to accept or touch money from Rufus' wallet – driving erratically with a great clashing of gears.

'Has this happened before?' Morgan asked over Rufus' lolling, dark-red head.

Bill nodded. 'Not so bad, of course. He – remembers – things when he's drunk, you know. Maybe he remembered something big this time. He always forgets again, and maybe that's just as well, too.'

Between them Rufus moved a little, murmured a word, not in English, and waved both hands in an abortive gesture of expansion, rather as if vast landscapes were spread before him. He laughed clearly, not a drunken sound at all, and then collapsed entirely.

They put him to bed in the big carved bedstead upstairs, among the purple curtains. He lay as limply as a child, his familiar-strange face looking curiously like a solid mask with nothing at all behind it. They had turned to leave him, both of them tight-lipped and bewildered, and they were halfway across the room when Bill paused and sniffed the air.

'Perfume?' he asked incredulously. Morgan lifted his head and sniffed, too.

'Honeysuckle. Lots of it.' The heavy fragrance was suddenly almost sickening in its sweetness. They turned. Rufus was breathing with his mouth open, and the fragrance came almost palpably from the bed. They went back slowly.

Deep waves of perfume rose to meet them as he breathed. There was no smell of liquor at all, but the honeysuckle sweetness hung so heavy that it left almost a sugary taste upon the tongue. The two men looked blankly at one another.

'It'd suffocate anyone else,' Morgan said finally. 'But we can't very well get him away from it, can we?'

'I'll open the windows,' Bill said with restraint. 'There's no way now to tell what's going to hurt him.'

When they left the room the curtains were billowing gently in a breeze from the windows; the walls shuddered all around the room with the motion. In the silence Rufus' perfumed breath was the only sound except for the stutter of the clock with its long jumping hand. Just as they reached the door there came a slight change in the quality of the fragrance Rufus was exhaling. Neither pleasant nor unpleasant, an indescribable shift from odor to odor as color might shift and blend from one shade to another. But the new odor was not like anything either man had ever smelled before.

Bill paused briefly, met Morgan's eyes, then shrugged and went on out.

Downstairs in the study, Morgan said, 'He's moving fast.' He was silent awhile, then, 'Maybe I'd better come in for awhile, Bill, until it's over.'

Bill nodded. 'I wish you would. It'll be soon. Awfully soon, I think. They grow so fast – you can almost *see* a child growing. And Rufus condenses years into weeks.'

Biological time moved like a river, swifter and narrower as it nears the source. And temporal perception ran clearer and slower with every passing day. Rufus returned unperturbed in mind to his first childhood – or perhaps his third, by actual count, though memory of that senile past had almost vanished now. In youth, as in age, forgetfulness clouded his tranquil mind, partly because the days of his age were so far behind him now, but partly too because his brain was smoothing out into the untroubled immaturity of childhood. Borne swiftly and smoothly along that quickening stream, he moved backward toward the infinities of youth.

And now a curious urgency seemed to possess him. It was like the reasonless instinct that drives an animal to prepare the burrow for her young; the phenomenon of birth, approached from either side of the temporal current, seemed to evoke intuitive knowledge of what was to come, and what would be needed for its coming.

Rufus began to stay more and more in his room, resenting intrusion, resisting it politely. What he did was difficult to guess, though there was much chalk dust about the table with the chessboard top. And he worked on the clock, too. It had four hands now; the face was divided into concentric circles and the extra hand was a blur that spun around the painted dial. All this might have seemed the typical preoccupation of the adolescent mind with gadgetry, had there not been that urgency which no normal child needs to feel.

It was not easy any more to determine what went on in his rapidly changing body, since he resented and resisted examination, but they did discover that his metabolism had accelerated unbelievably. He exhibited none of the typical hyperthyroid traits, but the small gland in his throat was busily undoing now all the pituitaries had governed long ago, in the growth of his first childhood.

Normally a 'hyperthyroid's' tremendous appetite is insufficient to keep up with the rate at which he expends energy, as his abnormally accelerated metabolism devours his very tissues in a fierce effort to keep pace with itself. In Rufus, that devouring metabolism worked inwardly upon muscle and bone. He was no longer physically a big man; he lost weight and stature steadily, from within, burning his own bulk for fuel to feed that ravenous hunger. But with Rufus it was impossibly normal. He felt no resultant weakness.

And with him, more secretly, perhaps the white corpuscles in his blood may have undergone change and multiplication, to attack his internal organs and work their changes there, much as the phagocytes of a pupa work histolysis inside the chrysalis, reducing what lies within to a plasma in which the imago to come lies already implicit in solution. But what lay implicity and hidden in the changing body of Rufus Westerfield was a secret still locked in the genes which time had so curiously disarranged.

All this was retrogression, and yet in a sense it was progress, if determined, orderly procedure toward a goal means anything. The time-stream narrowed about him, flowing backward toward its source.

'He's now, I should say, about fifteen,' said Bill. 'It's hard to tell – he never comes out of his room any more, even to meals, and I don't see him unless I insist on it. He's changing a good deal.'

'How do you mean?'

'His features … I don't know. Sharper and finer, not childish at all. His bones seem quite flexible, all of them. Abnormal. And he's running a fever so high you can feel the heat without even touching him. It doesn't seem to bother him much. He just feels a little tired most of the time, like a child who's growing too fast.' He paused and looked at his interlaced fingers.

'Where will it end, Pete? Where *can* it end? There's no precedent. I can't believe he'll just—'

'No precedent?' interrupted Morgan. 'I remember the time when you thought I was following Mephistopheles' footsteps.'

Bill looked at him. 'Faust—' he said vaguely. 'But Faust went back to a definite age and stopped there.'

'I wonder.' Morgan's voice was half sardonic. 'If the legend's all in code, maybe Mephisto's bill, when he presented it, had something to do with – this. Maybe what the legend coded as the loss of a soul was something like what's happening to Rufus now. Perhaps he lost his body, not his soul. Still, they were devious, those alchemists. "Body" for "soul" is pretty obvious.'

'Too obvious. We haven't seen the end yet. Before we do, we'll know. I'm willing to admit the moral now ... half-knowledge can be too dangerous to handle without losing ... well, something important. But the penalty ... we'll have to wait for that.'

'Um-m,' Morgan said. 'You say he isn't like a child now? Remember, I haven't been in his room at all.'

'No. Whatever kind of childhood he ... *they* have, it isn't much like ours. But I haven't really seen him very clearly. He keeps it so dark in there.'

'I wish I knew,' Morgan said longingly. 'I'd like very much to ... suppose we couldn't just walk in and turn the lights on, Bill?'

Bill said quickly, 'No! You promised, Pete. We're going to let him alone. It's the least we can do, now. He knows, you see. Reason or instinct – I can't tell which. Either way, it's no reason or instinct *our* species would understand. But he's the only one in the house who's sure of himself at this stage. We've got to let him play it his way.'

Morgan nodded regretfully. 'All right. I wish he weren't ... hadn't ever been Rufus. We're handicapped. I wish he were just a specimen. I'm getting some funny ideas. About his – species. Did you ever think, Bill, how different the child is from the adult in appearance? Every proportion's abnormal, from an adult standpoint. We're so used to the sight of babies they look human to us even from birth, but someone from Mars might not recognize them as the same species at all. Has it occurred to you that if Rufus went back to ... to infancy ... and then reversed the process and grew up again, he'd probably grow up into something alien? Something we couldn't even recognize?'

Bill glanced up with a sudden gleam of excitement 'Do you think that might happen?'

'How can I tell? The time-stream's too uncharted for that. He might run against some current that would start him back downstream again at any moment. Or he might not. For his sake, I hope not. He couldn't live in this world. We'll never know what sort of world he belongs in. Even his memories of it, the things he said, were too distorted to mean anything. When he was willing to talk about it, he was still trying to force the alien memories into the familiar pattern of his past, and what came out was gibberish. We won't know, and neither will he. Just as well for us, too, if he doesn't grow up again. There's no criterion for guessing what shape *his* adult form would have. It might be as different from ours as ... as the larva is from the butterfly.'

'Mephistopheles knew.'

'I expect that's why he was damned.'

He could no longer eat anything at all. For a long while he had subsisted on a diet of milk and custards and gelatines, but as the internal changes deepened his tolerance grew less and less. Those changes must by now have gone entirely beyond imagining, for outwardly, too, he had changed a great deal.

He kept his curtains drawn, so that toward the end Bill could hardly see anything more than a small, quick shadow in the plum-colored darkness, turning a pale triangle of face from the light when the door opened. His voice was still strong, but its quality had changed almost indescribably. It was at once thinner and more vibrant, with a sort of wood-wind fluttering far back in the throat. He had developed a curious impediment of speech, not a lisp, but something that distorted certain consonants in a way Bill had never heard before.

On the last day he did not even take his tray into the room. There was no point in handling food he could not digest, and he was busy, very busy. When Bill knocked the thin, strong, vibrant voice told him pleasantly to go away.

'Important,' said the voice. 'Don't come in now, Bill. Mustn't come in. Very important. You'll know when—' and the voice went smoothly into some other language that made no sense. Bill could not answer. He nodded futilely, without a word, at the blank panels, and the voice within did not seem to think a reply from him necessary, for the busy sounds went on.

Muffled and intermittent, they continued all day, along with a preoccupied humming of queer, unmelodious tunes which he seemed to handle much better now, as if his throat were adjusting to the curious tonal combinations.

Toward evening, the air in the house began to grow tense in an indescribable way. The whole building was full of a sense of impending crisis. He who had been Rufus was acutely aware that the end had nearly come, and his awareness drew the very atmosphere taut with suspense. But it was an orderly, unhurried imminence that filled the house. Forces beyond any control, set in motion long ago, were moving to their appointed fulfillment behind the closed door upstairs, and the focus of this impending change went quietly about his preparations, like someone who knows himself in the hands of a power he trusts and would not alter if he could. Softly, humming to himself, he prepared in secret to meet it.

Morgan and Bill waited in chairs outside the closed door as night came on, listening to sounds within. No one could have slept in that taut air. From time to time one of them called, and the voice answered amiably but in preoccupation so deep that the answers were haphazard. Also they were becoming more muffled, difficult to understand.

Twice Morgan rose and laid a hand upon the knob, avoiding Bill's anxious eyes. But he could not bring himself to turn it. He could almost think the tension in the air would hold the door against him if he tried to push it open. But he did not try.

As the hours neared midnight, sounds from within came at longer and longer intervals. And the sense of tension mounted intolerably. It was like hurricane weather, as forces high in the upper air gathered for an onslaught.

The time came when there had been no stirring for what seemed a very long time, and Bill called, 'Are you all right?'

Silence. Then, slowly and from far away, a reluctant rustling and the sound of a muffled voice, inarticulate, murmuring a syllable or two.

The two men looked at each other. Morgan shrugged. Bill in his turn half rose and reached for the knob, but he did not touch it. The hurricane was still gathering in the upper air; they might not know when the time for action came, but they could sense, at least, when the time was not.

Silence again. When Bill could wait no longer, he called once more, and this time there was no answer. They listened. A faint, faint stirring, but no voice.

The next time he called, not even a stirring replied.

The night hours went by very slowly. Neither of the two men was aware of drowsiness – the air was too taut for that. Sometimes they talked quietly, keeping their voices low, as if whatever lay beyond the door were still within reach of sound.

Once Morgan said, 'Remember, quite a while ago, I was wondering if Rufus was biologically unusual?'

'I remember.'

'We decided then he wasn't. I've been thinking, Bill. Maybe I've got a glimmer of what's coming now. Rufus, say, simply switched to another time-line as he retrogressed. Any human might. Any human almost certainly would. Your ancestors wouldn't have to be abnormal or nonterrestrial, and you wouldn't have any more mutation-possibilities than anybody else. It's just that by growing young, you cut over to another circuit. Normally we'd never even know it existed. The relation between our Rufus and the … the Rufus of that other place must exist, but we'd never have known about it.' He looked at the door without expression for a moment. Then he shook himself a little.

'That's beside the point. What I'm thinking is that the farther back he goes, the closer he's getting to the main-line track of that – other place. When he touches it—'

They knew, then, what they were waiting for. When two worlds touch, something has to happen.

Bill sat and sweated. *Has everybody got that potential?* he wondered. *Has Morgan got it? Have I? If anybody has, wouldn't I have? Inheritance. No wonder I felt Rufus was pulling me awry as he moved back along the track toward – what would I be like then? Not myself. An equivalent. Question mark.*

Equivalent. Ambiguous. Nothing I want to know about now. But maybe when I'm seventy, eighty, I won't think so. Without taste or teeth or vision, all senses dulled, I might remember the way – I might—

He was aware of a curious, secret shame, and shrugged the thought away. For a while. For a long while. For many years, perhaps.

They were silent after that. The night moved on.

And still the tension held. Held, and mounted. They smoked a great deal, but they did not leave the door. They could not begin to guess what it was they waited for, but the tension held them where they were. And the long hours of the night passed midnight and moved slowly toward dawn.

Dawn came, and they still waited. The house was tight and silent; the air seemed too taut to move through or draw into the lungs. When light began to come through the windows, Morgan got up with a great effort and said, 'How about some coffee?'

'You make it. I'll wait here.'

So Morgan went downstairs, moving with almost palpable difficulty that was perhaps wholly psychic, and measured water and coffee in the kitchen with hands that were all thumbs. The coffee had begun to send out its own particular fragrance, and the light was strong beyond the windows, when a sudden, perfectly indescribable *sound* rang through the house.

Morgan stood rigid, listening to that vibrating, ringing noise as it died slowly away. It came from upstairs, muffled by walls and floors between. It struck bewilderingly upon the ears and quivered into silence with perceptible receding eddies, like rings widening in water. And the tension of the air suddenly broke.

Morgan remembered sagging a little all over at that sudden release, as if it were the tautness in the atmosphere that had held him up during the long wait. He had no recollection at all of moving through the house or up the stairs. His next clear impression was of Bill, standing motionless before the opened door.

*

Inside it seemed quite dark. Also there appeared to be many small points of light, moving erratically, shining and fading like fireflies. But as they stared the lights began to vanish, so they may have been simply hallucinations.

But that which stood on the far side of the room, facing them, was not hallucination. Not wholly hallucination. It was – someone.

And it was a stranger. Their eyes and brains could not quite compass it, for it was not anything human. No one, confronted for one brief, stunned moment of his life with a shape so complex and so alien could hope to retain the image in his mind, even if for one evanescent instant he did wholly perceive. The perception must fade from the mind almost before the image fades from the retina, because there are no parallels in human experience by which to measure that which has been seen.

They only knew that it looked at them, and they at it. There was impossible strangeness in that *exchange* of glances, the strangeness of having exchanged looks with that which should not be looking at all. It was like having a building look back at one. But though they could not tell how it met their gaze – with what substitute for eyes, in what portion of its body – they knew it housed an individuality, an awareness. And the individuality was strange to them, as they were to it. There was no mistaking that. Surprise and unrecognition were instinct in its lines and its indescribable gaze, just as surprise and incredulity must have been instinct in theirs. Whatever housing the individual wears, it knows a stranger when it sees one. It knows—

So they knew this was not Rufus – had never been. But it was very remotely familiar, in a wrenchingly strange way. Under the complexity of its newness, in one or two basic factors, it was familiar. But an altered and modified familiarity which instinct rather than reason grasped in the moment they stood and saw it.

The moment did not last. Against the dark the impossible figure loomed for a timeless instant, its vision locked with theirs. It stood motionless, but somehow in arrested motion, as if it had halted in the midst of some rapid activity. The dark room was full of amazement and tense silence for one brief flash.

Then noise and motion swirled suddenly around it. As if a film had been halted briefly while the audience gazed, and now sprang back into life and activity again. For the fraction of a second they could see – things – in action beyond and around the figure. A flash into another world, too brief to convey any meaning. In the flash they looked back, unseeing, along the branching of the temporal track that leads from one line to another, the link between parallels along which alien universes go thundering.

The *sound* rang out again through the house. Heard from so near, it was stunning. The room shook before them, as if sound waves were visibly vibrating the air, and the four walls sprang suddenly to life as the curtains billowed straight out toward what might have been vacuum at the center of the room. The purple clouds threshed wildly, hiding whatever happened beyond them. For an instant the *sound* still quivered and rang in the air, the whipping of strained cloth audible below it, and the room boiled with stretched purple surges. And ceased.

Morgan said, 'Rufus—' and took a couple of unsteady steps toward the bed.

'No,' said Bill in a gentle voice. Morgan looked back at him inquiringly, but Bill only shook his head. Neither of them felt capable of further speech just then, but Morgan after a moment turned away from the bed and shrugged and managed a slightly shaken,

'Want some coffee, Bill?'

Simultaneously, as if sensation had returned without warning to their numbed faculties, they were aware of the fragrance of fresh coffee rising up the stair well. It was an incredibly soothing odor, reassuring, a link to heal this breach of possibility. It bound the past to the stunned and shaken present; it wiped out and denied the interval they had just gone through.

'Yeah. With brandy or something,' Bill said. 'Let's ... let's go on down.'

And so in the kitchen, over coffee and brandy, they finished the thing they had begun with such hopes six months before.

'It wasn't Rufus, you see.' Bill was explaining now, Morgan the listener. And they were talking fast, as if subconsciously they knew that shock was yet to come.

'Rufus was—' Bill gestured futilely. '*That* was the adult.'

'Why d'you think so? You're guessing.'

'No, it's perfectly logical – it's the thing that had to happen. Nothing else *could* have happened. Don't you see? There's no telling what he went back to. Embryo, egg – I don't know. Maybe something we can't imagine. But—' Bill hesitated. 'But that was the mother of the egg. Time and space had to warp to bring her to this spot to coincide with the moment of birth.'

There was a long silence. At last Morgan said.

'The – adult. *That.* I don't believe it.' It was not quite what he had meant to say, but Bill took up the argument almost gratefully.

'It was. A baby doesn't look like an adult human, either. Or maybe ... maybe this was a larva-pupa-butterfly relationship. How can I tell? Or maybe it's just that he changed more than we knew after we saw him last. But I know it was the adult. I know it was the ... the mother. I know, Pete.'

Across the fragrant cups Morgan squinted at him, waiting. When Bill offered nothing further, he prompted him gently.

'How do you know, Bill?'

Bill turned a dazzled look at him. 'Didn't you see? Think, Pete!'

Morgan thought. Already the image had vanished from outraged memory-centers. He could recall only that it had stood and stared at them, not with eyes, not even with a face, perhaps, as well as he could remember now. He shook his head.

'Didn't you recognize – something? Didn't it look just barely familiar to you? And so did I, to – it. Just barely. I could tell. Don't you understand, Pete? *That* was almost – very remotely almost – my own grandmother.'

And Morgan could see now that it was true. That impossible familiarity had really existed, a distant and latent likeness, relationship along a many-times-removed line stretching across dimensions. He opened his mouth to speak, and again the wrong words came out.

'It didn't happen,' he heard himself declaring flatly.

Bill gave a faint ghost of a laugh, quavering with a note of hysteria.

'Yes, it happened. It's happened twice at least. Once to me and once to ... Pete, I know what the code was now!'

Morgan blinked, startled by the sudden surprise in his voice. 'What code?'

'Faust's. Don't you remember? Of course that's it! But they couldn't tell the truth, or even hint it. You've got to face the thing to believe it. They were right, Pete. Faustus, Rufus – it happened to them both. They – went. They changed. They aren't ... weren't ... human any more. That's what the code meant, Pete.'

'I don't get it.'

'The code for soul.' Bill laughed his ghost of hysterical mirth again. 'When you aren't human, you lose your soul. That's what they meant. It *was* a code word, and it wasn't. There never was a deeper meaning hidden in a code that isn't a code. How could they have hidden it better than to tell the truth? Soul *meant* soul.'

Morgan, listening to the mounting hysteria in his laughter, reached out sharply to check him before it broke the surface, and in one last fleeting instant saw again the impossible face that had looked at them through the doorway of another world. He saw it briefly, indescribably, unmistakably, in the lineaments of Bill's laughter.

Then he seized Bill's shoulder and shook him, and the laughter faded, and the likeness faded, too.

HEIR APPARENT

Harding stepped from the pier to the little submersible's deck and moved instantly into the shadow, black velvet on moon-white steel. He could hear nothing except water lapping softly, the distant thud and throb of machinery, and very far away, the hollow bellowing of riven air, either a jet plane passing over from Java, or a spaceship blasting off from one of the nearer islands. Phosphorescent waves rippled in the moon-track and the strong tropic stars regarded Earth dispassionately. On the deck there was no sound at all.

Harding glanced once at the white jagged dazzle that was Venus near the skyline. That diamond dot represented sixty-one thousand troubled human beings – if you could call them human – whose relations with the mother-planet had once been Edward Harding's responsibility. Or a seventh of his responsibility.

He shook his head at the bright world in the sky. He would have to get over the habit of regarding the heavens as a chart with a glittering pin-head for each planet, and so many thousand Thresholders, ex-Earth-born, bred for the ecology of alien worlds, pinned up there upon the black velvet back drop for study and control. It wasn't his problem any more. Forget the Thresholders on Mars and the Secessionists of Ganymede and the whole tangled, insoluble mess that confronted the Integration Teams. Think about this current job, which was very simple now. Harding moved quietly toward the open companionway. Either the submersible wasn't guarded at all, or Harding was expected.

He was expected.

The big man in the tiny cabin below sat back in his chair and looked up to meet Harding's gaze squarely, the china-blue eyes watchful but calm. Billy Turner was a Buddha, solidly fat, solidly placid, the heavy face turned to Harding with an oddly innocent look of surprise.

'Something?' Turner asked mildly.

'You could call it that,' Harding said. 'Lay off, or I'll have to kill you, Turner.'

The fat man waited a minute, his gaze holding Harding's. Then he took the pipe out of his mouth, squinted at it, clucked a little and struck an old-fashioned kitchen match on the edge of the table. He sucked the flame downward into the bowl and exhaled a cloud of pungent violet smoke that smelled of the Martian deserts in full sunlight.

'Seems like I don't quite place you,' he said calmly to Harding. 'We met before?'

'We didn't need to,' Harding said. 'Wait a minute.' He stood perfectly motionless by the table, listening, his eyes going unfocused with the completeness of his concentration. It was a totality almost machine-like, both more and less than human. Then he grinned a tight, confident grin and pulled out a chair, sat down across the table from Turner.

Harding was a strongly built man with an incongruously academic look about him in spite of his stained and somewhat ragged clothing. He looked younger than his real years, and he looked ageless.

'No crew aboard,' he said to Turner confidently. 'Just the one Kanaka up forward. No guard. But you were expecting me, Turner.'

Turner blew out a cloud of aromatic smoke from a tobacco that hadn't grown on Earth. His china-blue eyes were watchful and expectant.

'Today,' Harding went on, 'I was fired. Incompetence. I'm not incompetent to handle a radar fish-location unit. If I were, it wouldn't have taken the fishery a month to find it out. O.K. You assume I'll try for other jobs and lose them – through your interference. I'll end up combing beaches with a home-made Geiger counter, you figure. Then you'll buy me for whatever dirty job you have in mind. It's your usual method, they tell me. It generally works. It won't work with me, because I'm one man in the Archipelagic who could figure out a fool-proof way to kill you.'

'Oh, you think so?' Turner asked, opening his blue eyes wide.

'You know what my job used to be,' Harding said gently.

Turner blew out smoke, gazed thoughtfully at it.

'You were with an Integrator Team,' he said.

Immediately, in the most curious way, Edward Harding's mind withdrew quietly into the middle of his head, pulling down blinds and closing doors as it went, receded along a lengthy corridor into the past that led by many closed episodes and half-forgotten things, until it came at the far end to a door. This was the door to a little square black-steel room called the Round Table. It was an entirely empty room, except for a tri-di screen, a chair and a table with a flat metal plate let into its surface.

Edward Harding in his mind's chamber sat down in the chair and put his palms flat on the plate. Instantly, as always, the tingling activation began. At first it was like wind under his hands, then water, then soft sand gently embedding his palms. He moved his fingers. Soundlessly his mind's image spoke. 'Ready, boys. Come in.'

Then in the chamber of memory the Composite Image moved slowly into being in the depths of the tri-di screen. Now the Round Table was open and the Integrator Team sat together at one table, no matter where the accident of their bodies placed them. Seven men made up the Team. Seven blended minds and bodies stood composite and whole in the screen of Harding's memory, as they stood perhaps at this very moment in the same screen, three thousand miles away before somebody else's watching face. Perhaps the Image spoke to somebody else as it had spoken to Edward Harding when he was … before he … well, in the old days. He wondered what the Image looked like now, with no Edward Harding in its make-up.

In the memory which Turner's careless words evoked, Edward Harding *was* in the make-up of the Composite Image. And as always, facing it anew, he looked for some trace of his own features in the blended synthesis of the seven Team-members. And as always, he failed.

Seven faces, seven minds – but you never could filter out the separate features of the men you knew so well. Always they blended into that one Image you knew even better than your own face in the mirror. The Round Table was open when you sat across the board from the Composite Image with the specialized knowledge of six other picked and long-trained Teammates literally at your fingertips, each man sitting in a chair like your own, each idly molding the test-pattern under his palms.

Doctor, lawyer, merchant, chief – biochemist, physicist, radio-astronomer – the needs of each Team met at the Round Table in the carefully chosen attributes of each member. And the needs could never have been fulfilled if all the men involved were actually in the same room, face to face. For knowledge had grown too complex. They talked a technical language made incomprehensible to one another by ultimate specialization. It took the Composite Image to integrate and co-ordinate the knowledge each member brought with the knowledge of each other member, and with the great Integrator itself.

But you could never find your own face in the Image, and you could never see the Image without your face blended into it. Harding thought of the Image as it had looked after George Mayall – left. By request. The first time the Team gathered at the Round Table with a new man in Mayall's place, how curiously flat and strange the intimate, composite features seemed with the new face incorporated. He had wondered then how Mayall felt, wherever he was, out in the cold, strange world after such a long time in the warm, intricately interlocking closeness of the Integration Team.

Well, Harding knew, now.

He thought as he had so often thought before, *What does it look like without me?* And he pictured the Composite Image cold and strange in the tri-di screen of the room no longer his, Doc Valley's face, and Joe Mall's, and the others, blending with the faces of strangers, linking with the minds of strangers, working on the old, complex, fascinating problems that weren't Edward Harding's any longer.

He slammed the door at the end of that long corridor of the mind, hauled his memory back past the shut doors and the closed episodes, and scowled into Turner's watching blue eyes.

'So let's get down to cases,' Harding said harshly. 'Make me an offer. I'm in a hurry. Six months from now, maybe you could pick me up off the beach and hire me for a bottle of gin. I won't wait. What are you driving at, Turner. Or would you rather I just killed you?'

Turner chuckled comfortably, his fat face quivering.

'Well, now,' he said, 'maybe we can arrange something. I'll tell you one thing that's been on my mind a while. I'm a busy man. I get around a lot. I got plenty of contacts. Been hearing about a fellow named George Mayall. You know him?'

Harding's hands closed on the table edge. His face went perfectly blank, like a clock's face, or a dynamo's. His eyes searched Turner's. Then he nodded.

'Mayall knows me,' he said.

'I'll bet he does,' Turner said, chuckling and quivering. 'I'll just bet. Hates you like poison, doesn't he? He was on your Integrator Team and he got kicked off. *You* got him kicked off. Oh yes, Mayall knows you, all right. Like to get his hands on you, wouldn't he?' The chuckles broke into a thick laugh that made Turner shake like a heavy and solid jelly.

'Very funny,' Harding said coldly. 'What of it?'

The jelly subsided slowly.

'Thought I'd hire you to pilot me out to Akassi,' Turner said, watching Harding. 'Trouble is, I don't think you're ready yet.'

'I'm no pilot,' Harding said impatiently. 'I don't know these waters.'

'Ah,' Turner said in a wise voice, cocking his head, 'but you know the Integrator. You could get me past the barriers around Akassi. Nobody else in the world could do that.'

'Barriers?'

'Acoustics, visual, UHF, scrambler,' Turner said in a comfortable voice, sucking his pipe. 'Playing dumb, are you? Never heard of Akassi, eh?'

'What about it?'

'Quiet place these days,' Turner said. 'Strong defensive system all around it. As if you hadn't heard. Ha. Nobody goes in, nobody goes out. You and I could go in and come out with more loot than this submersible would carry – or we could stay and play god, with your talents and training. Except for one little thing – George Mayall. He might not like it.'

Harding's eyes dwelt steadily on the fat, calm face. He did not speak.

'Didn't know Mayall was out here?' Turner asked. 'Never even heard a rumor?'

'Rumors, sure,' Harding said, and thumped the table with an impatient finger. 'But not just where. Not this close. What are you getting at? What's Mayall up to?'

'In short, what's in it for you, eh?' Turner said. 'Ah, that would be telling. Couldn't even guess, could you? What's likely to happen, when an Integrator man gets kicked off the Team?'

'He's given his choice of outside jobs, naturally,' Harding said with some bitterness. 'He doesn't stick with them.' (How could a man stick with an outside job, once he had known the tight-knit interperceptivity of the Round Table? Membership in an Integrator Team is an experience which few men attain and none willingly forfeit. It is a tremendous psychic and emotional experience, the working out of a problem on the Round Table. Afterward, ordinary jobs are like watching two dimensional, gray television when you've got used to full-color tri-di images. 'A man doesn't stick,' Harding said. 'He drifts. He winds up in a fishery in the Archipelagic and then a trader with a lot of influence gets him fired. And won't tell a straight story afterward. Come on, Turner, let's have it.'

'Don't like getting kicked out when you're on the receiving end, eh?' Turner said. 'What did they throw you out for, Harding?'

Harding felt his face grow hot. He set his teeth and held his breath, trying to force the heat and the anger down. Turner watched him narrowly. After a moment he went on.

'Don't try to tell me,' he said, 'that it's bare coincidence brought you here, this close to Mayall. Don't say you haven't an idea what he's up to. You know more than I do, don't you, Harding?'

Harding struck the table hard.

'If you want something, say so!' he said. 'If you don't, lay off and let me earn my living my own way. Coincidence? I haven't got any connection with Mayall any more. But I did once. We were picked for the same Team, and if you know what that means you won't think it's coincidence we drift the same way when we're free to drift. So we both wind up in the Archipelagic. What of it?'

'Mean to say you haven't been approached?' Turner asked keenly. 'You've been out here this long and haven't heard a murmur from – anyone?'

'Murmur of what? Come to the point, Turner!'

Turner shook his head doubtfully. 'Maybe they don't know about you. Maybe one Integrator man's all they needed. My good luck, anyhow. You mean the Secesh Thresholders haven't even tried to get to you?'

'Would I be here now if they had?' Harding asked reasonably. 'Go on.'

'Well, they got to Mayall. They set him up on Akassi with an islandful of machinery and he's feeding them all they need in Integration to organize a withdrawal from the empire. Big stuff. Now maybe you see how I could use you, if you were ready to throw in with me.'

'I see,' Harding remarked coldly, 'how *I* could get to Akassi and take over Mayall's work and cash in on the Secessionist deal for just about as much money as an Integrator could count. But I don't see where *you* come in, Turner.'

'Oh, Mayall works through me,' Turner said, puffing blandly. 'I've got my network spread out from the Celebes to the Solomons. The Archipelagic States couldn't hide a secret from me if their lives depended on it. Mayall needs outside contacts, and I'm the contacts.' He rolled ponderously in his chair.

'Thing is,' he went on, 'maybe I feel it isn't enough, just being contact man. Maybe I want a bigger cut. Maybe that's why Mayall put a roof over Akassi, just in case somebody like me got my kind of ideas. I couldn't do a thing about it – without you. You know how his mind works. You know what screens he'd dope out. But without somebody like me, Harding, you'd never even find Akassi.'

'I wouldn't? Don't be too sure.'

'If you could, you'd have done it before now. Maybe you haven't tried? Never mind. Mayall's no fool. He's dug himself a hole in the ocean and pulled Akassi in after him, if you want to look at it that way. The Secesh boys aren't paying him to set up an island the first stray radar beam could pick out blindfolded. Those barriers around Akassi – well, they erase Akassi, that's all. You can't see it. You can't find it. It isn't there – unless you work with Mayall and know his code. Even then you can't pass the barriers unless Mayall invites you.' He puffed violet smoke and squinted through it at Harding's face.

'You ready to risk your neck yet, my boy?' he asked. 'It'll take the two of us. But Mayall hates you. He'll kill you on sight. That means a risk on your part. I'll buy you higher than the bottle of gin it'd cost next January. I'd cut you in for half the take – if you get me ashore at Akassi and help me work out my scheme to take over from Mayall.'

'You'll have to have something pretty good to kick Mayall out a second time,' Harding said thoughtfully.

'Well now, I expect I will,' the fat man agreed. He took the pipe from his mouth and narrowed his eyes at Harding. 'Surprised?' he asked. 'You don't look it.'

'If you expect perfectly normal human reactions from me,' Harding said quite gently, laying his palms flat on the table with a soft, reminiscent gesture, 'you're the one who's in for a surprise. A man doesn't work ten years on an Integrator Team and stay entirely human. A gradual occupational mutation sets in. For example—' He looked up and grinned suddenly.

'For example, I know we've been under weigh for about three minutes now. There's no perceptible vibration and no roll, so how could I have guessed?'

Turner grunted, but the blue eyes gleamed.

'You tell me.'

'I *am* the boat,' Harding said, and laughed. There was no amusement in the laughter. 'I've got a score of my own to settle – with society. All right, Turner. I'm with you. Where's the control room?'

That was the question.

From Pluto to Mercury its echoes ran. From the New Lands mankind was molding into fertile red soil out of the stuff of fire and ice, on worlds where no man could have lived before technology brought the elements of life, from all the new colonies on the new planets that question went echoing endlessly. *Where is the control room?*

The artificial Threshold Experiments that mold humanity into shapes which can live on alien worlds had done their part. Thresholders inhabited the planets and the empire of Earth spun in a tight network around its sun. Interstellar drive was on the way. Paragravity was already a little more than theoretical. The enormous complexities of science sprang in century-long leaps across time. An engineering process would drag with it a dozen allied fields frantically trying to catch up, a biological method that could enable men to survive interstellar trips shoved rivals impatiently out of its all-important path, hustled other sciences along with it.

The web from Earth had spun out, intricate and tangled, through the Solar System. Now it stretched tenuous threads toward the tremendous macrocosm of the stars, and the moment the first star was reached – Earth could fall.

It could fall as Rome fell, and for the same reason. The New Lands beyond the stratosphere grew, young and strong and integrated, but for century after century Earth had been the control room. The controls grew so complex that unification became an almost impossible task. Only by absolute unity, by a complete and bonded sense of solidarity, could the intricate socio-technological system of Earth stay below critical mass. And it couldn't stay there long.

For Earth had grown to be too small a planet. And the other planets were not ready yet to take up their burden. They brawled among themselves and they complained against Earth. They threatened secession. The isolationism of the New Lands became a menace that threatened the unity of the Solar Empire as Thresholders tugged angrily at the cords which bound them to the Earth from which they had sprung. And desperately in the meanwhile man strove for one major goal – sanity, rational thought, system, organization – integration.

This wasn't the best method, perhaps. But it was the best one they had.

The Integrators were amazing things, electronic thinking machines that could be operated efficiently only by teams of specially chosen, specially trained men who lived a specially planned life. When you lived a life like that, you were apt to mutate in unexpected ways. You didn't turn into a machine, exactly, of course. But the barrier between living, reacting man and nonliving, reacting machine broke down – a little.

Which is why Edward Harding could be the submersible boat he was guiding.

It didn't have isotopic mercury memory units, like a differential analyzer. It didn't trigger electric circuits that punched out stored information and analytical reasoning for Harding to read. But in a way it nevertheless remembered—

And Harding's instantaneous reaction-time sense made him perhaps the one pilot alive who could have guided the submersible through the strong defenses Mayall had flung out around his island.

'We through yet?' Turner asked, up on deck. Around him the blue Pacific lay glittering emptily under a flawless sky. There was a faintly unpleasant smell in the air which the trades couldn't dispel. Turner puffed strongly at his pipe, studying the empty horizon that wasn't really empty. His eyes strained to find some break, as though the sky could tear like a veil, rift from top to bottom and let the real world show through. Mayall's world, Mayall's miraculously camouflaged island, impossible to find in spite of its plain markings on the charts.

In the control room below deck, Harding sat perfectly relaxed in a cushioned chair, his arms slipped into elbow-length metal gauntlets that glistened like wet snakes. Before his eyes hung a transparent disk, shaded like a color wheel. Harding moved his head gently so that his gaze looked through this section and that of the special lens. Before him, vertical on the wall, was the cosmosphere, a great half-globe than ran and bled and fountained with shifting colors and patterns. Radar and sonar made up only part of the frequencies that were the living chart of the cosmosphere. It showed the heavens above, the waters around, the reefs below – and most of the time now, it lied.

Harding said, 'We're not through yet. One more barrier – I think.'

On deck, Turner puffed violet smoke at the bland blue sea.

'Afraid of Mayall?' he asked the microphone.

'Shut up a minute. Tricky here.'

The false screen bled and flared, showing a clear, narrow passage through empty water. Harding moved his head around the varying shades of the lens, trying to find a frequency that checked accurately with another. Only this would keep the ship from sinking, this and the magnetic control panel.

Over the ordinary manual controls, a metal plate had been attached, corrugated and colored and marked into a pattern as dizzying as that which spun across the cosmosphere. But Harding knew it. He had used such controls with the Integrator. His gauntleted hands moved above the plate without touching it, while his glittering fingers played upon an invisible keyboard.

The varying magnetisms leaped a synapse from the ship across lines of force into the metal gauntlets, and Harding's own body-synapses snapped the messages instantly to his brain. His fingers responded as instantly on the keyless keyboard. And as his fingers moved, the ship moved, delicately, warily, perceptively, through wall after wall of frequency mirage where no ordinary compass or radar would operate sanely.

He was the ship.

'Afraid of Mayall?' he echoed Turner's question after a moment. 'Maybe. I can't tell yet. I've got to find out something first. So it all depends.'

'Find out something?' Turner sounded suspicious.

Harding cocked a sardonic eye at the round ear of the diaphragm. He said nothing. Presently Turner's voice came again. There was provocation in it.

'I've often wondered,' he said, 'why Mayall was kicked off the Team.'

'Have you?' Harding asked in a noncommittal voice. He paused. After a while he said, 'The important thing right now is that he blames me for it. So naturally, he hates me. He's afraid it could happen again. And it could. Oh yes, Mayall has the strongest reason in the world for hating me.'

His tone grew thoughtful. 'I'm a rival. I'm the heir apparent. And all he's got is Akassi. He'll be afraid of me. He'll try to kill me.' Harding meditated upon this thought. 'See anything up there?' he asked, after a moment.

'Nothing yet,' Turner's voice came down thinly. 'Sure he'll try to kill you. Wouldn't you, in his place?'

'I probably will anyhow. Try, I mean.' Harding made the modification of his verb in a meticulous voice. 'Akassi is – well, pretty tremendous. I hadn't actually realized it until now. These barriers are slightly phenomenal.' He considered, then laughed shortly. 'The defenses must be so complex that only something like this could have a chance. A direct, unexpected, outrageously simple attack. We'll have to—'

'Harding!' the diaphragm broke in with a sudden rasp. 'Look! I can see the island!'

'Can you?' Harding asked dryly. There was a pause.

'It's gone,' Turner said.

'Sure. And if we'd turned that way we'd be gone, too. Rocks. Wait.'

The glittering gauntlets performed arpeggios in the air. 'I think,' Harding said, watching the cosmosphere, 'I think we're through.'

'We are,' the voice from above said, more quietly now. 'I can see the island again. Different now. I can see buildings beyond the hills there. And a spaceship, ready to take off. Take her in shore, Harding. Ground her on the beach. We've got a jet-stern, you know.'

Harding had no idea what the beach looked like in a visual way, but the cosmosphere showed him all he needed to know of the strand he was approaching, the composition of the sand, what rocks lay under it, how far back the vegetation began. Under him the floor jolted upward as the ship's stern rose at a stiff slant, hesitated, grated motionless. A little shudder began in Harding's gauntleted hands and spread briefly through his body.

He took off the gauntlets.

He was no longer the ship.

He felt himself divide into two separate halves again, one flesh and blood, himself, the other mobile metal going inert as the life withdrew from it. For a rather horrible moment he wondered what it might be like some day if the machine he operated would not let him go. If the metal developed a taste for life, and the tool became the master.

'Harding?' Turner's voice called softly. 'Come up. Better bring your gun.'

Standing together at the rail, they scanned the peaceful, tree-fringed shore. Gentle green hills rolled upward inland a little way, and you could see rooftops over them, a high spider-web tower glittering against the sky, and farther back the unmistakable blunt, skyward pointing snout of a spaceship standing on its fins.

'It's quiet enough,' Turner said, regarding a spider crab that scuttled across the sand, its eyestalks twiddling convulsively. 'Have we sprung any traps yet?'

'No. I neutralized frequencies that would have tipped Mayall off. But I doubt if we can get to the settlement without announcing ourselves.'

'We may. Two men might have a chance where a small army wouldn't. Where's the best place to … to ring his bell?'

'Under the circumstances,' Harding told him, 'it's straight ahead, inland, toward those hills. Plenty of brush for cover here. The cosmosphere can't show everything, and Mayall's no fool – but spectral analysis showed that brush has had nonlethal frequencies used on it. There are microphone pick-ups, too, so—'

'So our trick ought to work, eh?' Turner said solemnly, tapping out his pipe over the rail. 'You call out your code phrase and Mayall will hear it. Don't see how we can miss. Only, don't go getting any funny notions, my friend. You and I haven't got a chance unless we stick together. I can't help remembering you and Mayall worked together for a good many years. I keep wondering how a man feels, once he's kicked off an Integration-Team.'

Harding laid his hands on the hot rail and slid the palms back and forth slowly. Then he tightened his grip so that every vibration of the boat carried up through his nerves to his responsive brain.

'A man misses it,' he said dryly. 'Come on. We're wasting time.'

The frequency caught them in the middle of the brush field. They had been only partially prepared for this. From now on everything would have to be played out free-hand, on the spur of the moment. Turner, who had been walking ahead, flung up a warning arm. Harding felt the beginning tremor a moment before Turner did, and with desperate speed he sucked air deep into his lungs and let it out again in a shout that must have made the hidden microphones planted along the shore rattle in their clamps.

'Mayall!' he roared. *'Mayall!'* And then he added a phrase that had no meaning to Turner, a quick, glib phrase which only an Integrator of Team Twelve-Wye-Lambda would know.

While he shouted, Harding let his muscles relax with a sort of frantic limpness, a lightning speed and control. Barely in time. The last syllables of his yell still hung in midair as he dropped into a crouch. The brush closed over his head and the vibration froze him motionless against the warm earth.

After that there was nothing but silence. The sky burned blue. The air hummed. His shouted words hung echoing in the stillness.

It seemed to Harding that he heard a sort of caught breath sough out of somewhere, hidden microphones catching the sound of it with a note of surprise. But Harding was almost instantly distracted by the urgent and immediate problem of Edward Harding, and the difficulty of staying alive.

First his eyes began to sting, because he couldn't blink. Almost immediately thereafter a frightening sensation of darkness and dizziness swept up from the brown earth and down from the clear blue sky, a shadow enfolding him from without which seemed to come hollowly and emptily from within at the same time.

He had stopped breathing.

That wasn't the worst, of course. The autonomic nervous system controls the heart, too. He hadn't anticipated this. The cosmoscope had revealed only nonlethal frequencies in this barrier field. Somehow it hadn't occurred to him that 'non-lethal' is a comparative term. He felt his heart lurch heavily in his chest, aware of its nonmotion as he had never been fully aware of its beating. Doggedly for a long instant, while that caught breath of surprise from some hidden throat echoed in the microphones, and the shadow of darkness hovered, he crouched helpless under this paralyzing power.

Then out of a dozen separate little mouths, vibrating tinnily low down in the brush, a harsh, familiar voice called out.

'Harding?' it cried incredulously. 'Harding, is it you? *Here?* Welcome to Akassi, Harding!' Sardonic menace sounded in the voice. It paused briefly and then rattled off a series of signal numbers that meant nothing to Harding. 'I'm cutting the paralysis,' Mayall's harsh voice said exultantly. 'I don't want you to die – that fast.'

Blood roared in Harding's ears. A sense of wide-opening distances lifted dizzily around him as the frequency-lock let go. The shadows from without and from within drew back, rose beyond the sky, sank deep into the earth, closed up like a black flower's petals and became a seed inside Harding again. Briefly and strangely he knew what death would be like, some day, Gigantic around him and tiny within him lay latent the enormous dark. Black seed within, black cloak without. When one swooped down to meet the other's swift unfolding, then the last hour would strike.

But not yet.

Someone was coming toward them through the brush. Crouched in hiding, Harding saw Turner's barrel-shaped bulk rise painfully to its full height directly between him and the approaching man. That was the plan, or part of it. He drew a deep breath, grateful anew for the air he breathed. The gun balanced delicately in his hand. He tightened his finger until it pressed cool metal hard. Then he was part of the gun. He couldn't miss.

He could still see nothing except Turner's back outlined against a clear sky, but he knew the familiar, harsh voice that spoke.

'Who are you? How did you—' There was a pause. Then, 'Turner! It's Turner! I didn't send for you!'

Turner spoke quickly. 'Hold on,' he wheezed. 'I know you didn't. Just let me get my breath back, will you? Near killed me!' He took a step sidewise and lurched heavily, rubbing his leg and swearing in a thick voice. Mayall turned automatically to face him, and now at last Harding saw his face.

It shocked him, somehow, to see that Mayall had grown a beard. He couldn't help wondering instantly, first of all, how the beard would show up in the Composite Image. If Mayall had a Team here – and he must have – would all those blended faces seem to wear it? Or would it be obliterated by the six other superimposed images?

Otherwise Mayall had not changed much. The hollow black eyes burned, under strong, meeting black brows. The gaunt body stooped forward. But Harding did not remember the eyes as quite so fiercely bright, or the mouth as quite so bitter and so violent. And the short, neatly clipped graying beard was a note of unfamiliarity that made Mayall somehow a complete stranger.

Turner muttered: 'My leg's asleep,' and bent to rub it, stumbling farther around so that he brought Mayall's back squarely toward the hidden Harding.

'Stand still,' Mayall snapped. 'You shouldn't have come. I'll have to kill you now, and I need you outside. Why did you do it, you infernal idiot?'

'Take it easy,' Turner said, painfully straightening. Harding could see through the leaves the outline of the gun in his jacket pocket. From here it looked as if Mayall were quite unarmed. One hand held a microphone, the other hung empty. Mayall could order the paralysis turned on again whenever he chose, of course, but surely it would trap him in the same field if he did. Frowning, Harding waited.

'Now let me say my say before you fly off the handle,' Turner was placating the bearded man. 'Won't cost you anything to listen, will it? I—'

'Shut up,' Mayall said, his voice sinking to a hoarse, angry whisper. 'Nobody joins me. Nobody! A machine doesn't need assistants, you fool! You haven't anything to say that I want to hear. Wait.'

He turned his head a little and Harding saw the thin mouth tighten to a grimace that was half grin and half snarl of pure ferocity. Harding was aware of a sudden shock at the violence that gleamed through the smile, so near the surface of the man's mind it seemed to glare white-hot through his grimace. Mayall was not perhaps really insane – but he wasn't sane, either.

'Wait!' Mayall said, and his breath came suddenly loud in the clear, sunny silence. 'You didn't come alone. I heard Harding's voice.'

Turner let out his breath in a heavy sigh.

'All right, Harding,' he said, keeping his eyes carefully away from the crouching man in the underbrush. 'All right, let him have it. Shoot, man – shoot!'

Mayall said, 'What?' and swung quickly around, raking the brush with eager glances in the wrong direction. The fat, swift hand on Turner's other side dropped toward the pocket where the gun lay.

'All right, Mayall,' Turner said in a satisfied voice. 'Stand still. We've got you now. Harding, shoot! Shoot!'

Harding stood up in the crackling brush, flicked his gun level and shot the revolver out of Turner's hand.

The bullet went cleanly through the fat man's wrist and whined into the brush beyond. Turner's thick fingers opened. His revolver fell spinning in the sunlight. There was an instant's total silence, broken only by the whispering sound of waves on the distant beach and the raucous scream of a bird somewhere inland, beyond the low hills. The wind brought a vagrant *thump-thump-thump* of machinery from the glitter of roofs half seen above the hill.

Slowly, slowly, Turner lifted his gaze to Harding's. He was gray-white with shock and disbelief, but as Harding met his eyes the whiteness vanished in a swift uprush of deep, angry red. Turner caught his breath and gabbled. There was no other word for it.

'Harding! Harding – I'm Turner! You've shot *me*! I hired you! What ... why did you do it? *Why?*' His eyes darted to Mayall and back. 'Is it a double cross? It can't be! You wouldn't dare! You know Mayall hates your guts!' His voice cracked. 'Why, Harding, *why?*'

Mayall's laughter cut into the disorganized babble. His eyes burned like hot coals deep in the sockets of his skull. His face had the half-demented ferocity of a tiger's, grinning over bared teeth.

'Because he couldn't help it,' he said. 'Right, Harding? This is wonderful. I never expected this!' He glanced at the shaking Turner, gripping his bleeding wrist with the other hand and still gasping for breath in the depths of his shock.

'You chose the wrong tool, Turner. So you got tired of playing second fiddle, eh? Thought you'd hire an Integration man and take over, didn't you?' He laughed harshly. 'There was one thing you didn't know. But—'

'Shoot him, Harding!' Turner cried, clutching his wrist tight and staring down at the welling blood. His hands were shaking like his voice, and a recurrent tremor ran over him so that his whole unwieldy body quivered like a large jelly. 'Go on, shoot!'

Mayall laughed. 'Go on, shoot!' he echoed in a mocking falsetto. 'Go on, Ed. Why not shoot me?'

'You know why,' Harding said.

'*Why not?*' Turner's voice was high with terror.

It was Mayall who answered him, with mocking politeness.

'You didn't know?' he demanded of the quivering fat man. 'Hadn't you heard about the posthypnotic compulsions they jinx you with when you join an Integration Team? Didn't you know that no Team member can ever injure another Team member, no matter what his provocation is?'

Turner stared stupidly at the man. His jaw dropped a little.

'But' – he swung toward Harding – 'You ... you didn't tell me! You let me think ... it's not true, is it, Harding? Go ahead and shoot, before he—'

'Go ahead, Harding, try!' Mayall's voice was ironic. 'Pull the trigger! Maybe you can do it. I'm not on the Team any more, remember?'

'Neither am I,' Harding said gently.

A slow grin spread over Mayall's haggard face. His eyes burned.

'Kicked off too, eh?' he said, exultation in his voice. 'That's good. That's wonderful! Kicked off just like me! How do you like it now, Ed? How does it feel?' The grin faded slowly. 'A little bit lonely, maybe? You don't fit in anywhere?' His voice softened reminiscently. 'You can't really think without an Integrator, you're an expert on an Integrator but you aren't allowed near one. You try joining lots of outfits. No good. What you want is the Team again, the chance to use your mind and your talents. You're lost without a Team.'

Suddenly and harshly he laughed. 'Well, I've got a Team!' he said. 'My own. My own backers, my own Integrator. Everything you tried to take away from me when you got me kicked out. Now you know what it's like. Maybe you think I'll take you in. I'm not the fool you think, Harding. I know you! You have to be top dog or nothing. But you've made the last mistake of your life.' He hefted the microphone and laughed his harsh, mirthless laugh.

'I've got the drop on you, even without a gun. You can't touch me, you fool. I see it in your stupid face. But I can kill you!'

Turner made an unsteady, bleating sound and swung round violently toward Harding, blood spattering from his wrist.

'It isn't true!' he said hysterically. 'You can kill him if you try! Pull the trigger, Harding! This is suicide if you don't!'

Mayall showed his teeth. 'That's right,' he said. 'But he can't do it. We were closer than brothers once. Cain and Abel.' He laughed. 'Any last words, Harding?' He lifted the microphone. 'All I have to do is recite a series of numbers into this,' he said. 'It's automatic. The field reacts to the same group only once, in progressive series, so you needn't bother trying to memorize it. Then the frequency hits you both. I may let you die right now, or I may—'

'You won't do a thing,' Harding said, smiling. 'You can't, George. It would constitute an injury to me, and you can't do it.'

Mayall flourished the mike, breathed gently into its black mouth. His eyes burned at Harding over the instrument. Everything was very still around them. Distant surf hissed upon sand, the brush rustled in a light breeze, machinery thudded like the beat of blood deep inside the arteries of the body, as if the island were alive. Three gulls sailing over on narrow wings turned curious heads sidewise to observe, yellow-eyed, the motionless men below. Beyond Mayall's bearded head the heaven-pointing muzzle of the spaceship loomed like a silver halo. Invisible above it hung Venus, blanked out by the blue dazzle of the day but swinging as if on tangible cord that linked it irrevocably to Akassi. Sixty-one thousand of the ex-Earthborn pinned high upon the chart of the heavens by a diamond pinhead waited, though they did not know it yet, the outcome of this conflict on Akassi.

'*I'm* free,' Mayall said, holding the mike against his mouth. 'I know when I hate a man. I can kill you whenever I choose.'

'You said that before,' Harding pointed out. 'Go ahead.'

'All I have to do is give the series into the mike,' Mayall said.

'Yes. Go on. Do it.'

Mayall drew an oddly unsteady breath and said into the microphone:

'Three-forty-seven-eighty... ah... eighty-two.' He paused briefly. 'Eighty-*five*,' he corrected himself. And waited.

Nothing happened.

The brush rustled. The surf breathed against the shore. Mayall flushed angrily, gave Harding a quick, defensive glance, and said into the mike, 'Cancel. Three-forty-seven-seventy-five—'

The breeze whispered among leaves. The distant throb beat like blood in their ears. But no shadow stooped out of the sky and no shiver in the air answered Mayall's command.

Turner laughed, a half-hysterical giggle. 'So it's true' he said. 'You can't!'

Mayall's face went dark with anger and a pulse began to throb heavily in his forehead. He shook the microphone, cursed the insensate macinery and stammered the numbers a third time into the diaphragm, stumbling twice as he spoke them.

For a timeless moment the three men stood motionless, waiting.

Then Turner laughed aloud and wheeled ponderously upon Harding. Ten feet of space separated them, and Harding had let his gun-hand drop—

The impact of the fat man's sudden onslaught caught him off guard and sent him staggering. The gun flew out of his hand as Turner's great, unstable bulk all but knocked him off his feet. They reeled together for an instant.

When they got their balance again Turner's huge forearm was locked across Harding's throat, blood from his wounded wrist trickled down Harding's shirt, and Turner's good hand pressed the point of a small, cold, very sharp knife against Harding's jugular.

The fat man was breathing hard.

'All right, Mayall,' he said with a painful briskness, though his voice still shook. 'My turn now. If this whole idea's a trick, let's find out about it! I don't know what you've got to gain by lying to me, but you can't kill me unless you kill Harding. Go ahead – turn on the paralysis again. But before you can give your signal, I can cut Harding's throat. Go on. What's stopping you?'

Mayall's face darkened terrifyingly with rage. The grizzled beard jutted straight out with the set of his jaw, and the pulse at his temple throbbed.

'Don't tempt me, Turner!' he said in a grating whisper.

Turner laughed again. 'Is it true?' he asked incredulously. 'I almost think it is! I almost believe you've got to save Harding's life! All right, then.' The knife-point pressed deeper. Harding felt the sharp twinge of breaking skin, and then a sticky trickling. 'I'll kill him unless you do as I say.'

'I wouldn't bet on it, Turner,' Mayall said in a choked voice. 'I—'

'I've got to bet on it,' Turner wheezed past Harding's ear. 'It's my one chance. I'm gambling for my life. And I'll win. You'd have turned on the paralysis by now if you dared. How do you walk through it, Mayall? No, never mind. I want to know first of all what this game is. No, Harding, don't move!'

He shook Harding a little. 'I want some answers! Are you working in cahoots with Mayall? Why did you come here, if you knew you couldn't protect yourself from him? Unless you're working together, I don't see—'

Mayall made a sudden, involuntary gesture of rejection.

'You think I'd work with *him*? You think I could ever trust him again?'

'Shut up!' Turner said. 'No – stop it, Mayall!' The knife-blade quivered at Harding's throat. Mayall paused rigidly, the microphone halfway to his lips, eyes on the knife as he struggled against almost unbearable compulsion.

The last thing Harding saw was Mayall's thin lips moving as he hissed into the diaphragm. Then darkness fell – total blindness, sudden and absolute.

For the second time in ten minutes Harding had a strong illusion of just having died. His first idea was that the knife at his throat had gone in, and this blindness was the first failure of the senses that presages total failure – but he could still hear. The surf still whispered on the far-off shore. Invisible gulls mewed overhead and Turner's wheezing breath caught with a gasp close to his ear.

He could still feel. Sunlight was warm on his cheek, and Turner's thick arm across his throat jerked with some sudden shock of astonishment. Turner grunted and the arm went a little slack.

Then all Harding's reactions snapped into instant alertness. Somehow Mayall had given him this one split-second chance to save himself if he could. Theoretically, he knew what had happened. Frequency juggling was a familiar trick, and phase-cancellation of vibration must have been the process Mayall's hiss into the mike set in motion. The frequencies of the visual spectrum-were being cancelled now, by a broadcast of other frequencies in the right phase. But visual only, since he could feel the sun's infrared heat on his face. If Mayall had an infrared viewing apparatus handy Harding would be clearly visible now.

He worked it all out neatly in a corner of his mind while his body sprang almost of its own accord into this instant's hesitation that slowed Turner's reactions. Harding's right arm struck upward and outward inside the curve of Turner's arm as it held the knife to his throat. He felt the pressure of the blade cease, and Turner grunted heavily as Harding's elbow drove into the pit of his stomach. For an instant they struggled fiercely together in the blinding dark. Then Harding sprang free.

Brush crackled and heavy feet thudded rapidly on the ground, diminishing in distance as Turner, gasping for breath, blundered away through the dark. Harding stood still, breathing heavily, feeling sunlight warm on his face as he stared about in the intense and total blackness.

The very completeness of it told him one interesting fact – there must be a roof over the island. It was almost impossible to create darkness in the open air. In all probability some intangible dome of ionization hooded Akassi in, something that could be varied at will, used to reflect downward any frequency-beams aimed up, a simple matter of angle-of-incidence calculation you could work out in your head. Somewhere on the island a device was broadcasting a beam in the right frequency to cancel the vibrations of light blazing down from the hot, invisible tropic sky.

Mayall's voice spoke out of the darkness, after a long, reluctant pause.

'Are you all right, Ed?'

Harding laughed at the note of hope in the question.

'Disappointed?' he asked.

Mayall's breath went out in a long sigh. 'I hoped he'd get you. I did what I could, but I was praying for the knife to go in. At least, I can get Turner.'

'Don't,' Harding said with some urgency. 'Let's have the light again, George. But don't kill Turner yet. I want to talk to you first. If he dies the whole espionage network he controls will fall apart, and we're going to need it. Do you hear me?'

The darkness went crimson before Harding's eyes, quivered, shredded and was gone. Day was blinding. He put up a hand to shield his eyes, seeing through his fingers Mayall's sardonic grin, the lips turned downward in a familiar inverted grimace.

'I hear you,' he said. He lifted the microphone and spoke into it, his eyes still holding Harding's gaze. 'Sector Twelve,' he said into the mike. 'Twelve? Mayall speaking. There's a fat man crossing the hills toward you. Kill him on sight.' He lowered the mike and showed his teeth at Harding. 'You've got maybe fifteen minutes to live,' he said. 'Just until I get my Team together and dope out a way to kill you. Maybe I can't beat the compulsion alone. But there are ways. I'll find one.'

'You're cutting your own throat if you kill Turner.'

'It's my throat,' Mayall said. 'I give the orders here. He can't get away.' Suddenly he laughed. 'This island's a living thing, Harding. A reacting organism with sense organs of its own and an ionized skin over it. I've got surrogate sensory detectors all over the place. They can analyze anything on the island down to its metallic ions and transmit the impulses back to … to headquarters. I've set up an optimum norm, and any variation will put the whole island in motion. Turner's like a flea on a dog now. The island knows where he is every second.'

'We're going to need him,' Harding said.

'You're going to be dead. You won't be interested.'

Harding laughed. 'Never very practical, were you, George? You were always a bright boy, but you theorize too much. You need somebody on your Team like me. Only luck kept Turner from drilling you. Luck – and me. Look at you, standing there unarmed. What was the idea, coming out like that? The island might have been crawling with Turner's men.'

Mayall grinned his wide, thin-lipped, inverted grimace.

'Ever have hallucinations, Ed?' he asked, his voice suddenly very soft. 'Maybe that's the real reason they threw you off the Team. Ever hear voices out of nowhere? Look at me closely, Ed. Are you sure I'm real? Are you *sure?*'

For a moment longer the tall, gaunt, stooped figure stood there vividly outlined in the sun. Then Mayall smiled and – faded.

The trees showed through him. The silver bullet of the spaceship towered visible behind the ghost of George Mayall. The ghost went dim and vanished—

Mayall laughed softly and unpleasantly out of nowhere.

Harding was aware for a moment of a tight coldness at the pit of his stomach. It couldn't happen. It hadn't happened. He had dreamed the whole thing, or else—

'O.K., George,' he said, trying to hide the sudden limpness of his relief. 'I get it. Where are you, then? Not far, I know. You can't project a tri-di image more than a hundred feet without a screen – or five hundred with relays. Let's stop playing games.'

Low down in the brush Mayall laughed thinly all around him. Harding felt the hair creep on his scalp. It was not the laughter of a sane man.

'Start walking,' Mayall said. 'Toward the settlement over the hill. By the time you get there, I'll have a way figured out to kill you. Don't talk. I'll ask questions when I'm ready.'

Harding turned in silence toward the gap in the hills.

From the hilltop he could see the settlement glinting in the sun. There was the square Integration Building with its familiar batteries of vanes on the roof, and the familiar tower thrusting a combing finger up against the sky. Long sheds lined the single street. There was a fringe of palm-leaf huts around the buildings, and farther off, over a couple of rolling green hills, the lofty tower of the spaceship balanced like a dancer on its hidden fins.

Still farther out were black rock cliffs, creaming surf and a lime-green sea with gulls wheeling over it. Brown figures briefly clad in bright colors moved here and there about the buildings, but Harding saw no sign of Mayall. Only the machinery thumping endlessly at mysterious tasks throbbed like the island's heart.

He started slowly downhill. A palm tree leaning stiffly forward over the path rustled, cleared its throat with a metallic rasp, and said:

'All right, Ed. First question. Why did they throw you off the Team?'

Harding jumped a little. 'Where are you, George?'

'Where you won't find me. Never mind. Maybe I'm in my getaway ship, all set to take off for Venus. Maybe I'm right behind you. Answer my question.'

'Rugged individualism,' Harding said.

'That doesn't mean anything. Go on, explain yourself. And keep walking.'

'I was kicked off,' Harding said, 'because I was so different from you. Exactly your opposite, as a matter of fact. You were the leader of the Team and you held the rest down to your level because you weren't adaptable – remember? It didn't show up because you *were* leader and set the pace. Only when a new man came in did your *status-quo* limitations show. The new man, in case you've forgotten, was I.'

'I remember,' the palm tree said coldly.

'You fizzled. I skyrocketed,' Harding said. 'I had too many boosters. They finally figured I was getting into abstract levels far beyond the Team, which is as bad as being too slow. So *I* was fired for undependable irrationality, which I prefer to think of as rugged individualism. Now you know.'

Ten feet ahead a flowering shrub chuckled.

'That's very funny. *You* were the stupid, unadaptable ones – you and the rest. You couldn't realize I was simply developing along a new line, a different path toward the same goal. I wasn't lagging behind. I was forging ahead of you. Look around you. This island's the living proof. You kicked me into a pretty unpleasant gutter and I pulled myself up by myself. Not easily. I built a living island here. You can have six feet of it, and that's all.'

The bush sighed. 'I've dreamed of killing you,' it said, rustling gently. 'But I'd have left you alone if you'd stayed out of my way. I've never forgotten, though. And I'm going to get even, when the time comes – with you, and the rest of the Team, and Earth. And Earth!'

Harding whistled softly. 'So that's the way it is,' he said to the empty air.

The moss underfoot said bitterly: 'That's the way it is. I don't care what happens to Earth now. Earth's overreached itself. Let it blow up. It and its Teams. I'll throw a shield around Venus that no power in the solar system can crack.'

'Maybe that's your trouble, George,' Harding told the moss. 'You think in terms of shields that can't be cracked. Sooner or later the pressure from within may force a crack. Growth can't be stopped. That was what went wrong on Team Twelve-Wye-Lambda, remember?'

The moss was silent.

'Anyhow, it checks,' Harding went on, trudging downhill. 'Central Integration when I ... ah ... left the Team, was sending out dope-sheets on an enormously complex plan under way on Venus. That would be you, George. Stuff too complex to figure out and counter without a lot of work among the Teams linked up in units. Obviously the Secessionists had themselves an

Integrator at last. It didn't take a Round Table session to find out who they'd subsidized.'

The moss laughed.

'It was a mistake to let me go,' it said. 'Do you want to know the real reason? It's the reason why no Integrator that Earth ever sets up can control Venus. The basic logic's wrong. Their key principles are based on Venus being a social satellite of Earth – and the balance has shifted. *I've* shifted it, Ed. Venus is no protectorate planet any more. That's Apollonian logic. Not a single Integrator on Earth is based on the Faustian viewpoint, which in this case is perfectly simple – Venus is the center of the new Empire!'

'You think so?' Harding murmured.

'I made it so! Every single premise the Earth Integrators base on a ... a geocentric society has got to turn out wrong. Or multiordinal, anyhow – valid only as long as the truth of Earth's power is maintained. I stopped believing in the old truth-concepts of the Earth Empire – and they threw me off the Team.

'But right here on Akassi is the only Integrator that works from the basic assumption that Venus is the System's center.'

'All right,' Harding said calmly. 'Maybe I agree with you.'

'No,' an airy whisper said above the whisper and rustle of a red-flowering vine that hung across the path. 'Not necessarily. How do I know you've really been kicked off the Team? How do I know you're not a Trojan horse?'

'There isn't much you can be sure of, is there?' Harding asked. 'Your Team here can't be very efficient. You've forgotten basic psych. Why do you suppose you've dreamed of killing me?'

'Prescience,' the vine said quietly.

'Displacement,' Harding told it. 'Who would you be wanting to kill? It couldn't be – yourself?'

Silence.

'What kind of a Team have you got, anyhow?' Harding asked after a moment. 'If it can't answer a simple question like that, it can't be worth much. Maybe you need me, George, even more than I need you.'

'Maybe I haven't got a Team,' the vine said behind him, in a die-away voice as the distance lengthened between them.

'You'd be a maniac if you hadn't,' Harding told the empty air flatly. 'You've got to have a Team, if you're operating an Integrator. One man couldn't keep up with it. You need a minimum of seven to balance against a machine like that. You have a Team, all right, but an incompetent one. I'll tell you exactly what you're got – either discarded misfits or untrained men. That's all there is available. And it isn't good enough. You need me.

'You're not wanted here,' a clump of bamboo said hissingly, rubbing its fronds together. 'If my backers had needed another Integration man, they'd have got in touch with you. I'm all they need.'

Harding laughed. 'Thought of a way yet to kill me?'

The bamboo did not reply. But presently a patch of gravel hissed underfoot and said, 'Go down into the village. There'll be a door open in the Integration Building.' And a lizard that looked curiously down at him from the top of a flat stone appeared to add in Mayall's voice, 'Maybe I've found a way—'

Harding pushed the heavy door wider and looked into the green-shadowed room. Sunlight filtering through leaves outside its broad windows made the dim air seem to flicker. Frond-shaped shadows moved restlessly upon banked controls which were the nerve-endings of the island.

In the center of the web George Mayall sat, his sunken eyes glittering, grinning above his beard at the door.

Harding stood still just inside the door and drew a long, deep breath. The smell of the room, oil and steel, the feel of it around him, the faint throb that traveled from the floor up his body and blended with the beating of his heart, made him a complete man again as he had not been for a long time now. He stood in the presence of the Integrator. He *was* the Integrator.

He closed his eyes for a moment When he opened them again he saw that Mayall's sardonic grin had widened and drawn down at the corners.

Harding nodded. 'Alone?' he asked.

'What do you think?' Mayall said, and his glance flickered once toward the inner door at his elbow – the door without a knob, but a flat plate inset where the lock should be. Harding could see through the steel panels as if they were glass, because he knew so well what the little black-walled room inside looked like, with its tri-di screen and its table and its chair.

'You've been here all along?' Harding asked. *'Are you here now?'*

Mayall only grinned. Harding took out a cigarette, lit it, inhaled smoke. He strolled forward casually toward the inner door, glancing around the big room as he crossed it. A control room is seldom as spectacular as the operational devices it controls. Most of the equipment looked familiar. It was what lay out of sight that interested Harding most. For this was only the antechamber to the Integrator.

'That's far enough,' Mayall said after a moment. Harding stood still, the smoke from his cigarette wreathing ahead of him toward the man behind the control desk. Mayall swung his hand edge-on, chopped through a swirl of smoke. His grin turned down farther at the corners.

'I'm real,' he said. 'Don't bother with smoke tests. Clever, aren't you? Stand still, Harding. Don't come any farther. I've got one more question to ask you and then – well, we'll see.'

'Fire away,' Harding said, looking at the door with the plate in it.

'Second question, then,' Mayall said. 'Second and last. Just what did you hope to accomplish by coming here?'

Harding blew smoke at him. 'It could be almost anything, couldn't it?' he said. 'Maybe I came to ask *you* a question. Could you guess what it is? Or would you rather I didn't speak at all?'

Mayall regarded him with narrowed eyes, burning black in hollow sockets.

'Go on,' he said after a pause.

Harding nodded. 'I thought you'd say that. Maybe you've been expecting somebody with – a question. Put it like this. You say all Integration has to fail that doesn't figure Venus as the center of the social system. Right?'

'I said that,' Mayall agreed cautiously. 'What's your question?'

'Why Venus?' Harding inquired.

'What?'

'You're not stupid. You heard me. *Why Venus?*'

Mayall licked his lips suddenly, with a quick, flickering motion, and glanced once at the big TV screen on the wall, nervously, as if the blank screen might be watching him.

'There are other Thresholders,' Harding went on. 'You just pointed out that if your backers had needed another Integration man they'd have got in touch with me. Well, maybe somebody did. Not necessarily your boys, but – somebody.' He blew more smoke. 'Shall I go on?'

Mayall did not speak a word, but after a second he nodded jerkily.

'What you've got here is priceless,' Harding said. 'The group you back has a chance to win independence from Earth. So I just wondered … now, you take Ganymede, for instance. A flourishing little colony they've got up there. Doing a lot of exporting these days. A very rewarding business. Plenty of money in it. What would you say, George, to setting up a little problem in the Integrator to see if you could figure Ganymede as a social center?'

Mayall did not move for a long moment. Then he drew a shaken breath.

'I don't believe you,' he said. 'You're lying. You're trying to trick me.'

Harding shrugged.

Mayall leaned forward over the control desk.

'What proof have you got?' he demanded, his voice hoarse.

Harding threw back his head and laughed. Then he took one final deep pull at his cigarette, threw it to the floor, ground it out under his toe.

'All right, Mayall,' he said crisply. 'You can step down now. I'm taking over.'

Mayall jerked back in his chair, startled and incredulous. His tongue came out again and touched his lip lightly.

'Like hell you are,' he said. 'You can't throw a scare into—'

'Shut up!' Harding snapped. 'Get on your feet, George. I mean it! Out of that chair and open the door for me. I've played it your way till now. But I know all I need to know. I'm a lot smarter than you ever were. I *can* take over, and I'm doing it. And you can't do a thing to stop me. You *can't* kill me! So I'm giving you one last chance – to join *me*.'

'You ... you're insane!' Mayall said, in a stunned voice. 'This is *my* island. I know every nerve-center on it. My men could—'

'Could do everything but injure me,' Harding said, and stepped forward briskly. 'So you lose. Let's put it to the test now. I'm tired of talking. You had your fun, and you've told me enough so I know who'll win this little game.'

'You're crazy!' Mayall cried, scraping his chair back. 'I'll have my boys kill you! I ... I'll send you off the island. I—'

'No you won't,' Harding told him, rounding the corner of the desk. 'Because you aren't sure. Maybe I've got that proof from Ganymede right here in my pocket. You want to bet I haven't? We'll call your Team together and see what—'

'Oh no you don't!' Mayall shouted, his voice shaking. 'You'll never see my Team!'

'Afraid I'll get you kicked off this one, too?' Harding asked ironically. 'Up! Out of that chair, George. You're going to work the trick lock on that door over there and open up your Round Table. Oh yes, you are. Then you'll call your Team together and we'll make a few trial runs. You needn't worry, George. You're perfectly safe. You and I couldn't hurt each other if our lives depended on it – and maybe they do. It doesn't make a bit of difference. Open the door.'

'You'll never get that door open,' Mayall said, stepping backward.

Harding snorted impatiently.

'Here, get out of my way,' he said. 'What kind of a code have you set it for? I haven't time to argue about it.'

He ran his hand experimentally over the surface of the metal plate set where the lock should be. Between plate and palm he felt the varying pressures slide soft and rippling. There was something familiar about the pattern of the pressure. It could hardly be the old cipher, the original team-code that had opened the doors to seven Round Tables, far away in time and space. It could hardly be that, and yet—

The door swung gently open under Harding's palm.

Mayall jerked around, his breath rasping with surprise.

'Who told you my code?'

Harding fowned at him. 'It's the old code. Didn't you realize that?'

'You're crazy. It can't be. I made it up, arbitrarily. Why should I have used the old code?'

'You've been fighting yourself all down the line, haven't you?' Harding said, and stepped through into the little black-steel room.

Mayall stumbled after him, stammering protests. 'It can't be! You're crazy! You found it out – somehow.'

Wearily Harding said over his shoulder: 'You must have flunked basic psych, George. It's the old cipher, but it unlocks a different door now, no matter what your unconscious had on its mind when it set up Twelve-Wye-Lambda's key. *That* door will never open again for you. Or me. This one will have to do, and it's good enough for me. Now let's have a look at your Team. Who are they, George? Where are they?'

Mayall laughed, a high whinny of mirthlessness.

'You'll never know. I'll kill you first.'

Harding snorted. 'Think so? You're welcome to try.'

'You can't get to my Team!' Mayall shouted. 'They ... they're all on Venus. They're—'

Harding swung round and regarded the excited man with a sudden, quickened surprise. 'Don't talk like a fool, George. Of course they're not on Venus. What's the matter with you?'

'They *are* on Venus!' Mayall cried. 'That's it! And if you call them together to talk about Ganymede – you know what they'll do, don't you? So you can't do it, Ed! You can't!'

Harding turned around completely and looked at Mayall with a frown between his brows.

'What's wrong with you, George? I think you really are a little crazy. Are you *jealous*, George? Is that it?' He laughed suddenly. 'Maybe I've got something there. You think you *are* the Integrator, is that the trouble? Well, George, my friend, I may not be able to kill you even if my life depends on it, but – *I can dismantle your Integrator!* How would you like that?'

Mayall drew a whistling between his teeth. He stepped backward into the open doorway, leaned to grope toward his desk, his sunken eyes not moving from Harding's. Then he let the breath out in a sigh and straightened. There was sweat on his face and he was breathing hard.

'Stand back, Ed,' he said grimly. 'Get away from that table. Now I can do it! Now I know I can kill you!'

Harding looked down into the black eye of the pistol trained upon his middle. He lifted his gaze to meet Mayall's murderous stare.

'Go ahead,' he said. 'Try.'

Sweat trickled down Mayall's forehead. His beard jutted. Ridges of tendon began to stand out on the back of his gun hand. But the crooked finger inside the trigger guard didn't move at all. He lowered his head, staring at the gun. Then he brought his left hand forward to grip his right in reinforcement. Both hands were shaking badly.

'Threshold reactions happen inside the body,' Harding said. 'What good will that do?'

Mayall's breath whistled through his teeth more sharply than before. He looked up at Harding, a white, frantic glare. Suddenly he closed his eyes, squeezing the lids shut. Panting, he tried to pull the trigger.

His gun hand quivered – quivered and began to swerve. Slowly it moved until the gun muzzle pointed beyond Harding, toward the wall.

Now the gun cracked, six times, six sharp explosions that blended into one. Mayall's eyes stayed shut. His gun hand dropped.

'I did it,' he said in a whisper. 'I've killed you. I—'

Slowly he opened his eyes and looked into Harding's. Then his gaze went farther, resting upon the six silvery star-shaped holes in the black wall.

Harding shook his head gently. He turned his back upon the man in the doorway, dismissing him. He pulled out the chair that faced the tri-di screen and sank into it.

Then the chamber of memory slid softly over to superimpose upon this real chamber. The little square black-steel room was suddenly a part of Harding, as close and warm as the domed walls that shielded his living brain.

He laid his palms flat on the metal plate.

At first it was like wind under his hands, then water, then soft sand gently embedding his palms. Soundlessly he spoke. 'Ready, boys' he said. 'Come in.'

'You can't do it, Ed,' Mayall said behind him. 'You can't—'

In the outer room a sudden crash sounded. A sudden voice shouted with a wheeze in it, 'Mayall! Harding! Do you hear me? Turner speaking! Mayall, answer me!'

Harding twisted in his chair, glancing up with a startled face to meet Mayall's eyes. Mayall swung up his empty gun and spun too, toward the door. The antechamber was empty, but Turner's harsh breathing filled it with sound. And on the wall-screen Turner's sweating, unstable face glared blankly at the unoccupied room.

'Mayall!' the fat man shouted. 'I know you're there! Step out where I can see you, or I'll blow the whole island sky-high!'

Harding said softly, with derision in his whisper, 'So Turner couldn't get away, eh? Just like a flea on a dog – you know where he is every minute. Oh, sure. Now what? Is he bluffing?'

'Harding! Mayall!' Turner's voice made the antechamber echo. 'I know you're there. I saw you both go into the Integration Building. I'll blow up Akassi and everything on it unless you do as I say! I mean it! I'll give you a ten-count, starting now. One. Two. Harding, do you hear me?'

'All right, Turner,' Harding called, not stirring from his chair. 'This is Harding. What do you want?'

The wheezing voice sighed with relief.

'Step out where I can watch you, Harding. Mayall, too. I—'

'Where are you?' Harding interrupted. 'You're bluffing.'

'I'm at the relay station on the hill. There's a lake south of me and I can see the village. I can see the Integration Building from here, and the door to it, Harding. I'll blow you up! I mean it!'

'You couldn't blow anybody up,' Harding said, and moved his fingers urgently on the table. In a whisper he urged the tri-di screen, 'Come in, boys! Come in!'

'It's no good, Harding,' Mayall said, also in a whisper. 'I told you. You can't work it. Nobody can but me. And I won't. You'll never see my Team!'

'Listen to me, Harding!' Turner's voice insisted from the antechamber. 'Step out here and look. You'll see! I've got a UHF beam pinpointed and focused right in the middle of the fuel tanks of the spaceship. You know what ultrasonics can do, Harding?'

'I know,' Harding said flatly. 'If that spaceship blows, you go with it. Or do you mind?'

'How long would I live if I'm caught?' Turner asked logically. 'Now do as I tell you, or—'

'It's a bluff,' Harding said laconically, aloud, and bent over the table, his palms molding the test-pattern with frantic speed. *'Come in, come in, boys!'* he cried in an urgent whisper.

Mayall laughed sardonically and very softly at his shoulder.

'It's not a bluff!' Turner shouted, his voice thick. 'Look here! I broke into the relay station. I got the beam up fast through the hot frequency into UHF – so fast the fuel didn't have time to blow. Then I pinpointed it right in the middle of the tanks. I've got my hand on the lever. As long as I hold it there, O.K. But if I let go, or if I'm killed – what happens?' Triumph wheezed in the fat man's voice. 'The beam runs down the scale. On the way it hits the hot frequency. In the fuel tank! I can drop it to hot as fast as I can move my hand. Now, am I bluffing?'

'You'll never do it,' Harding called. 'I don't believe you.'

Turner was silent for a hard-breathing moment. Then he shouted suddenly:

'I've got it! You'll *have* to do as I say! Harding, are you listening? You can take the chance with your own life if you want to – *but can you take it with Mayall!* He's in there – I saw him go in. Mayall, do you hear me? You've got to do as I say or Harding will die with everyone else on Akassi! Come out, Mayall! Harding, come out! I mean it. I'll finish the ten-count and then the whole island goes. Three ... four—'

Harding met Mayall's eyes. He shrugged reluctantly.

'He's got us,' he whispered. 'Unless—' Suddenly he shoved back the chair and jumped to his feet, laughing in soft triumph. 'Unless *you* call together the Team, George! Maybe I can't, but you can and you've got to ... to save my life! Here, sit down and get at it, quick!'

For an instant longer Mayall only stared at him, blank-faced. Then—

'All right!' the bearded man snapped. 'I will!' His manner changed abruptly and completely. Faced with a threat he could counter, his mental indecisiveness vanished in a breath. He flung himself into the chair and slapped both hands down hard on the plate.

'Seven ... eight—' Turner called from the screen. 'Harding, you've got about three seconds left to live. Step out here, or—'

'Go on, step out,' Mayall said softly over his shoulder, his voice crisp with new decision. 'I've got an idea.'

'Oh, no,' Harding whispered. 'I want to see your Team. I'm going to—'

'You're going to die if you don't! He isn't bluffing. Listen, now! Go out and keep him quiet while I figure out an answer with my Team. You haven't any choice, Ed! *My* life depends on it, too!' He flashed a sardonic glance upward. 'Look, Ed – tell him I'm dead. Tell him you killed me. Otherwise he'll insist I come out too, and I can't. Go on, quick!'

'Nine—' Turner called. 'Harding, are you listening? On the count of ten the whole island blows. Mayall, do you hear? I'll—'

'Hold on, Turner,' Harding said laconically, and stepped out of the door into full view. 'Mayall can't hear you. He can't hear anything. I ... I've just killed him.'

Turner glared down at him from the wall. His fat face was scratched and trickling with blood from the underbrush he had run through. His clothing was torn and he had tied up his wounded wrist with a soaked rag. His good hand rested above his head on a poised lever. He was leaning heavily upon the face of the TV screen, so that he seemed to rest against empty air in the wall above Harding. Beyond him, through a window, a blue lake twinkled, and a road wound down through thickets, among trees and valley to reappear as the village street. Harding could see the image of the Integration Building clearly, with its open door. He had a moment's dreadful impulse to step to the door and wave at himself.

'Dead?' Turner repeated, and sighed gustily. 'I thought ... I thought you couldn't kill him.'

'So did I,' Harding said dryly, with a glance at Mayall through the inner door. 'Up to the last minute. Then I had to. You can relax now, Turner. Mayall's dead. There's just two of us now, and we'd be fools not to work together.'

Turner laughed.

'I trusted you once,' he said, 'Come out of the Integration Building and walk north. Head for the relay station. You'll spot it when you get to the top of the hill. We'll talk a lot better when I'm pointing a gun at your belly.'

'Everybody keeps pointing guns at my belly,' Harding said mildly. 'I'll develop a stigmatic target if this goes on. Relax. I could blow up the island too, if I felt like it. This building's the control center for the whole setup, and I know practically every gismo here. Wait a minute, Turner. I want a cigarette.' He turned his back to the screen, searching upon the desk top as if for matches. 'Mayall, get busy!' he whispered, rolling his eyes sidewise. 'What's the delay for? Call your Team!'

'Harding,' Turner said from the wall. 'Turn around here. I don't trust you. Come out of that door and start walking north. I mean it!' His fat hand quivered on the lever.

'All right,' Harding said. 'Take it easy. Can't I light a cigarette first?' He cupped a match in his hands, and in their shelter looked anxiously at Mayall. The bearded man had taken his hands off the Round Table plate and was scribbling busily in large letters on a pad.

'No time for the Team,' he whispered. 'Look – read this.' He held it up. Harding blew smoke and scanned the lines of writing. He nodded very slightly, turned to face Turner on the screen.

'Relax,' he said. 'I'm on my way. Just take it easy – we need each other now. I'll play along with you.'

'Have you got any choice?' Turner demanded angrily.

'Maybe not. Any last instructions? Because after I leave this building we can't talk. I'll be beyond reach of any TV screens.'

'Get going, that's all. If I don't see you before I count to—'

'Hold on!' Harding said. 'I've got some ... some stairs to climb before I reach the door. This room is two flights underground. I'll be outside in about twenty seconds. Don't be rash!'

'Twenty seconds, then,' Turner said. 'I'm starting to count now.'

Instantly Harding turned away and stepped toward the inner door, outside the range of the screen.

Mayall moved ahead of him, on tiptoe, every gesture precise and accurate now that he had a definite job to do. But Harding didn't like the suggestion of a satisfied smirk half hidden by his beard.

'Mark time!' Mayall said urgently. *'Mark time!'*

He had swung open a section of the wall, revealing within, between parted chain mail curtains, a little cubicle hung with glittering, swinging mesh from floor to ceiling. A shove sent Harding staggering into the shining tent. The curtains closed behind him. Mayall's whisper sounded disembodied from outside.

'Mark time – but stay in the same place. Like a treadmill.' A switch clicked loudly somewhere behind the curtain. 'You're on. He can see your image. Start moving, Ed.'

Suddenly, without having moved a step, Harding found himself facing the village street. In perfect reflection upon the swinging walls around him he saw dusty roads patterned with sun and shadow, the sheds across the way, the Integration Building looming behind him, its door swinging open. Then the street swung smoothly from right to left before him, lay out straight toward the vanishing point between two distant hills. It was exactly as if he and not the street had turned.

'Mark time, you fool!'

Harding belatedly began to walk, swinging his arms a little, moving his feet, almost taken in by the illusion of what he saw around him. It seemed strange that the breeze which made the leaves move soundlessly did not ripple his own hair.

To all intents and purposes he was actually outdoors, walking at a leisurely pace toward the hills beyond which the spaceship towered. Overhead was the clear sky and the sun. Around him, stereoscopic and in perfect perspective, lay the village. Again the images swung dizzily and he was facing in a new direction as the path turned itself under his feet, sliding backward below him at the rate of a man's normal walk.

'Don't stop for a second,' Mayall's voice said from the other side of that unreal curtain which looked like the airy distances between Harding and the hills. 'Keep walking, and keep in the path. Your image is being projected outside – like a mirage. Turner's watching you. It's a moving mirage. Your image is being moved forward across the island at a slow rate of speed, but you've got to keep your feet treadmilling or Turner may get suspicious. Can you see your way?'

'Just as if I were outside,' Harding said, marking time. 'Is it all right to talk?'

'For a few minutes, yes. You're still too far away for him to see your lips move, and I've got the sound cut. I've set the projection for straight on down the road and over the two hills to the relay station. It'll take care of itself now as long as you guide your course so you don't seem to be walking in the air or through the houses.'

'Nice work,' Harding said admiringly. 'I've seen something like this done before, but only under restricted lab conditions. How do you do it?'

'Wouldn't you like to know?' Mayall said mockingly. 'This whole island *is* a lab. Or a theater. All I need is a specially sensitized frequency beam reflected down from the ionized island roof, to serve as light-sensitive cells. I've got projecting devices, carrier and receiver, two sets of them, one for you here inside and one for the outdoor illusions. Two-way visual projection, plus a mobile unit, chiefly a series of relay zoom lenses. But the details are my business, naturally. All you need to know is that you'll keep marking time with your feet for about ten minutes before your projected image comes within clear sight of Turner, and he comes in sight of you – exactly as if you really were walking through the village. Only, this way I can keep my eye on you.'

'Get busy, then,' Harding urged the blue hills before him. 'Make it fast. Turner *will* use that hot sonic once he finds out he's being tricked.'

'I'm calling the Team now—'

Harding turned sharply toward the sound of the voice. His steps on the sliding road faltered. He glanced back at the curtains through which he had entered, meditating possible action.

'Don't you do it!' Mayall's sharp voice snapped, as if the hills had spoken. 'I'm watching you. You can't do a thing but stay put and keep walking. If you step out of line, we both die. Remember, my life depends on you!' He laughed. 'The Team's coming in now. Don't strain your ears. You won't hear a thing. I've got that sound cut.'

'You may not need the Team,' Harding said, trudging in one spot doggedly. 'Why not order the spaceship to take off? Then Turner can't—'

'On no. That's my insurance. Without it, I'm immobilized. Besides, it wouldn't work – you see why, don't you?'

Harding nodded. Of course he saw. The usual slow-starting take-off would give Turner time to keep his beam focused on the fuel tanks while he exploded them, and a top-speed take-off, never used on Earth, would blast the entire village. Space flight, to be safe, was a job for boosters initially, and that inevitable, fatal slowness was the final wall of the trap in which Turner had caught them. But—

'Phase?' Harding suggested.

'That's the only out,' Mayall said flatly.

'It'll take a good Team.'

'I've got one.'

Harding was silent, turning over possibilities in his mind, marking time briskly as the dusty way glided under his feet. Tension was tightening in him. He wanted to start running. But he was trapped in a squirrel-cage helplessness that kept him immobilized while Mayall hatched schemes with his mysterious Team in Round Table session. Who could guess what murky plans moved in that strange, unstable mind?

The visual mirage around Harding was perfect. So perfect the impulse to test the nearest tree with a questing finger was almost irresistible. Was he really indoors? Halfway he disbelieved it. Only the ghostly silence of the world he walked through attested to its unreality.

The fringes of the village slipped away behind him. Now he was climbing the first hill, remembering to bend forward a little as the ground seemed to rise steeply before him. The domed relay station where Turner waited dropped below the hilltop and vanished for a moment. Until he reached the rise of ground ahead, he would be hidden from Turner. But that did no good. If he didn't reappear on schedule at the hilltop, Turner would certainly suspect a trick. And if he did suspect, he was very likely to act. A man with a bullet through his wrist is apt to be impulsive.

The spaceship would blow, and the island with it. Or at least, a good part of the surface of the island, along with whatever life forms happened to be there at the time.

Phase. Phase was the answer. Harding kept walking automatically across the grassy rise, tilting his body forward to compensate for the slant. No, he needn't bother yet with that. Turner couldn't see him. He stopped walking. There was no need. Eerily, the landscape still moved backward around him at a walking pace. Once, a little while ago, he had crossed this island's hills and talked to its trees, hearing the leaves reply in Mayall's bitter voice. Now he glided in utter silence where sight was the least reliable of the senses.

He looked ahead, deep into the illusion, estimating the distance to the rise. The landscape flowed by around him. Tentatively he reached for the curtains upon which all this unreality unrolled itself. His hand touched woven metal, invisible in midair. He waited, listening. No sound came from Mayall. If he were really able to see into the cubicle, he was not looking now. He sat at his Round Table, facing the Composite Image of his Team.

Moving swiftly, Harding stepped backward on the gliding path and slipped out between the curtains of sunny air. The shadowy control room lurched violently underfoot as the slanting hillside seemed to give place to level floor. On the wall, visible at an angle, the TV screen from which Turner had spoken still showed a foreshortened and flattened relay chamber, and Turner's broad back leaning toward the window that opened in its far wall.

Turner's hand was on the lever. He was stretching to watch the village, the path along which Harding's illusion moved leisurely. His intentness as he stared at the hilltop was so compelling that Harding himself could not be sure his own image would not in the next moment come strolling into view.

Soundlessly, hugging the wall to stay outside the TV screen's range in case Turner should glance back, he slid toward the door of the Round Table room. It was closed. Quietly he laid his hand flat on the lock plate. The vibrations rippled softly under his palm, but he did not manipulate the code of the lock. He put his ear to the panels instead, listening. He could hear only an inarticulate murmuring from inside.

He dared not interrupt.

Absolute concentration would be necessary to work out the phase method that could counter Turner's threat. Phase. He had used it himself, getting through the barriers around the island. But this was a more precarious matter – the sending out of a frequency from another relay station that could cancel Turner's was easy enough, but timing was another matter. When the UHF started slipping down the spectrum, the other frequency would have to slip down too, at exactly the same pace, so that the phase cancellation would operate while Turner's beam passed through the dangerous hot band which would explode the ship's fuel unless the controller beam nullified it.

Only an Integration Team was capable of the enormous concentration that could ensure perfect coordination with Turner. It called for faster than instant perception and reactivity. And Harding thought it extremely doubtful whether many Integrator Teams could manage it. Only the best, the ones who had worked together for years, developed a Composite Image that was an absolute projection and synthesis – and what was Mayall's Team like?

Turner in the TV screen shifted his feet noisily on the floor, exhaled an impatient breath. Harding glanced up, alarmed. Clearly it was time for his projected image to come over the top of the hill. Past time, perhaps. Turner's hand was quivering on the lever already.

Harding flattened himself to the wall once more and slid back rapidly toward his cubicle. Just before he ducked inside he measured the distance between the probable inner wall of the Round Table room and the room where the metal curtains hung. They were side by side, sharing a single wall. Bullets would pierce that wall.

There was no time to waste now. Harding slipped between mesh hangings that swayed like the curtains of reality, blue sky and green grass shivering, warping space, settling again into the illusion of a solid world. The ground glided past fluidly under him. Bending forward as if against a steep slope, Harding began to mark time again as the top of the hill slid level with his feet.

He began to descend the hill. Now he could see the domed building again, and the lake below. He thought of Turner, a white shape dimly visible at a window under the dome, letting out a loud wheeze of relief as his image came into view. The disorienting sense of doubled projections everywhere made Harding's head swim when he tried to think.

'Harding?' The blue lake seemed to speak in Mayall's voice as Harding's path carried him smoothly down toward the shore. 'Everything all right?'

'So far,' Harding said, moving his feet dutifully as the path skirted the water's edge. 'How are you doing?'

'I think we're getting it,' Mayall said, apparently out of the rushes around which soundless water lapped.

'You'd better,' Harding said, thinking grimly that if they didn't, this ghost of himself might go on gliding for years to come over the desolate island, always supposing the projective equipment survived, by some miracle. Or no – no, the man himself had to stand here before the ghost could walk.

'Harding,' the rushes said, half hesitantly, 'we've got a few minutes. I want to talk to you. Suppose we succeed. I've got a paralysis beam set upon Turner now. The moment we cancel his hot sonic, the paralysis goes on. Turner's a dead man already, as far as his chances go. But afterward ... Ed, what about this Ganymede deal? Have you got *proof?*'

Harding chuckled.

'Do you take me for a fool? Once Turner dies, do you think I don't know the next question you'll put to your Team? *"How can I force myself to kill Harding?"* Maybe it's set up already, just waiting until they're free. They'll give you an answer, too – if we survive. If they're good enough to cancel Turner's beam, they'll be good enough to tell you how to get rid of me. If I die, George, you'll never know the truth about Ganymede.'

The rushes were silent. The whole ghostly world was silent, for the distance of a dozen paces. Harding trudged on around the edge of the phantom lake under a phantom of sunlit sky. At the top of the next rise stood the phantom of a domed building where a phantom Turner waited to recognize a phantom.

'Ed, tell me the truth,' a phantom of Mayall's voice said out of air. 'Are you from the Ganymedans?'

'Why not ask your Team?' Harding mocked him. 'Maybe I was lying. Maybe I'm just a washed-out Team member trying to muscle in on your racket.'

'Or maybe you *weren't* washed-out,' Mayall said. 'Maybe the Team sent you to stop me, because they couldn't stop me any other way.'

'That would be a joke, wouldn't it?' Harding said, chuckling. 'Building up Integrators and Teams to such a pitch of complexity they cancel each other, and we have to go right back to the old prehistoric days of man against man, unarmed – without even weapons against each other, George! Because we can't hurt each other with *any* weapons. Yes, that would be very funny – if it were true.'

'Is it true?'

'Ask your Team,' Harding said again cheerfully. 'There's another possibility you may not have thought about. What if Venus sent me, George?'

'Venus?' Mayall echoed in a startled voice.

'They might have. They may have been waiting and watching for just such a man as me, George. They snapped you up when you were bounced off the Team. O.K. Maybe they snapped me up, too. I've never *said* I wasn't approached, have I?'

'But why?' Mayall's voice was bewildered.

'Lots of reasons. Maybe they were curious to know if you'd sell them out when a better offer came along.' Harding chuckled again. 'Well, they'd know the answer to that, wouldn't they, once I got in touch with *my* backers again?'

'You won't leave this island,' the green hillslope said grimly. 'Ever.'

'One of us won't. That's sure. But maybe you'll be the boy who stays. Do you really wonder why Venus might want you kicked off this Team too, George? Maybe for the same reason Twelve-Wye-Lambda had to. What disqualified you for one Team might disqualify you for another. Might? It would!'

'There's no reason—' Mayall sounded a little choked.

'There's every reason. Why is it Venus hasn't made any offensive moves against Earth for ... how long has it been now? ... six months? Eight? All Venus does is counter Earth's aggressions – successfully, but defensively. Only defensively. Things are settling down to a *status quo* – another Hundred Years' War. I wonder why?'

'Why?' Mayall asked harshly.

'Because the top brass always hates for a war to end. And you're top brass as long as Venus depends on your Integrator. Why, you've put up such defenses yourself nobody could get in to stop you, until I came along. Maybe for a long time now your backers have wanted to change things on Akassi. But how could they? They've set up a Frankenstein's monster.

'Did you pick out an incompetent Team on purpose, George? One you could boss around the way you bossed Twelve-Wye-Lambda until I came along? Or have you got 'em drugged or hypnotized? It looks like a draw between Earth and Venus, infinitely prolonged, because Earth's too vitiated to expand and reconquer, and Venus just isn't asking any questions.

'That's what wins any fight, George – asking questions. That's what progress and growth is. Not answering questions so much as asking 'em. And it's the one thing a thinking-machine can't do.'

'I suppose you know all the answers, Ed,' Mayall said coldly. 'I suppose—'

'Nobody knows all the answers. Nobody can. The only way a machine could know them all would be to draw a circle and destroy everything outside it, everything it couldn't handle. And that's what you're doing, George. You're not *using* your Team or your Integrator or yourself. The one thing nobody wants is *status quo* right now. Only a machine's at optimum at *status quo* – and you're a *status quo* man from away back, George. It's why they threw you off our Team. It's why Venus *might* have sent me to Akassi.'

The landscape unrolled silently when Harding's voice ceased. Mayall said nothing. The lake wheeled away behind and the pathway, straightening itself ahead, swung the whole island around with it until the domed station where Turner sat waiting lay directly before Harding, at the top of the nearing hill.

He grew tense as the time drew out and still Mayall did not speak. What was happening behind that illusory veil upon which the world reflected itself? Whatever was happening, it couldn't go on much longer. Already Harding could see the thick white shape of Turner leaning at the window eagerly, watching him – watching his illusion – toil up the steep hillside toward the dome.

Something was going on. In the square, small room on the other side of the wall, where Mayall sat at a table before a tri-di screen, something was certainly moving to a climax. It had to. Because in another two or three minutes Harding was going to reach the door of the relay station – no, not Harding, but Harding's phantom. Just how convincing it looked Harding had no way to guess, but sooner or later the limits of illusion would have to be reached, and then—

Then Turner would pull the lever and the whole game would be canceled on Akassi.

Now Turner was leaning over the windowsill, waving to the oncoming ghost. Harding could see his quivering, fat face with the blood streaks on it. He saw the mouth open and knew Turner must be shouting to him. But since this illusion of Akassi was silent, he didn't know what Turner was saying. It might be a command to halt. It might be an invitation to come in. It might be a question upon whose answer all the lives on Akassi depended. But he could not answer if he could not hear.

He said, 'George!' in an urgent undertone, pitching his voice low because of the irrational feeling that Turner *must* hear him if he spoke aloud. He was so near now – he was looking up at the fat man in the window from so close he could see the sweat beading the heavy face. The closed door of the relay station rose up within a hundred feet of him, and he was nearing it with every step.

When he got there, what would happen? His hand was solid and the door *looked* solid, but the width of the island lay between them, and once the unreeling illusion swept him irresistibly into contact with the door, Turner would see the truth.

'George!' Harding said again, his eyes meeting Turner's eyes.

From the other side of the illusion, he heard the hillside laugh—

It was Mayall's voice, and it did not speak a word, but the laughter was a freezing sound.

Between one step and the next, Harding knew the truth.

He stopped dead still, stunned for an instant by the knowledge of what was happening in the black steel room – what had already happened, while he plodded blind and lost through the mirage.

He should have known when Mayall first spoke a few moments ago, after the long silence of concentration upon the Composite Image and its problem. Mayall would not have broken silence *before* the problem was solved.

That meant the Team already knew its answer to the question of Turner. And that meant the Team was free to give Mayall the second answer upon which his life depended. He must already have asked that final question, and the Integrator must be answering it in this very moment. *'How can I kill Ed Harding?'*

No wonder the hillside laughed at him.

Smoothly the pathway swept backward beneath his unmoving feet. Smoothly the ghost of the domed building glided toward him. At its window Turner leaned, staring down anxiously. Harding made his feet move, striving for illusion to the last. For the fat man's hand quivered on the lever. He sensed something wrong, though he did not yet see what.

'George!' Harding said desperately, putting up a hand to hide his mouth so that Turner would not realize the ghost's lips moved soundlessly. 'Look, George! I'm almost there. Are you watching?'

The hillside laughed again, the same chilling sound.

Of course Mayall would make no move – yet. There were still several seconds left, and as long as Turner stayed alive, Harding was trapped in his little treadmill of mirage. He dared not break the illusion while Turner could still be held by the last slow-running moments of it. But while Harding plodded in his trap the Integrator gave Mayall the answer that was all he needed to extinguish Harding forever.

'George!' Harding shouted suddenly and desperately. 'George, look' And with frantic resolution he snatched the revolver out of its holster at his side.

The hillside gave its freezing laugh again. 'You can't shoot me,' Akassi said to Harding. 'All I need is half a minute more, and—'

'I'm not trying to shoot you,' Harding said, taking careful aim. 'George, if you aren't watching we're all dead! George – I'm going to fire at Turner!'

The ghost of Turner shouted soundlessly in its window just over Harding's head. To that ghost, the man and the gun below looked desperately real. Turner lurched backward clumsily, mouthing shouts that made no sound.

The fat hand tightened on the lever.

The lever moved.

'George!'

'All right!' Mayall snarled from the other side of the hill. The air began to fill with a strange, thin singing sound too far above the threshold of hearing to impinge except as a stinging and tickling in the ears.

But Harding knew what it was. The Team and the Integrator, working as one tight-welded unit, were bending every iota of their blending efforts to cancel Turner's UHF as it slid down the spectrum toward explosion. It would take full concentration from Mayall and his Team and his Integrator – for a few seconds.

In those few seconds, Harding had to act.

He thought, *If I can ever kill him, the time is now!*

He saw through the window just above him the deadly lever dropping under Turner's hand. While the united Team rode the beam downward invisibly Harding was safe – and only that long. Then their full concentrated attention would go back to the problem of Harding's death.

The mirage was vividly real before him – but he knew it for a mirage. He knew that where open hills and a lime-green sea seemed to stretch before him in the sun there was really only a mesh curtain, and beyond that a steel wall which bullets could pierce, and beyond that – George Mayall.

He swung his gun around toward the spot on the wall where he knew Mayall would be sitting. Even if Mayall were watching him now, he couldn't move from that spot. He had to focus his full attention upon the screen and the Integrator. If Harding *could* fire, then the game was his.

If he could fire.

Until this moment he had not consciously tried to kill Mayall. He knew the strength of the compulsion that forbade him to shoot, and he had not wanted to build up defeat-patterns until he made his final effort. But it was now or never.

He thought. *I can fire a gun at nothing. And there's nothing in front of me. Nothing but empty air. The bullet will clear the corner of the relay station and go out over that hill and drop into the ocean when it's spent. There is no mesh in front of me. There is no wall. There is no George Mayall. I'm shooting into midair—*

The revolver was a part of himself, an extension of his outstretched arm. The new synapse waited to be bridged between the crook of his finger and the smooth, cool trigger it pressed. He *was* the gun.

The gun responded as his arm responded to conditioned reflex. The gun felt pain.

Sensory hallucination is an old story. The gun had symbiotic life that was one with the gunner's, and how real is psychogenic pain? Harding knew this sharp, increasing burn was purely imaginary. But it hurt. Moving backward from the muzzle, the pain burned through the steel and the hand, up his arm, contracting the muscles until the pistol wavered. He was suddenly frightened. The symbiosis was terrifyingly complete. *Could he let go when the time came?*

He made one desperate, determined effort to squeeze the trigger. And all his muscles locked. For an instant absolute rigidity held him. And for that instant he fought hard against the frightening illusion that the awareness he had projected into the gun had been seized by the gun. The tool seized the man, merged with him, might never let him go.

Then every muscle from the shoulder down went limp. The arm dropped helpless to his side. He couldn't do it. He couldn't shoot Mayall. He was conscious at the moment only of relief.

Above him in the window he saw Turner at the lever go suddenly rigid. Paralysis had struck him motionless in the middle of a gesture as the Team moved in. He saw the back of the man's thick neck go red with congestion as the breath stopped in his frozen lungs. That meant the UHF was now dropping and the Team with it, in full, fast action. Within the next few seconds they would succeed – or fail. If they failed, probably Harding would never know it. If they succeeded, then Mayall would get his answer to that other question in a matter of minutes.

There might still be one chance for Harding. If he could hear the answer—

His rebellious arm was perfectly obedient when he sent the impulse downward to holster the gun. Rubbing the numbness from his muscles, he whirled in the illusion of the sunshine and tore the universe apart like a painted veil.

Blue air and lime-colored sea separated to let him through.

On the wall of the control room the TV screen showed Turner still rigid, back to the screen, his neck purple now. He was probably quite dead already.

Walking fast, Harding crossed the room, laid his hand on the lock plate of the inner door. He watched the door slide open.

Then he stepped into the little, dark-walled metal room, and the conflict ended as it had begun, with an image on a screen.

Mayall sat with his back to the door, leaning forward over the table, his hands flat on the plate. He was staring hard at the tri-di screen, and out of it the Composite Image of himself and his tools looked back.

It was beautiful and terrible – and the answer.

It was something Harding could not believe, and yet it came as no surprise, for given George Mayall as Harding knew him, what other answer could there have been but this?

The Integration Team was complete – seven thinking brains and the Integrator. But George Mayall was the only human being on the Team. The Composite Image glittering before him on the screen blended his outlines and theirs, merged his mind with their minds. But the six minds that met with Mayall at the Round Table on Akassi were machines. And Harding knew vividly the danger of machines.

Six mechanical brains, stored with knowledge out of human brains. But not humans themselves. Not beings who could ask questions or demand accountings from the one living human on the Team.

No one man had ever before controlled an Integrator single-handed, single-minded. No one man had ever dared try. And no sane man could do it. George Mayall had tried, and in his way succeeded. But his success was a failure more terrifying than any defeat could be.

Perhaps the most terrible thing of all was his attempt to create a Round Table with his seven mechanical storehouses of human knowledge. It would have been bad enough had he simply stored the knowledge away on tapes and drums. Even then it would be fearfully dangerous to draw upon it blindfolded, as he had to, because one man's mind can hold only so much, and it takes seven minds at least to balance an Integrator. Not seven storage drums of recorded fact, but seven human minds, alive, active, perpetually posing questions and arriving at flexible decisions as no mechanical brain has ever yet learned to do.

The mechanical brain *must* be balanced by human minds, or spin out of control. Or else it must draw a circle at the limits of arbitrary control, and destroy all growth outside the circle.

Out of the tri-di screen an Image looked back at Harding which made his mind go numb. It was the most beautiful thing he had ever seen. He hated it more than anything he had ever seen.

The Image had no face, and it had no eyes. But Mayall's burning black gaze looked out of it – somehow, impossibly – blended with the glittering masks of the machines in a synthesis so perfect no watcher could decode that total linkage. Seven component parts made up the Image. It glittered, it was smooth and shining, its fine, functional lines and perfect proportions made it a thing of unthinkable beauty. But you could not separate what of that Image was human and what was machine. The steel was one part flesh, the flesh six parts steel.

A man cannot blend and merge with machines and remain sane. Nor should the machine look back at its watcher out of human eyes, with rage and terror showing in lines of passionless steel. If it were possible for a machine to be mad from too close a contact with humanity, then these machines were as mad as the man who had forced them into the impossible unity of the Composite Image.

But the machines had their revenge. They had seized the man.

It was this Image which guided the lives and fortunes of sixty-one thousand humans upon Venus, and threatened the Solar Empire.

Out of the Composite Image George Mayall looked despairingly at Harding, trapped and desperate in his inchoate prison of steel. The man in the flesh sat three feet away from Harding, but the man in the Image was the real George Mayall. And Mayall *was* the machine.

Drowned, lost, hopeless in the steely beauty of the Image, Mayall's face looked back at Harding out of the bright, burning, multiple mask of the machines. There was helpless terror in the look, and a desperate appeal.

For Mayall had set up upon Akassi too strong a Team. He had laid out his defenses too well. And no one could break through to rescue him from the monster he had made and merged with. Mayall was the ultimate secessionist. He had seceded from the race of man.

Not now nor ever could Harding allow himself to injure a man who had once shared a Composite Image with him. But he lifted his revolver with a steady hand. It was no injury he was about to do Mayall now. Not any more. The time was long gone when death would be injury to George Mayall.

'I meant to tell you, George,' Harding said to the Image in the screen, 'why I'm here and who sent me. But it doesn't matter now, does it?' He centered the pistol upon the back of Mayall's head in the chair before him. *That* wasn't Mayall any more. Harding spoke only to the composite thing in the screen. 'It makes no difference at all who sent me. It only matters that I'm here, and that I should win. And that you should die, George. This was what you wanted, wasn't it?'

He *was* the gun. The trigger pressed backward of its own accord.

On the screen, steel suddenly shattered outward and blood gushed over the hard, bright face of the metal Image and spread down the metal breast.

The screen began to dim. The fading face upon it was all steel now.

When the last trace of humanity melted from the metal, and the last trace of the Image from the screen, Harding put his gun back in the holster. He had been in time, then. Mayall was merely the first.

He closed his mind to that terrifying thought, that inevitable possibility. It might not happen. It might never happen, as long as men were willing to accept defeat rather than win conquests at a cost which all mankind must pay.

Man is a rational animal that can ask questions, and fail, and go on again from failure. But Mayall had come close to creating a machine which could not fail. It could maintain optimum – an eternal, functional, inhuman optimum, guarding its charmed circle with perfectly adaptive defense against all attacks from men – as long as men lasted.

No, surely it was impossible. That blinding, beautiful foreshadowing upon the screen had been a promise and a threat, but fulfillment must never happen. Now or ever. Harding would have a job of destruction to do – dismantling of the robots, so the Integrator might function normally, harnessed and guided by a human Team which he could get from … no, that didn't matter. All that mattered was this.

Harding lifted his hand and touched his forehead gently. There the real Integrator lay. Once, a very long time ago, premen in the days of their unreason carried under their skulls brain-mechanisms of potentially great capacity. But at first they did not use them. Not until – something unknown – happened, and the flame of reason kindled in the waiting Integrator of the human brain. *Homo sapiens—*

Machina—?

Harding shook his head angrily. He turned toward the door, but on the threshold he paused to look back once, doubtfully, at the empty screen that was like a closed door on the wall.

GATEWAY

C.L. Moore (1911–1987)

Catherine Lucille Moore was born in Indianapolis in 1911. Prolonged illness when young meant she spent much of her time as a child reading the fantastic tales of the day, a background that no doubt spurred her on to become a writer of science fiction and fantasy herself. Moore made her first professional sale to *Weird Tales* while still in her early 20's: the planetary romance 'Shambleau', which introduced one of her best-known heroes Northwest Smith. She went on to produce a highly respected body of work, initially solo for *Weird Tales* and then, in collaboration with her husband, fellow SF writer Henry Kuttner, whom she married in 1940, for John W. Campbell's *Astounding Science Fiction*. Moore was one of the first women to rise to prominence in the male-dominated world of early SF, and paved the way for others to follow in her footsteps. Moore ceased to write fiction after Kuttner's death in 1958, concentrating instead on writing for television. She died in April 1987 after a long battle with Alzheimer's Disease.